Lorenzo's Rising

Book Five in the Medici Warrior Series

by Emily Bex

Foundations Publishing Company
Brandon, MS 39047
www.foundationsbooks.net

Lorenzo's Rising
Book Five in the Medici Warrior Series
By: Emily Bex
ISBN: 978-1-64583-061-0

Cover by Dawne Dominique
Edited by Laura Ranger

Dedication

This book is dedicated to all the loyal readers and hopeless romantics who are on this journey with me. Your enthusiasm and love for these characters makes the long hours spent in front of the computer screen writing and re-writing worthwhile.

Acknowledgements

This series could not have been written without the help of my collaborator, Johanna Morisette. Johanna had dabbled in fan fiction, and dragged me reluctantly into a world of vampires, encouraging me to write. She had the initial vision for Shade and was instrumental in the development of that character. Throughout the seven years it took to write this series, she remained a sounding board for the development of the storyline. These characters, and this saga, would not exist if not for her constant support and input which kept me motivated to keep pushing forward.

Table of Reference

Lorenzo's Rising Part Two

Italian to English Translation

Addio	Good-bye
Alzati guerrieri	Stand-up warriors
Amica	Friend
Amore	Love
Bambino(s)	Baby/babies
Bastardo	Bastard
Bel	Beautiful
Beleeza	Beauty
Bellissimo	Very beautiful
Bravado	Brave
Buonasera	Good evening
Cazzo typically interpreted as fuck	Generic curse word
Ciao	Hi/Hello
Dipendenzo	Addiction
Dolce	Sweet
Dormire guerrieri	Sleeping warrior
Familia	Family
Figlia/Figlio	Daughter/Son
Fino ad allora	Until then
Fratello	Brother
Grazie	Thanks
Guerrieri	Warriors
Impavido	Fearless

Lei e il mio vero amore	She is my true love
Madre	Mother
Meile	Honey
Mi/Mio/Mia	My
Coraggioso	Courageous
Moltobella	Very beautiful
Nostra Figlia	Our Daughter
Padre	Father
Per Favore	Please
Per Sempre	Forever
Rosso	Red
Scusi	Excuse me
Si	Yes
Signorina	Young Lady
Sorella	Sister
Stupido	Stupid
Ti Amo	I Love You

French to English Translation

Ma belle immortelle	My beautiful
immortal	
Ma belle ami	My beautiful
friend	
Bon soir	Good evening
Sante’	Health
Oui	Yes
Mon ami	My friend

Lorenzo's Rising

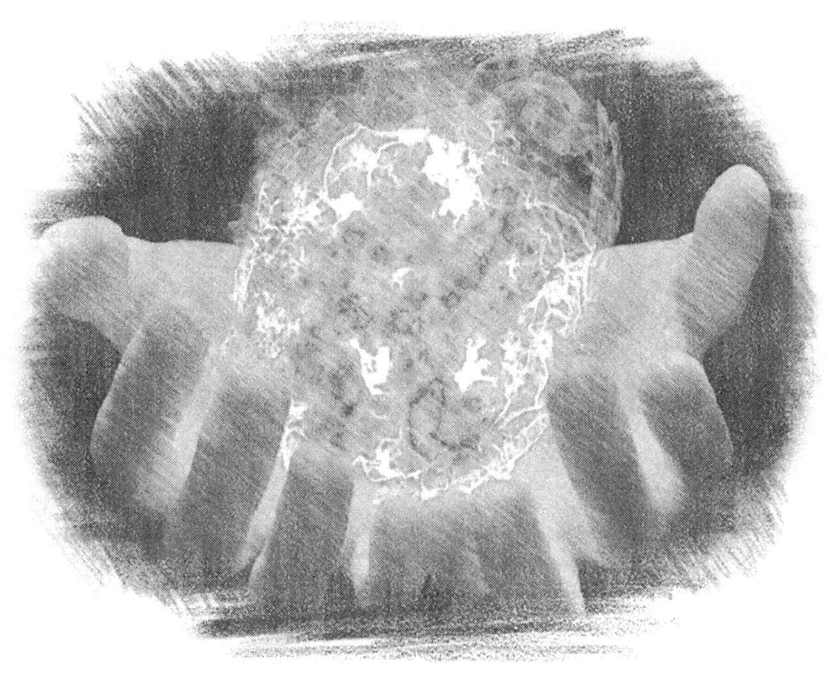

1

Standing at the window, Lorenzo looked out over the grounds of Castello. The sun was setting, and his father would wake soon. He was ten now, and they'd come to Florence for him to begin officially training as a warrior in the camp, under Marco's direction. He felt both excited and nervous to begin this journey. On one hand, he couldn't wait to join the other young boys, and to train in earnest. Of course, he'd practically grown up in the camp in Bel Rosso, but he'd never been allowed to engage in mock combat with the adult warriors. He did have his private lessons with Skelk to master his fire-throwing skills, and his father's help with mastering the sword. Now coming to Castello meant leaving the comfort of his family. His parents and his sisters, Sophia and Natalia, would all return home to Bel Rosso, after he was settled in. At least he'd have Zeus here. His father had promised to have his pony shipped back to Florence for him. Although, Lorenzo would soon outgrow him and need to get a horse.

He'd visited Castello many times since his birth, and his father had made it clear he had strong obligations to the coven. Lorenzo would be allowed to live inside Castello, as opposed to living in the barracks. Other than that one concession, his father had told him to expect no favors from Marco. He'd be treated the same as the other boys in the camp and expected to excel. Lorenzo's wet feeder, Nita, would live at Castello. He wouldn't require the services of the adult female feeders until his puberty, which unlike mortal children, he wouldn't reach until around eighteen to twenty years of age. He'd no longer have his beloved nanny, Theresa. She'd return to Virginia with the rest of his family. Instead, Carlos had been assigned as his private butler.

Yesterday, he'd met Uberto, who would become his new tutor here in Italy. Enzo too would remain at Bel Rosso, teaching his sisters. Lorenzo felt like he was being ripped from everything, and everyone, he'd known in his highly guarded life. He was aware now, of how different he was. He'd been taught the differences between the mortal and immortal world. Although, he'd found that lesson hard to grasp. He'd been made aware of how, and why, it was necessary to protect himself from mortals, while growing up in a household with two mortals. His half-brother, Cory had plans to marry a mortal girl. He understood Cory would never have been able to mate with an immortal. He accepted but didn't understand why his species rejected the half-breed. He couldn't imagine his life without Cory. And Madison presented no danger to him. Cory's mortal mother would come to visit from time to time, and she was always welcomed into their home with loving arms.

There was, of course, his Uncle Luca and Aunt Shannon. His auntie had been turned now and was mated to Luca. For most of his life, he understood Shannon had been mortal. Of course, he knew his own mother was once mortal, even though Lorenzo never knew her as such. One thing was for sure, there were no mortals at Castello, and currently no female warriors either. His Uncle Marco was strictly old school, and this camp was run much differently than the camp in Virginia.

As he watched the sky turn pink with the setting sun, he heard a strange sound, like the clip-clop of horse's hooves echoing down the long hallways of the castle. He turned to see his sister, Sophia, pushing open the massive door to his bedroom. Lorenzo rolled his eyes at the sight of her. Not only was his six-year-old sister wearing their mother's heels, but she had somehow managed to get inside the vault where the royal jewels were stored. Sophia had the coronation crown for the queen, sitting lopsided on her small head, slipping down over one eye, and had on the large twenty carat diamond necklace, which was hanging almost to her waist.

"Sophia! Mom has told you to stay out of the vault."

"Be quiet, I can wear a crown whenever I want. I'm a princess!"

Lorenzo had learned already that arguing with Sophia was a waste of time. "Okay, but don't look at me when you get in trouble."

Sophia stuck out her tongue, before turning to clip-clop out of the room and ran right into her mother.

Kate shook her head in exasperation, as the willful child with red curls was once again breaking the rules. "Hold on, missy. Where exactly do you think you're going?"

Sophia put her hands on her hips. "Are you going to take my crown?"

"Indeed, I am, and the necklace. Now, hand them over."

The child stomped her foot, as she shouted, "But I'm a princess!"

Kate knelt down in front of the girl and locked eyes with her. "And I'm a queen. Hand them over now."

With a sigh that could be heard the length of the hallway, the child reluctantly removed the crown and the necklace, returning them to her mother.

"Thank you. Now the shoes."

"Mommy!"

"The shoes, Sophia."

Sophia stepped out of the designer heels, her chubby bare feet dancing on the cold marble floor. Kate summoned Emma who arrived quickly to take the jewels back to the vault.

Kate issued the last request to the child. "Could you please be quiet until your father and sister wake from their slumber? They will be up shortly."

Sophia shrugged. "I don't know why they can't sleep at night, like we do. This is very inconvenient."

Kate laughed. "Inconvenient is it? Did Enzo teach you that word? And you know perfectly well why they sleep during the day. Your father and Natalia weren't born with the gift of day-walking."

"Will Natalia have the gift of Animalism like us?"

Kate shook her head. "We haven't seen her gifts yet, Sophia. We only know she's not a day-walker. We'll see her gifts emerge as she gets older, just as we saw yours. Now head back to your room and put on your socks and shoes. These floors are too cold."

Sophia turned and started to skip down the hall toward her room, singing at the top of her lungs.

Kate called out, "Quietly, please."

Sophia looked over her shoulder and giggled. "I forgot."

Kate muttered under her breath, "I doubt it," and heard Sophia giggle even louder. She stood in the hallway until she saw her daughter enter her bedroom, then turned and tapped at Lorenzo's open door. He'd watched quietly as the drama played out between mother and daughter. A scene he'd gotten quite used to in the last six years.

"Hey, Mom."

Kate entered the room and sat on his bed. Looking at this miniature version of Shade, a boy on the threshold of moving out of childhood, she swallowed hard. He'd been brave about this move to Florence, but she knew his apprehension around all the change. She'd not add to it by making him carry the burden of her own sadness. She couldn't believe ten years had passed so quickly, and now during the next phase of his life he'd live apart from her. "Are you okay?" she asked.

The boy nodded yes, his black curls bobbing, just as they did when he was such an impish toddler. "I'll be fine. Alfie is here, and Uncle Marco. Besides, you'll come visit, and I'll come home from time to time. I want this. I want to train. I have a warrior's blood, and people will depend on me."

Kate smiled at her son who'd been raised with the understanding of his responsibility, the burden he must bear for the coven, and the legacy of Medici. "True, many will depend on you, and you're born to greatness. You'll be a warrior to equal your father, but foremost, you'll always be my son."

Lorenzo felt a wave of emotion and quickly turned back toward the window, the sky now dark, as the sun slid below the horizon. "You'll keep my room for me at Bel Rosso, right?"

Kate stepped up behind him, kissing the top of his head. "Always."

2

Rolling over in their bed, Shade knew, without looking, the space beside him was empty. As if their life wasn't hectic enough, their third child wasn't born with the gift of day-walking. Now, Kate shared some of her day hours with Lorenzo and Sophia, and some of her night hours with Natalia. Somewhere in between, she always found the time to lie beside him when he slept, but it was rare for him to wake anymore, and find his *bel* next to him. The demands of their children took much of her time.

He could feel the sun setting and knew it was time to move out of this bed. Tonight, would be Lorenzo's first official night of training, and his nervousness for his son was heavy on his mind. Swinging his long muscular legs over the side of the bed, he stood and stretched his arms, flexing his chest and broad back muscles. Casually strolling to the settee, his leathers were already laid out, his boots sitting on the floor, waiting for him. Smiling, he was definitely at Castello, no one laid out his clothes at Bel Rosso, and after all these years, he still had to rummage through the drawers to find what he was looking for. Once dressed, he sat and laced his boots, when he heard the door open and Kate walked in. He could tell from her expression she'd been with their son, and he could feel her emotions. She was his queen, putting on a brave face, even though she was crying inside. "How is he?"

"He's fine. I'm the one who's a mess. He's a little nervous, to be sure, but he's eager to follow in his father's footsteps." Her eyes followed his motions as he bent forward to tie the laces on his boots, looking as handsome as the day she'd first seen him.

Lifting his head to look up at her through his dark curls, he grinned. "Well, I am a bit nervous myself, to be honest. I want him to be a great warrior, and he is well on his way. This experience will be the true test of his skills."

He stood his full height, with his chest stretching the black tee shirt to its limits. He crossed the room and took her in his arms, this precious crimson jewel of his life. "He will be fine, once he gets down on the field, sees Alfie and the rest of them. It won't take him long to adapt."

She molded herself against him, accepting the protective hug that had always made her feel so safe. Laying her head against his chest, she sighed. "Oh, before I forget, your daughter got into the vault again. She was wearing the coronation crown and your mother's twenty carat diamond necklace."

"*Cazzo*. Can I not have one moment alone with you without us speaking of the children, or what they have or haven't done?" He chuckled deep in his chest. "She is but six, *mi amore*. She is only playing and having fun, she gets bored very easily. Castello is a treasure trove of rooms and things to discover. Has my Nattie awoken yet?"

Kate thought he indulged their older daughter too much, and wished he'd take a stronger hand with her, but Sophia had him wrapped around her little finger since the day she was born. "She's awake, and with her feeder. Do you want to see her before you leave to take Lorenzo to camp?"

Pulling her tighter to his chest, he could feel her relax a bit. Talking about their flock always calmed her. "No, we keep the same hours. I will see her before I go to bed. Not sure yet if I will stay with Lorenzo all night. If he wishes me to, I will. But if not, I may sneak back here to see Nattie and ravish my woman."

The knock on the bedroom door was subtle yet strong, and they both turned their heads to the door to see their son.

Shade nodded. "Come in, Lorenzo."

Lorenzo stepped into his parent's bedroom, wearing a set of leathers Cory had made for him. It was his going away present from his half-brother, and his first official set of Medici leathers. "How do I look, Dad?"

Shade couldn't wipe the grin from his face, as he nodded his head with approval. "Impressive, you look like a true warrior. I think today is the day I must stop calling you little warrior. Are you ready to go?"

Kate was biting her lip, as she looked at their son. The leathers made him look older and drove home the reality of what lay ahead for him. She felt concern for him grip her heart, as Lorenzo answered his father, holding his sword in his hand. "May I take my sword with me? The one you had as a boy?"

Shade held Kate tight in his arms. He didn't let her go, knowing that seeing her son for the first time in leathers was overwhelming. "You can take it along, but to be honest, Marco is calling the shots, son. He may wish for you to take up a sword from the lots we use for practice. He doesn't always allow beginners to the camp to use their own swords. He tests the true weight and length of your practice sword, based on your skills the first months you are in training. You may end up getting a new sword out of this ordeal. Though it is easier to start training with a sword you are used to, you need to be able to pick up any weapon and know your limits with it, *si*?"

"Yes sir, I'll take it just in case."

Lorenzo effortlessly sheathed the sword in the strap that ran across his back, then looked up when he heard his sister coming down the hallway toward the bedroom.

At the top of her lungs, her voice creating an echo in the high ceilings of Castello. Sophia shouted at him, "You got leathers! How come you get to wear leathers and mommy took back my crown?"

Busting into her parent's bedroom, Sophia ignored the rule to always knock before entering. "If Lorenzo gets leathers, then I want a princess dress."

Kate gave her daughter a stern look. "Sophia, you have a closet full of princess dresses and crowns."

The petulant child flopped down on her parents' bed. "But they're toy crowns, not real. Lorenzo has real leathers. I want a real crown."

Kate gave Shade a look that said, *She's your daughter. Do something.*

He smiled at the red-headed tornado that whirled into the room, and immediately sent sparks flying. Shade had grown immune to the temper tantrums. His feisty crimson haired daughter always created drama wherever she went. Releasing Kate, he strolled to the bed and stared down into the most beautiful blue eyes he'd ever seen, as he held out his arms to her. "Come, princess, *padre* needs to have a few words with you, *si*?"

Sophia stood up on their bed and jumped into his arms. She loved being the center of his world. Between Mommy, Lorenzo, Natalia, the camps, and the vineyards, she had to work hard to get his undivided attention. Her tiny arms surrounded his neck, as she kissed him on the cheeks, leaving a wet smear of slobber.

"*Grazie* for the kisses. But first, you broke a rule. You need to knock first because privacy is very important. So, remember please." Kissing her tiny button nose, he smiled into her eyes. "And that crown you wear on your head is not yours, but your Mommy's. It is much too big for you, and it may fall off your head and become damaged. Then you will not have a crown to wear when you become a queen, *si*? Daddy will make you a deal. You want to know what it is?"

Her eyes lit up with excitement, and she clapped her hands. "What, Daddy, tell me!"

Kate chuckled at the two of them. The children adored him, almost as much as she did.

"If Daddy has a special crown made just for you, you have to leave Mommy's crown alone. I will have a Medici jeweler come to the house, measure your beautiful head and make a crown that is a perfect fit for you. He will bring lots of jewels, and you can pick what you like. Mommy can help you, but you must first promise to leave Mommy's crown alone, *si*?"

Kate didn't approve of his tactics of rewarding their daughter's bad behavior, but the promise of the gift was out there now. She wished he'd spoken to her before offering their daughter such an extravagant gift, as a bribe to do something she should do anyway. It wasn't the first time he'd spoiled her, and she doubted it would be the last. Kate said nothing but gave him a disapproving glance.

Shade didn't miss *bel's* disapproval, as he placed Sophia on her feet, bent down and kissed the top of her head. "Now, be my good princess and run along, and tell Theresa your news. Mommy and Daddy need to get things moving with Lorenzo."

The child skipped from the room, her voice ringing loud and clear, as she sang, "I am the princess," over and over.

Shade changed the topic, as he looked back at Kate. "Okay then, I think we need to get Lorenzo to camp, don't you? I'm sure Marco is wondering where his new student is."

He turned to his son, giving him a wink. "Say goodnight to your *madre,* then I will meet you right outside this door."

Lorenzo gave his mother a hug, and she looked at him with pride, holding back her tears. "You have a good first night in camp."

He gave her a tight squeeze. 'I will, Mommy...Mom."

Her heart skipped a beat, as he called her mommy. She watched her son turn and walk from the room, his back straight, as he stood at his full height, proudly wearing the leathers. He'd stopped calling them Mommy and Daddy when he was about eight, because he said it made him sound like a baby. He heard Cory calling them Mom and Dad, so he shifted to calling his parents by those names as well. Just one more sign for Kate her child was growing up. The tiny slip today only showed his nervousness about leaving home and moving here on his own. He closed the door behind him, and Kate turned to face her mate.

"He is growing up, *mi amore*. This is his destiny." Taking her in his arms, he kissed her softly. "I love you." Snuggling into her neck, he whispered into her ear, "He will always be your Lorenzo. He will always love you above all other females. Please save your tears until I leave with him. I feel what is in your heart, and I understand your pain, but do not let our son see your tears."

Letting her go, he walked to the door but turned before he exited, speaking loudly, more for Lorenzo's benefit than for Kate's, "Your warriors are off for the night, my queen. Don't fear for him, or for me. Within us beats the heart of the Medici, and we are both born from strong Medici females."

Shade closed the door behind him, as he and Lorenzo teleported out to the camp. It was time to begin his son's journey into manhood.

3

Teleporting with Lorenzo, Shade took them onto the large field outside the barracks. The facilities in this camp were very old and different than those at Bel Rosso. Marco maintained an old school mentality when it came to training and hadn't changed much in the centuries he'd been here, training warriors. Despite Shade's prodding, Marco rarely accepted any female recruits in this camp, and the environment here was much the same as it was hundreds of years ago, when he and Shade were students.

They had modernized the buildings with the times, adding electric, and better plumbing, but there was nothing plush about the barracks. All in all, the basics of what was being taught to the warriors today remained the same. It was the first night of training for the new class, and as they walked toward the group of young recruits, the young boys started to become aware of Shade's presence among them. The boys turned, and dropped to one knee, honoring their king and prince. Some of the boys had come from other territories and had never seen Shade before, in person, but they all knew immediately who he was. They also knew it would only take one word from him, and they could be banished from this camp.

Marco witnessed the boys, as they dropped to their knees and turned to see his oldest friend approach. He raised his hand in acknowledgment and yelled across the field, "You are late, old man!"

Shade could feel Lorenzo bristle beside him. He knew Lorenzo was hoping Marco wouldn't hold him responsible for his tardiness, when he was held up by his parents. Shade laid his hand on his son's shoulder, as they quickly approached Marco and the young warriors. "Relax, son, Marco is just giving me a blast of hell, not directed at you."

Marco and Shade embraced, laughing and slapping each other on the back.

Shade turned to this new class of warriors, who were taking their first steps in their journey to becoming a true Medici. "Arise, warriors."

He eyed them all, stepping in to speak briefly to each boy, and shaking their hand. It was rare for Shade to be here when a new class began. Marco stood with his arms across his chest and eyed Lorenzo carefully. He was anxious to see just what he'd learned at the Bel Rosso camp. He was about to understand Marco would grant him no favors, nor show him no mercy. Marco didn't care if he was the prince, he'd work him hard, if not harder. No one in the class would have more to prove than Lorenzo, and it was up to Marco to make sure he did just that. This would be his ultimate accomplishment as SIC, to make the Prince an even better warrior than his father.

Marco held his hand in the air and the crowd went silent. "Tonight, we begin with some simple sword skills." He pointed to the small cart that sat to the side. "Choose a sword from the lot. Leave your own weapons on the ground beside it. This is a test of skill level, using a weapon you are not used to. Later tonight, the older warriors will come out and join you. Everything you ever thought you knew about fighting and defending yourself, will be wiped away when they get here. Move!"

As the warriors scrambled, Marco turned to his best friend. "You get to keep your mouth shut, stand back, and watch. Open it, and I will shove my fist down your throat, with pleasure, of course."

Shade roared with laughter. "That will be the day."

Marco was the only vampire on the planet who could speak to him in that manner and live to see another moon. Shade slapped him on the back and walked over to the barracks, leaning up against the building. He'd watch his son from a distance, as he was faced off to compete for the first time in his life. Lorenzo had grown up in the camp at Bel Rosso, and worked with many of the warriors there, but that was more play than work. This was for real.

Lorenzo walked tall, aware that every boy, among the new class of warriors, was watching him. He knew coming to camp would be a challenge, and he'd have a lot to prove, to both his father and to Marco. He'd never considered he'd also be constantly critiqued by his fellow students. At Bel Rosso, Marcello and Skelk always looked out for him, and the other warriors were always helpful but protective. He learned things from his father as well, but he was in the camp enough to see how the warriors really trained. It was no holds barred, and sometimes a new recruit, or even an experienced warrior, would get hurt in training. They trained with real weapons, and they fought to win. They stopped short of a kill, but otherwise, they went at each other full force.

Lorenzo swallowed hard as he realized this was no game. He was standing in his father's shadow, and it would be a lot to live up to. He resisted the urge to return to his father, to chuck the leathers, and ask that they all return back home to Virginia. He stood at attention as he and the other recruits listened to Marco's instructions. His father had already warned him he might not be able to use his own sword.

Falling in with the other boys, he walked to the cart. He knew if he pushed forward, they would part for him, and let him have first pick. He was also smart enough to know the boys would hold that against him. He was born to privilege, but here, he must learn to be one of them. He must earn their respect through his actions, not because of his birthright. He let the other boys all choose first and took the remaining sword. It was bigger than his sword, and heavier. It was left for last on purpose. He wouldn't complain. He picked up the sword, and swung it over his head, loosening the muscles in his shoulders, as he'd seen his father do hundreds of times.

Marco was amused as he observed the young boys adjusting to their new swords, and couldn't help but notice Lorenzo held back, letting the others have their first pick, leaving him with the heaviest sword. He always threw that sword into the mix. It was much too large and too heavy for any of them. But he was always interested to see if any would step forward and take on the challenge. Lorenzo ended up with the sword through default, not choice. He waited to see if he'd hear a complaint, but Lorenzo had accepted his luck of the draw, or in this case, his bad luck of the draw.

For their first task, Marco would have the warriors run laps around this field. He shouted out the instructions, letting them know to run five laps with the sword held across their chest, and then five more with the sword held at their side, with the one caveat, the sword had better not touch the ground.

The other boys cast glances at Lorenzo, he knew they were waiting for him to complain, but he held his face emotionless. He'd carry this sword around the field until his arm fell out of socket before he'd quit. This was his first test, for them, as well as for himself, and he'd not fail. He fell in with the group, as they started to run the track that encompassed the full training field, while he clutched the heavy sword to his chest as instructed.

He had run through the vast acres of Bel Rosso since he was old enough to walk. He regulated his breathing and went inside his head as he started the run, like his Uncle Luca had instructed him. Luca had taught him not to focus on how far there was to go, to stay focused on the next step.

Despite the sword that was heavy enough to make a grown man sag under its weight, Lorenzo kept pace with the other boys. He completed the first five laps and heard Marco bark out at them to switch positions, hold the sword with one hand at their side, and not allow the sword to touch the ground. Lorenzo ran and felt the sweat as it ran down his brow. He didn't wipe it away but remained focused. He was aware the boys were paying more attention to him than they were to the assignment, and a few allowed their swords to drag against the ground. One boy dropped his sword, quickly retrieving it, and then scrambled to catch up. Lorenzo felt the pain in his shoulder from the weight of the sword, but maintained his pace, breathing through his mouth, focusing on one step at a time.

All the boys were dragging now as they finished up the tenth lap and thought they were done. Marco shouted out they must hold the swords above their heads and run another five. There was a collective groan from the group, but Lorenzo remained silent as he lifted the sword. He could feel his muscles tremble under the weight, and he was the first one to start this lap. Some of the boys had lowered their swords, and were rubbing their shoulders, before lifting their swords above their heads to start running again. One boy had dropped out of the pack, letting his sword fall to the ground, as he bent over, hands on his knees, trying to catch his breath.

Lorenzo wanted desperately to look at his father. To see or hear some words of encouragement, but he wouldn't look away from the task at hand. Besides, he couldn't afford to break his focus. For the first time in his ten years, he uttered the word he'd heard from his father's lips since the day he was born. "*Cazzo*!"

The muscles in his shoulders burned with an intensity he hadn't felt before, and his arms shook. Still, he ran. His breath was ragged, and his lungs ached. He remembered another trick taught to him by Luca. In his head, he traveled to Bel Rosso. He visualized his tree house, and the rolling hills, running with Warrior and Aegis at his side. It was a distraction from the pain. *I can do this.* He pushed himself, as he led the pack, the other boys dropping further and further behind him, even though they carried a lesser burden. *I can do this!* He repeated the affirmation in his head, over and over, as his feet hit the ground. *I. Can. Do. This.*

He saw the finish line and crossed it. He dropped the sword to the ground and lowered his arms, as the pain shot through both shoulders. His face showed nothing of the pain he felt. He walked slowly, cooling down, letting his breath return to normal. The other boys straggled in behind him, looking at their prince with a newfound respect.

Marco stood back and watched as they completed the laps, slower every turn, except for one. By the time their laps were finished, he felt an inner pride with Lorenzo's performance. He'd feared Shade had coddled his son too much, and Kate had been overly protective, and the son would never live up to the father. But this kid had what it took. He knew it deep in his gut. His old man, and the warriors at Bel Rosso, had found a way to condition him and prepare him for what was ahead. This was only the beginning of their journey. There'd be many long days and nights ahead for all of them, before they earned the right to call themselves Medici warriors.

"Walk it off, warriors. Damn bunch of runts. Let this be a lesson to you. Before your warrior ass walks out on this field every night, it might be a good idea to warm up your muscles."

Marco walked past Lorenzo and nodded, the only sign of approval he'd receive. "Line up in parallel lines, warrior across from warrior."

The boys scrambled to assemble into two straight lines, facing off against each other.

"Here is the drill. You will toss the sword in your right hand to your opponent, while catching the sword he is throwing at you, in your left. As soon as you catch the sword, move it to your right hand and taking one step down, repeat the process with your new opponent for the next round. When you reach the end of the line, you must run as fast as you can back to the beginning and start again." As Marco barked out his instructions, he walked between the two rows, checking each boy, adjusting their spacing.

"Now, this is not to kill your brother, keep that in mind. It is a toss of the sword, not a throw. This exercise will teach you how to grasp a sword being thrown to you by your brother during battle, should you lose your own. It will require coordination, and help you build strength in both arms equally. Begin!"

Stepping back, Marco glanced at Shade who was no longer so relaxed, leaning against the building. Shade had been observing Lorenzo closely, and could tell when his son went into his own head to escape the screaming pain in his muscles. He was tempted to telepathically speak to him, send him encouragement, but he held back. This was Lorenzo's trial, his own burden to bear on his way to manhood. Even coaching him mentally would be an unfair advantage. Shade had drilled into him time and time again, he could never expect his coven to follow if he couldn't lead, and he couldn't ask a warrior to perform a task he wasn't willing and able to perform himself. If he expected the warriors to follow him, they must respect him, and respect was earned.

He remembered well this next drill Marco had assigned, and he crouched down to have a clearer view. He kept his eyes on Lorenzo, as he easily tossed the sword with his right hand while simultaneously catching his opponent's sword with his left. The boys started out slowly at first but picked up speed as they got the hang of it. He was focused on Lorenzo's eye-hand coordination, when he saw a wild throw from Lorenzo's opponent. He almost called out a warning, but Lorenzo caught the sword before it grazed his cheek. *Cazzo, Kate will kill me if Lorenzo comes back from his first night of camp with a gash across his cheek.*

There was another boy in the crowd Shade took notice of. Even though all the boys were about the same age, this one stood a full head taller, and had a stockier build than the other boys. He had his hair pulled back in a long braid down his back. Whenever Lorenzo stepped in front of him, the boy tossed the sword with more force than necessary. At first, Lorenzo was caught off guard, and almost lost his footing. Shade stood and paced, watching as the exercise played out.

Lorenzo had hoped they'd take a break after running the laps, but Marco sent them right into the next round. He was tired, but remained focused, his eyes never leaving the swords as they flew across the divide between the two rows of warriors. He was almost knocked off balance when a boy, taller than him, threw the sword with unnecessary strength. Lorenzo wasn't sure if it was by accident, or by intent, but no matter, he was ready for him next time, steadying himself, tightening his core, as once again the taller boy threw the sword with force.

Lorenzo glanced up quickly and made eye contact. He could tell by the glint in the boy's eye, he was doing it on purpose. He was trying to knock Lorenzo off his game. Lorenzo had watched the warriors at Bel Rosso sparring, goading each other, especially after a few rounds of Midnight spent around the fire pit. Their goading was frequently under the guise of fun, when, in reality, a warrior could be seeking revenge for a slight. The next round he was ready for the boy, and gave as good as he got, throwing his sword with more power, and watched as the boy caught the sword but staggered backward unexpectedly from the force of the throw. Lorenzo locked eyes with him when the boy looked back in surprise, and Lorenzo gave him a smirk that said, *Bring it.*

Marco was keeping a keen eye on the rivalry. He'd not interfere. Every warrior, especially Lorenzo, would need to learn to stand his ground. He saw Lorenzo caught off-guard when the larger boy threw the sword with force and waited to see how it would go down. He knew their small arms were aching, and they were getting tired, but he'd make them complete the exercise. Lorenzo circled again, and stood in front of the larger boy, and sent him a message loud and clear with a powerful toss of the sword that staggered the larger boy. Marco had to hold back a laugh as he saw a little of the queen's stubbornness and temper emerge from Lorenzo. He shook his head, knowing the Medici and his mate had both given him traits that would make him a formidable foe.

Lorenzo glared at the taller boy as the exercise came to an end. If he thought for one minute he'd be intimidated, he could think again. If anything, he'd learned from Raven you didn't have to be bigger than your opponent to get the best of him, just faster and smarter. He didn't want an enemy in the camp, but he wouldn't be bullied either.

"Halt!" Marco watched as the warriors responded to his order, dropping their arms, and Lorenzo cast a glare in the direction of the larger boy. His message was clear, the larger boy took a step back and looked at his feet. Marco smiled to himself, when he heard a ruckus coming from the other end of the training field. The young warriors looked down-field, to see the teens emerging from their barracks and marching toward them, tall and lean, dressed in their leathers. The older boys taunted them.

"So, you think you're warriors? You're nothing but grunts!"

Marco smirked as the teens shouted their intimidation. It was a ritual as old as time. The teens harassed the young boys, the men harassed the teens. Marco would enlist the teens in training the grunts, pushing their skills to the limit.

Lorenzo scanned the new group of older boys, all in their teens, and saw Alfie. The two boys locked eyes as Alfie gave him a wink, and Lorenzo got a burst of confidence, as he saw his friend take the field.

4

Kate had finally gotten Sophia in bed, with help from Theresa, and would like nothing more than a hot bath when she heard Natalia. The four-year-old had dressed herself, and exited her bedroom, shoes in hand. "Mommy, I need help with my shoes, please."

Natalia was the last of their children. Kate had been able to see all three of her children, long before they were born, with a view of their unique personalities. Lorenzo would have a warrior's spirit, eager to follow in his father's footsteps. Sophia would be their willful and stubborn princess, overly spoiled by her father. Last, but not least, Natalia. Their youngest was quiet and curious, always asking questions and seeking answers. Enzo said she was already reading at a twelfth-grade level and would be moving into college courses at age five. Natalia was more interested in books than toys. The one thing Kate hadn't been able to see was what gift their children would inherit. So far, they'd all acquired Kate's unique quality of possessing two gifts. Lorenzo was born a day-walker, as well as with the rare gift of fire-thrower. Sophia was also a day-walker, and shared Kate's gift of animalism. With Natalia, the only thing they knew for sure was she hadn't been born a day-walker and went to her death slumber every morning at sunrise, just like her father. She was still young, and it was too early to tell if she'd possess yet another gift.

For Kate, this had presented yet another challenge, in trying to find time each day to dedicate to each child, and still have time for her mate. As a day-walker herself, she required less sleep, but there were days when she could literally fall asleep standing up. She'd been with Shade for eleven years now, and as tired as she was some days, she wouldn't trade one minute of it. She picked up Natalia and carried her to the master bedroom, tossing the girl on the large king-sized bed, as she melted into a puddle of giggles. Kate took the child's bare feet and nibbled on her toes, until Natalia squealed, "Mommy, it tickles!"

Kate sat on the bed and pulled the child onto her lap, and was helping her put on her shoes, when she heard Shade on the stairs.

***

Shade could hear the giggles of their youngest daughter. Natalia looked nothing like the first two children. Nattie's hair was a rich brown, long and straight. Her eyes were an even darker brown, looking large in her face against her peaches and cream complexion. Her eyes reflected an innocence and vulnerability, much like her mother's eyes. Her level of intelligence was off the charts, and he wondered what she'd accomplish in her life. She had a gentle and loving spirit, just like his beautiful *bel*. But Nattie would be their last child, and her birth had been emotional for both Kate and him.

There'd been a time when he would have found it hard to imagine raising children. Now he couldn't imagine his life without them. He quietly entered the bedchamber to find two of his females in a muddle of giggles and tickles on their huge bed.

Natalia spotted her father in the doorway and held her hands out to him. "Daddy! Come play with us."

The grin spread wide across his face. "My Nattie!" He quickly grabbed her up and spun her around in his arms. Her squeals of delight filled the room, and he laughed out loud at her glee. "What are we playing, and can I win?"

Natalia placed her hands on either side of his face. "I let you win at chess already."

Kate laughed. "You know, it's quite humbling when your four-year-old is smarter than the both of us together."

Shade made a fake pout. "Mommy is making fun of Daddy. What should be her punishment?"

Natalia scrunched up her face. "No, Daddy, no punishment. Guess what I found yesterday?"

Shade looked as if he was in deep thought. "Well, I know it wasn't Mommy's jewels, your sister found those. Was it an old book?"

"Yes! I was in the Castello library, and there was a book on all the Medici's. It said the Council kept records of our family that goes back many centuries. Could I see that book? The one the Council keeps?"

Pausing before he answered, Shade cast a questioning glance at Kate. "Well, I don't see why not. There is no rule that says you are not allowed. But Daddy will have to make an appointment, you can't just walk into Council and demand things, they have rules. I will call Malachi and see what we can arrange, perhaps a small tour as well. Would that be satisfactory?"

Natalia clapped her hands. "Yes!" She planted a wet kiss on his cheeks. "I knew you would find a way, Daddy."

"That's right, anything for my Nattie."

Kissing her softly on the cheek, she smelled like the night air on a spring evening. "I have left you two new books in the library, you may be interested in. Get Theresa to take you down, I beg you give me some time alone with Mommy. I promise, once we are done, I will tuck you in when it is time for your death slumber, *si*?"

She squirmed to the floor, heading for the door to make her way to the library. "Thanks, Daddy."

Kate watched their daughter as she scampered from the room. The girl was still only four. Although she had the physical and emotional development of a four-year-old, her intellect grew exponentially. Kate rolled over on their bed, making room for him as he lay down beside her.

"You know she'll present as big a challenge for us as Sophia, right? With Sophia, it's hard to keep her focused and sitting still long enough for Enzo to get her through her classes. With Natalia, we'll be stretched to make sure the lessons are increasingly difficult. But enough about that, how did Lorenzo do on his first night?"

Shade turned to her on the bed and pushed an errant crimson lock behind her ear. "He did well, *mi amore*. It is good he will be trained by Marco. I would find it difficult to be objective, and I had to restrain myself from praising him and sending him encouragement."

Kate sighed, she'd felt Lorenzo's spirit all night, a combination of nervous energy and pride, so she knew he was feeling good about his first experience. "Did he see Alfie? He was hoping he'd be there."

"Yes, he saw him alright. Alfie was caught off-guard when Lorenzo did a backflip over his head and took him out from behind. Damn, Kate, you should have seen him, he was incredible. I wanted to run out there, hug him, and tell him how proud I was. It will be hard to let him go."

He rolled off the bed and stood looking at her, as she stared back at him with a bewildered look. "It is time, woman, we need to get naked, and into the bathtub. This is one of those rare moments when we are alone."

Kate jumped out of bed and grabbed his hand, leading him to the bathroom and the huge marble tub. "I can't even remember the last time we did this." She turned on the water, poured in bath salts, and let the tub fill as she slowly undressed for him. "Can I still entice you? Or have you grown weary of me?"

Watching her undress, his eyes caressed every inch of her, from head to foot. She was as beautiful to him as the first day he saw her, and his cock grew harder with each piece of clothing she discarded. He pulled the t-shirt over his head and tossed it aside. With his eyes still glued to her, he unbuckled his belt and removed it, but not before snapping it across his thighs, still covered in the soft leathers. Unzipping his pants, he hooked his thumbs into the waistband of his leathers and peeled them slowly over his hips, as his dick sprung free. "Take off my boots, *bel*, it's time we took care of each other for a change."

Kneeling before him, she unlaced his boots and he stepped out of them. He treated her as his equal, but he was still her master, and she willingly submitted. She understood him, knew his soul and knew for them, her willingness to submit, to follow his lead was something that sparked their beasts. A rumble erupted from deep in his chest, as she slid her hands down his long legs. She nipped at his thighs and flicked her tongue along his bare legs as she lowered the leathers to the floor, before flinging them unceremoniously into a corner. Still on her knees, she slid her hands the length of his legs, stroking his thighs, and cupping his balls in her hands. She heard the sharp intake of his breath, and she gently drew her nails across his balls. Stroking his cock with her hand, she slipped the slick purple head into her mouth, and ran her tongue across the hard, smooth skin. She felt his hand in her hair, gripping hard as he guided the motion of her head, fucking her mouth. She looked up at him, and his icy blue eyes never left her face. She was his for eternity.

Wrapping his hand in her hair, he pulled her to her feet, and lowered his mouth to hers. His kiss was slow yet searing and claimed what was his. Kate lifted her legs, wrapping them around his waist as he stepped into the huge tub, the kiss never broken. He slid down into the scented hot water, leaning his back against the tub as she straddled him.

"This feels so good, *mi amore*. Alone."

She ran her hands down his chest, beneath the water line, until they settled at his hips. His eyes never left hers. "Alone," she whispered.

Leaning forward, she turned her face up to him, seeking the heat of his mouth on hers. He bent his head to her, their lips connected, and he devoured her with his kiss, his tongue probing inside her mouth. He always came to her, both of their bodies demanded it, but it was usually just before his death slumber. They rarely had the time, or the privacy, to enjoy spontaneous sex. He deepened the kiss, and Kate could feel the passion in him, undimmed. His body was as familiar to her now as her own, but she never grew weary of him, and never stopped wanting him.

As she broke away from his kiss, he grabbed the bath sponge that lay on the side of the tub, and slowly washed her, stroking her pale, soft skin. He could feel her body relax under the careful ministrations of his skilled hands. She leaned her head back, as he lifted the sponge above her head and squeezed, the water cascading over her head, running in rivulets down her body, dripping from her hair and slowly over her luscious breasts. Bending over her, he took a nipple into his mouth, and heard her soft moan, as her hands gripped his hair.

"*Ti amo*. You are so beautiful. I never tire of your beauty nor your love."

Her back arched, to accommodate his mouth at her breast, as his tongue flicked across her nipple, sending an electric current straight to her core. Her sharp intake of breath was audible in this room of marble, the sound bouncing off the walls. He pulled away, and the air felt cool against her nipple, making it harder.

"And I never tire of you, lover. There's never enough of you to go around." She slid forward on his lap, her hands still tangled in his hair, responding to her need to feel closer.

Snuggling into her neck, he inhaled deep and felt his beast beating on his chest. Gripping her hips, lifting her, he settled her with aching slowness onto his now throbbing cock. His eyes were locked on her face as he was buried inside her. The lust for him played across her face, and she was more erotic than any painting he'd ever beheld. Her eyes glowed a soft red as he felt her beast come alive. "Let her out to play, *mi amore*, I need you."

As he slowly impaled her on his cock, she dropped her head back, the moan escaping her lips. She felt the ache in her gums as her fangs pushed through. She felt his hips thrust forward, as waves were created on the surface of the water. She snapped her head forward, her wet hair hanging in tendrils, as she laid against his chest, clinging to his shoulders, matching the rhythm of her hips to his.

The dance began, their movements were slow and rhythmic, practiced, and yet new. He knew what she liked, and how she'd respond. His hips thrust deeper, as she matched him thrust for thrust. He could hear the water splashing to the floor as the motion of their bodies sent water over the side. Her head lay on his chest, and he could feel her blood singing to him, urging him to feed, to claim her, protect her.

"I cannot wait, *bel!*"

His fangs punched through, long and sharp, aching for the essence of her. He sank them deep into her neck, pulling her uniqueness inside his body as he swallowed every drop. His body crackled and popped, her blood lighting him up from the inside. He felt his balls tighten as the pressure to have her built.

As his fangs pierced her skin, she responded to the sweet sting that brought both pleasure and pain, as she felt the heat between her legs, burning with a fire only he could extinguish. Her arms encircled him, holding him close as he fed. She felt their bond, strengthened over the years with their feeding. Her connection to him now was unbreakable. She was as much a part of him, as he was of her.

He pushed harder and deeper inside her, as if he could climb inside her skin and never come back again. Gripping her hips, he slammed his dick into her, and she rode him with equal measure. He drank heavily, needing all of her.

She knew his heart, felt his emotions, and heard his words before he spoke them. His hands slid easily up and down her back, before settling on her hips, steadying her as he thrust deep. She rode his pounding cock, as her tongue snaked out, following the vein in his neck, before sinking her fangs into the muscles of his shoulder. She growled slightly when the blood hit her tongue, and she closed her lips over the wound, drawing his blood into her mouth.

Their blood mingled, and their beasts danced. He gripped her tight as she came with him, and his guttural growl rattled off the walls, shaking them both. They gasped for breath, and her blood trickled down his chin. His arms encircled her like a shelter from the storm. Her head lay on his shoulder as her breathing slowly returned to normal, their hearts beat in unison.

He held her close with his eyes still closed when he heard the breathing of another. He opened his eyes to find Sophia staring nonchalantly at the door.

Kate felt the intrusion at the same moment and lifted her head, turning to see their red-headed daughter, her hands on her hips, scolding them both. "Who's going to clean up all that water?"

Kate spoke sharply to her, "Sophia! You've been told to knock. How long have you been standing there?"

The child shrugged. "Back to when you were talking about being alone. I thought I should be quiet until you finished."

Kate looked at her. "Finished?"

Sophia nodded. "With the mating stuff. We read about it in biology."

Shade felt the anger building inside Kate and softly rubbed her back, calming her, not that he was doing a good job at controlling his own anger. He locked eyes with his unruly daughter and held her in his gaze. "I should get out of this tub and punish you like there is no tomorrow. Did you also learn in your biology class that mating is a private act between two partners? Haven't you been told to knock, Sophia?"

Sophia shrugged again. "It's no big deal, Daddy."

He was ready to explode, but instead took a deep cleansing breath. He needed to handle this appropriately. Kate carefully slid off him, as he stood and grabbed a towel, wrapping it around his waist.

"Let me tell you something, you little imp. You just disrespected your mother and me. So, let me remind you who sets the rules here. No crown for you, you do not deserve it, so that is shelved. I would suggest you march your ass back to your bed, before I physically take you there myself, *si?*"

Shade stepped out of the tub and slammed the door shut, leaving his daughter on the other side. He leaned against the door, his eyes closed, taking several deep breaths.

Sophia shouted at him from the other side of the closed door, "Fine! I didn't want a stupid crown. And I'm telling Emma about all the water on the floor." She turned and stomped off toward her room.

Kate stepped from the tub, pulled a towel from the bar and wrapped it around her. She walked to him as he stood with his back against the door, and she could tell he was fighting his anger.

She gently stroked his cheek. "Well, at least we contributed to her biology lessons. I'm sure Enzo will be pleased with her progress."

She opened her towel and laid her body against him. "Come back to me." She kissed his bare chest, the water still running off him, and puddling at his feet.

He slammed his hand against the door behind him. "She tests me, constantly testing me. I am so angry at her, *mi amore*. I want to just throttle her where she stands."

He wrapped his arms around Kate and snuggled into her neck with a heavy sigh. "What will I do if she pushes me too far?"

"She'll test us both, every day. And your beast knows she is your flesh and blood, just as your beast knew I was your mate. The beast will always protect what is his, even if she drives him mad in the process. Come to bed with me. I'll have Theresa punish her with time out, but please don't let her steal away what little time we have together."

Lifting her in his arms, he knew she was right, as he carried her to their bed, and laid her down gently. He climbed in beside her and drew the blankets over them, as she curled up on his chest. He rested his hand on her beautiful ass and squeezed. "*Ti amo*, my walking sin. I worry about you, you are tired."

"I'm never too tired for you. I'll always find time for you."

He rubbed her back until he felt her body relax. "Sleep, *mi amore*. It is not yet sunrise. I will check on the children. I'll return to our bed before the slumber takes me."

Before he could finish his sentence, she was breathing softly, her eyes closed. He smiled down at the female who owned his heart and soul. Sliding gently from the bed, he knew she'd feel him leave. She always did. He slipped on his jeans and a tee shirt and walked out of the room, closing the door behind him. He had two daughters to check on.

5

Making his way to Sophia's bedroom, Shade passed several servants along the way, Castello never slept. He peeked in to find his daughter in her bed, but he knew she wasn't asleep. All his children had their own bedrooms in Castello. Sophia had picked the one that had a huge queen-size bed, with a headboard of gilded 14k gold. Her small frame was curled up in a ball, and she was hardly visible in the bed, if not for her bright red hair peeking out above the pure white sheets. He walked to her bed and crouched down beside her head, letting his hand play in the soft curls. "We need to talk, princess."

Sophia pulled the pillow over her head, her voice muffled. "Don't talk to me."

Shade held back his laugh, Sophia had always been headstrong and petulant, and presented a challenge for Kate and him. Lifting the pillow from her face with ease, he kissed her cheek. "I'm sorry you are angry. But you know the rules, *si?* You must learn to respect the privacy of others."

Staring back at him, she pouted. "You made a big mess. I get scolded when I make a big mess. I told Emma, and she said I should mind my own beeswax and not be such a busy body. I told her I was a princess, not a busy body. This is my castle."

"Sophia, this castle belongs to the whole family and supports the rule over the coven. We have a responsibility to every member of the coven. They will need you to lead them, to carry the legacy into the next generation, just as Lorenzo and Natalia will be required to do. You are born to royalty, and with that privilege, comes great responsibility. You need to really think about that. Now, come, give me a kiss and tell me you are not angry with me anymore. You will break my heart if you stay mad at me."

Sophia gave him a hug. "I'm not mad anymore, Daddy. Will I live here when I grow up? I like it here."

Shade smiled at his daughter. "The day will come when you will seek a mate, and when you do, you will live with him. Who is to say where that will be? Perhaps you will live in another castle here in

Italy, or somewhere else in Europe. Or you may find your mate in the States. That is a long way off, I hope, because I am not ready for my princess to leave me. You will be given some of my territory as your dowry, and that will be combined with the wealth and territory of your mate. You will be required to mate a master, someone of great standing among our species, to ensure the long-term survival of our coven."

Sophia gave his words some thought before responding, "But will I still wear a crown? Will I still be a princess?"

He ran his fingers through her red curls. "*Si*, you will always be a princess. That is your birthright. If you mate with royal blood, then you would become a queen, like your mommy."

She nodded her head. "Yes, then I can wear a crown every day if I want to. Daddy, can I still have a crown?"

Hugging her tight, he smiled. "Can you leave Mommy to sleep without interruption?"

She shrugged her shoulder. "Well, unless I have an emergency."

Standing, he walked to the door and took a deep breath. "Let's try not to have an emergency then. Let your mommy rest and I will think about a crown. I will go to my death slumber soon, so you have a good day. *Ti amo*."

Sophia knew she had him wrapped around her little finger, and just what it would take to melt his heart. "I love you, Daddy."

He closed the bedroom door quietly and teleported to the library to check on Natalia. He found her studying, her face filled with wonder. He stood in the doorway, leaning against the doorjamb watching her, and felt a hand on his shoulder. It was his *madre*, Portia. She was watching over her grandchild. Shade was momentarily saddened that, as the children had aged, they could no longer see their grandparents. Lorenzo said he could still hear them from time to time, but only he and Kate could see and speak to them. "*Madre*, I have missed you."

Portia smiled at her only son, who had grown to be such a powerful warrior and strong master over this coven. He had exceeded even her dreams for him. "She is a beautiful child, *figlio*, and she will bring to this coven something even you cannot fathom."

She kissed him gently on the cheek and disappeared before he could question her. He looked at Natalia and spoke quietly. "Did you like the books I left for you?"

Looking up from her books, Natalia gave him a huge smile. "I did, Daddy. This one has an inventory of all the art pieces inside Castello, which artist painted them, and what year. There is a whole section on the royal jewels. I better not show that to Sophia."

Shade laughed and walked to her, lifting her from her chair, taking a seat and sitting her on his lap. "I agree. So, tell me, are you now going to be an explorer and find all these great pieces of art within Castello?"

She nodded her head. "I was going to take the book with me until I could find every piece. I already know where some of them are. Uncle Luca said he'd help me, if I needed."

"That is a great plan. In the classroom where Lorenzo studies, there is a huge map of Castello, all of the rooms, a blueprint. I am sure we could make a copy you can take along. Mark all the places as you find them."

"Did you ask about visiting Council, Daddy?

"Not yet, I'm going to my office, and I'll call before I go to my death slumber."

Looking up, he found Anya, Natalia's wet feeder, standing in the doorway, waiting to get the child ready for bed. "Anya is here to do your bath and get you to bed. Mommy is sleeping, so she will not tuck you in this night. I have some things to do in the office, and I want to speak with Lorenzo when he comes back from camp, so will you give me a kiss and hug before you go?"

She hugged him tight, and kissed his cheek, wrinkling her nose at the whiskers on his cheek. "But you come tuck me in, Daddy, even if I'm asleep okay?"

"Always, my sweet Nattie, always. We are two of a kind, you and I, sleeping in the day. I rather like that we keep each other company in our dreams." He hugged her, kissing her cheek. "*Ti amo.*"

"I love you, Daddy." The child took Anya's hand and followed her back up the stairs to the bedrooms.

Shade watched her go and sighed. "Two down, one to go. *Cazzo*, how the hell does Kate do this?"

Teleporting to his office, it was one of his favorite rooms within Castello, and yet it held memories of his most humiliating moments. His *padre* sat at this same desk, building the coven, and admonishing Shade for not being strong enough. He knew Lorenzo would be done with his first night of camp soon and he wanted to be here waiting for him. He phoned the Council and spoke with Malachi, arranging a meeting for Natalia and himself. He wasn't surprised at Malachi's hesitation, but his request was granted. He felt Lorenzo approaching long before he saw him, feeling both his tiredness and his jubilation.

***

Lorenzo had thought earlier in the day he wanted to stay at the camp and sleep in the barracks with the other boys. But his body was tired, his muscles ached. He was looking forward to a hot bath and the comfort of his large, plush bed. He felt depleted, and he'd need to feed from Nita tonight. Walking through the halls just before dawn, he knew his father could still be awake. He sought him out in his office and found him seated behind the massive desk. "Dad?"

"Come in, son. Sit down, before you fall down. Talk to me."

Lorenzo curled up in a chair near the desk, his eyes feeling heavy. "Do you think I did all right? Did Uncle Marco say anything? I tried really hard."

"All right? Hell, you kicked some ass, son. And that move on Alfie, he didn't see that coming, true Medici."

Shade stood and poured himself a Midnight. Walking to his son, he laid his hand on his shoulder. "Marco was impressed, but he won't make this easy on you, neither will I. Learn, practice, and remember one thing, I love you. Becoming a warrior is a long journey. You will have success and you will fail. It is all important in learning to become a warrior's warrior, *si*?"

The boy nodded his head yes, blinking slowly. He was a day-walker, but there was no way he could stay awake today.

Shade almost laughed out loud, the boy was completely depleted. "Get to bed, you will end up falling asleep on Nita before you replenish."

Taking Lorenzo's hand, he pulled him up and hugged him tight to his body. His pride in his son overwhelmed him. "*Ti amo,* Lorenzo, you make me so damn proud."

Lorenzo returned the hug, basking in his father's praise. "I'll be just like you, Dad, I promise."

The boy left the study and made his way up the long marble staircase, his sword clanking on each step. As he got to the top of the stairs, he turned toward his bedroom then hesitated. Looking over his shoulder, he saw the door to his parents' bedroom slightly ajar. Heading for the door, he peered in and saw his mother asleep under the covers. He tiptoed to the side of the bed and whispered, "Mommy?"

Kate stirred and opened her eyes. Sitting up slightly in bed, she looked at him with concern. "Lorenzo, are you okay."

He hesitated before answering. "I'm a little bit scared."

She pulled her child to her, as he climbed onto the bed. "What scares you?"

He buried his face in her red hair, hiding his face. He wanted to be brave like his father, and he didn't want to show weakness. "I'm scared of when you and Dad leave, and I'll be here alone."

She kissed the top of his head. "You'll never be alone. Not ever. Medici blood runs through your veins, and your father and I will always feel your presence, even from Bel Rosso, just as you will feel ours. You are my brave boy, and it's all right to be scared. Being brave is doing what needs to be done, even when you're scared. It doesn't take courage to tackle something that doesn't scare you. I love you so much."

She held him tight and didn't tell him she would be just as afraid to leave him behind.

***

Shade downed the Midnight and could feel the pull of the sun rising, he needed to get his ass back to his woman and his bed. As he turned to set the empty glass on the desk, his *padre* appeared at the desk, as if he was still in charge. He spoke to Shade without looking up.

"You are too soft on him, *figlio*. Much too easy, you need to toughen him, make him a warrior."

Shade laid his hands palm down on the ancient desk, leaning across it, making eye contact with his father. "He is my son, and he will become a warrior under my guidance. There is nothing weak about him, and there was never anything weak about me, either. Someday, *Padre*, you will discover him to be a warrior like no other.

Now, I am off to my bed, as I suggest you do as well. *Madre* will be missing you. Good day."

Turning to leave, he stopped at the door when he heard three simple words from Christofano. *"Ti amo, figlio."*

He turned back to his father. "*Ti amo, Padre*."

Rushing up the stairs, he tucked in Natalia as promised, kissing her forehead, and pulling the soft blankets around her sleeping form. Looking into Sophia's room, his day-walking daughter was already gone from the room, and under the supervision of Theresa. He was heading to Lorenzo's room when he passed his own bedchamber and stopped short when he saw Lorenzo sleeping next to *bel*, his sword lying on the floor by the bed, still wearing his leathers. Kate held her son in a soft embrace, her head bowed to his, both of them soft and warm in the bed. She was just like his own *madre*, giving Lorenzo courage, and soothing his darkness with her light. He tiptoed in gently, dropping his clothes to the floor by the bed as he slid in next to her. He would grant his son this one last night to be a child before he was left here at Castello alone.

6

Waking from his death slumber, Shade felt refreshed. He found both Kate and Lorenzo gone from their bed. Sliding from their bed, he shuffled into the shower, sending Anya a message to prepare Natalia for their visit to the Council. He was hoping to get the Council meeting over quickly, so he could get back to see Lorenzo at camp before the night was over. Stepping out of the shower, he toweled off and dressed quickly in leathers that bore the Medici crest on his chest. He had almost finished dressing when Kate entered their bedroom with Sophia in tow.

Sophia saw her dad was awake and ran to greet him, hugging him around his knees. "Daddy! Do you have time to play with me today?"

"Not right now, angel, Daddy is taking a trip with your sister. Natalia has a meeting with Council, so you need to mind your mommy and behave. Can you manage that for me?"

Sophia sighed heavily, as she answered, "I guess so."

"Kate, Nattie requested to see Council. I asked Anya to get her ready. We shouldn't be long. Can you please do something with my hair, I need it tied back."

Kate pulled some leather strips from the dresser, as he sat on the side of the bed. She drew her hands through his hair and created a lose ponytail at the nape of his neck. "Natalia is going to Council? What's that about?"

"*Grazie, mi amore*. She asked to see the ledgers that hold the history of the Medici genealogy. I called Malachi and set up the appointment, to which he reluctantly consented."

Kate laughed softly. "I bet this is the first time Malachi has been summoned by a four-year-old." She kissed his neck, and nibbled on his ear, whispering, "Don't stay too long."

Sophia listened to the exchange. "Can I go too?"

He gave Kate a quick kiss before answering his daughter, "Not this time, Sophia. I don't think Malachi is prepared to handle the both of you." Shade stood and looked in the mirror, and then turned and smiled at Kate.

Sophia was starting to pout when Natalia entered wearing a dress, white ankle socks and patent leather shoes. Her hair had been brushed to a high sheen and held back with a bow that matched the color of her dress. Sophia stomped her foot. "How come she gets to dress up?"

Kate took her oldest daughter's hand. "Come on, Miss Thing. Let's see what we can get into tonight." Kate looked over her shoulder as she left the room with Sophia and addressed Shade, "You owe me one."

Shade winked at Kate and responded, "I owe you more than one, *mi amore*. I owe you more than I can ever repay."

Bending down on one knee, he took Natalia's hand. "Princess Natalia, will you please accompany me this evening to Council? It would be a great honor." He lifted her tiny hand to his lips and kissed it gently.

Natalia giggled. "You're like the man in the fairy tales, Daddy."

Shade cocked his head to the side. "Am I? Well that will be our little secret. Now, we are going to teleport, and you can hang on to me. It is a short trip. Can you manage that?"

She nodded her head as she wrapped her arms around his neck, and he lifted her up. With her head resting on his shoulders, he teleported her into the Council compound. Natalia had only seen pictures of the compound in the old books she found in the library. Still, she was caught off guard by the majesty of the large building, surrounded by high walls. A fortress, protected from the outside world, where the Council members would live out their entire lives. She was excited and eager to make this visit. There were no pictures of the Council members. She'd read they relinquished the names they were given at birth and assumed the age-old names that were assigned to each member who had worn the robe before them.

Shade landed gently, holding his smallest daughter in his arms. He could feel her excitement rolling through her. Sitting her down, he walked with her to the waiting room outside the Council chambers. "We will be announced and then led inside the chamber, Nattie. You will meet Malachi. Do not be frightened of his robe. All the Council members wear one. You must mind your manners, do not speak until spoken to."

Natalia nodded, she'd read that each Council member had a special area of responsibility, special gifts and skills that allowed them to rule their species, protecting the ancient traditions. Malachi was named for the malachite stone, the protection stone. Its green color represented life and growth, and was sometimes called the eye stone, believed to enhance great visionary powers. They were believed to provide for the security and protection of children. She had read it was for that protection that Malachi was present at the birth of any royal child.

She held her father's hand as he stood before the closed doors, waiting to be announced to Council. She heard the warrior call out their names, as another warrior opened the door for them to enter. She knew the warriors that served here were all trained in the camp at Castello, and like the Council, would serve here for life. As the huge doors swung open, her father led her down the wide carpeted aisle to the dais at the far end of the chamber. Seated behind the long table was Malachi.

Shade could feel a moment's hesitation from his daughter. "It is okay, Nattie, do you wish me to hold you?"

"No, Daddy. I'm big."

He pulled out a huge chair for her and lifted her onto the seat. She could barely see over the massive table, so she tucked her feet under her to give herself more height, as her father sat down next to her. Malachi waited patiently for the Medici and his daughter to get settled.

"I must say, Medici, this is a rare request. What is the purpose of your visit today?"

"*Grazie*, Malachi, for taking the time to see my daughter and me." Shade cleared his throat before proceeding. "Princess Natalia has requested to see the ledgers that contain the Medici ancestry. She is much interested in our lineage."

Malachi nodded his head and turned it in her direction. "Princess Natalia?"

Natalia's eyes were glued to the man in the green robe, his hood pulled forward so much of his face was in shadow. She spoke up, her voice echoing in the chamber. "Do you live here?"

Malachi nodded once and answered. "Indeed, child. The other council members and I reside here. It is rare for us to leave. What is it you wish to know?"

Natalia lifted herself up higher in her seat by rising to her knees. "I was looking at some books at Castello, and they said the Council keeps records of every vampire family. You have records of every birth and death that goes back for thousands of years. Do you have records for my family?"

Malachi nodded again. "Indeed. We not only keep records, we are present for the birth of any vampire born of royal blood, such as yourself."

Natalia looked back at him, trying to see his face without much success. "You were at my birth?"

Malachi had no idea where this line of questioning was going. He slipped the hood from his head, so he could face the child directly. "I was at your birth as well as your sister and brother, and I was there when your father was born, and your grandfather."

Natalia looked at him wide-eyed. He looked even older than Gi. "I was wondering if I could see the records, my whole family, as far back as your records go."

Malachi creased his brow and paused before he answered. He turned toward Shade to give his answer. "Medici, the Council is aware of the advanced intellect of this child, so I am not surprised by her curiosity. To that I would say, she will see the pattern, and what has been seen cannot be unseen. The records are not secret, and if you wish her to see them, then we will, of course, open the ledgers for her, but I would suggest we wait until she is older, perhaps approaching her puberty. It is your call."

Shade knew what pattern Malachi referred to. They held the one secret he had kept from Kate. When he first met her, he withheld the information because he didn't want to lose her. Now he feared she'd feel betrayed and trapped. If Natalia saw the pattern, he'd have to ask her to keep the information to herself. To hold the secret that he'd held was too heavy a burden to place on a child so young. Shade nodded to Malachi.

"Your guidance and advice are well taken. I do believe we shall wait until later in her life."

Shade turned to his daughter, placing his finger under her chin, he spoke softly to her. "Nattie, Malachi and I wish for you to see the ledgers when you are older. I promise you once older, we will return. Please understand I do not think it is the right time for you to view them, *si*?"

Natalia looked confused but nodded her head yes. She knew her father would keep his promise to her. "Okay, Daddy. Can I ask another question then?"

Shade nodded. "Of course, you can, Nattie. Malachi will answer whatever you wish, but you must remember, we cannot use a lot of his time."

Turning back to Malachi, Natalia addressed him again, "I read in the book at Castello you can tell what gifts a vampire has by tasting their blood. Is that true?"

Malachi nodded his head. "Yes, it is true. It is part of my gift. We generally wait for the gifts to manifest on their own, but there have been occasions where I was able to accurately taste the gift. I tasted your mother's blood at her coronation, after she was turned, and I was able to see she would have two gifts, day-walker and animalism. Is that what you wanted to know?"

The small girl nodded her head yes. "But I want to know my gift, and if I will also have two. Can you tell me, please? My brother and sister know their gifts already, and I want to know mine."

Again, Malachi looked to Shade for direction. "Medici? Do you wish this as well?"

Shade looked at his daughter with surprise. "Nattie, are you sure you want to know? I would think you would want your mommy with us when you discover these gifts. But if you wish it now, you may go to Malachi and he will tell you."

She nodded her head eagerly. "I want to know, Daddy."

Malachi summoned an assistant who brought him a scoring ring, and a chalice, and asked the child to approach. Natalia slid off the chair and scampered up the dais, holding out her arm to him. Malachi took her arm and scored her wrist, letting her thick, red blood run into the chalice. When he thought he had enough, he released her arm and told her to lick the wound. Natalia lifted her wrist to her mouth, careful not to let the blood drip on her dress. She tasted the metallic tang of her blood as she licked at the wound, and Malachi sent her back to her seat.

Eager to hear the answer to her question, she rushed back to her father, and climbed up in his lap, watching carefully as Malachi took his first sip. The old vampire closed his eyes, as her blood settled on his tongue and he let the visions come to him. He nodded his head once. "There will be two gifts."

Natalia turned to her father and beamed. She'd been hoping for two.

Malachi took another sip of her blood, again closing his eyes, savoring the taste. "You will have the gift of dream-walking."

Natalia clapped her hands. "Like you, Daddy!"

Shade beamed. "*Si*, my angel. I told you we are together in our dreams. Now, hush, let Malachi concentrate with his vision."

They both sat anxiously, waiting for Malachi to reveal her second gift.

Natalia leaned across the table, watching Malachi's face, eager to hear what her second gift would be. When Malachi opened his eyes, he almost laughed at the eagerness in her face.

"Your second gift will be the power of the Third Eye. It is my gift as well, young Natalia. It means you will be able to see into the future."

Natalia looked at him wide-eyed. "I can tell the future?"

Malachi hesitated. "Not exactly, child. I'm afraid it is more complicated than that. There will be things you see, flashes of information. You cannot summon it at will. So, you have no control over what you will see, or what you will not. For example, I know your brother Lorenzo will be a great warrior, and he will lead the coven with honor. He will fight and win many battles. But I can't see when those battles will occur, or who he is fighting. The details may or may not become clearer, as the events become closer in time. Do you understand? I must be careful, because while I have been given this gift to see into the future, it does not show me all. I must be careful not to assume I know the outcome of all things."

Natalia nodded her head yes. "Can you see my future?"

Malachi spoke softly, "I do, if you wish to hear it."

She nodded her head yes. "Yes, please."

Shade pulled Natalia closer, holding her to his chest. "Nattie, I am not sure it is wise for you to know what is to come." He felt his heart racing and wished *bel* was here.

Natalia returned his hug. "It's okay, Daddy. I want to know, really."

Shade looked in her eyes and knew she wouldn't be satisfied until she got her answer. He raised his eyes to Malachi and nodded.

Malachi proceeded to answer her. "I do not see great detail, child, for you are still very young, and your future is developing, but I know you will have a great impact on our species. You will have the power to change the course of our kind."

Natalia looked at him quizzically. "Like a warrior?"

Malachi shook his head no. "You will not live on the battlefield, like your father and brother. Your power comes not from a weapon, but from your intellect."

Natalia shrugged. "I don't know what that means."

Malachi gave her a soft smile. "And so, you see the blessing, and the curse, of this gift."

Natalia nodded, acknowledging his words. "But is it good? Do I change it for good?"

Malachi thought before he answered. "As you grow and learn to use these gifts that will be an easier question to answer. But you see the dilemma, yes? Because I have lived many years, and I know your family and the history of the Medici, I can assume the changes you bring will be good for our kind. But like you, I must wait and see. Our gifts can sometimes be a burden, child. Take your time, and do not jump to conclusions. You will become more skilled at interpreting what you see."

Natalia nodded. "I think it will be good. I wouldn't want for bad things to happen. Will I be able to taste other vampire's gifts, like you?"

He nodded yes. "That is part of the gift, yes."

Natalia appeared to give this some thought, and then gave a sharp nod. "Okay then."

Malachi waited to see if she had more to say, then asked, "Do you have any further questions?"

She shook her head. "Not today."

He held back a smile as he dismissed them. "Then we are adjourned here. Good night to you." He stood and pulled the hood of his green robe back over his head as he left the chamber.

Shade was so impressed with Natalia he couldn't speak. He sat there like a stone, trying to take in all that had happened in such a short period of time. He looked at Natalia, who seemed pleased and had a big smile on her face. "Did you get what you came for, Natalia?"

"Well, except for seeing the ledgers. But I'll wait for that. I'm a dream-walker, Daddy! Aren't you excited?"

Shade felt overjoyed with the blessing of this child, the happiness she displayed over her gifts. He'd always feared she'd be unhappy that she wasn't a day-walker, like her mother and her siblings, but she'd never complained. Lifting her in his arms, he held her high in the air. "Oh *si*, very excited. For once, I can help one of my children with their gift. We must travel home now. You will want to tell Mommy, *si*?"

She clung to his neck and kissed his cheek. "I can't wait to tell Mommy!"

7

Teleporting back to Castello with Natalia in his arms, Shade was proud of his daughter and how she'd conducted herself with Council. She was squirming with excitement at the knowledge of her gifts and could barely contain herself. As he landed in the grand foyer, Natalia wiggled free and started to run up the stairs, eager to tell her mother the news. Shade laughed at her excitement as he followed her up the stairs.

She rushed ahead to the door of her parents' bedroom, turning the doorknob and sticking her head inside to find her mommy napping. She felt her father step up behind her as she entered the room. Shade hated to wake her, but he knew he wouldn't be able to contain Natalia's excitement over this news.

He asked Natalia. "Should we wake Mommy, or let her sleep?"

Natalia was already running toward the bed. "Mommy wants to know now!"

Kate heard the ruckus in their bedroom and woke from her nap. She was taking advantage of these night hours when Sophia was asleep, and Lorenzo was in the camp. A quiet house was something she rarely experienced. As she sat up, Natalia scrambled onto the bed.

"Mommy, guess what?"

Shade followed the child across the room and sat down on the bed next to her. Kate smiled at her daughter. "Did you see the ledgers, Natalia?"

She shook her head no. "Malachi said I had to wait till I was older, so I didn't see them, but guess what else. I asked if he could taste my gifts and he said yes, so he tasted my blood."

Kate cast a quick glance in Shade's direction, trying to read the expression on his face, but he gave up nothing. They knew Natalia hadn't inherited the gift of day-walking like their other children, but she hadn't exhibited any signs of what her gifts would be yet. "And did he tell you, Natalia?"

She nodded her head, a smile spreading across her face. "Two gifts, Mommy. I'm a dream-walker, like Daddy."

The little girl was bouncing on the bed as Kate laughed. Natalia was always such a serious child. It was a pleasure to see her respond with such joyfulness. "That's wonderful! Your father can help you to channel that, like I can help Sophia with animalism. I think it is a perfect gift for you. And the other gift?"

Natalia beamed at her. "I have the Third Eye. I'll be able to see the future, but maybe not all of it. Malachi said it will take time for me to learn to interpret what I see. Isn't that exciting, Mommy?"

Kate kept the smile on her face but wondered if the gift of seeing into the future was really a blessing or a curse. But then, every gift seemed to have its drawbacks. "Very exciting."

"Can I go tell Theresa?"

Kate nodded. "Of course. She'll be excited to learn of your gifts."

The girl slid off the bed, and took off running across the bedroom, when Kate admonished her, "Be careful on these floors, Natalia, the marble is slippery."

"I know, Mommy," she answered, as she headed out the door and down the hallway.

After they were alone, Kate turned to Shade. "I thought she was going to see the ledgers on the Medici ancestry."

"Malachi thought perhaps it better if we wait until Nattie is older. She took it well. I was impressed with her questioning of Malachi. It was not an unproductive visit."

Kate listened to his explanation about delaying Natalia's exposure to the ledgers. "Does Malachi understand how advanced she is? She wouldn't have any problems deciphering the Medici family tree. She probably already knows more about the Medici's than the Council. I think they're not used to dealing with vampires as young as her. It's no big deal, I guess, the information will be there for her when she gets older. I'm glad we know her gifts. It may make it a little easier. Certainly, you'll be able to help her with dream-walking, but the Third Eye? I don't know a lot about it. I know Fiamma had it to a small degree. I guess we'll need to wait to see how Natalia's gift develops. How do you feel about it?"

Shade was relieved she didn't probe further into the reasons for delaying Natalia having access to the ledgers, but he too had mixed feelings about her second gift. He stood up from their bed and walked to the window, staring out into the night. He could feel her eyes as they stared at his back. Finding his voice, he answered her. "Fiamma had a version of the Third Eye. She could not truly see into the future, nothing like Malachi can. But she could see where a person was, as if looking through their eyes. She could describe in great detail the person's surrounding. She was an amazing warrior, *mi amore*, and I miss her. She would have loved our children."

He placed his open palm on the window, his sigh filling the room. "Nattie's Third Eye will be different, as she will see events in the future. She may not know the outcome of the event, or exactly when it is coming. Malachi warned her she would have no control over what was shown to her, and what remained hidden, but as she hones her skills, she will become more adept at interpreting what she is seeing. She will have to be strong of heart to manage such a gift."

Kate felt him wrestling with his own emotions over the news of this gift. "It sounds like a burden, Shade. I don't think it's always good to know what the future holds. Can she change the future? If Natalia had been alive when Cory and Madison were abducted, if she'd seen that event, could we have prevented it?"

Shade hung his head, shaking it. "No, *mi amore*, she cannot change the outcome, nor can she prevent it. It will happen no matter. She is like the herald. She can only give a warning to help those it affects. Do you understand?"

She nodded her head. "So, maybe you could've gotten to California earlier, maybe it would've been easier to find them, but you couldn't stop Max from taking them. He would have found a way, if not that day, then another day. This means our child will see many things, some good, and some very bad, and she'll have to live with the fact she can't stop these things from happening. She'll be able to give us an early warning, so we're better prepared, maybe limit the damage. That's what you're telling me?"

Shade turned to her and could tell from her expression she felt his unease with Natalia's gift. Returning to the bed, he knelt before her, his hands on either side of her legs as she sat on the side of the bed. Laying his head in her lap, he told her what he knew.

"I don't know. Malachi is the only one I have ever met with this gift. Nattie is so intelligent, far above others her age. It is possible she could do more with her gift. Our children all have such rare gifts; fire-thrower, animalism, and now the Third Eye, and with them come great power. It puts all our children in great danger and makes them targets for others. I do not tell you this to scare you. They are strong, or these gifts would not have been bestowed upon them. It is the power of our blood together that has produced these gifts in our children. They will each learn to harness the power of their gifts for the protection of the coven." He snuggled into her lap, as his arms went around her waist, holding her tight. "I love them so damn much."

She hadn't considered her children would be in danger from others as a result of their gifts. She'd always felt concern for how they'd manage them, learn to control them. To hear him speak of them as targets immediately brought her beast to the surface. Her babies! No one would fucking hurt her babies.

"I'll tell you this, Shade, as long as I draw a breath, no harm will come to these children. There is no master I'll not stand toe-to-toe with and no warrior fierce enough to break through my defense of them. No one. Do you hear me?"

She stood up from the bed, walking away from him. How did this get so complicated? She already had concerns about leaving Lorenzo in the camp, living here alone, without her, without Shade, or the protection of Luca. "Lorenzo needs a new protector. Before we leave, I want it done. I want the protector inside Castello when Lorenzo is here. I won't leave here until it's done."

Shade rose from his knees as she barked her commands to him. "Lorenzo is now a warrior, *mi amore*. *Cazzo*, he is in the middle of the damn camp. This place is not easily penetrated by anyone. You cannot be serious? Will you stop this train of thought and think about how this will make him feel, having a protector when he is now a warrior?" He threw up his hands as he paced around the room. "You need to accept the fact he is now a warrior, Kate, no longer your baby."

Kate turned quickly to face him; her hands balled into fists. "There is a camp at Bel Rosso, and he had you at Bel Rosso, as well as Luca. What's different? He's a prince, and the heir to this coven. He has a rare gift that makes him a powerful threat. He's the son of the warrior's warrior! Don't tell me what he needs and doesn't need! He's not yet a warrior, and he'll always be my child. He's not some pawn to be moved around on the chess board just to increase the size of your kingdom. When you lived here, you came home to your father. He'll come home to nothing!"

Shade stopped pacing and locked eyes with her. "Understand this! I would never use any of our children as a pawn. This is our coven, and they protect all of us. They will fight long and hard to get through me before any fucking bastard is able to get near any of the children. The coven reveres the children, and understands their future lies in their survival. And the day Lorenzo walked into this camp, he became a warrior, plain and simple. He now rules here. This is his home, no longer mine. He will reign here. It is what he was born to do. He will never again live at Bel Rosso, woman, so you better fucking get that through your head. He belongs here now. A warrior does not have a protector. He will build a bond of brotherhood with his fellow warriors. Assigning him a protector sends a message he is weak. That he is not able to rise to power. Is that what you want? I am your king and master, and I still rule here. You will not do this to him, Kate. No!"

She was taken aback by his anger. They had never fought like this. They rarely fought at all since the early years when she was learning to adjust to this life. She covered her face with her hands and sobbed. He was her mate, and her master, but was this the right choice for their son? She'd known, since the day Lorenzo was born, that this was his destiny. He'd train at Castello, live at Castello, and she knew it would be hard to leave him. She'd hoped that ten years of preparing would have made it easier. Their children had led such secluded lives, never out of their view, or protection. She felt like her heart was breaking.

"Lover, this is so hard."

The anger left him immediately, as he felt her heart breaking. He opened his arms to her. "Kate, you knew from the beginning this was his fate. Our son is a warrior, he will kill, and he will destroy and conquer. Just like me. I am sorry but he belongs to the coven now. And you must trust the coven we have built and protected to now protect our son. Lorenzo will rise to rule and lead them, as will his sons. I'm sorry."

She allowed herself to be embraced by him, to feel the protection that always came from being held by him. She'd been tested many times, and now she must make the ultimate leap of faith, and leave her son behind, placing her trust in the coven.

Laying her head against his chest, the tears still on her cheeks, her throat felt tight with emotion. "Tell me he'll be okay."

Rubbing her back, he swayed with her softly. He'd done this so many times to calm her, assure her to trust his judgment. "Relax. I cannot promise you he will never be scared. But I can tell you he has some of the fiercest warriors in the world at his disposal. Marco, and every warrior in this camp, will die for him. Nothing will get near him, *mi amore*. He is a Medici. That name alone strikes fear in the most hardened masters across this world. They fuck with our son, they fuck with us, and no master is that damn stupid. If they are, they will soon lose. Have we not proven that already? *Si*, he will miss us, and we will miss him. It is time to let go, *bel*."

She closed her eyes as he rocked her back and forth, his voice softer now, as he calmed her. She wiped away the tears and nodded her head. "I'll do as you ask. If you say he doesn't need a protector, then I'll accept that. I told you to lead, and I'd follow."

"*Si, mi amore*, just remember, when the burden becomes too heavy to bear, I will carry you. My death slumber calls me. Come sleep next to me, like in the beginning, when it was just your savage lover and his lily-white."

8

Lying in bed, staring at the ceiling in his bedroom in Castello, Luca was lost in thought. He felt Shannon roll over, curling into him, and her arm sliding across his chest, as he softly kissed the top of her head. He'd turned her not quite a year after Natalia's birth, knowing there'd be no more babies for Kate and Shade. She'd been mated to him through the blood covenant since right after Sophia's birth, six years ago, but they'd waited another two years until Natalia's birth before he turned her.

Shade had come to him to feed during each of Kate's pregnancies, which meant he wouldn't have been able to feed Shannon as well. They'd wanted to avoid further complicating the relationship by having to force Shannon to go to a feeder when Luca made himself available to Shade. They'd made a lot of sacrifices to be together, and he acknowledged her burdens had been greater than his. He didn't regret his choices, and he'd worked hard to make sure she had never regretted hers. He couldn't have asked for a better mate or a better life for himself. His role as protector to the queen and her off-spring grew over the years as the children had arrived. Protecting Kate was crucial, but protecting the children born of royal blood, who'd ensure the future of their coven and the continuation of the Medici legacy, was vital for the survival of them all.

After ten years, he was about to give up some of that responsibility, at least on a full-time basis. They'd all be going back to Bel Rosso soon, and leaving Lorenzo behind. He'd been responsible for Lorenzo's safety from the day of his birth, and now he must turn him over to Marco. He knew the prince would have visits back to the States, but for most of the time, he'd live here in Florence, train to become a warrior, and remain under Marco's protection. He had no reservations about that. He knew Marco had the responsibility for every boy in the camp, but this was different. When Luca had grown up in the camp, he'd been personally trained by Shade. It was Shade who'd taken him under his wing, and Luca knew he'd always been given special attention, and had advanced further than the other warriors because of it. It was one of the many reasons he remained so loyal to his master. Even now, he lived inside Bel Rosso with a mate of his choosing, instead of the lonely life of most warriors who lived in the barracks and sought out feeders.

Luca couldn't help but have mixed feelings about letting go of some responsibilities, and he was wondering if Marco was up for the challenge. He knew he wouldn't sleep until he got this off his chest. He slid from the bed, trying not to wake her, but Shannon lifted her head from her pillow, her eyes heavy with sleep. "Is everything okay?"

He kissed her soft lips, running his hand through her thick mop of brown hair. "Shh, *mia belleza*. I'm going to the camp to speak with Marco. I'll be back shortly. Go back to sleep."

She nuzzled back into the pillow, as he tucked the blankets around her. Pulling on jeans and a sweater, he sat on the side of the bed and laced up his boots, listening to the soft sounds of her breathing. He kissed her cheek one last time, before teleporting out to the camp. Landing on the training field, among warriors of all ages, engaged in a variety of weapon training exercises, he scanned the field. It was easy to spot Marco, barking out orders, as his lieutenants scrambled to break up the warriors into smaller groups by age and skill level. Luca approached slowly, waiting for an appropriate break in the action to approach him. When Marco looked up, Luca was lighting up a cigarette, and offered the pack to Marco.

"Got a minute, brother?"

Marco banged the pack of smokes at the base of his hand, and then lifted the pack to his lips, slipping one of the cigarettes between his teeth. He handed the pack back to Luca and lit up. "What the hell is eating you? I know you well enough. You aren't here to inquire about my health. I bet standing on this sacred ground brings back memories."

Luca smiled as he looked at the training field, and the memories of his own time spent here flashed through his head. "It doesn't seem like that long ago, brother. I remember it well, my life in the barracks, and the hours on this very field. I wouldn't trade those years for anything, yet I'm glad they're behind me. Can we walk to the barracks?"

Marco grunted, as he turned in the direction of the barracks and Luca dropped in beside him. "You looking for some peace and quiet away from the *bambinos*?"

Luca drew deeply on the cigarette and exhaled, as the smoke escaped his lips, catching the wind. Luca chuckled. "Oh, they can drive you mad sometimes, no doubt. But they're good children. I know Shade has used a lighter hand with his children than his father used with him, but he and our queen make sure they each understand their greater responsibilities to the coven. It's a burden they've carried since birth, and none greater than Lorenzo. He lives in the shadow of a great warrior, and he'll always feel the pressure to be as good as his father. We've all helped him in the camp at Bel Rosso, preparing him for this day; Shade, Marcello, Skelk, myself. All of us have spent long hours with him, helping him gain confidence and master skills that would give him an edge when he got here. Shade understood more would be expected of him, and the other children would look at him to outperform. It's not an easy path for our prince, Marco."

Marco listened as they walked, wondering where in the hell this was going. As they entered the barracks, they walked to Marco's office. Marco pointed to the chair opposite his desk and pulled out a bottle of Midnight from the desk drawer. He opened it and took a swig, no glasses needed. This was a fucking warrior camp, not the castle. He flopped down in the worn leather chair and shoved the bottle toward Luca.

"You don't have to fucking lecture me about the prince. I trained and battled alongside Shade most of my life. He was a prince once too. Christofano was a bull-headed son of a bitch when it came to Shade, he'd cut him down to nothing. Made him the warrior he is today. But what the hell is eating at you, brother? You got a plush assignment, so you'll get no sympathy from me. Get to the damn point." Marco sat back in his chair and stared at Luca hard.

"I'm not here to complain about my position, brother. I'll gladly serve my master until I draw my last breath. I'll give up my life for him, our queen, or any of their children. I know Shade's father raised him with a heavy hand. I wasn't alive then, but I've heard the stories, but the point is, his father was here, as was his mother. When Shade was a boy, and he finished up in the camp every night, he went back to Castello, to the comfort of family. Times were different then. Children were raised differently. It was a harsher time, and the children had to survive it.

"Lorenzo, for all the extra training he's had, has been raised with gentle guidance. When we leave here, Lorenzo will return to Castello every morning, not to his parents, to me, and to Shannon. He won't have his family around him like Shade did. He'll return to a castle full of servants. He's always known the comfort that comes from seeking out his family. I know your style, Marco, and you have an unblemished reputation for turning out warriors of the highest caliber, or our master wouldn't have you here. But I think you need to be aware, at least, that Lorenzo's circumstances will be different, and in some ways, more difficult than what Shade endured."

Marco crossed his arms over his chest, leaning back in his chair, as he laughed out loud. "Well, let me put it to you this way, Luca. Every single warrior that comes through this camp is my responsibility. It's my job to make sure the bastards keep their heads. Lorenzo is now in my hands. Don't ever think Shade won't be on top of it either. He may be going back to Bel Rosso, but I assure you, he'll be checking up on Lorenzo's progress weekly, if not more often. Give the boy credit. Medici blood runs through his veins and a little fire from his mother too. Lorenzo will be fine. Shade was challenged early and had to step into his father's shoes way too soon, but he rose to the challenge. Lorenzo will face his own challenges, and he too will rise to conquer them. I got his back, brother. But I'm not going to make it easy on him."

Luca tipped back the bottle of Midnight, tasting the sweetness of the grape, and the jolt of the blood, as it slid across his tongue. He knew Marco understood his responsibility here. He'd probably lost count of the number of warriors who'd been trained by his hand.

"Sorry, brother, I'm finding it hard to let go of him. He's been my responsibility for ten years, living under the same roof with him. He calls me uncle. Perhaps I'm the one who needs reassurance, *si?*"

Marco looked at Luca, and recalled his years here in the camp, and how quickly he excelled and responded to Shade's tutelage. He'd turned out to be one of the best. *Cazzo, where did the time go?* "Our prince was born of a warrior and carries those instincts inside him. Just like you. Go home, take care of the females and your king. Don't worry about Lorenzo. This is a brotherhood. Lorenzo needs to be here to develop and understand that bond."

"You're right, brother. He's in good hands. Can't help but worry about him, you know. I love him like he's my own." Standing up to leave, Luca tossed the pack of cigarettes into Marco's lap. "Here you go. I know how much more you appreciate a cigarette when it didn't come from your own pocket, you cheap bastard. Now take good care of my boy."

Luca left the barracks and breathed in the cool night air before teleporting back to his bedroom, and his mate.

9

Castello was abuzz with activity as everyone was packing and getting ready to go back home to Virginia, all except Lorenzo and his feeder, Nita. The servants were running from room to room, completing their assigned tasks. Shade always left coordinating their departure to Kate. They'd been here many times, and she knew what she wanted, and how she wanted it done, and he felt like he was just under foot. They were both trying to keep busy, and not focus on the fact they'd be leaving their son behind. After their argument, he knew *bel* understood there was no need for Lorenzo to have a protector, but he could tell she was putting on a brave face and throwing herself into the business of packing up this crew and getting them all home. He easily made his escape from the chaos around him and went to Lorenzo's room, tapping lightly on the closed door. He couldn't leave without making sure his little warrior was going to be all right.

Lorenzo had retreated to his bedroom to escape the chaos. He knew they were all leaving to go back to Bel Rosso, the only home he'd ever known. How many times had he been part of that chaos of packing and preparing to leave, listening to his father complain about flying? It was less painful to hide away in his room, and not watch them all as they hurried about. He stood at the window that looked out over the formal gardens, with the camp in the distance. This was his home now. He blinked back his tears, as he heard a tap at the door. Quickly wiping his eyes, he called out, "Come in."

Shade entered to find his son standing at the window. Closing the door behind him, he stepped into the room, walking to stand behind Lorenzo and laying his hands on his shoulders. "It helps you think looking out at all that is Medici, *si?*"

Lorenzo nodded. "I guess so. I don't really think of it as mine, though. I mean, I didn't really earn it, I inherited it. There's a difference, Dad. I have a lot to prove. I just hope I'm up for the challenge."

Shade chuckled. "*Si*, you inherited it, but you also earned it through your birthright. You will earn it through your performance in camp. It will seem like a long journey, son, but when you walk out of it, you will know who you are. It is a rite of passage. We have all been through it. You have nothing to prove to anyone, but yourself. This journey is as much about learning the skills of a warrior as it is about discovering who you are. Make the most of it, it won't be easy. Nor should it be."

Lorenzo stared back at him with wisdom well beyond his ten years. "I don't want it to be easy. I already hear the whispers of the other boys. They know I grew up with a privileged life and being born Medici is just my luck of the draw. I'm no better than them, and yet, I'll have to find a way to set myself apart, earn their respect, so they'll follow out of loyalty, not obligation. That's what you did. Now it's my time to figure this out. I don't want to let you down, or the coven. I know there are a lot of people depending on me."

Shade ruffled the top of his curly head. "My little warrior, you already seem to have grown up right before my eyes. This is not easy for me either. And do not worry about what others say about you. It is of no concern. Earning respect comes with time, and from your actions. It comes from the respect you show others. It comes from the respect you have for yourself. Part of camp is making the mistakes here instead of when your life depends on it outside these walls. Marco can take any damn vampire and teach him skills of warfare. It takes what is inside your heart and soul to make you a warrior. You need to forget, for now, about your obligation to the coven. Concentrate on you. No one will ever let you forget you are Medici, especially your brothers. But as the days turn into years, you will grow into your role, and they will stop the teasing and begin to follow. Bond with your brothers in the camp, and that includes fights, taunts, and everything that comes with growing up."

Shade took him in his arms and hugged him. "I'm not really leaving you, Lorenzo, so don't shut me out. You can call me whenever you need me. I can teleport here if you need me for anything. I need you to understand that, *si?*"

Lorenzo accepted his father's hug. "I know that, Dad. I've always known it. I promise not to let you down."

Shade pulled back from his son and looked him in the eyes. "You cannot let me down, Lorenzo. You are my son, and I will love you no matter what. Loving you is not something I can ever turn off. *Cazzo*, I will miss you. Do you want to ask me anything?"

Lorenzo thought for a moment if he'd left anything unsaid and shook his head. "I told Mommy to keep my room for me at Bel Rosso, okay? So, I can visit?"

Shade grinned. "Of course. And besides, I don't think your mother would have it any other way." Shade leaned down and kissed one cheek and then the other. "I love you, Lorenzo. Just be yourself. You've already won many hearts, without even knowing it. I am proud and I look forward to the day we fight side by side. *Per sempre* Medici!"

Walking to the door, Shade opened it and stepped outside, closing the door behind him. He leaned against the wall, his hands over his face. He'd waited so long for this day to come, for his son to join the camp, and begin his training, but he'd never expected it to be this hard. He teleported to camp and went in search of Marco.

Lorenzo stood in the quiet of his room after his father left. His head was filled with the memories of years of walking to the camp in Bel Rosso, holding his father's hand, learning to handle the sword under his father's direction. His father had been a strong and ever-present influence in his life, and he wasn't sure he liked this feeling of independence. Opening his bedroom door, he stepped into the hallway, with servants rushing past him, carrying luggage and boxes that would be taken to the private plane, the plane that wouldn't be taking Lorenzo with them this time. Walking down the hall, dodging the activity, he wandered into his parents' bedroom to find his mother, holding a checklist in her hand, as she marked off the tasks that needed to be taken care of before they left.

"Mommy?"

Kate heard her son and spun around to face him. "Lorenzo! Are you okay?"

He nodded his head yes, but his face said otherwise. She knelt down, opened her arms and he ran to her. In the camp, he felt almost like a man, holding his own against the warriors in training, but here, he was just a boy.

Kate held him tight, wondering where the time had gone. "I'll miss you, my beautiful boy."

He squeezed her tight. "I'll miss you, Mommy."

Gripping his shoulders, she held him away from her. "You're going to be okay, Lorenzo. You're strong and brave, like your father. You're like him in so many ways. You've been schooled by Enzo, and trained at the hand of your father, as well as Luca, Skelk and Marcello. Your father made sure, from the day you were born, you were being prepared for this day. Never doubt yourself. Never doubt what you can achieve. And even though we are separated by the miles, we're family. You're my son and will always be my son. I couldn't love you more if I tried."

She kissed his forehead as he nodded and responded in a soft whisper, "I love you too, Mommy."

She stood and took his hand. "Would you like to escort me downstairs? You can say goodbye to the family one last time." He nodded, as they walked together down the hall and down the large staircase into the grand foyer, filled with people and luggage, and lots of noise. Shannon was the first to look up and see them come down the stairs.

She smiled softly at him and moved to the bottom of the stairs to give him a hug. She whispered to him, "Do me a favor, and raise a little hell while you're here, okay? This place could use some livening up." Lorenzo laughed and told her he would.

Luca stepped up behind her and waited his turn. As Shannon stepped aside, Luca knelt, so he was eye-level with the boy. Luca locked eyes with him. "On the day of your mother's coronation, I took an oath to protect her, and her children. I took her blood, and that oath is as solid today as it was then. I'll protect you with my life, brother, with my life."

Lorenzo blinked several times. This was the first time Luca had called him brother, and the significance wasn't lost on him. Luca stood quickly, not wanting the boy to feel overcome with emotion, and spoke to Kate, "I think we're ready here. This is the last load to be taken to the plane."

As Luca moved away, Theresa stepped forward, and Lorenzo fell into her arms. He'd fed from her, and she'd slept in his room until Sophia was born. She'd been as much a part of his life as his parents had been. "I love you, Theresa."

She held him tight and fought back her tears as she answered him, "And I love you, my Prince. Now go make us proud." She stood and hurried away, gathering up luggage and carrying it outside.

Lorenzo walked across the foyer, weaving his way around the boxes, looking for his sisters. Natalia was sitting quietly, holding a book from the Castello library she planned to take back home. She looked up as he approached and flashed him a bright smile. "Are you excited, Lorenzo?"

He nodded. "Sort of. I'll miss you, though." He leaned down and gave her a hug, which she returned.

"I'll miss you too. But Mommy says you'll get to come home to visit, and we'll still come back here. It will be okay."

He nodded and looked around the room. "Where's Sophia?"

Natalia shrugged. "Who knows?"

Lorenzo looked confused, as he looked across the grand foyer, and didn't see her anywhere. He headed down the long hallway of ancestors, looking into the many rooms, trying to find her when he picked up her scent and followed it. Past the grand ballroom, lay the throne room, which remained locked except for coronations and other rare occasions, like royal births. He noticed the large double doors were ajar and peeked inside. Seated on her father's throne, wearing her mother's crown, was Sophia. She held a solid gold scepter in her hand and was addressing an invisible crowd.

"From this day forward, you will kneel when I pass, and place your forehead on the floor. You will not make eye contact with the Queen!"

Her voice echoed in the room. Lorenzo pushed the door open, and the loud creak made her jump. "Lorenzo!"

He shook his head, trying not to laugh. "Sophia, this room is off limits, and I know for sure that crown is off limits. If Dad finds you in here, you'll be in time out until you're thirty!"

She slid off the huge throne, and the priceless crown almost toppled from her head. She caught it with one hand, trying to balance the scepter in the other. "Don't you tell, Lorenzo. Don't you dare tell!"

Shade and Marco had come from the camp and were walking through the long hallway back to the foyer. Shade slapped Marco on the back. "You better take care of him or I will bust your ass from here to hell and back!"

Marco chuckled, as they both had shared a few Midnights. "Take it easy, old man. I value my balls too much. Your son will be safe here."

As they passed the throne room, they heard the last of the conversation between Lorenzo and Sophia. Shade grabbed the double doors and flung them open wide, hearing them slam against the walls. Both of his children turned and gave him startled looks. Shade strode forcefully to the front of the grand room, where the thrones were situated, standing over his daughter.

"Lorenzo doesn't have to tell on you, princess, you told on yourself. You know very well, this room is off limits, as well as the vault you have clearly raided again. Put the crown and scepter on the throne, right now!"

Sophia startled when she heard the doors bang open, and Lorenzo backed away, as his father marched up the center aisle of the huge room. Sophia listened to her father's admonishments and figured she was already in trouble, so why not go for it. "Did you hear me? I said you must bow down. Do not look at me!"

"Oh, I will look at you as much as I damn well please, female! You have broken more rules in one hour than Lorenzo has his entire life. It is about time that brazen attitude of yours is set straight. Speak to me like that again and you won't sit down for a week, so I suggest you do as your king and master commands, or you are in for a fight. I have backup."

Shade turned to Marco, who closed the doors and stood spread-legged baring any exit, when Shade shouted, "What's it going to be?"

Sophia looked at Marco, who was guarding the door, his face stern. She knew she'd pushed it too far this time. She put the crown and the scepter on the seat of the throne. "Just kidding. Jeez, chill out will ya?"

Shade towered over her. "No one threatens me, princess, not even you. You want to take on the Medici King? I suggest you rein in that mouth or you will lose your tongue. Now, move it to the foyer. No side trips. Move!"

Sophia stomped her way to the door and Marco stared her down, and then opened the door for her. She marched out with head held high and started skipping down the hall. The old warrior bent over, roaring with laughter. "I've never seen a female you couldn't handle, but I do believe she is the first one to challenge your ass."

Lorenzo remained quiet and followed his father and Marco down the hall. Shade sighed. "*Cazzo*, she'll be the fucking death of me!"

10

Lorenzo stood with his manservant, Carlos, outside of Castello as his family loaded into the cars. The first car held Luca, Shannon, Theresa, Ghita and Anya. As it slowly pulled away, Lorenzo watched as Luca saluted him and Shannon blew kisses. He saw Theresa wipe away tears before waving goodbye. He waved at them and forced himself to put a smile on his face. The second car, driven by Dante, turned in the driveway before pulling away. Natalia smiled and waved, as Sophia smashed her face against the glass, making a face that made him laugh despite himself. He waved to his sisters and called out goodbye. He caught his father's eye and held it, as Shade spoke to him telepathically. "**Be strong, my little warrior.**"

He nodded in acknowledgement before looking at his mother. She was biting her lip and put the palm of her hand against the glass, as Lorenzo read her lips. "I love you, my beautiful boy."

He reached out his hand and placed it over hers on the window. "I love you, Mom."

The car pulled away, and he followed it with his eyes. He could see Sophia bouncing in her seat, and his father trying to settle her down, but his mother turned her head and looked back at him and held his gaze until the car was no longer visible to him. He swallowed hard, as he turned to go back inside, Carlos beside him. He knew Carlos would be with him now for the rest of his life, just as Gi served his dad.

Carlos rushed ahead and opened the massive door. Lorenzo stepped inside to the grand foyer, and for the first time in his life, he was here alone. He knew the castle was filled with servants, but they'd remain invisible to him unless summoned.

Carlos stood nearby. "Is there anything I can do for you, master?"

It took the boy a moment to realize Carlos was speaking to him. It was the first time he'd been addressed as master. He was the master here now. He shook his head no. "No thank you, Carlos. I think I'm going to the camp for the night."

***

Marco had all the warriors on the field, the young grunts, the juniors, and the seasoned seniors, working them hard. There was no sign of Lorenzo, but he wasn't expecting him tonight. He was aware that Shade and his family were leaving for the States, and Lorenzo would be left behind for the first time. Marco had the warriors split into groups by age, as they each tackled different skill sets. He couldn't help but notice Alfie was constantly looking in the direction of Castello, keeping his eyes open for Lorenzo. Alfie had taken Lorenzo under his wing, and with each visit over the years, the two boys had grown closer, despite their age gap. Lorenzo would enter the camp as a 'grunt', along with all the other ten-year-old kids. Alfie had already advanced to the juniors and was sixteen now. Marco caught some movement from the side of the long training field and looked up to see Lorenzo. He threw up his hand in acknowledgement and walked over to the perimeter of the field to greet the boy. He lit up a smoke as he approached Lorenzo, who was already dressed in his leathers and boots.

"Bored already, son?"

Lorenzo saw Marco approach and stood taller, pushing out his chest, as he carried the sword that once belonged to his father. "Not bored. I just didn't want to stay in Castello by myself. Not yet, anyway. Better to keep busy. Do you have an assignment for me?"

Marco glanced at him sideways and shook his head. *Cazzo*, if the kid didn't look just like Shade when he was at camp, that mop of black hair and his damn chest puffed out. "I know your father has trained you on the sword, but let's see what Skelk has taught you on the crossbow. Alfie is a damn good shot, but I will make you a bet, if you're the gambling type, warrior."

Lorenzo was glad for the distraction, and glad Marco wasn't ribbing him about being lonely already. "I'll take that bet. What do you want me to do?"

"Alfie has some years on you, are you willing to take him on with the crossbow? Let's see you go head to head. I'll set up the targets for 50-yards, and we'll see which of you can hit six out of six shots dead center. If you can beat him, you choose, either you can stay here one night in the barracks or Alfie can go to Castello. If Alfie wins, we let him choose the prize. You think you can handle that, warrior?"

Lorenzo nodded his head. Between his father training him with a sword and Skelk training him on crossbow, he knew his skills were much more advanced than the other boys in his group. But Alfie was a junior and had been in the camp six years already. Still, Lorenzo was ready to bet no one here had crossbow skills like Skelk. He knew he'd learned from the best. "You're on!"

Marco fist bumped Lorenzo. Walking onto the field, he halted the activities. "Listen up, you grunts. I've laid down a challenge for Lorenzo to go up against Alfie with a crossbow at 50-yards. Best six out of six wins."

Marco didn't miss the smirk on Alfie's face. "I wouldn't be too damn sure of yourself Alfie, the grunt can shoot."

Alfie moved to the center of the field as the other warriors, grunts and juniors surrounded them to watch. Marco grabbed the crossbow from Vanni and handed it to Lorenzo with six arrows. "Show us what you got, grunt!"

Vanni bristled when his bow was taken for the prince but knew better than to say anything in front of Marco. He'd been resentful of the prince's presence since the first night he'd arrived, and Vanni had challenged him in the exercise with the tossing swords. Lorenzo took the crossbow, and moved to the center of the field, joining Alfie. Alfie greeted him with a hardy slap on the back.

"You go first, Alfie, so I can see what I'm up against."

Alfie laughed. "No problem, brother."

Alfie took his stance in front of his target and pulled a bow from his quiver, taking careful aim. The young teen got serious and focused his attention, as he fired the first arrow, hearing it whistle in the air as it flew toward the target, hitting the bullseye with a solid thud. Alfie looked over at Lorenzo and winked. "Piece of cake, brother."

Lorenzo smiled back at him. "Five more to go, Alfie, don't count your winnings yet."

Marco stood back and watched. He wasn't worried. The prince had been personally trained by the best crossbow warrior he'd ever laid eyes on, and he was damn sure the queen put her two cents in as well. Marco expected Lorenzo to take this challenge easily, and he knew Alfie could take the ribbing he'd inevitably get from his brothers if he lost. He liked how Lorenzo worked with the older warriors. He teased them as well, but he didn't display a false bravado. He was fucking Medici to the bone.

Alfie proceeded to fire the next four arrows with precision, but the final arrow was caught by the wind, and landed in the outer ring of the target. Alfie muttered '*cazzo*' under his breath as he stepped aside.

Lorenzo shook his head. "Tough break."

He wore his hair longer than his father, and the wind caught it and blew it across his face. Reaching into his pocket, he pulled out a leather strip and tied his hair back in a loose ponytail so it wouldn't be a distraction. "Always compensate for the wind, or the rain, brother. Skelk taught me that."

Stepping in front of his target, Lorenzo knew he must deliver now. Skelk also taught him not to trash talk unless you could walk the walk, or the experience would be humbling. Pulling his first arrow from the quiver, he took careful aim, measuring the impact of the wind gusts, and let his arrow fly. It landed dead center of the bullseye. Lorenzo had done this a thousand times, as Skelk drilled into him that practice was the only path to perfection, and there was no substitute for hard work when it came to mastering a skill. Alfie nodded in approval but reminded him he had five more shots to go. Lorenzo placed the next arrow in the crossbow and took careful aim, firing once again, as the second arrow split the first arrow, and he heard a collective gasp from the young warriors watching them.

Alfie laughed. "Lucky shot!"

Lorenzo kicked his boot in the dusty ground, before looking up. "I don't believe in luck." Pulling his third arrow from his quiver, he fired the arrow, splitting the second arrow, as it fell to the ground. Again, he heard the murmuring of the young warriors as they watched their new prince.

Alfie laughed out loud. "Damn, brother, I've been set up!"

Lorenzo smiled at him as he quickly fired shots four and five, then pulled the final arrow from his quiver. He twirled the arrow in his hand, the way a drummer twirls a drumstick, before loading it in the crossbow and taking his final shot, landing all six in the bull's-eye.

Alfie slapped him on the back. "Makes me glad I'm an ally and not an enemy. I especially like that rock star move at the end."

Lorenzo laughed. "Skelk taught me that. He also taught me if I spend too much time showing off, I could get my ass beat."

Marco knew Lorenzo would be good but *cazzo*, the kid knocked it out of the fucking park. The reaction from the grunts didn't escape his notice either. Walking out to the middle of the field, the warriors were all crowding around the target to get a closer look.

"Enough gawking. Break it up and get back to work. Alfie, Lorenzo, come with me." As the warriors moaned, Marco barked loud and clear. "If I hear that bullshit one more time, you'll be doing twenty laps around the training field before you sleep."

Taking the two boys aside, he looked at Lorenzo. "Good job, Lorenzo. Now, tell Alfie what the bet was. You won hands down, grunt."

Lorenzo hoped Alfie would be excited about the bet. "Marco told me if I won, I could invite you to stay over at Castello in the morning, instead of you going back to the barracks. But I won't hold you to it if you don't want to."

Alfie looked at him wide-eyed. "Are you kidding? That would be awesome, brother!"

Lorenzo beamed back at him. "I know it's just sleeping there, and I'll still have to go to class, but I've got some video games. My brother Cory taught me a lot of video games."

Alfie had never been inside Castello, and was eager for a break from the monotony, and lack of privacy from the barracks. "Dude! It'll be great, are you kidding?"

Marco shook his head at the two of them, sometimes forgetting they were still kids. "Enough blathering like girls, get your asses back on the field. I want both of you on this damn field warming up tomorrow night before my old ass gets out here. And Alfie, get back in time to feed, you need to replenish. Lorenzo, before you got here, we were working swords. Have someone in the juniors set it up for you. Now move, the pair of you!"

The two boys hurried to take up their next assignment, as the other young warriors returned to the field. Lorenzo carried the crossbow back to Vanni and handed him the bow. "Thanks, brother."

Vanni snorted, grabbing the crossbow and jerking it hard from his hand. "You aren't a brother yet, spoiled little prince."

Lorenzo was caught off guard, as the junior yanked the bow from his hand, flinging the insult in his face. His father had warned him he'd meet with opposition, and he'd have to prove his worth. He knew he'd been raised in a life of privilege, and not every boy here came from homes that offered many advantages. It stung to think they saw him as spoiled. He'd worked hard at his skills, but he bit his tongue, and took a deep breath, letting the slur slide off his back, before returning to the task Marco had assigned.

11

They had been home for a month now, and Kate had secretly Skyped with Lorenzo every day. Shade had asked her to give him space and let him get used to being on his own, but she'd had a hard time cutting the apron strings. He was doing well and was making friends with Alfie. Alfie went up to the castle to stay with him a few nights each week, and she knew Lorenzo occasionally stayed in the barracks. He seemed to be adjusting well and seemed excited about the skills he was learning. He'd had a few run-ins with one of the juniors, but said it was nothing he couldn't handle. Kate heard Shade enter the house, returning from the camp as the sunrise approached, and she quickly blew a kiss to Lorenzo and closed the laptop, pushing it aside just as Shade entered the bedroom.

Shade started stripping from his leathers as he came through the door. Flopping down in the armchair, he unlaced and kicked off his boots. "So, what were you doing on the laptop this time of morning?" He strolled to her, buck ass naked, giving her a look that usually sparked more than her blood.

"I was checking market prices on sunflower oil. Everything has been harvested. Shannon said we had an exceptional crop this year. She's working on some sunflower bath products to add to the line." Technically, it wasn't a lie, as Kate rationalized her response. She had been checking market prices before she'd Skyped with Lorenzo. "And how was your night?"

Chuckling, he rolled his eyes and climbed up to her from the bottom of the bed on all fours. He crawled right between her legs and kissed her, growling deep in his chest. "My night was a long one. I am ready to relax in your arms, go to my death slumber with your kisses still lingering on my lips."

Kate slipped down in the bed, opening her arms to him. "Then come to me, so I can take care of you before you sleep."

He climbed over top of her, lowering his weight onto her as her arms encircled his broad shoulders. His mouth sought out hers, and he locked her in a kiss. She felt his hands slip beneath her, lifting her body to his, they molded together as one. He broke the kiss, his lips seeking out her neck and she turned her head to allow him to feed, when the door opened, and Sophia burst into the room.

"Poppy is cold!" Sophia slipped the full-grown chicken under the covers before climbing onto the bed beside them. "I went outside to feed him, but there was frost on the ground. He needs a warm bed."

The chicken was flapping and clucking loudly. Sophia pulled the covers over top of him.

Shade heard the squawking of a chicken and felt the creature struggling to flap his wings beneath the blankets, as feathers started to float through the air.

"Sophia! How many damn times do we have to tell you not to enter this room without knocking? And what the hell?"

Reaching down, he grabbed her pet chicken, Poppy, by the back and held it up as it struggled to get free. "This is a farm animal, not a house pet!" Looking at Kate, he closed his eyes, trying to keep his temper under control.

Kate was caught between laughing at the absurdity of a chicken in their bed, and scolding Sophia for breaking the rules...again. Trying to sit up, with Shade half on and half off her, she struggled under his weight. "Sophia, get Poppy out of our bed, and take her back outside. Now! She has feathers to keep her warm, and she has her own coop."

The child resisted. "Mommy, Poppy is cold!"

Theresa frantically entered their bedroom. "So sorry, master. I will take care of this."

Theresa scooped up the chicken, now squawking loudly, and grabbed Sophia by the arm, leading her away. Sophia struggled to get free, but Theresa had a firm grip, as she led the child from the bedroom, closing the door behind them. Kate looked at Shade and bit her lip, trying hard not to laugh as she saw the anger behind his eyes. "Well, talk about a mood killer."

Shade released a loud growl. "A chicken! Seriously? Now I feel..." He stopped mid-sentence and looked at her biting her lip trying not to laugh, and he burst out laughing as a feather came floating from his hair and he blew it out of the way. "Where does she come up with this stuff? It is as though she has radar whenever we get naked."

They collapsed in laughter, knowing they'd have to deal with her misbehavior later when he woke from his slumber.

Kate spoke through her laughter. "Sophia lives by her own rules. I pity the poor man who mates with her." She kissed him again, rolling him over, so he was now beneath her. "Now...where were we before we were interrupted?"

"Don't even mention her mating. *Cazzo*, I am not ready to contemplate that yet."

As she lay atop him, he pushed back the crimson locks from her face. "She gets this from you, because I would never do such a thing." Slapping her ass hard, he snuggled into her neck.

Kate laughed. "Of course, you were such an angel."

She felt his mouth, hot and wet, as it explored her neck, seeking out her vein, and the laughter stopped. His hands explored the curve of her hips, as he sank his fangs into her flesh and the moan escaped her lips. He swallowed long and deep, as he lifted her onto his steel hard cock. She rode him slowly, letting her hips tease, until his hands gripped her tightly, and his thrust demanded more. She bit into the strong muscle of his shoulder, and felt the jolt that traveled straight to her core, the heat building between her legs until she felt him release inside her, as they both rode the waves of passion that washed over them. She lay on his chest, her heart pounding, and waited until her breath returned to normal, before sliding off him.

He pulled her close, her head on his shoulder, as she felt him slip away from her into his death slumber. She lay quietly, her own eyes heavy, and thought about their life. Between the camp, and the vineyards, the businesses she ran with Shannon, the children, the animals, the responsibility to the coven, and the chaos of this house, they somehow always found each other. It was the only constant in their lives. She smiled, as she felt sleep drag her down, her hand resting on his chest, her leg thrown casually across his.

"*Ti amo*, lover."

12

Lorenzo picked up his sword and began the walk back to Castello. He'd been here a month now, and thankfully, Marco kept them so busy in the camp he was too exhausted to think much about his family and his home at Bel Rosso. He'd take a quick shower, check in with his mom on Skype, then head for class with Uberto. After class, he'd seek out Nita to feed, and then drop into his bed for a few hours of sleep before he started it all over again. Entering his bedroom, he tossed the sword on the bed and slipped out of his leathers, stepping into the steaming hot shower. He'd made some new friends, but Alfie was still his best friend here, and Marco had allowed him to sleep over several times. When he exited the bathroom, wrapped in a towel, he found Carlos waiting.

"Master, you have a visitor."

Lorenzo looked confused. "Is it Alfie?"

Carlos shook his head, his face expressionless. "No, master, it is Mistress Donatella."

Carlos had laid out his clothes for him, and the boy quickly dressed in jeans and a tee, pulling on a pair of boots. He rubbed the towel across his hair, still wet from the shower, before brushing it back from his face with his hands. "Is this protocol, Carlos? Did I miss something?"

Carlos told him no. "The visit is without invitation, master. Unless you summoned her?"

Lorenzo shook his head no. "Well, no, I didn't summon her. But when I lived at Bel Rosso, she wrote to me on a regular basis."

Carlos left and let him know he'd take Donatella to the parlor. Lorenzo looked at the laptop that was sitting on the table by his bed. His mother would be expecting him to log on, and he hesitated a minute, wondering if he should tell her he had company. He grabbed his cell phone and sent a quick text, telling her he was running late, and he'd catch up with her later.

Without waiting for a response, he slid the phone in his jeans pocket and headed downstairs to the parlor to find Donatella seated, sipping a Midnight. She stood when he entered and opened her arms to him. "Look at you! You are the spitting image of your father. Oh my, how this takes me back."

Lorenzo accepted her hug, which she held a little too long for his comfort. As he broke away, she patted the seat next to her. "Sit down, Lorenzo. I am so eager to hear about your training, and how things are going."

Lorenzo was glad for her company and sat next to her, as he gave her the details of his nights in the camp. She had a carrier at her feet, and he heard a scratching noise coming from the box. She giggled as she ran her hand through his damp hair. "Well, I can't keep this a secret, can I?"

She pulled the carrier over closer to him and prodded. "Open it."

Lorenzo bent forward and opened the carrier to find a fat yellow puppy, all wiggles and warm tongue, as he reached in to free him. Donatella beamed at him. "I know you had a Golden at your home in Virginia. I understand he was getting old and your family didn't think it was a good idea for him to come with you. This dog can't replace your dog in Virginia, but I thought you'd like a new companion. I'm sure you must get lonely here."

As Lorenzo lifted the dog to his face, the dog covered him in kisses and the boy laughed with a sense of abandon he hadn't felt since moving here.

Donatella watched the boy as he bonded with the dog, and knew she'd chosen well.

"Thank you! You didn't need to do this. But I'm glad you did."

She smiled back at him, pleased with his response. "Lorenzo, don't think for one minute I don't understand how hard this must be for you, to be away from your family, living here at Castello alone. It is a lot for anyone to adjust to, but especially for one as young as you. I want you to know you can call on me for anything while you are here. I know I can never replace your mother, but I care deeply for you. The Alizzi and Medici families go back many generations. If there is anything I can do for you, please don't hesitate to ask. I hope you do not mind, but since you are living here now, I'd like to visit instead of writing. Do you think that would be okay?"

The puppy continued to squirm and lick at Lorenzo's face, as he smiled at her. "Of course, mistress. You're always welcome here."

She placed a hand on his knee. "Oh please, call me Dona. We don't need to be formal."

Lorenzo nodded. "Dona, okay."

She removed her hand and sipped at her Midnight again. "Now then, we need to come up with a name for this puppy."

Lorenzo held the squirming ball of fur, looking him over. "What do you think, boy? Thor?"

Donatella clapped her hands. "Perfect! I love that name for him. Every warrior should surround himself with the Greek gods. Now, I won't keep you. I know you have a busy schedule. I'll stop in about once a week and check on you. And remember, if you need anything, no matter the time, you call me."

Lorenzo put the puppy on the floor, as she stood to leave and gave her a hug. Carlos appeared from nowhere, ready to escort her to the door. Lorenzo thanked her, once again, for the puppy as she took her leave. Grabbing the puppy under his arm, he raced up the stairs and climbed on the bed, as the puppy started to sniff and explore. Lorenzo flipped open the laptop, logged on, and called his mom on Skype. He waited a few seconds for her to answer, and then excitedly held the puppy up in front of the monitor for her to see.

"Look, Mommy! Donatella brought me a new puppy. We named him Thor."

Kate stared at the image on the screen, her son's happiness evident on his face, as he held the puppy up for her to see. *Donatella?* Kate was well aware of her son's affection for Donatella, and she'd certainly done nothing but show kindness to their son, but she wasn't happy that she'd take such liberties without discussing it first with her nor Shade. Perhaps Shade was aware and had forgotten to tell her.

"I...wow, he's really cute, Lorenzo. Does Donatella visit you there?"

He shook his head no. "Well, not before today. But she said she'd be checking on me, and I could call her anytime. That's really nice of her, don't you think?"

Kate didn't want to lay her own negative view of Donatella on her son's shoulders. "Of course, very nice. Now tell me about camp."

Her son excitedly described his training, and his friendship with Alfie, as well as his progress in class with Uberto. He wrapped up his call with her, holding the puppy in front of the monitor again, and waving the puppy's paw at her. She blew him a kiss as his image disappeared from the screen. She knew her son was lonely, and she should be happy there were people there who were looking after him, but she'd resented Donatella from the first time they'd met and felt uneasy about the relationship.

Shade teleported inside Bel Rosso from camp and began the trek up the stairs. It would soon be time for his death slumber. As he neared the top of the stairs, seated in the small alcove that led to the second staircase to Cory and Madison's suite was Natalia, curled up on one of the steps with a book. She immediately felt his presence as she looked up from the book, giving him a big smile. She squealed and ran to him.

Gathering her up in his arms, he made his way to the master bedroom. "Let us see what Mommy is up to."

Kate was closing the laptop when Shade entered with Natalia on his hip. It was almost sunrise, and the two of them would be slipping into their death slumber, just as Sophia's feet would hit the floor. Kate smiled up at them, as he sat Natalia down on their bed and she climbed over next to her.

"Lover, did Donatella contact you?"

As he walked toward the armchair to sit and remove his boots, he stopped mid-stride and turned to look back at her. "Dona? Why would she contact me? Is something wrong?" He plopped down in the chair, exhausted from the camp, and pulled off his boots.

"No, nothing wrong. I just spoke with Lorenzo. She brought him a puppy."

Natalia perked up. "Can I have a puppy?"

Kate shushed her. "We'll talk about that later, okay?"

Walking back to the bed, he pulled the shirt over his head. Picking up Natalia, he sat on the bed and held her on his lap. "Nattie, I need you to find Anya right now, so she can prepare you for your slumber. Be a good princess and go." As she kissed his cheeks, she squirmed down and left the room. Shade looked at *bel*. "I don't see any harm in him having a dog at Castello, keeps him company, gives him something to take care of. Do you have a problem with it?"

Sliding over next to him, she laid her head on his shoulder. “It's not the dog. I'm fine with him having a dog. It will be good company for him. I think I’m uncomfortable with the fact she made the decision without asking either of us. I know her coven is an ally, but I never trusted her. Sorry, I know this is my jealousy talking."

He slid his arm around her, kissing her cheek. "*Mi amore, si,* Dona is an ally. But keep in mind she too, is lonely. She has no master, no children. She is just being a good friend, keeping an eye on Lorenzo. Besides, he is the son she never had. Don’t hold that against her. Did Lorenzo seem happy?"

Kate laughed. "He was so excited over the puppy. He loves camp, and he’s becoming closer friends with Alfie. He says Alfie sleeps at Castello whenever Marco will let him."

"So, you see, Dona is just helping Lorenzo make the transition. The Alizzi coven borders our own. Without a master, without warriors, they rely heavily on the Medici for their own survival. If we were to fall, they would surely follow. Dona is simply protecting her own coven by maintaining her alliance to Lorenzo. He is master there now. Do you understand?"

“You're right. It's just a puppy. I’m making too much of it. Now come to me quickly, before the slumber takes you."

13

It had been too long since Shade had taken Impavido out for a ride. He enjoyed the solitude of riding the horse alone across Bel Rosso and having the free time to ride was a rare treat these days. Riding helped clear his head, and took his mind off things, especially Lorenzo. Leaving Lorenzo at camp hadn't been easy, but it had to be done. Only Shade knew the burdens his son's shoulders would have to bear as he grew older, but this place wasn't the same without him. Heading back to the stables, Shade waved off Antonio, preferring to water and rub down Pavi himself tonight. The huge horse shook his head and let out a snort.

"I know it wasn't a long ride, Pavi. I never seem to have enough time."

The horse snorted again and pawed at the ground, as Shade dismounted and started to remove the saddle. Looking up, he saw his son, Cory, entering the stables. "To what do I owe this visit?"

Cory slipped his hands in his jeans pockets and waited, as his father dismounted the horse. As Shade started to remove the saddle, Cory grabbed a brush and started brushing down the magnificent animal, his black coat gleaming. "If you have a minute, there's something I'd like to talk about, Dad."

Pleased that his son still came to him whenever he had something on his mind, Shade smiled at him, and nodded. "You certainly have learned a lot about horses since Madison came into your life. So, spit it out, what's on your mind?"

"Well, Madison and I have been talking. I mean, we've been together a long time now. Her shop on the downtown mall has been doing really well. We feel really, you know, established. I know I can't turn her, Dad. I understand that's not an option for us. She's fed from me, so we're bonded in that way, but it's different for us. You know, she's still mortal, and that will never change, and we straddle both worlds. We're thinking maybe we could, you know, maybe have a mortal marriage? Just family, of course. Nothing big. But it would mean a lot to us. What do you think?"

Shade paused and stared at Cory. He wasn't expecting this. He knew the two of them were committed to each other, and their relationship had been a very close one in the years that Madison had been living here. "Marriage is our version of mating. It means forever, your vow must mean the same thing, Cory."

Cory gave his dad a look that translated to 'seriously Dad?' as Shade held up his hand.

"I know, I know, I only want to make sure. I love you both, we all do. I think a wedding is a great idea. And you know Kate and Rachael will be over the damn moon arranging a wedding, so, of course. Have you thought about children?"

Cory kept brushing Pavi as he answered, "We've talked about it, but you know, Dad, my childhood sucked. I know if Madison and I were to have kids it would be different, because they'd be raised here, and they'd be accepted by the coven. But that's only because of you. The bottom line is, they still wouldn't belong in either world. I understand with each generation, there'd be less and less vampire in their DNA. Our children would only be a quarter vamp. But what does that mean? How would it affect them? I think it would still place limitations on them. We think it's just best if we don't have kids."

Shade peered over the horse's back, watching his son's face. "Of course, they'd have limitations, each of us does, vampire or mortal. But family..."

His voice drifted off, as he contemplated his son's dilemma. He felt a bit sad, knowing this was their decision, but understanding, on some level, their hesitation. He grabbed a handful of treats from the bin and offered them to the horse. "So, you already made that decision together then? You could come to change your minds later, I suppose."

Cory nodded. "Yeah, we could change our minds, I guess. But, Dad, it's not about whether we would love them. I know they'd be surrounded with love here. Still, they may have to be confined here. Like me, and like Madison. Madison is mortal, and yet, she has to live this double life, keeping so many secrets. Our children would be the same. You can't know my life. None of you can. All my life, I've wished to be either fully vamp or fully mortal. Don't misunderstand me, I love my life here. But if you hadn't found me, I think we both know I'd be dead by now. Compared to how I once lived, this is a paradise, but it's still a paradise with walls. You know what I mean?"

Not for the first time, since discovering Cory was his half-breed son, did Shade feel guilt wash over him. Cory's life choices were limited because of him. Shade took a seat on a bale of hay, running his hands through his hair, his voice softer than normal. "This is my fault. These walls exist because of me. I can't tear them down, Cory, without exposing us all. I did what I thought was best for both of you." Shade stood and looked long and hard at the man who was his son. He was so proud of how far he'd come.

"Dad, no! Finding you was the best thing that ever happened to me. You and Kate, bringing me here, I finally have a home and a purpose. I would've died on the streets, like the other half-breeds. I love my life, and I can't believe my luck to have found someone like Madison. But a day doesn't go by that I don't try to remind myself of what she had to give up to be with me. I know Kate did the same for you, and I try to never take that for granted, you know? I mean, Madison has a lot of freedom. She goes into town every day to work in her shop, she loves her pottery workshop, and she loves our life here. But we have to be careful. We can't get too friendly with other mortals. We can't let anyone get too close. We don't make friends outside of Bel Rosso, because we know we can't invite people here. We have to be careful, but that's not just me, or Madison. It's all of us. I'm not complaining. I'm just stating our reality, and why, for us, I don't think we'll have kids. That's all."

Shade listened to his son, relieved at least that he didn't have regrets. "Kate gave up her life for me as well, and I make damn sure every single fucking day she does not regret that. I know Madison has probably felt she fell into this without a lot of options, but the two of you can have a good life. Our world is small here, but you won't find this kind of love anywhere in the world. What we have here, our family, is rare, mortal or vampire. Family is all you have in the end. You can have all the friends from the outside you want, but when the storms come, it is your family standing in that fucking storm with you."

Looking up, he locked eyes with Cory. "I know the walls restrict us, Cory. Don't ever think I don't. I have had my own struggles dealing with the restrictions of this life, but I made those walls work for me. I made sure that even though I had walls, my family was inside them, my coven, my brothers. I understand how you feel. But your love will get you through. Madison is by your side and so is your family. I feel your love for me. I just hope to hell you feel mine."

"I have felt your love, and Kate's, and everyone here. I feel accepted here, and so does Madison. We just want to seal our bond to each other, in a way that is most meaningful to us. Like you are bonded to Kate, and Luca is bonded to Shannon. You made your bond official in the eyes of the coven. We can't do that, so this is what this marriage means for us. We don't have eternity, but we know we want to spend our lives with each other. I know it's likely I'll outlive her. We've talked about that as well. I'm hoping my blood gives her something, some longevity, anything that will allow her to stay on this earth a little longer. But whatever lies ahead for us, we want to face it together. I know you get that."

Shade chuckled. "Well then, I suppose you better ask that blonde you are so fond of to marry your half-breed ass. Make it official. But do me a favor. Buy her a ring that shows her she belongs to you. And call Rachael. Looks like there is going to be a wedding."

"Thanks, Dad, but, we have to also think about Madison's parents. We've visited them a few times in Oregon, but they've never been here. I know it will present some problems, but we could put them up in a hotel, and have a car pick them up. Madison really wants them to be here. If we have the wedding at night, here, in the gardens, we could pull it off, don't you think?"

Shade threw back his head and laughed. "More mortals at Bel Rosso? Would not be the first time. A night wedding sounds romantic. I have no problems with them being here. We know how to lock it down tight for the mortal company. Hotel is the best idea since Sophia and Nattie are a bit much for mortals. That would be the safest bet all around. Have Madison coordinate with Kate, get a date together. We will fly in her parents. And, of course, we will have to bring Lorenzo home for this."

Cory tossed the brush aside and hugged his father. "I knew you'd understand. I can't wait to tell Madison. We'll wait until spring, when the gardens are in full bloom. This is going to be so great!"

Shade hugged his son to his chest. His happiness was all he cared about. "Well then, I get to call you an old married man."

14

Shade left the stables, knowing he should return to camp, but his mind and heart had been struck by his son's words. He and Madison wanted to get married, but there would be no kids. His son's words played through his head, particularly his statement about living behind walls. Shade understood they all lived behind a wall of deceit to the outside world. They had to protect their true nature for their race to survive. Walking back to the house, he worried over how much this had impacted Cory's life. The rules were in place for all of them, and as master, his highest priority was to protect the coven. Entering the house, he made his way to the master bedroom, finding it empty. He flopped down on the huge armchair that sat at the window. Staring out at the beautiful early dawn sky, the trees would soon become vibrant with color and the weather chillier. He could feel *bel* in the house, attending to one of their daughters, and knew she could feel him as well. He sat quietly in the dark room, staring at the Blue Ridge Mountains as the moon shone down on what would always be home.

***

Kate checked on Natalia, who was sleeping soundly, already pulled to her death slumber. Theresa was sleeping lightly on the sofa bed in the room. She pulled the soft blankets over her daughter's shoulders and lightly kissed her cheek. Theresa sat up in bed and whispered, "Is everything all right, my lady?"

Kate smiled and sat down on the bed next to her, speaking softly, "Everything's fine. I finally got Sophia settled down in class for Enzo, and I was just checking on Natalia. You know, she's old enough now you probably don't have to sleep in her room."

Theresa nodded. "I know, but it is hard to give them up. I have slept in the room with one of the children for over ten years now. They have grown up so fast."

Kate smiled at the woman who had helped raise her children and had become so invaluable in her life. She took Theresa's hand. "That's why we look forward to having grandchildren."

She stood to leave the room when she felt Shade's presence, and his turmoil. She scrunched her brow, wondering if he might have heard something from Lorenzo, and headed toward their bedroom. As she pushed the door open, she saw him slumped in the armchair, staring out the window before the blinds sealed them in for the day. She walked to him, and sat on the floor at his feet, resting her head against his thigh. "Lover? What's bothering you?"

Shade looked down at the most beautiful female he'd ever laid eyes on. If they lived a thousand years together, she'd still take his breath away. He laid his hand gently across her cheek. She always knew when he needed her. Only Kate could clear his head, take the muddled darkness and turn it into light.

"Cory came to talk to me. It has left me with a heavy heart. Unfortunately, the things that burden him I cannot change."

She placed her hand over his. "Is he okay? Is Madison okay? What's wrong? I saw her yesterday when she left to take new pottery pieces to her shop. She was in a hurry, so we didn't have time to talk."

Placing his thumb over her lips, he traced them, feeling their soft plushness against his rough thumb. "Shh. They are both fine. Cory and Madison want to get married in the spring, here at Bel Rosso. They want a night wedding in the gardens. We definitely have some of the most beautiful, fragrant gardens in Virginia. Madison wishes for her parents to be present. Cory and I decided to put them up at a hotel in town. It will be a small affair, family only."

He wasn't smiling as he spoke, and he dragged his hand through his dark raven hair, tangled from riding. Sighing heavily, he looked at her face and could already see her planning the wedding in her head. He looked out the window. "Tell me, what are your thoughts?"

She sat upright, her hand on his thigh. "I think that's wonderful! He can't turn her, so it's their way to seal their commitment to each other. Why are you concerned? Is it having the mortals here?"

Shaking his head, he looked back at her. Taking her hand in his, his fingers massaged her hand. "I have no objections and told him so. It was just..." Shrugging his shoulders, he laid his head back on the chair. "Just his words, the things he told me. They have decided not to have children because of what he referred to as walls. Damn, *mi amore*, I never knew he felt so confined. I understand it, in a way. But I never had to straddle two worlds where I am not accepted in either one. He said they can't make friends on the outside. They can't invite mortals into their lives. He said Madison does not connect with mortals in the way she should because she has to keep so many secrets. Do you ever feel like this?"

With a sigh, Kate laid her head back on his thigh. She was well aware of the walls. And Cory was right, for all the love and beauty in their lives, for the freedom the money brought to them, for the gifts that allowed them to live longer, more special lives, there was also a price to pay.

"Lover, of course, I'm aware of the walls. I know, for you and the others who were born vamp, you know nothing else, but for me, for Shannon and Madison, and even for Cory, there was another life, a different life. I could've chosen that path, but to do so meant I would've had to leave you behind. That wasn't an option for me. I couldn't imagine a life without you, and I've never regretted my choice. I know Shannon feels the same, and I've never heard Madison speak with any regret. She and Cory have always seemed very happy to me. But I understand their decision about children. We can keep our children well protected inside the confines of our vampire community. For Madison and Cory, it's different. Madison will always be mortal. Her pregnancies could be troubled, and any children born to them would be another generation removed from the vampires. Cory is loved dearly, but he knows his acceptance in this world comes through you. He's found a place where he fits, and his skills are valuable to the warriors, and he's happy here. But where would his children fit? They really are caught in the middle, so I understand their choice. Of course, they'd be loved, and they'd always have a place here, but if they wanted more, if they wanted to leave Bel Rosso...you know that could never be. Is that your worry? That they won't have children. They can be very happy together, have a very productive, happy life here, even without children. Shannon has said, many times, that she and Luca have discussed children, and they both think it may not be a path for them and look how happy they are together."

Her words made him ache even more. Lifting her onto his lap, he buried his head into her hair and the scent of roses. "It hurts me that I can't make this better for them. How can I make them feel free inside the walls, knowing I can never tear them down? His words are like an arrow to my heart, *mi amore*. Cory assured me they were happy here. He said it is a paradise, but a paradise with limitations. I struggle to figure out how to lift those limitations without increasing their risk. I almost lost them once and it will not happen again. He is my son, and I must bear the burden of the life I have condemned him to. And Madison, she has done nothing but love my son. What can I do, *bel*?"

With his face buried against her neck, he gently kissed that pulsing vein. She was his strength and his greatest weakness, and as he was fast becoming aware, so were his children.

Kate allowed herself to be enfolded in his embrace and absorbed his pain. There was nothing she wouldn't do for him. "We can't remove the walls, lover. The walls protect all of us. But perhaps, for Cory and Madison, we could build them their own place, here on the property, of course. A cottage built on the other side of the vineyards. Maybe having their own place would allow them to live more like a married couple, instead of living under our roof. We could build that and have it ready for them after they marry. Our gift to them."

Shade inhaled sharply, it was the simplest solution and yet, it took his soul mate to make him see the answer. His smile spread wide across his face. "I love you, woman! That is perfect. *Cazzo*, this house must seem like a bunker to them at times with all the activity. They need a house of their own and the freedom to be who they are. They can come and go without having to see the whole family to get to the door. How could I have not seen this? Yes, it is perfect."

He pulled her close, kissing her as if the stars and moon arose around her. His tongue probed and tangled with hers. She was his queen and she'd always follow wherever he led, but he could never again lead without her on this journey of their life.

15

Lorenzo stretched his hands over his head, rolling his head and stretching his neck. They had practiced with swords all night, and the muscles in his back were aching. Picking up his sword, he headed back to Castello, thinking there was nothing he wanted more than a hot shower right now to ease the pain. He'd been at Castello for several months now, and every time he thought his body had been pushed as far as it could go, Marco pushed it farther. He wasn't complaining. He liked the strenuous training, and he could see his skills improving every day. As he headed toward the gates of the camp, he saw Alfie gathering up his gear to return to the barracks.

"Hey, Alfie! Wait up!"

At Lorenzo's shout, Alfie turned to see him running toward him. "What's up, brother? Something wrong?"

Lorenzo caught up to him, slapping him on the back. "Wanna come up to Castello? You can stay in Luca's room again and use the big shower. I'll have Carlos send your feeder up if you need her, then we can play some video games before we crash."

Alfie exchanged a fist bump with his friend. "That sounds good right about now. But what about Marco? Did you check with him first? I'll stand by you in battle any day, brother, but I'm not willing to break the rules and go against Marco."

Lorenzo laughed. They all knew better than to cross Marco, and not even Lorenzo got a pass when it came to following Marco's rules. "I'll ask him, brother."

Lorenzo darted off across the field where the man he called uncle was stuffing weapons into a duffle bag, ready to wrap up for the night. "Marco, would it be okay if Alfie stayed at Castello tonight?"

Marco looked up when he heard Lorenzo approach. Standing at his full height, he towered over the boy, and gave him a stern look before answering. "You both need a damn good cleaning and some decent rest. And you punks better get some feeding in. Don't stay up all day playing those damn games. I want you rested when you come back to the field. Go on, the pair of you, before I change my mind."

Lorenzo smiled back at him, his smile lighting up his face. "Thanks, uncle." Running back to Alfie, he gave him a thumbs up. The two boys trudged toward the castle, caked in a layer of dust from a long night of skirmishes on the training field. Winding through the formal gardens, they entered the grand castle, as Thor bounded to greet them. Lorenzo squatted down to rub the fast-growing puppy that slept faithfully on the foot of his bed. They were quickly greeted by Carlos.

"Master, I must inform you that Mistress Donatella is here to visit. Would you like me to have her wait in the parlor while you two clean up?"

Lorenzo looked up, as the puppy stood on his hind legs, licking at his face. "Uh...yeah, I guess. I wasn't expecting her." He turned to Alfie. "Donatella is the mistress who owns Umbria. She's a friend of the family. I'll introduce you. She won't stay long."

Alfie looked at him quizzically. "Maybe I should go on back to the barracks and come another time. I didn't know you'd have company."

Lorenzo stood, as the puppy danced around his feet. "No, don't go. She's a longtime friend of the family. She's known my father since he was a young boy like me. She brought me Thor and she's been looking in on me since I moved here, you know, just checking on me since my family isn't here." He turned to Carlos. "Have her wait in the parlor and get her some Midnight, please. Let her know we'll be down as soon as we shower."

Turning back to Alfie, he tugged at his arm. "Come on. She won't stay long, then we can feed."

Alfie wasn't sure this was such a good idea. He knew of the Alizzi and had heard stories of the Medici's past with the Alizzi coven. He knew Lorenzo's father had at one time been promised to her, and he found it odd that she was visiting Lorenzo without invitation. But it didn't seem to bother his friend, so Alfie shrugged it off. "Sure, but I'm going to have to borrow some of Luca's clothes again, no way am I meeting the Alizzi in this condition."

Lorenzo laughed. "Luca won't mind. Come on."

They hurried up a back staircase to the second floor where the boys discarded their leathers and grabbed a quick shower, washing away the dust and sweat, and slipped into jeans. Meeting up in the hallway, they headed down the grand staircase and into the parlor, where Donatello sat waiting. She stood when they entered, tall and regal, in a dress that was blood red, her long dark hair worn loose, her wide gold cuff bracelets gleaming against her dark olive skin. She held her arms out to him.

"Lorenzo! It is so good to see you. Look at you! I could swear you are taller than when I last visited, and clearly, Marco is building your strength."

Lorenzo accepted her hug, which always seemed to go on a little too long, before he stepped back. "Donatella, this is my best friend, Alfie. He's in the class ahead of me in camp."

Donatella extended her hand to the teenage boy, locking eyes with him. "Alfie. I am delighted to meet you. What an honor for you, and for your family, that you have been accepted to train here."

Alfie wasn't often nervous about anything, but he felt nervous about meeting her. The woman who stood before them was tall, elegant and dressed with classic good taste, if not a little too revealing. She was beautiful, and hugged Lorenzo, as if he were her own son. Alfie stood taller in her presence, squaring his shoulders and puffing out his chest. As the woman spoke, her voice was melodious. He was somewhat dumbfounded and found himself locked in her gaze. Finally finding his voice, he reached out and lowered his head, as he took her hand. "*Grazie*, Mistress Alizzi. It is a great honor to meet you. I'm a proud Medici warrior."

His mouth felt dry when he felt her release him from her gaze and he shifted his eyes to Lorenzo.

Dona could sense the older boy's nervousness around her. He was young, and handsome. He was clearly older than Lorenzo by several years, standing tall, maybe 5'11". He'd be a junior and would still have a few years to grow to his full height. He was muscular, but still slender, and he'd fill out as he matured. He wore his light brown hair shorter than a lot of the warriors, in a more modern style. Dona could tell from his scent he still fed from a wet feeder and had yet to reach his sexual maturity. Her feminine wiles would have little effect on him, but she still understood this boy had a lot of influence on Lorenzo.

"And a great warrior you will be, young Alfie. The Medici has helped to protect the Alizzi territory for centuries, and I am sure you will continue in that proud tradition."

She turned her attention back to Lorenzo. "I asked Carlos to bring Midnight for both of you. I am sure you must need nourishment after your training. I know Marco cuts you no slack. Please, sit down and relax while we chat. I will not keep you long."

As Carlos entered the room, he held the tray to Alfie who took the glass of Midnight. He'd never tasted the liquid the older warriors sometimes drank. He doubted they should be having this drink, but he couldn't show disrespect to the Alizzi. He took the smallest sip and felt the ruby liquid go through his whole body. It wasn't the same as feeding, but it felt good. He looked up to see the Alizzi was watching him with beautiful eyes and he looked at Lorenzo to escape her stare. He quickly took a seat across from her and didn't speak until spoken to.

Lorenzo took the glass from the tray and hesitated slightly, looking at Donatella for approval. "We've never had Midnight before."

Dona looked back at him with surprise. "Really? Oh, my darlings, you must try it. All things in moderation, of course, but this elixir sustains us. The Medici family has held the secrets to this drink for centuries, and the rest of us are just glad for the relief it brings."

She held her glass out in a toast. "To us, the Medici and the Alizzi. Long may we rule!" She lifted the glass to her lips, sipped, and watched as the two boys did the same.

Alfie knew if he didn't partake, he was being rude to a mistress. He nodded and took a slightly bigger sip. This felt good, soothing, satisfying the edginess of hunger that always lay inside of him. Taking a larger sip, he felt his blood come alive, stimulating something inside him that made him want to go out into the night and hunt. The vampire inside him slowly arose. He looked at the glass and wanted more, and took a long, deep draw from the glass and smiled. Medici was a fucking genius.

Lorenzo tipped the glass and let the thick elixir slide across his tongue and down his throat. It was the first time in his life he'd consumed anything other than the blood of his mother, his father, Theresa, or Nita. This blood was different. It was mortal, not vamp.

He knew it was pure, and filtered, to remove any contaminants. He knew from his years around Luciano, who'd overseen his father's vineyards for centuries, the process for selecting the human blood was a stringent one. Luciano had his own legion of Medici warriors who reported to him. They sought out the humans, fed from them in their sleep, and returned to regurgitate the blood before it could be absorbed into their own bodies. The blood was tested, then processed and filtered, before being blended with the wine. For every human who ever woke up feeling more tired than when they went to sleep, they had probably contributed to the Medici wealth. For every human who'd ever had an orgasm in their sleep, attributing it to their erotic dream, their blood was being extracted to serve the needs of the vampire community. Lorenzo had grown up with an awareness of the process, and knew it was a carefully guarded secret. He liked the taste of this mortal blood, and the alcohol warmed him, relaxing the tight muscles in his shoulders. He took another sip, deeper this time, and felt the alcohol quiet his mind. It soothed him as he relaxed back in the chair.

Donatella watched as the two boys experienced the impact of the Midnight for the first time and smiled. Setting her glass aside, she stood and walked behind the chair where Lorenzo sat. She reached over the back of the chair, and slowly massaged his shoulders, feeling the tension release under her fingertips. "So many pleasures wait for you both. So much to look forward to."

Alfie watched as the Alizzi began to massage his friend. He watched her mouth, her lips a deep red, when she said pleasures await, and he knew all too well what she meant. He'd watched the older warriors leave the camp for the hunt, and he couldn't wait to experience the pleasures females could bring. He shook his head to try and clear it, but the Midnight was having a strange effect on him. His body felt warm and relaxed, his heart was beating faster, and his tongue was loose.

"Battle! Being a warrior and seeking adventure outside the gates of camp. Those are things I look forward to." His eyes widened as he realized he'd spoken without being asked a direct question. He lowered his eyes and his head.

Donatella chuckled. "Oh, my sweet warrior, there is so much more than battles that await you. I promise you will find more to entertain you outside of camp than battles. There is nothing like the pleasure of the hunt, the seduction of your conquest, and that first bite into mortal flesh and the sexual ecstasy that follows. You have a few years yet, but trust me, it will push any thought of battle from your mind."

Lorenzo relaxed under her touch, his eyelids getting heavy as he took another drink, emptying the glass. Carlos appeared in the doorway, clearing his throat. "Mistress, they are still boys."

Donatella stood up straight, removing her hands from Lorenzo's shoulders. "Of course. I am quite aware. No harm here. It is time they taste the elixir."

Carlos informed the boys that their feeders were waiting for them but remained standing in the doorway. Donatella looked at him with some annoyance but knew she may have crossed the line. Returning to her seat, she asked Lorenzo about the dog, and he told her how much he'd grown and how he slept on his bed. She inquired if there was anything he needed, and he assured her he was fine.

"I know you two boys had plans, so I won't keep you. Please call me, Lorenzo, if there is anything you need. And feel free to visit me anytime."

Carlos escorted her out, leaving the two boys slumped in their chairs.

Alfie was conflicted when Carlos stepped into the room and intervened, cutting the Alizzi's visit short. He was pretty sure Marco wouldn't approve of them drinking Midnight, but the view! She was by far the most stunning female he'd ever seen. She moved like a cat, slowly, sensuously. It had a way of mesmerizing him. Finally, as she left, he looked at Lorenzo who was already almost asleep.

"Lorenzo, get up, we need to get to the feeders. I need my feeder. How do you feel?"

Lorenzo slowly opened his eyes, heavy with sleep, the aches from his sore muscles gone. "What? Oh...I feel...good."

He stood up and staggered slightly before gaining his balance. Carlos returned to the room, taking each boy by the elbow. "Upstairs. Now. You both need to feed, then sleep."

The tone in his voice was clear. The servant, used to taking orders, would, on this night, give the orders, and he wouldn't accept any arguments. The two boys were led upstairs without protest.

16

Alec was making sure he had the business plan and the real estate information he needed to have the discussion with Shade. For the last six years, he'd been living in a house in San Francisco, and paying rent to Shade. He'd had to remain inside, for the most part, and make sure to disguise his appearance when he did leave. After the failed campaign, the Council had stripped him of everything, and he'd been forced underground. Initially, the press was in a fury, trying to figure out where he was and what had happened to the Senator, but after about a year, they lost interest. Every now and again, there was a newspaper article, or something online, speculating on his whereabouts, or the latest conspiracy theory, but the public seemed to have all but forgotten him. He'd received protection from the Medici warriors here, in California, led by that fruitcake, Raven. And Raven had set up a schedule for feeders to visit regularly, so he had no need to leave, but after six years, he was going stir crazy. He knew the Council had exiled him for a hundred years, so any mortal alive during this time period wouldn't recognize him if he was seen out in public, but Alec thought he had an idea for how he could remain unseen, and still get out of this fucking house. He'd asked Shade if they could meet, and promised he'd teleport to Bel Rosso, remaining unseen by mortals. Shade had agreed. Alec made one last check of his papers before tucking them in his sport coat pocket and teleporting out.

Shade heard Gi moving quickly to the front entrance and knew Alec had arrived. He poured two large Midnights just as Gi entered the office and announced Alec.

"You sure as hell look better than the last time I saw you, brother. Take a seat and tell me how things are going for you on the opposite coast." Shade slid the Midnight across the desk and took his seat in the leather chair.

Alec dropped into the large armchair across from the desk, and gratefully accepted the Midnight. He'd not teleported any distance in a long time, and his energy felt low. He quickly downed the liquid and set the glass back on the desk. "Thanks for seeing me, brother.

I heard from Raven that Lorenzo has gone to Florence to live now. You must be very proud."

Shade nodded his head and grinned. "Proud does not begin to cover how I feel about my son. He is doing well at Castello. It will be his home now. I have two beautiful daughters as well and I have to tell you, they do try my patience at times. But it is all part of being a father. I can't believe how fast the time has gone since I first arrived here. But I am pretty sure time seems to be dragging for you."

Alec ran his hand through his hair. "You have no idea, brother. It already feels like a hundred years. I have an idea, something I'd like to try, but I'll need your approval, and your help."

Shade spun the glass of Midnight slowly around on the desktop. *This could be interesting*. "Idea? The last time you had an idea, you ended up losing everything. Better be a damn good idea, Alec."

"I know you are skeptical, brother. But I've met with some lawyers, and some real estate people. I've thought about it long and hard." He pulled the papers out of his pocket and spread them on the desk in front of Shade. "Just keep an open mind. Let me explain my idea before you discard it."

Shade glanced down at the papers Alec spread across his desk. "Go on, I'm listening. Tell me what this is about."

With a sigh, Alec began his explanation. "I've been looking at the number of vamps in San Francisco. The place is a mecca for vamps. And there are a lot of very rich masters there. The underground clubs are plentiful, but they're all designed to appeal to the younger crowd and attract a lot of mortal kids from the Goth sub-culture. Not exactly my cup of tea, and I'm betting it's not a place where the masters with more refined taste want to go for a night's entertainment."

Alec pushed the blueprints for a large mansion-style home on the outskirts of San Francisco across the desk. "This property is outside the city, located to the south near Half Moon Bay. It's a large walled estate. I still have my money. It's the only thing the Council didn't take. I could buy this place, and with an investment of cash, do some renovation, and install some real state of the art security systems. I could live there, but more importantly, I could open a business there. Brother, you know when we had the Gorean sex cult there was no lack of interest. I'm picturing something similar, but higher end. It would be exclusive, members only. Private rooms, instead of the dungeon we had at Castello. Each room would be designed to appeal to a different fantasy. Members could bring their own partner, or I could supply them with a partner. Membership fees would be exorbitant, and I'd have a fucking job! Something to keep me busy. We'd need protection, of course. Not sure how many, but we'd need Medici warriors to keep things under control. I'd remain underground, not visible to the mortal world, so I wouldn't be breaking any of the Council's rules."

He laid the business plan on top of the blueprints. "I met with an accountant. We laid out the business plan, what I'd have to invest, how much to charge, and what the return would be. Help me on this, brother, and I'll cut you in on the profits. Twenty percent. And you know it will be a fucking gold mine. There's nothing else out there like it."

Shade never saw this coming. But he should have known, this was Alec, after all. He remained quiet, listening and looking at the paperwork and blueprints that lay in front of him. He bristled when the Gorean sex cult was mentioned. That was a time in his life he hoped never to return to again. He sat hunched over the desk, examining what was before him. Finally, he sat back in his chair and looked at Alec.

"It looks good on paper. The financial plan looks sound. There is nothing like this anywhere in the States, that I know about. I think there is a market for it." Shade stood up and paced the floor. "My warriors, protecting an exclusive sex club, I have to say, that is new territory. The Medici warriors have never been associated with such ventures. *Cazzo*, Kate will have something to say about that."

He kept pacing, a good fifteen minutes, before sitting back down. He withdrew his smokes and lighter from the drawer in his desk and lit up. "If you need warriors, I want thirty percent. You're not the most popular vampire around right now. How in the hell do you propose to convince them to come to this set up, brother? Your name alone exiles you from most."

Alec leaned back in his chair. He could tell from Shade's response he was cautious but interested. "Well, brother, I'm sure as hell not going to put my name on it. This will be low key, word of mouth. I'll use Colin to help me bring in the clientele. He's well connected. He and Elana can bring their friends, and we'll let the word spread from there. Members will have a contract, guaranteeing their anonymity. No cameras or cell phones allowed; other than the ones I have installed. The warriors will screen the patrons before they come inside. And whatever happens in the club, well, that's no one's business. Complete freedom, brother. You know it will work."

Shade nodded his head unconsciously as he thought. "It will work. I just have to convince Kate that loaning the Medici name to its protection is worth it. I have done some wild things in my day, but I now have children who bear my name and it not only reflects on me, but them as well. Once this gets out, you are going to be busting at the seams, if it's done right. But there is one other thing that may make this work in my queen's eyes."

Alec leaned forward in his chair, his arms resting on his knees. "And what's that, brother?"

Shade picked up the decanter of Midnight and filled Alec's glass. Holding it up, he grinned. "The magic of Midnight. I have been working diligently with a new formula, one that makes the Midnight more powerful. It is almost ready to be marketed. It is harder to produce, so it will not be mass marketed like Midnight. I was thinking more of targeting masters who own a private stock, or exclusive clubs. But it's not cheap. Your club would be the perfect place to introduce it. I guarantee you, once they taste it, your clientele will definitely want to buy it for their personal stock."

Alec's eyes lit up at the possibilities. "Make it exclusive to my club...our club. They can order it for their homes, but they can only buy it at the club. That will draw clientele in from all over the States. That's a great idea!"

"That's what I am thinking, brother. I won't have to market this at all. I can make it exclusive to the club and for sale to the clientele only. This is a perfect setup. I am interested, but I have a lot to coordinate and think about. How long before you think you can have this up and running?"

Alec was too excited to remain seated. He stood up, feeling energized to finally have some direction in his life. "One phone call, brother. The mansion has been on the market for some time. I can call my realtor right now and have him put in an offer. The renovations shouldn't take more than a few months."

"Look, need to be honest, Alec, I need to discuss this with Kate. I don't do anything without conferring with her. She isn't going to like it, but I think I can convince her. I also need to check on the progress of the Red Moon. That's the name of the new wine. We should have enough ready to stock you up within months. I also need to coordinate with Raven. He will have to see the facility, figure out what you need for protection. Can you give me a week here?"

Alec reached out to shake his hand, when the door to the office swung open, and a small red-headed tornado entered the room, holding a chicken that was wildly flapping his wings and squawking.

"Daddy! I tried to put a dress on Poppy, and she pecked me."

The chicken broke free, and started to run around the office, looking for an escape.

"Sophia! How many damn times do I have to tell you this chicken belongs outdoors, not in this house? You try my patience, female!"

Shade was trying to corner the frantic bird, wearing a doll's dress that was half on and half off. Poppy was fast and in a panic. Shade grabbed the chicken as it flailed helplessly. Trying to hold the frightened bird against his chest, he glared at his daughter. ***"Bel*, get to my office now!"**

Kate heard the command in her head, along with the wave of anger and frustration he was feeling. She rushed down the stairs to his office. Entering the room, she saw their daughter, Sophia, bent over in laughter, and Shade holding the panicked chicken, one wing caught in a doll's dress. Kate rushed to the chicken. Her hands immediately calmed the bird, as she untangled the frightened chicken from the dress. "There you go, Poppy."

She took the bird from Shade and cradled it in her arms, letting her own energy calm the creature. Turning to Sophia, she leveled her with a stare. "And you, miss thing! How many times have you been told Poppy lives outside? Now take her, and return her to the coop, then get back here. I will be thinking about the appropriate punishment while you're gone."

Sophia took the bird but pointed in Alec's direction. "Who's he?"

Kate turned around and noticed Alec for the first time. "Oh, I'm so sorry. I didn't know you were here. Please excuse the interruption. Our house isn't usually this chaotic...well, not true, our house is always this chaotic. It's good to see you again, Alec. This is our daughter, Sophia. She was just a baby when you moved away. Sophia, this is Master Alec Canton. He is a friend of your father's."

Sophia tucked the chicken under one arm and wiped her hand on her jeans before extending it to Alec. "I'm a princess, but you're not in our coven, so you don't have to bow."

Alec was watching the whole scene unfold and couldn't believe his eyes. This was a far cry from the Shade he'd once known when they'd hunt together. The child approached him after being introduced by her mother, extending her dirty hand for him to shake. Alec looked at her momentarily, wondering whether to ignore her gesture, but realized he had a business proposition at stake, so he took her hand. "I'm honored to meet you, Princess Sophia."

Sophia lifted the chicken up to him. "Wanna hold Poppy?"

Before he could answer, Kate had both hands on the girl's shoulders and was leading her out of the room. "I'm so sorry, Shade. I'll take care of this."

Kate closed the door behind them, as she left with the child, and the room was suddenly quiet again. Alec looked at Shade and shook his head. "Brother, you really need this club. Your reputation depends on it. You've gone from a bad ass warrior to an ineffective chicken wrestler."

Shade struggled to get his temper under control. One of these days, he was going to strangle that female. "Oh, I am still a bad ass warrior, and one you need at the moment."

He slammed his fist down on the desk, as the feathers flew. "And my reputation is still very much intact. Call the damn realtor. I will call Luciano and Raven. Get our lawyers on this immediately with contracts." Shade extended his hand to seal the deal.

Alec shook his hand, and quickly gathered up the papers on the desk. He knew when the deal was sealed, wrap things up quickly before the negotiations started again. "I'll call as soon as I get back home. You won't regret this, Shade. Set up a meeting with Raven. I'll show him the property, and then he can figure out what we'll need in the way of protection. I can tell you're busy here with your family, so I'll take my leave."

Stuffing the papers in his pocket, he gave Shade a quick nod before teleporting out.

Shade flopped down in his chair, his elbows on his desk, and his hands in his hair. *Cazzo*, what had he done? He'd just broke a vow he'd made to his mate, that they'd decide everything together. He knew already she wouldn't be happy with his decision to be a partner in a sex club. He'd let Alec's taunt get to him. He, too, wondered at times what had happened to the warrior he'd once been. In frustration, he swept his arm across the desk, sending the desk lamp crashing to the floor. **"*Mi amore*, we need to talk when I get home."** He didn't wait for her answer but teleported out to camp. He needed to release his frustration on something, and he had warriors to help him do that.

17

Kate handed off the pet chicken to Theresa, who apologized profusely for the child getting outside to the chicken coop. Kate waved it off. "Please, don't beat yourself up. None of us can keep up with her."

She marched Sophia upstairs and back into the girl's bedroom. "You should be sleeping. Theresa has already put you to bed once." She leveled her daughter with a stern look. "Now lie down, and quiet your mind. We'll talk about this tomorrow. And I suggest you stay clear of your father for a while until he cools off. Don't push my patience any further, Sophia."

The child rolled her eyes, and with a heavy sigh flopped back on her pillow. "Bear!"

Kate retrieved the stuffed bear from the floor and tucked it in her arms. "I think 'bear, please' would have been nice, young lady."

Sophia rolled over, turning her back to her mother. "But I'm not feeling very nice right now."

Kate kissed her cheek. "That makes two of us. Now, sleep."

As Kate turned to leave the room, Sophia called out, "I sure hope Poppy doesn't freeze to death."

Kate looked over her shoulder. "It's fifty degrees out, Sophia. I don't think anyone will be freezing tonight." She stood in the doorway, looking at her daughter's mop of red hair on the pillow, the covers pulled over her tiny shoulders as she clutched the bear. She looked so tiny, and so beautiful, how could such a small bundle create so much havoc? "I love you, Sophia."

"I know, Mommy. I try to be good, but all the fun things are bad."

Kate bit her lip. "Yeah, life works like that sometimes."

She closed the door and headed back to their bedroom. She'd felt the energy shift when Alec left their home, followed by the sound of a crash and breaking glass, and the sensation of Shade leaving, followed by his message in her head. She knew he was blowing off steam in the camp. She stood still for a moment, wondering what prompted this visit from Alec. Shade hadn't mentioned he was coming. She returned downstairs to his office to find the broken lamp on the floor, and Gi sweeping up the mess of glass and feathers.

"I'm so sorry, Gi. I can get this?"

He shook his head, as he swept the debris into a dustpan. "Do not concern yourself with such, my lady. It is not the first time I have swept up broken lamps and I doubt it will be the last."

Kate looked at him bent over at the waist, as he brushed up the glass and feathers. "Bet it's the first time for chicken feathers, though."

Gi chuckled. "*Si*, my lady, I must admit, the chicken feathers are a first."

Kate turned to go back upstairs, but she could feel Shade's anger, and had no doubt their middle child was the cause of all of it.

***

Shade was a mad man on the field, letting out all his frustrations on his new warriors and they were feeling their master at his best. He was angry that Alec had goaded him into making an impulsive decision that broke his promise to Kate.

Marcello watched him closely, wondering what had him so riled up. He kept his eyes peeled. The warriors had been working out for some time now and were getting tired. If they made one mistake, Shade could lope off an arm without thinking. Marcello barked a stop order, and all the warriors dropped their weapons. Shade looked up, and if he could have slayed Marcello with a glare, he would have. Throwing up his hands, sword still in his fist, he snorted and kicked the dirt beneath his feet. He was just getting warmed up. He stormed toward Marcello to find out what in the hell he was doing.

Marcello stood his ground. "Not sure what set you off, master, but the recruits are tired, and not deserving of your ire."

Shade tossed his sword point into the earth, his voice booming loudly. "Heading back to the damn house!"

He stomped back to the house, pushing his curls, wet with his sweat, away from his face, as he tried to calm his breathing. By the time he hit the back door, he was calmer but had no damn idea how to approach this subject of a sex club with Kate. *A little too late to be pondering that now!* He took the steps two at a time as he headed to their bedroom, walking through the door in dusty boots and leathers. She looked at him as he entered, and he knew he needed to calm down before he opened his mouth.

She felt him before he entered, his emotions rolling off him. She looked up when he walked in, and it was clear he'd been working off his anger. "Come with me," she beckoned, and led him to the bathroom where she turned the water on in the tub. As the tub filled with steaming water, she started to undress him, peeling the formfitting leathers from his skin. Dropping to her knees, she untied his boots, and pulled them free, tossing them aside. Looking up at him through her red bangs, she grasped the waistband of his pants, and worked them down his hips, and pulled them down over his thighs until they were low enough for him to step out of them.

He stepped into the tub, and settled with his back against the marble, resting his head and closing his eyes. She removed her clothes, and stepped in with him, her back at the opposite end, so she could face him. They sat quietly together, as she let him calm down, the hot water relaxing his muscles. She watched his face and decided tonight wasn't the best time to discuss Sophia and what punishment might be best for her.

"Feeling better?"

He looked back at her and those large brown eyes, and felt his body relax. Her small foot lay next to him and he reached out, lifting it from the steaming water. He kissed her toes, one by one, and then massaged her foot as he stared at her. "Better, *si*. We need to talk. Serious talk."

"If it's about Sophia...I know she's a handful but let that go for tonight. We can talk about it later."

Sighing heavily, he had to tell her. "Oh, we will talk about her, but you are right, it will be later." He pulled her foot to his mouth, and with the tip of his tongue, licked her foot from the heel to her instep and then to her toes. His eyes never left her face. "Alec presented me with a business proposal. Something he is quite intrigued about and should keep him busy for the next hundred years."

His tongue along her foot was sending signals straight up her leg and causing a rippling sensation in her belly. Her breath quickened, as she tried to keep her mind clear to what he was saying. "Alec? I wondered why he was here. What kind of business? He has to stay underground, doesn't he?"

He knew his hands and mouth were distracting her, as he'd hoped. He lowered her foot in the water and sat up straighter in the tub. He couldn't romance her while he did this, it wasn't fair to her. "Before I tell you, I need you to promise me you will remain calm until I tell you everything."

His seduction stopped abruptly as he released her foot, and she opened her eyes and stared back at him, confused, and wondering what he was going to say. "Okay. Well, this doesn't sound good. What's going on?"

"Alec and I are going to be business partners. He is investing his money, not ours, into a mansion in California. It is a...do you remember when I took you to California? The club where I met Cory?" He felt her anger go straight from zero to a thousand in the blink of an eye.

"A club? An underground nightclub? Shade...why would...I don't understand. The decision is made then? You didn't even discuss it with me?"

He held her gaze, placing his hands on her shoulders. "Listen to me. It is not going to be anything like that club. This will be an elite club, members only, to appeal to the very rich masters. No mortals. He will need protection and will require the services of Medici warriors. I also think it will be a good way to sell Red Moon. It will be exclusively sold at the club, and available for the masters who may want it for their private stock. This will not be some sleazy underground club. He is buying a mansion, modifying it to accommodate his members. A very private resort."

He released her shoulders, preparing himself for her fury.

She stared back at him as he finished explaining this plan. She was so angry with him, she dared not release it. In a quiet voice, she responded, "So, it's decided. And I'm supposed to be okay with it apparently."

She stood up and stepped from the tub, wrapping herself in the large towel, as she left for their bedroom. "Let me know how that works out for you."

He'd expected anger and wasn't prepared for her calm rebuke. But his beast was angered by her response, as she walked away from him. Bolting upright out of the water, he stepped from the tub as water dripped to the floor. “Do not walk away from me. You will talk to me about this. And you will do it now, woman!"

He followed her across the floor of their bedroom. Grabbing her, he spun her around. "I was planning on discussing this with you until a red-headed demon blasted through a closed door with a fucking chicken!"

She turned on him, releasing her fury. "Oh, so, now it's Sophia's fault? Really, Shade?"

"Not all of it, but she is out of control with her damn insubordinate behavior. She made me look like a damn fool. And Alec didn’t help with his fucking remark of how far I have fallen from bad ass warrior to chicken wrestler. I had had enough and shook on the deal without thinking. I know I broke a vow to you. But this deal will work.”

"So, it was your male pride speaking. I didn't realize you needed to compete with Alec, of all people." Kate dropped the towel and slipped on a robe before sinking into the armchair, placing her head in her hands, trying to calm down. “Shade, this is getting us nowhere. Tell me about this...deal. I don't understand. Why would you agree to a sex club? That's what we're talking about, isn't it? A glorified version of the dungeon that used to be in Castello. I thought you’d left all that behind. Is that where you’ll spend your time now?"

Rushing to her, he knelt so he was eye level with her and grabbed her shoulders. "No, *mi amore*. I will not be a part of his business. My warriors provide protection, under Raven’s supervision, and we sell Red Moon there. Beyond that, it is Alec’s business to run. In exchange, we make thirty percent of a very lucrative business. I don’t need to be there. This is about keeping my warriors employed, keeping our coffers filled, and our coven protected.”

Kate knew in her heart he’d never stray from her. They were bonded in a way that made them one and the same. But the memories of that chamber in the bowels of Castello flashed through her mind, the darkness, the soulless sex, the pain and torture. How could they be a part of this?

"I don't understand. How can we be associated with such a place? I walked through the dungeon at Castello, the memories there haunt me still. I could feel the fear inside that room. People were brought there against their will. What message does that send to our children? Is this what we want to leave them?"

His head snapped up, and he stared at her. "No, it is nothing like that. The sex cult was about controlling and hunting helpless victims. This is much different. They come willingly, masters with their mates. Or if a master does not have a mate, Alec will provide them with partners who are willing. It is a place to act out their fantasy, in privacy and safety.

"Our coven grows every day. It has never been this large, and our people are employed and protected. But that means I must constantly find ways to generate more wealth, and more jobs. We are the Medici. We do warriors and wine. The basis of this decision was not about the sex but money, and resources for the coven."

Her sigh was a heavy one, as she tried to reconcile his reasoning with her vision of this place. She'd seen much in the twelve years she'd been with him, and she knew their culture viewed sex very differently than her mortal roots. There was a freedom, a complete abandonment of the rules, if there even were any rules, when it came to sex and feeding. But she knew there was loyalty as well. She had his loyalty, and she saw Luca's loyalty to Shannon. And even as Velia had serviced many, her heart belonged to Gi.

"I don't want our children to ever see this. You sell him the new wine and provide protection. That's what you do. But beyond that, I don't want us involved. Can you give me that?"

Standing, he lifted her from the chair and held her so tight he thought he'd break her. "I will do as you ask. *Grazie.* I will call Alec next evening. This business will be discreet. And I know it will be successful. I craved for such in my younger years, but there was nothing. I have no use for it now, but I know many masters who would prefer something more refined than the Goth underground clubs that exist today."

She wrapped around him, feeling the strength of him, as she laid her head on his shoulder. "Please don't make me regret this choice."

"I try every day to make sure you never regret the choice you made in choosing me as your mate. My whole life was spent finding you, and nothing will ever come between us, not even a certain princess."

She kissed his neck, his dark hair still damp from the bath, brushing across her nose. "I can only tackle one problem at a time, lover. Can we not talk about our daughter until tomorrow? Take me to bed, and finish what you started with my feet."

Chuckling softly, he licked the vein that pulsed in her neck. "Oh, I intend to finish a lot of things this night, *mi amore*."

Walking to the bed, he laid her down and melted into her. Princess Sophia forgotten, Alec Canton and his sex club forgotten, but his love for her would never be forgotten.

18

Lorenzo rolled over in his bed. The fire in the fireplace had burned down to hot embers. The castle had central heating, but the rooms were so large, and there was so much stone and marble in the house, it never felt warm here. As they moved into winter, Lorenzo missed the warm coziness of his home in Virginia. He reluctantly slipped out of bed, and the comfort of the warm covers, to find his leathers laid out for him. He quickly got dressed and walked down the hall to the room Alfie occupied. Tapping on the door, he stuck his head in to find his friend still buried under the blankets. Donatella had visited them again today, and they had shared their usual glass of Midnight. Their bodies were adjusting to the alcohol, although Lorenzo still limited himself to one glass. Alfie would sometimes have more, with Donatella's encouragement. Both of the boys knew they were breaking the rules, and if Marco ever found out, he'd kick their asses.

"Alfie! We're going to be late."

Alfie had fed heavily from his feeder. He always seemed to need the comfort of the wet feeder more after a visit from the Alizzi, and she seemed to be here a lot. He heard Lorenzo calling to him and grunted. "It's warm in here, brother. Shit." He threw back the covers and growled. "Why didn't you wake me up earlier? My head feels like I've been battling all night."

He grabbed his leathers, struggling to get them on and flopped on the bed to strap on his boots. "How do you feel?"

"Better than you, brother. You need to slow down on the Midnight. Donatella isn't the one who'll have to face Marco if he finds out. And I don't even want to think about what my dad would do."

Alfie rolled his eyes to Lorenzo. "No one will tell him, will they? Like the servants, or even her?"

Lorenzo sat down on the un-made bed. "Nah, Carlos is cool. He's got my back. And Donatella knows my dad would never let her come back. Nobody is going to say anything. But still, you show up with a hangover, Marco's no fool, Alfie. Dad told me when I left to come here that anything I could possibly think of pulling off, Marco has seen a hundred times."

"More like he and your dad experienced it together a hundred times. Come on, don't just sit there, we need to get moving and fast."

Alfie grabbed his sword and they headed outside to camp. "Brother, do your parents know the Alizzi comes to see you so often?"

Lorenzo shrugged his shoulders. "I guess. I mean, they know she visits. I don't tell my mom every time because I can tell my mom doesn't like her much. She doesn't say it, you know, but I can tell. My dad just says the Alizzi's are allies, and Donatella is lonely because she never found a mate, never had her own kids. They wouldn't like that we're drinking Midnight, though."

"I don't think anybody would."

As they approached the field, Marco was gearing up for a night of cold weather and pushing them hard. The senior warriors were on the field tonight and warming up with the juniors and the grunts. Alfie moaned. "Great, this looks like a bad night to have a hangover. Next time I want more than one glass, hit me in the head."

Lorenzo playfully slapped him upside the head and ran to his group, laughing. "Okay, but just remember you asked for it."

Alfie squinted and scrunched up his face, as the headache banged inside his head. He chased after Lorenzo and by the time he caught up with him, a small group had assembled to perform some easy exercises to warm up for sword play. Alfie lunged at Lorenzo playfully and the two of them went at it, getting their muscles warmed up. They were both laughing a bit too much, when Alfie realized they were drawing attention. He stopped laughing and signaled to Lorenzo. The last thing he wanted was to draw attention to himself and Lorenzo. Marco would know something was up. As Lorenzo lunged at him, Alfie spun away, avoiding the sword, and Vanni stepped into place, sparring with Lorenzo. Lorenzo was holding his own against the much larger boy, so Alfie stood back, and didn't intervene. He didn't like Vanni, and it was clear Vanni had it in for Lorenzo, but Alfie knew if he stepped in every time, he'd just make Lorenzo a bigger target.

Lorenzo was caught off-guard when the play fight turned into a real fight, as Vanni became more aggressive. "Get off me, Vanni!"

Vanni laughed at him. "What's wrong, cry baby? Can't come to camp without your big brother to protect you? You afraid of the long walk by yourself, or are you too puny to teleport?"

He lunged at Lorenzo and Lorenzo countered but Vanni was ready and swung his sword low at Lorenzo's knees. Lorenzo jumped high enough to avoid the blade but lost his balance and fell backward on his ass. He scooted away, fast as lightening, out of range of Vanni's sword, and regained his footing, taking a stand against the bully.

Vanni laughed harder and taunted him, "Want to call your protector now? Did it hurt?"

Lorenzo's temper flared, as the older boy got the best of him. He caught him off-guard, but Lorenzo was ready for him now. "I don't need a protector, Vanni, but you might by the time we're through."

Lorenzo defended himself against the not so playful jabs from Vanni's sword. His sword skills were advanced, well beyond his years, thanks to the hands-on training from his father. He could easily take the older boy down, but this was another Medici warrior, not an enemy. Lorenzo tried to rein in his anger and continued to fight a defensive battle only.

Marco saw something was brewing and entered the fray. It was clear Vanni wasn't sparring to warm up but fighting with intent. "Enough! Step down, you bastards, right now!"

Everything came to a screaming halt at the sound of Marco's voice, as he pushed through the crowd that had gathered to watch the fight. He marched up to Vanni, pulling him by his long hair and shoving him toward the barracks. "Get the hell inside and I will deal with your ass later. Move!"

He turned to look at Lorenzo, hands on hips. "What the fucking hell was that about?"

Lorenzo wasn't going to throw a fellow warrior under the bus, even if he deserved it. "Nothing. Just goofing off."

Marco growled. He wasn't about to take this bull one more second. Yelling at one of the senior warriors, he told him to carry on with the exercises. "You and Alfie, in my office, now!"

Marco marched toward the barracks and Alfie looked at Lorenzo, swearing under his breath, "Shit."

Lorenzo cast a sideways glance at Alfie and whispered, "Stay cool, brother." They followed Marco into his office, and stood, waiting for further orders.

Marco slammed his desk drawers, looking for his smokes. He lit up and turned to look at the two young warriors. "If you two would stop diddling around up at the house, you might make it here on time. I let Alfie go there to keep you company, Lorenzo, and so the both of you can get some decent rest, and obviously that is not happening." He flopped down at his desk. "Damn it, Alfie, you saw what was going on, why didn't you step in?" His eyes bored into Alfie's.

Alfie gulped, if he got busted for anything, he could be thrown out of camp. "Lorenzo has asked me not to, sir. He can handle a sword much better than Vanni. They were just warming up, no harm was done, sir."

Marco laughed and his eyes turned to Lorenzo. "You will back him till your dying day, just as your father does for me. I admire that, but I am in charge here. Don't ever forget that. Did you feel threatened in any way?"

Lorenzo's heart was pounding, but he stood tall. "I don't need Alfie to stand up for me. I can stand up for myself. And I didn't feel threatened. I was just pissed off because I was caught off-guard. That's my own fault."

Marco admired this kid. He'd worried Shade had been too soft on him as a child, and he wouldn't stand up to the rigors of camp, but he was more than holding his own. "Well, let's get one thing straight. Every damn time your ass walks into this camp, someone is going to piss you off. You handled yourself fine this time but do me a fucking favor. The next time you want to goof off, don't." Marco stood with his arms crossed over his chest. "And I don't know what the hell is going on up at the castle when you two leave here, but don't make me find out. You are warriors, act like it. Get out."

Both boys mumbled, "Yes, sir." and scrambled out of the room as quickly as possible before Marco could change his mind. Once outside, they had to suppress their laughter. Lorenzo headed toward his group of grunts.

"I'll see you later, Alfie. I better go join my team before Marco drags me there by the hair."

Alfie laughed, but he knew in his gut he had to be more careful when he went to Castello and the Alizzi was there. Lorenzo couldn't get thrown out of camp, but he sure could. Alfie wasn't jealous of Lorenzo, he'd been his best friend here, but there had been times when he wished he was in Lorenzo's shoes, to live the life he did. But that wasn't his fate. He sprinted out to his brothers who were already practicing, and they ribbed him and congratulated him for getting called into Marco's office. He was the first of his group to receive the official reprimand, and it was a badge of honor among the warriors.

19

Cory had gone with Madison to her shop in town to deliver new pottery pieces. Kate took advantage of this time at the end of the day, to summon in the contractors to work on a home for the couple. It had been a few years since they'd made any modifications to the estate, and they'd need to keep this project under wraps. She'd already taken the contractor over to the plot of land where the new house would be built, and now they were back inside Bel Rosso, going over several floorplans the contractor had brought for her approval. Kate had the plans spread out across the long counter in the kitchen, so she could see them all simultaneously.

"This one is too grand, too large. It will just be the two of them. They prefer cozy to opulent. I want something with more of a cottage feel, but still Tuscan."

The contractor pulled out his pencil and a ruler and started making sketches over top the original floorplans. "No problem, my lady. We could remove this wing, add a covered patio maybe?"

Kate scrunched up her face, taking the pencil from his hand to add her own sketches. "And maybe put the kitchen back here, with an eat-in section. Remember, they both eat mortal food."

The two of them were so engrossed in the floorplans they didn't hear Shade when he came in.

He stood in the doorway, still in his leathers and boots, admiring her ass as she was bent over the counter, making sketches on the blueprint. He chuckled as she took charge, and both Kate and the contractor turned their heads in his direction. "You will learn to do as she says, or you won't have a job for long. My *bel* knows what she wants, and usually gets it, one way or another."

Walking up behind her, he wrapped his arms around her waist and peered over her shoulder. "So, what are you working on, *mi amore*?"

"Lover, I want this to be their home. To feel like it was something they would've picked out for themselves. They both prefer something simpler than Bel Rosso, but I want them to have room to expand, room to do what they want, but it needs to feel cozy, and quaint. I was thinking I'd only put minimal furniture inside, so they could move in, and then let them decorate it however they pleased. Do you like this floorplan? I'm leaning toward this one."

Shade watched her face as she drew over the contractor's plans, creating the house in her head. He knew her impeccable taste, and whatever she created, Cory and Madison would love. He glanced at the blueprint in front of him, looking it over carefully. "Where is Hyde's suite? He is moving in with them permanently, no argument from anyone, *si*."

"Hyde! I didn't even think about that. He'll need his own suite, like Luca's."

Kate quickly freehand sketched the bedroom, living room and bath to the side of the house. "This will be good. It's on the opposite end of the house from their bedroom. They'll have some privacy. Does Hyde know? Be sure he keeps the secret."

Crossing his arms over his chest, he made a face of surprise. "What do I look like? An amateur? I have done this before. And *si*, he does know. He's their protector. Don't worry. He knows if he lets out the secret, he will have to deal with your wrath and not mine. None of the warriors are up for that." He slid the blueprint around and looked at the sketches. "Something else I want for this house."

She stepped back as he lifted the blueprint from the counter to examine it more closely. "And what is that?"

Shade's brows scrunched up as he examined it more closely. "Cory said he was restricted by walls. Give them windows, more windows. They can both walk in the sun, and the light will give them more freedom. Install the electronic shades, for other vampires who may visit, but both of them need light to make them feel as though there are no walls. Tell me your thoughts."

Kate was a day-walker, but she'd lived with him for so long now, she'd almost forgotten what wide-open windows during the day could feel like. "Of course! Big windows, floor to ceiling, or with arches, and French doors that open to the outside. They can both enjoy the sun. I picked a plot of land on the other side of the estate, on that extra land we bought. They can see the vineyards, and the flower fields, but they can't see the camp. It will be very private for them. We'll have to extend the access road as well."

He looked down at her face, filled with happiness and determination. She loved taking care of their children, and his warriors. He leaned down and kissed her, ignoring the presence of the contractor. "Do as you wish, *mi amore*, everyone here knows that, without you, I would still be sleeping on a mattress on the floor. We will give them a credit card to purchase everything they need for the house. I just want them happy, and feeling like it is their home, and perhaps not so restrained by walls."

She turned and placed her arms around his waist, squeezing tight, feeling giddy with excitement. "I can't wait for them to see it! I'll make this special for them."

"Now, I have need of you for something. Can you wrap up here and come with me?"

She gave him a quizzical look but rolled up the blueprint and returned it to the contractor. "Go with this one, please. We may tweak it as we go. I'll stay in close contact throughout the build, and remember, it must be completed by March. I want time to put in landscaping and get it started before the wedding." The contractor took the blueprint as Kate summoned Gi to escort him out. Turning back to Shade, she inquired. "Now what can I do for you?"

He smiled wickedly and winked. "Show me this plot of land you have chosen to build the house on. We have not been on the horses in a long time. You can ride with me on Pavi or you can ride along on Bravado. What will be your choice, my queen?"

"Let me ride beside you on Bravado. I don't get out riding as often as I should."

Taking her hand, he strolled casually with her out to the stables, sending Antonio a message to get the horses saddled and ready to go. On their entrance to the stables, Pavi and Bravado stood ready to ride, as Antonio held their reins. Shade grabbed a heavy saddle blanket and tossed it over Pavi's neck in case the night air got too cold. He helped Kate to mount and then mounted Pavi.

"You will have to lead us, *mi amore*. Show me where we are building this house."

She led the horse out of the stables at a slow trot, into the open and he followed. Pavi snorted as he wasn't used to following, and

Shade rubbed the massive stallion's neck. "Calm down, boy, you don't always get to lead, console yourself with the view." Even though it was dark, he could see her silhouette as she sat astride the horse, and he loved every inch of her.

Kate looked over her shoulder at him and extended her hand. "Ride next to me."

Shade grinned and lightly kicked Pavi to pick up the pace as he moved alongside her. Reaching out, he took her hand as they rode. "It is a beautiful night. Listen to the quiet."

She laughed softly as he held her hand. "I love our children dearly, but I do miss this, lover." She guided Bravado around the dirt road used by the farmworkers, across the vineyards and the flower fields into an area of open pastureland. The wood line was in the distance, with a great view of the mountains. "Here, on that slight rise. That's where I want to put the house."

Shade looked in the direction she indicated and smiled. "It is beautiful. You can see the vineyards from here, and the flowers will make their surroundings a pleasant spot." Pavi pranced a bit and Shade pulled the reins to calm him down. He looked at her as she held her face up to the sky and closed her eyes. Her long crimson locks were tied up on her head, with a few tendrils hanging around her face. He reached out and pulled the clip that held her hair in place and watched the crimson waterfall, as her hair fell around her shoulders. He moved Pavi closer and held out his arms to her. She obliged him as he lifted her to his horse and helped her settle in front of him on the saddle. He wrapped the large saddle blanket around his back and covered them both from the night chill.

"I just realized something, *mi amore*."

"And what's that?"

He wrapped his arms around her, pulling her close, the scent of her rose perfume drifting on the night air. She felt so good in his arms. It had been a long time since they were out, under the moon, with no one around. He could actually hear the sound of his own breathing. "Well, this is the first house you have had the pleasure of designing from the ground up. All our other homes were built already. You just needed to do some renovations and decorating."

"True, although there was the camp, and the feeder compound. Not quite the same, though."

"*Si*, not the same. I would never trade this life for anything, you make it all worthwhile. But I wonder sometimes, if this is what you envisioned when you were still mortal."

Kate laughed out loud. Her laughter carried on the night breeze. "I could never have imagined any of this, not in my wildest dreams. Not until a certain dream-walker entered my dreams and turned my world upside-down."

Snuggling into her neck, he breathed in her scent. He hoped there was never a day she came to regret her choice. "Once I saw you, I could never have left you. There was nothing I ever wanted more in my life than you. Will you ride back with me on Pavi?"

"Of course. Give Bravado a slap on the rear. He knows the way home."

He laughed as he slapped Bravado on the rear flank. "And if you slap my ass, I suppose you think I know my way home." He heard her giggle as he gently kicked Pavi, and the horse headed back across the fields. Their ride home was a long one, but he didn't want the night to end. He wanted to ride forever with her in his arms. Living with her was like living inside a fairytale. Tonight, was like the old days, before the children, and the camp, and the house full of servants, when it was just *bel rosso* and her savage lover. He rode with her wrapped in his arms, until the sky started to lighten, and he knew it was time to go back to the house, take care of their children, and keep the legend of Medici rolling forward.

20

Making one last check in the mirror, Marco adjusted his dress leathers. Donatella had sent a courier with a special letter, requesting to meet with him. She gave no indication as to what the meeting was about. He was very much aware of the frequency of her visits to Castello since Lorenzo had moved here and assumed this would have something to do with the boy. Marco had never been particularly fond of Donatella, although he was aware, she had Shade's blessing when it came to visiting Lorenzo and acting as his surrogate mom. Shade had rejected the mating contract with Donatella that his father had arranged, but he'd never rejected her, and had maintained a close relationship throughout the years. But Marco could see Dona had never given up on the prospect of mating with him.

Shade was his best friend, but there was a limit to how far even he could push things. He felt the Alizzi was spending more time than necessary with Lorenzo, although the boy seemed to really like her. Even Kate seemed resolved to her visits, so Marco had kept his mouth shut. He shouted out some final commands to his Lieutenants, then teleported out to the Alizzi mansion.

Donatella had the servants cleaning from sun up to sun down, until her sparse palace sparkled. There was a time when her home was as opulent as the Medici's, back when her father was still alive. The Alizzi's and the Medici's had presented a very strong united front. But after Shade's refusal to honor the mating contract, she hadn't found another royal mate as her father had wished. Now, her parents were deceased, and she'd watched her finances, and her coven, dwindle. Staying aligned with the Medici's was her only means of holding on to power. She'd been courted through the centuries, but not by a master of wealth and power, not by royalty, and she refused to give up hope. She'd sent a message to Marco and was expecting him any minute.

The fine crystal glasses were removed from the cupboard, and the cork had been popped on the Midnight. She stood anxiously at her window, waiting for him, when she saw him appear in the driveway outside her villa. She scurried to the parlor, and sent her lady-in-waiting to answer the door and escort him in. As he entered, she bowed discreetly.

"Marco, it has been too long, *si*? Please, have a seat. Allow me to pour you a drink."

Marco hadn't been inside her palace in years and was taken aback by its sparseness. It was clear she'd been selling off many valued pieces just to make ends meet. "*Grazie*, Donatella." He took a seat on an elegant yet aged settee, as he accepted the glass of Midnight. "What's this about?"

She sipped demurely from the wine glass and looked at him over the rim. She was well aware of her beauty, and her power to seduce, and she never failed to use it. "You are looking well, Marco. The years have been kind to you. I regret that we have not kept in touch. But I know you are a busy man. As you are probably aware, I promised Shade and his mate I would keep an eye on young Lorenzo. He is alone at Castello, and misses his *madre, si*? Shade had the comfort of his own *madre* when he was a young boy in the camp, but Lorenzo is making his way alone. You are aware I gave him a pony many years ago, but he is much too old for a pony now. He is on the path to becoming a warrior, to follow in his father's footsteps, and I want him to have the same advantages Shade had. You, of all people, understand how much I depend on the Medici for my protection, and maintaining goodwill is essential. I have acquired a young Friesian horse, and I wish to give it to Lorenzo. With your permission, I would very much like to invite Lorenzo here, to give him the horse. I do not wish for there to be any false impressions, so please, feel free to include the young Alfie. I know they are best friends, much like you and Shade when you were young boys in the camp, *si?*"

Marco didn't miss the coy look she bestowed on him. She was a fine woman, but one way above his station. He took the Midnight in one gulp and carefully set the crystal on the table beside him, breaking his eye contact with her. Turning back to her, he threw his arm over the back of the settee, before answering her. "Mate would be the wrong term, she is our queen. I would be obliged if you would address her as such in my presence. She is revered and has earned that title. Shade paid you for that pony, Dona, do not think I don't know the details. Have you informed Shade of your intentions?"

She was caught off-guard by his defensiveness. "I have not, as of yet. But I assure you, I have every intention of asking his permission. I thought it only right, I check with you as well, since Lorenzo has been left in your charge. We share responsibility, do we not? You provide the firm hand, guiding the young prince, and I, perhaps, provide comfort in the storm, a soft place to land when he has had a rough go of it. He can't show his vulnerability in the camp, Marco. But he is still a child, carrying the burdens of a man. Our Lorenzo has much to live up to, does he not?"

"*Si*, we both have a responsibility to protect Lorenzo, and prepare him for the throne. But you don't shoulder that responsibility alone. There are many who will carry him to greatness. He is never alone in his struggles. He is not a child, but a young man in my eyes, and one who is just discovering his full potential. He represents the best of both The Queen and The King. He is going to be something to behold, I can tell you that." Marco stood and walked to her side, placing his hand over hers. "Dona, he is not Shade."

She was taken aback when he laid his hand on hers but didn't pull away. "No, he is not. But Shade's blood runs strong in his veins. I can see he is different in many ways, and yet, much the same. But I see what you do not. He will always present himself as strong when he is around you. He is well aware his every move is being measured in the camp. Well aware all the other boys watch him, looking for a crack in the armor. That is a lot to ask of a young boy. With you, and the other warriors, he must be a man. With me, and with Alfie, he can, for a short time, revert to being a boy. He can forget, for a moment, the weight of the responsibilities his shoulders must bear, and how many will come to depend on him. It is his legacy, and he can't escape it. Like Shade, it is his fate, and like it or not, it is what his future holds. He was born to great privilege, but don't forget, with that privilege comes great responsibility. The horse, it will look like his father's. The horse is young, and Lorenzo can train him, just as Shade trained Pavi. His horse is named Eredita...Legacy. I beg you, Marco, allow me this."

Marco knew she spoke the truth, and he could see she understood Lorenzo better than he'd thought. He let his hand slide away from hers as he stepped behind her chair, gripping it with both hands.

"You make a hell of an argument. Your *padre* would be proud of you. Call Shade. If he is agreeable, then tell him to contact me immediately. I will not stand in the way. Besides, the boy needs a horse. He has outgrown the pony. I will let Alfie come along as his escort. It looks more presentable." Marco leaned over the chair and spoke softly in her ear. "Begging is so beneath you, Dona."

Donatella smiled to herself. She knew she had him hooked. Turning her head slightly, bringing her lips in close proximity to his, she answered softly. "Am I begging, Marco? I do not wish to appear so. But it is not often I am in the company of such a strong and powerful warrior. I am afraid my skills of interacting with men, such as yourself, are quite lacking. Perhaps I have not shown my appreciation for all you have done for me."

Her voice was seductive and soft as a purr and her beauty hard to ignore. He could feel his blood pulsing through his veins. She was still the temptress and he thought it best to make his exit as quickly as possible.

"You have done enough." He winked and turned on his booted heel, heading for the door. "No need to see me out. I will expect a call from my master. *Buonasera,* Mistress Alizzi."

Marco left her palace and, once outside, teleported back to Castello. Donatella watched him leave, knowing if she had Marco's blessing, it would go a long way in convincing Shade. She retreated to her bedroom and propped herself up on her bed, thinking of the man she should have been sharing it with as she checked the time difference before making her call. Shade should be up and about. She hit dial on her cell and hoped it wouldn't go to voicemail.

Shade was getting ready to leave for the camp when his cell phone rang on the nightstand and he grabbed it, seeing it was Donatella. "*Mi amore,* it is Dona." Taking the call, he hoped nothing had gone wrong. "Medici."

Dona let the purr come through in her voice. "Medici, so formal. I hope I am not interrupting anything, Shade."

His eyes went to *bel* as he answered. "No interruption, I was just leaving for camp. I'm putting you on speaker, trying to get ready to leave here. Is anything wrong?"

Dona hesitated, wondering if his mate was in the room. She'd have to be careful. "Oh, nothing is wrong. Quite the contrary. I only wanted you and your lovely mate to know your son is doing well. I check on him and his friend, Alfie, as often as my schedule allows. He is adjusting well to life in the camp. You would be so proud of him. But I did call for a specific purpose."

He continued to gather up his gear as he talked. "We are grateful for your attention to our son. He speaks often to his mother and me. Tell me your purpose."

"I have just met with Marco, to secure his approval as he is responsible for the Prince, and now I seek your approval. I have a gift for Lorenzo, and I need your blessing. I have found a young Friesian who looks like Pavi. I wish, so much, for Lorenzo to have him. You know he has outgrown the pony, and it is time he learns to break in his own war horse. He is of purebred stock, and I have named him Eredita. I thought long and hard for such a name, for he is your legacy, is he not?"

Shade ran his hand through his hair, casting a glance at Kate. "Marco gave you his approval? Dona, Friesians are an expensive breed. This is a lavish gift. Are you sure you can afford such an expense?"

Donatella sighed loud enough for him to hear over the phone. "Please, I don't have the wealth of the Medici, but I am not destitute, Shade. I have not taken to begging in the streets quite yet." She chuckled, but he was right. She had sold off some of her jewelry to be able to afford this horse.

"Consider this gesture as a small repayment for all the protection your warriors have provided to the Alizzi through the years. We could not have held on to Umbria without it. I am begging you. Allow me this small pleasure, to bring joy to the young boy's eyes. I have never had my own children to spoil."

Shade plopped down in the armchair, laying his head back and closing his eyes. He could think of no reason to deny her the pleasure of giving this gift. Lifting his head, he looked at Kate. "Your thoughts, please."

Kate didn't completely trust this woman, but Donatella's intentions appeared above board. "Lover, I can see no reason to deny Lorenzo this gift. He's worked hard at camp, and I know he puts on a brave face for me. You have our approval to present this gift to the Prince."

Dona was giddy with joy. "Thank you, Shade! And thank you to your queen. I spoke with Marco about this. I want to invite Lorenzo here, with Alfie, of course. I would invite them to visit my estate, and see the horses here, and then surprise him with Eredita. You will call Marco? Let him know you have given your approval, *si?*"

"Si, I will call him. *Grazie*, Dona. You will make him happy. Well done. As always, our allegiance remains solid. Good night." Shade grabbed the phone and ended the call. "I am proud of you, *mi amore*. She means well. And Lorenzo needs a horse, not a pony. I can't be there to help him choose, and Donatella is an excellent horsewoman. She knows the breed and will have chosen wisely. Lorenzo will need a horse, and it is important he learn to break him in. She is doing us a great favor."

Kate had listened without comment to the whole conversation. "I don't want my jealousy to cloud my judgment, and certainly don't want it to negatively impact Lorenzo. He'll be responsible for protecting Umbria someday, and I understand he needs to secure those alliances. Still...I have my reservations. Not about the gift. I agree it's time for Lorenzo to have a horse. He's outgrown the pony. But in my heart, I can't help but question her motives."

He took her in his arms, kissing her softly. She'd always have reservations when it came to any female, especially one she knew had a connection to his past. "He is our son. Not hers. She can't steal Lorenzo away from you. He is a smart boy, *mi amore*. Now, I need to get my ass to work and make a phone call to Marco. You are all right with all this?"

She returned his kiss, reluctantly letting him go. "I'm fine, lover. Finish up in the camp, so you can come back to me."

"Your warrior returns to you every night. And this night will be no different." He slapped her ass, as he laughed and headed out the door, leaving his lily-white.

21

Excited about the visit, Lorenzo and Alfie got dressed to go see the Alizzi. Lorenzo had never been to her home before, but Marco let them know she'd extended the invitation, and his father had approved. The two boys were excited to get away from the camp for a while, regardless of the reason. Stripping from their leathers, and taking quick showers, the boys changed into jeans as they prepared to leave. Alfie called to him from the hallway, "I'll meet you in the foyer."

Lorenzo called back, "No, I'm ready!" He exited his bedroom as the two boys headed down the stairs to the grand foyer. Carlos greeted them and gave Lorenzo final directions for teleporting to Donatella's estate in the nearby region of Umbria. Carlos had his own suspicions about the boys being allowed to go to the Alizzi's and felt the need to issue a warning. "I have held my tongue, master, when it comes to the Alizzi's visits. I hope you will use discretion."

Lorenzo knew he was referring to Donatella's habit of sharing a glass or two of Midnight with them. "Don't worry, Carlos." Turning to Alfie, he asked, "You ready?"

"Yes, I'm nervous, though. Do I look okay? Is this sweater good enough?"

Lorenzo laughed and punched Alfie in the arm. "We're not going on a date. You look fine. Come on, let's go!"

The two boys teleported out over Tuscany, passing into neighboring Umbria. Lorenzo checked his coordinates, as they landed in front of the palace that belonged to the Alizzi. It was nice, though not as grand as Castello. Looking over his shoulder to make sure Alfie was still with him; he walked to the door and used the large brass knocker to announce their presence. The door swung open as they were greeted by house staff that welcomed them in. They were led to the main parlor. "Please be seated. I will let the mistress know you are here." The two boys entered the room, looking around as they took their seats.

Alfie took note of the simplicity of the Alizzi's home. It was much smaller than Castello, but still elegant in a shabby sort of way. Straightening his sweater, he looked at Lorenzo. "I just thought of something. We should've brought a gift. Like Midnight or flowers or something. You're supposed to know this stuff, brother."

Lorenzo smiled. "What makes you think I didn't?" He slipped his hand into his pocket and removed a piece of pink quartz, cut in the shape of a heart, polished and smooth.

Alfie was a bit shocked. It was a heart. He questioned whether that was the best choice but shook it off. "Wow, you never cease to amaze me."

As Donatella appeared, the boys immediately stood up to greet her. Alfie's eyes roamed from her head to her toes. She might be the most beautiful woman he'd ever seen, and his blood raced every time he saw her.

Dona had brushed her dark hair to a high sheen. She was wearing jeans and riding boots. Her white blouse had been left unbuttoned at the neck, with one too many buttons opened, exposing the tops of her ample breasts. Her golden skin glowed in contrast against the white of her blouse.

"And here are my handsome boys! Look at you both. You grow taller every time I see you. Come, give me a hug."

She opened her arms to Lorenzo, who gave her a motherly hug before extricating himself from her grasp. Dona turned to Alfie, opening her arms. "And you? No hug?"

Alfie had a lump in his throat and swallowed hard. He always felt nervous around her. He smiled and nodded, approaching her as she embraced him, holding him close against her breasts. His arms slid around her waist, returning her hug before he backed up. He looked at Lorenzo and took a deep breath. Her scent was enticing. He wondered if all females smelled like this.

Dona felt Alfie's self-consciousness. She knew he'd not yet reached his sexual maturity, and still fed from a wet feeder. But his reaction told her he was getting close to making that change, where feeding and sex would go hand in hand. She released him reluctantly.

"I am so glad you were able to visit. Let's have a drink first, *si?* Then I have a surprise for you, Lorenzo."

Her house maid was already entering the room with three goblets filled with Midnight as the drink tray was lowered before them. Lorenzo flashed Alfie a look, as he removed his own glass from the tray.

Alfie smiled when the Midnight arrived, he needed a drink to calm his nerves around Donatella. He took the glass and nodded to the Alizzi, taking a hefty swig, it went down smoothly. He liked the taste and the warm feeling that spread through his body. He'd not yet been trained to hunt, but the drink brought images in his head of hunting, and feeding, and stirred other feelings that made him uncomfortable. His eyes lingered on her breasts. Her blouse strained against them, outlining their plumpness, and he took another swig.

Alfie responded awkwardly, "You have a lovely palace, mistress. I'm honored to be invited."

Dona took the remaining glass and sat down next to Alfie. She took a sip from the goblet, leaving her lipstick stain on the rim as she peered at him over her glass. "Why, thank you, Alfie." She placed her hand on his thigh. "You are welcome here any time. I could not have survived all this time without the aid of the Medici warriors. If there is ever anything, I can do to repay you..." She left the sentence unfinished but gave him a wink over her glass.

Alfie was finding it hard to breathe. She peered at him over the rim of her goblet. His eyes saw only one thing, the print of her lipstick on the glass. Without thought, his tongue darted out as he licked his lips. He felt the warmth of her hand on his thigh, as if he didn't have jeans on. It scorched his skin and sent his blood slamming into his heart. He cleared his throat. He needed another drink. He liked the feel of her hand on his leg. She winked and he had a desire to touch her hand. He took a deep breath to clear his head, but her scent filled his nose and made his head spin.

Dona liked the effect she was having on the boy. It had been a long time since she'd flirted with a male. She flagged down her house maid to bring Alfie another drink as she turned to Lorenzo. "And how have you been, Lorenzo? You know if Castello gets too lonely the two of you are welcome here."

Lorenzo thanked her, but said they'd been doing fine. "We have a lot of fun, actually. But thanks for the invitation. I brought you something." He slipped his hand in his pocket and removed the pink quartz heart, holding his hand out to her. "I know this isn't much, but I wanted to thank you for being my mom away from home."

Dona placed her hand at her throat and smiled at him. "Lorenzo! How sweet."

Unlike Alfie, Lorenzo was still a few years from his sexual maturity, and Dona saw the innocence of his gift. She had a flash of what it might have been like...what it should have been like, had Shade mated her, and she'd had his children. She'd never experienced this, a child offering a gift of love to his mother. She held out her hand as Lorenzo stood and placed the polished stone in her palm.

Lorenzo blushed. "It's nothing, really."

She took his hand. "Not so. It is everything. You honor me. Now, would you like to see your surprise?"

Lorenzo glanced at Alfie as both boys nodded. She stood and waved her hand. "Well, follow me then."

The boys stood, and Alfie downed the last of the Midnight before following her. She led them outside, in the direction of the stables. Lorenzo called out to her. "Are we going riding?"

She looked over her shoulder, a radiant smile on her face. "Maybe."

As she reached the stable door, she waited for the boys to catch up, then stepped behind Lorenzo and placed her hands over his eyes. "Follow my lead, and no peeking."

She guided him inside as Alfie followed along beside her. She positioned Lorenzo in front of the stall holding the young Friesian. Leaning down, she whispered in his ear, "Ready?"

Lorenzo nodded, and she removed her hands. Lorenzo looked with surprise at the young horse that would grow to be the size of Pavi. His coat had been brushed until it gleamed, and his long black mane hung in waves. "Can I ride him?"

Dona laughed. "You can do more than that. He is yours. His name is Eredita. That is Italian for legacy. That is what you are, Lorenzo. The Medici legacy, the warrior your coven has been waiting for."

Lorenzo spun and gave her a tight hug before climbing over the stall. The horse responded, a little skittish at the intrusion, and

Lorenzo quickly calmed him. Dona turned to Alfie. "How about you, Alfie? Do you have a horse?"

Alfie smiled at his friend's happiness, as he answered her, "Oh no, mistress. My family could never afford such a beauty as this. I've been taught to ride, of course, every warrior is taught to ride. But owning a horse is a luxury."

Donatella looked back at him. He showed no jealousy or envy over the gift Lorenzo had been given. He understood his position in the hierarchy, but Donatella was touched by his loyalty to the prince. "Well that will never do, will it? I mean, you are the best friend to the prince. You are to Lorenzo what Marco is to Shade. They are like brothers, *si?* You train together, you ride together. Every warrior needs a war horse. Pick the one you want. I rarely ride anymore."

Alfie quickly raised his hands, holding them palms out. "Me? Oh no, mistress. I couldn't accept such an expensive gift. I couldn't repay you, and when would I ride, or have time to tend to the horse?" Alfie walked up to the stall, watching Lorenzo check every inch of the Friesian.

Dona smiled back at him. "Alfie, do you not understand the concept of a gift? You do not repay me. And you ride when Lorenzo rides. You can board the horse in the stables at Castello. Medici has full stables, and plenty of stable hands. Your horse would be cared for."

Lorenzo stopped patting down Eredita and looked up at Alfie. "It's okay, Alfie. You can board your horse at Castello. We'll ride together."

Dona slid her arms around Alfie's broadening shoulders. "See? No argument. Now pick out the horse you want."

Alfie felt torn. He knew he shouldn't accept but his heart couldn't let this go. A horse of his own! He'd never had anything of his own. He felt her arm around his shoulders, and he wanted to lean into her. He missed his own mother's arms, but this felt very different. He liked when she touched him. Turning toward her, he caught and held her gaze. "Will you help me choose?"

She flashed him a smile that would melt butter. "I would like nothing better." She dropped her hand from his shoulder and took his hand, leading him from stall to stall. She stopped in front of a stall and stepped up on the rail, pulling him up beside her, as they looked at another breed of horse. He, too, was solid black.

“I like this one. He is Peruvian Paso. They are known for their calm disposition. They don't spook easily and this one has already been broken in. His name is Corridore. What do you think?"

Alfie felt like he could walk with her all day and night, hand in hand. Her smile made his heart do flips, and other parts of him ache. The Midnight had kicked in and he didn’t care if what he felt was right or wrong, he just knew one thing. She was beautiful and amazing.

"Corridore means runner. I like that. What a beauty he is."

Climbing over the stall, the horse immediately nuzzled into his hand. Alfie looked at her and smiled. He’d only felt this happy once before, when he was ten and learned he’d been accepted in the Medici warrior camp. He hopped back over the stall and hugged her.

"*Grazie*, mistress. *Grazie*. It’s the best gift I’ve ever been given, and I’ll take great care of him." He held her tight and didn’t let go. She felt so soft in his arms. Best day of his life.

Dona held the boy to her breasts, and slowly slid her hand up and down his back. He was almost as tall as she was, and he was losing the rail thin body of his youth, as he developed the muscles he’d carry as a man. "It is my pleasure, Alfie. Trust me, my pleasure."

Alfie reluctantly let go and stepped back, feeling embarrassed and overwhelmed. He looked down, kicking his boot in the fine dust on the floor of the stables. "Hey, Lorenzo, come meet Corridore!"

Lorenzo climbed over the stall gate and ran to see his friend’s new horse. “He’s awesome, Alfie! He’s fully grown. How old is he, mistress?"

Dona ruffled his hair. “Please, call me Dona. Corridore is three, and Eredita is only about six months, so you will have to train him, Lorenzo."

Lorenzo nodded with excitement. “Can we ride now?"

She laughed. "Of course!" She flagged down a stable hand who would get the horses saddled and bridled so they could ride.

The stable hand led the horses from the stables as the three of them mounted. Donatella led with her horse, Belleza, as Alfie easily mounted his new stallion. "He seems calm."

Dona nodded. "He is broken in and used to being ridden. He will not give you any problems."

She laughed as she looked back at Lorenzo, as Eredita danced about while Lorenzo attempted to mount the horse. "Eredita, on the other hand, has only begun to be broken in. He will take some work, Lorenzo."

Lorenzo finally got atop the horse and pulled in the reins, stroking the horse's neck. "No problem. Dad taught me how to ride, and how to break them in. We'll ride as one soon enough."

Dona led them across the rolling pastures. It was late fall, and most of the leaves had already fallen, and the air was cold and crisp. Dona took in a deep breath. She usually rode alone and was happy for the company of the two young boys. They started out in a trot, letting the horses warm up, before giving them lead to run. The three of them raced across the field, Dona's dark hair caught in the wind, flowing behind her. Alfie was able to keep up with her, while Lorenzo, on the younger horse, fell slightly behind. She flashed a warm smile at Alfie as they raced.

Corridore sat easy beneath Alfie, and he loved the feel of this horse already. He could tell Donatella was a skilled rider, as she easily maneuvered her own horse. He looked over his shoulder to see Lorenzo struggling with his new Friesian but knew Lorenzo would get control. Catching up with the Alizzi, she beamed at him with a smile that lit up her face, and he smiled back.

Alfie issued a challenge, "Race you to that line of trees. Let's see how well you do keeping up with a Medici warrior." Alfie kicked Corridore in the sides and the horse responded immediately, taking lead over Dona. He felt free and happy, and he could hear the horse hooves pounding behind him.

Dona wasn't surprised when Alfie took the lead, pulling ahead of her. She'd grown up around warriors, and she knew how competitive they were. She laughed as she kicked her mare but knew her horse was no match for the stallion she'd given to Alfie. She kept her eyes on this man-child, as he moved with ease and grace sitting atop the horse. The muscles in his thighs were more prominent as he used them to direct the animal beneath him, the muscles in his shoulders flexing as he guided the horse along the tree line. She caught up to him as they both slowed down, letting the horses cool down. Lorenzo caught up quickly on the still young Friesian. Dona knew the Friesian would be massive when he was fully grown, and Lorenzo would have grown with him.

"You both look like you were born to ride. I am so happy you like the horses."

Lorenzo smiled back at her. "I don't know how to repay your kindness, Dona."

She reached across to the boy, her hand under his chin. "Your time with me is payment enough. It is a joy to have you here. I hope you will come anytime." She shifted her gaze to Alfie. "Both of you."

Alfie didn't miss her specific attention to him. He felt honored and special that she purposely included him. No one had ever given him this much attention. Corridore stepped around restlessly, nuzzling at her horse.

Dona spoke to Lorenzo, "What do you think? Is Eredita going to suit you?"

Lorenzo laughed out loud. "We were made for each other. Right, boy?" He patted the horse's neck. The horse snorted and pawed at the ground. "Dad said Friesians are spirited but very loyal. Once he's used to me, we'll be fine."

Dona laughed. "The same could be said of your father, spirited but loyal."

Both boys laughed and Lorenzo spoke through his laughter. "That's putting it mildly!"

Dona looked lovingly at the boy, and once again, felt a pain in her heart. She couldn't help but think he should have been hers. Turning her horse, she looked at the boys. "Ready to head back?"

They nodded as she took off. "Last one back has to serve the drinks!"

Lorenzo kicked at Eredita, spurring him to run, but knowing he had no chance against the older horses. "No fair, Dona!"

She laughed as she looked back at him. "Life rarely is, my darling boy!"

Alfie laughed at their banter and let Corridore run free, kicking him to take her on. He knew Lorenzo would never beat them back.

Alfie leaned over the mane and spoke to the stallion beneath him. "Come on, boy, let's show her."

He easily raced beside her and took the lead, both of them laughing. They went fast and hard all the way back to the stables. Dismounting quickly, Alfie took Dona's horse's bridle and pulled him around, offering to help her dismount. "May I, mistress?"

She needed no assistance dismounting, but she loved that Marco had instilled in all the warriors the tradition of old-world manners. She'd seen the young mortals and even some of the young vamps when she went into town, and they showed so much disrespect. She extended her hand to Alfie, and allowed him to help her dismount, making sure her body brushed against his as she slid to the ground.

"Thank you, Alfie. And it looks like the prince will be serving our drinks. Come. Let's get back to the house and you two can quench your thirst before you must return to camp."

22

It had taken a few days to get the horses ready to transport to Castello, and now Dona needed to confront Marco. The boys had been concerned when they'd left that he'd be angry about her gift to Alfie, and she had no doubts he would be. It would take considerable charm on her part to sooth him. The horses had been loaded in a horse trailer and were enroute, when she teleported ahead, hoping to prepare him for their arrival. Arriving at Castello, Carlos informed her that the boys were both in the camp. She let him know it was Marco she wished to see and asked if he could please summon him here. He nodded, having her take a seat in the parlor and ordering her a glass of Midnight before going to the camp. Carlos couldn't remember the last time he'd gone to the camp. The house staff rarely had a need to visit there. Entering the enclosed training field, he skirted around the edges, trying to avoid the warriors involved in their training exercises. He spotted Marco, barking out orders at a group of juniors, and waved frantically trying to get his attention.

One of the warriors nodded to Marco, directing his attention to Carlos, who stood in his black waist coat and bow tie on the edge of the training grounds. "Looks like someone is lost or has an emergency."

Marco turned to see Carlos, flailing his arms about and looking completely out of place among the warriors. "*Cazzo*, what in the hell does he want? Take over and keep things moving until I settle this mess." Marco made his way over to Carlos, shaking his head as he watched the manservant nervously fidgeting with his black waist coat. "Carlos, what in blazing hell are you doing here?"

"I am so sorry to disrupt you, but Mistress Donatella is here and has asked to see you. I left her in the parlor with a glass of Midnight. Shall I tell her you are too busy?"

Just the mention of her name brought a scowl to Marco's face. He couldn't imagine why she'd need to see him. He turned to see Lorenzo fully entrenched in his exercises and shrugged his shoulders. "No, Carlos, I'll handle her. Return to the house, I'll be there shortly."

As Carlos skittered away as fast as he could back to Castello, Marco gave his orders to one of the senior warriors and let him know he was leaving the field for a while. Wondering what the hell she wanted now, he teleported up to Castello, and walked into the parlor with a stride that was a mix of business and frustration.

"Donatella. Want to explain to me what in hell is so important as to pull me away from my duties?"

She looked up with a startled expression. "Oh, Marco! I do hope this is not too much of an intrusion, but it is important I speak with you." Standing, she took charge, as if this was her parlor. "May I have Carlos bring you a glass of Midnight? Please, be seated." She waved her hand at Carlos, indicating he was to bring another glass.

Marco grunted unceremoniously. He had no time for her games. "Just tell me why in hell you're here. What is so damn urgent? Seriously, mistress, you try my patience. I have a camp to run, now get on with it!"

Dona tossed her hair over her shoulder, sitting back down as she crossed her long legs. "You are aware, of course, I was giving Lorenzo a horse. He is being transported here now, as we speak. But when he and Alfie came to my home, and I gave the boy the horse, it seemed so...unfair. I don't ride as much as I once did, so I made a decision on the spot, to give Alfie a horse as well. It is an excellent horse, Marco, a Peruvian Paso. I know I should have checked first, but it was a spontaneous gesture. I hope you will not deny the boy this gift."

Marco had taken the seat across from her. He lowered his head and looked her in the eyes. "Let me understand this. You not only gave Lorenzo a horse, but Alfie as well?" He slapped his hands hard on his leathered thighs, the sound reverberating across the room. "You told Shade one horse, not two. And I don't give two flying fucks if it was spontaneous or not. You aren't going to tell me you didn't have this planned. Do you have any idea the situation you put Alfie in?"

His response wasn't unexpected, and she was prepared. Reaching over, she placed her hand on his knee. Her voice was as soft as a kitten's purr. "Marco, please. Calm down. I had not planned on it but think for one minute. Surely, you, of all people, know how it feels to live in the shadow of a royal. Alfie is Lorenzo's best friend, but he can never be Lorenzo. One boy gets a gift of a new horse, and the other must stand and watch? When would Alfie's family ever be able to afford such an extravagance? You know the answer is never. Now the two boys can ride together. I know it was impulsive on my part, but I beg you. Please. Let him keep the gift."

Marco looked at her hand on his knee. It had been a while since he'd tangled with a woman, and this one was far above getting her way than most. "There are other horses at Castello. If he wanted to ride, there was no problem. You know this."

Flinging her hand off his knee, he stood and paced, his temper rising. She was above him, so his reactions called for a level of diplomacy. " Alfie will get teased by his brothers, even more than he does now. They already think he gets special privileges being friends with the prince. And I know damn well how it feels. I lived with it my whole fucking life. Still do. There's much rivalry among the warriors, especially the young ones. Do you ever think about anyone but yourself?"

She tucked her head, as if deferring to him. If logic wouldn't work, she'd try other feminine wiles. As a tear slid down her cheek, she raised her hand to wipe it away. "I'm so sorry. I meant no harm, Marco. You know I have no children of my own. I only wanted the boys to be happy. If you could have seen them, if you could have seen Alfie's face! I admit, my decision may have been selfish, because it gave me such pleasure to be able to give a gift to both boys. But what would you have me do? Take back the gift? Tell the boy you are refusing him? Please don't do that." She looked at him with doe eyes, wet with her tears.

Marco stared back at her and sighed. Damn females and their crying. "No, I won't deny him. But *cazzo*, Dona, a puppy, now horses. What in hell are you going to give him next?"

He downed the Midnight that had been left by Carlos, tossing it back. Turning quickly, he stared at her, long and hard. "There's another matter which I want to speak to you about. You are here far too much for my liking. Lorenzo does not need a mother. He already has one. I know you have no children, but you can't adopt him. Lorenzo needs to be tough, he is warrior and prince, for hells sake, woman. Back it down on the visits."

She tucked her head again. He was giving in on the gift of the horse. She'd deal with the issue of visits another time. "Of course, Marco, I never wish to displease you. I am grateful for all you do."

He sat back down in the chair opposite her, crossing his leg on his knee. "Are you? Grateful? You've been interfering in this family for a long damn time, Dona. You still have all the beauty and charm to attract a master worthy of Alizzi. Shade will never leave our queen. Give it up."

She looked up startled. "Marco! How can you even think that? I can see with my own eyes how much he adores her. There is no female who would ever tempt him away from his queen, of that I have no doubt. I know him too. Maybe not in the same way you know him, but Shade and I have shared much. He is a man of his word, and his integrity, his loyalty, they will not be compromised, *si?* We both know that. I promise you; I have no designs on Shade. But we share a history, and the least I could do for him, and for his queen, is offer to look after their son."

Marco was taken aback by the sincerity in her expression. Maybe he'd misjudged her. "Just making a point, letting it be heard. My apologies if I offended you. I'm used to dealing with warriors, not females of your class. I'm an old warrior, and to be honest with you, Dona, never thought my old ass would survive this long. But my days running this camp are numbered. Lorenzo will rule here, and Alfie will step into my shoes as Second-In-Command. It's my job to make sure they are both ready when the time comes." Chuckling, he smiled at her. "It is one of the reasons I look out for Alfie as much as I look after Lorenzo. The times are different, but Shade needed me as much as I needed him. Alfie is good for Lorenzo, he gets grief over it, but he handles himself well. I just regret it will make them hard inside, like me."

She looked up at him, giving him a soft smile. "My dear Marco, you have given so much to this family, to your coven. Please do not underestimate the contributions you have made. I don't think they have made you hard inside, but quite the contrary. You love Shade like a brother, and you would lay down your life protecting this coven. You will ensure that Lorenzo will be ready to rule when his time comes, and Alfie will stand beside him, just as you stood beside your king. I do not see a hard man, I see a strong man, with a good heart. It is quite different, *si?*"

He scoffed. “I am not sure many here would say the same, Dona. I hate to end this meeting, but I have warriors who need to be groomed." Standing, he reached for her hand. "Please allow me to escort you to the door. Be assured the horses will be taken care of."

As she took his hand, he squeezed it softly. "Just make me one promise, Dona."

"You may ask me anything, Marco. If it is mine to give, I will give it."

She was so close to him he could feel her breath on his face. "If Lorenzo has a problem, you will let me know? There may be things he won’t tell me, because he doesn’t want to appear weak. I want to understand whatever he is dealing with, at least if I know about it, I can help, in a way he won’t notice, *si?*"

"Of course, I will let you know if I see anything that is concerning to me." She lifted his roughened hand to her lips and gently kissed it. "Thank you for not denying me the chance to give Alfie the horse."

"Females and your wiles, I will be damned if I ever get used to it." Leading her to the door, he knew he needed to work with her, even if just to keep an eye on her. With an impulse he didn’t see coming, he hugged her softly. "Safe journey home."

23

Emma and Gi had been working diligently to get the house spotless for the wedding. The house would be filled to capacity once all the guests had arrived. The guest bedroom had been prepared for Rachael's arrival tomorrow, and they were expecting the arrival of Lorenzo and Alfie shortly. They'd let the two boys share Lorenzo's bedroom. Shade had sent the jet to bring them home and arranged to have their wet feeders brought home as well. The wet feeders would reside in the staff quarters, and Nita was very excited to be reunited with her sister, Ghita. Lorenzo had pleaded with Shade to allow Alfie to join them, and Shade had finally relented, thinking the exposure to the second camp might be a good experience for the boy.

Kate and Shannon had taken on the responsibility for getting the gardens in top shape for the wedding. It had been a beautiful spring, and the flowers were in full bloom. The irises, peonies, roses, and lavender were abundant throughout the gardens. Kate and Shannon had chosen a perfect spot to place a curved trellis, and had it covered in fresh wisteria, intertwined with pale ivory tulle and small white lights. The garden path had been lined with candles that would be lit right before the ceremony. There would be a cake and champagne for the mortals.

Kate was still feeling nervous about Madison's parents. They'd arranged for them to stay in a hotel in Charlottesville, and Dante would pick them up and escort them wherever they wanted to go while they were here. Still, having mortals in their home was always a risk. Kate checked the time, and decided to wrap up, brushing the dirt from her hands.

"I'm going to go back to the house, Shannon. I need to get cleaned up. Lorenzo should be here soon, and I think Shade and I need to talk to the kids."

Shannon was on her knees in the garden, putting in some new plants, as she wiped her hand across her face, smudging a streak of dirt across her cheek. "You go ahead, I'm almost finished here. Tell Luca I'll be up shortly."

Kate gave her a kiss on the cheek. "I don't know what I'd do without you." Walking back to the house, along the meandering garden path that Madison and Cory would walk together, Kate gave everything a last look. Pleased with how it all looked, she entered the house and kicked off her garden clogs by the back door. The sun was dropping behind the mountain range as dusk settled across the estate. She called out to Shade. "Lover, are you up?"

Shade emerged from the shower, dripping wet, and wrapped a white towel around his hips. The house had been bedlam the last couple of days as everyone had been preparing for the wedding. He zipped up his jeans, slipped on a tee shirt and was preparing to put on his boots when he heard her voice. "Upstairs, *bel.*"

Kate took the stairs, hearing him call back to her from their bedroom. She entered to find him with his hair still wet from his shower, lacing up his boots. "Looks like I missed the fun part. I should have gotten here a little earlier."

He looked up at her through the damp tendrils of hair hanging over his forehead, as he winked at her. "Never too late." Standing up, he ran both hands through his hair, pushing it back from his face. "I've missed you."

"Do you miss me enough to hug me, even though I'm covered in dirt and you're all clean?"

He laughed and took her into his arms. Tucking a red lock of hair behind her ear, he kissed her softly. Licking his thumb, he wiped the smudge of grime off her face. "You trying to hide from me?"

She laughed. "I'm just glad you can find me at all under all this dirt. Lorenzo and Alfie will be here soon. I was thinking we should talk to the kids. Remind them of how careful they must be around Madison's parents. As for Alfie, I know nothing about how much exposure he's had to mortals. Madison's parents have met Cory, but he's used to walking that thin line between mortal and immortal."

"Si, they will be arriving within the hour." Walking to the dresser, he dragged a comb through his still wet hair and made eye contact with her in the mirror. "But a meeting with the children is good. Can you get Sophia to sit quiet long enough? Because she is the only one, I am truly concerned with. Alfie and Lorenzo are taught about the mortal world in camp, as are all the warriors, and Nattie, she will do whatever we ask of her."

Kate started to strip off her garden clothes. "Give me a few minutes to shower. You can check on the camp, and by then, Lorenzo and Alfie should be here. We'll get the boys settled, then gather all the kids." She gave him a quick kiss before heading to the shower.

Shade headed to camp, and before he got there his ears were assaulted with the sound of very loud music. "What in the hell is going on now? Damn fucking warrior dance party?"

He could see flashes of swords as they flew through the air, high above the wall surrounding the camp, the bright lights that illuminated the training field catching the metal and glinting. It looked like a fucking circus act, with warriors flying and flipping through the air. Entering the gates, he saw the cause of the commotion, triple somersaulting in the night sky, wielding a sword, as his hair, black as the night sky flowed behind him. "Raven, I should have known."

He heard a loud squawking and looked up to see that damn bird. Wherever Raven went, Poe wasn't far behind. Making his way around the training field, he could only grin at the acrobatics and the sword play. All his young recruits were standing back in awe at this display. As the steady beat of the music finally ended, Raven landed on his feet, hair flying, and yelled to the warriors, "And that's how we do it Medici California style!"

As Raven headed in his direction, Marcello and Aislynn began to gather the warriors, getting them assigned to their training groups for the night. Shade met him halfway. Raven walked with a long stride and a wide grin on his face. They embraced, pounding each other hard on the back.

"Boss-man! I thought the place needed livening up."

Shade threw back his head, laughing. "When the hell did you get here? Welcome home."

Raven cocked his head to the side. "I came in early to see my brother while he's still single. How's Cory doing?"

They walked to the barracks and lit up some smokes. "He's good. Be sure to go to the house and see him. How is Mica?"

Raven nudged him hard in the shoulder. "Mica's fine. We both are. Alec is a pain in my ass, though. He seems to have a problem with my dress code. You need to speak to that uptight vampire."

Shade grinned. "He has been through some rough times lately. Provide him with warriors and all will be smooth sailing. I need to get back up to the house, Lorenzo is due in. Make sure you pay your respects to your queen before the wedding."

Shade headed back to the house, shaking his head. It was good to see his warriors happy, no matter where in hell they were stationed. But now, it was time to get serious. As he approached the house, he saw the limo sitting out front. His son was home. His step became a bit lighter and his stride faster.

Lorenzo loved the camp in Florence, so he was surprised by how excited he was to be home. Alfie had hardly slept on the flight over. He'd never flown on a plane before. His mom had met them at the door and smothered him in kisses. He had to laugh as Alfie looked a little embarrassed by it all. Gi and Dante carried in their luggage and Kate followed him upstairs to his room.

"We put an extra bed in your room for Alfie. Sophia and Natalia are in class with Enzo, but I'm sure they won't be able to stand it for long once they know you're home. You boys get settled, and then join us in the living room please. There are some things we need to discuss before Madison's parents arrive. Alfie? Are you okay? Do you have everything you need? Your feeder will be in the staff quarters. Just let Gi know when you wish to see her."

Alfie felt honored to be a guest of his master and king and stammered slightly when he answered his queen, "No, my lady...I'm fine, my Queen. *Grazie.*"

Kate gave the boy a hug. "Please, just call me Kate. Put your things away, then join us downstairs."

Kate was about to leave when she heard the sound of pounding feet down the hallway and Sophia and Natalia burst into the room. Sophia flung herself at her brother, practically knocking him down. "Lorenzo!"

Natalia stood back, waiting her turn to greet her brother. She extended her hand to Alfie. "Hi. I'm Natalia. You must be Alfie."

Alfie had seen the princesses from afar when they brought Lorenzo to live in Florence, but he'd never met them in person before. Alfie took Natalia's small hand in his own and bowed. "It's an honor and privilege to finally meet you, Princess Natalia."

Natalia nodded, speaking with a maturity well beyond her years. "You don't need to call me princess, Natalia will be fine. Sophia, on the other hand, will insist on it. Welcome. We've heard a lot about you. Lorenzo talks about you all the time."

Sophia finished greeting her brother and proceeded to jump up and down on his bed, while Kate scolded her to get down. Sophia looked at the tall boy her brother had brought home with him.

Natalia stepped in to give Lorenzo a hug. Natalia asked, "Are you learning new things, Lorenzo?"

Lorenzo returned her hug. "We have class every day, just like here, plus we have training in camp. How about you, little sister?"

She nodded her head. "I'm ahead of Sophia in class. Enzo is teaching me physics and calculus now. It's okay, kind of boring. I like history best."

Lorenzo smiled and shook his head. Natalia seemed more at home in the classroom than on a playground. Sophia squealed as Kate finally grabbed hold of her, lifting her from the now disheveled bed.

Sophia shouted, "I'm gonna go get Poppy!"

Kate shook her head no. "No, you're not. We need to have a family meeting. You too, Alfie. Come on, we're going to the living room."

Sophia broke free and ran for the stairs, as Kate and the other children followed. Sophia saw her father as he entered the house, returning from the camp, and launched herself at him. "Daddy! Lorenzo is home. Can I bring Poppy in to see him?"

Shade caught Sophia as she landed in his arms. "*Si*, princess, your brother has returned. And no, we will not be inviting Poppy to join us." As he set her down on her feet, he saw his son coming down the stairs. "Damn, you have grown taller!" He opened his arms to his son, his heart racing at the sight of him.

Lorenzo hugged his dad and felt his father's pride. It made him stand taller. "Marco keeps us busy, that's for sure."

Shade hugged him tight. He was beginning to look like a warrior now. Ruffling his dark curls, Shade put his arm around his shoulders. "He better, he gets paid a lot of money to turn you into a warrior."

Shade turned to Alfie. "Welcome to Bel Rosso. We are happy to have you join us. Come, let us go to the living room and get settled in."

As everyone made their way to the living room, Shade poured himself a Midnight and threw it back in one shot. "By the way, *mi amore*, Raven has arrived."

She laughed. "Well, that explains the music we heard from the camp earlier."

He took a seat in the oversized armchair and she nestled in next to him. Lorenzo took a seat on the sofa, and when Alfie joined him there, Kate could see how much their son had grown. The two boys took up all the room on the sofa. Sophia plopped down in the other armchair, while Natalia sat on the floor by her father's feet, her arms wrapped around his leg.

Kate made sure she had the children's attention. "Kids, we wanted to remind you that while Madison is mortal, and used to our ways, her parents have no idea what we are. It will be important they're not exposed to anything that will make them question. Your father will shut down the camp. The warriors will remain in the barracks or feeder compound. They won't train the night of the wedding. Luca and Shannon will be there, as well as Raven. No teleporting. No tricks. No display of fangs. The mortals will be eating cake later. We'll cut a slice for you as well, but you're to walk away with it, pretend to eat, and discard it in the garden. Aegis and Night Stalker will take care of it. It won't last long. And they know to remain out of sight."

As Kate finished, Shade cleared his throat. "Now, I have some instructions. And I expect them to be followed. There will be punishment if you do not." His eyes landed on Sophia who was already squirming in the chair, her feet hanging over the arm, as she moved her head from side to side. "Sophia!"

"I'm listening, Daddy. I just got music in my head."

"Could you possibly turn it off? I need you to hear me, *si!* There will be no chickens inside this house, out in the garden or anywhere near the ceremony. All of you will be on your best behavior. Mortals do not understand our culture. You are Medici. You will act and behave as such. Manners and etiquette are expected, and I will know if you do not heed my word. This is not a request, understood? If you have a problem, you come to me or your mother. We will handle anything that arises. You will welcome the Barnes' into this home with grace and dignity. Does anyone have questions?"

The kids sat silently, shaking their heads no, as Sophia looked from face to face. "Daddy! Poppy wants to come to the wedding. I already told her she could go."

"Princess, what in the hell did I just get done saying? I know damn well underneath that mop of red curls you have ears. Repeat after me. Poppy will not be attending the wedding. Do it!"

With an exaggerated sigh, she flopped back against the chair. "Okay! I'll tell Poppy you hate her guts and she can't come. But don't blame me if she runs away from home."

Shade sighed and had to calm his temper. "I did not ask for your smart comment, I asked you to repeat. Now, repeat. No Poppy anywhere to be seen at this ceremony."

Sophia sat upright in the chair and looked back at him. "No Poppy anywhere at the ceremony. Jeez, this will be so boring."

Alfie was biting his tongue trying not to laugh at the antics of Lorenzo's sister. Lorenzo just shook his head. "You'll get used to her."

"*Grazie*, princess. And if you do not listen, there will be a problem. Raven is visiting from California, and he has brought Poe with him. I have given instructions to Poe not to eat the chickens, but I can easily have all of that retracted. So, if I were you, well..."

Sophia's mouth flew open. "No! Mommy would never let Poe hurt Poppy. Would you, Mommy?"

Kate looked at their red-headed terror. "Sophia, could we have one night without drama."

Sophia pouted and kicked her feet against the chair. "I guess so. But it won't be easy."

Kate smiled at her. "I'm sure it won't, but you need the practice."

Sophia slipped out of the chair. "Can we go now? I have to go break the news to Poppy."

As much as she tried his patience, he loved his daughter's spirit. "*Si*, you are excused. Love you."

Sophia blew him a kiss as she scrambled from the room.

Natalia stood to leave. "I will never understand her, Daddy. She gives me a headache."

Shade laughed at his youngest daughter. "Give me a kiss, Nattie, and go with Mommy. Daddy and these two fine warriors are going to camp."

24

Hank and Janis stood outside the doors of the hotel, waiting for the limo. They'd spent all day yesterday with Cory and Madison. They'd showed them around Charlottesville, taking them to Madison's store on the mall, and visiting the historical sites. They'd both been a little surprised they hadn't met Cory's parents yet. Cory explained his dad was away on business and wouldn't be home until late, but his parents were looking forward to seeing them.

The Barnes liked Cory, and thought he was a good match for their daughter, and clearly, she was happy and had done well with her business. They knew Cory's father had had a hand in getting her shop financed, and she'd always spoke highly of them, but in the seven years they'd been together, not once had they met the Medici's. They'd chalked it up to the fact they lived in Oregon, and how much Cory indicated his dad had to travel as a result of his vineyards being located in different countries.

The limo pulled up on time, and the driver jumped out, opening the door for them. They slid into the back of the opulent car, as the driver got back behind the wheel. Janis had been surprised when they'd been picked up at the airport two days ago to learn the limo wasn't rented but was owned by the Medici's, and the driver was their employee. They sat back and enjoyed the ride through the Virginia countryside, as they drove in the direction of the mountains.

Janis leaned forward to speak to the driver. "Have you worked for the family very long?"

Dante glanced over his shoulder; well aware he was transporting mortal passengers. He'd like to see her face if he answered her correctly and said he'd been working for Shade for about 300 years. Instead, he nodded as he responded, "Yes ma'am, a number of years now."

They drove in silence. As they approached Bel Rosso, and he turned onto the long private drive, Dante could hear the woman as she exclaimed, "Oh my!" And he thought to himself, *you haven't seen anything yet, lady.* It was mid-afternoon when they arrived, and he knew his master would still be in his death slumber, so his queen would have to handle this bunch on her own.

He pulled up in front of the house and slid out of the car, opening the door for them. The Barnes emerged from the car to see Cory was there to greet them, along with a lovely woman with red hair who looked about the same age as Cory. They were wondering if she might be another wedding guest. Janis was out of the car first and rushed to give her soon to be son-in-law a hug, as her husband stood patiently. Janis stepped back, Cory hugged Mr. Barnes, and then introduced the redhead. "This is my step-mom, Kate. Kate, these are Madison's parents, Hank and Janis."

Kate greeted them warmly as the two exchanged quick glances at each other. "Welcome to Bel Rosso. I'm sorry we didn't have room for you to stay here. But our other son came home from Italy and brought a friend, and Cory's biological mom is already here as well. Please come in."

She turned to walk back to the house, where Gi stood with the door open for the guests. Janis leaned into her husband and whispered, "She looks the same age as Cory."

Hank was looking around the estate as he answered back, "Trophy wife, Janis."

Cory could hear them but decided not to comment. Things would be weird enough around here as it was.

Kate led them into the house, Cory was a bit nervous. He knew they tried hard to keep mortals out of the house whenever possible, and he was just hoping nothing went wrong. As they entered the living room, Rachael stood to meet the Barnes.

Cory introduced her. "This is my biological mom, Rachael. Mom, these are Maddie's parents, Hank and Janis." Cory looked at Gi, and it was easily understood he needed a drink. Gi was already opening a few bottles of wine for the mortals and was filling the glasses on the tray.

For Rachael, this was a day she never thought she'd see. "I'm so glad to meet you. We all love Madison so much. We couldn't be happier about the wedding."

Janis gave the woman a hug and wondered if Rachael was comfortable here with her ex-husband's much younger wife.

"We're both happy to finally meet you as well. I understand you also live on the west coast."

Rachael nodded. "I do. I'm in California. I don't like to travel much, though. Cory and Madison come out to see me from time to time, but I rarely come here."

Janis was thinking she understood why. Gi served a tray of white wine to the mortals and indicated a table where he'd set out hors d'oeuvres for them. Janis held up the glass of white wine. "Is this from your vineyards?"

Gi nodded. "It is, indeed, madam."

Cory took a glass of the white wine as well, although he'd much prefer the Midnight about now. When Kate didn't take the wine, Hank gave her a wink. "No wine for you? Not old enough, eh?"

Kate smiled back at him. "I have so much to do to get ready. I don't need anything to slow me down."

Janis was looking about the well-appointed room. "And Mr. Medici. Will we be meeting him soon?"

Kate nodded, already feeling tense. "Yes, of course. He had to go down to the stables, but he'll be here. Madison is getting her hair done now, so why don't you all have a seat. Eat whatever you want. I have a lot to check on. I'm sure Madison will want your help with her dress later. Please excuse me?"

Kate hurried from the room, speaking to Cory under her breath as she passed him, "You got this?"

He looked at her with a glint of panic in his eyes. "Guess we'll find out."

Cory couldn't believe Kate was leaving him, but he understood why. He looked quickly at his mom and she winked. "Please everyone, take a seat and get comfortable." Shrugging, he smiled. "It takes women a while to get ready for their wedding day. At least the weather is cooperating. The garden looks great. Kate grows lavender and sunflowers here. She has her own business apart from Dad's." He was searching for anything to talk about to fill the time and hoped it wouldn't be long before his dad woke from his death slumber.

Hank sipped at the wine as he popped a shrimp in his mouth. "Must be a good business. You never mentioned how, uh, young your stepmother was. Not that it matters, of course."

Cory tensed up. They hadn't even thought about that. His biological mom looked about the same age as Madison's parents, but Kate and his dad weren't aging. They never paid attention to it, but he realized now that to Madison's parents, he and Madison must look about the same age as Kate. His father would look slightly older, but not nearly old enough to have a son who was twenty-seven. "Uh, well, she's a little younger. But she's really active too, stays in shape."

Raven entered, and Cory was glad for the distraction. Raven stayed true to form and was wearing a leather suit. The lapels of the suit jacket had been covered in studs. He looked like he was getting ready to give a rock concert and his outfit took the conversation off how young Kate looked. He had a ring on every finger, and his hair hung long and unfettered down his back. Raven gave him a hug.

"Well, little brother, it's the big day. Congratulations, you made it."

Cory had never been so glad to see Raven in his whole life. "Thanks, brother. Let me introduce you to everyone. You know my mom. And these are Maddie's parents, Hank and Janis. They flew in from Oregon."

Raven walked to Rachael and lifted her hand and kissed it. "My pleasure to see you again, Rachael. Looking good, I might add."

Rachael had met the extravagant warrior several times before, and knew he'd played a key part in rescuing Madison and her son when they'd been kidnapped by Max. She gave him a bright smile. "It's always good to see you, Raven."

Janis looked at her husband and spoke under her breath, "Raven? What kind of name is that?"

Her husband shushed her. "Probably a nickname, Janis. Look at his hair."

She huffed as she took a sip of the wine. "Looks strange to me."

Raven turned to the mortals. He could hear every word they'd said. He knew Hank was here for the free ride, sucking up the luxury and the free food and wine. Madison's mother was a house mouse. And she'd have one hell of a lot of gossip to tell her book club when she got home. Walking to Janis, he bowed slightly. "A pleasure to meet you. Beautiful night for a wedding, don't you agree?"

Janis had met some of her daughter's bohemian friends before, but this one seemed a little more over the top than usual. "We're looking forward to it, aren't we, Hank?"

Her husband had almost single-handedly emptied the shrimp platter. "What? Oh, sure...looking forward to it." He wiped his hand on a napkin before extending it to Raven. "Good to meet you. So, you're Cory's brother too?"

Raven grinned, shaking his hand with a grip that told the mortal he was treading in enemy territory. "Not by blood, but close in every sense of the word. I work for Cory's father. My partner and I run the vineyards and inn in California. I lived here a while before I was transferred to California. Cory and I became close then."

Raven was distracted and looked up as Luca and Shannon entered the room. "Luca!"

Raven and Luca hugged and pounded each other's back. Raven looked at Shannon and bowed. "You look like you just walked out of a designer magazine."

Shannon couldn't believe how nervous she was. With the exception of Madison, she was rarely around mortals anymore. She found it hard to even remember some aspects of that life. Luca led her into the room on his arm, and Cory introduced them. "This is Luca. He's going to be my best man. He works for my dad as well, and this is his mate, uh, wife, Shannon. I told you about her. She's in business with Kate."

Janis was taking in the handsome young couple, and thinking, once again, they all looked so young. She was expecting the adults to be more her age. "I'm so pleased to meet you. Madison mentioned you were going to be her Matron of Honor."

Shannon shook her hand. "Yes, and I couldn't be happier."

Hank greeted them both, shaking their hands. "So, you live nearby?"

Luca looked quickly at Shannon before answering. "We live here, actually."

Hank nodded. "You mean in the country?"

Luca shook his head. "No, here, in this house."

Frank gave him a quizzical look and Luca felt the need to explain. "Shade is often absent, so I manage things here when he's gone."

Hank looked at Shannon from head to toe. "Well, that's not a bad job."

Gi entered with a tray of Midnight and the vamps all quickly grabbed up a glass, Cory and Raven downed their glass as Shannon and Luca sipped more slowly. Hank nudged Luca, pushing him in the direction of the table laid out with food. As he started on the small crab cakes, he looked at Luca. "You eatin'?"

Luca stepped back. "Not yet. I had a big lunch but help yourself."

Hank looked him over. "So, you stay here with your wife and the redhead while he's out of town?" Hank laughed to himself before looking up to see Luca leveling him with a deadly stare.

"Careful, Mr. Barnes. We wouldn't want to get off on the wrong foot."

Hank swallowed the half-chewed crab cake. "No. Uh, no, I was just joking around. I mean, you here alone, with two beautiful women. Can't be too hard a job, now, can it?"

Luca stared back at him without answering and the man felt a chill down his back. "Sorry, no harm meant." He stuffed another crab cake into his mouth and made his way back to the couch.

25

Kate and Theresa were trying to get the girls dressed for the wedding. The girls had matching dresses of the palest pink, little lace-topped socks, and white Mary Jane shoes. Theresa had made headbands with fresh flowers from the garden. Natalia was dressed and looked like a porcelain doll.

Kate directed her daughter. "Please sit over there, Nattie, while Theresa puts the headband in place. Sit quietly until we're ready to go downstairs, so you won't soil your dress or scuff your shoes."

Natalia checked out her image in the mirror and gave a single nod of approval before sitting in the chair. Sophia had slid under the bed, complaining that she didn't like the dress. Kate grabbed her by the ankles and pulled her out. Sophia grabbed the bedrail, hanging on for dear life.

"No! I hate that dress! I want to pick out my own dress."

Kate sighed and took a deep breath. "Sophia, you helped pick out this dress. Now, stop it. I don't have time for this."

She freed the child from the bed and stood her upright, as she wrestled the dress over her head. "If I behave can I bring Poppy?"

Kate got the dress on the child and was buttoning the small buttons up the back. "Sophia, if you don't behave, I may serve the Barnes' Poppy for dinner. Now, settle down."

Sophia looked at her with her mouth open. "Nooooo, Mommy! Please don't hurt Poppy."

Kate looked at Sophia and shook her head. "You know I won't hurt Poppy. Please, this is Madison's day. Can you please not spoil it for her?"

Sophia shrugged. "I guess."

Kate finished buckling her shoes, as Theresa adjusted the headband on her hair. Sophia looked at herself in the mirror. "That looks stupid. Can I wear my crown?"

Theresa, usually very patient, knelt down in front of her and placed her hands on both shoulders. "Today, Madison is the princess, and you are her flower girl. Today is about Madison, not you. Understood?"

Sophia tilted her head to the side and put both hands on her hips. "All right. I get it. *Cazzo!*"

Kate leveled her with a stare. "Young lady! You've been told time and again about using that word."

Sophia shrugged again. "It slipped."

"Well, make sure it doesn't happen again. I don't want to have to explain what you said to Madison's parents."

Sophia was picking at the dress. "I'm pretty sure they've heard the word fuck before."

Kate sat down hard on the floor, and closed her eyes, counting to ten.

***

Shade rose from his death slumber and remembered this was the night he'd have mortals in his home. He inhaled deeply, and realized they were already here. He could smell them. He rushed to the shower and washed up. As he returned to the bedroom, he could feel the chaos. Kate was about to explode with frustration. He didn't bother getting dressed for the wedding but slipped on his jeans and headed in the direction of all the noise. Standing outside Sophia's bedroom, he overheard the argument between mother and daughter, and he had to bite his tongue not to laugh. He heard Sophia utter the profanity as Kate gave up in frustration.

Stepping into the room in his bare feet, arms crossed over his chest, he towered over his red-headed daughter. If he hadn't known better, he'd swear she was spawned by the devil himself. He bent down and placed his hands on either side of her face, holding her firmly as he growled, "You are so far out of line this time, Sophia. You have made your mother upset, and do you know what that does to me?"

Sophia knew when she'd pushed too far, and now was one of those times. She could wrap her father around her little finger, but when he lost patience with her, she knew it was time to reel it in. "It makes you mad. I'm sorry, Daddy. I'll be good."

He picked her up and sat her on the bed. "Do as you are instructed. I will not tolerate this madness in this house. You keep pushing and you won't be going to the ceremony, and you won't be leaving this room for a long time." He reached down and helped Kate up from the floor. "I'm sorry you had to go through this alone.

Go on and get ready. I will meet you in the bedroom shortly, I got this."

"I'm fine, lover. We're almost finished here, and she'll settle down now. If you don't mind, could you go check on the boys? I haven't had time to help Lorenzo, and I think Alfie may be too embarrassed if I went into their room." She planted a kiss on his lips. "I don't know what I'd do without you."

He smiled softly at her. "That I can do." Heading to Lorenzo's room, he tapped lightly and heard his son say enter. Walking in, he found the two boys helping each other, making sure their attire was impeccable. "Well, glad to see I don't have to admonish either of you two fine looking warriors. I swear that female is going to be the very death of me. I would kill for a damn drink."

Lorenzo laughed. He didn't need his father to explain which female he was referring to. "Some things never change, Dad."

When Alfie gave him a quizzical look, Lorenzo responded. "My sister, Sophia. She makes up her own rules."

Alfie laughed. "Yeah, I sort of noticed that."

The two boys looked dapper in their dark suits, white shirts and ties. Alfie looked to Shade. "Thank you for the suit, master. I never wore a suit before, just jeans or leathers. I hope I look okay."

Shade nodded. "You are welcome, Alfie. You look like a proper Medici in that Italian suit. I am sorry for all the chaos. I have way too many females and not enough warriors inside this house to keep things balanced."

Shade looked at his son and took in a deep breath. "Can you keep an eye on your sister for me at the ceremony and afterward. If she looks like she is going to break out the chicken, please stop her. I need to get back and get myself presentable. And remember, mortals."

"We got this, Dad. Don't worry."

Shade nodded as he headed for the door. "Oh, and one more thing, if you have a brain in your head, neither of you will come out until someone comes to get you. It's a damn three ring circus out there." He left, closing the door behind him and hearing their laughter. Entering the bedroom, he found Kate getting ready. "Boys are fine. Ready to roll. So, while we get ready, how do the Barnes' come off to you?"

Kate slid into the peach-colored sheath dress and backed up to him to help her with the zipper, pulling her hair aside. "Oh, uh, well, she seems to be the type that judges everything, and is a little bitter, and he seems to have an eye for the ladies. I didn't really feel a connection between them. I understand, now, why Madison never seemed interested in going back home."

Zipping up her dress, he kissed the nape of her neck. "Mortal men, need I say more? Hank and Janis, right?" He hurriedly pulled on his dress pants, slipped on a white dress shirt and reached for the peach tie with black stripes that matched her dress. She helped him with his cufflinks.

"Our son is growing up, *bel*. Scares the fuck out of me. The boys look handsome as hell. Camp is doing him good." He stood before the mirror and tied his tie, then ran his hand through his hair. "What do you think? Tie it up, or leave it down?"

She was slipping her feet into her shoes and looked up at him. He looked delicious, and she regretted they had to go downstairs to greet guests. "Oh, I say we go all out and create a real scandal. Leave it down."

Walking to him, she stood on tiptoe and slid her arms around his shoulders. "Lorenzo has grown so much taller, and he hasn't been there a whole year yet. I can't believe how much...older he acts. I know I was afraid to let him go, but the camp has been good for him. Still...I hate letting go of my beautiful little boy."

Looking down at her, she still took his breath away. "He is growing up, *mi amore*. He will reach maturity soon. Alfie is almost there. I should probably talk to Lorenzo before that happens."

"Yeah, that's a talk I'll leave to you."

He smiled as he kissed her, lingering over her, knowing they'd be rushed once they stepped outside their door.

She broke the kiss before it got out of hand. "Keep that up and we'll miss the whole wedding. I think Luca was going to help Cory. He was going to get dressed in Luca and Shannon's suite, so he wouldn't see Madison in her dress. But I should probably go check on Madison. Shannon is helping her get dressed, but I want to make sure she's okay. You could send her mother up when you take the boys down, okay?"

"With pleasure, my queen. And just for the record, once this wedding is over, there is no camp tonight. So, you better be prepared to have a honeymoon night of your own." Slapping her ass, he winked as he headed out the door for the boys.

As she followed him out, she flashed him a look that said she was up for the challenge. "I'll hold you to that."

Rushing up the stairs to the third floor, she tapped lightly before entering. Shannon was helping Madison with some last-minute touches. Madison had found a vintage wedding gown, the lace slightly tea stained with age. She'd worked with Cory to remake the dress, so it fell off her shoulders. Instead of a veil, she wore a halo of fresh flowers from the garden, matching the flowers in Natalia's and Sophia's headbands. Her hair had been curled in long, loose tendrils. She looked like a garden fairy.

Kate exclaimed when she saw her, "Oh, Madison! You look perfect."

***

Shade gathered the boys and grabbed Emma along the way. He needed her to stand by to escort Mrs. Barnes back upstairs to Cory's suite. "Okay, boys, the show is on."

As they entered the living room, the three of them stood tall, warriors all in a row, dressed to the nines. Hank and Janis both stood up when he entered the room with the younger boys. Shade approached Hank and extended his hand.

"Good evening, I am Cory's father, Shade Medici. I apologize for taking so long to join you. Welcome to Bel Rosso. I hope you have been comfortable while waiting for the festivities to begin. Allow me to introduce my youngest son, Lorenzo, and his friend, Alfie. Both are home from school in Italy."

Janis was shocked when she saw him. This was Cory's father? She looked back at the middle-aged woman sitting on the sofa, who must be a good thirty years older than him. Her daughter Madison was twenty-seven now, and she knew Cory was very close in age to her, and this man only looked about ten years older than Cory. She'd have guessed he was about thirty-eight. She extended her hand.

"You're...Cory's father? His biological father?"

Shade gave her a bright smile, as he locked eyes with her. He was going to charm her a bit; use a little vampire magic just to make sure this line of questioning was halted immediately. "Yes, I am Cory's biological father. And you must be Madison's mother. I see where she gets her beauty from. It is a pleasure to meet you, Janis."

Lifting her hand to his lips, he kissed it quickly and released it. Turning to Rachael, he smiled, and leaned over to her, kissing her softly on the cheek. "It does my heart good to have you with us today."

Turning to face everyone, he smiled at Lorenzo. "Lorenzo, would you and Alfie please escort Rachael back to Luca's suite, I am sure she would like some time alone with Cory before the ceremony."

Lorenzo stepped forward, taking Rachael's arm to escort her to visit with her son. Shade turned his attention back to Janis. "Now, Janis, I do believe the ladies have asked for your assistance with your daughter. Emma will escort you upstairs to the proper room." Taking her hand, he turned her over to Emma, leaving the two men alone.

"Hank, let me refill that drink for you, what is your poison?"

Hank had watched the interaction between the suave Italian and his wife. No wonder he had women of all ages at his feet. He'd take advantage of that situation himself. As Janis was escorted away, he held out his glass. "The wine is great, really. But if you have something stronger? A little scotch or bourbon, maybe? Some Jack Daniels if you have it."

"Jack Daniels it is. Gi, please get Mr. Barnes a Jack Daniels, straight up, and I will have my usual. Please, Hank, sit down, relax."

As Gi rolled his eyes, he made the drinks, served them and Shade had to hold back his laughter as his manservant kept up this masquerade.

"Madison is a beautiful woman, Hank. She is loved in this family. I want you to have no worries about her safety or welfare. I am able to make sure all my children live a good, productive life and want for nothing. My son is a gentleman, and he loves Madison very much. Do you have any questions for us?"

Hank accepted the drink from the butler and took a healthy swig. "No concerns. No sirree. We've met Cory before when he visited with Madison, and the wife and I were very impressed. He treats her good, and she told us how you helped her get her shop financed. Really appreciate that. Nice spread you got here."

"Madison is a true artist, and I was happy to invest in her future. She and Cory are a good match for each other. May I inquire what line of business you are in, Hank?"

Shade took him in while he talked, tapping into his thoughts. Mortals could be harmless fools, but he could tell Hank was enjoying the views of not only his estate but the females as well.

Hank was wondering just how generous he was willing to be with all that money. "Me? I'm an accountant. Work for a firm. Thought of going out on my own a few times, but you know...the money situation. We had to make sure we had the money for Madison to get through college, so it didn't seem like a good time to take the risk, you know."

Shade nodded. He didn't miss the subtle hint. "Finances are something I leave to my accountants. But, perhaps now that Madison is through with her college, you can go it on your own. They are both working, do well in their craft. But be assured, Hank, my son needs no help from anyone in providing for his wife. We take care of our own. Do you smoke?"

So much for that, Hank thought to himself. Well, at least he wouldn't have to worry about Madison's expenses anymore. "You got cigars? I love a good cigar. The wife won't let me smoke in the house, though."

Shade chuckled. "Well then, we have something in common. Come, let us step outside onto the patio and have a cigar and get some fresh air. I have some Havana's that are excellent for two fathers ready to launch their children's future."

26

Kate made one last check on the girls to find they were all dressed and ready. Shannon would stay with Madison until the ceremony began. Gi let her know the justice of the peace had arrived, and the string quintet had set up in the garden.

"Keep your fingers crossed, Gi."

"My lady, they have been crossed all evening."

Kate sent Sophia and Natalia up to Cory's suite to wait with the bride, and then headed down the stairs. Cory was waiting nervously in the living room with his dad. Shade had Lorenzo and Alfie at his side, as he and Luca sipped at a glass of Midnight. Kate gathered them around.

"I think we're ready to move outside. Mr. Barnes, you'll wait here. Shannon will bring Madison down and you'll be able to escort her out. Just stand near the bottom of the stairs."

He emptied the last of his Jack Daniels and moved into position. Kate slipped her arm through Shade's, as he offered his other arm to Janis. She smiled graciously and took his arm. "Not often I get to escort two beautiful ladies, *si?*" He gave Janis a smile that made her weak in the knees.

Kate had to bite her lip, as she saw how smitten Janis was with Shade. He could charm a snake if he needed to.

Raven offered his arm to Rachael. "I hope I'm not a disappointing escort."

Rachael laughed out loud, a sound they rarely heard. "That would be impossible." He gave her a wink, as she slid her arm through his.

Luca, Cory and the boys followed behind them, as Gi, Theresa and Emma moved outside as well. The staff had gathered discreetly under the large oak tree, where they were close enough to watch the ceremony. After all, Cory felt like their child too. The justice of the peace stood beneath the trellis, and Cory and Luca stepped forward. Luca had never participated in a mortal ceremony before. He wasn't used to a celebration that didn't include swords, but he'd been instructed all he needed to do was pass the ring to Cory. Cory was shuffling his feet and looking about nervously. Luca whispered, "Too late now, brother." Then heard Cory's soft laugh.

Shade made sure Janis got seated, leaving the seat next to her empty for Hank, and then sat next to *bel*. Raven took a seat next to Rachael, sitting next to Shade and Kate. Lorenzo and Alfie slid into the seats behind them.

Alfie whispered to Lorenzo, "I've never seen a mortal wedding."

Lorenzo laughed as he answered, "That makes two of us."

Kate shushed them, as the quintet began to play Pachelbel's "Canon in D Major".

As the music drifted through the night air, the crowd was watching as the Princesses appeared in their matching gossamer dresses of the palest pink, walking side by side. They each held a basket of pale pink rose petals, mixed with sprigs of lavender, which they dropped on the garden path as they walked slowly to the music. Kate placed her hand to her lips, as a tear rolled down her cheek. There had never been two more beautiful children. She leaned her head on Shade's shoulder and he kissed the top of her head.

The two girls were about halfway down the path when they heard the clucking. Walking behind Sophia was her pet chicken, pecking away at the petals as they were dropped. Picking them up and discarding them before running to the next. Sophia turned to look behind her and saw the chicken. "Poppy! I told you to stay." She looked back at her mother; her face full of innocence. "I told her to stay."

Kate waved her hand at her and mouthed, "keep walking," as she listened to the giggles through the crowd. Kate looked at Shade and shrugged. "Could be worse."

"What the hell should we do now? That damn bird will flap and squawk if we try to catch it." He was trying to keep a straight face, more amused than he cared to admit.

Kate smiled back at him. "Go with the flow, lover. What's a wedding without a pet chicken?"

The girls took their place under the trellis, as Poppy continued to peck at the ground, oblivious to the ceremony.

Shannon appeared a good bit behind them, carrying a bouquet of lavender and sunflowers, dressed in a pale lavender dress. She was lit by the candles that lined the path, and the lanterns that hung from the trees. Luca took one look at her and fell in love all over again. He locked eyes with her as he mouthed, "*mia belleza*." She smiled back at him.

The crowd had turned to watch the wedding party, and Kate saw her best friend, saw her eyes go to Luca, and the love Shannon felt for him was written on her face. She squeezed Shade's hand, and he lifted her hand to his lips, kissing it lightly. **"I know what is in your heart, *mi amore*."**

Alfie took one look at Shannon in the dress, surrounded by the candlelight and said, under his breath, "Wow, she's hot!"

Lorenzo smiled and nudged him hard. "Better not let Luca hear you say that, brother." Shade cast a sideways glance at both the boys, and they settled down.

As Shannon took her place under the trellis, facing Cory and Luca, she held Luca in her gaze. The crowd turned back around to see Madison, on her father's arm, as they walked down the path. She was a vision in her vintage gown she and Cory had worked on together. Her father looked proud but might have had one too many drinks, as it looked like Madison might be giving him more support than he was giving her.

Cory took one look at his bride, and the crowd could hear him as he said her name, "Maddie." She smiled back at him, as she walked with her father to join Cory under the trellis. Hank handed off his daughter to his soon to be son-in-law, and turned to take his seat next to Janis, who was already wiping her eyes.

The justice of the peace performed the simple ceremony, and asked Cory if he had a ring. Luca slipped the ring to him and Cory placed it on Madison's hand, and spoke his vows to her.

"I take you to be my partner for life. I promise, above all else, to live in truth with you, and to commit myself to you fully and fearlessly. I give you my hand and my heart, as a sanctuary of warmth and peace, and pledge my love, devotion, faithfulness, and honor, as I join my life to yours."

Kate felt the tears on her cheeks and squeezed Shade's arm. She looked over at Rachael, who held a tissue under her nose, the tears falling freely. The two women shared a love for this boy, one they both called son. Kate reached over and took her hand, and Rachael accepted the show of affection.

Shade's eyes never left Cory's face. He knew deep in his heart he'd made the perfect choice in a female for himself. As Cory placed the ring on her finger, then spoke his vows, Shade's own heart felt fulfilled. This son he'd found, missing for most of his life, had found love and happiness. He might be the most infamous bad ass warrior in vampire history, but the tears still filled his eyes. He was surrounded by his family on this day of celebration. He leaned his head softly to Kate. "*Ti amo, bel.*"

Shannon handed a ring to Madison, who slipped it on Cory's hand. "On this day, I give you my heart, and my promise that I will walk with you, hand in hand, wherever our journey leads us. Living, learning, loving. Together, forever."

The justice of the peace placed his hand over theirs and looked out into the crowd. "By the power vested in me, by the state of Virginia, I now pronounce you man and wife. You may now kiss your bride."

Cory scooped her up in his arms and kissed her, twirling her around, as she hung on to the floral halo on her head. The crowd stood to clap for them as they turned and walked back down the path, both of them smiling.

Luca extended his arm to his mate, as Shannon slipped her hand around his elbow. Shannon looked up at him. "Makes me want to mate you all over again."

He gave her a wink. "That can be arranged, *mia belleza*." They followed the couple back into the house, as Sophia and Natalia fell in behind them.

Sophia looked in her basket and shouted, "I still got petals left!"

Kate shook her head, as she watched Sophia empty the basket on the path, letting the petals fall in a heap. She and Shade stepped out into the path and herded the children back in the house. Sophia looked up at her father. "Did I do a good job, Daddy? I didn't bring Poppy, I promise."

Shade smiled down at her. "You did a good job, princess. Let us see if you can continue to do so until this is completely over."

Sophia smiled back at him, as she watched her brother Lorenzo slide out into the aisle. She'd never seen him in a suit before. "You look nice, Lorenzo."

He looked down at her with a smile. "Thanks, little sister."

As the Medici parents walked ahead, with Natalia in tow, Alfie stood from his chair and eased his way onto the garden path to stand next to Lorenzo. He was a good head and shoulders taller than Lorenzo. Sophia looked up at him, as if seeing him for the first time. "You look nice too, Alfie."

He flashed her a smile. "You look pretty good yourself. Good job up there. I especially enjoyed the chicken."

Sophia blushed at his attention and couldn't take her eyes off him. Lorenzo looked at her strangely. "You okay, little sister? I think we have to go in now and mingle with everyone."

Sophia was pulled from her trance, as her brother spoke to her. "Oh, sure. Let's go." She turned for the house, but stayed close to the boys, walking next to Alfie.

27

Both families gathered inside the house for the reception, where the mortals drank champagne, and the vamps drank Midnight after faking a drink of champagne following the toast to the new couple. Gi served cake to everyone, and the kids were great about slipping away with their plates and discarding the cake in the kitchen or the garden. Although, not before Sophia stuck her finger in the icing, and tried a taste. Her eyes lit up with the burst of sweetness, but it was quickly followed by a sharp pain in her belly. Kate remembered well the sweet taste of delicious pastries and candies and felt a momentary pang of guilt that her children would never know that pleasure.

Hank reverted to his Jack Daniels after the champagne toast and seemed particularly smitten with Shannon. He remained close throughout the evening, and Luca kept a close eye on him. As the hour grew late, the young couple hinted they had honeymoon plans, and Madison's parents prepared to leave. Janis was still not sure about this family, Shade especially. She was stuck on how this man had any interest in a woman of Rachael's age, let alone had a child with her. It was a story she was sure she'd never hear the truth about.

As the Barnes' were escorted out, Dante was waiting by the limo to take them back to the hotel. Tomorrow, they'd fly back to Oregon. As they pulled away, Kate let out a sigh of relief. She hadn't been fully aware of just how tense she'd been until they'd left, and thankfully, everything went as smoothly as they could expect, under the circumstances. Taking Shade by the hand, they turned to go back in the house.

"Lover, I wasn't aware Cory and Madison had made plans for a honeymoon. That will spoil our surprise."

He chuckled. "They didn't. Cory was just ready for them to leave."

Kate laughed. "Oh, he is so much his father's son."

As they walked back into the house, everyone had scattered, the children feeling released from the bondage of having to hide their true nature. Luca and Shannon were in deep conversation with Cory and Madison, as Rachael clung to her son's arm. Shade smiled, it was a good feeling to know after all these two had been through, they were happily united.

He announced loudly. "I would like to see everyone in the living room." Taking her hand, he led *bel* into the living room, as the adults joined him.

"First of all, I extend congratulations to the new couple. Madison, you are a beautiful bride. And son, I am proud of you. For Kate and I, there is nothing more special about this evening than being together as a family. But there is something Kate and I think you are missing. I remember distinctly a conversation you had with me, son. It was one that struck my heart deeply. You spoke about walls, and I realized walls can enclose a soul. You are starting your lives together, and you need space, air and sunshine. Walls that are your own, not mine. So, with that said, Kate and I would like to give you the keys to your own home. Because love is something that grows every day, we want you to have a place of your own, where it can grow as it should."

Cory looked shocked, as did Madison. "Dad! A house? You didn't have to do that. This is too much!"

As Kate clung to Shade's arm, she smiled at her stepson, and new daughter-in-law. "You need your own space, your own home, as you start your life together. You're still on the property, but far enough away you'll have your privacy. There's a suite for Hyde, just as we have for Luca. Since you're moving out of this house, and away from the protection, your father insisted Hyde would have his own suite. But I think you'll find you're happier on your own now."

The young couple stepped forward to be hugged by Shade and Kate, as tears slipped down Madison's cheeks. Shade stepped back, breaking the love fest as he invited them to see their new home. "I think we should all take a walk on this beautiful night and see if these keys work. I am sure your mother would like to see where you will be living."

Rachael locked eyes with him, mouthing 'thank you.'

He slipped his arm around her waist and bowed his head to kiss her cheek. "I promised you he would always be loved here."

Taking her hand, he grabbed Kate and led the way out of the house and through the gardens, across the fields of lavender and sunflowers. It was a long walk, and the women removed their shoes, preferring to make the journey in bare feet as opposed to heels. Shade was enjoying the night air, as well as the chatter of those he loved the most in this world.

As they approached the warrior camp, Cory stopped dead in his tracks. Lining both sides of the road were the Medici warriors, standing at attention in their dress leathers, each holding their sword. Cory looked at his father. "Dad?"

Shade winked at him. "The warriors were having a real problem with not being able to come to the celebration. They are your brothers and sisters. So, they asked to honor you and your new bride in the only way they could. The warriors wait for you."

With Madison on his arm, Cory stepped forward and, together, they walked down the drive, as each warrior raised their sword, crossing tips with the warrior that stood across from him. The clanking of metal against metal was loud and echoed off the Blue Ridge Mountains. It was the warrior's ultimate show of respect, and typically reserved for their master, and the best way to show Cory and his mate, they were one of them.

As the couple made it through the arch of swords, the warriors dropped to their knee as one, shouting in unison. "*Per sempre* Medici!" Then they all stood and issued a war cry that carried over the hills. Cory could feel the tears in his eyes and the lump in his throat. He never thought he'd be accepted by anyone, but these warriors had taken him in and now he didn't know what he'd do without them. He'd come such a long way from the streets of San Francisco. The warriors slapped him on the back or offered fist bumps, as they left to return to camp.

Back on the road, they continued to the crest of a hill where they got their first glimpse of their home. With the lights on inside and outside, the Italian villa, constructed of stone with a red tile roof, sat nestled among a crop of trees. Madison squealed with delight and she and Cory ran to the front door.

Shade threw Cory the keys, so he and Madison could be the first to enter their new home. Cory unlocked the door, and scooped up his new bride, carrying her over the threshold. Kissing her before he set her on her feet, he whispered, "You're a Medici now."

Other than Kate, none of them had seen the completed project. Shade stood next to her as they watched Madison and Cory, rushing from room to room, exclaiming over what they found. Shade smiled as they rushed past him again. "I take it you approve?"

Madison squealed, "We'll never fill all this space!"

Kate laughed. "You'd be surprised. There are three bedrooms for you, and two bathrooms, plus a kitchen, dining room, and living room. You'll have a room for your potter's wheel over there, so you won't have to work in the garage anymore. Hyde's suite is separated on the far side of the house. I designed it much like Luca's suite, so he has a bedroom, living room, and large bath. You'll have a great view of the property out every window. It's sparsely furnished, so you two can decide for yourself how you want to decorate."

Rachael was charmed by the cozy cottage feel of this house, and knew it wouldn't take them long to make it a home. "This is perfect for you, Cory. You and Madison will be very happy here." Cory stopped his tour long enough to kiss her on the cheek. "And there's room for you whenever you want to visit."

As the couple peered into rooms and opened closet doors, Shade let them know the kitchen had been stocked. Cory returned to his dad and hugged him. "I don't know what to say."

"You don't need to say anything. Just love her, live a full life and be happy." Reaching into his pocket, he removed a packet and slipped it to Cory. "Tonight, you can spend the night here in your new home, but tomorrow, Dante will fly you both to our home in Paris. I must insist Hyde accompany you, but you can stay as long as you wish. You need a real honeymoon. Inside the packet are the keys to the Paris house, and a credit card. When you get back home, furnish your home however you wish."

Madison had heard about the Paris house, but had never seen it. It had always been a dream of hers to see that city. She could never have imagined such a honeymoon. They would have been content to just stay here. She first hugged Kate, then Shade. "I can't thank you enough. This is so unexpected."

Shade returned her hug. "Love can take you to unexpected places. We got off on the wrong foot, you and me. But I told you I would always protect you, make things right for you. Thank you for standing by my son. You make his life complete. I have two daughters, but today, I gained another. There is no difference in my heart, Maddie. I am here for you, as is Kate."

Madison wondered what she'd ever done to deserve this family. She wasn't vampire, she'd never be vampire, and yet, they embraced her as one of their own.

Shade took Kate's hand and looked deep into her eyes. He wasn't sure how they had gotten this far in such a short period of time, but he wouldn't trade a moment of it. "I do believe it is time to let these newlyweds alone. Love is in the air tonight. Let's be on our way."

As everyone said their goodbyes, they left the newlywed couple, and began the walk back to the main house. Shade held Kate's hand as they slowly strolled back home, with Rachael walking alongside Shannon and Luca.

"*Mi amore*, do you regret we did not have a wedding?"

She looked up at him with surprise. "We had a wedding, when I became the first to ever feed from you, and when you turned me. That was our wedding day."

He smiled back at her. "But not a honeymoon. I remember something about having a honeymoon all our own this night?"

She gave him a sly smile. "You think I'd forget that? Come with me, lover."

She led him off the main road and back along the foot path to their property, letting the other adults walk on ahead. She'd asked Emma to move the candles that had been laid out for the wedding to create a new path that led to Lorenzo's old tree house. She climbed the ladder to the tree house, looking over her shoulder at him. Emma had covered the floor of the tree house with plush blankets, fur throws, and lots of pillows.

Standing at the bottom of the ladder, he gazed upward as she climbed, her silhouette illuminated by the moon and the lanterns in the tree. Kate climbed on all fours across the floor before stretching out. "What's taking you so long?"

"Oh, I was just admiring the view. And wondering exactly what you might have on under that dress." He climbed up the ladder behind her.

She giggled as he crawled across the floor towards her. "Well, I guess there's only one way to find out."

"*Si* and find out I shall!" Growling, he slid his hand under the hem of her dress and lowered his lips to her slender ankles. He kissed her ankle, before running his tongue up her calf, nipping at her knee, and kissing the soft, smooth flesh on her inner thigh. He heard the sharp intake of her breath and chuckled. Pushing the dress up over her hips, he exposed the delicate white lace of her panties. The growl rolled out of him from deep in his chest, as he lowered his mouth to tug at the lace, his tongue seeking out her sweetness. He pulled against the fabric with his teeth, as the panties slid off her hips, and he gave them a sharp yank, tossing them aside.

Kate slid her hand into his hair, as his tongue lit a fire between her legs, when he stopped and stood, towering over her. He threw his jacket out of the tree house. Slowly, he proceeded to strip bare, tossing his clothes to the ground below.

"Do you need this dress for another event, because I have no intentions of waiting until it comes off?" With a lightning fast move, he bent down and ripped it off her with his bare hands, as the sound of the cloth tearing away was carried on the night air. "You need to answer a bit quicker, woman!" She giggled as the dress was tossed over the side of the tree house.

He knelt between her legs, sliding his hands up her thighs, before lowering his mouth to lick at her sweet nectar. “I believe I have found my treasure."

As he leaned over her, his dark hair fell forward around his face, his features were illuminated by the flickering candles. Her breath quickened as his mouth and tongue teased and tantalized, exploring between her legs before he moved to her breasts. Her arms encircled his shoulders as she pulled him down on top of her, her mouth seeking his. His lips covered hers, as she felt his tongue probing her mouth. Sliding her hand down the warmth of his back, she never failed to notice the strength of him, and be aroused by it.

Her kisses fired him beyond waiting. Sliding his cock inside her, he held and moaned. She was warm, dripping with honey. Throwing back his head, closing his eyes, he felt her wrap herself around him. "Mine."

"Always." She felt his breath on her neck, hot against her skin. She loved the feel of him, his weight on her, as his hips moved in sync with hers.

He felt the rush of his beast, rising to claim her. He knew her body better than he knew his own. He knew where she wanted to be touched, where she loved to be kissed. He knew what would make her shiver, and what would make her moan. He could take her to the edge, and pull her back, tease until she begged for release. They moved as one, in a rhythm that was born of the many nights he'd made love to her, and yet always remained as exciting and new, as the first time he took her. He felt her body respond beneath him, her thighs gripping him as she clung tight to his shoulders. He thrust deep and hard, filling her need as he pushed them both to their peak. His fangs punched through and he sank them into her vein as it pulsed in her neck, calling his name. He drank deep and his desire for her was fulfilled.

The power of the sensation his feeding brought never faded, and she felt his fangs penetrate the soft skin on her neck, followed by the explosion of heat between her legs, and the desire to possess him completely. Her hands gripped his shoulders as she reveled in the sensation, before biting hard into the muscles of his shoulder. She loved the feel of the firm, taut muscles under her lips. His blood spilled across her tongue, and with it, she felt the full power of the beast.

Her beast joined his, and their dance was never ending. Only an immortal can understand the truth of souls entwined in the covenant of blood. For both of them, it was the ultimate bonding, as the orgasm washed over them in waves, their bodies lost in the grip of passion. They fed, as he released his seed inside her, and they moved as one. The sensations slowly receded, as Shade rolled off her, pulling her on top of him. His breathing still labored, his hands squeezed her ass and he moaned. The vortex had taken them both, spun them around, and dropped them back to earth.

"No one could ever love me like you do, *mi amore*."

She laid her head on his chest, listening to the pounding of his heart, as his arms held her close. She closed her eyes so she could savor him, focusing on the feel of skin on skin. "No one," she whispered.

***

Alfie went upstairs to Lorenzo's bedroom after the reception to change out of the suit. He slipped out of the expensive Italian made garments and was grabbing for his jeans when a motion outside the window captured his attention. Out of curiosity, he walked to the window in time to see a torn dress flutter down from the tree house. The lanterns hanging in the tree provided a soft illumination to the two bodies, joined in passion. Alfie recognized his master as he possessed his mate, and he felt tightness in his belly as he backed away from the window. He understood the mechanics of sex. All of them had been taught that, one day, they'd leave their wet feeders, and the need to feed would be accompanied by a powerful sexual desire that must be satisfied. He felt his heartbeat quicken at the sight, as his cock grew hard. Leaning against the wall, his breath ragged, Alfie knew his own time to hunt was near.

28

Lorenzo had packed up his things and managed to say goodbye to all his family again. He'd enjoyed coming home, seeing everyone, and staying in his old room, but he'd found that when it was time to go back to Florence, he was ready. Alfie had been quieter than usual, as they were preparing to leave, and Lorenzo was wondering if maybe the trip made him miss his own family. The flight back to Italy with Dante was uneventful, and again, Alfie seemed withdrawn. It was such a contrast to the excitement he'd displayed on the flight over.

As they were preparing to land, Alfie woke from a short nap. Lorenzo waited for him to speak, and when he didn't, he inquired. "You okay, Alfie? You've been quiet this whole trip home. Do you miss your family?"

Alfie smiled. He wasn't ready to share the fact he might be transitioning. Not that it was a problem. It was just a matter of him advancing to a different level, one which Lorenzo wasn't mature enough to experience yet. He hoped their age difference, and his transition, wouldn't place a strain on their friendship. "Just something on my mind. No big deal. It was a good trip. I enjoyed it a lot, but I'm glad to get back to Florence and camp."

"Me too! I thought I might be sad to come back. I do miss my family, but camp feels like family now too. My dad said that would happen. The warriors would become my brothers. Do you feel like that too?"

Alfie shrugged his shoulders. He looked out the plane window, as it prepared to enter the hanger. "We are family, Lorenzo, warrior family. But my family is nothing like yours. Not even close. There's no big celebration when I visit. My family is part of the coven, but we're not royalty, or live in the luxury that you live in. I feel closer to my brothers at camp than my own family."

Lorenzo listened to his friend describe his home life. He'd never met Alfie's family, or seen them visit him at camp, and he rarely went home to visit them. He had a hard time imagining it. They left the plane as their luggage was thrown into the trunk of the car. The boys slipped into the back seat and Dante drove them back to Castello.

Lorenzo nudged his shoulder. "I hate to tell you, brother, but I think my sister Sophia has a crush on you. She couldn't stop staring at you when we were saying goodbye."

Alfie rolled his eyes. "Sophia? She's just a baby. She'll have a hundred crushes before she finds her mate. And I can't imagine why she'd have a crush on me. She'll have many nobles to choose from."

Lorenzo laughed. "We're as protected at Bel Rosso as we are in the camp. Our mother tried to build a paradise for us there, so we wouldn't be lonely, and we'd have a lot to do. I was in the camp daily, but for my sisters, the camp is off-limits. Beyond my dad, Luca, Cory, and, of course, Gi, you're probably among only a few other males my sister's ever seen. But you're right. My sisters will be expected to marry a master, and royalty, if possible. Just as I was expected to be a warrior, a master and eventually king. My sisters understand their obligation. But I'll tell you now, Sophia has a mind of her own, and like my father, she'll follow her heart, and throw the rules out the window. I'm sure you're right, she'll fall in love a hundred times."

Alfie shook his head, as a single lock of hair fell over his eyes. He was different than most of the warriors his age who preferred to wear their hair longer. "Yeah, a million times."

The flash of the master and his mate in the tree house rolled through his head and something inside him rumbled as well. Love, he didn't know if love would ever be in his future, but he knew what he needed now was more than any wet feeder could possibly give him.

As they pulled up the long drive to Castello, Dante stopped at the entrance, and Carlos emerged to help unload the luggage. "Welcome home, master."

Lorenzo smiled back at him. "Good to be home, Carlos." Turning to his friend who was gathering up his luggage, Lorenzo extended the now familiar invite. "So, you want to stay here? We'll have to report in at camp first, but then we can come back here afterward."

Alfie grabbed his luggage. "Thanks, brother, but no. I want to get back to camp, and I need to speak to Marco about something.

Thanks for inviting me home with you, Lorenzo. I won't ever forget this trip." He turned and walked away, toward camp, never looking back. His mind could think of one thing only, relieving this aching thirst.

Lorenzo was taken aback. The invitation was a formality, as he fully expected his friend to say yes. Alfie had never missed a chance to stay with him. He wondered if he'd said something to offend his friend.

Dante had felt the boy's restlessness and hunger as he walked past him, and understood Alfie was transitioning now. The blood of his wet feeder would no longer soothe him. He saw the confusion on Lorenzo's face. "He is fine, master. Give him some space."

Lorenzo looked up at him. "Space?"

Carlos exchanged a glance with Dante over the boy's head. Carlos moved to distract him. "Come inside, master. A bath has been drawn, then you can report to camp, and let Marco know you are home."

Alfie made his way back to the barracks and dropped off his luggage. His bunk mates greeted him with fist bumps and high fives, teasing him good heartedly about how he was living the high life now. He returned their jabs, realizing how much he'd missed them. They'd all be expected on the field in a few hours, and Alfie wanted to find Marco before training started. Changing quickly from his street clothes into his leathers, he felt more like himself. Heading to Marco's private quarters, he beat on the door with some impatience. "Marco, its Alfie, can I come in?"

Marco was on the phone with Terri. She told him about the activities that had been going on at Bel Rosso, and he was laughing his ass off at the episode with the chicken at Cory's wedding. He heard the knock on the door as Alfie called out to him and told Terri he'd call her back. If Alfie had sought him out in private, then something was wrong. "Come in."

As Alfie entered, Marco picked up his scent, and knew before the boy spoke that he was transitioning. Marco had seen it a thousand times in his years. "You look a bit worse for wear, warrior. Tell me you kept your ass in shape while traveling the world."

Alfie was shuffling from one foot to the other. He was nervous, but he knew Marco would know what to do. He waited, as Marco lit up a cigarette and flopped down in a chair. He pointed to the chair opposite him, and Alfie obliged.

"So, you want to tell me what this is about?"

Alfie looked down at the table between them. "I don't think I can manage on the wet feeder any longer. Her blood will no longer sustain me, and I feel balled up inside. I have trouble sleeping. And, uh, well, other stuff. I need your guidance."

Marco made no jokes. He knew this was a challenging time for a young warrior, and something that needed to be handled with dignity. It was a rite of passage.

"It is your transition. It makes you feel like hell, you can't figure out if you want to eat it or fuck it or both. Nothing settles you completely, not even swinging that sword. What you're feeling is normal, Alfie. You just need someone to lead you, show you a few tricks, teach you to hunt, and then you'll be fine. That beast can become agitated when not fed properly. I am going to assign an experienced warrior to you. I have several here in the camp who have done a damn fine job of helping the young ones through the transition. They will teach the skills you need, and the etiquette as well. We don't kill, and we don't leave behind any trace of our feeding when we hunt. Learning how to properly hunt mortals, so we are not exposed is vital to our survival. I am going to give Diego this assignment. He is one of my best hunters, knows the area well, and can help show you how to lure the females. You fine with Diego?"

Alfie gave him his undivided attention, relieved to know he'd have help. "Yes, Diego is fine, I know him, thank you. I feel confused about how this makes me feel. I get urges I can't explain. I haven't acted on them yet. I just want it to stop. I want to feel full and satisfied."

Marco chuckled. "Oh, you are going to feel full and satisfied, warrior. Once you have a female beneath you there's no going back. You will start with a feeder. They are trained to help in your transition as well. I will assign a feeder to you. Then, after a few nights, Diego will start teaching you how to hunt. You must learn how to survive outside this camp, and when there is no access to a feeder."

Alfie looked at him and nodded, feeling better already. "I'm getting my own feeder?"

Marco stood up, laughing. "Welcome to manhood, Alfie. You will need to move out of the barracks with the juniors, and into senior barracks. Diego will assign you times to go to the feeder compound. Stick with the feeder that is assigned to you for now. Later, if you want to change up things, you can select another who is more to your liking. A good feeder will hold your secrets. They not only feed your hunger but offer much comfort to a warrior."

Alfie had mixed feelings about leaving his brothers in the junior barracks behind. He'd grown up with all of these boys. But it was also a badge of honor to move to the senior barracks.

Marco leaned across the table. "You are no longer a boy, Alfie. You're a full-fledged warrior now. You have a lot to learn yet, but this is the next step toward your freedom, and the day you will leave the camp. Be proud of your hard work."

Leaning back in his chair, Marco took a long drag on the cigarette. "You know this will put some space between you and Lorenzo. Shade and I were closer in age. We transitioned about the same time. Lorenzo is far behind by several years. Have you talked to him about this?"

"No, I didn't understand it all myself. I haven't said anything to him. I know it will be different, but he's like a true brother to me, Marco."

Marco nodded. "I understand that, but once you have a feeder, you won't be going to Castello as often. We could send your wet feeder to the castle, but we can't let the adult feeders leave the compound. You won't need to feed every night, but training will drain you a lot. Your body will change more rapidly now, your size, your strength. Tell your brother you are transitioning, so he'll understand the changes he sees. Now, go get your gear and get your new bunk. Then find Diego, he'll take you to your feeder. By tomorrow this time, you will feel much different and one hell of a lot more settled."

Alfie stood to leave. He was ready. He just wanted to feel better, get his life back to normal. He was both nervous and excited. He'd heard the seniors bragging about their feeders, and their sexual prowess. He'd heard the stories of their hunting, and how they seduced their prey. He knew the seniors would subject him to another round of teasing, as he learned the ropes.

29

Alfie had moved into his new barracks with the senior warriors and had been introduced to his new feeder. She was beautiful and patient and she tasted like heaven to him. She'd introduced him to the pleasures of sex that accompanied his feeding and was teaching him the art of seduction. He knew it would be a while yet before he went with Diego to hunt, and he was still learning to adjust to the transition. He'd not had the chance to talk to Lorenzo privately since he'd moved to the senior barracks. Marco had kept them on grueling training schedules, and the seniors didn't often interact with the grunts on the training field.

Walking out of the barracks and onto the training field with his brothers, his stride was a bit cocky. He warmed up his arms and shoulders with the sword and then ran laps for endurance. He could feel Lorenzo's eyes on him as he ran. He needed to find some time in his schedule to go to Castello and talk with him. He knew Lorenzo would already have heard that he'd transitioned, and knew he'd been moved to the seniors, but he still owed his friend an explanation. As they finished their laps, the seniors strolled over to the other groups on the field to get their assignments for the night. Marco barked out group assignments, and placed Alfie with Lorenzo. Finally, he'd get a chance to talk to his brother while they trained

***

Lorenzo had, at first, been surprised when he saw Alfie had been moved to the senior group with all the adult warriors, but even more surprised that he'd seen almost nothing of him since the move. As Alfie approached him, Lorenzo walked away from his group, meeting him halfway.

"You okay, brother? You got moved to the seniors. Haven't seen you much since then."

Lorenzo feared his friend might feel he was too young for him to hang out with now. Perhaps he'd be embarrassed by Lorenzo's youth, and would need to move on.

Alfie gave him a wide smile. "Better than I've felt in a while. I'm sorry, Lorenzo, a lot of changes. You know about transitioning, right? So, I had to be moved to the seniors and got a feeder." Alfie saw the concern on Lorenzo's face and read his emotions. "It doesn't change anything between us, Lorenzo. You'll catch up. I'm just older than you, that's all. You okay?"

Lorenzo nodded. He knew a little about transitioning. He was still a few years away, but he knew that was when he'd leave his wet feeder, Nita, who'd been with him since birth, and he'd be free to go to any feeder, and would be taught to hunt. "Yeah...I'm okay. Does this mean you won't come to Castello anymore?"

Alfie punched him on the shoulder. "And give up that comfortable bed and all the games? Hell no, brother. It just means I can whip your scrawny butt faster now."

Lorenzo laughed out loud, relieved to know his friend didn't feel like he'd outgrown him. "Well, you can try."

The two boys laughed, and quickly fell back into their routine. Marco kept them paired together for the entire night. As they wrapped up their training, Lorenzo extended the invitation to Alfie to join him at Castello.

"Sorry, brother, another time."

Lorenzo nodded and walked alone back to the empty castle.

***

Shade was back at Castello to check on the production of his new wine, Red Moon. He planned to put the first bottles into Alec's new underground club, which would be operational soon. While he was here, he'd check on his son's progress. It had been a month since Lorenzo had come home for the wedding, and Marco had informed him Alfie had transitioned. Shade knew this would be something Lorenzo would need to adapt to. Sitting in his office, going over the financial figures for the coven based here in Florence, he spent a portion of his night meeting with some of his coven, hearing their complaints and settling matters. Didn't matter where in the hell he was, there was always work to be done. He didn't realize the time, when he heard Lorenzo come back from camp and he wondered how his night had gone.

"Son, I'm in the office, come in."

Lorenzo heard his father call to him and ran to the office. "Dad! I didn't know you were coming."

Shade stood grinning, walking to meet his son, hugging him to his chest. "Well, sometimes a surprise is good. I just needed to check on the vineyard production and a few coven affairs. So, how's camp treating you? Learn anything you could teach your old man yet?"

Lorenzo accepted the hug then flopped down in a chair near his father's desk. "Nah. I don't think I'll ever see that day. I love camp, but, you know, Alfie's not around much anymore. The seniors don't train with us much, and he doesn't come back to Castello with me. I'm okay, though."

Shade walked back to his desk, poured a Midnight and stared at his son. "Well, you're not that okay with it because you brought it up. Have you talked to Alfie?"

The boy shrugged his shoulders. "Not much. He's not around much. I mean, we're still friends. But..." He was reluctant to say he got lonely here by himself. He didn't realize how much he'd relied on Alfie's company to help him adjust to life away from his family.

"Lorenzo, we need to talk, son. I know you love being at camp, but you also miss home, and you miss the companionship of having someone who understands what you go through. You miss your brother, and that's normal. But Alfie is transitioning. It is something every vampire must do as they mature. It can be a confusing time. You know you can talk to me about it, ask me whatever questions are in your head, *si?*"

Lorenzo had been taught about the transition, but he felt he didn't understand enough to know what questions to ask. "How did Alfie know? I mean, he didn't say anything to me about feeling different. How will I know when it's time for me to transition?"

Shade swirled the Midnight around in his tumbler and smiled. "First of all, you will start to take notice of females in a different way. How they smell, how they look, the shape of their bodies. Your body will respond to them. Your beast begins to emerge, taps on your insides and makes things a bit more interesting. Then you'll notice that no matter how much you feed from your wet feeder, you can't beat down the hunger. The hunger lingers, along with a feeling that something is missing. Nita will no longer be enough. Your beast feels agitated, and you will sleep poorly. For me, I felt my anger building, and I thought I would go mad I was so restless."

Lorenzo scrunched up his face. "I think I understand. But, you know, there aren't many females to take notice of around here. How will I feel more attracted to females when there aren't any to see? That's what I wonder about Alfie too. I mean, we don't see any females, except Dona. She visits us some."

Shade laughed. "It only takes one. Trust me, you will notice. Then you will be assigned a feeder, she will help you with your transition. Afterwards, one of the warriors will teach you to hunt. If you don't have access to a feeder, hunting is your only option to feed. It is a skill as vital as learning to use your sword. You can't leave camp until you have learned to hunt. The key to the hunt is learning how to charm, to seduce, and leaving the mortal female unharmed, and erasing her memory. There can be no evidence of your feeding, or you risk exposing us all. When I finally left home, Marco and I went out together. I would never give up those days, Lorenzo, learning to survive among mortals. When the time comes, you will know. But I think we have a few years before that happens."

Shade looked at his son's concerned face. "Alfie is just adjusting son, takes a bit of time, but you haven't lost his friendship. It is hard to comprehend until you go through it yourself. But trust me, I know that bond between you is tight. Nothing will come between it. He will be your brother for life."

"Did Mom come between you and Marco?"

Shade chuckled. "No, son, she did not. Marco was not fond of your mother because she was mortal. Marco is old school. One of the reasons you don't see many females in this camp. But Marco and I had a tangle over a certain female once. After that, we made an oath to each other as brothers. If I chased, he backed off and left her alone and vice versa. Luckily, we had different tastes in females."

Lorenzo nodded. "I'll make that pact with Alfie, then. I wouldn't want to lose his friendship over a female."

"Good idea." Shade stood and pulled his son out of the chair, hugging him. "I'm just glad you haven't outgrown giving your old man hugs yet. Just remember, Lorenzo, your time will come, and you will know when it does. You can't force it. So, give Alfie some breathing room, support each other. I love you, son. I could never have talked to my *padre* like this. I am glad you have confided in me and feel good about talking things out with me. Now get some sleep, I'm heading out before the sun rises, I can't be away from your *madre*, she misses me."

30

Alfie sat on his bunk in the barracks, waiting for Diego. He wouldn't attend camp tonight but go out with Diego instead to learn to hunt. He'd begun to adapt to his feeder, and she'd guided him well, and for the most part, he was feeling quite confident. Diego had taken him hunting only once before. They'd found a mortal female, walking alone at night, with no other mortals around. Diego said she was easy prey, just take her and erase her memory. He said there'd be times when we'd need to feed, and we wouldn't have time to seduce. He called it a snap and grab, the mortal equivalent of 'fast food.' Alfie didn't find it easy. He found it impersonal, even though it did provide relief for his hunger and his cock, and nothing more. He'd learned to shadow himself, to quickly subdue her, to feed without draining her, and to use her body's unbidden response to his feeding to have sex with her. He then erased her memory completely. He'd fumbled a lot during the sexual interaction, but he was nervous knowing Diego was watching him. Once he was done, Diego assured him it would get easier, and more efficient. But tonight, Diego had asked him to leave his leathers behind, and to dress casually. Alfie's mind was whirling with questions, as he wondered what Diego had in mind for his next lesson.

Diego stepped into the barracks to see the young warrior looking like a scared rabbit, sitting on his bunk. "Relax, brother, this is supposed to be a learning experience. Tonight, will be more fun. You'll learn some interaction and the pick-up."

Alfie stood up as his heart lurched in his chest. "The pick-up?"

Diego slapped him on the back. "Look, you're a Medici warrior. Act like one. We're heading into Florence, into the heart of the city where we'll mingle with the females. Let you work on developing some skills to charm your prey, so she'll come with you. Just find one you like, then move in, seduce, go from there. Lure her in and convince her all she wants is you."

Alfie gulped and looked at Diego like he was an alien. "Me? I never picked up a female before! How the hell am I supposed to do that? I don't even talk to females much."

Diego laughed. "You need to feed and fuck, don't you?"

Alfie nodded his head. "Oh yeah."

Diego slid his arm around his shoulder. "Then trust me, you'll figure it out soon enough. This is Florence, brother, plenty of females out late, drinking, looking for a guy. They're not going to fight you."

They took off, teleporting to Florence and the nightlife. Diego had already arranged a set-up ahead of time. He wasn't going to let the young warrior fail. He had a beautiful female he tapped often, and tonight, she was meeting him and bringing along a friend. The girls were older than Alfie, but it would be a chance for him to interact with them, and a chance for Diego to keep an eye on him.

They landed in a small alcove off the Via de' Benci, near the Basilica of Santa Croce. It was in the heart of the old city, with lots of tourists and locals. As they merged into the crowd, Diego took this chance to fill in his brother on their plans for the night. "Look, Alfie, I'm meeting a female I've fed from in the past. She always welcomes my visits, and she's bringing along a friend. Just follow my lead, talk to her, charm her. By this time of night, they've already had enough wine to make them pliable to your will. Just flow with it, brother, you'll know when the time is right to strike. And for fuck's sake, relax!"

Alfie nodded and followed him with his heart in his throat. Diego made it sound so easy, but he got tongue tied around females. They turned the corner and walked to a small bar called Moyo. Some people were seated, and others stood at the bar, as the chatter and laughter inside the bar made conversation difficult. Diego looked around, then saw the girl he was looking for seated at a table outside, enjoying the night air. He threw his hand up to wave to her, and she motioned him over to her table.

"Okay, brother, here we go. Turn on the charm."

Alfie turned to see Diego hurry to the table, taking a seat next to his friend. Alfie took in the other female at the table, and she made his knees weak. Her dark hair hung to her hips, and she wore a flowing skirt with an embroidered blouse, a modern peasant look. Her brown hair shimmered like a beacon to him and when she looked up at him, her eyes were the softest doe brown, reflecting the candlelight that adorned every table. Alfie wanted to hug Diego, maybe he *could* pull this off.

Alfie took the seat beside her and introduced himself. Her name was Calynda and Alfie was already entranced. As the night progressed, he followed Diego's lead. Diego bought them more wine and they sat outside and talked. Calynda was a cousin of Diego's friend, Maria, and she was visiting for a week. She lived in northern Italy, near Lake Como, and as they conversed, he found her interesting and easy to talk to. Her laugh was beautiful, and he wanted to be with her. She flirted with him, laying her head on his shoulder when she laughed. Her eyes sparkled when she talked to him and she kept placing her hand on his thigh. As the girls stood up to go to the ladies' room, Diego nudged Alfie and smiled.

"You're in, brother. Listen, Calynda is staying with Maria. She's asked me to walk them back to her place, so we're going to walk them home. Don't worry, they'll ask us inside. You got this one. Take your time. I'll be with Maria, so no worries. Relax."

Alfie couldn't believe this was happening so easily, but he knew he wouldn't have had it this easy if Diego hadn't been along. "She's beautiful. I'll follow your lead, brother."

As the girls returned, the warriors stood and Diego offered his arm, telling the girls they'd make sure they goet home safely. Calynda turned to Alfie and smiled, taking his hand, and he couldn't stop looking at her, as they walked to Maria's small apartment.

Once they arrived, Maria asked them to come inside and Alfie felt Calynda pulling him along, without even asking. She'd had a lot to drink and seemed more than obliging. As Diego and Maria headed straight for the bedroom, Alfie felt at a bit of a loss as to what he should do next. Calynda pulled him to the couch and Alfie curled up beside her. The streetlights cast a soft glow through the open windows, leaving the room dimly lit. He leaned in to kiss her and was surprised when her tongue slipped into his mouth. Her hands were in his hair and he felt his heart pounding in his chest. He couldn't get his clothes off fast enough and she responded in the same way. She sat up and pulled the blouse over her head, exposing her bare breasts, before helping him remove his shirt. He was more than happy to let her lead and let her do whatever she wanted.

This was very different from the 'snap and grab'. Calynda wanted him! Alfie could feel his fangs aching and knew his eyes would give him away soon. She unzipped his jeans and he wiggled out of them, as she quickly removed her skirt, and shimmied out of her panties. He wasn't able to think about anything except being inside her. His heart was hammering, and his blood was rushing through his veins. He took the lead and laid her on the couch. His beast wanted her blood, her sex, and she wanted him. She grabbed his cock as he snuggled into her neck, kissing her. He plunged inside her warmth, so wet and soft, and he thought he'd lose his mind. He was overwhelmed with the urgency, and the intensity of what he felt. She moaned and followed his rhythm, as his tongue sought out the vein, pulsing in the soft flesh of her neck. He waited until she was thrusting hard against him before sinking his fangs into that tender flesh. Diego had warned him she'd struggle at first, and he'd need to calm her. She squirmed and cried out slightly as she sank her nails in his back. He held her tight, knowing she was surprised by the momentary pain of his teeth piercing her skin, but as he took his first swallow of her blood, he felt her body respond beneath him. His veins crackled and hummed as her blood energized him. She dropped her head back in ecstasy, as she wrapped her legs around him and he took her. He didn't want this feeling to stop but knew he must be careful not to drain her. When she came, he held her tight, releasing his seed into her, as she shuddered beneath him. Unlatching, he licked the wound, and watched as it healed. He'd never felt anything like this, not even with his feeder.

Neither of them spoke a word, and he slid off her, finding a narrow slice of the sofa to lie next to her, as he let his breathing slowly resume its normal rate. He could hear the moans from the bedroom, and knew Diego was enjoying the same pleasures. Alfie realized Calynda wasn't moving and he panicked, as he quickly scrambled off the couch to look at her more closely. She was out like a light. He closed his eyes and breathed a sigh of relief. He thought for a moment he'd killed her. Standing, he quickly got dressed and covered her up with a soft blanket.

Alfie wandered around the room, staying quiet as he waited on Diego. As Diego emerged from the bedroom, he had a big grin on his face. "You erase her yet?"

Alfie shook his head. "Not yet. She's out, brother."

Diego slapped him on the back. "Look, last time on the snap and grab, we erased the memory completely, but if you like this girl, and you think you want to see her again, then you want to be more selective." Diego knelt down next to the sleeping girl, motioned for Alfie to join him. "You can leave the memory of you in there, your time at the bar, and you walking her home. You just need to erase any memory that would make her suspicious, if she saw anything, heard anything, and definitely the feel of your fangs at her throat. Leave the good stuff, brother. Never know when you might see this female again, and that makes for an easy, fun night, *si?*"

Alfie knew one thing for sure, if he ever saw Calynda again, he'd want to be with her. Diego took his hand and placed it on her forehead and placed his own hand on top. "Feel what I do, brother, and then you know how."

Alfie left her with the memory of him, his face, and the sex, but everything else was gone. Diego double checked her memory, then made sure her wounds were healed, and nodded. "Let's get back to camp, brother. Job well done. Just a few more times and then I'll cut you loose."

They teleported out and Alfie knew he'd taken a step closer to becoming the vampire he was born to be, followed by an odd feeling of loneliness. A warrior lived a very solitary life, unless he found a mate, and for many warriors, mating was unlikely. Most warriors never mated but served their master their entire lives. He was still young, he still had a lot to learn about females, but he wondered if he'd ever have one to call his own.

31

It had been a long, hard night in camp. The grunts were paired with the juniors and they'd been running a series of mock battles. It was late in the summer, and it was hot and humid. The night had brought little relief from the heat. Lorenzo was tired, and they still had a couple of hours to go before dawn. All he could think about was standing under a cool shower, washing away the dust and sweat, and climbing into bed. He could see Alfie training with the seniors. At least he was in camp tonight. Since Alfie had transitioned, and had been trained to hunt, he was frequently absent from camp, and absent from Castello as well. Lorenzo missed his friend. One thing he didn't miss was Vanni. Vanni had always been a thorn in his side, but since Alfie had been advanced to the seniors, Vanni had taken advantage of Lorenzo's isolation. He'd been on his ass all night, and the warrior in charge of their platoon had looked the other way, leaving it to Lorenzo to figure out how to handle the situation. He understood the reason. He couldn't count on others to bail him out. He'd have to learn on his own how to deal with the bully.

Vanni kept his eyes on the prince. He hated the attention the prince received and was glad Alfie had been advanced to the seniors and was no longer around to watch his back. He liked the group they were assigned to tonight. The Lieutenant had turned a blind eye to Vanni's taunts and had pretty much ignored the prince. It was about time. He was tired of everyone stepping around Lorenzo like he was something special. If Vanni had his way, he'd make sure he went down hard. They were running another mock battle and it was easy pickings for Vanni to get to him. So much was going on around them, and Marco kept moving from group to group, so Lorenzo was an easy target. He saw the prince battling another warrior as Vanni stepped in, pushing the other grunt aside, and faced off against the prince, swinging his sword close to Lorenzo's face.

Vanni shouted yet another taunt, "You should know by now never turn your back in a battle. Piss poor fucking warrior you are."

Lorenzo heard the blade of the sword as it whistled through the air and spun out of the way a fraction of a second before the blade would have struck him. These were mock battles, but even in mock battles, warriors got hurt. The injuries were accidental, but with Vanni, it wouldn't be an accident.

"What the fuck, Vanni! You aren't even paired up with me. Get back to your station."

"What, you afraid to take me on? Thought so. You can't battle without your babysitter beside you. You make me sick. You couldn't lead a fucking herd of sheep, let alone warriors."

Vanni growled and dove at Lorenzo with a vengeance. Lorenzo blocked the strike with his sword, feeling the power of the blow as the pain traveled up to his shoulder. Vanni kept pushing, forcing Lorenzo to back up, as he remained on the defensive. Vanni felt his advantage and wouldn't be content until Lorenzo's ass hit the dirt where he belonged.

Lorenzo tried to ward off the blows. His father had told him not to let the bullying get to him, and for the most part, he'd been able to ignore it. He didn't want to strike Vanni and hoped the bully would tire of this game. He kept coming at him, as Lorenzo held his own, blocking every blow. The muscles in his arms and shoulders were already tired, and they were now screaming for relief from the weight of the sword, and the power of the strikes. He looked quickly in the direction of the Lieutenant, who had his back turned. The momentary lapse in concentration cost him, though, as Vanni lunged forward with the blade, and Lorenzo leapt back quickly to avoid it, losing his footing and falling to his ass.

Vanni watched him go down and stood over him, holding his sword as if to strike a killing blow, and laughed. "Aw, did the prince fall down? You going to go up to your castle and call your mommy? Ask her to call her dogs now?"

Lorenzo jumped to his feet, shoving Vanni hard in the chest, as he spoke through gritted teeth, "I don't need my mommy, Vanni, but you might."

The other boys were starting to take notice of the skirmish and formed a circle around them, wanting to see how the conflict played out. Lorenzo saw the Lieutenant walk away, leaving him on his own.

Vanni laughed in his face then spit on the ground. He threw down his sword and crossed his arms over his chest as he circled Lorenzo. The other warriors had gathered to watch and Vanni enjoyed having an audience. "That the best you can come up with, grunt? Did your daddy teach you hand to hand combat? Or did your sisters teach you?"

Lorenzo turned slowly, always facing Vanni, as he continued to taunt him. "My father never taught me hand to hand combat, Vanni. I had to learn from another warrior, his name is Skelk. Pretty sure you don't want to see what I learned. So back off."

Vanni looked at the other warriors and grinned. Narrowing his eyes, he leaned in close to Lorenzo. "Oh, I heard about Skelk, and a few others. Like Raven. You into boys, too? Did he teach you that, pretty boy?" Vanni went nose to nose with the prince, lowering his voice. "Or are you doing the Alizzi, because she seems to like giving the pretty boys' presents."

Lorenzo shoved the older boy, but he wasn't backing down. "Shut up about her! You protect the Alizzi, as do all Medici warriors."

Vanni shoved back, and hard, making Lorenzo stumble. "Did I hit a soft spot? We might protect her, but she never gave me a horse." Vanni watched as Lorenzo caught his balance. "Maybe you do like boys. You got a thing with Alfie? Is that why he spends so much time at Castello? He's a pretty boy, just like you."

Vanni rushed him and threw a punch, connecting with Lorenzo's mid-drift. As Lorenzo clutched his stomach and doubled over, Vanni planted his foot against Lorenzo's backside and shoved him face down in the dirt. "Who's the pretty boy prince now?"

Lorenzo heard the whispers of the young warriors circled around them, a few in surprise, a few who laughed. He slowly got to his feet, looking up through his long hair at Vanni, who was relishing his moment in the sun, smiling back at the circle of warriors. Lorenzo had never revealed his gift. His father had instructed him before he came to camp to keep it under wraps. With the exception of Marco, no one here knew he was a fire-thrower. Day-walker was the only gift they'd seen. As Lorenzo's temper boiled over, the palms of his hands tingled and burned. Standing at his full height, he faced off against Vanni.

"You want a fight with your prince? You dare to stand against one of your own? I'll show you the power of Medici."

Lorenzo raised his arm over his head, as if to throw a baseball, and flung a ball of fire instead, landing at Vanni's feet. The fire quickly licked up his legs, as the boy danced around, slapping at his legs, trying to put out the flames. The crowd backed up, as a collective gasp could be heard. None of them had ever seen a fire-thrower. It was a gift many believed was pure myth. The Lieutenant heard Vanni's screams and ran back into the fray, wondering how the fuck Vanni caught himself on fire.

Vanni had watched in disbelief as the prince threw fire from nowhere. Immediately, he could feel the pain of his skin burning. He felt someone throw him to the ground and roll him around, as his screams echoed in the night. Alfie heard the commotion and ran to the crowd, only to see Vanni on the ground, screaming and on fire. He looked at Lorenzo to see his fangs bared and his eyes glowing red.

"What the hell happened, Lorenzo?"

One of the boys, his eyes big as saucers, looked at Alfie and answered, "Oh man, the Prince just created a ball of fire with his hands! He threw it at Vanni. What the fuck is that?"

Alfie looked back at Lorenzo who remained silent, when they heard Marco screaming for them to get Vanni to first aide immediately. Alfie's brain was spinning. *Fire- thrower? Lorenzo is a fire- thrower?* He didn't think they really existed.

Marco sent everyone to their bunks for the night, clearing the training field. "Get to your barracks. Now, all of you! This fucking show is over."

He stood beside Alfie, as they both looked at Lorenzo. "What in hell were you thinking, Lorenzo? Why in hell didn't someone call me over here?"

Lorenzo looked back at Marco defiantly. "I won't apologize to you, or to Vanni. He pushed too far. I've held him off now for almost a year. He's not a Medici. I want him out of here. Tonight!"

Marco stood over the boy, taken aback by the commands delivered by the Prince. He needed Shade here, and fast. **"Brother, you need to get your ass to Castello and pronto, I need backup here. Lorenzo just set one of the warriors on fire, and now he is giving me orders. Move it!"**

"Well, I do not think, my prince, that you will be seeing Vanni on this field any time soon. But I will tell you, The King is on his way, and until he gives me a direct goddamn order to take my commands from you, I am still SIC of this camp."

Shade was just beginning his night in the camp when he felt Lorenzo's burst of anger. Then he heard Marco in his head that all hell was breaking loose. **"On my way, brother. Keep him calm."**

Shade teleported to the house to let Kate know he was leaving, and then moved like lightening to Florence.

32

Shade hovered over the deserted training field at Castello, seeing only Marco, Alfie, and his son. Marco had filled him in on the events telepathically during his teleport. The dust rose around his feet as he landed near Marco. Looking at the three of them, he asked in a stern voice, "Alfie, you involved in this?"

Alfie shook his head. “No, master.”

"Then get back to the barracks, this doesn’t concern you."

Alfie locked eyes with Lorenzo communicating sympathy, and telepathically sent him a message of luck. "Yes, master." As he walked away, he knew his prince would need his friendship and support when this was over.

Shade began to pace in a slow circle around Marco and Lorenzo. "The first thing I want to know, son, is why you gave Marco an order. That is insubordinate. You do not make demands to your SIC."

Lorenzo had had time to get his anger under control, and knew he’d gone too far. "I'm sorry, Marco. What I said to you is a conversation we should have had in private. I apologize for speaking out in front of the other warriors. It was disrespectful, and I mean you no disrespect. But it doesn’t change how I feel."

Marco stood silently, letting Shade take charge. Shade stopped pacing and stood beside Marco, his arms crossed over his chest, standing to his full height. "You do not give him orders in private or otherwise, but you have apologized, acknowledged the gross disrespect to a man that has spent his life protecting this coven and serving his king. Marco, do you care to respond?"

Marco nodded his head to Lorenzo. "Grazie for the apology, accepted warrior to warrior."

Shade looked at his son for a good minute. "Lorenzo, Marco has accepted your apology. As a warrior under my charge, shake hands and this matter is settled between the two of you."

Lorenzo extended his hand and locked eyes with Marco. "You guide my hand in all things, and train me to be the warrior I was born to be. I will always look up to you, as I look up to my father."

Marco took his hand and pulled him to his chest. "We are Medici, and warriors, you learn as you go, Lorenzo. But this is the easy part. You have to deal with your old man now." He released Lorenzo and walked to Shade as they hugged as brothers.

Shade patted Marco's shoulder. "See to Vanni's injuries. Contact the family. Relay to them I will speak with them as soon as possible, once I have all the details sorted. If he is able to be moved, send him home. They will be worried. His padre is one of our warriors. Let him go home with his son."

Marco left the field, feeling sorry for the kid having to deal with Shade's temper, but he knew Lorenzo could handle it.

Shade ran his hands through his hair and was acutely aware of the coming dawn. "Get inside the house, now."

Lorenzo walked alongside his father. He was ready to face whatever punishment his father dealt out, but not before he said what was on his mind.

As they entered the castle, Shade headed straight for the huge office. He poured himself a double Midnight and kicked it back in one shot. He poured another and set it on the desk. He felt like throwing it at something but knew that wouldn't solve anything. He sat down in his chair and nodded. "If you want something, get it."

Lorenzo remained standing. Today, he was in this room as a warrior, not as a son. He'd stand as a warrior before The King. "No, sir."

"Well, glad to see you are taking this seriously. Let me say my piece. You will have your chance. First of all, your *madre* is upset. I will calm her when I return, but you must deal with her as well. Secondly, you seriously injured a fellow warrior, your brother. There are some very serious consequences for doing such. As for me, I must now face his family, a family who left their son in my charge to learn and be protected as he was being trained. On top of that, his *padre* is one of my trusted warriors. So, I suggest you tell me what in the hell this all is about."

Lorenzo hung his head. He hadn't thought about the long-term ramifications of his actions, or the position he'd put his father in. "Dad..." he paused. This wasn't a discussion between father and son. This was a discussion between warriors. "Master, I didn't think about how this would affect you, or Marco. That's a burden I must carry on my own. But Vanni is not Medici. He doesn't reflect the values of our warriors, or the values his own father displays. He doesn't act out of honor and integrity, as you have taught me. He's disrespectful of many. I couldn't trust him to have my back in a battle. But I understand I overstepped. The decision as to whether he stays or goes is not yet mine to make. I can only tell you I won't go into battle with him."

Shade held him with his eyes. "No, you did not think. And you will carry this burden, for a very long time. There will be many things that will anger you, push you beyond your control. You cannot respond to every situation by throwing fire. You did not solve a problem today, Lorenzo, you created one. You claim your brother has no honor or integrity, that he displays disrespect. Those are some pretty high charges. Give me an example of why you think this of your brother."

"He taunts and teases all the grunts. Tries to keep them down, belittles them. He walks among the juniors as if he is better than them. He thinks, because his father is a warrior, he has automatically earned a spot here. He is brother to no one, and especially not to me."

Shade sat back in his chair, steepled his fingers together and nodded. He saw the intensity of his son's aggravation. He didn't doubt his son's word. Lorenzo, if nothing else, had always been honest with him. "Do you feel, because your *padre* is King you automatically earn a spot here?"

"No, sir. I must earn my place and earn the respect of my brothers. I know it's my birthright to be a prince, and a warrior. But being born of royal blood doesn't mean I'm owed their respect. That's something I must work for on my own. Loyalty should never be given blindly. I would hope to be worthy of their loyalty. If they're willing to die for me, then I must also be willing to die for them."

"*Si*, a warrior can never demand respect, it must always be earned, as must a king, or a prince." Shade sighed heavily as he stood and paced. "I have seen Vanni's attitude, and not all warriors are meant to rise. Father to son, I am beaming inside with pride. Master to warrior, I must deal with you on several levels. You attacked a fellow student, when you should have used your head. You were insubordinate to your SIC. And more importantly,

Lorenzo, they all know your gift now. Your greatest weapon, son, is your gift. And when I tell you everyone in this land will know it now, it is the truth. I cannot stop the gossip that will travel from this camp. By this one act, you will now have enemies, as your gift will create fear. They all know what you can do now. The only vampire safe from a fire-thrower is another fire-thrower. And I know of no other. You can burn them to the ground, while you remain immune to the flames. Lethal damn gift to carry, son."

Lorenzo hung his head. "I understand what I've done. You asked me not to display my gift, and I've kept it a secret from them all, even Alfie. I let my anger get the best of me, and now I've put all my brothers at risk, and my family as well. I accept whatever punishment you feel is appropriate. If you need to make my punishment public, announced in front of all the warriors, to show you do not show me favor, then I understand that as well, master."

Shade stood with his back to his son. He was proud that Lorenzo was accepting responsibility and blaming no one else for this lapse in judgment. He got a glimpse of the powerful warrior his son would grow to be.

"Speaking to you as your master, several punishments are due. You will be expelled from camp for a week. You remain inside your quarters, no visitors. Complete isolation. It will give you time to think about what you have done." With a deep sigh, he continued, "You will apologize to your brother, once he is recovered. When you return to camp, you will speak to all your brothers and Marco, make your apologies known."

Turning to face him, he walked to Lorenzo, hugging him, holding him tight. "Speaking as your *padre*, I know you were pushed beyond your limits. But getting control of this gift is vital. I am proud of the warrior you have become, son."

Stepping back, he looked into his eyes, his hands on his shoulders. "Remember, and heed my advice, use words first, then sword, and then your gift as the last resort. Your gift is designed to kill. They cannot fight your gift and win, they die. Remember that."

"I never meant to bring shame to you, master. I accept your punishment. If it matters at all, I was able to gain control, and threw the fire at his feet. I didn't want to kill Vanni, but I did want him to know I wasn't taking any more of his shit."

Shade laughed as he released his breath. "Spoken like a damn Medici Prince, if you ask me. You don't need to feel shame, just own what you have done, and learn from it. I have heard from Marco how much hazing you have taken from this boy. Marco had already spoken to him about his behavior, but he did not heed the warning. When I speak to his father, I will let him know Vanni brought this on himself. The shame will lie with Vanni, not you. You are dismissed. Your punishment begins at sunset tomorrow. All other matters, I will handle. But you have one other task, call your *madre*. If she hasn't pulled every hair out of that beautiful head of hers, she has worn a hole in the floor from pacing. Ease her mind. I will be here for a few nights attending to this. Go, now."

Lorenzo turned to leave the room. He hadn't meant to bring shame on Vanni's family. Vanni's father was a trusted warrior, but Vanni was nothing like his father. He stood in the door and looked over his shoulder. "I'll call Mom now. I love you, Dad."

"I love you too, Lorenzo, always and forever."

Shade watched him leave then sat back down in the chair. He suddenly felt a presence and looked up to see Christofano standing before him. Shade held up his hand. "Not tonight, *Padre*, I beg you. No lessons and arguments this night."

Christofano stepped behind him and laid his hand on his shoulder. "You have raised a strong prince, my *figlio*. I feel only pride." He disappeared as quickly as he came, as Shade laid his head back and closed his eyes.

"*Si, Padre*. I only hope I live to see the day he reigns over all we have built." He stood and headed for his bedchamber. Castello would hold two warriors whose sleep would be restless, but whose bond was stronger, as warriors, and as father and son.

33

Alfie slipped into a pair of leather pants, and one of his nicer shirts. The shirt was starting to pull across his broad shoulders, as his musculature continued to develop. He'd need to buy new shirts soon. Unlike the prince, his wardrobe options were limited. He checked his appearance one last time in the mirror, running his hand through his light brown hair, cropped close on the sides, and only slightly longer on top. He preferred the shorter, more modern, hair style to the long hair worn by most of the warriors. He was just shy of six feet and would continue to grow in height now that he'd transitioned. Most of the seniors in his barracks stood at six foot three, or four.

He was heading to the Alizzi palace. Donatella had invited him for a visit. He usually went with Lorenzo, but for the past month, he'd not had the free time to spend with his friend and hadn't enjoyed the frequent visits the Alizzi made to Castello. He felt a bit odd going to visit her alone, but Lorenzo was still in lockdown at the castle. Alfie wasn't allowed to even talk to him. Just as their master had warned, the news of Lorenzo's gift had traveled fast, and Alfie was sure the Alizzi had questions.

Standing at the door of her villa, he used the huge knocker to announce his presence, waiting for the staff to greet him. He looked himself over one last time and tried to calm his nerves. He was feeling slightly more confident around females now that he was hunting.

***

Dona had sent her house staff out, so she'd be alone with Alfie. She'd finished primping in front of the mirror, applying the dark red lipstick, when she heard him at the door. Wearing a sheer gown in red, and a matching robe, the thin fabric floated behind her as she rushed to open the door. Swinging the door open, she greeted him with a big smile, and a tantalizing view of her toned body through the sheer gown of silk and lace.

"Alfie! I'm so happy you could make it. Please come in. I'll pour us some Midnight."

Alfie felt his mouth go dry as she opened the door, standing before him in the sexy negligée, the gown and matching robe just brushing the top of her satin slippers. He could see her body through the sheer fabric, the red color a compliment to her skin, the color of coffee and cream, and her thick black hair that hung down her back. He was speechless and could only stare for a moment, before he realized he was standing like an idiot outside the opened door.

The Alizzi turned, sending the gown in a swirl, as she walked away from him, her backside swaying as she headed to the bar. His eyes were glued to the swing of her hips and how her hair fell gracefully down her back, her silhouette visible through the gown. He stepped in, taking a deep breath and closed the door behind him. Walking with a cocky gait, he followed her to the parlor where she was pouring drinks, and damn if he didn't need one.

"Did I interrupt your sleep, mistress?"

"No, my darling. Why would you think that?" She handed him a tumbler, filled to the rim with Midnight.

Alfie took a gulp of the drink before answering. "Well, you have on your dressing gown and robe. I thought perhaps I'd come at the wrong time. You look beautiful though."

Dona sat across from him with a drink in her hand, and crossed her shapely legs, leaning forward slightly to give him a view of her ample cleavage. "I wore this for you, Alfie. I thought you might appreciate it. I'm glad you like it."

Alfie choked slightly on his Midnight, coughing as he tried to regain his composure. *She wore this for him.* "For me?"

He kept looking at her red lips. He could imagine kissing her, and quickly banished the thought from his head. Looking away from her lips, all he could focus on were her luscious, plump breasts. Licking his lips, he made himself look into her eyes, but that didn't help much either. Her dark eyes bored into him with an invitation, and he felt his leathers getting tighter in the crotch. What the hell was it about this female that made everything in him crackle and pop? "Well, umm, I, uh, I'm glad you invited me because there's something I needed to tell you about Lorenzo."

Dona kept her eyes locked on his and could easily see the impact she was having on the inexperienced man-child. "Yes, please. I had heard something about the prince being a fire-thrower. Could that be true? Come sit next to me and tell me everything."

Alfie reluctantly got up and sat beside her. "Well, there was a skirmish during a mock battle. One of the warriors has been provoking him ever since he came to camp. Lorenzo has been putting up with it, but on that night, he just lost his shit, and now Lorenzo has been expelled from camp for a week. He can't have visitors or leave Castello." Sitting next to her, he felt dizzy from her intoxicating scent.

Placing a hand on his knee, she leaned in close to him. "So, is it true? Is he a fire-thrower? That is a most unusual gift."

Alfie looked down, as her hand lay on his knee. "I really can't say. I didn't see what happened. I was on another part of the field. I've been moved up in the ranks." He patted her hand that lay on his knee. "But Lorenzo is fine. No need to worry."

She leaned back against the sofa, making herself comfortable, as she sipped at the Midnight. "Well, I am glad to hear it. And you, tell me how you're doing. You have transitioned, *si?* I can tell by your scent. They would have assigned you to a feeder by now. Have you been trained to hunt?"

"Yes, mistress, I've been training to hunt. I like it. And my feeder is beautiful and sweet. I've moved from juniors to a senior's rank. Lorenzo and I haven't had as much time to ride. I have more responsibility now in training the others." He noticed how her body was draped over the sofa, as languid as a cat, looking very exotic. "May I pour you another Midnight?"

"Yes, my darling. And refill your own glass as well." As he sat back down next to her, she accepted the glass, making sure to touch his hand as she did. "Now, tell me, who is teaching you to hunt?"

Alfie pushed the errant lock of hair from his eyes. "That would be Diego. He's pretty suave with the females. He's giving me some great tips." Shrugging, he smiled. "I really like hunting better than a feeder. I guess that's normal."

"Of course, it is. It not only satisfies your hunger, it satisfies your need to stalk your prey. You know what I have always found so amusing, is they pair the young males with an older male, to teach him how to lure in a female. I have always found that so odd. I mean, who knows better what a woman likes, than another woman, right?"

Alfie threw his arm over the back of the sofa behind her. "Well, I never thought about that, but you have a good point. But you know, we don't have any female warriors in our camp. When I was visiting at Bel Rosso, they had females." Without even realizing it, his fingers were playing gently in her beautiful raven hair and he quickly moved his arm back down to his side. *What in the hell is wrong with me?*

Dona smiled. "Ah, yes. Marco still holds to the old traditions, does he not?" She giggled like a young girl. "He always was a bit of a stick in the mud. You know, of course, Shade and I used to hunt together?"

Alfie laughed. "You really went hunting with the master? I bet that was an education. He has a real reputation as a Casanova. Where did you hunt?" He turned toward her, eager to hear her stories. "Tell me about it, please?"

She placed her hand on his thigh as she laughed. "He would kill me if I told all our secrets. This must remain between the two of us. I am sure he would not want to remind his queen of his days as a young vampire. Needless to say, he was quite the catch. Shade Medici never had to work very hard when he was hunting. For him, it was more a matter of eliminating the ones he didn't want, rather than finding one who would respond to him. I would tease him about that. While the other males would be lucky to find a single mortal in a night, he would have gone through three or four. Now that is who should be teaching you to hunt."

Alfie felt the heat of her hand through his leathers. This female was so exciting, so knowledgeable, and he had all her attention this night. "I'm not sure I'd feel comfortable hunting with the master." He smiled at her. "But I bet you had to fight off the males as well. You're so beautiful. They'd have been swarming all over you as well." He pushed back a long strand of her black hair that hung over her shoulder.

The Alizzi continued to weave her web, knowing she already had him snared. "Well, I think now that he is older and mated, and carrying so much responsibility for the coven, your master no longer has the need, or the time to hunt. But I could certainly help you, darling. I believe a female should train the young males anyway. The way it is, never made sense to me."

She placed her forefinger on his full lips. "I mean, who knows a woman's body better than a woman, *si?* Who knows what will make her pulse quicken, and her breath ragged with desire? The man always thinks he knows, but you know how he learns? Trial and error. I can teach you so much more. You want a reputation with the females like your master? Would you like to go back to the barracks at sunrise, having sated your hunger with as many females as the hours would allow? Or do you want to follow Diego, and go to the same one or two he has shown you are willing?"

Alfie heard the seduction in her smoky voice, the way she crooned as she talked to him, and her body was so close. He could feel her breath on his face when she spoke. Her finger was warm and soft on his lips, and he wanted to open his mouth, and wrap his lips around her finger. His own breathing was getting ragged and he was about to burst out of his leathers, they'd grown so tight with his erection. He wanted to touch her and wanted to be touched by her. He was wondering how she'd taste, how it would feel to sink his fangs into the soft flesh of her neck. His voice was broken and raspy as he answered, "*Si*, mistress."

"So, let us begin. You have had your first lesson without even realizing it. Don't go to the bars and the clubs. You will find a willing subject, but there is no skill involved. Go to a quiet restaurant, an art gallery, a park. When you see someone you like, approach her as a gentleman, begin small talk, put her at ease. Make eye contact. Hold her in your gaze. Talk softly, and tell her she is beautiful, *si?* Or that she smells sweet, or you love her hair. Move slowly, Alfie. Let her come to you, and she will. Offer to buy her a drink, because the mortals become easily muddled by the alcohol."

All the while she was speaking to him, she brushed her fingers lightly through his close-cropped hair, and across his shoulders. "Sit across from her, not next to her. Engage her in a conversation, and when she seems relaxed, take her hand in yours, raise it gently to your lips and kiss the palm of her hand, letting your tongue flash out ever so quickly, so she will feel the heat."

Taking his hand, she demonstrated for him, and heard the sharp intake of breath, as her tongue caressed his palm. "Do not linger.

Let go of her hand. Apologize for being so forward. Tell her you were transfixed by her beauty and you could not help yourself, *si?*"

Alfie couldn't believe he was actually here, alone with her, and she was showing him how to seduce. He wanted to lay her back on the couch like he'd done with Calynda. He stared at her, hanging on her every word, she had transfixed him. *"Si."*

"Should I continue, young Alfie? I don't wish to make you uncomfortable, but to share with you my own knowledge of hunting. I think it will help you."

"*Si*, please don't stop. Diego never told me these things. He just said to relax, talk to them, they would come easily." Looking down at his hands in his lap, he felt the depth of his inexperience. "I don't have much experience with females, not even to talk to them. I've been at camp since I was ten. I want to learn with your guidance." He looked up at her then, taking her hand in his and kissing it gently, letting his tongue dart out softly in her palm. "I'm a good student."

Dona gave him a sly smile, as she felt the heat of his tongue against her palm. "Good student indeed. I like a quick study. Once you have kissed her palm, and teased her with your tongue, watch her reaction closely. If she pulls away, she may not be ready for an adventure. You may want to seek another. You will learn quickly how to spot the mortals who will respond to your advances, and which ones will flee. If she is thrilled by your touch, hold her hand to your face. Move closer to her, but not too close. Let her come to you, understand?"

Dona took his hand in hers, and held it against her cheek, letting the back of his fingers brush across her smooth skin. "Her experience will be quite different. She will feel the light stubble of your facial hair."

Dona kissed his knuckles and slid closer to him. "Is she beautiful? Then tell her. Tell her what you see. Is it her eyes that speak to you? Her lips? When I look at you, young Alfie, I see a strong vampire, broad shoulders. I see pale hazel eyes that capture me in their gaze. See what I mean? Now tell me, Alfie, what do you see?"

Alfie listened to her, tried to pay attention to her every word as they slid from her red lips. He felt the heat of her body as she moved closer, her soft hand on him. He swallowed hard, as he looked into her eyes. "What I see is a mistress who is so beautiful she makes the sunset dull in comparison. Your eyes have a sparkle of life. And those lips..." He leaned in and kissed her gently. "These lips were meant to be kissed." Letting his hand slid into her hair, he moaned. "Raven black hair, silky and soft. There could be no vampire who could resist you." He pulled his hand away and laid it in his lap. He looked away from her, embarrassed by the words he'd said. "How was that?"

"That was very good, but you must not call me mistress. I am a girl, a young girl you have encountered in the park. Call me Dona. And remember, you are seducing mortals. You must never say vampire or do anything that implies you may be vampire." Her hands explored his shoulders, feeling the strength of the young warrior. "Also, be sure your mortal is ready for a kiss. Lean in slightly, so she will know your intent. See if she leans toward you. Say to her, I want to kiss you. I want to taste your lips."

Focusing, he looked at her lips, so red and plump, and then up to her eyes. Leaning closer, he spoke softly. "Dona, let me kiss you, taste your lips so red."

She leaned into him, meeting him halfway. "A young girl may not want to appear so forward. She will want to appear to be protecting her virtue. If she leans in, responds to your request for a kiss, she is granting permission, *si?* So, then you should kiss her. Lightly, at first. Feel the softness of her lips. Do not move too fast. Follow the kiss with smaller kisses, touching at the corners of her mouth, teasing, *si*? Now show me."

"Should I close my eyes, or keep them open?"

"Close your eyes, young Alfie. Some parts of the sexual experience are a feast for the eyes and fire your passions. Others, you want to savor, and focus only on the sensation. Close your eyes and feel the kiss."

"*Si*." Closing his eyes, he leaned in for the kiss, and focused on the sensations of her lips, so soft, plump, and juicy sweet. He wanted more. He opened his eyes, remembering he should kiss her on the sides of the mouth. His lips touched her softly, at the corners of her mouth, first the left, then the right, soft, easy, delicate kisses. He sat back, licking his lips. "What do I do next?"

"Do not pull away. If she responds to your kiss, slide your hand into her hair, and kiss her again, more deeply this time. If her lips are soft and yielding, if you hear her breath quicken, her pulse race, then slide your tongue between her lips, gently at first. She may pull back. If so, you want to slow down, if not, then explore. Let her tongue battle with yours."

Alfie's smile grew. "May I try?"

"Of course. You cannot learn seduction from a book. You learn from doing."

"*Si*, I'm learning so much more from you than Diego." He kissed her softly on the lips, once, then twice, pulling her closer. He kissed her again, letting the kiss linger, deepening its intensity. His hand glided through her hair, and around her neck. He felt her respond then, her mouth hungry for more. He felt her lips part slightly and he slowly put his tongue in her mouth. *Cazzo, it's so warm and sweet!* He could feel her breasts against his chest, as he rolled his tongue around hers, and felt her do the same. He could barely breathe. His head was spinning, and his cock was aching. He stopped the kiss and quickly stood up. "Sorry, umm, I need a drink." Grabbing his glass, he made his way to the bottle of Midnight and poured a glass full and slung it back. His breathing was still ragged. "I'm so sorry, maybe I was too forward. I feel like I'm going to explode."

Dona laughed softly. "And isn't that the point, young Alfie?" She stood up as he refilled his glass and brushed past him, glancing over her shoulder as she went, the gown flowing behind her as she walked. "Are you going to follow me? Or stand there gawking with your mouth open?"

"*Si*, mistress." Alfie set the glass down and followed her, his eyes glued to the sway of her hips.

Dona led him up the stairs, her hips moving seductively, knowing his eyes were glued to her ass. She took him to her bedroom, and untied the sash of her robe, letting it slide from her shoulders and drop to the floor as she continued to walk toward her bed. She sat on her bed and looked back at him demurely.

"Pretend we are in the park. That I am sitting on a blanket under a tree. You have just kissed me. I have responded to your kiss. Come here and join me on this blanket beneath the tree."

He climbed on the bed, and leaned in and kissed her, as his arm encircled her. He felt her tongue inside his mouth, and he fenced with it, swirling it around and around. He pulled away, speaking breathlessly. "Dona, you're so beautiful."

"And you, are my Adonis, my Greek god." She ran her hands up his chest, and slowly unbuttoned his shirt. Her eyes drank him in, the firm, hard muscles of his chest, the tight muscles of his abdomen. She'd watched the warriors train, watched their bodies glistening with the sweat of their toil. It had been a long time since she'd lain with a warrior. She tugged the shirt free of his waistband and didn't miss the bulge in the tight leather pants. She slid the shirt over his shoulders, stroking him as she did.

"Does this feel good? Do you like how my hands feel on you? Undressing you?"

Alfie closed his eyes, as her hands explored his body. "*Si*, Dona. It feels good to have soft hands on my body. My muscles get tired and ache." His head dropped back, and he took a deep breath.

Dona scooted back, so she was in the middle of the bed. "Pull off those leathers. They cannot be comfortable and lay here beside me." She stretched out on the huge bed, patting the empty space beside her.

Alfie opened his eyes and seemed unsure of her request. "I'm not sure I can do that. I shouldn't be in your bed. What if Marco finds out? I'd be disgraced, thrown out. I'd shame my family and lose my best friend."

"Do you see Marco in this bedroom? Do you think I would tell him this? I would never betray you, Alfie. Do not forget, I am a great friend to your master. He would expect me to help you. You protect me, *si?* This is how I repay you, warrior. I will teach you the art of seduction, so you may become a warrior as powerful as your master." She sat up and slid the sheer gown over her head, now completely nude before him. "No shame, Alfie. Now come to me."

His eyes took in all of her. She was a vibrant mistress, with much power, and he did protect her. Everything she said made sense to him. But he knew she had lain with masters, and he was nothing like his master. He was just a young warrior. He gulped hard, and hoped she wouldn't laugh, hoped he wouldn't disappoint her. Bending down, he unlaced his boots. Kicking them off, he slowly removed his leathers and stood before her.

Dona drank him in with her eyes. "My magnificent warrior, you are a Medici. Look at you, such power and strength. You do not yet even know your full power, but you will. You will be the one who stands at the side of the prince. You will rise to greatness."

She slithered to the edge of the bed, and slowly slid her hands between his legs, cupping his balls, as her mouth slid over the head of his rigid cock. Her tongue flicked and twirled, before she slid her mouth down the long shaft, then slowly retreated. Holding his erection in her hand, she looked up at him. "Has any woman showed you how she can pleasure you with her mouth?"

Alfie felt his body shake. He watched her and felt her mouth on his cock, and he wanted to roar. He felt his erection grow larger, and with it, a throbbing for release. He wanted relief from the ache in his cock. He shook his head. Was she talking to him? "What? No, no. Show me, please." His breathing was so rough he felt like he'd pass out, but he didn't care.

Dona pulled him down on the bed next to her, as he lay on his back. She liked him naked, he was her warrior! She crawled over top of him, softly raking her nails over his balls and feeling his body tremble beneath her. Sliding his cock into her warm mouth, she swallowed him, pushing him deep into her throat, before slowly releasing him. Sucking and nipping softly, she stroked with her hand, and then swallowed him again, beginning a slow rhythm of stroking his cock with her lips and tongue, as the young warrior writhed and moaned in pleasure.

Alfie had no idea females could do this! But he sure as hell was glad to discover they did. Diego never told him this. He moaned and felt his dick hit the back of her throat. His body moved without him telling it what to do, and his beast was loose. His fists clenched the bed covers and his knuckles were white, when he felt his balls tighten. He had to cum now, he couldn't stop it. She was sucking him so deep into her mouth. "No, no!" He tried to scoot back and escape, when he came inside her mouth. His whole body shook with the release and he turned his head into the pillow, ashamed and embarrassed that he couldn't wait.

She'd laugh at him now.

He was no warrior.

Dona licked away his cum, lapping at it as if it were his blood. "So good, warrior. You are delicious, just as I knew you would be."

She nipped at the hard muscles of his abdomen, as she crawled over him, and lowered her mouth to his. Kissing him deep, her tongue snaked into his mouth and she felt him grow hard again. Her hands sought out his cock as she stroked him. "You are warrior, young Alfie. Your appetite for blood and sex is never completely satisfied. As soon as you cum, you will always be thinking of the next conquest." She straddled him as she lowered herself on his rigid erection, and slowly started to ride.

He was surprised. She kissed him like nothing was wrong, like it was a reward. He kissed her back, hard and deep. He felt his cock go hard again almost instantly, as she continued to tease his body.

He knew from his feeder that females liked to be touched during sex, and his hands reached out, cupping her breasts as they bounced in front of him. He wanted to give her as much pleasure as she was giving him. He dropped his hands to her hips and squeezed her ass, as she rode him. She was soft yet strong. Her hair hung down in his face like a blanket of soft silk. He was lost in the feel of her, his hunger beating at him. He felt lightheaded. He raised his hips to meet her thrust, driving deeper inside her. He was buried in the hot, wet depths of her, and it was like nothing he'd ever felt before.

She knew he'd last longer this time, and she rode him hard. She was tired of being courted by ancient vampires who were looking for a mate as a breeding mare to save their dying covens. It had been so long since she'd ridden a young buck like this one. She felt her fangs punch through, as she expertly guided her hips to create the maximum friction against his steel hard cock. "You cannot hurt me, warrior. Follow the demands of your body and do what you want."

His fangs punched as the soft red glow from his eyes lit up her skin. He stared at her like he was ready to eat her alive. He wanted all of her. Sitting up, he suckled her nipple, biting and nipping, his other hand behind her neck. He raked his fangs along her neck, he wanted blood. He wanted powerful blood to feed his warrior body. He'd never felt anything so intensely before, every cell was alive. Pushing her raven hair from her neck, he licked her vein, feeling it pulse beneath his tongue. He growled deep in his throat.

Dona rolled with him, so he was now on top of her, and wrapped her legs around his hips, so he could plunge deeper. She tilted her head back, baring her neck. "Feed from me, warrior. Take the blood of a mistress. Feel my power in your veins. No mortal will ever make you feel like this. No feeder's blood has the power of a mistress. Feed, warrior. Your master has fed from me. Feed."

He didn't hesitate and kissed her vein softly before sinking his fangs deep into her vein. He drew deep and hard, and her blood spilled across his tongue. As he swallowed, he felt her power and his body responded. He felt stronger with each mouthful, and he drew deeper, filling his mouth. He gripped her by the hair, and groaned as he drank, her blood driving his passion as he pounded his hips into her. His beast was in charge now, and he took her harder, giving himself up to the sensations, as he released into her, and his roar filled the villa.

Dona felt him sink his fangs into her flesh, and felt his body respond to the power of her blood as he drove deep and hard. The unsure boy was gone, replaced by this warrior who'd take what he wanted. Her orgasm hit her, and she screamed out, clawing at his back as she clutched him, feeling him release into her. He lay on top of her, heart pounding. She smiled to herself, knowing he'd be back. Mortal blood wouldn't satisfy him the same way hers did. It was how she'd kept a hold on Shade for so long. Stroking her hand through his hair, she whispered. "Those mortal girls will thank me now, young warrior. Once you fuck them, all others will pale by comparison."

Alfie rolled off her, trying to regain his senses. He'd just fed from and fucked the Alizzi! He rolled to his side and she stroked his hair. "Will it always feel like this with an immortal?"

"An immortal will be able to handle your beast better than a mortal. But you won't need to hunt an immortal. They will come to you freely, or not at all. That is the thrill of the mortal. The hunt, the seduction, and knowing you hold their lives in your hand. But no immortal's blood holds the same power as a master or mistress. My blood will make you stronger, as strong as your prince. Come to me when you want, and you will stand out on the training field. The others will notice your strength. Your master fed from me before battle. It gave him an edge. It was why our fathers wished to see us mated, but that was not to be. But I serve you now, warrior. You feed from me whenever you want."

"You give me a great gift. You make me feel amazing." He reached out and slid his knuckles along her cheek. "Did I disappoint you? Did I give you pleasure as well?"

She kissed his lips lightly. "Young warrior, you have no idea."

Alfie sat up then, throwing his long legs over the bed, feeling her hand along his back. "I'll always protect you, Donatella, for the gift you've given me. And I want to come back, learn more. Your beauty and power are something I could never find elsewhere. Thank you for sharing with me."

He stood up then, his shyness gone, as he stepped into his leathers. "I need to get back to camp."

"I understand, young warrior. And know that you need no invitation to return. Come when you need me, and I hope it is often. This is our secret, Alfie. None will know of this, I promise you."

He sat on the bed, lacing up his boots. Nothing would stop him now. He looked for his shirt. "None must know. I'm dead if anyone finds out about this. But I want to be your warrior."

He slid his arms into the shirt sleeves, and then knelt at her feet as she sat on the bed, still naked and her skin glistening. She smelled like sex, their sex. He looked up into her eyes. "You are so beautiful. And you taste like heaven. I'll come back."

He kissed her softly on the lips, and then kissed each corner of her mouth. Standing, he walked out the door, never looking back. As he went outside, he howled into the night and teleported out. Tonight, he was a vampire, a man, and a Medici warrior. Nothing would ever top this night.

34

Shade had stayed at Castello several nights to attend to the business of Vanni and his family. He had to get back to the States and to his *bel*. He missed her deeply. Even his death slumber was restless. Neither of them was used to being separated for long. He finished up all the paperwork and coven issues, scheduled the first shipment of Red Moon wine to California for delivery to Alec's establishment, and downed the last of his Midnight. He decided to have one last talk with his son before he left. He wanted Lorenzo to know the outcome of this episode with Vanni. Deep in his heart, Shade knew Lorenzo was worried about Vanni. He knew his son's heart, and while he'd let his temper get the best of him, Lorenzo wasn't the type to cause anyone injury and pain unless it was on a battlefield. He walked the long hallways of Castello, his boot heels hitting the marble floors, and echoing in the high ceilings. Rapping on Lorenzo's door, he waited to hear his son's voice.

***

Lorenzo hadn't left his bedroom since his dad had issued the punishment. Carlos checked on him from time to time, and brought Nita to him when he needed her, but otherwise, he'd existed in solitude. At night, if he stood at the window, he could hear his brothers practicing on the training field, and he wished he could join them. He'd asked Carlos about Vanni, if he knew how he was doing, but Carlos didn't have any information for him. Lorenzo was at the window, his eyes glued to the lights coming from the camp when he heard the rap at his door. He didn't care who it was, he was happy to have a visitor for any reason. Looking back at the door, he called out, "Come in!"

Shade heard the loud command and smiled. He opened the door and entered to find Lorenzo looking out the window toward camp. He'd remained behind closed doors as Shade had required and hadn't once asked if he could leave. Shade hadn't seen him since the night of the incident on the field. He was proud of him. "Missing camp?"

"Yes, sir. A lot."

Shade settled himself on the couch inside his room. "I am here as your *padre*, Lorenzo. Address me as such please. If you are missing camp, that tells me a lot about you. All of it good, I might add. Come, sit with me, I have some things to talk to you about."

Lorenzo left the window and took a seat by his father. He hadn't asked for any leniency in his punishment, and he wouldn't ask now. He'd follow his father's direction and accept his punishment.

"I am proud you have taken this punishment of solitude seriously. I know you miss being in camp. That tells me you understand how vital it is in your life and in achieving your destiny. I am also damn sure you miss Alfie. Solitude gives you time to reflect on the importance of the people in your life, brothers, family and your dedication to those you serve." Shade threw his arm around the back of the couch behind his son. "This night, I go back to Bel Rosso. Missing your *madre* is wearing on me heavily, missing my daughters as well. Do you have any messages for them?"

Lorenzo nodded. "I talked to Mom on the phone but tell her I'm really sorry. I lost my temper, and I didn't think things through. I don't want her to be disappointed in me. Tell Mommy I love her. And... would you talk to Skelk? I don't want him to be mad at me either. He worked so hard to train me how to use my skills as a fire-thrower. This isn't his fault. He was the best trainer ever. Because of him, I had control of the fire. I was able to redirect it, so it landed at Vanni's feet. Is Vanni going to be okay, Dad?"

Shade patted him on the shoulder. "Well, son, Vanni is home. I can tell you his injuries will heal, and he'll have no lasting effects, so rest your mind on that. I visited his family. It seems Vanni confessed his deeds to his *padre*, explained to him why you lashed out at him. His father is a great warrior who has served Medici well, so I never wish for you to hold the father responsible for his son's deeds. His *padre* is a good man, Lorenzo. Vanni has brought great shame to him. And for that, his *padre* has pulled him from the camp. He will never return here, his life as a Medici is finished." Shade looked at Lorenzo. He wanted him to understand the magnitude of these events. "Tell me your thoughts, son."

Lorenzo shrugged. He felt a mixture of feelings swirling inside. "I guess...this feels so confusing. I know Vanni must feel bad now that he's been removed from camp, and his family must feel bad too. If I put myself in his shoes, I wouldn't be able to stand that feeling of bringing shame on my family, and I'd never want to disappoint you in that way. So, I feel really bad for Vanni and his family. And I feel bad I was the cause of it. But I also know in my heart Vanni wasn't a Medici. He didn't live up to the standard of conduct expected of our brothers. His father is a strong warrior, and a proud Medici, but Vanni...that's not who he is." He leaned against his father's shoulder. "How can something be right and wrong at the same time? I can't feel good about it, and I can't feel completely bad about it. But I know my part in it was wrong. "

Shade wasn't expecting these words from his son. Lorenzo had used his solitude to his advantage, and his thoughts were deep. "Learning to become a prince and leader is a trial of victories and defeats. You make great advances and you make errors. Let me tell you, son, I have made plenty of both. You were a threat to Vanni for some reason. Vanni missed the key lesson of being a warrior, especially a Medici warrior. His end would have come whether this happened now or not. But the lessons you have learned through it are important to take with you into your future. Not all who present themselves as allies can be trusted. Vanni did not show respect, did not honor you as a brother, let alone as his prince. Everyone deserves a chance, Lorenzo, and you gave him plenty. A warrior's true colors will eventually come through, if you pay attention. Seeing beneath the guise of friendship and loyalty could save your life one day. Trust me, I have been betrayed by those I thought to be loyal to me as well."

Lorenzo sighed. "I knew that instinctively, Dad. That's why I said Vanni would never have my back in a battle. If he saw me cornered, he'd stand and gloat, not come to my aid. That's why I struck out at him and gave the order to Marco. I know I overstepped. I shouldn't have thrown fire, and I shouldn't have given a command to Marco. You know I love and respect Marco, but my instincts told me, even then, Vanni would never stand beside me in battle."

Shade nodded. "Vanni's father saw that deceit as well. I did not have to throw Vanni out of camp. His father removed him of his own accord. He knew Vanni did not display the integrity of a Medici. So, you see, a true Medici warrior is always about the good of our kind, and always your brother. Vanni was not, nor ever shall be, a brother. I am impressed and pleased with the time you have taken to reflect on this. You have used your solitude wisely."

Lorenzo pulled his knees to his chest, resting his chin on top of his knees. "I wish I could take it back, though. Marco would have seen what I saw eventually, maybe he already had. Vanni would never have made it all the way through training. Throwing fire was not the wise choice, and I'll always regret it. How do I let Vanni's father know my actions were wrong, and I'm sorry for what I've done? It's not enough to say I am sorry. They're just words. What can I do for him, or for his family? They're still in our coven, and still our responsibility. In that, I've failed as their prince. The coven should never fear their prince."

Shade pulled his arm from around his son and stood, walking to the window and looking out at the view his son had been looking at earlier. When had Lorenzo grown up? He'd left a child here and now he talked as though he'd lived a hundred years. "Just remember, Lorenzo, you can never take back what you have done, once done. It will always linger in someone's heart and soul. It is the reason I am so strict in teaching and guiding you. My own heart holds the scars of many mistakes I can never take back. I hope you can learn from me, and perhaps your heart will not hold such pain."

Shade sighed heavily. "You are a young prince. You have failed no one. Vanni's family will survive. His *padre* provides well for his family. Your job is to learn to be fair and evenhanded with your coven, provide protection, and provide for their welfare. At some point, you may encounter Vanni again, when that happens, your conscience will tell you what to do. As for this coven fearing their prince, remember that the next time you want to burn down the fucking field. Gifts can be used as deadly weapons or saving graces." He turned toward his son and walked to him, crouching down, so their faces were level. He took Lorenzo's face between the palms of his hands and smiled. "Such serious business for one so damn young. I cannot tell you how to repay them. That is something you need to figure out yourself. It means nothing, if I tell you, *si?*"

Lorenzo looked into his father's eyes. The burdens of being a warrior, a prince, and the eventual king lay heavy on his shoulders. "I'll find a way to make it right. I don't know the answer yet, but I'll find it." He sighed heavily. "Sometimes... I wish I could just be a boy. Back at Bel Rosso with Mommy, and my sisters, when my biggest problem was how to get Sophia's chicken out of my bedroom. But don't worry, Dad. I'll figure this out."

"*Cazzo*, son, I am still figuring out how in the hell to get that blasted chicken out of our bedroom!" They both hugged and laughed. "I will deliver your messages to your *madre* and Skelk. Both will understand, Lorenzo. Now, you learned well in your solitude. I am pleased with the progress. So, I will grant a small convenience. You are still not allowed to leave, still no technology, but the night before you go back to camp, Alfie can come visit. He cannot stay over, just visit. I think it will be good for you both to talk about what happened before you go back to camp. Have you figured out what you are going to say to your brothers and Marco yet?"

"Thanks, Dad, I've really missed Alfie. And I've thought about what I need to say, but I'm not sure words are enough. They all know I'm a fire-thrower now. There's no way to take that back. I'll have to earn back their trust. Whatever ground I gained, I know it's been lost, and I'll have to start over. I guess that's what I'll tell them. I expect nothing, I'm owed nothing, but I'll work hard to regain their respect and their trust."

Shade ruffled his shaggy mop of curls. "Sounds like the words are already there, just say what is in your heart. They are your brothers and not all will have lost trust. Some will be in awe of your gift. Just look them in the eyes, tell them how you feel, your heart can speak loud."

Standing up, he stretched. "Damn if I don't miss my bed and your *madre*. She is all that holds me together sometimes. My light in the darkness. Someday, son, you will understand all of this, why it happened and for what reason. You will have a mate and queen of your own, as well as a son, perhaps many sons. So, I must head home. If you need me, you know where I am. I am so proud of you, Lorenzo. You are a good son, a good prince, and you will be a great king. I love you so damn much."

Lorenzo stood, taller now, but not nearly as tall as his father. His father could do no wrong in his eyes and remained his hero. Lorenzo threw his arms around him. "I love you, Dad. I'll make you proud of me."

"You already do, son, you have nothing to prove to me." He turned and left the room, walking back down the corridors of Castello, looking at the castle with new eyes. This was Lorenzo's now. He'd rule here. He found Carlos and informed him Alfie would be calling on Lorenzo and he was to let him enter. As he headed out the door, he heard the sounds from the camp, as they drifted through the Florence night, and for the first time, he wasn't sorry to leave it behind. This was his son's realm, his son's warriors, and he had no doubt about Lorenzo's ability to lead them. He had his own home and warriors to attend to. **"On my way home, *mi amore*. I have missed you so, I ache for you. *Ti amo*."**

35

Alfie changed into his jeans and a simple tee shirt, and sat on his bunk, lacing up his boots. Marco had informed him that master was allowing him to visit Lorenzo before he came back to camp. It had been a long week, but one Alfie would never ever forget. He'd been with the Alizzi, laid with her, made love with her, fed from her and he'd never felt better in his life. He knew no matter what, he could never reveal this secret to anyone, not even Lorenzo. It would be hard to not share such exciting news with his best friend, but he knew he'd put them both in jeopardy if he talked. He was her warrior now, and that secret needed to be kept buried. He walked to the castle, eager to see his friend. He knew this must be tough for Lorenzo, but he'd support him no matter the outcome. As he raised his hand to knock, Carlos answered the door and led him inside. "*Grazie*, Carlos, is Lorenzo in his room?"

Carlos nodded, opening the door wide for him to enter. "*Si*. He is expecting you."

Alfie bound up the wide marble staircase, taking the steps two at a time. He got to Lorenzo's room and pounded on the door, making it rattle. "Bro, let me in!"

Lorenzo leapt from his bed and pulled the door open, a wide grin on his face. "Alfie!" He hugged his brother, slapping him hard on the back. "Come in, before someone changes their mind."

Lorenzo led his friend back into his room, where he climbed back onto his bed. "I'd order us some Midnight, but I don't think Carlos would respond to my commands the way he responds to the Alizzi." He fell over laughing on the bed. "Sit down, tell me about camp. I've missed everyone, but especially you."

Alfie didn't laugh at the comment about the Alizzi, he just nodded. "Slow down, one thing at a time, warrior."

Alfie sat on the couch and crossed his ankle over his knee. "Camp is good, you're missed there, but I have to tell you, some of the brothers are buzzing with the fire throwing thing. Where the hell did that come from? Why didn't you tell me?"

Lorenzo sat up. The smile gone from his face. "I'm sorry, I couldn't tell you. We discovered my gift when I was about four, I think. I was trained how to use it in the camp at Bel Rosso. Skelk trained me. Remember him? He's not a fire-thrower, but he'd worked with a fire-thrower a long time ago. He's a good teacher. My father told me I must keep my gift a secret. That exposing the gift would only alert our enemies to my power and make us a bigger threat. My anger got the best of me with Vanni. I shouldn't have responded as I did, but...*Cazzo!* He makes me so angry. My father told me he'd no longer be allowed to train as a Medici. Do my brothers hate me now?"

Alfie shook his head. "Brother, that's some wicked gift you have, just too damn awesome. I didn't see you do it. When I got there, Vanni was rolling around on the ground and Marco was screaming at everybody." He stretched out on the couch, his long body covering the length of it as his booted feet hung over the end. "Lorenzo, I don't think they hate you. Some mixed feelings going around. Some of them are scared as hell of you now. They won't even say your name out loud. But it's mostly the grunts. The juniors seem fine with it. But the senior warriors, hell, it's all they talk about. They want you to be moved up to the seniors. They're in awe of you, brother. They understand the power of that gift."

Lorenzo had mixed feelings about his response. It made sense that the seniors would understand and accept his gift more readily, but he'd have some work to do to repair his relationship with the others. "No, I won't advance. I don't think my father would allow that. I need to move through the ranks, just like all the others. They already think I get special treatment as it is. You're not afraid of me, are you, Alfie?"

Alfie looked at him and laughed. "Me? I can still kick your ass, little brother. Hey, while you've been in exile, I went to see the Alizzi."

Lorenzo looked at him wide-eyed. "You did? Did she know about me? Dad said the whole coven would hear about the fire-throwing."

Alfie nodded. "I went over there to tell her not to visit for a while, but she already knew what had happened. She tried to get me to admit you were a fire-thrower, but I didn't exactly tell her yes or no. I said I didn't see what happened, which is the truth. She said she'd heard about it and she thought it was exciting."

Alfie swung his legs down to the floor and sat up. He didn't want to talk about Dona, less chance of questions being asked, so he changed the subject. "You know, this could change a lot for you now. Covens begin to hear about your gift, masters will come after your ass. It's a dangerous thing to have, Lorenzo. But it can be an advantage too."

"Yeah, a blessing and a curse. I understand. It was foolish of me to expose it, but it can't be undone. If I could take it back, I would. It should've been exposed on a battlefield, to catch my adversary completely unaware. I'll never have that advantage now. And I may have put a target on my back, on *our* back. Are you sure you still want to stand beside me, brother?"

Alfie stuck out his fist. "To the end, brother, till the end." They fist bumped and Alfie knew his destiny lay with this prince. "I sure will be glad when you get back to camp and everything gets back to normal. It's been a weird time for me. Hey, can you aim that fire? I mean, like how in hell does it work, can you show me sometime?"

Lorenzo shrugged. "Yeah, I can control it. I can aim it as precisely as I aim an arrow. I can make the ball of fire small or large. I can throw it in a close battle, with my enemy only a foot away, or in a long battle, where my enemy stands sixty or seventy yards from me. I can throw it farther, but I lose precision in my aim. If I hadn't held back, if I hadn't reined in my temper with Vanni, I could've thrown a ball of fire large enough it would have consumed him in a flash. It's a lethal gift, and I don't think my father would approve of me putting it on display. Maybe at Bel Rosso, someday, when I'm working with Skelk. Maybe you can watch us."

Alfie took it in. He may be older, but he was completely in awe of Lorenzo. He didn't envy his friend and all that would be expected of him. It must be a heavy burden to be the Medici Prince. "Yeah, I'd like to see it, brother. I'm curious. If I battle by your side, I want to know how it works. That will help me help you."

Alfie stood and stretched his arms above his head, rolling his neck from side to side, loosening up. His tee shirt pulled free of the jeans that hung low on his hips, exposing his bare belly. "Marco has really been pushing us hard. I think to stop all the talk about you.

But there is rumor in the seniors that he's going to let some of us go to the outposts for a week to check it out."

Lorenzo looked hard at his friend. His body had changed dramatically since he transitioned, and he looked even more powerful now, his muscles filling out the contours of the tee shirt, his abs looking hard as steel, the six-pack evident. His best friend was more man than boy now, and Lorenzo hoped he wouldn't outgrow him, or feel foolish hanging around with him. And now he might be assigned to an outpost.

"Really? That's exciting for you, Alfie. It's a great opportunity to learn, as well as to display your leadership skills. Marco will make you a Lieutenant soon. Just don't grow up so fast you leave me behind, big brother."

"It's just for a week to observe. And I just got moved up, so I doubt I'll be chosen. To be honest, I'd rather hang out here more in camp, be around you. But you know since I transitioned, I'm released from camp a few hours to hunt. So I may not be able to visit as much as I once did. But don't worry. I'll never leave you behind. Someone has to keep your fire throwing ass in line!"

Lorenzo grinned at his friend. "Someday, brother, we'll hunt together. We'll make our own legends, like my father and Marco." Lorenzo collapsed on the bed in laughter. "Oh brother, I can see us now."

Alfie laughed and jumped on to the bed, wrestling with his friend. "And what do you see?"

"I see me having to beat off the females, and you'll have to settle for my leftovers." The two boys laughed as they wrestled. "I've heard all the rumors too, how my father had two and three females a night. Can you keep up with that, brother?"

Alfie stopped wrestling as he looked at Lorenzo. "Well, at this point, no. I'm lucky to get one. But Diego is a good teacher, so I'm learning a lot." Alfie hung his head. Shit, he didn't want to talk about this. There was only one female he wanted right now, and he couldn't tell his brother. "But since I have a head start on you, by the time you transition, heck, I'll be a pro."

Lorenzo was still laughing. "Well, learn everything you can, brother, and pave the path for me."

"You have to pave your own path, and you aren't sharing mine. Trust me, you'll have females groveling at your feet. You're a prince."

There was a knock at the door and Carlos informed Alfie he must now leave. Alfie slid off the bed and fist bumped Lorenzo. "See you in camp tomorrow night, brother and don't worry, it'll work out with the warriors."

Alfie left his friend and headed down the stairs. He needed to get back to camp. He felt the gnawing hunger inside that triggered his need to feed, and knew it was going to be a long night.

36

Kate was tucking Natalia in bed, kissing her on the forehead. "Get some sleep now."

Natalia rolled onto her side, clutching a book. Kate went to remove the book from her hands. "Natalia, wouldn't you rather have a doll, or a stuffed toy?"

"No, Mommy. I love the words."

Kate shook her head, a soft smile on her face. "And what words are you reading?"

Natalia held up the large book with two hands. "It's by Charlotte Bronte, *Jane Eyre*. Have you read it, Mommy?"

Kate took the book and flipped through the pages, smiling. "I have, but I was a bit older than five."

Natalie smiled back at her. Her small hands folded as if in prayer, as she slid them under her pillow. "It's a good story, isn't it? It's a love story, Mommy. Like you and Daddy. Jane is young, and Mr. Rochester is a lot older, and people thought he was mean and scary, and Jane loved him anyway."

Kate handed the book back to her daughter who clutched it to her chest. She brushed the hair back from the child's face. "A very good story, indeed."

Natalia beamed back at her. "You believe in love, don't you, Mommy?"

Kate kissed her cheeks, as she pulled the covers over her shoulder. "With all my heart."

Natalia giggled softly. "I can tell."

Kate stood and turned off the small table lamp. "I love you, my precious one. Now sleep."

As Kate left the room, Natalia called out to her once more. "Mommy, when Daddy gets home, will you tell him to come kiss me good night? Even if I'm asleep?"

Kate looked over her shoulder at her youngest daughter. "I promise you, Natalia, he won't need any reminders from me. Your father will come kiss you good night."

Natalia smiled back at her, as she clung to the book and closed her eyes.

Walking to Sophia's bedroom, Kate saw the aftermath of the red-headed tornado getting dressed. She had clothes strewn all over the bedroom. "Sophia? Is this necessary?"

Sophia was in her closet, tossing out dress after dress. "I can't find the pink one!"

Kate looked about the room at the pile of pink. "Which pink one?"

Her daughter put her hands on her hips and looked back at her with surprise. "My favorite pink one! Oh wait, here it is." She pulled the dress off the hanger and started to pull it over her head. Kate sat on the side of her bed and waited for Sophia to come to her so she could button up the back of the dress.

"Why so fancy today? You don't usually wear a dress for class."

Sophia held her hair up on her head while her mother buttoned the dress. "But Daddy's coming home. Maybe Lorenzo will come too, and Alfie."

Kate ran her fingers through her daughter's hair before grabbing a brush from the dresser, and brushing out those brilliant red locks, so much like her own. "Well, yes, your daddy is coming home tonight. But I'm pretty sure Lorenzo won't be coming with him. Lorenzo has training at camp."

Sophia looked over her shoulder at her mother. "And Alfie?"

Kate took her daughter by the shoulders and turned her around to face her. "Why would your father bring Alfie home with him?"

Sophia shrugged. "Maybe he liked it here."

Kate looked at her quizzically. "I'm sure he enjoyed his time here, Sophia, but Alfie is a young warrior in the camp. He's training every day, just like your brother."

Sophia nodded her head in acknowledgement. "Do you think he gets lonely sometimes?"

Kate found a pair of white socks with pink lace from the dresser drawer and gave them to her daughter to put on. "Your brother?"

Sophia was sliding her feet into the socks as her mother looked for her shoes under the pile of dresses. "No, Alfie!"

Exasperated, Kate sat down in the heap of dresses. "Sophia, what's this obsession with Alfie?"

Sophia tilted her head to the side as she held out her hand for her shoes. "I don't know what obsession means. I just think he's cute. Do you think I could write him a letter?"

Kate tucked her head and bit her lip. She didn't think she'd be dealing with boy crushes for many years yet to come, and here was one daughter reading *Jane Eyre*, and the other wondering about writing love letters. "I'm sure Alfie would love to hear from you."

Sophia's smile took up her whole face. "I think so too."

Kate got off the floor, looking at the pile of dresses and shaking her head. "Hurry now, Sophia. Enzo is waiting."

***

Shade teleported outside Bel Rosso, landing on the expanse of green that faced the house. He stood and lit up a smoke before going inside, looking at this house that held the people he loved. He could feel the activity inside and it made him smile. He was glad to be home, and glad to finally be rejoined with his *bel*. He hadn't fed in days, and his body ached for her. He heard a rustling in the woods behind him, and didn't have to look back to know Aegis was checking in. She took her place beside him, nudging his hand with her nose, as he scratched her head. Finishing his cigarette, he tossed the butt on the ground, and put it out with his boot before going inside.

Gi greeted him at the front door. "Welcome home, master, shall I pour you a Midnight?"

Shade shook his head. "No, but *grazie*, Gi. I have something else to quench my thirst, and my heart aches for the sight of her."

Gi nodded as Shade headed upstairs. His first stop was Natalia's room. He knew she'd be tucked in for sleep at this hour. The sun would be up soon. He opened the door and slipped inside the room. He leaned over and kissed her cheek and her eyes fluttered, opening wide.

"Daddy, I stayed awake just for you." She wrapped her small arms tight around his neck, kissing his cheeks as the large book tumbled to the floor.

"My sweet Nattie. I missed you so much." He felt her soft sigh against his neck, and her scent was so soft and delicate. "Now, get some rest. We will visit when you wake, I promise." He put the book back on the bed, tucked in the blanket, kissing the top of her head and heading to her door.

"Daddy, I'm glad you're home."

Shade blew her a kiss and closed the door. He adored this beautiful child with her huge heart, and it scared him how damn intelligent she was.

Sophia was squirming in her seat in the classroom as Enzo showed her mother some of her latest work. She heard her father's footsteps in the hallway and couldn't wait for him to get there. She darted out of her seat and threw open the door, launching herself down the hallway toward her father, in a whirlwind of a fluffy pink dress and red hair. "Daddy!"

Shade squatted down just in time to catch her. "Who could ask for a better welcome than that? So, how is my princess? I have missed you. What are you learning today?" Shade held her tight while he could. She was hell to keep still, even with hugs and kisses.

"I haven't learned anything yet. Enzo is talking to Mommy. Did you bring Alfie with you?"

"Alfie?" Shade scrunched up his brow. "Why would I have Alfie?"

She looked at him with confusion. "Because he likes me, Daddy. I can tell. A girl knows these things. Mommy says you can tell when a boy is interested in you, and I think Alfie is interested."

Shade looked at her wide-eyed, his fingers stroking his chin. "I see. And why would you even be thinking about boys already? You should be more concerned about your studies. So, let me look at this beautiful dress you have on, did you wear that just for me? Spin around, let me see."

He was trying to think of anything to keep from talking to his daughter about boys. *Cazzo*, he was only gone a few nights and comes home to Sophia crushing on a warrior.

Sophia was more than happy to comply with his request and completed numerous spins, loving the way her skirt swirled around her. She squealed. "This is my favorite dress!"

He finally reached out and grabbed her around the waist. The small girl staggered a bit, dizzy from all the spinning. "Whoa, my head is still going around."

"Well, how about you aim your head for the classroom. Better yet, let's go together, *si?*" Picking her up, he carried her inside the classroom and lost his heart all over again. Kate turned and smiled at him and his knees went weak. He loved that her smile never grew old to him and always had the same effect.

"Look what I found while wandering down the hall. A beautiful pink princess."

Kate set the papers aside and immediately went to him, standing on tiptoe to kiss him, as he held Sophia in one arm. "Lover, I've missed you."

Sophia piped in, "Me too", and patted her father on the cheek.

Enzo cleared his throat. "Lady Sophia, we are late for class. In your seat, please."

Sophia looked at her father with an annoyed look. "He always says that."

Shade set her down and she reluctantly took her seat and turned on her computer. Looking back at her father, she inquired, "Could I go to camp instead? Like Lorenzo?"

Kate answered, "And give up pink dresses and crowns?"

Sophia scrunched up her face. "No, I'd still wear those. Can I, Daddy?"

"Your destiny is not to be a warrior, so no, you cannot go to camp. But you can sit here and study, and become an intelligent young lady, worthy of your title, *si*."

Sophia made a face. "I hope it doesn't take too long."

Enzo prompted her, "Lady Sophia, open your history book. Let's start with the Renaissance period."

With a heavy sigh, Sophia answered under her breath. "Let's not."

Kate suppressed her smile, as Shade scooped her up and left the classroom.

"Hurry up before she follows us." He ran with her in his arms for their bedchamber.

Kate laughed. "Enzo said he's going to put a seat belt on her chair. He's been tutoring for over a thousand years, and never had a student as hard to keep in class as Sophia. How is Lorenzo? Is he okay? And Vanni?"

Shade set her down in their room, kicking the door closed behind him. "No words yet, woman." He bent his head to hers and kissed her like he hadn't seen her for months. Her arms were around his shoulders, as his hands sought out her ass. The kiss was long and sweet, and he felt her hands tangle in his curls.

"*Cazzo*, I have missed you so badly. I can't sleep without you on my chest. I love you to the depths of my soul, woman."

"And I've missed you. This bed is much too big and empty when you're not beside me."

"Then I suggest we get naked and lay there together, then we can talk, *si?*"

He began to undress her, and she returned the gesture, both of them like crazy teenagers, fumbling and in a hurry. As they lay in the bed, he pulled her to his chest. "Damn it feels good to hold you. So, I have messages for you from our son. Do you wish to hear them now?"

She laid her head on his chest, her hand caressing the smooth, hard muscles in his shoulders, her leg thrown across his legs. She'd never get tired of him, lying next to him. His arm protectively encircled her, and his voice vibrated deep in his chest.

"Tell me, lover. I've been worried about him. He called me and told me what happened. He feels bad about letting his temper get the best of him. He says he's fine, but I also hear a change in his voice. Our little boy...he sounds like, I don't know, like he's growing up really fast. Tell me he's okay."

His hand ran through her crimson locks. "He did what he needed to do, *mi amore*. It was impulsive, and he understands that, understands the ramifications of his actions. He was pushed, and when backed in a corner, Medici's push back. Lorenzo is growing up fast, but he struggles with his duty, his obligations. He is smart, he will figure it out. His message to you was very simple in its love and sincerity. He said to tell you he is very sorry. He lost his temper and didn't think things through, and he does not want you to be disappointed in him. I might add he used the word mommy the entire time."

Kate quickly wiped away a tear. "He always calls me mommy when he's worried, or nervous. Doesn't he know he could never disappoint me? I love him to the very core of my being. He'll be a man before we know it. I could already see a big change when he visited here. Alfie is good for him, a good older brother. Lorenzo looks up to him. Alfie will be his brother, like Marco is yours." Lifting her head, she looked at him through strands of red hair. "Speaking of Alfie, your daughter has a crush."

He chuckled. "So, I was informed. What in hell sparked this crush?"

Kate giggled as she laid her head back on his chest. "I think it was at Cory and Madison's wedding, when he was dressed in a suit. She was following him around like a lost puppy. Get used to it, lover. I fear Sophia will fall in love a thousand times."

He groaned loudly. "I am in no hurry to deal with males sniffing around my daughters." Rolling her over, he kissed her softly. "Can we stop talking now? I am starving for you, my heart and soul ache for you, *mi amore*."

"I left Enzo a note to lock the classroom door, and Theresa is on guard. We won't be interrupted, and I'm all yours."

37

Lorenzo's week-long expulsion from the camp had ended, and tonight, he must face the warriors. He was feeling quite nervous, and wishing his dad was here to help pave the way. He'd be expected to address the warriors and begin the process of earning back their respect. Dressing in his leathers, he left his room and headed down the massive staircase into the grand foyer. Carlos was waiting for him, gave him a once over, and told him he'd be fine. Lorenzo wasn't so sure. Leaving Castello, he began the long walk to the camp. As he entered the camp onto the enclosed training field, Alfie stood waiting for him. He knew he could count on Alfie.

"Hey, brother."

Alfie nodded. "Brother. Take a deep breath, Lorenzo, everyone here is on your side. No one holds what you did to Vanni against you. Remember, we all knew him and saw how he acted. Marco is waiting for you. He has everyone gathered."

Lorenzo looked a little surprised. "Everyone?" He blew out his breath, and then walked alongside his friend. "Okay, then let's get this over with."

The two boys walked together across the well-lit training field, as Lorenzo took in all the warriors, gathered in the center of the field. Marco turned to see him approaching and walked to meet him half-way.

Marco could see the boy was nervous, but this was an issue he must face on his own. "Good to see you back, Lorenzo. The master has asked that you address your brothers, so let's get this done and get back to the business of becoming warriors. Come."

Marco walked ahead of the two boys, as Alfie fist bumped Lorenzo before running ahead to join the seniors. He was confident that, no matter what Lorenzo said, he'd always have their allegiance. Marco whistled to quiet the crowd and drew their attention. "Listen up you bone-heads, Lorenzo is returning to the ranks tonight, and he has something to say."

Marco stepped aside and nodded for Lorenzo to come forward, as the warriors gather round.

Lorenzo stepped forward and looked at the faces of all the warriors staring back at him. He swallowed hard, and his mouth felt dry. "Brothers, I owe you an apology. I let Vanni get the best of me, and in doing so, made an unwise choice. That's not a luxury any warrior can afford. I know my actions have let you down. I want to make it clear. You owe me nothing. My birthright put me here, but only your loyalty can keep me here. As your brother, I failed you, and I commit to you I won't make that mistake again. I'll work to earn your trust and your loyalty, for only then can I be worthy to lead. It's also no longer a secret that I'm a fire-thrower. I'll never again raise my hand against one of my own, and the only time you'll see me use my gift is in battle against our enemies. I'll strive to be a warrior of honor and integrity, like my father, and like Marco, so each of you will be proud to say you're a Medici."

Alfie was listening to his friend's words while his eyes roamed over the faces in the crowd. He could read from their expressions they accepted him into the fold. As he finished his speech, all the warriors dropped to one knee, lowered their head and shouted. "*Per sempre* Medici!"

Alfie felt in his heart these warriors would always follow Lorenzo into battle, and he hoped this show of respect and acceptance from his brothers gave Lorenzo the same feeling. As they all rose, Marco stepped forward, and without fanfare, barked out orders for the warriors.

"All right, all of you get your asses into your groups and let's see what in hell you can manage tonight. Move it!"

Lorenzo walked to Marco and nodded his head. "I know I said this already, but I should never have issued a command to you. I have much to learn, and I hope you'll guide me to be the warrior they need me to be."

"That matter is settled, warrior to warrior. You stumbled, and it won't be the last time. That's how you learn. Your mistakes bring the biggest lessons, just as they did for your father, and for his father. Be honest and fair with your warriors, and they will follow you. No one expects you to be perfect, Lorenzo."

Lorenzo looked back at him with respect. "Yes, sir. Do you have my assignment for tonight?"

Marco looked at the warriors on the training field, separated now by age group. “The grunts are a little edgy. You scared the fuck out of them. The juniors and seniors, well, let’s just say, their asses would follow you to hell and back. You choose where you go tonight, where you think you need to do the most work to improve your own skills."

Marco walked away from him and headed into the group of seniors, shouting out orders. He turned to look back at Lorenzo as he stood there thinking, and chuckled. "Damn kid. Have to make faster decisions than that or you will kill us all!"

Lorenzo was taken aback when he was given the choice, but it didn’t take him long to know where he belonged. His actions didn’t merit a move up in rank, and he needed to regain the trust of the grunts. Casting a glance in Alfie’s direction, the older boy winked at him, as Lorenzo returned to his group, and immediately fell into the night's exercises led by the lieutenant.

38

Shade pulled out his iPhone. It was time to contact Alec and let him know the Red Moon was scheduled for delivery. Alec's club appeared to be well underway, and the perfect place to test out his new Red Moon wine. There was little doubt that once they had a taste, they'd come crawling back for more. It was much more potent than Midnight and would soothe and excite in equal measure. He called and waited for Alec to answer.

L'Adventure had been open about a month, and Alec's client list was expanding far beyond what he'd anticipated. He'd been right about his gut instinct that the older, more sophisticated male wanted a very different club experience than the pounding music and the Goth mortals, who clung to the edge of their culture. His establishment was vampire only, no mortals, and offered privacy, secrecy, and a means to pursue their every sexual fantasy in a refined environment. The new business was keeping him busy, and, of course, he didn't miss the opportunity to indulge in a few fantasies of his own. He'd just given the sweet receptionist the appointment list for tonight's clients, along with the list of which fantasy room they'd requested. As she left his office, providing a view of her ample curves poured into the black latex bodysuit, he was distracted by the ringing of his cell phone. Grabbing at the phone, he answered. "*L'Adventure.*"

"Medici here. What the hell is going on in California, brother?" His smile was spread across his face as he chuckled into the phone.

Alec leaned back in the plush leather chair behind the massive mahogany desk. "Business couldn't be better, brother. We've been booked every night. I'll need to make a decision to either expand or turn away prospective clients soon. How about you? Any news on the Red Moon?"

"Well, there is good news for both of us. The Red Moon has left Florence and should be delivered within a few days. Five cases for right now, the rest are being bottled as we speak. Full production is already in the works. So, you need to get busy pushing it. I have no doubts it will fly once they get a taste. How is the security working out?"

Alec chuckled. "I'd say they're quite happy. We've not had any incidences that have presented threats, and several of our patrons have been quite taken with your warriors and invited them to join in a ménage a trois."

"*Cazzo*! I need to speak with Raven, not acceptable behavior for Medici. What the hell is going on out there? This sounds like I need to make a trip and have a meeting to dress down a few warriors, including the one in charge."

"Hey, no harm done, brother. There are several warriors on duty, so the place is still guarded, and my whole business model is based on fulfilling fantasies. If a couple wants a hot, young warrior to join them, I think that's completely appropriate. And it's a fringe benefit for the warrior. You should be pleased. But feel free to visit anytime. I'm sure you have a few unfulfilled fantasies, yourself, by now."

Shaking his head, the only fantasy he had was to be alone with Kate for a full night without interruption from the children. "I should be out in about a week. By that time, you should have the Red Moon, and a good idea of how your clients like it. Just need to convince my mate she should accompany me. See you then."

Alec leaned back in his chair. "Get here right at sunset. I'll give you a full tour. I can even reserve one of the rooms for you. Are you sure you want to bring Kate? There are plenty of females to choose from, brother, and your mate may not be ready for all that goes on in this house."

"Brother, don't proceed to tell me what my mate can handle. Her beast is the perfect match to my own. I have no use for other females. Kate is all I will ever need. We will see you soon, and Alec, congratulations. It's good to see you back on top of your game."

Alec chuckled. "Whatever pleases you, brother. Just never thought I'd see you so domesticated. I'll let the guards know you're coming."

Shade ended the call as he tossed the phone on the table. "You should damn well be used to it by now." Right now, he had another task to arrange, he needed to convince *bel* to go with him to California, and make sure his daughters were taken care of for the night. He stood quietly and concentrated on her whereabouts. Kate was having a talk with Nattie, so he headed for the classroom.

Enzo was writing a calculus equation on the whiteboard, and Natalia had the answer before the ink was dry. Kate could only shake her head. She'd had trouble balancing her checkbook when she was mortal. Kate looked at her daughter in awe. "That's excellent Natalia!"

Natalia shrugged. "I think the math is kind of boring, though. I still prefer history."

Kate kissed the top of her head and wondered where this child would find a mate who'd be her intellectual equal, when she heard Shade enter the classroom. They both looked in his direction as Natalia flashed him a huge smile.

"Hi, Daddy!"

The smile alone made his heart leap, as his eyes absorbed the beautiful child of their creation. "Calculus, I see. Math was not a good subject for your *padre*. I was more interested in the art of war." Walking to Natalia, he crouched down beside her, "Give Daddy a kiss. I need your *madre* for a bit, will you let me borrow her while you finish your studies?"

Natalia wrapped her small arms around his strong shoulders and gave him a tight squeeze and a very wet kiss on the cheek. "Daddy, since Sophia has a chicken, I was wondering if I could have a kitty. I'll take care of him. It won't be any extra work for the staff, or Mommy, I promise. Please, Daddy?"

Brushing back her long brown hair, he couldn't deny her anything. "I think a kitten would make a good pet. She can curl up with you when you read, and nap next to you when you sleep. Just make sure she does not agitate Poppy; we both know that chicken is crazy enough as it is!" Kissing her soft cheek, he loved the look on her face as she beamed back at him.

"Thank you, Daddy! Thank You! I'm going to name him Lord Byron, after the British poet."

"Perfect." Standing, he took Kate's hand and they exited the classroom as Enzo resumed his class.

"Come along, woman, let's take a walk outside, *si*? Something I want to discuss with you." They walked hand in hand outside and Shade led them casually through the garden path. He had no destination in mind, but if she was going to give him grief, he didn't want to disrupt the whole household. "You are a wonderful mother to our children, *mi amore*, and a beautiful one at that. But I think you need a break. One night, alone with me, would you be interested?"

"The two of us alone? Without interruption? Let me think when the last time that happened. Oh yes, I remember. That would be eleven years ago, right before Lorenzo was born. Of course, I'd be interested. We created the Paris house and the California house, we converted Max's mansion into the inn in Virginia, there are the small cottages in the vineyards in France and Greece, and we never have time to visit any of them. I'd like nothing better than time alone with you."

He lifted her up to sit on the rail fence and stepped in between her legs so they were eye to eye. "I must admit, it is a business trip, but one I will find time for our pleasure. Alec has invited us to see his new club, *L'Adventure*. I have a shipment of Red Moon scheduled for delivery, and I am interested in client feedback."

She started to speak, and he put his finger to her lips. "Let me finish, *si*? I have already informed Mica to prepare our rooms at *Touch of Tuscany*, so we will spend the night there. But this is important to our production of Red Moon, and I feel we need to oblige Alec. This is nothing like *Under the Coffin*, and besides, we could use some kink in our routine." He chuckled but she wasn't laughing.

She pushed him away as she slid off the top rail of the fence and started marching back toward the house. "Routine? That's what you call it now? Routine? Well, I'm sorry I've been such a disappointment to you."

She stopped in her tracks and turned sharply on her heels, as he almost bumped into her. "But I'll tell you this! If you think, for one minute, you're going there alone, you're mistaken, Shade Medici!"

And there it was, her beast rising faster than lightening. Damn, he thought she'd be happy to get away together. "Please, will you listen to me? I did not mean it in that manner, Kate. I don't want to go there alone. I want to make this an evening for both of us? I apologize for the use of those words."

She glared back at him, her eyes emitting a soft glow as her temper simmered. "Oh, I'll go! It's a house for fulfilling fantasies, and I'm sure there are a few who wouldn't mind including you in some of those fantasies. We'll visit as you request, so you can see how the new wine is accepted, then return to our own place in Napa. But if this is your idea of a romantic getaway, think again."

She turned and stomped back to the house, looking over her shoulder as she screamed out at him. "Routine? Really! You need some kink? I'll show you some kink!"

Shade watched her strut back to the house, her crimson locks blowing in the breeze. His voice was low, but he knew she could hear him in her head. "Oh, I am sure you will, you fiery woman. But rest assured, it is time this vampire shows you who is your master."

His eyes never left her ass as it switched angrily back to the house and his mind wandered. She'd just fired his beast up good, already anticipating this trip with the only female he'd ever want to have there.

39

Shade stood in their bedroom and sighed as he adjusted his tie in front of the mirror. He wasn't sure what to wear to *L'Adventure*. Deciding to skip the tie, he remained casual in his dress slacks and shirt. He'd slip on his jacket before teleporting out. Running his hands through his hair, he decided this would do. He'd received the cold shoulder from Kate all week, after his unfortunate choice of words about their sex *routine*. He'd tried to explain to her she had misinterpreted his meaning, but his explanation fell on deaf ears as she continued to fume.

She'd been getting the children settled with Theresa, when she came roaring through the door, slamming it for the hundredth time. He gritted his teeth and didn't respond. The entire house would need the doors rehung if they had to wait another week. Every time he was near her, she was mumbling under her breath about 'routine' and she'd show his royal ass the meaning of kink. He had no doubts she could, but he was, after all, a master of kink. He'd had several hundred years of experience on her, but that wasn't what this night was about. He loved her, she was his mate and he'd reclaim what was his. He'd let Alec know which room he wanted, and what he wished to have set up inside the room, but she was the main attraction.

"We must arrive just at sunset, are you ready?"

"You tell me!" She was wearing a dress in his favorite color of red, cut low in the back, and a pair of black Louboutin heels, with their trademark red soles. "Is this dress 'too routine' for you? Maybe I should change into leopard skin, or would you prefer nude with a few chains. I'm sure I could find a dog collar and leash around here somewhere."

He let her rant and refused to take the bait. "You look beautiful, *mi amore*, and if you are quite done berating me, I suggest you teleport beside me." Sliding on his jacket, he took her hand, and gripping firmly, teleported out.

Kate was startled when he teleported them out so quickly, she barely had time to grab her purse from the bed. He'd ignored her irritation all week, not responding to her constant smart remarks, and ignoring the slammed doors, although everyone else in the house had been staying out of her way. He looked so handsome dressed in the suit. They both rarely had any reason to get dressed up. He gripped her hand tightly and she tried to free herself, but without any luck, then realized she had no idea where Alec's club was anyway, so she stopped the struggle.

Shade grinned. "About time you settled down." He controlled the teleport, landing them just outside the gated mansion, still gripping her arm. She straightened her dress as he made a final appeal.

"Please be accommodating with Alec this evening. He is my conduit for getting Red Moon introduced in the U.S. market. I would appreciate if you could keep the smart-ass remarks to a limit while in his company." Taking her arm in his, he kissed her cheek. "Ready?"

She sighed heavily as he spoke to her. She knew her behavior had been totally unreasonable this week, but every time she heard the word 'routine' in her head, she got angry all over again. "I'm sorry. This is business, and I'll conduct myself accordingly. I'm ready."

"Well, not all business, *bel rosso*." He gave her a wicked grin.

As they approached the guardhouse at the gate, he recognized Robbie and Riley who greeted him and led them inside. Both had started out in his camp in Virginia and were now assigned here in California.

"Master Shade and my lady, welcome to *L'Adventure*. Master Alec has asked me to escort you both inside to his office."

Shade nodded and fist bumped Robbie. "Good to see you, warrior. You as well, Riley. How are you adapting to your new post?"

Riley grinned and Shade was praying like hell he didn't say anything about 'the benefits.'

"Master, never thought I'd see myself in California, but I truly love it here. Enjoy your evening." He winked as Robbie led them inside.

The receptionist, dressed in her latex bodysuit, greeted them at the door, her pale blonde hair a sharp contrast against the shiny black. She was already tall, and the four-inch heels placed her eye level with Shade as she greeted him.

"Master, how might we serve you tonight?" She slipped her arm around his. "Your pleasure is our only concern. We have a new wine selection called Red Moon. May I get you both a glass?" Her voice was soft and breathy, and dripped like honey, as she clung to him. "Will it be just the two of you? Or would you like company? We can arrange whatever you desire."

Kate huffed beside him and spoke through her gritted teeth. "Guess I should have worn the chains."

Smiling at the beautiful blonde dressed in latex, Shade knew whatever he did or said would inflame an already ignited Kate. "*Grazie*, but I am expected by Master Alec. Will you please announce our arrival? Master Shade Medici and his Queen."

The blonde let go of his arm. "Oh, of course. So sorry, Master Medici. Right this way. He's expecting you."

She turned and walked ahead of them, making sure he had an unobstructed view of her ample ass, poured into the latex, as she swayed her hips. As she got to Alec's office, she turned and flashed him a smile as she opened the door for them. "Be sure to let me know if you need anything, and I *do* mean anything."

Alec stood from behind his desk, calling out to him. "Brother! Welcome. Come in and have a seat. Bree, bring us all a glass of Red Moon please."

Kate observed the look that Alec exchanged with the blonde and knew Bree brought him more than just wine. Bree smiled seductively at her master. "Of course, master, whatever you desire."

Shade smiled as he saw Alec. It had been some time since the two of them had seen each other face to face. Shade quickly turned to Bree. "If I might request, we skip the Red Moon for me and my mate. Please bring us Midnight."

He led Kate to a comfortable seat and clapped Alec on the back. "Damn good to see you again, Alec. Gorgeous place you have here and very friendly staff. Saw Robbie and Riley outside at the gate."

Alec took a seat as Bree returned with the wine, placing the glass in Alec's hand, and bending over more than necessary to give Shade a good rear view. Turning to Shade, she handed him the two glasses for him and his mate, and leaned in, exposing her cleavage, as she asked, "Is there anything else?"

Shade wasn't oblivious to the blatant display or to the cold stare from Kate. "*Grazie*, Bree, I believe this will suit us well for the moment."

As she left, he handed Kate her glass of Midnight, and raised his glass to Alec. "Here is to a prosperous future and to new beginnings with old friends." He looked at Kate and added, "And to love." They all sipped their drinks after the toast. "So, how is the Red Moon doing? I know it hasn't been that long yet."

Alec sipped from his own glass of Red Moon. "It's been a huge hit. I'd say ninety percent of my clients prefer the Red Moon over the Midnight. We'll need to look at the numbers and shift my future orders accordingly. Business is booming, my friend."

Shade nodded. "I can see why. If the whole place operates like this, you will have a waiting list of masters. The shipment of Red Moon is easily adjusted. We are in full production now. Selling it here exclusively should ramp up business for you as well, but I am sure, by the looks of Bree, you need no help in that area. Speaking of business, is anyone interesting coming in?"

Kate heard his comment about Bree, and removed her hand from around his arm, turning slightly away from him as he spoke, sipping at the wine. She'd promised him she'd behave, but he was pushing every button. *Fucking routine. I'll show him fucking routine.*

Shade looked at her as she slipped away, and Alec answered. "We've had a number of interesting guests, Colin and Elena are regulars. That's no surprise." He chuckled as he saw Kate bristle at her mate's acknowledgement of Bree. *Once a mortal, always a mortal.*

"No surprise at all, brother, Colin is almost as sick as you. But I rather prefer being mated to my *bel*. Having *bambinos* and ensuring my blood line is vital for Medici. But beyond that, I have never felt so loved in all my life." Grabbing Kate's hand, he squeezed hard, well aware of the cold shoulder he was getting. "Your mate should always give you her all, satisfy your beast. I am the luckiest vampire in the world to have found that in Kate. Could I request a small tour? I'd like to see what you have here."

Alec stood. “Of course, brother, I’m more than happy for you to see the place. I'm rather busy at the moment, so I'll have Bree show you around."

As he extended his hand, Shade took it, and Alec passed off the key card to the room he’d requested. He needn't be discreet about it, because Kate had already turned her back on the whole thing. Alec smiled. "Good luck, brother. Looks like you may have your hands full."

He chuckled softly." *Grazie*." They both hugged and slapped each other on the back as Bree entered the room, smiles galore.

"*Mi amore*, I do believe our tour guide is waiting. Let’s see what Alec has created."

Kate flashed him a glance that could melt steel. She wasn’t the least bit happy about Bree giving them a guided tour. Shade winked at her and slipped his arm around her waist, ignoring her anger as they followed Bree down the long hallway, as she began to explain their surroundings.

"We have a central room, where the guests can all gather and drink, and there are monitors that allow them to watch what’s going on in the private suites, but only if the vamps in the suite request it. This room is a bit of a free for all, and there’s frequently a lot of exchanging of partners."

Bree opened the door into the large room, furnished in low seating that accommodated a number of people. The room had monitors mounted on the walls, and the option to hear as well as see what was taking place inside some of the private suites. The tangle of bodies on the seating and the floor made identifying any one individual almost impossible, as the bodies writhed like a pit of snakes. Kate took a step back, feeling the firm pressure of Shade's hand against the small of her back. Bree pointed out the blank monitors.

"The people in the private rooms can turn the cameras off if they don't want to be viewed. This is a fun room. I come here a lot myself. Anyone can join in, at any time. It's still early. It will get really busy as the night goes on." They turned to leave, and Kate thought to herself, *Okay, maybe I am routine.*

Feeling her doubt as he read her thoughts, he leaned in and whispered in her ear. "There is nothing routine about you, *mi amore*."

They followed Bree along as she guided them away from the central room, and down a long corridor that looked much like a hotel, with doors lining either side. Bree pointed out the light above each door. "If the light is on, and the light is red, the room is occupied, and they don't want to be disturbed. If the light is green, the room is occupied, but they are open to others joining them. No light means the room is empty."

Bree opened the door onto an empty room. "This is the mirror room, as you can see, mirrors on all four walls, and the ceiling, so you won't miss anything."

Moving to the next room, she swung the door open to reveal a tall woman, clad all in leather, and holding a whip. Bree laughed. "And for our bad boys...They like this room. That's Lady Grace, she's our dominatrix." Bree flashed Shade a smile. "She'd be happy to beat your ass, master."

Kate gritted her teeth as she spoke to him under her breath. "That makes two of us."

She heard him chuckle as he squeezed her closer. Bree continued her tour, opening a door with a green light. "This is our shower room. All tile, and shower heads at every angle."

The couple inside were busy soaping each other up, as the female turned and waved them in. Bree looked at Shade who showed no interest in wanting to join the fun. She shrugged to the couple and called out, "Just touring", and closed the door. Moving down the hall, she opened another door that looked like a bedroom, decorated in black. "This is our live webcam room. You can have sex in here, and broadcast it live on the web. It shows you how many people are logging on to watch."

Kate shuddered as Bree closed the door and led them down the hall to the next room. "Sometimes, we get special requests. If people want to role play, we'll find costumes and props and set the room up in advance." Opening another door, she looked in. "Oh yeah, this room shows porn. They have a whole menu to choose from, girl on girl, guy on guy, anal, oral, rape fantasies, whatever gets you off." She winked at Shade as she closed the door. "I believe, master, that this next room was reserved for you. The Shibari room?"

Kate looked at him with surprise. *He reserved a room for us in this place? And what the fuck is Shibari?*

Shade followed along on this tour. He'd seen it all before, plus some, but he was impressed. The extravagance of the rooms was perfect for masters. If he'd had something like this when he was still sowing his wild oats, he would have paid any price. "*Grazie*, Bree." He slipped the key card from his pocket and opened the door as he instructed her to make sure the red light was on and the cameras were turned off.

Bree flashed him a smile as she slipped inside. "I'd be more than happy to." She immediately flipped on the light switch that triggered the red light above the door. "There's a tiny red light here by the switch, so you know the light is on. You can also lock the door from the inside if you wish." Walking to another panel installed on the wall, she deactivated all the cameras. "Are you sure? I love to watch."

Shade led Kate inside the room, her eyes as large as saucers as she took it in. Shade chuckled. "Most sure, Bree, what I do behind closed doors belongs to only one." Removing several hundred-dollar bills from his jacket, he slipped them to her. "Please make sure we are not disturbed. Thank you for your assistance."

Kate stepped into the room, the walls heavily sound-proofed and covered in a red brocade fabric. There was a large circular bed in the center of the room, and a separate room with red tiles, and a large marble tub, big enough for two, as well as a separate shower stall. But what caught her eyes were the well-stocked cabinets along one wall, stocked with every imaginable sex toy. Hanging from pegs on the wall was an assortment of whips, chains, and ropes. She swallowed hard as the memory of the sex chamber beneath Castello flashed through her head. *Is this what he wants?* On a table by the bed was a bottle of Red Moon, chilling on ice, along with several bundles of rope, a blindfold, feathers, candles, and a flogger. He was dismissing Bree, and she heard the door close and lock behind her. *This is definitely not routine.* She swallowed hard as she turned and looked at him, as he turned the dimmer switch down on the lights. "Lover?"

Shade felt her temper drop to zero as she took in the room and its contents. The tone of her voice changed from annoyed to confused. He turned to her as he slipped off his jacket. "*Si, mi amore*?" He knew this wasn't their thing, but he also knew, if he approached this correctly, they'd both enjoy their evening inside this room. "So, did the tour scare you? Give you any ideas? Conjure up questions in your head? Talk to me, *si*?"

She knew he'd never hurt her; despite all the things she saw in this room that could be used to inflict pain. She knew he'd never force her to do anything she didn't want.

"Scare me? I wouldn't say it scares me. But I don't understand it. I don't understand people wanting to share their experience, or have others join them, or watch them. It's not a judgment. I just feel like what we have, what we do together, it belongs to us. Do you... do you need something different?"

"My culture is very diverse because we live so long, *mi amore*. We have experienced much. I do not judge as well, and whatever I choose, I choose with you. It is only a room, *bel*. We can explore, or not. The choice is yours to make."

Kate walked slowly around the room, letting her eyes roam across a lot of equipment she had no idea how it would be used. Walking to the table by the bed, she poured them both a glass of the new wine, and handed him a glass, as she sipped from her own. Walking over to the wall, she ran her hand along the leather belts, whips, and floggers, setting them in a slow, swinging motion. There was one whole panel of ropes, made of different materials and colors, different thicknesses, different textures.

"Lover, I don't know what most of this stuff is. I mean, I sort of know... I don't understand how it can bring pleasure."

He observed her actions closely, as she was showing more curiosity than fear. He could understand how the items on display in this room could incite fear in any female who didn't fully trust her mate. "Well, the ropes you are looking at are used in the art of Shibari. It is an ancient Japanese art of rope tying. The word means 'to tie'. The arrangement of the ropes and knots on your body are designed to stimulate pressure points, very similar to Shiatsu, a form of Japanese massage. Many believe the experience enhances your sexual pleasure. This is not the chamber at Castello, *bel*. I will do nothing you do not choose to experience. Choice, and trust, without both, there is no pleasure."

He sipped at the Red Moon, feeling it relax him immediately. "I know you trust me. Show me something you see that sparks your interest, something you wish to explore."

She laughed. "I don't know what any of it does." Running her hands over the rope, she looked up at him with a sly smile. "Do you want to tie me up?"

He stood next to her, kissing her. Laughing, he slid his hand through her crimson waves. "Sometimes, *mi amore*, I want nothing better than to tie your ass down and keep you under me forever."

She downed the rest of the wine and felt the burn of the alcohol in her throat, before setting the glass down. She lifted her hair and turned her back to him, so he could unzip the dress, looking at him over her shoulder. “Then do it."

Unzipping her dress, he slid it off her shoulders and watched it float to her ankles in a pool of red. Beneath it, she wore a red lace bra, and a hint of a thong, as his beast licked his chops. "Step out of the dress."

She kicked the dress aside as she felt his fist in her hair. He leaned into her, inhaling her rose scent as he licked her neck. Leaning into her ear, he whispered in a husky voice. “My lily-white.”

Standing behind her, he slowly released her bra, letting it drop, as he cupped her breasts in his hands, and nipped at her shoulder. She dropped her head back against his chest, and he slipped his hand under the elastic of the thong, and with a quick snap, tore them away.

He walked around her slowly, the growl low and deep in his chest. "Come, take off my clothes for me."

He held her in his gaze as she slowly unbuttoned the buttons on his dress shirt, sliding her hand inside the shirt to feel the smooth hard muscles on his chest. He helped her as he pulled the shirt free of his waistband and dropped it. She grabbed the front on his pants and yanked hard, pulling him forward, as she lifted her face to kiss him. As his lips meet hers, she unbuttoned his pants, and slowly lowered the zipper. Her hands moved swiftly, sliding the pants over his narrow hips, and letting them fall around his ankles.

He growled. "You make me want to devour you, but you already know that, woman.“ He smiled at her and lifted the coiled, red rope from the wall. He held it up and looked at her, and she nodded yes. Taking her hand, he led her to the bed. "Sit down, *mi amore*. Hold out your hands, wrist to wrist.”

She sat on the bed, wearing only her Louboutin heels, and held her arms out to him, as he wrapped the rope around her wrist. Once her wrists were secured, he lifted her gently and laid her on her back across the bed, lifting her arms above her head as he kissed her. Breaking the kiss, he looked down at her, his beautiful captive.

"Can you tie my ankles? Not together like this, tie my ankles to the bed."

"So, my minx is ready to play? Spread your legs for me." He walked around the circular bed and stepped on a switch in the floor, activating small steel poles that rose up from the floor with holes in the ends to anchor the ropes. He slid off her heels one at a time, and quickly and efficiently tied the rope around her slender ankles, leaving her spread eagle on the bed.

She held his gaze as she spoke to him. "Now I'm at your mercy. Will you show me any mercy?"

From the foot of the bed, he climbed over her on all fours, until they were face to face and he kissed her again. "Perhaps I will be lenient, *si*?" Reaching over to the table, he held up the blindfold, and once again, she nodded yes. Straddling her, he tied the black silk around her eyes. "It is all about trust now, *bel rosso*."

She nodded. "I trust."

She felt his lips on her again for a split second, and then could feel him shift his weight to the side of the bed. She could hear him moving things on the table, and then startled when she felt something cold and wet, as he poured it on her belly. He leaned over her, his tongue lapping at the wine. The heat of his mouth was a sharp contrast to the cold of the liquid. His tongue explored, following the rivulets of wine that had run between her legs and her body involuntarily responded to the cold liquid as it splashed against her skin, followed by the heat of his tongue, and she squirmed beneath him.

"Talk to me, *bel*."

"The cold, and the heat. I like it."

"Can you keep your hands over your head? Or must I tie them down?"

"Tie me."

He quickly secured her bound wrists to the bed frame and sat back down next to her. He kissed her deeply, and she could taste the wine on his lips. Then he was gone again, and she could hear him arranging things on the table. She heard the strike of a match and smelt the pungent odor of the sulfur dioxide from the burning match. She listened intently and could hear the clinking of ice against the ice bucket, her senses were on overdrive. Her heart rate picked up, and her breathing was shallow as she waited in anticipation of what he'd do.

He lit a single candle, and held it over her bare breast, and watched as the hot wax pooled ever so slowly before dripping down on her pure white skin. The nipple hardened instantly, and he heard her sharp gasp, and slight cry of pain. He placed the ice cube in his mouth, and lowered his mouth to her breast, soothing the burn, and heard her moan. He kissed her again and transferred the ice cube to her open mouth.

"Tell me, *mi amore*. Stop? Or more?"

"More," she whispered.

He repeated the process, letting the hot wax drip on both breasts, and her belly button, always followed by the cold ice. Her body tensed each time the hot wax hit her skin, and she cried out softly, only to relax, and moan with pleasure when his lips followed with the ice. When he was done, her body was splattered in the wax, now solid and hard on her skin. He blew out the candle, and she could smell the acrid smoke, and knew this part was over. She felt him stand up from the bed and walk away. She listened intently, trying to figure out what he'd do next, when he returned and sat back on the bed next to her.

She felt the cold hard steel skim across her skin, and he hushed her. "Shh, lie still, *bel*. It is my blade. Lie still and I will remove the wax."

He'd retrieved the blade he'd always worn in a sheath at his waist. She'd seen it many times. It was sharp enough to split a single hair. She lay perfectly still, as he whittled the wax from her skin.

"Trust, *mi amore*."

"I trust, lover."

"I would never leave a mark on my lily-white. There, good as new."

She felt him stand and leave the bed again and heard the clang of metal as the knife hit the table. She could hear his footsteps in the room and could tell he was at the wall. She was trying desperately to remember what was hanging there when she heard him return. He didn't sit down but remained standing by the bed. She was holding her breath when she suddenly feels a light flick of pain on her thigh and she jumped. "What is it?"

"A riding crop, *bel rosso*. We have them in the stables. I can't tell you how many times I have wanted to swat your ass with one." He dragged the leather tongue of the riding crop along her inner thigh so lightly it tickled. "Yes or no, *mi amore*."

"Yes."

He smiled to himself, as he looked down at her. She was completely vulnerable to him. Open to him. His cock was throbbing to be inside her, but he wasn't finished torturing either of them yet. He slowly dragged the leather tongue between her legs and saw her tense up. He snapped the crop lightly with his wrist against her sex, with enough pressure to create a mild sting. She flinched, and drew her breath in. He snapped the crop again, and she made a sound that was somewhere between a cry and a moan.

"No pleasure without pain, *bel rosso*."

He dragged the crop over her belly, and across her breast, watching as her nipple hardened again. He snapped his wrist, bringing the leather tongue down hard against her nipple, and watched as she arched her back, and threw her head back on the pillow, her mouth open, gasping for air.

He lowered his mouth to her breast, and drew the nipple into his mouth, circling with his tongue, when he heard her whimper. "Does my captive need mercy yet?"

"Don't stop, lover."

"*Si*, as my lady wishes."

He climbed onto the bed and straddled her chest. Dipping his fingers into the wine glass on the table, he ran them over her lips. She opened her mouth, sucking at his fingers, tasting the wine. "More," she whispered.

He took a big gulp from the glass, holding the wine in his mouth as he kissed her, releasing the wine into her mouth. She swallowed, and licked her lips, and it drove him insane with want. Holding his cock in his hand, he touched the smooth head to her lips. She parted her lips, and he slid his cock into her hot, wet mouth. Placing his hands on the bed on either side of her head, he slowly fucked her mouth. He had to fight his own beast and worked hard to control his movements. Her tongue swirled around the head of his cock, and her lips sucked and pulled at him, and he wasn't sure who was tortured more.

His fangs punched through and he withdrew from her mouth, sliding down her body, licking at her as he went, until he was between her legs. He tortured her now with his mouth as he kissed and licked and suckled her clit until it was hard and throbbing. His tongue probed deep inside her and he sucked her sweet honey, and she squirmed beneath him, panting, begging.

"Please, lover."

She felt the sharp sting of his fangs as they sank into the tender flesh of her inner thigh and a loud moan escaped her lips and grew louder as the orgasm washed over her. She was bound, hand and foot, and completely under his control. The spasms shook her as she arched her back, pushing her hips forward, when he suddenly pulled away. "No!"

He left her breathless and needing more. He slid off the bed and walked back over to the cabinets. She was gasping for air and pulling at her restraints when he returned to the bed with the flogger. Holding the flogger over top of her, he dragged the leather strips over her belly and between her legs, brushing it against her sensitized clit. He watched as the goose bumps rose on her skin.

He let the flogger trail softly along her inner thighs, and down her legs. He struck the soles of her feet and her body jerked against the restraints. "Mercy, *mi amore*?"

Her breathing was rapid as he teased her body with the flogger, testing her limits, exploring her response. She squirmed beneath the restraints and felt a shock of pain as he struck the bottom of her feet. Her gasp was audible. "No mercy."

He untied her ankles, rubbing them gently to restore the circulation. She was wondering if the game was over. She didn't want it to be over. He released her hands, and again, rubbed her wrists, kissing her palms softly. He pulled her upright and kissed her passionately and left her sitting blindfolded on the side of the bed. She could hear him walk away again, followed by the sound of the soft whir of a motor. He returned and removed the blindfold.

"Want to play with me on the harness swing?"

Kate looked at the contraption of straps and ropes suspended from a scaffold on the ceiling. *A swing?* "Show me."

Taking her hand, he led her to the scaffold. "You sit in the suspended swing. Your legs go through the straps, and I have control. The swing has ropes, so you can hold on, but I control your motion. I prefer you to wrap your legs around me, so you can lean back but still hold on, *si*?"

He lowered the harness, and she stepped into the straps as he slid them up her legs, securing them around her thighs. She grabbed the ropes as he raised her in the air and stepped between her legs. She smiled back at him. "Can you put one in our bedroom?"

He smiled and slapped her ass. "Where has this minx been hiding?"

She felt the sharp sting of his slap, and her skin felt hot. The look she gave him was smoldering. "I've been here the whole time, waiting for you."

"Then I won't make you wait any longer."

He slid his hands into her hair, and pulled her close, kissing her, their tongues exploring. She wrapped her legs around his hips, and he teased her with his rock-hard cock, gliding it along her sex, hot, and wet for him. He was barely able to breathe he wanted inside her with such urgency. "Lay back, my walking sin, I have you."

As she lay back, her hands slid along the ropes and her hair hung almost to the floor. He slid inside her, and stood still, as he slowly rocked her on the swing. He could control how deeply he'd penetrate her, and how fast or slow he'd move the swing, giving him total control of the device and her.

She closed her eyes and gave herself up to the experience of him, as she felt his cock glide in and out.

After teasing her body, he needed release, and his beast was impatient. His fangs punched through and he began to pump the swing more aggressively, filling her to her depths. He threw his head back and growled loudly. He pulled her upright and gripped her ass with both hands, pushing hard into her. He ran his fangs over her neck, his breath hot against her skin. "Let me taste you."

Holding tight to the ropes, she dropped her head back, exposing her neck to him in a clear invitation to feed. "Feed, lover. Drink in all of me."

Sinking his fangs into her, his body jerked as her blood flowed across his tongue. Her beauty and blood brought his beast to the surface, as he gripped the harness, and pounded his hips hard against her, driving his cock as deep as he could. He wanted her to cum with him, feed from him, in the bond that held them together for eternity. She was his, every inch of her, and he'd never let her go.

She felt his body convulse as their bodies teetered on the edge of the abyss. As he fed, she bit into his shoulder, feeding from him, completing the circle. The power of his blood, and the pounding between her legs, pushed them both into the free-fall of their orgasm as she felt his primal growl against her neck. She swallowed his blood as she felt his hot seed filling her, and the room was lit in the soft glow of red from both their eyes.

He felt her unlatch and he did the same, still holding her close to his body. "I love you, *bel.*"

She licked at the wound, slowly and seductively. "And I love you."

"Let me get you out of this thing and we can take a long, hot bath together, *si*? And if you like, we can stay longer or travel to the inn in Napa. I don't want this all the time but tell me you enjoyed this."

She laughed as he helped her out of the harness, and willed the tub filled with hot water. "Oh, I enjoyed it. And I haven't given up on the idea of installing this thing in our bedroom."

Chasing her to the bathroom, he caught her as she squealed, and he lifted her into the tub with him. "Be careful what you wish for, my queen, you know I can deny you nothing."

40

Enzo was attempting to teach Sophia Italian. All the children had been raised speaking English, and Shade was adamant they be taught Italian and French. He had strong business interests in those countries, and it wasn't clear which of the children would end up running which of the businesses. Lorenzo had taken quickly to the other languages when he was still Enzo's student, and Natalia excelled, as always. But Sophia was another matter. It wasn't that she wasn't smart. It was more that she wasn't interested.

Enzo turned from the white board, where he'd been conjugating verbs in Italian, to see Sophia diligently writing. He watched her a few seconds, realizing she never looked up at the board. Whatever she was writing had nothing to do with today's lessons. "Princess Sophia, what are you writing?"

Sophia looked up startled and slid her hand over the paper. "Nothing."

Enzo looked at her over his glasses. "I would propose that it is impossible to take pen to paper and write 'nothing'. Bring me the paper, please."

Sophia frowned and folded the paper in half. "This is my personal stuff. You can't have my personal stuff."

Enzo gave her a stern look and held out his hand. "Then I suggest the princess not write personal stuff during class time. Now hand me the paper."

Sophia rolled her eyes and slid from her chair, as she stomped to the front of the classroom and shoved the paper in his hand. "Are you happy now?"

He nodded his head and pointed her back in the direction of her seat. He glanced at the paper and saw it was a letter, *'My dearest, dearest Alfie.'* Enzo left the folded letter on his desk and returned to the white board. After class, Sophia was dismissed, and she asked for her letter back.

"I think not. You may write letters to your dearest, dearest Alfie when you are not on my time, understood?"

Sophia sighed and put a hand on her hip. "You know you are standing in the way of true love."

Enzo suppressed a smile. “Ah, princess, if you have been reading your literature assignments, then you know that true love always finds a way."

Sophia stared him down, thinking hard on her response. He could almost see the gears turning in her head when she shouted back, "Well, it didn't work out so well for Romeo and Juliet, now, did it?"

With that, she turned on her heels and stomped out of the classroom. Enzo bit his lip as he answered. "Touché, princess."

He cleaned up the classroom and got things in order for the classes he’d teach to Natalia when she woke from her death slumber. Before class, he carried the letter to Kate. "My lady, it may be of no concern to you, but I thought I should bring this to your attention. Sophia was writing a letter in class today." He handed Kate the folded paper.

"A letter? To whom?" She unfolded the paper and saw the salutation and giggled. "Thank you, Enzo. I'll have a talk with her."

Kate tucked the letter in her pocket and walked outside to find her daughter playing in a large pile of leaves. Poppy was running behind her, keeping right on her heels. "Sophia, where is your jacket?"

Her daughter looked up with leaves caught in her red hair. "What? Oh... I put it on the swing."

Kate shook her head. “Could you put it on yourself, please?"

Sophia climbed from the leaves, walking to the tree swing, and reluctantly put on the jacket. Kate sat down on the grass beneath the tree, and patted the ground beside her, inviting her daughter to sit next to her. Sophia looked at her doubtfully.

"Am I going to get yelled at?"

Kate looked back at her. "Have you done something I need to yell about?"

Sophia thought hard. "I don't think so."

Kate smiled and patted the ground again. "Then come sit with me."

Sophia skipped over to her mother, Poppy running behind her, and sat down next to Kate. Kate smoothed her daughter's unruly hair, picking out some of the leaves, as she talked. "So, Enzo came to see me today."

Sophia jerked her head up. "Did you read my letter?"

Kate slipped the letter from her pocket. "No, I didn't. I'll never read your private correspondence without your approval, but I'd very much appreciate if we could read it together."

Sophia blinked her eyes several times, eyes the same piecing blue as her father's. "But....it's a secret."

Kate held the folded letter in her hand. "Then I'm sad you feel you must keep secrets from me, Sophia. There should never be anything you fear to share with me, or your father."

Sophia scrunched up her face as she thought about her mother's words. "Well, not like a real secret, like considential."

Kate thought a minute. "You mean confidential?"

She nodded her head. "Yes, that's the word, confidential."

Kate smiled in acknowledgement. "Do you trust me to keep your confidences?"

Sophia thought hard and could think of no reason not to trust her mother. "But...I might be embarrassed."

Kate pulled her daughter close. "Don't be. I'm your mother, and no one will ever love you the way I love you, or the way your father loves you. Now, can we read this together?" She handed the folded paper to Sophia, leaving the decision in her hands. Sophia took the paper and unfolded it, glancing up at her mother one last time, then took a deep breath.

"Okay, tell me how this sounds." Kate nodded, and her daughter started to read out loud. *'My dearest, dearest Alfie'...*"I said dearest twice because one didn't seem like enough."

Kate nodded. "I understand completely."

Her daughter continued reading. *'I hope you are doing well in camp. I hope you like camp more than I like school. I hope Marco is not as grumpy as Enzo.'*

She looked up at her mother. "Do you think Enzo read that part?"

Kate was trying hard not to smile as she answered her daughter. "Enzo is a gentleman. He would never read a lady's private correspondence."

Sophia nodded, and continued to read. *'Do you think you can visit Bel Rosso again soon? I really liked it when you came here to visit. If you come in the spring again, maybe we can ride horses together. Or maybe I can visit you in Florence. Anyway, I miss you a lot. I hope we can see each other again soon. I know you are busy doing warrior stuff, but do you ever think about me? I think about you all the time. My daddy says I am too young to think about boys, but my brain doesn't listen. I might love you, maybe. But only if you love me back. If you don't then, never mind, pretend I didn't say that. Write back to me if you want to. Then I will know if you think about me. Love, Sophia.'*

She folded the paper over then looked up at her mother. "What do you think?"

Kate leaned back against the tree. "I think it's a beautiful letter, Sophia. And I'm sure Alfie will be happy to get a letter, but you know, Alfie is ten years older than you. For adults, that's not much difference, but for children, ten years is a lot. I'm sure Alfie is fond of you, but what if he's not in love? Are you prepared for that? Can you be good friends if he's not ready for love?"

Sophia looked disappointed but thought about what her mother said. "I guess so. I mean, I won't stop liking him, but Mommy, I really, really love him."

Kate smiled back at her. "Sophia, you're seven. Something tells me there will be many, many boys that you fall in love with before you mate. You're the daughter of a master, a king. You're a true princess of royal blood, and your father will be introducing you to the sons of masters, and possibly the sons of other royal families."

Sophia listened intently but shook her head no. "But Natalia said I'd mate a warrior, not a master, and I think it's Alfie."

The smile left Kate's face. "Natalia said that?"

Sophia nodded vigorously as Kate contemplated whether Natalia had seen Sophia's future. "Well, I guess we'll see."

41

It felt cold in the house, and Kate felt him stir beside her, as he woke from his death slumber. He eased out of the bed as she pulled the covers up over her shoulders, burrowing into the pillows.

He smiled as he watched her wrapping herself in the blankets. "Perhaps you need to have Gi call someone to check the heating system."

She eyed his back, as he walked nude across their bedroom, accompanied by the sound of the whir of the electronic blinds. He started opening drawers, looking for his clothing and she sat up on one elbow to watch him, wondering how many drawers he'd open today looking for his clothes.

Shaking her head, she finally directed him. "Top drawer, socks. Second drawer, tee shirts, folded, on the right. Leathers hanging in the armoire. Boots in the closet." She heard him chuckle.

She knew him like a book; he could never find a damn piece of clothing, no matter that she put his things in the same place every time. "I think I am finally getting used to the blasted cold here." Pulling open the top drawer, he spied the heavier socks, folded to perfection. "Socks!"

"Shade, do you have a minute to talk before camp?"

He pulled the long sleeve tee shirt over his head, sliding his arms into the sleeves, pushing his head through the neck opening as his dark curls tumbled around his face. "*Si*, make it fast, I have a lot to do tonight. What the hell did she do now?"

Kate laughed. "Now how did you know it was about Sophia? Actually, it's nothing bad. You know she has a crush on Alfie. Well, this week, she was writing a letter to him during class time. Enzo took the letter away from her and gave it to me. We read it together, and it's innocent enough. It's her first crush, and I'm sure not the last. I did try to prepare her for the fact that Alfie may not feel the same way she does. She seems to understand, I just thought you should know."

Pulling on his leathers, he was half listening, trying to dress. Why do women always want to talk when you are in one big ass hurry? "*Si*, a letter, no harm done. Alfie is a warrior. He may not even respond. Boy has duties in camp, did you tell her that?"

"She acknowledged his responsibilities in the letter actually, that he may be too busy. But there's one thing..."

Somehow, one thing always ended up being a thousand in this house. Looking up at her, he grabbed his boots and sat down to lace them up. "I have mock battles tonight, the first major ones we have had with this group, there are bound to be injuries. I need to get my ass down there. One thing, *mi amore*, just one, and I'm gone. Besides that," He threw up his hands, shaking his head. "She is still a child, with schoolgirl crushes, love letters...it means nothing."

Kate sat up on the side of the bed. "I reminded her that she's a princess, daughter of a master, and a king, and she'd be introduced to the sons of masters...she said...she'd talked to Natalia, and Natalia had told her she'd mate a warrior."

He stopped lacing his boots as his head snapped up. "What? Nattie told her that? Why in hell would she..." He left the sentence hanging and thought he needed to pay more attention to this conversation. "Come here." He patted his lap.

Kate slid from the bed and shivered slightly as she climbed in his lap. He wrapped his arms around her, keeping her warm.

He held her close to his chest. "You need to understand Nattie's gift. She can see the future, but not always details. She is very young still, and although she is brilliant, I do not think she has a full grasp on her gift yet." Kissing the top of her head, he sighed. "Does this bother you?"

"I'm not bothered, I just found it curious. Sophia is certain that Alfie is 'the one'. I told her she's only seven, and she'd have a million crushes before she was grown. I know, as a child, it's hard to envision yourself as an adult. But then, when she said Natalia told her she'd mate a warrior, it made me stop and think. I know you have a plan for her, and who she mates. Not in the same way your father did with you, but an expectation that she'll mate into another royal family, or at least the son of a master."

Standing, he lifted her up as she wrapped her legs around his waist. "*Si*, her choice of a mate is important to the coven. I will not tell her who to mate, like my father, but I will make sure she meets the right people. I do not know what Nattie may have seen, she may even have been influenced by Sophia's response to Alfie when he was here. But I am warrior, *si*? It is possible to mate a master *and* a warrior. I am not concerned."

Kate smiled, thinking Natalia had seen more, that her gift was telling them more, but that was years away, and no way to tell what the outcome would be. "I'm sure you're right. Alfie did look handsome in his suit though, enough to turn any young girl's head."

Kissing her softly, he grinned. "All Medici look handsome in a suit and in leathers. Once I start arranging to have young masters come to see her, trust me, she will forget about Alfie." He slapped her ass, growling. "Now let me get to work, woman. I am late as hell and I need the warriors with all their extremities."

42

It had been a grueling night, Marco was working them into a frenzy, and Alfie was tired and dirty. He was looking forward to a long hot shower and then some rest, but he had a few things to do before he slept. He'd been out hunting the previous night and he felt great. He was easily tackling anything Marco threw at him lately, since he'd taken Dona's blood. Walking back to the barracks, he heard a familiar voice and turned to see Lorenzo running in his direction, yelling for him to hold up. Alfie grinned, he hadn't been spending a lot of time with Lorenzo, and he missed his company.

"What's up, brother? You need some special training lessons?" Alfie laughed as they bumped fists.

Lorenzo grinned back at his friend. He'd chosen to remain with the grunts, based on his age, but it was clear to everyone he could easily surpass any of the juniors, and could hold his own against a few of the seniors. "Nah, just hadn't seen you in a while. You doing okay?"

"Sure am. How about yourself? You're kicking some ass out there, but I expected nothing less. What do you have planned for the rest of the night? Let me guess. Games? Feeder? Studies?"

"All of the above, and some sleep. You want to come with me back to Castello?" Lorenzo walked beside his friend, as he headed for the barracks housing the seniors.

As they walked, Alfie thought about the things he needed to do and decided they could definitely wait. "Sounds like a plan, brother. The showers at Castello are much better than here. And you can be in the shower for hours without losing hot water. Three minutes here in camp and your balls are blue from the cold water." Lorenzo followed him into the barracks. "Come on in, I need to grab some clean clothes and stuff them in a duffle."

Lorenzo plopped down on Alfie's bed, waiting for his friend to gather his things. As Alfie stuffed his clothes in the duffel bag, Lorenzo noted the corner of a folded paper sticking out from under the pillow. The rules for how a bed was made in the barracks were strict and didn't allow for any deviation. Lorenzo pulled the paper from under the pillow and unfolded it. He quickly scanned the note, recognizing his sister's handwriting. He took in the salutation, *'My dearest, dearest Alfie'*, and saw her signature, *'Love, Sophia'*.

"Dude! You're writing letters to my sister?"

Alfie's head snapped up. "*Cazzo*, Lorenzo, didn't you learn to not read other people's personal letters? No, I haven't written back to her yet, but I intend to. She's just a little girl with a crush. If I don't write back, that's rude. Besides, she's funny. And the things she does, like that chicken, just sweet. Don't tell anyone."

Lorenzo fell over on the bed laughing. "Oh man, I knew she had a crush on you! I could tell by the way she was following you around at Cory's wedding. Your secret is safe with me, bro." Lorenzo folded over in laughter. "Sophia and Alfie, oh man, would you have your hands full!"

Alfie tossed his smelly socks at Lorenzo. "Don't you tease me around the other warriors. I get enough grief hanging out with you. But if they knew I had one of the princess's hot on my heels for this amazing warrior body, all hell would break loose. All I need is for Master to find out."

Lorenzo sat up, handing his friend the letter. "I suggest you put this in a safe place, and brother, nothing happens at Bel Rosso my father doesn't know about. I think it's safe to say he's aware the letter was sent. Trust me, if he had a problem with it, you would've heard from him by now."

Alfie took the letter and locked it inside his footlocker. "It's just a crush anyway. Let's face it, I'm a warrior with not a lot to offer any female, and nothing to offer a princess. She'll be required to marry a master, or someone of royal blood. Do any of the warriors at Bel Rosso have females?"

Lorenzo thought a minute. "Most just go to the feeder compound. My dad only gives select warrior's permission to hunt. Marcello hunts a lot, but he doesn't have any one person. There's one warrior named Robert. He has a mate, and both of his kids, Robbie and Rebecca are in camp too. Of course, there's Luca and Shannon. In California, Raven is mated, but to a guy." Lorenzo shrugged. "I guess that's it."

Alfie shook his head. "Just wondering. I guess you start to think about that stuff once you transition and start hunting. I always knew having a mate was probably not in the cards if I became a warrior. You, on the other hand, will have a shit load of females to pick from." Alfie knocked him over on the bed and laughed.

Lorenzo chuckled lightly. "Yeah, but that's a burden too. I mean, warriors are usually single for a reason. My dad waited a long time before he mated. When I'd listen to warriors in the camp at Bel Rosso, most of them were happy to be single, and free to go wherever they wanted. They said a warrior's life didn't accommodate a mate. I don't know, brother. It's too far off for me to even think about."

Alfie didn't spend much time thinking about a mate, but he sure spent a lot of time thinking about the Alizzi. He loved his time with her. She was beautiful, and sexy, and her taste was something he couldn't find anywhere else. "Me too. We have a lot of adventures before we even think about females and settling down. Hell, you'll probably have six babies before I even find one female that will talk to me!"

Alfie tossed the duffle bag over his shoulder. "And in the meantime, I'll write to this red-haired princess. It isn't like I get a lot of letters anyhow. Come on, I need a shower. Are we going to the house or are you going to lie around here the rest of the night?"

43

Sofia watched the commotion in the laundry room, as both Theresa and Gi were trying to coax Natalia's new kitten, Lord Byron, out from behind the dryer. She shook her head in disgust. Poppy would never do anything that stupid. Turning on her heels, she headed outside, grabbing her coat that hung by the door. Poppy immediately responded to her presence and ran to follow her.

"Come on, Poppy. Let's go on an adventure."

Tucking her chin against the cold, Sophia headed through the garden, and cut across the vineyards to the road that led to the camp. The camp was off-limits unless accompanied by her parents. As she approached the high walls, covered in ivy, she stood before the massive gates. With her eye pressed to the narrow space between the two gates, she peered inside. The training field was empty during day hours, and most of the warriors were either asleep or in the feeder compound. She looked to the sky and saw the sun would be setting in about an hour, and then the camp would be filled with activity. It was now or never. Looking down at Poppy, she said, "I'm going in."

She pushed against the massive gates, but they didn't budge. She knew she'd have to teleport over, which meant she'd have to leave Poppy behind. "I'll be right back, Poppy. You stay here." As she lifted herself to teleport over, Aegis ran at her, nipping at the hem of her skirt as she cleared the wall, and Sophia laughed. "Too slow!"

The wolf paced outside the gate, as Poppy clucked nervously. Sophia walked across the empty training field, so quiet she could hear the wind in the nearby trees. As she approached one of the barracks, she pushed open the door to find a long narrow room, with bunks lined up on either side. Each bunk was filled with a hulking warrior, snoring loudly, caught in their death slumber. She tip-toed silently through the room. Her eyes were wide, her heart pounding, when she spotted something of interest. Leaning against the wall next to one of the beds was a guitar. She carefully slipped between the two beds as she kept an eye on the sleeping hulks and grasped the guitar. Looking around to make sure no one had seen her, she tip-toed back out of the barracks, carefully closing the door behind her. She let out a big breath, unaware, until now, that she'd been holding her breath the whole time. Holding the guitar up in the air, she ran as fast as she could for the main gates, and quickly teleported to the other side. She landed with a thud, and fell on her butt, as Aegis issued a soft growl of disapproval and Poppy started to cluck loudly.

"Shh. You'll wake up the whole joint!"

Jumping to her feet, she brushed the dirt off her skirt and started running back to the house, with Poppy on her heels. As she entered the back door off the kitchen entrance, she stood quietly and listened. She could still hear Theresa and Gi in the laundry room. With any luck, she could make it to her bedroom unseen. Rushing up the stairs, she moved quietly to her room, and slipped inside, closing the door behind her.

***

Shade stirred and stretched, as Kate burrowed deeper under the covers. He kissed her lightly as he said, "Shower." And left their bed.

Kate was thinking she'd sleep a little longer when she heard an unfamiliar sound. She sat up and listened, finding it hard to distinguish over the sound of the running water coming from the bathroom, she pulled on a robe and stepped into the hall, following the source of the sound to Sophia's bedroom, where the door was closed. Kate opened the door, to find Sophia sitting on the floor, strumming on a large guitar almost as big as she was. "Where did you get that?"

Sophia looked up startled. She hadn't heard her mother come in. "Uh...it's a present."

Kate looked at her with a confused expression. "A present? Who gave you a present?"

Sophia tried to strum the guitar, making a very distracting racket. "One of the warriors."

Kate didn't like the sound of this. "One of the warriors? Which one? And when?"

Sophia stopped strumming as she tried to come up with a story, but her mind felt muddled. "Uh, I don't remember."

Kate sat on her daughter's bed. "Sophia, someone gives you a guitar, and you don't remember who? Now tell me what's going on. Right now!"

Ignoring her mother, Sophia began strumming vigorously as she sang loudly, "Taking care of lizards. Every day..."

Kate removed the guitar from her hands. "First of all, it's 'taking care of business', not lizards, and secondly, I want to know, right now, where this came from."

Sophia shouted loudly, "Okay! I just borrowed it."

Still in the shower, Shade felt Kate's anger building. He sighed heavily. Could he have one night without a confrontation in this house? Quickly grabbing a towel, wrapping it around his waist, he could feel her temper rising. It had to be Sophia. Rushing down the hall, dripping wet, he heard the argument going on inside Sophia's room. Walking in, he saw the guitar and he knew, right away, who it belonged to. He stared at her and his eyes flare red.

"You had better start telling the truth, because right now, my hand is about ready to beat your little ass."

Sophia looked up as her father stormed in and tried a diversion tactic. "You're dripping on my floor!"

Balling up his fists, he was in no mood for her attitude, this was serious. Growling deep in his throat, gritting his teeth, he looked at *bel*. "You better keep a tight rein. I am very angry."

Kate lifted Sophia from the floor and stood her on her feet, so they were eye level. "Now listen to me. You'll tell us, right now, when and where you got the guitar. This is no joke, Sophia!"

The child sighed. "Okay! It's no big dealio. Jeez! I just went for a walk, and I *accidentally* ended up in camp. And while I was there, I thought I might as well explore. I borrowed this guitar. The warrior was sleeping. It's not like he was using it or anything. I was going to take it back."

Shade closed his eyes, trying to regulate his breathing. He was tired and pushed to his limits with her willfulness. "Why? Why would you do this? You know this is wrong! This is not Medici behavior."

Sophia shrugged. "It was just an adventure. You and Mommy were sleeping, and Nattie was sleeping. It was boring in here."

Shade roared and walked toward her, reaching out to grab her, but slammed his fist through the wall instead. Every word she spoke angered him more. "You lied to your *madre*, and to me. You stole it, Sophia. There is no other word for it. How dare you show such disrespect for me, your *madre* and my warriors who are sworn to protect you. You have pushed me to the edge! Never in my life..."

Sophia squatted down next to the bed, cowering from her father. She'd never seen him this angry. "I'm sorry, Daddy."

Kate stood from the bed. "Shade, get control." With her hand on his chest, she backed him out of the room. Looking back over her shoulder, she issued instructions to their daughter. "You stay put, missy! Do not leave this room. We will discuss this later and decide on your punishment."

Sophia looked back at her wide-eyed and nodded her head yes. Entering the hallway, Kate led him back to their bedroom. "Calm down please. She needs to be punished, and she needs to understand what she's done won't be tolerated. But I don't want her to behave out of fear, she needs to behave because she understands the right thing to do, and knows actions have consequences."

He leaned back against the wall. "Do you have any idea what she has done? She has broken every rule of Medici in one swift move. I cannot tolerate this. She never listens to either of us. She needs to be fucking scared of me!"

Kate laid her head against his chest, stroked his cheek, and calmed him. "Shh, like your father? That's not what you want. You don't want her to fear you. She's spoiled and gets away with far too much. But she's such a willful child. I think you must take her hand and walk with her back to camp. Make her give back the guitar and apologize to the warrior she took it from. She'll feel humbled and ashamed of her actions. Then we must decide what her punishment should be."

Images flashed through his head of his own *padre* dressing him down, bellowing loud enough to bring down Castello. He remembered his own fear, his own feelings of low self-worth when it happened. He remembered how his *madre* would come to him, sooth him, just like his *bel*. He wasn't his *padre* and never wanted to be like him. His temper left him immediately, and he hugged her tight.

"I am sorry, Kate. I am not my *padre*. I never want her to be afraid of me, but she needs to understand, she can't push me like this."

He was a warrior, and a king, but this one small female broke through all that and provoked him beyond his limits. "Let me dress and go to her."

44

Shade had calmed down considerably with Kate's help, and now he had a task at hand. He needed to talk to Sophia calmly, he'd scared her and that wasn't how he wanted to leave things. He made his way back to her bedroom, and taking a deep breath, tapped on the door lightly before opening it.

Sophia was sitting in the rocking chair by her window, waving her hand, and tapping on the glass. "It's okay, Poppy, I'll never leave you."

Stepping inside, he closed the door behind him. His anger under control, he still knew with Sophia, he couldn't be soft. "Sophia Medici, we need to talk. Stay in your rocking chair and look at me when I speak." He sat down on the floor in front of her and was amused she continued to rock.

"You have done something that is wrong on many levels. You are old enough to understand right from wrong. Your actions show disrespect for me, your *madre* and the warriors, and it will not be tolerated. You went somewhere you have known since a *bambina* you are never to go without supervision. You invaded the warriors' private space. They have very few personal items, and you stole from them." He stared at her for a moment or two, making sure she was listening to him. "You have disappointed me. This hurts me, and I am sorry I lost my temper with you. What do you have to say for yourself?"

She stared back at him, wide-eyed. She knew she was good at manipulating a situation in her favor, but she'd seen his anger earlier, and now his voice was stern. She considered tears, wondering if they'd make him go easier on her, and decided she might have pushed things too far already.

"I didn't think about the disrespect part because I think of words that are disrespectful. Like I told Enzo learning Italian was stupid, and he said I was being disrespectful with my words."

She kicked her feet against the bottom rung of the rocker and glanced out the window before looking back at him. "But I know I'm not supposed to go in the camp. And I know I'm not supposed to take stuff. But I really was going to put it back when I finished playing with it. I just get ideas in my head to do something, and I just do it. Mommy says I need to think before I act."

"Your *madre* is correct in saying that to you. If someone came in and took Poppy and you could not find her anywhere, how would it make you feel, Sophia?"

Her eyes grew larger. "Poppy! I would cry, Daddy."

"Well, you took something from a warrior that is like Poppy to you. He is far from home, Sophia. That guitar is how he copes with missing his home and family. It brings him comfort. It helps him to relax when he plays the songs of his home. It brings friendship to him when he is with the other warriors. You took something he loves."

Her bottom lip quivered as the tears flowed for real. "I didn't mean to hurt anyone. I'm sorry, Daddy."

His hand automatically moved to brush back her tears, but he pulled back. She must learn these lessons. "You hurt a lot of people with your actions. So, I suggest you make amends, *si*?"

"How do I make one?"

"I have not yet accepted your apology to me. We will see what you do next before I decide to accept it. But to that warrior, you must apologize with your heart. Not just empty words, Sophia, but you must truly feel sorry for your actions. We will take the guitar back to the warrior. You will return it with a heartfelt apology and explanation of why you did it." Reaching out, he took her hand.

She nodded her head, as she wiped her nose across the back of her hand. "I need a tissue."

Shade got her a tissue from her little vanity table, and wiped away the tears, and made her blow her nose. "Now get the guitar, and we will walk to camp, *si*."

She picked up the guitar that was propped in the corner and held her arm up in the air, so it wouldn't drag on the ground and took his hand.

As they walked to camp, he said nothing. He'd sent Marcello a message to gather all the warriors inside in the meeting room. It was important Sophia learned what it was like to face those she'd wronged and explain herself. He was determined to make this female understand what being a Medici meant. As they approached the gate, the outside lights were on, but not a soul was outside. Opening the gate, he led her inside, making sure the guitar wasn't damaged.

"Are you ready to make your apology?"

She nodded her head. "Is that the same thing as amens?"

Shade bit his lip, holding back a chuckle. "No, Sophia, making amends means you will make it right." He led her inside the doors of the main barracks, and it was eerily quiet.

"Where're we going, Daddy?"

"To the meeting room. The last time you were in there was at Natalie's presentation to the warriors. Come along."

She was still holding her arm high, so the guitar didn't drag on the ground. "Okay, but my arm is getting tired."

"That arm didn't get tired when you stole it and carried it all the way back to the house."

The doors were closed, and he gave her no warning when he flung them open to a room filled with his warriors. All the warriors stood as they entered, his leaders lined against the back wall.

"Proceed to the front and the small dais, Sophia. Just carry the guitar up the aisle between the two rows of warriors."

"Are they going to kill me?"

Shade heard the nearest warrior cough, trying to hide his chuckle. "No. They will die to save you, but your actions, this day, have surely made them doubt if you are worth such a sacrifice."

He led her down the aisle but made her carry the guitar. As they approached the dais, he took the guitar from her and helped her up. "Please sit in the chair until I am finished. I suggest you do not open your mouth until I ask you to speak, *si*?"

She climbed into the chair and faced him, making a motion that pantomimed zipping her lip as she nodded her head yes.

Aislynn and Olivia stood side by side at the back of the room with all the camp leaders. Aislynn leaned in and whispered, "Terror."

Olivia put her hand over her mouth to stifle her giggle. "I think if she wasn't born a princess, she'd make one hell of a warrior."

Marcello grunted and gave them both a stern look as Shade finally had Sophia settled in her chair. Shade stepped forward, facing his warriors. "There has been an incident today where a warrior's personal property was stolen. I know it has caused a lot of turmoil inside this camp. I will not apologize to you, because I did not do it. But the culprit of this deed sits before you."

He stepped aside and raised his hand to Sophia. "Princess Sophia Medici has broken the rules. She was disrespectful. She did not follow the simple rules of any Medici, honor, respect, and courage. Her punishment will be determined by the queen and me. Invading a warrior's personal space is not something I approve of, especially by my own blood. I can tell you I am disappointed in her actions, as well as her attitude. I do believe Princess Sophia has something to say. Would you agree to hear the princess?"

The group nodded and Shade went to Sophia, taking her hand, and helping her from the seat. He marched her to the front of the dais. Leaving her standing alone, he returned to take a seat. "I do believe you have something to say. Proceed."

Sophia had been shifting nervously in her chair as her father spoke to the warriors. They'd look at her father, and then shift their eyes to her. There was nowhere to hide from their scrutiny. She had no idea which of them owned the guitar.

"Uhm, I was thinking it was a good idea to go to the camp, cause Theresa and Gi were getting Lord Byron out from behind the dryer, and Daddy was still in his death slumber, and Mommy was sleeping too."

She looked at their faces and saw some confusion. "Oh, and Lord Byron is a kitty, not a person. We didn't have a person stuck behind the dryer."

She looked at her shoes and scuffed one toe of her patent leather shoes over the other before remembering her mother had told her not to do that. "So, I came to the camp and everyone was asleep, and Aegis tried to stop me, but I teleported over the gate before she could get me. I'm not supposed to come to camp without supervision, and I've been told a million times, but I was on an adventure, so I told myself it was okay, since it was an adventure. But Daddy said it wasn't okay. And then I went in the barracks and you were all sleeping, I tip-toed so I wouldn't wake you and then I saw the guitar. No one was using it, so I took it and went back home, but Daddy asked me how I would feel if someone took Poppy and I said I would cry, so now I understand it hurts the person if you take things that don't belong to you. So, now I'm really, really sorry I took it, and not just because Daddy yelled at me, but because I wouldn't want to make anyone sad. Amen."

Standing, he went to her side and reached down to take her hand. She grasped it tightly. "Do the warriors accept this humble apology?"

Many of them were trying like hell not to laugh, but they'd been warned to keep it stern. He was damn sure they'd had a good laugh before they arrived. The warriors responded with a loud "yes", as they all stood and dropped to one knee. "*Per sempre* Medici."

They rose and Shade cleared his throat. "I do believe, princess, the warriors will save your life if necessary. Piers, would you please come forward. The rest of you are dismissed. Get your asses to work, I will join you shortly."

Piers was a young warrior. He'd been in camp for two years and he was French. Shade knew the minute he saw the guitar it belonged to Piers. He entertained the warriors often with his playing and singing. As the room emptied, he picked up Sophia in his arms. "Princess Sophia, please meet the warrior who owns the guitar you stole. This is Piers. I believe you have something to say to him."

Sophia felt ashamed that she'd taken his guitar. "I'm really sorry I took your guitar. Daddy explained it was not mine to take, or even borrow, and the guitar probably helped you not be homesick. If you feel homesick, you can come play with me and Poppy any time."

Piers nodded to the small, curly-haired child. He knew she was a handful and had heard many stories of her antics from the warriors. "I accept your apology, Princess. I'm honored to serve you and your family as a Medici warrior. My family is far from here, in France. I miss them and I sing and play the guitar to help me. Remember, Princess, to mind your parents, for they have a great deal to teach you. I am still learning from my parents."

Sophia looked confused. "Your parents still tell you stuff when you're old?"

Piers smiled. "Oh, yes. You will be learning from them all your life. We have chickens in France, too. I had many chickens when growing up. And I understand a young girl wanting to go on an adventure. I accept your apology."

She smiled up at him. "You do? I think I got Poppy in trouble too. She's been clucking outside my window all night."

"You have a curious nature, Princess Sophia, and it can sometimes get you into trouble. "

"Mommy says I have a problem with listening. And Enzo, my tutor, he says 'Lady Sophia, you're not listening.' I say, 'Yes I am', but I was really thinking about something else."

Piers laughed at the child. "I have a request if you will oblige me?"

She shrugged her shoulders. "I don't know what oblige means."

"It simply means, will you accept what I ask of you. And I would ask if I may have a hug from a Medici princess before I go to learn my lessons at camp?"

She spread her arms wide as the warrior gave her a hug. "I hope Marcello doesn't fuss at you as much as Enzo does at me."

Hugging her softly, he smiled. "If I listen and do as Marcello asks, I find he does not fuss so very much. Thank you for giving me my guitar back. This was my father's guitar, and the one I learned to play on, so it is something I love very much."

He retrieved his guitar and left the meeting room. Shade kissed his daughter on the cheek. "I am proud of what you did this night. Do you still love me?"

"I always love you, Daddy. I can't help myself. It just flows right out."

Shade threw back his head and laughed. "*Si*, the same thing happens to me. Let us go back to the house. I do believe Mommy and I have some punishment to give to you. And I will make sure Mommy knows you did a very good deed in returning the guitar to Piers."

"More punishment? Daadeeeee!"

"Oh, my beautiful princess, this was just making apologies. The punishment is yet to come."

He teleported them back into the house as she huffed in disgruntlement. He knew it would be hard to change her. But there were some things he could always count on, and one of them was her willfulness and her spirit.

Lorenzo's Rising

Part Two

2-1

Lorenzo walked back to Castello after another grueling night in camp. He and Alfie had the whole weekend off, and they were planning to go into the city. He'd lived at Castello now longer than he'd lived at Bel Rosso, and it felt like home. Their basic skills training was behind them, and he and Alfie were frequently assigned to different outposts to enhance their leadership skills. He was twenty-five now, and Alfie was thirty-one. The age difference that seemed so dramatic to them as boys now seemed insignificant. Lorenzo was as tall as his father, but slenderer. He wore his hair long and had lost all the curls of his youth. Hunting was no longer a challenge for either of them. It was more a matter of selecting. In addition to inheriting his father's good looks, he'd also inherited his charm, and women, mortal or immortal, tended to seek him out. It had become a source of constant ribbing among his fellow warriors, and he took it in stride. He was almost back to the castle when he heard Alfie running up behind him.

"Brother, wait up!"

Lorenzo stopped and turned, waiting for his best friend. "What's the rush? We have the entire weekend off. So, what's the plan?"

Alfie slapped him on the back. Lorenzo was now taller than him, but Alfie could hold his own against him. Lorenzo was solid muscle, but still looked slim for his age. "We're legends in town, according to all the warriors. We might as well live up to it."

Lorenzo chuckled. "Didn't have a plan, brother. Just thought we'd enjoy the time off and see what we could get into. Maybe we can get a hotel room in Florence. I don't like bringing mortals back to Castello. Dad said that was too risky. Even if you wipe their memory, they remember some aspects of the night, and where they were, and they come back for more. Best to keep them on their own turf."

Alfie laughed. "Yeah, well, he's the expert." They trudged back to Castello, ready to shake off the night's work and think about their time off. "Florence is good, but I think we've hit pretty much everything there."

Lorenzo laughed. "There may be a few I've missed, and we always have fresh targets with tourists. Why? You want to go somewhere else? Somewhere on the coast, maybe? Naples?"

Alfie stopped walking and shook his head. "Damn, brother, your parents own huge estates all over the world. I have a taste for...Greek!"

Lorenzo shrugged. "Dad has a small cottage in Santorini, near the vineyards. We can sleep there. Sure, Greece is fine."

Alfie looked at him with question. "What's eating you, Lorenzo? Is there a female in Florence you really want to revisit?"

"I'm good, brother, getting away is probably good. Dona has been calling me a lot. She's been good to me, you know? She was there for me when I was a kid and I missed my mom, but she needs to cut the apron strings now."

Alfie remembered all the nights he'd spent with her. All the things she'd taught him, the sex, and the feeding. He'd learned a great deal from the Alizzi, and he used those skills every time he hunted. Females adored him, but he was no Lorenzo, hell that was just in his blood. He'd pulled away from the Alizzi over the years. He enjoyed the hunt and the fun of being out in the world and finding females closer to his own age. But Dona had sunk her claws into Lorenzo, and whenever she was at Castello, Alfie tried to steer clear. He'd never told a soul about his affair with the Alizzi, and he'd die with that secret.

"Then Santorini it is. Beaches, bikinis, and alcohol. And since we don't live there, we can take them back to the cottage. But I understand what your father's saying. Remember that female? What was her name? She drove around Castello for weeks looking for you." Alfie laughed and nudged Lorenzo. "That's a story you can tell your sons."

Lorenzo shook his head. "I can tell my sons, as long as my mother isn't within hearing distance. She's not amused by my exploits with women. I think it reminds her too much of Dad when he was young and unattached. Come on, let me pack some stuff, and Carlos will let the staff in Santorini know we're coming."

As they walked into Castello, Carlos was waiting for them as Lorenzo gave him instruction. Alfie immediately made his way to the office Shade now shared with Lorenzo, as he learned the business of running the coven. Marco and Shade were still in charge of everything, including the camp, but Alfie knew Lorenzo would be expected to over-see it all at some point.

Alfie headed for the stocked bar and poured a glass of Red Moon. It was their preferred drink now. He flopped down in the large side chair and pulled the letter he'd received yesterday from his pocket and read it again. It was from Sophia. He hadn't seen her in a good six months, but they'd remained in contact all these years. She was the most gorgeous female he'd laid eyes on. She was twenty-one now, of mating age. It made him sad to think of that. He had no chance in hell of ever mating her. He was just a warrior, of common blood, and nothing more. The Medici expectations for her mating a royal blooded master with wealth and lands were made clear.

Lorenzo followed him into the room to found him sprawled out in the chair and chuckled. "Make yourself at home, brother."

He poured his own glass of Red Moon before sitting in the large chair behind the desk...his father's chair. Propping his booted feet up on the desk, he saw Alfie reading the letter. "You got it bad for my sister, and don't tell me you're just being polite to answer her letters after all these years. You know my father is already setting up dates for her with the sons of other masters. He said he won't arrange her mating but let her choose, but he expects her to choose a master. Makes no difference to me, brother. And just between the two of us, Sophia would be a handful anyway. She's not exactly the obedient type, if you get my meaning." He looked hard at Alfie. "Seriously, brother, what are you going to do?"

Alfie folded the letter and stuffed it inside his boot. Shrugging, he looked up at Lorenzo. "Not much I can do. It's wrong of me to want to be with her, I know it's pointless." Standing up, he poured another Red Moon. "Fuck, Lorenzo, she's so damn beautiful. I know she's a handful, but I love her spirit. And when she writes to me, or when she's here at Castello on visits, it's so easy to talk to her. Believe me, I know the day will come when she falls hard for some master, who can give her the life she's become accustomed to, and she'll forget she ever knew me. Should I just stop writing her?"

Lorenzo downed his drink and jumped up to take the bag Carlos had brought him. "Nah, as long as she's writing to you, and you know the score, keep writing. I think if you stop, it will hurt her feelings. Just be realistic about it, that's all. Come on, let's go to Greece and you can drown your sorrows in wine, women, and blood."

He slapped his friend on the back as they teleported out.

2-2

In Santorini, the night air was warm still, even with the breeze off the ocean. The young people strolled through the narrow streets, stopping at the local bars. Alfie found the women here very open, friendly, and extremely sexy. Their skin looked bronze, and their delicate sundresses and soft sandals left a lot of skin exposed to admire. He sat at a table outside a café, downing his Midnight, with two very beautiful women on either side of him. The drink had been easily flowing all evening, and it was clear he wouldn't be required to make a choice between the two women, he could have them both.

He looked over at Lorenzo, surrounded by women, who touched his hair, or ran their hands over his shoulder, tugging at his hand to join them to dance on the street, as the music wafted from inside the café. Alfie had never been to Greece before, but he knew Lorenzo had been here many times. Alfie downed the last of the contents of his glass as he thought to himself, *life is good.*

Lorenzo was surrounded by women, and all four of them were beautiful. Why choose when he could have them all? He cast a glance at Alfie, who had a girl on either side of him. "Why don't we take this party back to our villa? We have plenty of wine there, and we'll be more comfortable."

The women exchanged glances, giggling as they stroked his arms and chest. Lorenzo winked at Alfie, as he started to walk down the shell covered path back to the vineyard. "It's not far." He looked over his shoulder at Alfie. "You gonna sit there all night?"

Alfie grinned. "The more the merrier I always say, brother."

With the women in tow, Alfie trudged happily back to the villa, following Lorenzo. What could be more fun than six eager females and two very hungry, hot warriors? The girls laughed and talked incessantly, as they clung to the two men, open to whatever the night brought. They entered the house and the girls squealed, as they all ran for the outside pool, stripping off their clothes and diving into the cooling water. Lorenzo gave Alfie a look, and they both stripped bare as they headed for the pool and the large outside lounge that overlooked the ocean.

The two young warriors traded off the women, slowly working their way through the six females, who willingly went to each of them. Before the night was over, they'd fed and fucked them all. Before sunrise, Alfie and Lorenzo wiped their memories clean, and left the girls sleeping in the lounge chairs around the pools. Lorenzo was thinking now it had probably not been a good idea to bring them back to the villa.

"Come on, brother. Let's get out of here before they wake up. If we're not here, they'll just wander back to the village."

Alfie stretched and yawned. He'd like nothing more than to climb into bed and sleep, but knew it was best to let the women leave first, or they'd never get rid of them. Patting Lorenzo on the back, he draped his arm over his shoulder as they headed back into town, not sure what they'd find at this hour. Lorenzo stopped suddenly in front of a shop and Alfie turned to see what had caught his eye. He shook his head.

"No way, brother, you can't be serious?"

Lorenzo nudged him. "Come on, let's go in."

They were standing in front of a tattoo shop that was apparently open twenty-four hours a day. Lorenzo wandered into the darkened establishment, where a sleepy-eyed woman looked up at him with interest.

"Can I help you?"

Lorenzo gave her a sly smile. "Maybe."

She came from behind the counter and looked him over. He stood over six feet, with the dark complexion of the people of Greece, but his accent was wrong. "Where you from?"

Lorenzo looked her over from head to toe. She was no beauty queen, but on a slow night, he might give her a go. "Italy," he answered. He walked around the room, looking at the displays on the wall. He wasn't interested in the traditional rose or dagger through the heart tattoo, but the tribal designs appealed to him. He took in the image of a man with a sleeve that extended onto his pectoral muscles. "How much for this one?"

The woman stood close behind him. "For you, I think we could work out a deal."

Alfie wandered around the shop, flipping through a few books that displayed designs and overheard the conversation. Walking over, he looked over Lorenzo's shoulder at the design he was considering and laughed. "When you do it, you go big. You really can't be serious? Marco will kick your ass."

Lorenzo picked out the design he wanted. "Come on, Alfie. Don't you want a tat?"

The girl led him to a table where he pulled the shirt over his head and stretched out. She wiped his skin down with alcohol before asking if he was sure this was what he wanted. She ran her hand over his firm, hard chest as he placed his free hand under his head and crossed his feet at the ankles.

"Just don't fuck it up."

She smiled at him seductively. "I promise you a masterpiece."

Alfie took a seat, watching the female go to work when another female emerged from the back of the shop, shielded by a curtain. She sidled up beside him.

"You got a real nice body too, come on, don't you want to have a tattoo like your handsome friend here?"

Alfie looked her over. "How do I know you even know how to do this? Show me your work." He heard Lorenzo laugh.

"Sure, come here." Walking behind the counter littered with thousands of designs, she pulled out a photo album. "Here is my work." She flipped through the pictures of her patrons wearing the completed images of her art.

Alfie admired her talent and looked for some type of tribal design that appealed to him. She stroked his arm. "I can customize it for you. Come on, you know you want to."

Alfie shrugged. "Okay, let's do this."

Lorenzo closed his eyes as the girl worked her magic, creating a template to place over his arm, shoulder, and pec muscle on his right side. She spoke softly too him. "Take a look before I start. Make sure this is how you want it."

Lorenzo opened his eyes and nodded. "Looks good, go for it."

The woman turned on the pneumatic needle gun and began to apply the ink. "You know, this is a large area. A lot of people get this done in stages because it can be painful."

Lorenzo answered her with his eyes closed, as he slipped into a light sleep. "I'm good."

He could hear Alfie in conversation with the other female, and knew he was getting his own tattoo. He called out to him. "I don't want to see any puppies or rosebuds, warrior. Don't you embarrass my ass."

Alfie tried not to laugh as the artist was working on his back. The tattoo would go across his shoulder muscles. "And if I see your naked ass walking around with the word "Mom" spread across it, I'll make sure every damn person at Castello knows, brother." He bit his tongue trying not to laugh. "Hell, the first person I'm telling is your sister."

Lorenzo chuckled. "Sophia would be right here beside us, if she thought she could get away with it. I'm afraid my dad has her on too tight a leash for that to ever happen."

Lorenzo lay quietly as the woman finished her work, the hours passing by. Alfie had finished and joined him, pulling up a chair. Lorenzo asked to see his tat, and Alfie turned to show him his back. Lorenzo smiled. "Looks good, brother."

When the woman finally finished the tribal sleeve design, she dabbed away at the fresh ink, and placed an ointment on the raw skin. "You'll need to be careful. It will take a few days to heal."

Lorenzo smiled back at her. "I heal quickly, don't worry about me."

She gave him a wink. "Anything else you want?"

Lorenzo understood her meaning, but he'd already had more than his fill of blood last night. "Maybe another night?"

She smiled back. "Any time."

He looked around the room at the walls plastered with images of tats and piercings. Pointing to a picture of a nipple ring, he said, "How about that, on the left side?"

She shook her head. "You are a glutton for punishment, aren't you? Are you sure?"

He smiled. "Why not? I'm here."

She shook her head as she grabbed the piercing gun and ran her hand over his nipple until it was erect. "Just warning you. It hurts like hell."

He smiled back at her. “Pleasure and pain, right?"

She continued to rub her hand over his nipple. “Now you sound like my kind of guy."

He gave her a wink and said, "Another night."

She swabbed his skin with alcohol, then placed the gun over his nipple and pulled the trigger, piercing the flesh and inserting the ring, and he didn't flinch. "I'm going to hold you to that."

Alfie shook his head. "The next time you go home, all hell is going to rain down on your ass. You're on your own, brother!" As the woman finished the piercing, she turned toward Alfie who knocked over his chair, he stood so fast. "No way, sister. You keep that thing aimed at him."

She giggled as the female who'd done his tat played with his hair. She whispered in his ear. "So, where are you off to after this?" Alfie turned and smiled at her. "It's been a long night. Home, bed, sleep. If I can get wild man out of here before he gets a ring through his cock. Are you done now?"

Lorenzo sat up from the bench. "A ring through my cock. Now that's an idea."

The woman ran her hand over his thigh, covered in his tight jeans. "I'd be happy to oblige."

Lorenzo slid off the bench and gave her a quick kiss. "I'll think about it. If I decide to go for it, I'll save it just for you."

They both paid their bill and left the establishment as the sun was up, and the early morning people were filling the cafés for coffee. Lorenzo looked at his friend. "Think it's safe to go home yet? Better teleport over and see if the girls have left the pool."

"I hope like hell they have, my ass is ready for bed, brother."

They took off, teleporting to the villa and checked out the scene. The girls were gone, and they landed outside by the pool, as one of the staff was picking up stray clothing and empty glasses and bottles.

Alfie nudged his friend. "Lorenzo, I need to ask you something."

Lorenzo stretched his arms over his head and yawned, ready to climb into bed after a night of carousing. "Ask away, brother."

Alfie walked over to the pool and lifted up a bra floating on the surface of the water. Holding it up, he inspected it and looked at Lorenzo. "Do you ever come home and wish you had the same female here waiting on you?"

Lorenzo laughed as he headed for his bed. "I have a smorgasbord, why would I want to put myself on a diet. Someday, brother, but not today. Don't tell me you want to become domesticated?"

Alfie followed him into the house, away from the heat of the sun. Lorenzo was his best friend, they did everything together, but he sometimes found the flood of different females unfulfilling. He wanted nothing more than to be a warrior, but there was a part of him that wanted to find that one special female he could bond himself to for all eternity.

With a false bravado he answered. "Hell no. I was just wondering if you'd ever get tired of this." Swinging the bra around his finger, he clamped his other arm over his brother's shoulder. "Always an adventure, brother. Let's get some shuteye and call it a night."

2-3

Checking in with Marcello, Shade confirmed that Alfie's accommodations in the warrior's barracks were ready for his arrival. Shade had spoken at length with Marco, and it was time Alfie gained some training and experience in leading a larger brigade in his path to becoming Second-in-Command. It was inevitable Alfie would assume this role for Lorenzo when the time came. Coming to the States to train with his warriors, and spending time working at the Dead House would be great exposure to a more urban area. Florence, and the surrounding area of Tuscany, though filled with tourists, was a bucolic setting, almost stuck in time. The atmosphere in D.C. would give him a totally different experience in urban guerilla warfare.

Both Lorenzo and Alfie had completed their time in camp, and were now canvasing the globe, honing their skills at living among the mortals. It was also the time a young vampire sowed his wild oats, getting it out of their system before they settled into the more disciplined life of a warrior. As Shade laughed to himself, he knew exactly the shit they were getting into, hell, he'd done it all himself. He was happy his son had this time in his life, and a friend who was like a brother to him to share this experience, but it did make him feel old.

Although Alfie's move would be a more extended one, Lorenzo would be coming along for a short visit home. Shade was aware that Kate was already at work to get Lorenzo's old room ready for his homecoming. She was anxious to have their son home again, even if it was only for a brief time. Sophia and Nattie were also eager to see their brother. It was rare that Lorenzo had the time to come back to Bel Rosso these days.

Pushing away the papers on his desk, he downed the Midnight from his glass and decided to find his mate and see if she was still scurrying around, preparing for their son's visit.

***

Kate and Theresa had packed up all of Lorenzo's old things, the clothes and toys of his youth, and moved them to the attic.

Although both of her daughters still lived here, she'd never really gotten over the fact her son had spent more years away from her than with her. He was a man now, and she felt like there was so much of his life she didn't share. His visits were rare, and there was so much time between stays, she felt like she had to get to know him all over again.

"This looks good, Theresa. It at least looks like a boy's room, if not a man's room. I don't even know what he likes."

She felt Shade before she saw him and looked up to see him as he stood in the open doorway. "What do you think? This looks nothing like his rooms at Castello."

He looked around the room and then smiled at her. "*Mi amore*, Lorenzo is a grown man now. He takes no notice of such things. It looks perfectly fine. It is just a place for him to rest. He will be busy as hell while here, but I will speak with him. I wish for him to have some intimate time with both of us, to share his life. It is a rare occasion for him to come home these days."

Shade looked down at his feet and chuckled. "But it will be nice to have another damn male inside this house of beautiful and willful females."

Getting off the floor, surrounded by the boxes, she went to him, sliding her arms around his waist. "And when have I ever known you to grow tired of beautiful females?"

He smiled down at her through his curls. "There is no answer to that question that will not land me in hot water." Kissing her softly on the lips, he raised his head and winked at Theresa. "But I must admit, I am running out of options in trying to find a mate for Sophia. Our daughter is a rare beauty, and there are plenty who are interested in her, but she turns her nose up at all of them. She is as obstinate now as when she was a child. What the hell am I going to do, *bel*?"

"She's young. Don't be in such a hurry to get rid of my children. Look how long you waited before we found each other. Besides, she'll know him when she finds him. You can't arrange love. You should know that by now. Look at us, and Luca and Shannon, even Cory and Madison. Our girls will find their mates, and I promise you, it will be on their own terms, no matter how much you try to arrange things."

"It is my job, *mi amore*. I am still master of this coven. And although I found love in the most extraordinary place, with the most extraordinary woman, I need to make sure our girls are taken care of properly. The demands on them will be different than what is expected from Lorenzo, but they still have obligations to the coven. They need to have mates with position and power, in their own right. I don't want to go to my damn death slumber every morning worrying about their safety. Speaking of which, where are they? Too damn quiet."

"Natalia's with Shannon. Shannon has an idea about expanding our business into olives. There's a lot of property that hasn't been developed in Tuscany and in Santorini. The soil isn't right for vineyards, but Shannon thinks it will support olive groves. The last time we were there, checking on the limoncello production, she noticed a lot of olive trees were thriving in that soil. Natalia is helping her with some research. And Sophia said she and Madison were going riding. They both like to ride at night to avoid the heat. She knows we're expecting Lorenzo tonight, so she won't be gone long."

"All my girls out and about except for you." He picked up several boxes. "And where do you want these, my lady?"

"I've been storing the children's things on the third floor, in Cory's old rooms. Not sure what I'm saving them for."

She followed him up the stairs, as he carried the boxes to the now empty suite where Cory had once lived. Kate looked around the empty rooms. Cory and Madison had taken some of the furniture to their new home after they married, and Kate had sold what they didn't want. She walked through the now empty space. "It's hard to believe it's been more than twenty years since he moved here with us. That our own babies are grown."

She leaned against the window, looking out over the estate, the outline of the mountains clear against the night sky. She turned and looked back at him. "Is it what you expected? What you wanted? I remember when I had the vision of our babies, and knew we'd have three. Three seemed like plenty to me, but now that they're young adults, and we're still...young. Lorenzo is twenty-five. I was twenty-seven when I first met you. How is that possible? I've been turned for less than thirty years, but for you, what does this feel like? I try to imagine your life sometimes, living through centuries, and I still can't fathom it. I look in the mirror and see the same girl that stumbled over her words when she saw you the first time. It's gone by so fast."

Sitting the boxes down, he thought about her words. Thirty years was nothing to him, a blink of an eye, and he'd been looking at the same face in the mirror for centuries. He forgot, sometimes, that she was ever mortal, that there were things about their life that still caught her off-guard. Walking to her, he slid his hands around that tiny waist and laid his head on her shoulder. "*Si*, it has gone by fast. In an immortal life, a childhood is but a flash in time. But we will see them grow, and find their mates, and have their own children. With any luck, we will see their children's children, and the generations that follow. Protecting the Medici name, and the coven, ensuring the future of our species, it is what we all fight for, yes? You have raised them well. We gave them everything, prepared them for life, and protected them. Do you regret we only had three? Did you wish to have more?"

She leaned her head back against his chest, his body unchanged by the years, as she chuckled. "I'm not sure we could survive another Sophia. But no, I know there are no more children for us. And the three were a handful at the time. It's just...there was a time when we were constantly adjusting this house to accommodate more people. First, we added the staff, and Luca, then Cory and our own children, then Shannon and Madison. Now it feels like the opposite. Lorenzo went to train in Florence and will most likely live there his whole life. Enzo is gone. Cory and Madison have their own place. Someday, our girls will find their own mates, and they'll leave. This house has seen a lot, yes?"

Laughing, he kissed her cheek. "I am surprised the house survived. But above all, *mi amore*, it has seen so much love. And that is what matters. We can't look back, *bel*, we must keep looking forward to what is yet to come. To be honest..." He spun her softly in his arms and let his hand wander through her silky mane. "Well, to be honest, I am looking forward to being alone once again. I know that is selfish, but I admit there were times I grew tired of sharing you. It is time we returned to lily-white and her savage lover again." Just as he leaned down to kiss her lips, he heard the ruckus in the foyer, and felt their son's arrival. The Prince had come home. "See what I mean?"

She laughed softly at the interruption, something they'd both grown used to. "Some things never change. Come, let's go see our son. He grows so much I hardly recognize him."

She took his hand as they descended the stairs to the first floor. She could hear Luca's voice, as he laughed and talked with Lorenzo, and quickly recognized Alfie's voice as well. They entered the living room together, to see Luca and the two young men standing close. Alfie turned and gave her a broad smile, and Kate went to him, giving him a hug. "Welcome back to Bel Rosso. I hope you're not worrying about coming here to live. I know it will be a big change for you."

Alfie returned her hug. "I'm looking forward to it. All the warriors at Castello are jealous."

Kate turned to hug her son and stopped in her tracks. He was wearing a loose-fitting tank top over his jeans, and his hair was even longer than when she'd last seen him. It hung well past his shoulders. But what she noticed first was the tattoo that covered his arm from wrist to shoulder and disappeared inside the tank top. As he turned to face her, he ran his hand through his hair, in a mannerism that looked exactly like Shade, and exposed the pierced ear. He wore multiple leather strips around his wrist and a chain at his neck. She stared dumbfounded as she took him in, noticing the outline of the nipple ring beneath the fabric of his shirt.

"Lorenzo..."

He looked at her and saw the blank look on her face. He'd debated about whether to wear a shirt with long sleeves to cover the tattoo, but figured it was better to just get it over with. "Hey, Mom." He took her into a big bear hug, ignoring the expression on her face. As he stepped back from her, he watched her eyes as they scanned his body.

"Lorenzo, what were you thinking?" She turned to Shade. "Did you know about this?"

Alfie gave his friend a look that said, 'you're on your own here, brother.'

Shade looked at their son and could feel the shock roll through Kate. He was never into tattoos himself, but he knew they held great appeal to the younger warriors. Luca wandered over to him and whispered, "This should be interesting." Shade elbowed him in the side. He was sure there was a story attached to the tattoos, and pretty sure Kate didn't need to hear the details. He looked at Alfie, who had no visible signs of body art or piercings.

"I had no idea, *bel*. But our son is a grown man. He is old enough to make his own decisions, and mistakes." Walking to Lorenzo, he hugged him, pounding his back. "So, your journey went well? Is that a nipple ring?"

Lorenzo slapped his dad on the back. "Yeah. It was an impulse. Alfie wanted to go to Greece for a long weekend, so we stayed at the villa there. Found this place in town that did tattoos...and piercings. No big deal. Besides, the females like it. Went back later and got the earring. I was thinking about a nose ring, or maybe a lip ring."

Shade crossed his arms over his chest and cocked his head to the side. "Really? Well, I doubt your *madre* likes it much. Tell me the house in Greece is still standing."

Lorenzo laughed. "The house is fine. It survived you, I'm sure it will survive me. And if you want to get matching tats..."

Kate screamed out, "No! Don't even think of it." She looked at Alfie. "So, you were along for this little adventure? How did you manage to use your common sense and remain tattoo free while my son did this?"

Alfie cleared his throat as all eyes looked at him. "Well, uh, I didn't. I got a tattoo. It's just not as visible. It's across my upper back and shoulders. No holes in me, though. I did try to stop him. But I've learned he's like his father. Once Lorenzo sets his mind to something, there's no talking him out of it."

Shade threw back his head and laughed. "Well said, Alfie. Let's have a drink, *si*. Midnight all around."

Lorenzo spoke up. "Can we have Red Moon instead?"

Kate was shaking her head, deciding it best not to probe for any more details of the long weekend that ended up with tattoos and body piercings.

Shade stopped and turned his head, staring at his son. "Red Moon, is it? Yes, you have definitely turned into a true Medici. This stuff is meant for celebratory occasions. But I will grant you, your homecoming is a celebration."

Shade looked at Alfie. He nodded and responded, "Red Moon for me as well."

Luca shook his head chuckling. "I'll stick with Midnight."

Shade walked to the bar and poured out glasses of the liquid that had brought them much fortune. Passing out the drinks, he raised his glass, and they all followed. "*Per sempre* Medici. Welcome home, son."

He took a sip and watched as both Lorenzo and Alfie downed the drinks like shots. Oh hell, these two definitely needed to be separated. Memories of his escapades with Marco when they were that age streamed through his head. "So, tell me, Alfie, are you ready for this new adventure?"

Alfie and Lorenzo took a seat, stretching out on the sofas. "*Si*, master. I'm looking forward to learning to take command. I've been to several posts in Tuscany, and I enjoyed my time there. But I have to admit, based on what I've seen of D.C., it will be a challenge, and I'm more than prepared for it."

Shade nodded. "That is what I want to hear. Your rooms are prepared over at the barracks. You will have a private room upstairs, with the leaders. Aislynn is in charge of the feeder compound. She will set up a schedule for you. The feeders are not allowed to leave the compound, and other than the female warriors, I allow no females in the camp. The leaders are also free to hunt. But remember, this is different than Europe, so are the females. Best to have Marcello show you the ropes before you hunt alone."

Alfie exchanged a glance with Lorenzo, as he chuckled. "Yeah, I've been told."

Alfie wondered if he should ask for a refill when Madison and Sophia entered the room. It was clear they'd been riding, as they were both wearing the tight-fitting riding pants and knee-high boots. He couldn't help but notice Sophia's curves. She was much taller than Kate, but she had her mother's pale skin, and he could see a lot of similarities in her face. She had the piercing blue eyes that both she and Lorenzo had inherited from their father, but her hair was long and wind-blown, like her mothers, and the same impossible red. Her hair had lost the wild curls she had as a child. She'd continued to write to him, telling him the details of how her father continued to arrange dates for her with the sons of masters who ruled both here and in Europe. She never failed to mention what a disappointment she found them to be. Her letters had evolved over the years, and the schoolgirl crush, where she'd always expressed love for him, changed into a friendship. He'd become the person she could confess things to, the person she could share things with when she didn't want others to know her true feelings. Looking at her now, he began to fidget, wishing he had more alcohol in his glass.

Sophia headed straight for Lorenzo. "Oh my god! You get away with everything. Take off your shirt so I can see the whole thing."

Lorenzo pulled the flimsy tank top over his head, exposing the full extent of the tattoo. Sophia shook her head. "That's awesome!"

Kate responded to her immediately, "Don't get any ideas, Sophia."

Sophia giggled as she tweaked the nipple ring. "Oh brother, you really went for it. Dad would kill me. Seriously...kill me."

Shade chuckled. "*Si*, I would."

She laughed, as she turned away from Lorenzo to greet Alfie, and plopped down on the sofa next to him. "So, warrior, I understand you're moving in. Guess I can just hand deliver my letters now."

Alfie was stunned when he looked into her eyes, and her smile made his heart pound in his chest. "No females on the premises, your father just said so. So, unless you have special privileges, I do believe you will have to have a male deliver your letters."

Sophia's laugh could be heard all over the house. "Alfie, don't you know by now, the rules don't apply to me. The harder Dad pulls on the reins, the more I resist. If I want to deliver a letter, trust me, I'll find a way."

Madison snickered, deciding not to add fuel to the fire, but knowing it was true. Sophia would find the loophole in every rule.

Shade walked over with the decanter of Red Moon and leaned down to fill Alfie's glass. He stared hard into his daughter's eyes. "Do not push me, princess. Alfie has come to learn and work, not to be bothered with your misbehavior. And you wonder why no eligible master will have you. Pay her no mind, Alfie."

Alfie looked at Sophia and smiled. "I pity the master who has to tame you."

Sophia shot back, "And what makes you think I can be tamed?"

They all laughed, knowing whoever took on Sophia would have a handful, as Natalia and Shannon walked in. Natalia went immediately to her father and gave him a hug. Shannon sat on the floor at Luca's feet, leaning her head against his knee, and his hand gently stroking her hair.

Natalia turned her attention to her brother. She scrunched up her brow as she took in the tattoo, and the pierced nipple. "So, how much Red Moon did you drink, brother?"

Lorenzo laughed. "Not enough, apparently."

Natalia nodded to Alfie, as she squeezed in on the other side of her brother. She laid her head on his shoulder. "It's good to have you home."

Lorenzo kissed the top of her head. "Good to be home. Can't stay for long, though."

Kate slid into Shade's lap, as she looked at their grown children, and wondered where the time had gone.

Shade nodded to Natalia. "Your *madre* tells me you were with Shannon checking out olive groves. Come up with anything interesting in your research?"

Natalia nodded, getting serious. "It's very profitable. Most of the olive oil from Italy comes out of the Tuscan region, so the soil and climate are ideal. You have land that isn't cultivated, so why not make it turn a profit? Luciano said the soil wasn't right for the grapes, but it would work for olive groves. There are a lot of trees growing there already, but they aren't cultivated. I couldn't find anything in our research that would suggest this would be a bad move financially."

Shannon leaned forward. "We already have brand awareness in the mortal world with the wine and the limoncello, as well as all the bath and beauty products from the sunflowers and lavender. We have an established reputation for producing high-quality goods. In addition to adding olive oil for food consumption, we can add olive oil into our bath and beauty products as well. I'd really like your accountants to run some numbers for us, look at what we'd have to invest, and do some revenue projections. What do you think?"

Shade looked at this circle of brilliant women who had managed to increase his coven's wealth hand over fist. "I like the concept, Shannon. It is useless to have land that cannot be turned into profit. I mean, look at what the two of you have done with Bel Rosso. I like the idea the olive oil can be used for many purposes. Any production that is not food grade can be used for bath products. I will have my accountants look this over and get together with you once I get back their findings."

Shade scanned their faces. This was his family, together at last. It was a rare occasion to have them all together. Just as his thoughts were going there, Cory walked in the front door.

Cory shouted out, "I was wondering where you were, Maddie. Hey, Lorenzo!"

Lorenzo stood, pulling the shirt back over his head as he hugged his half-brother. "Brother! The warriors at Castello send their regards, along with a bunch of new orders for you. I'll bring them to you later."

Cory shook his head. "They definitely keep me busy. I should go and visit sometime, but it's hard to get away. When you come to my shop, I'll show you some of the new designs I'm working on. Nice art, by the way."

Cory stood behind the chair where Madison was seated and kissed the top of her head. Shade snuggled *bel* closer to him. "You are awfully quiet, my queen. All of your *bambinos* sit before you. Is there anything we have to discuss as a family while we have them all here?"

She curled into his chest, watching as their children planned for the future, and smiled. They were all happy, and healthy, each pursuing their own paths. Their wealth would give them every advantage in life, and despite their independent spirits, they were all smart, and generally showed good judgment. She knew that, together, she and Shade had built a strong foundation for them to move forward.

"Nothing, lover. It's just good to have them all at home."

2-4

Alfie woke up in his new room and took a few seconds to get his bearings. He'd unpacked his gear, and gotten settled in, finding that Bel Rosso warriors had a more luxurious barracks than anything he'd ever seen at Castello. He'd been assigned upstairs, to a private room with the other leaders, Marcello, Skelk and Aislynn. It was comfortable, and roomy. Aislynn had taken him to the feeder compound and introduced him to Velia and set up a schedule for him to feed. Everything looked great, but still, he felt a bit lost. It had been a few days, and he was more homesick than he cared to admit, and he missed Lorenzo. He sat up in his bed, his head in his hands. Lorenzo had returned to Castello after his short visit with the family, and for the first day in fifteen years, the prince wouldn't be a part of his life.

Standing up, he shook his head. "Get your shit together, warrior, you're a grown ass vampire." Taking a shower, getting himself prepared for the long night of camp, he knew he'd shake off this funk eventually. The one trade-off to living here was the closer proximity to Sophia. But he also knew he had to watch his step. She was off limits, and he doubted he'd get to see her often. Maybe that was a good thing.

Walking downstairs, his sword strapped to his back, he took to the field. Seeking out Marcello, he was ready for the night to begin. Marcello was already barking out orders as he approached.

"So, what are we into tonight, Marcello?"

Marcello looked up to see the young warrior approach. He'd settled in quickly and seemed well accepted by the crew here. Marcello liked his easygoing attitude. He'd been afraid that, having grown up with Lorenzo, Alfie might feel entitled, but he showed nothing of the sort.

“Hey, brother. I'm going to have Aislynn take you out tonight. I want her to show you the surrounding areas, including Charlottesville. That's the hunting grounds for the warriors allowed to hunt. Then, tomorrow night, I'll have Skelk start taking you into D.C. You won't have a specific assignment in the Dead House yet, it will take you a while to learn the layout, and Skelk is the most knowledgeable. I don't want you leading any of the recruits until you're familiar with the territory. You good with that?"

Alfie nodded. "That'll be fine. Aislynn seems to know her business. We didn't have any females at Castello, so it will be different for me working with the females. I'm fine with it, though, nice change up."

Marcello slapped him on the back. "Master has a different attitude about the female warriors than Marco. He keeps pushing Marco to add females to the ranks, but I think it's a lost cause. Since you haven't worked with them before, the only advice I can give is to not treat them any differently. If you try to help them, or imply they aren't capable of doing the job on their own, you'll find yourself on your ass, brother. They're trained to the same standards as the males. Master doesn't give them any slack, nor do they want it."

Marcello flagged Aislynn down, and Alfie looked up to see the tall, shapely female, clad in black leather and the long black braid that extended down her back. Aislynn approached, and extended her hand for a fist bump, which Alfie returned. She nodded her head. "You ready, warrior?"

"As ready as I'll ever be. Just take the lead."

As Aislynn and Marcello talked for a few moments, Alfie turned to check out the activities on the field. Several of the young females were staring at him, their heads together as they talked about him. He'd been given the rules, no mingling with the female warriors and vice versa. The female warriors held no attraction for him, but he was interested to see how they held their own in a battle.

As Marcello walked off, Aislynn tossed her arm nonchalantly over his shoulder. "Here's the plan. I'm going to take you into C'ville. There's a large university there, and it's the primary hunting ground. Target rich environment. You read the handbook, so you know the rules. When you hunt, you take no one by force. Use your powers of seduction and let them come to you. Be sure you never drain them, and always wipe their memories. No rough stuff. We haven't had any problems with the town's people, and master wants to keep it that way. Understood?"

Alfie grinned. "Completely. Same rules at Castello. So, you're hunting too? I apologize, I'm just curious. We don't have female warriors in Florence. Do I call you sister or brother?"

Aislynn threw her head back and laughed. He'd been hoping she'd see the humor in his question. He didn't want to get off on the wrong foot. She looked like she could kick his ass.

"Sister, please. I don't think anyone would ever confuse me as a brother. Oh, by the way. I've got something for you." She slipped her hand into a pocket in her leather jacket and pulled out a sealed envelope. She gave him a sly grin as she held the envelope under her nose and inhaled.

"Someone asked me to deliver a letter. Better not let Daddy find out." She handed him the letter with his name on the envelope in a handwriting he immediately recognized.

Alfie took the envelope and quickly jammed it into his boot. "Oh, uh, yeah, thanks." *Damn Sophia, she has more balls than half the warriors in this camp!* He didn't want to wait all night before he could read the letter. "Hey, give me a few minutes. I don't think this sword strapped to my back is a good idea if we are going into C'ville. So, let me re-adjust my weaponry before we go."

She grinned and nodded, and he took off for his room in the barracks. Getting inside, he quickly took off the sword, throwing it on the bed, and retrieved the note inside his boot. Holding it up to his nose, he closed his eyes and could see her face before him. Opening it quickly, he began to read and found his heart was pounding. He hoped this wasn't a goodbye letter.

In her flowing hand, she'd written.

> *Dear Alfie, I thought maybe I was over you, but after seeing you in person after all these years, it's clear I'm not. Aislynn has agreed to be our go-between, so feel free to give her any letters you have for me. It's difficult for me to get inside the camp unseen, but you'll have plenty of opportunities to leave. Aislynn said she'd have you back tonight by 4:00 a.m. at the latest, so we'll have some time before sunrise. Meet me in the hay barn behind the stables. Yours always, Sophia.*

Alfie grinned. You had to love a woman like Sophia. She just kept on coming, no matter the risk. But Alfie knew he could be setting himself up for heart break. Master would never allow this. Sophia was a princess, and she'd be expected to mate a master. He had nothing to offer her, but he knew he could love her like no one else. Re-reading the letter again, he hid it in the writing desk in his room. He quickly gathered a small knife that could slide into the pocket of his jeans. It might be a good idea to feed tonight if he was going to meet Sophia. It would help if his hunger was gone. He just needed to be careful as hell with her. He returned to the field, meeting up with Aislynn.

Aislynn teleported with him into town and gave him a tour. He was amazed at the number of young people roaming the campus. The school was teeming with beautiful females. The pace in Italy was relaxed, but here, everyone seemed in a hurry. They checked out the downtown pedestrian mall, and Aislynn pointed out Madison's shop. After showing him the general layout of the small town, she asked if he was okay. He assured her he was, and she patted his back before taking off back to Bel Rosso.

"Good hunting, brother."

He had no problem roaming the campus and attracting a beautiful female. She invited him back to her dorm, where he fed, had sex with her, and wiped her memory before teleporting back to Bel Rosso. Landing inside the camp, Marcello asked him how it went. Alfie shared a few details, then faked a yawn and said he was headed back to his room, but he had no plans for going to bed. He stripped off his clothes, and stepped into the shower, removing the scent of the mortal. Quickly drying off, he pulled on clean clothes and teleported straight to the hay barn.

***

Sophia left the house with no problem, calling out to her mother that she was going riding for a while. Her mom was busy with Auntie Shannon, and her dad had gone into D.C. She hurried to the hay barn, skirting the stables to avoid Angelo. Aegis followed on her trail. As she got to the barn, she turned, and shooed the wolf away.

"Will you please not hound me? I'm fine."

The wolf backed off but stayed close by. Sophia slipped inside the dark barn to wait for him, hoping he'd gotten her letter. She paced as she checked the time on the cell phone. It was already five minutes after four and she was wondering if maybe he wouldn't come, when he teleported into the space.

"Alfie! You came!"

"Of course, I did, Sophia. Seriously, you took a big risk to get this letter to me, then to meet me. I assumed it must be important?"

She looked at him, her hand on her hip. "Important? You're expecting some big announcement? Alfie, I really like you. What don't you get? My father keeps pairing me up with a bunch of masters' sons and keeps waiting for the sparks to fly."

She flopped down on a hay bale and patted the bale beside her, indicating she wanted him to sit. "He says he won't force me to mate anyone I'm not attracted to that he won't tie me to a contract like his father tried to do, but this feels a lot the same. He's started trying to pair Natalia up as well, but she really has no interest, and told him so. I know it's frustrating for him. He only wants what's best for the coven, and he thinks if we can find a mate who's powerful, in their own right, it will strengthen the coven. I mean, I get it. Really, I do. But look at him! He mated a mortal! I just wish he would back off and let me find my own path."

As she beckoned, he sat beside her, but kept his hands to himself. "Sophia, we've known each other since we were children, and you know I have feelings for you. But your father makes a good point. He's worried for the future of the coven. I know you have a responsibility to do what's right. Your name alone is a heavy burden. I've seen it with Lorenzo."

She stood up quickly, pacing back and forth in front of him. "I mean, look at Lorenzo. He goes out on his own. He doesn't live at home. He's free to find his own mate. He has the same expectations on his shoulders. He knows Dad wants him to marry the daughter of a master, and if she's also royalty, then he hits the mother lode! How come Lorenzo has the freedom to find his own way in the world, while Natalia and I must live at home and wait for our father to find us a suitable partner? I complain to Mom, and she just says we're young yet, not to fret over it. I feel like I'm in a prison, Alfie."

Reaching out, he took her hand and softly squeezed it. "Sophia, relax. You know males dominate our culture, and the customs and old ways still exist. Be thankful you weren't matched up when you were five or something. You could have been stuck with some old goat of a master." Releasing her hand, he stood. "But I have to admit, selfishly, I'm glad you haven't found anyone to your liking, because I know when you do, the letters will stop."

He looked down into her face, so beautiful and willful. He'd always loved her spirit. "Someday, one of them will sweep you off your feet, and you'll never look back. You'll find yourself living the life you want. He'll come when you least expect it."

She sighed heavily. "Yeah, I guess." Reaching out, she took his hand. "Natalia says she sees a change, where our culture will evolve, so it's not so patriarchal. I asked her when, but she said she couldn't see the details. I mean, Dad can be progressive in some things. He has the female warriors here, and I know Marco rarely let's a female into camp, despite how hard my dad pushes him. I don't understand how my dad can be open minded about the female warriors, and so close minded about his own daughters. I want to see the world, Alfie!"

He smiled at her. "I've seen some of that world, and I wish I could take you on that journey myself. It would be fun to watch you discover things for the first time. But I think we're very lucky if we're on the cusp of change for our world, Sophia. I can't change it much, but you can. You're a Princess of Medici. You and Lorenzo and Natalia can make great changes for our entire race. It's exciting to think about, *si?* What would you change if you could? The first thing."

"The first thing? That's easy. I wouldn't be held prisoner in my own house. Dad still makes us use our wet feeders. We haven't been trained to hunt. Can I go out with you some night, Alfie?"

"Whoa, you want me to get killed? No, I can't take you out to hunt. Master would lop off my head." Sighing heavily, he hugged her close, and heard the soft growl coming from Aegis. Turning his head, he saw the wolf pacing outside. Sunrise was close, as he noted the lightening sky on the horizon.

"It's time for me to get back to the camp. Someday, someone will love you for who you are. So, don't worry so much about it."

She turned to leave but looked over her shoulder. "What about you, Alfie? Do you love me for who I am? Or am I just the sister to your future master?"

He saw the look on her face, and he still held back his true feelings from her. Walking to her, he laid his hands on her shoulders and kissed her cheek softly. "I love you, Sophia, and your adventurous spirit. You aren't just a sister to my best friend. You're *my* friend."

Her heart dropped a little. She couldn't remember a time when she didn't love him, but she knew he was off limits. "Yeah, you're a good friend, Alfie." She stepped outside and Aegis fell quickly into step with her, as she walked back to the house.

Alfie watched her walk away. She knew, as well as he did, that he was just a warrior. But he also knew no one would love her as much as he did. He longed to share adventures with her and show her the world. He stood and watched until she made it back to the house safely. His need to protect her was like nothing he'd ever felt before, and it scared him. She'd always be out of reach, but how the hell would he ever let her go? No mate would allow such a friendship with a male such as himself. Teleporting back to his bunk, he stripped and lay down on the bed. He slipped into a troubled slumber, filled with visions of red hair, blue eyes, and a smile that warmed him to his core.

2-5

Natalia tossed the book aside, sighing loudly. She'd brought home all the books from Castello that dealt with the Medici history, both mortal and immortal, but still couldn't find some of the pieces to the puzzle in her family tree. It was so frustrating, because she knew every detail was locked in the vaults of the Council. Sliding off her bed, she went in search of her father. It was almost sunrise, and they'd both be pulled to their death slumber soon. She loved she wasn't a day-walker, and she was like her father in his need to escape the sun. It was becoming rare to see young vamps that were susceptible to the killing rays of the sun. Most had evolved now to be able to walk freely among the mortals. She found him as he entered the house from the back patio, stomping the mud from his boots.

"Dad, do you have a minute?"

Shade looked up to find Natalia waiting for him. "I have all the time in the world for you, Nattie. You look frustrated, what in hell did Sophia do now? Come on, let's go into the living room, I need a drink and you can talk to me alone."

Throwing his arm around her shoulder, they walked to the living room and poured drinks. Taking a seat, he beckoned her to sit beside him. "Now, come tell your *padre* what is wrong."

Natalia sat down next to him. "This isn't about Sophia. Dad, remember when I was a girl and you took me to Council? I wanted to see the books that recorded all the births and deaths of the Medici, but Malachi thought I was too young. That made no sense then and makes even less sense now. You both said when I was older, I'd be given access to the Council's records. I've read everything that's at Castello. I've researched every resource, but there are huge gaps in the data. I want to go back to Council."

Shade took a long drink, avoiding eye contact with her. He'd known this day would come. He took a deep breath and released it. "Nattie, why is this so important to you? I know you have a curiosity and desire to learn. There is nothing wrong with that, but there are so many other things for you to pursue. You are a Princess of Medici. You have an amazing gift, an ability to see into the future! You are still learning to channel that gift and interpret what you see. You have a brilliant mind; beyond anything I could ever have imagined. And yet, you are like your sister in that you seem to have no interest in mating. You have rejected all the young males I have arranged for you to meet. Perhaps it is time you put down the books, look around you, and see there is life outside the printed page."

Natalia rolled her eyes. "Oh please. Don't start. You keep pushing Sophia to find a mate with a master's son, and I've already seen her fate. She loves Alfie, she'll always love Alfie. But don't worry yourself. Alfie is an honorable warrior, and he won't take liberties." She sighed. "You know it's the twenty-first-century, right? I have a brain. I can figure things out for myself, and I don't need a male to control and direct my life. This culture is so antiquated. You keep saying the Medici keep their females on a pedestal, well, I have news for you. We don't want to be on a pedestal. We're perfectly fine taking care of ourselves. If I find a mate who'll let me stand as his equal, then maybe I'll be interested, but it's not my priority."

Shaking his head, his daughters continued to both amaze and frustrate him. "Well, first of all, Alfie is a warrior, nothing more. And Sophia knows what I expect of her, what the coven expects of her, but enough of that." Shade shifted his weight on the sofa. *Damn, I thought that thing between those two was long over, and now I've moved the warrior back into her life.*

"As for you, you seem to forget something. You are not able to defend yourself. You have little to no skills at defense. Having a mate helps secure your safety. And I am sure there are masters out there that will let you stand as an equal. It may take time to find him, but he is out there, waiting on your beautiful mind to snare him. I know my thoughts on this are old school, princess, but my time on this earth has been long. Loving someone and having someone in your life who loves you back, is vital. I just want you to be happy, whatever you do. I don't understand it. Neither of my girls want to mate and give me grandchildren." Shrugging, he slid his hand through his hair. "I am trying to grasp your line of thinking,

Nattie, I truly am, but I cannot see you in the future without a mate."

"Relax, Dad, you'll have grandchildren. I can see them for Lorenzo and for Sophia, so you get your wish. Malachi said I'd never be able to see my own fate, but I could sometimes figure things out by what I saw happening to those around me. But, once again, you've managed to steer the conversation away from what I want to talk about. Why is seeing our family's ancestry such a big deal? I want to establish our family tree, and the Council has everything!"

Clearly, she wasn't going to give up on this. He fiddled with his glass. He knew what she'd find, and he still wasn't sure she was ready. "Why is that so important to you? It is ancient history. Why can't you focus on the future, and what lies ahead, instead of what happened in the past?" He was somber and quiet, his eyes looking straight ahead, but seeing nothing.

She flopped back on the sofa. "Oh my god, you are so melodramatic! I want to study and learn. There's no end to learning, Dad. I'm not a warrior. And I can't be happy with Mom's life. I can't be happy fixing up homes and taking care of kids, and I have no interest in the businesses that Mom and Shannon run. I don't know what's ahead for me. Perhaps Malachi knows, but I'm willing to let things unfold and see what lies ahead. Why are you blocking me from seeing this information? I don't understand. It's a family tree. Do we have some relative you don't want me to know about? Some illegitimate child who laid claim to a crown? Jeez!"

Her words hurt him as she rejected the lifestyle he had with *bel*. "Stop, Nattie." He felt the pain in his heart. It was time to let her go to Council, meet with Malachi, and learn what he'd kept from them all. She was an adult now, and she didn't need his permission to go, and blocking her would only cause dissention.

"I will arrange for us to go to Council. I will speak with Malachi." He stood up and walked from the room, never looking back at her. "Your *madre's* life was one she spent loving and raising you. My life was one of loving and protecting you. Never forget where you came from, and how you got where you are." He walked out of the room and headed to his *bel*.

"Dad, wait!" she called out to him, but he didn't turn around. He thought she didn't appreciate her life, but she did. She knew that, for them, no sacrifice was too great for their children. But she'd grown up in this patriarchal culture, where the females, unless they were warriors, were led by the males. Her mother was strong and had more freedom than most females in their culture, but Natalia had still watched her mother defer to her father's decisions or use her feminine wiles to sway him. How many times had she heard her mother say, "You lead, and I'll follow?" She knew her father respected his mate, but he also expected a level of compliance and subjugation. It was subtle, but she saw it, and it wasn't the life she wanted for herself. She'd rather stand alone than stand in someone's shadow.

***

Shade heard her call out to him, but he kept a steady pace up the stairs, his heart and mind in a tangle. Walking into their bedroom, Kate was already in bed. He headed straight for the showers, never speaking a word. He stood beneath the hot water for a long time, thinking, trying to clear his mind, but his mood wasn't changing. He felt so conflicted about taking her to Council, to the books that would reveal all. Stepping out of the shower, he dried off and walked naked to the bed. Climbing in beside Kate, he lay quietly, waiting for the slumber to take him.

Kate turned toward him, placing her head on his shoulder and draping her arm across his chest. She was silent but she could feel his turmoil. "Lover, what's bothering you?"

He was lost in his thoughts, but began to speak, giving them voice. "My children have become strangers to me. I don't seem to fit into their lives anymore. I can no longer fix all the wrongs. I have to let them go. Even my little Nattie has grown beyond my reach. I question my whole purpose in their life. They see me as old, and not understanding of their time. How did I not see things have changed? My daughters want to follow a path in a world so different than the one I know. I have to open their cages and let them fly, and it's breaking me inside." He sighed heavily. "I have become the old king, with old thoughts and methods." He laughed, but not from joy. "My *padre* would give me hell right now. He would think me foolish."

Kate stroked his chest. "Our daughters have been raised in a bubble, even more so than Lorenzo. At least Lorenzo left home and was forced to grow up quickly. He's out in the world, learning to live among mortals, and learning how to manage the coven. But our girls...they rarely leave Bel Rosso without us. They see the young mortals their age, who are living on their own. They talk to Madison about her life before Cory, when she left her parents and went to the university and lived in her own apartment. They're both young women, they're sexually mature, and yet they still have their wet feeders, and you've refused to teach them to hunt. Even the female warriors who come to camp every spring have more experience of this world. They're not strangers to you. They're just no longer children. We have to let them go at some point. They have to find their own way in this world. Assign them a protector if need be but loosen your grip on them. You'll find if you don't hold them so tightly, they'll come to you willingly."

"No, I am their protector until they mate. And you think I should teach them to hunt? Allow them to go out in a world that would kill them, if it knew what they were? Should I teach them weaponry as well?"

He sat up abruptly, as her arm slid off his chest. He held his head in his hands. "They are females and letting them find their own way is not acceptable to me. I will not lose them to mortals, Kate. Never! They have no idea of the danger, even among our own. The Medici name alone puts a target on their backs. Lorenzo comes home with tattoos and piercings, Sophia refuses to even accept she must find someone her equal in status, and Nattie, she wants to disappear behind her books and wants nothing to do with a mate. She doesn't want our life. She wants no *bambinos* and has no business interest. What in hell am I to do?"

Kate watched him fight against the inevitable. "Why are your daughters different? Lorenzo hunts. The female warriors hunt. You haven't allowed them to train, to learn even the most basic skills in weaponry. You're leaving them more vulnerable, not making them stronger. They're only safe when they're here at Bel Rosso because you haven't taught them to live in the world of mortals. I've taught Sophia how to channel her skills with animalism, and that's something at least. Let them train. Let them learn to hunt. Let them grow up, Shade."

He turned and stared at her. Suddenly, something clicked inside his head. He'd held them down. He'd made them vulnerable. He took her face in his hands. "Where have I been, *mi amore*? What have I done? I need to teach them how to survive without me. But I don't want them hard, like warriors. They are not warriors."

"Lover, I'm a master with a crossbow, my skills taught by Luca, and honed by Skelk. I can kill if I need to. Do you find my heart hard?"

He smiled at her. "Never. They are right, I have been a fool. I love them so much. I have been afraid to let them go. To let them live. How could I have been so stupid and wrong? I am going to fix this. I am going to make them Medici females, with strength and power and heart. How is it you always know the right path for me?"

She pulled him down beside her. "Lay down. Sleep. You can save your daughters tomorrow."

2-6

Shade was up long before the electronic blinds opened. His death slumber had been restless, and his mind refused to release him into the slumber he needed. This only happened when something had him in turmoil, and the previous night's revelation from his youngest daughter was definite turmoil. His talk with Kate had given him a dose of reality. He needed to better equip them with the skills they'd need to move about the mortal world. They were grown women, and he still viewed them as small girls.

Kate was still sleeping when he slid from the bed, and pulled on a pair of jeans, quietly leaving their bedroom. She'd know he was gone, she always did, but she never followed him. She knew he needed to work this out on his own. He'd worked out a plan in his head, now he needed to go to the one person who could help bring it to fruition, Luca. He rapped lightly on the door of the suite Luca shared with Shannon, and hoped he wasn't interrupting them.

Luca heard the light tapping and lifted his head from the pillow. He and Shannon both patterned their sleep around Shade and Kate. Shannon still slept soundly, curled up next to him. He kissed her cheek, and gently slid his arm from under her. Slipping out of bed, he grabbed a pair of jeans and pulled them on, as he headed for the door. Opening the door, he saw Shade. Looking over his shoulder at Shannon still sleeping, he closed the door behind him, so as not to disturb her.

"Master? What's up?"

Shade led them into his office where they could speak in private. He closed the office door behind them, knowing it was a sign that no one was to disturb them, a rule even Sophia now obeyed.

"I'm sorry to interrupt your time with Shannon, but there are things that have come to my attention that disturb me. I have a plan, but I need your help. Sit down and relax. You want a drink?"

Luca ran both hands through his hair, wiping the sleep from his eyes as he tried to clear his head. "Uh....not right now. What's the plan?"

Shade sat in his huge leather chair, now worn in spots. "It has all happened so quickly, Lorenzo coming home with tats and piercings, Sophia fighting me on choosing an appropriate mate. But I think it truly hit me when Nattie told me she doesn't want to mate, and to have *bambinos*. She has no interest in taking over any of the businesses. She wants to dedicate her life to learning. I realize I must let them go, live their own lives. The girls, especially, want their freedom in a world they know little about, and I have not taught them to protect themselves in that world. Kate pointed out there should be little difference in how I prepared Lorenzo for the mortal world, and how I prepare my daughters. They need to learn to hunt and feed. They need to learn to use weapons. You taught Kate; can you help me with our girls?"

Luca stifled his chuckle. "I was wondering when you'd let them go. You still have them with their wet feeders. I can train them on the basics, like I did for Kate. Let them figure out for themselves which weapon they want to master. But I think the best approach for teaching them to hunt is to pair them up with the female warriors. Aislynn is strong willed. She can handle Sophia. Rebecca is softer spoken. She'd be a good match for Natalia. In the meantime, wean them off the wet feeders, and send them to the feeder compound. I have to say, I don't have any experience at teaching a female to hunt. Shannon and Kate were both shielded from it."

Shade listened and contemplated all he'd said. It made sense to him. "I don't have any experience teaching females to hunt either. I've been with many females on hunts, but I didn't have to teach them. Aislynn and Rebecca will be good, I can easily arrange for that. But the damn feeder compound? I don't know, Luca, too damn many warriors in there."

Luca shook his head. Some things would never change. "I know Kate doesn't want the feeders to come to the house, but we could probably arrange a schedule for them to come to the staff quarters, and let Natalia and Sophia go to them there. I doubt Kate would want the girls in the compound when the warriors are there either. This seems like a good compromise. If you want, I can talk to Velia about having new feeders brought over, who are reserved for the princesses. They'd be off limits to the warriors. And for the record, I've taught Shannon the basics as well. She just prefers a handgun, but I put her through the same drill I created for Kate years ago. You know they're so protected it's not likely they'll need it, so it is just a precaution."

Shade turned his chair, so he was looking out the large window. He rarely let his thoughts travel back to the events of that night. "We left her alone in this house. Cuerpo almost killed her, and would have, if she did not have the skills you taught her, Luca. If we were attacked today, she and Shannon are the only females in this house with a skill to take down a warrior and never look back. My girls are immortal, but they have never killed a thing, or had anything challenge their life. I can't pretend anymore. It is not enough."

Shade spun the chair around, facing Luca once again. "Then let's do that. Arrange with Velia to bring in two new feeders to the compound just for them, and they will go to the staff quarters when my girls need to feed. Talk to Aislynn and Rebecca for me. Ask them to teach the girls to hunt. I will talk to my daughters and let them know what I plan. I will leave it up to you to meet with them and set up a schedule of training. Agreed?"

Luca nodded. "Just let me know when you've talked to them, and I'll get started."

Shade stood and walked to Luca. Embracing him, he wondered what he would have done without Luca. "*Grazie*. I could not survive without everything you do for me. I never take it for granted."

As Luca left, Shade stood at the window looking out. It was time he talked to his daughters. It was time to give them wings.

2-7

It was dusk, and Shade could hear the noises coming from the camp, as the warriors took to the field for the night. He knew the house would soon begin to wake. As the children had grown, the house wasn't as noisy as it had once been. There were far less people here now. He telepathically asked Kate to gather the girls and bring them to the office at once. He wanted to speak with all three of them together. He was about to lay before them a small window of freedom and could only hope this was the remedy that would satisfy them both.

Kate was sleeping lightly when she heard him in her head. Lifting her head from the pillow, she focused on his message. Rolling out of their bed, she dressed and walked barefoot to Natalia's room. Kate woke her gently. "Natalia, your father wishes for us to join him in the study. Get up and get dressed, please."

Natalia brushed her thick mane of dark brown hair from her face, pushing back the covers, dropping her feet to the floor. With a big yawn she asked, "What's this about?"

Kate stroked her cheek. "Not sure, my darling, but your father was quite upset after the two of you spoke."

Natalia looked back at her mother. "Yeah, well, that makes two of us."

Kate looked at her a moment before responding. "It's hard for him to let go. Everything he does for you; he does out of love."

She sighed. "I know, Mom. I get it. Really, I do. But it's still frustrating."

Kate turned to leave. "Get dressed and join us downstairs. I'm going to get Sophia."

Kate walked to Sophia's room to find her already dressed. As a day-walker, she kept her own schedule. "Your father wants us to join him in the study."

Sophia had hoped to sneak out and find Alfie before things got busy in the camp. "Now?"

Kate gave her a stern look. "Now, Sophia. Why, do you have other plans?"

Sophia sighed. "Well, not anymore!"

Kate headed down the stairs with the girls following in her footsteps and led them into the study. The two girls took a seat on the large leather sofa. Natalia sat demurely, her feet crossed at the ankles, and Sophia collapsed in the corner, her leg thrown over the arm of the sofa. Kate flashed her a look of disapproval and Sophia dropped both feet to the floor. Shade was standing, facing the window, and waited until he heard they were settled before turning.

As he faced them, his face was stern. He walked to Kate and kissed her on the lips. "Thank you for doing this. It shouldn't take long."

Shade propped himself against the edge of the desk and crossed his arms over his chest. "I have made some decisions in regard to a few things both of you have talked to me about." His eyes went from Natalia to Sophia.

"The first thing is your inability to hunt and feed. I have arranged with Luca to set up some lessons for each of you. Sophia, you will be going with Aislynn, and Nattie, you will be going with Rebecca. You both will be weaned from your wet feeders and, in conjunction with hunting, you will both be assigned to new feeders from the feeder compound in the camp. Velia will have two feeders brought in from Florence, especially for you, only for you. Your schedule will be set up, so they will be available to you in the staff quarters. You will not go to the compound. Any questions?"

The two sisters looked at each other, unable to hide the look of surprise on their faces. They looked at their mother who shrugged her shoulders, indicating she was hearing this for the first time as well. Sophia looked at her father. "Wow! No disrespect, Dad, but it's about time."

"So, I have been told on numerous occasions, princess." Turning to look at Kate, he smiled. "I will leave it up to you to dismiss the wet feeders and arrange their departure when necessary." Turning back to Natalia, he directed his eyes to her. "No comment?"

Natalia looked back at him; aware their conversation was what sparked this turn of events. He'd been angry when he walked away from her. "I know this is hard for you, Daddy, but thanks."

He simply nodded. "Let me make this perfectly clear to you both. You will not go out hunting alone until my female warrior's report to me that you can handle it. They will be reporting to me on your progress, but if you have problems, please feel free to come to me with anything regarding that."

He sighed heavily. He hated this. But he could tell his daughters were appreciative as they both sat up straight, listening attentively. "Secondly, both of you are incapable of defending yourselves in any manner. With that being said, I have arranged for Luca to teach you weaponry and self-defense. He taught your *madre* the skills that saved her life. He has the damn patience of a saint and has agreed to take this on. You cannot go out into the mortal world and hunt if you cannot defend yourself. Luca will be reporting to me as well, on a daily basis. I do not expect you to become warriors but choose a weapon that fits you and learn to excel in it. Develop enough skills that you can defend yourself until someone can get to you. So, do you have questions? Comments? Feedback?"

Sophia perked up. Training might give her more opportunities to run into Alfie. "That's a great idea, Dad!"

Natalia seemed less enthused, training held no interest for her, and would only take her away from her books, but she saw the logic in it. She nodded her head. "Yeah, okay, as long as it doesn't take up too much time."

Shade walked around the desk and sat down. He ran his hand through his curls. "Look, I know my ideals are old. I'm trying to move ahead and see things through your eyes. This is not easy, to give you wings, and let you out of my grasp. I've spent your entire lives loving and protecting you the best I know how. I'm doing my best to provide you a safe way to break free and become who you both want to be."

Kate bit her lip; she knew how hard it was for him to let go. It was the same struggle she'd felt when Lorenzo was sent to camp. Shade had seen that separation from their son as natural. It was how he'd been raised. But he'd never had sisters, and his view of raising daughters was caught in a time warp.

Natalia was the first to speak. "Daddy, I think the things I said to you made you think I don't appreciate what you've done, or that I don't appreciate the life we've been given here. Nothing could be farther from the truth. We're both aware we've been raised with every advantage, and we've traveled the world with you and Mom.

Our futures are open to every possibility because of who you are. It's time to trust we can make the right decisions, and when we don't that we can pick ourselves up and start over. We're Medici, after all."

Sophia nodded. "What she said."

Shade felt the corners of his mouth go up a bit, but his heart was hammering. She was right. "Your *madre* and I have given you all we could. You both were born from love, and all we want is the best for you. Medici works as a *familia*. It is why we have survived for so long when other royal bloodlines have died off. I know you have the skills to achieve whatever you want in this life. These are the last lessons I can give to you. The rest, you need to learn on your own. So, I give you access to learn to survive among mortals. I can't make either of you go down a path you do not wish. I know, deep in my heart, you will choose a destiny that is your own. If there is nothing else, Sophia, you may leave. I wish to speak with Nattie and your *madre* alone, please."

Sophia looked surprised but took advantage of the fact her family would be preoccupied and maybe she could say hi to Alfie before camp. "Okay, see ya." She bolted out of the room and Kate shook her head. Natalia curled her legs under her on the sofa.

"What is it, Daddy?"

He stood from his chair and went to her, crouching down in front of her. Tipping her chin up a bit with his finger, he looked into her eyes. "I owe you an apology. I was upset last evening. I walked away from you, but I did so because I was afraid any words I spoke, might be something I could never take back. And I want to thank you for showing me I need to let go, give you and your sister more freedom. Will you forgive your old *padre*?"

Natalia wrapped her arms around his shoulders and hugged him tight. There was never a day that any of them had ever doubted his love for them. She knew, without a doubt, her parents would lay down their lives to protect their children. "Daddy, there's nothing to forgive."

"I love you, princess." He stood and walked to *bel*, grabbing her in his arms as he stood behind her. "Nattie has asked to return to Council and view the family history there. Malachi told her she could return when older, and she has asked to go. I have agreed and will be calling him tonight to arrange a meeting. I wanted you to know. Give me your thoughts, *mi amore*."

Kate smiled as his arms encircled her. "Your daughter has an unquenchable thirst for learning. Maybe she'll be a great teacher, like Enzo, and teach the children of other masters. I think you must let her follow her heart."

He snuggled into her neck. He only hoped his daughter was ready to handle what the records revealed. "*Si*, Nattie, you may go. I will let you know when we leave for Florence."

As his daughter left the room, he kissed Kate's neck, never tiring of her rose scent. "I will miss you when we go."

She turned so she was facing him. "Will you be gone long?"

"A few days perhaps, but I want to take her alone. After our disagreement, I think it will be good to spend time with her."

She nodded. "There's nothing for me to do at Council, and Shannon and I are working on the plans to expand the olive groves. Go, be with your daughter."

"*Si*, when you have finished your research, we will all travel to Florence together, check out the properties, and see what we need to start the olive groves, and you get another visit with our son." Kissing her long and passionately on the lips, he smacked her ass and smiled. "Now, go to your business, I have to call Malachi and set this up, and then I am going to camp."

2-8

Shade watched her hips sway as she walked from the room. Damn woman could still make his cock hard as steel after all these years. He picked up his cell phone and dialed up the Council. He took a deep breath as he heard the phone begin to ring.

Malachi heard the phone and sighed loudly. He missed the days when they could only be reached by a letter, written out in long hand, and delivered by messenger. Now the covens could reach the Council any time, with the infernal jangling of the phone that broke the silence of these sacred halls. Picking up the phone, he saw it was Shade Medici, and hoped there were no problems.

"Master Shade. Malachi here. How can I help you?"

"*Buonasera,* Malachi. *Grazie* for taking my call. I have a request to set up an appointment for myself and Princess Natalia. She wishes to view the family history." Shade closed his eyes and waited.

Malachi sat down, pushing the green hood back from his face. He remembered the visit from the young Natalia when she was but a small girl, and his request that she not be shown the books until she was older. She'd be about twenty now. "*Si,* of course. The books in the archives are the property of the covens we oversee. I think she is old enough. Does her mother know your history?"

Shade felt his heart beating rapidly and let out his breath slowly. "Queen Katherine does not know, and I do not wish her to. But I can think of no more excuses to deny Natalia access to those records. I will talk to her after she has completed her research, to make sure she understands she must guard the secret."

Malachi nodded his head. "So, your queen does not know. Then yes, there will be much that we will need to discuss. I will set up some time, and young Natalia can spend as much time as she likes reviewing our archives. There is one thing...."

Shade heard the hesitation in his voice. "What, Malachi? What is it?"

Malachi waved his hand. "Probably nothing. I have had a vision. I am still not sure of its meaning. I hesitate to bring it up until I understand it better. We will discuss it when you are here. No danger, so do not be alarmed."

Shade gave little thought to Malachi's vision. "On the topic of gifts, if you might spend some time with her while we are there. She is beginning to have her own visions, and she needs someone who can guide her in what she sees."

"Of course, Master Shade, I will be most happy to help the princess with her gift. Any guidance I can offer to her would be a privilege."

Shade laid his head back on the chair and felt grateful that Malachi would help her. "*Grazie* Malachi. From my heart, I thank you. Please let me know when you have the time, so we can arrange to be there."

"We will pull the Medici records from the archive. Ivor should have them ready in no more than two days' time. We will see you then, Medici."

"*Grazie*, Malachi, my graciousness to Ivor as well." Shade ended the call and looked out at the moon in the sky. It had begun. He could only hope she'd understand the need to keep what she learned to herself.

2-9

Shade waited for Nattie to finish dressing before they left for Council. He'd learned to be patient in this situation. Being mated, and having two daughters, he'd grown used to the extended preparation time. He finished his glass of Midnight and stepped outside of Castello as he waited. They had an appointment with Malachi this evening, and Natalia would finally be given access to the archives. He'd never visited the archives himself, he'd never had much interest, but he knew Nattie could probably hole up in there for days. He also knew there were things she'd learn that would create as many questions as answers. He was prepared, or at least he hoped he was. He soaked in the moon as he waited.

Natalia rushed to finish dressing and grabbed up a briefcase full of notes she'd made with the questions and gaps she was hoping to find answers to in the Council archives. She was so excited that her father, and Malachi, had finally agreed to give her access. She walked quickly down the long hall to her parents' bedroom and peeked in the door to find the room empty. Heading down the marble staircase, she encountered Antonio, who informed her that her father was outside. Tucking the briefcase under her arm, she walked outside into the gardens, and found him in the rose garden. She knew this was where her grandparents had died. That was one part of her family's history that had been shared with her and her siblings. She saw him standing quietly in the warm night air.

"A penny for your thoughts, Daddy."

Her soft lilting voice made him smile, and he turned to find his youngest daughter looking very much a woman. He had to accept his children were all grown now. "You look beautiful, as always." He hugged her softly. "My thoughts were in the past, I must admit. I was thinking of your grandmother, working here, in her rose garden, and of your madre. Kate always comes here when we visit, and makes this garden come alive. And now, seeing you all dressed up and so beautiful in the moonlight, I do believe this memory will be with me as well. Are you ready? Do you have everything you need?"

"Ready. I haven't been back to Council since I was a little girl. I'm excited to see their archives."

He chuckled softly, remembering that visit and her excitement. "Well, I must say, you have never lost the glow of enthusiasm. It still plays across your face. Malachi will give you full leave of the archives. I want you to take your time, Nattie, there is no rush. Ivor will be there as well, to assist you. When you are done, we will talk, si? I want you to understand everything you see."

She looked at him quizzically. She'd wondered about the family records stored inside those archives since she was four. There was something there both her father and Malachi had been reluctant for her to see. "Okay, Daddy. I will. Shall we go now?"

"*Si*. Let us teleport there on this beautiful Florence night."

Her smile was beaming brighter than the moon, but he knew once she found the answers to questions she sought, that smile might not be so bright. As they teleported, she sped past him and he could hear her giggle float through the air. He couldn't help himself from smiling. As they landed outside Council, it was a short journey and he took her arm and led her inside. They were greeted by a Medici warrior, who nodded to his former master, and led them straight to Malachi's office. The guard opened the door then took his leave, as Shade laid his hand on her shoulder. "Take a deep breath, your journey is about to begin."

Before she could respond, Malachi was on his feet, walking to greet her. "Ah, our lovely Princess Natalia. How good it is to see you again. I have heard many accounts of your great intellect. If you are ready, I'll escort you to the archives. Medici, do you wish to go with her, or would you like to wait here in my office?"

"I will await here." He smiled at Natalia and kissed her cheek. "Enjoy."

Natalia followed behind Malachi, his green robe dusting the floor, as he led her down a long hallway. "How long have you lived here, Malachi?"

He slowed his walk until she was beside him and looked at her from under his hood. "My dear, I have so little sense of time, but it has been over a thousand years now, I think. I moved here as a young adult male, around twenty-five, as soon as it was discovered

I was born to Council. We will live here until our death. Our immune systems eventually fade, and even the Medici's warriors can't save us from that inevitable end. So even we die, my dear. Jasperion is over 2,000, and Onyx is only 200. He is our youngest. Our previous Onyx passed away when he was around 2,500 years. He developed an infection in his lungs we could not heal. And then the new Onyx emerged."

She stood still beside him, as she thought about what he'd revealed. She knew that the immortal were not actually immortal, only that their lives could be extended for an undetermined length of time, with records showing some vampires survived as long as 5,000 years. "But I thought you were chosen to serve."

He nodded his head. "Yes, chosen, but through birth. We are the rarest breed of vampire, those born to serve the Council."

He retrieved a key from his pocket and opened the massive door, pushing it inward. "Come, follow me, I'll show you where your records are stored."

Natalia was still trying to absorb what he'd revealed when she followed him into the massive room. There were rows and rows of shelves, holding thick tomes of ancient text. She followed him through the dusty records and saw leather bound books with dates that extended back centuries before the time of Christ. She saw the names of some of the great families, Alizzi, Rothchild, Hapsburg, Borgia, Plantagenets, Ferragamo, Tudor, Valois. These families still ruled, and her father had introduced their sons to both her and her sister. He turned a corner and stopped in front of a large section, dedicated to the Medici. He pulled out a chair from the ancient table.

"You can set your things down here, Princess. Take as much time as you need. We guard these records. They are our sacred trust, our history and our heritage. But they belong to all of us. I will let Ivor know you are here. He will be able to help guide you in your search. If there is nothing else, I will leave you to your research."

Natalia was looking at the massive number of documents, knowing it would take years to get through all of them. "Yes, send Ivor, please." He nodded and turned to leave her.

Malachi sent a telepathic message to Ivor, letting him know the Medici princess was in the archives, and she had requested he join her. He heard the acknowledgment, as he walked back to his office to join Master Medici. As he entered, he saw the Medici standing at the window, gazing out, the lights of Florence in the distance.

"It is still a beautiful city, our Florence, is it not?"

"*Si*, Malachi. It has changed, and yet, remains the same. Is my daughter settled?"

Malachi took his seat behind his desk and extended his hand, indicating the seat for Shade. "*Si*, she is settled in, and Ivor will be joining her. I am sure there will be questions she will need answered before this night is over. There are things I wish to discuss with you. But first, would you like a Midnight?"

Shade took a seat in the old office. He chuckled. "Of course, Malachi, I would enjoy having a Midnight with you. I know you mentioned a vision of my daughter, and that has played on my mind. I am concerned as to what it entails. Your visions are seldom wrong."

A servant appeared with a bottle of Midnight and several glasses on the tray, silently placing the tray down on the desk and departing. Malachi filled two glasses and passed one to Shade and sat back with his own glass.

"*Si*, even after all these years, I must be careful with my visions. As I have explained to Natalia, it is a powerful gift, but the visions are not always clear. It is important not to jump to conclusions about what you see. It is why I have delayed sharing them with you." He took a sip of the thick wine, and cleared his throat, unsure of how to begin, or how the Medici would react.

Shade raised his glass and took a sip but stopped mid drink. It wasn't like Malachi to tread so lightly. He glared at him over the rim of the ancient crystal. He could feel Malachi carefully calculating his words before he spoke. Shade sat the glass down carefully on the desk.

"So, this is about Nattie. You know something, and you fear I will not like what I hear. Just speak, Malachi." Shade shifted about in his chair, suddenly nervous, a small thread of fear rolling through him.

"*Si*, it is your youngest princess. Do not fret. I see nothing that brings her harm. Quite the contrary." He took another sip of the wine. "My vision of Natalia, I have had it many times now, it will not go away. It pushes at my brain, forcing me to acknowledge it. But I see her in the white robe, Medici."

Shade leaned forward in his chair, his hands together. White robe? He was impatient as hellfire and he could make no connections in his head about his daughter in a white robe. "I do not understand the significance of the white robe, Malachi. Talk to me."

Malachi set his drink down and pushed the hood back from his head. His hair was grey, and the wrinkles marred his face. "She would be the first female of our kind to wear a robe, Medici. Your Natalia is born to Council. She will wear the white robe. She will be Ivor. But our Ivor is young yet, only 700 or so, and I have not seen visions of his passing. I have thought long and hard about this. It can only mean there is to be a third Council, a Council for the United States. Centuries ago, we broke off to develop the Eastern Council, for the Asian families. With our expansion into the States, I believe my vision is showing me the development of a third Council, a Western Council. Your Natalia will serve that Council and will live her life inside the safety of its walls, guarded by your own warriors. She will wear the white robe and record the history of the covens there." He stared back at the Medici, waiting for his response. "She will be the first female to ever serve Council in all our history."

Shade sat silently for a long time, his face a mirror of confusion, realization, and then amazement. Somewhere in the thoughts flying at a blistering speed through his brain, he felt both pride and anxiety. He shook his head several times, was he dream-walking? Was this truly happening? He held up his hand, as if to stop Malachi, and stood, shaken by this incredible news.

"My Nattie, Council? I don't know...I'm lost for words."

He paced across the office, his hand running through his raven curls. He gripped the back of his chair, facing off against Malachi as he remained seated behind his desk.

"So, you are telling me, there is going to be a Council in the United States, and my Nattie is going to be the recorder of history for the covens there. She is female. How is that possible, Malachi?"

He began to pace again, back and forth across the ancient floors, which had seen much traffic in its centuries. He flopped down in the chair. He felt as though he'd just fought a battle.

"Natalia Medici, a Council member. I'll be damned. I knew there was something unique about her. But she was female, and it never occurred to me that something of this magnitude could lay in her future. She is brilliant, of course, and her gifts are rare, but I never envisioned this. Have you told her?"

Malachi shook his head. "I wanted to talk to you first. With this great honor, comes much sacrifice. She will not be mated. She will not have children. But her contribution to our people will alter our course, our culture. We have been a patriarchal culture since the beginning of time. We have had covens led by females, like the Alizzi, but they have found it difficult to sustain their coven without mating, and most of them die off. We have always relied on the males to lead. The princess, being born to this role, indicates a shift. It is a small beginning, but make no mistake about it, this will change how the females are perceived over time. I can see a day when females hold equal power to males."

He felt both joy and heartache. He knew Natalia had resisted his attempts to have her meet the eligible young males from the other covens. She'd already informed him she didn't want his life, or her mother's life. She'd said she'd never subjugate herself to a male and become a breed mate for some master. She had no interest in learning to run the Medici businesses. And as much as it had hurt him to hear those words from her, it all made sense now. This was her destiny. She would lead their species and its females into a new era.

He sat quietly for a very long time, and Malachi didn't interrupt his thoughts. He'd have to tell Kate. How the hell would he tell her? He couldn't think of that yet. His daughter, rising to Council, and ruling all covens in this newly established territory. A Medici had never risen so far. Yet, all of his children were born to greatness, with unique gifts. He knew Lorenzo's path, and now he knew Natalia's. She'd never know the joy of love for her mate, and its incredible light. She'd never know the sound of laughter from her own child. His thoughts were many, and they came so fast. But he had no doubts. She was born to this, and he knew she'd embrace it. How could he ever be sad, when he knew it was a life she'd willingly choose for herself, and not see it as a sacrifice?

"Our world is changing, Malachi. It continues to change faster than we can even imagine. Everything around me seems strange and out of place sometimes, like I have fallen asleep for a very long time, only to wake to a world I no longer understand. My children help me see this new place, when I view it through their eyes. But they are also the ones who are driving the speed of the changes. This world has the largest number of vampires we have seen in centuries. If we are to thrive here, we must evolve with the times, and my princess will be there to guide us through those changes. She brings such pride and honor to the Medici name. I wish for you to explain to her what you have seen. Tell her all you know, Malachi, and help her transition, for I can be of no use to her in this role. She will need your hand to guide her."

Malachi nodded his head in respect. "It is a mission I accept with great humility. It will be my honor to direct her, as will Ivor. She will not enter the Council until she is twenty-five, and she will be called Ivory."

***

In the archives, Ivor was pulling down the ancient books that held the secrets of the Medici. He laid the books on the table before her and watched as she put on the white gloves to turn the brittle parchment pages. She took notes on the earliest members of her ancestral family, reaching back to 1147. In vampire culture, her family was still considered a young one, not even a thousand years. She recorded the information from the book on the first emergence of the Medici vampires, noting the first mating, the births, and the deaths. She looked at details of the early beginnings of the coven, its size and scope.

Ivor helped guide her to the next generation, and the next, as they moved slowly forward in time. Natalia made careful notes, writing down everything, not sure what would be important to her research. As they worked through each generation, she started to see the pattern, and found it odd, but said nothing. Ivor pushed the first book aside, as they opened the second book, and she began once again to make notes, generation after generation. She looked at Ivor, but his face was blank, he had no expression. They completed that book and he pulled another in front of her, and then another, and then the final book. As they worked through the pages of the final book, she saw the birth record for her own grandfather, Christofano, his footprint as an infant, in blood on the page. She saw the document recording his mating to her grandmother, Portia. She'd never known them, but she'd heard about them all her life. She knew her mother and father could see them at Castello, and speak with them, but she and her siblings had only occasionally heard them, as if from a distance. She'd seen their portraits in the halls of Castello, along with those of her great grandparents, and the generations before them. She saw the records for her father's birth in 1472, and a short twenty-five years later, the deaths of both her grandparents, when they were burned alive during the bonfire of the vanities. She was well aware of the story, but it carried an even greater meaning now. Her father had shown them all where their grandparents were killed in the rose garden at Castello. She saw the record of his father's mating, and her mother's turning, and the subsequent birth of her siblings, including the insertion of Cory as the son of the Medici, all the way to the last page, which displayed her own birth. But she couldn't deny what she'd seen now. The pattern was clear, and she stared ahead, her eyes blank.

"He never told us."

Ivor closed the last book and put it back on the shelf, brushing the dust from his white robe. "I never understood why I must wear the white robe. So impractical, working in these archives."

She looked up at him. "What?"

"Nothing, my dear, just the ramblings of an old man."

She repeated again. "He never told us."

Ivor looked back at her. "And why would he? What will it change?"

Natalia blinked her eyes several times. "Nothing...or everything? Did you know, Ivor?"

He nodded his head. "*Si*, the Council knows." Ivor also knew her fate, as Malachi had shared his vision with the Council. "Are you finished here, Princess?"

She wiped away a blood tear on her cheek and answered in a whisper. "Yes." He nodded and led her from the archive, back to Malachi's office.

2-10

Natalia was lost in thought as Ivor led her back to Malachi's office. "Does Malachi know?"

She saw his hooded head bob up and down. "*Si*, Princess, all Council knows the content of the archives. We hold the history of all the covens."

She repeated again. "He never told me."

Ivor stopped and turned to look at her. "You were but a child. It is a lot to absorb. He brought you here to learn when he thought you were ready. Talk to him, Princess, but I will tell you now, he will not be able to reveal much more than you have already learned for yourself."

They reached the door of Malachi's office, and Ivor tapped lightly before opening the door for Natalia. She stepped inside and Ivor closed the door behind her. He knew she'd learn more today than what she'd read in the archives, she'd learn her future as well. Malachi had shared his vision, and the Council had already begun the search for the other six vampires who were born to serve the new Council in the West.

Natalia entered the room, and both her father and Malachi turned to look at her. As soon as she locked eyes with her father, she felt the tears fill her eyes. "Daddy."

Standing, he went to her and held her, crushing her into his chest. Petting her beautiful hair, he tried to calm her. "Shh, it is okay. I am sorry, my beautiful *figlia*, but not all discoveries are pleasant."

Natalia released all the emotions she'd held at bay and sobbed against his chest. "Do you know when, Daddy?"

"No, I do not. But it could be centuries." Laying his head on top of hers, he rocked her softly as her sobs tore him apart inside.

"Or it could be tomorrow." She wiped at her tears and looked to Malachi. "You know, don't you?"

Malachi shook his head. "No, Princess, I do not. Just because I have the gift of third eye, does not mean I see everything. You will find this gift we share can be quite frustrating. It reveals some things, but not all things. I am often caught by surprise when events unfold about which I have had no warning. Sit down, Princess. Let me pour you a glass of Midnight. It will calm you."

He handed her a handkerchief to wipe her tears and poured her a glass of the wine as she took the chair next to her father. Natalia dried her tears and took a sip of the liquid that had brought her family great wealth. She looked at her father. "Does Mommy know?"

Shade sighed heavily. losing his eyes, he shook his head no. His icy blue eyes locked with her deep brown ones, so much like her *madre's*. His voice remained calm. She must understand fully what he was about to tell her. They couldn't leave Council and return home until he was sure she understood what he was about to ask of her. "Beyond Council and I, only three others know, Luca, Marco and Gi. Your Mommy does not know. Your brothers and sister do not know."

He knelt before her, gripping her delicate hands, his eyes holding her gaze. "They must never know, Nattie. You can never speak of it again. I thought about it a long time before turning your mother. I agonized over whether I should tell her before she was turned and decided I could not. It was selfish on my part, I know that. I feared she might back away. Afterwards, I regretted I had not told her, but it was too late. To tell her after the fact, felt like a betrayal. I made the decision, and I cannot look back, understand? You must keep this locked inside, as I have done. I don't know if this was the right decision or not, and I ask you not judge me. Besides, it is done now, and she must never know."

Natalia listened to his plea. She thought about the information she'd learned and wished she hadn't seen it. He was right. It was a secret that was better left buried. She nodded her head and her voice cracked as she answered him. "I'll never speak of it. I promise."

Shade nodded, giving her the smallest of smiles. "I will take the word of the Princess of Medici any day." Kissing her on the cheek, he stood and returned to his seat. "As if you have not learned enough today, Malachi has had a vision. I will let him explain further. He has much to speak to you about."

Malachi cleared his throat. "As I said, young Natalia, this gift we share is unpredictable. I have no control over what visions appear to me. I am not able to pull them forth on a whim. They come as they come, and then I must learn to interpret them."

Natalia nodded her head. "Yes, that's how it is for me as well. I can't make the visions appear either, nor can I choose their content."

Malachi watched her face closely. She'd already taken in a lot tonight. "For some time now, my visions have been about you. I have moved slowly, made sure my interpretations were correct before I revealed what I know to your father. And now, if you are ready, I will reveal to you."

Natalia looked at him with concern. "Is it bad?"

Malachi had the slightest smile. "Well, I do not think it is bad, and your father did not think it was bad, although he was taken by surprise. I hope you will not think so. Do you wish to hear it now?"

She casts a glance at her father, and he gave her a reassuring nod of his head before she turned back to Malachi. "Yes, please."

Malachi looked deep into her eyes, this daughter of the Medici who would create a fault line in their culture that would forever change their course. "Princess Natalia, you were born to Council. You were born to wear the white robe and keep the history of the covens."

She looked at him with confusion. "But Ivor?"

He nodded. "There is to be a third Council, one that rules in the West, in the United States. It will be based in the capital, in Washington, D.C. You will wear the white robe, and you will be called Ivory. You will enter the halls of Council at the age of twenty-five, and you will reside there the rest of your life. We are currently looking for the other six members and scouting for the best property to build the enclave that provides maximum protection. The Council will, of course, be guarded by your father's warriors, as they have done for centuries. Those warriors will be chosen by your father, and they, too, will serve there for life. You will be the first female Council, young Natalia, and your legacy will be reshaping our culture, to give the females a greater voice."

Natalia felt dizzy with this news. "Me? Are you sure?"

He nodded. "It has been seen, daughter. You are one of us."

The smile spread slowly across her face until she beamed back at him. All the pieces of the puzzle fell into place for her. She'd never felt drawn to follow in her mother's footsteps, to subjugate herself to a male, and bear his children. She'd never been able to see herself in that role and was chafing at her father's insistence to find a suitable mate. She'd always rejected the patriarchal structure of their culture and felt the females should be able to rule with equal power. She didn't want to inherit the vineyards and run the businesses her mother and Auntie Shannon had built. This felt right. This was her path.

"Yes, I am one of you."

Shade watched his daughter's face intently and saw the acceptance, and the joy. Her path wouldn't be a traditional one. There would be no mate, no children. She'd be dedicated to Council, and all covens. He slowly reached out and took her hand, letting his thumb slowly caress her knuckles. "I am so happy for you. My heart is bursting with pride. You are the rarest of the rare, and you will bring great change to our culture, Nattie. It is the highest honor to be born to Council, but to be the first female. You bring such honor to the Medici name! I could never have imagined this. But you understand, you will never mate, never leave the interior of those walls?"

She had tears in her eyes again, but tears of joy. "I'm so glad you approve. This feels so right to me, Daddy. And I didn't mean to sound ungrateful when I rejected the idea of being mated, of having babies. I know it sounded like I was rejecting you and Mommy, but that's not the case. We all know how much we're loved, and both of you have worked so hard to ensure we'd have the best there was to offer. We had a sound foundation for moving forward. Sophia, Lorenzo, and I, when we get together, we can only speak of our childhood, and the joy we experienced, and how grateful we are to have this family. But this is right for me, I feel it, and I'm so happy you approve. Do you think Mommy will be okay with it?"

"Mommy will feel the same. She wants you to succeed, find your destiny. We both want you to have an eternity filled with what you love. She will be shocked, as was I, but she will accept your path."

Natalia smiled back at him and wondered how it was possible that on this night, she had learned both the saddest and the happiest news of her life.

2-11

Returning home to Virginia, Natalia had time to think about what she'd learned. It would be hard to face her mother, knowing what she knew, and having to keep it to herself. She hoped her excitement over the news about being born to Council would cover any emotions she was feeling about what she'd discovered in the archives. Her father stayed close during the teleport, and they landed together behind the house, as Aegis leapt to her feet to greet them. Natalia scratched the wolf behind her ears. "Hey, old girl. Did you miss us?" The wolf sniffed her over carefully, before walking away. She turned to her father. "Well, now or never, I guess."

"*Si*, some things now, but do not forget, some things never." He threw his arms around her shoulder and laughed. "Want to make a bet with your old dad?"

She smiled back at him. "Sure. What's the bet?"

"I will bet you your mommy is standing right inside that door, and she has worn a path in the floor since we left. She does not have her *bambinos* to chase after anymore."

***

Kate felt them both as they neared the house and she rushed down the stairs. She stood still a moment to hone her senses, until she knew they had landed near the patio. She rushed to the back door and pulled it open before they could reach for the doorknob. She had never been separated from Natalia this long before, and even though she was with her father, she worried about her the whole time. "My baby!"

She opened her arms and Natalia walked into the hug. She squeezed her mother tight, closing her eyes and blocking her thoughts. "Mommy, I missed you."

Kate kissed her cheek. "I missed you more." As she let go of her child, she smiled at Shade. "And you...I always miss you."

Shade winked at Natalia. "See, I told you." He grinned and took Kate into his arms. "I hope you aren't going to hold out on the hug for me." He held her close, inhaling her familiar scent as she nestled into his chest. "Come along, Mommy, we have much to tell you."

Kate allowed herself to be swallowed up in his hug. "It was a good trip then? Natalia found what she was looking for?"

He nuzzled his nose into her hair. "*Si*, and much more, but I think she would prefer to tell you." He held her hand and led her to the living room. Pouring them all a glass of Midnight, he handed out the glasses as he took a seat in the big armchair. Kate curled up on the sofa next to Natalia, reaching out to hold her hands.

"So, tell me, what did you find in the archives that has you so excited?"

Natalia gathered her thoughts quickly. "Well, the archives were interesting, for sure. So much history there, and I was able to complete the family tree the way I wanted, but that's not the exciting part. We met with Malachi afterward, and he had a vision for me."

Kate looked puzzled. "Malachi had a vision that involved you?"

She nodded. "Don't look worried, Mom, it's all good. He said I was born Council. There will be a U.S. Council and I will be the keeper of the archives here. Mommy, I'm Ivory!"

Kate sat back on the sofa, absorbing the news. "A U.S. Council?" She looked at Shade to gauge his response. "But, the Council...they live in seclusion. Natalia, this is what you want?" Even before she asked the question, she knew the answer. Her daughter's face was bright with excitement.

"Yes! I'm the first female born to Council, Mommy!"

Kate nodded, and put a smile on her face. "That's...I'm so happy for you."

Natalia jumped up. "Can I go tell Sophia?"

Shade had said nothing but kept his eyes on Kate. She was putting on a brave face, but her heart just got slammed with news that they'd be giving up their youngest child to the Council. He felt her emotions and understood her mixed feelings. He had to be strong for her. "You may go tell your sister, go share your news, Nattie."

Kate waited until Natalia had run up the stairs before turning to Shade. "Lover, tell me this is good news. She'll live at Council? They rarely leave. I know she'll be safe, but...she'll be so isolated. She won't mate nor have children. How is this a good thing?"

Standing, he took her hand and lifted her from the sofa. "Come, let us take a walk. I think we should do this outside, no ears around."

Putting his arm around her, he led her outside, and down the long lane that led to the main road. They walked a bit before he spoke. He wanted no distractions. Stopping, he lifted her up and sat her on the fence railing, as he slide comfortably between her legs. Looking into her eyes, he didn't have to tell her how he felt about all this, she already knew, but there were words she needed to hear.

"She is going to be fine, *bel*. This is her destiny. This is where her gift and her brilliant mind have taken her. *Si*, she will be isolated, but also protected. She will be the first female to Council. The Council is the highest honor any vampire can achieve. It feels scary, I know, but you must see this future through her eyes. She does not want our path. She has no desire to run the Medici businesses. Natalia has always been happiest when she can escape inside her books. And imagine what she can accomplish inside those walls. Malachi says she will shift our culture."

She nodded. "I'm proud of her. I've always been proud of her. And to be the first female in Council, I understand the significance of it. My response is a selfish one. It's just not what I envisioned. Will we be able to see her? Can we visit? Can she come home?"

He smiled softly as he returned her gaze. "She will not be allowed to come home often. The role of the Council is so important to our species, we keep them sequestered, and highly protected. They are our ruling body, as well as the keepers of our history. They are the rarest among us, born to this role, and must be protected at all cost. But we may visit her on occasion, although we may have to make an appointment. Malachi said she will not leave us until she is twenty-five years of age, so you have time to prepare. She will be traveling to Florence a great deal before that time. Malachi and Ivor will take her in hand, I have Malachi's word. He is quite excited, if you can imagine that, to have this vision of a new Council emerging in the West. They will rule over all the covens and new territories growing here in the States."

Kate leaned against his chest. "She'll be very powerful. She'll re-shape our world. I'm glad at least she'll be well protected. And if this is what makes her happy, then I have to let her go, and be happy for her. Her life will be so different than ours. It is hard to imagine."

"*Si*, but you are on the right path. She was born to this. It is not an honor that can be earned or given. We have given her a strong foundation. Look at it through her eyes; see the joy in her heart. That is how I console myself. This is what she wants."

He held her tightly as he stood between her legs, feeling them wrap around him. "The dream of having grandbabies at my feet is getting slimmer by the moment, *mi amore*."

She laughed softly as her arms encircled his shoulders. "Don't give up. We still have Sophia and Lorenzo."

He grunted. "At this rate, with Sophia, I am beginning to wonder. And what is wrong with my sons? Cory wants no children. And our prodigal son, Lorenzo, what damn female is going to want to mate with him with that black canvas tatted across his body? Am I missing something? I mean, do you find that sexy?"

Kate laughed. "It doesn't appeal to me, but he's young, and for his generation, the girls will find it appealing. I hear him talking with Alfie sometimes, and it doesn't sound like either of them has to work very hard at finding women. I fear he'll be much like his father, and we'll both be ancient before he settles down."

Shade felt his heart slam hard in his chest. He'd never thought about that. "Perhaps it will not take him as long to settle down. I would give all my wealth to know his female was out there waiting. One of our children better be giving us little ones to cuddle and love. I miss it."

It broke her heart that she couldn't give him another. They lived an eternity, so why should their breeding be so limited? And there were so many that didn't breed at all. No wonder their race was so limited. "I miss it too."

He took her beautiful face into his hands. "Well then, I propose we go back to the house. We can pretend we are making another. Come along, woman, I have need of you and your love tonight."

2-12

It had been months now since Alfie had been assigned to the States, and Lorenzo was on his own. He, too, had taken numerous assignments in various outposts in Tuscany, gaining exposure to all the members of the coven, as well as learning the territory. He'd led the brigades in Siena, Pisa, Livorno and Volterra, managing the warriors there, as well as meeting with the coven, and listening to their needs. The breadth and depth of the responsibilities he'd be expected to carry was finally sinking in, and he hadn't even begun to learn anything about managing the finances of the coven. He'd learned from his father that Natalia would be going to Council, and while that was great news for the Medici coven, it made Lorenzo a little sad as well. He'd hoped, with her great mind perhaps Natalia could one day manage the businesses, and just leave him with the responsibility of running the camps.

His father's assets were massive now, covering many countries, and while he had many people who helped to manage these businesses, his father made the final decisions on the vineyards, and Kate made the final decisions on the flower fields. Now, Lorenzo learned they were planning to expand into olives. Luca ran the lemon groves, and Shannon was Kate's business partner in the flowers, and soon, the olives, but he'd be expected to understand all of these businesses as well, and be able to step in should something ever happen to his parents.

His family was wealthy, but that wealth also supported a large coven, and their wealth was as vital for their success moving forward as the protection of the warriors. Now, the burdens of managing the coven would be shared with Sophia, and he could only hope she found a strong and powerful mate.

He was back in Castello for a short break, and the rooms had never felt emptier. The staff usually communicated among themselves telepathically, so the massive halls were deathly quiet. His footsteps echoed in the great emptiness as he made his way to his bedroom. He met with Marco on his return, and was told after a few days of rest, he'd be sent to Umbria, the neighboring territory, owned by the Alizzi. Umbria didn't belong to the Medici, but since Donatella never mated, and she held strong ties to the Medici family, there had been an agreement between Christofano and Donatella's father, that the Medici would provide protection. Of course, it served the best interest of the Medici as well, since Dona's territory bordered theirs, and maintaining a strong alliance with the Alizzi was a sound strategic move. If Dona were to decide to mate with a master who wasn't on good terms with the Medici, it would place an enemy at their doorstep.

Carlos was waiting for him when he entered the room, to find his bed turned down. "Master, do you wish to bathe before you sleep? Or do you wish for me to send for a feeder?"

Lorenzo handed him his sword and eyed the bed. He looked down at his dust-covered leathers and decided he should probably shower before climbing into those clean sheets. He'd lived in the barracks at all the outposts, sleeping in a narrow bunk, and the comfort of his own bed, and a long hot shower, was a luxury he'd missed. "Shower first."

Carlos nodded as he took the sword, and Lorenzo peeled off the leathers. Carlos gathered the soiled clothes, which would be cleaned for him, and fresh leathers would be laid out. Lorenzo stood under the shower, letting the hot water pour over him, as he closed his eyes. He was well aware of his father's past, and he had a new understanding as to the number of women who'd passed through his father's bed. Of course, it served his need to feed, and it provided sexual pleasure, but more than that, it momentarily filled the loneliness. A warrior's life was not his own, his future uncertain, so he rarely took a mate. A warrior's bed was filled with a parade of nameless, faceless women, both mortal and immortal. But he would be a master, and one of royal blood, so a mate was more than expected, it was required. Lorenzo hadn't found a female who spoke to his heart yet, but he was hoping it wouldn't take him 500 years, like his father. He was already tired of the loneliness.

He emerged from the shower to find a stack of fresh towels, and he dried off, walking back into his bedroom. Carlos was waiting, looking apologetic.

"Master, I know you are ready to sleep, but the Alizzi is here. She has brought you a feeder from her coven. Do you wish for me to send her away?"

Lorenzo sighed. He was tired to the bone, but he did need to feed. Wrapping the towel around his narrow hips, he pushed the long-wet strands of hair back from his face. "No, I don't want to offend. I'll accept her gift, and besides, I need to feed. Send her up, please."

Carlos nodded and left to deliver the message. Lorenzo dropped the towel, and climbed into bed, waiting for the feeder. He planned to make quick work of it, feed and fuck, and send her on her way, so he could get some much-needed sleep. He was surprised when he looked up to see the feeder, who looked like a young version of the Alizzi, and Dona both enter his bedroom.

"Dona! I didn't expect you. I'm sorry, I'm not dressed."

Donatella led the feeder to his bed, as she slithered under the covers and molded her body to his. Dona climbed on top of the bed, on his other side.

"Don't be foolish, Lorenzo. Do you have any idea how many naked Medici's I have seen? I wanted to bring you a gift, and also to talk. I understand you will be assigned to my territory soon."

The feeder slid the covers from Lorenzo, leaving his body exposed, and Dona's eyes took him in. She was startled by the tattoo that covered the arm and shoulder on his right side. As the feeder slid between his legs, her hot, wet mouth swallowed him up, and he felt Dona's hands stroking the tattoo on his arm.

"Oh my, look at this. It is magnificent, Lorenzo. So, befitting a warrior."

Her fingers traced the outline of the tribal design that covered his arm and shoulder, and he found it difficult to respond, as the feeder worked her magic on his cock. Dona's hand slid over his chest and stopped at the nipple ring. Her fingers toyed with the ring, tweaking it gently, as the feeder crawled up his body, straddling him, and began a slow seductive ride on his cock. Lorenzo needed her blood, and pulled the feeder down onto his chest, sinking his fangs into her neck, drinking deeply. Dona sat back, and watched as he quickly rolled over, the feeder clinging tightly to him, so he was now in control. She smiled as she watched him savagely take her, the feeder's face expressing ecstasy, as they rode out the orgasm that shook the bed. He unlatched from her throat, the blood still on his lips as he rolled to his back, leaving the feeder at his side. Dragging his hand across his lips, his eyes felt heavy.

"Dona, I am tired. I'm in no mood to talk now. I thank you for the gift, but I must sleep."

"Of course." Her voice was a soft purr, as she shooed the feeder from his bed. She covered him up, tucking the blankets around him, and softly ran her hand through his long, dark hair. "Rest now. Think nothing of it. We have plenty of time to talk." She gently kissed his cheek. "Goodnight, my prince."

She slipped from his bed, as his body relaxed into sleep and looked back over her shoulder at his sleeping form. *You look so much like your father. It breaks my heart*.

Carlos escorted her back downstairs, where Antonio was waiting, as he stood with the feeder. He thanked her for coming as he escorted them to the door. She bid him goodnight as they teleported back to Umbria. *Someday, Lorenzo, Castello will be my home too. If I can't have the father, I will have the son.*

2-13

Sophia had been sending letters to Alfie on a daily basis for months now, and Aislynn had been her courier, delivering her letters, and bringing Alfie's responses in return. Occasionally, they'd meet in the hay barn, but it didn't give them much privacy, and there was always the risk that one of the stable hands could walk in at any minute. After her father gave them permission to hunt, she'd go out with Aislynn, and when he was able, Alfie would sneak away from camp to meet her. Her father had wanted her to only feed from females, as he thought it would be safer, and so far, she had complied. There was only one male she was interested in anyway.

She'd finally taken her half-brother, Cory, into her confidence, explaining her frustration, and sharing that it was Alfie she loved, not the rich and powerful sons of other masters her father kept parading in front of her. Cory and Madison had both been sympathetic, understanding more than most that love strikes indiscriminately. She was ecstatic when they said she could bring Alfie to their house, if she promised to be discreet.

She dressed casually in jeans and a sweater. They were moving into fall, and the vineyards had been harvested, the lavender was dormant, but the sunflowers were still in bloom. The trees were starting to turn, and there was a nip in the night air. Pulling on a pair of boots, she hurried down the stairs and shouted out to her mother. "Going to see Madison and Cory tonight. I might be late getting home."

Kate and Shannon were on the phone with Luciano, who'd been coordinating some of the early plans for the development of the olive groves and purchasing some existing groves. Kate stepped out of the office. "Do you want Luca to escort you there?"

Sophia rolled her eyes. "It's just over the ridge, Mom. I think I can teleport there safely."

Kate smiled back at her. "Then give them my love."

Sophia bolted out of the house before she was faced with any more questions. "I will!"

She teleported into the lane leading to the villa where Cory and Madison had lived since their wedding, looking at the warm glow of the lights in the windows. She knocked on the door, and Madison opened it immediately, giving her a hug before pulling her inside.

"Thank you for doing this."

Madison shook her head, her blond hair pulled back in a single loose braid. "I can't believe Cory said yes. Just be sure your father doesn't find out."

***

Alfie spent his nights in camp, or at the Dead House, patrolling the streets of Washington. He had learned much since he came to the States. Still, he was restless. He loved being closer to Sophia, but their opportunities to see each other were limited. She was all he wanted, but he never forgot, for a minute, that she was royal blood, and off-limits to him. As he returned to camp from a night in D.C., he saw Cory's light on in his workshop. As he walked into the shop, Cory looked up. "You ready, brother?"

Alfie was more than ready. "Appreciate this, Cory."

Cory shrugged, he understood. "Just stay quiet about it. If my dad finds out, who knows what he'll do. Come on."

They headed down the long, winding lane to the house. Alfie felt a bit gritty, and wished he'd had time to shower before seeing her. Entering the house, he saw her sitting with Madison, chatting quietly. Cory nodded to the bar in the kitchen. "Midnight is there, help yourself. Our home is your home."

"Thanks, brother."

Madison made eye contact with Cory as she stood up. "I think we should leave these two alone. Come on, we'll watch some TV in the bedroom. Have fun, and just make yourself at home."

Sophia was on her feet as Alfie entered the room, her smile covered her face, as she extended her hand to him, and he took it. Turning back to Madison as she and Cory left the room, she shouted out, "Thanks, you guys!" Taking Alfie's other hand, she stared into his hazel eyes. "Well, here we are."

For Alfie, it seemed like he'd waited months to look into those big blue eyes. The smile on her face told him all he needed to know. She was just as excited as he was to be alone.

"Here we are, red, just the two of us. I can't stay very long. They'll notice I'm not in the camp." Pulling her into his arms, he hugged her, his hands sliding up and down her back. Pulling her down beside him on the couch, he kept her hand in his. "So, where are you supposed to be, and what are you supposed to be doing?"

"I'm exactly where I'm supposed to be. I told Mom I was going to Cory's, and here I am. Mom and Shannon are working, and Dad is in D.C., and I told Mom I'd probably be late, so we're good."

His eyes roamed every inch of her face, as he took a long tendril of her red hair and twirled it in his fingers. "Good. Cory and Madison can only cover our asses so much. They won't lie to him if questioned, and neither will I."

He knew what they were doing was wrong, but the need to see her overcame his judgment. "I've missed you, Sophia. I wish we didn't have to sneak around. Is he still pushing you to mate?"

She rolled her eyes. "Yes. He sets up a meeting about twice a month. And seriously, it's a meeting. We go to their home, so he can check out their estate, and we meet the whole freakin' family."

She flopped back on the sofa. "Even if I found any of those guys remotely attractive, does he honestly think we're just going to look at each other and the sparks will fly? It's the most awkward thing ever. I hate it. He scolds me after every meeting, telling me no one is going to pick a mate who is surly and ill-tempered, and I just laugh and say, 'Good!' I know he's frustrated too. Why can't he just let me find my own way?"

He loved when she got riled up. Her face turned a beautiful shade of pink, and she could go from zero to a hundred in about two seconds flat. Sliding his arm around the back of the couch, he pulled her to his shoulder. As her head rested there, he snuggled into her red hair and breathed in her scent. He didn't know when he'd be able to see her again and treasured every second to take in all he could.

"He loves you, very much. He won't be satisfied until he knows his princess is with someone who can give her the life she's accustomed too. Master is a warrior at heart, but he fell in love his own way. I thought, once he knew your true feelings, he might back off, but with your sister going to Council, he seems even more adamant in his search. Lorenzo says once he gets something in his head, he doesn't let up. But he also told me your mother can sometimes get through to him. You and I both know you won't find a son of any master to suit you. At least, I hope you never do."

Sophia enjoyed the closeness, the feel of him, and the sound of his voice. She'd been attracted to him since she was a little girl, and the attraction had only grown through the years. He was her soul mate. "I never will. My father is stubborn, but I am even more so." She turned her head on his shoulder, so her lips were close to his face. "I already found what I'm looking for."

"So have I."

Alfie thought she was the most beautiful creature he'd ever laid eyes on, and she tempted his beast like no other. He felt her warm breath across his face and the warmth traveled all the way to his groin. It was a struggle to not move forward with her. He knew in his heart she was his but feared she would be pulled away from him by the one force he couldn't fight. Bending his head to hers, he kissed her lips, soft and lingering. He watched her eyes flutter shut.

She was caught off guard by the kiss. They'd danced around each other ever since he was stationed here. He'd hold her hand, and occasionally hug her, but it was their first real kiss. She slid her hand across his chest and kissed him again. It made her heart pound, and she pulled back quickly, surprised by how powerful her emotions were and how intensely she felt drawn to him. She wanted nothing more than to be with him. It would be so easy. It felt so right.

"Alfie, would you be surprised...if I told you I love you?"

Alfie wasn't expecting that response from her. He stood up quickly, tempted to just take her, teleport away with her. If only it were that simple. "No, I'm not surprised. But you can't love me, Sophia. I'm not good enough for you. I can't provide for you as your parents wish. I'm simply a warrior in your coven. It can't happen, red."

Turning to face her, his breathing was unsteady, and his heart was breaking. "I love you too. And if I could, I'd make you mine. I'd protect and love you, like no damn royal-blooded master ever could. But that choice isn't mine to make."

Sophia looked back at him; her mind made up. "But it's mine to make. You're my soul mate, Alfie. And you *can* take care of me. Daddy said he wouldn't force me into a mating I didn't want, and I want you, Alfie. What if we just did it? It's not like it can be reversed. If we feed from each other, then it's done."

Grabbing her shoulders, he squeezed them tight, his eyes locked with hers. "No! Sophia, listen to me. You deserve better. You're royalty. Everyone expects you to mate someone of equal station. You're at the top, I'm at the bottom. Do you hear what you're saying?"

He let go of her, his body aching to accept everything she said. He'd spent nights dreaming of her, and the taste of her blood on his tongue. "*Cazzo*, I want what you want, but how the hell will we explain it to your parents? I'm to be your brother's Second-in-Command. I could be banished, no longer a Medici."

"Alfie, if we're mated, you could never be banned. My dad would be angry for a time, but he'd never ban you, because in doing so, he'd have to ban me as well. You'll be my brother's SIC. You'll be the top-ranking warrior, second only to my brother. You're not at the bottom. I don't care if you're not a master, and my family doesn't need more money. Just think about it, okay? I mean, only if you want me. Do you want me, Alfie?"

Alfie stared at her like he was seeing her for the first time. *Did he want her? He'd take on legions of warriors to have her. And she was right. Master would be angry, but he'd not deny his daughter for long.* He'd grown up surrounded by this family, and he loved the woman in front of him and was ready and willing to give up everything for her. Rushing to her, he kissed her, like she should be kissed. His lips claimed her as his, his hands tangled in her hair. He kissed her long and passionately, and he was going to show her just how much he could love her. "Does that answer your question?"

She was startled by how quickly he moved to her and pulled her to him in a tight hug. She returned his kiss, feeling her blood rushing through her veins, her knees growing weak, and she clung to him for support. *This is how love is supposed to feel.*

"Yes, it answers all my questions. I want you to think about this, Alfie. Make sure it's what you want. I don't want you to ever feel regret."

Kissing her forehead, he smiled. "The only regret I'll ever have is not claiming you sooner. I was in love with you while I was still at Castello, and it's only grown since being here with you. There is nothing to think about."

Kissing her again, he moaned softly against her mouth, his cock aching to have her, and to feel her blood singing through his veins, but he knew they must wait. Breaking the kiss, and tugging at her hair, he chuckled. "Make sure you want a warrior. If you think you'll pull that temper tantrum shit on me, think again, red. I'll keep your beautiful ass in line."

Sophia laughed. "Really, warrior? You think you can tame what my father can't? I'd say make sure you're ready to take on a stubborn female who won't be so quick to obey. Make sure you're up for the challenge."

Alfie laughed, and it felt good to laugh with her, have her in his arms and know she'd never stray from him. Slapping her ass hard, he grinned. "This warrior is definitely up for the challenge. Never doubt that, red."

Pulling her down on the sofa next to him, he stretched out, and she lay beside him. "We have to think this through. It has to be planned, Sophia. We need time to be alone, and not rushed. We have to wait for the perfect opportunity, *sí*? Can you wait?"

"I can wait, but don't make me wait too long. You know my father has only allowed me to feed from females, even when Aislynn takes me to hunt. You'll be my first, and my last."

Winking, he took her face into his hands. "You're mine, Sophia. This is as it should be. It's getting late. People will notice I'm not in the barracks. We don't need to do anything that draws attention." Kissing her one last time, he made it last, sliding his tongue deep in her mouth, rolling it with hers. "I love you, Sophia Medici."

"And I love you. Get used to that name, Alfie. You'll be Medici now too, and not just because you serve the Medici as a warrior. My blood will run through your veins. You'll be my prince, and a Medici by blood."

You could have hit him with an ax. Alfie had never given much thought as to what it would actually mean to mate with her. He'd be a Prince. He'd be recorded as a full-fledged Medici. Not just a warrior but mated to a princess in the Medici royal blood line. A taste of fear ran through him wondering what Shade would think about it.

"I never thought that deep into this, Sophia. Damn, we'll need support here, because your father is going to fight this. Lorenzo knows I care about you. I must tell him what we plan, or he'll feel betrayed. If he supports this, he may be able to help us when the time comes to tell your parents."

Sophia shrugged. "You can tell Lorenzo. He'd never snitch on me. Don't freak out on me now, warrior! Besides, Natalia has already said she sees the two of us together. And I think my mom will be okay with it. She is already telling Daddy not to push me so hard. He won't kill you, Alfie. You'll be mated to me."

He chuckled uneasily. "Easy for you to say. He'd never lay a hand on you. Me, I've seen his wrath. He reacts first and thinks about it later. We can't afford that, red."

Cory came out of the bedroom, and Alfie and Sophia sat up quickly on the sofa, Alfie's cheeks turning red. Cory just shook his head. He knew the complications of hiding a relationship.

"Alfie, you need to get out of here now. Dad just asked if Sophia was over here and when I told him yes, he said he was sending Luca down to bring her home. Get out now, before Luca comes."

Alfie didn't think twice, kissing Sophia quickly on the cheek and teleporting out.

Sophia threw both hands in the air. "Well that's just great. We can't ever find the time to see each other. Just once I'd like to see him where I didn't feel like there was a clock ticking off the minutes."

Cory smiled at her. "You're young still, be patient."

Sophia huffed. "Patience. I wasn't born with that gift."

Luca appeared suddenly and gave her a sympathetic look. He was well aware of how tight a leash Shade had both his daughters on. "You ready?"

"I guess so."

Madison entered the room and stood next to Cory, slipping her arm around his waist. "Come back any time, Sophia. You know the door's always open."

She smiled. "I'll take you up on that if I can escape from prison. Come on, Luca. Do you need to hold my hand too?"

Luca gave her a half smile. "I am not your jailer, Sophia, just following orders."

They teleported out together, leaving Cory and Madison standing in their living room. Madison looked at him. "So, what do you think? Where's this going?"

Cory chuckled. "I don't know, but my money's on Sophia."

2-14

Another fall season was upon them, and the days were becoming shorter, the colors vibrant, and there was woodsy aroma in the air. Shade was awake. He loved the longer night hours, giving him more freedom and time to spend with his family. As soon as the electronic blinds opened, he slipped from bed and dressed, heading down the stairs to his office. He looked over the stacks of paper on the desk that detailed the plans and progress for the expansion into olive production Kate and Shannon had been working on. Luciano had done a good job of negotiating the purchase of some existing groves, which would allow them to jumpstart their business.

He heard their giggles and looked up to see his two daughters walking past the door. Gathering the papers, he placed them back inside their folder, and placed the folder inside the desk drawer. He'd finish looking at them later, but right now, he needed to speak with Sophia. He called out to them.

"Excuse me, but your *padre* sits alone in his office, working his ass off, and all the two of you can do is giggle and keep moving? What has both of you in such a hurry?" He heard Sophia sigh loudly as the girls stuck their heads in the doorway.

Sophia peered in at him. "We just assumed you were working. You're always working. I was going to see if Luca would escort me to Cory and Madison's for a while, since you never want to leave me unattended."

Steepling his hands together, with his elbows on his desktop, he nodded. "*Si*, I am always working, but that does not mean you need to not speak to me. Good evening to the both of you. And you, Nattie? Any plans for the night?"

"I was planning on doing some research on some of the other great covens and completing the family tree with the information I got from Council. And I was thinking I should write a letter to Enzo."

Shade smiled. "Always with your head in the books. Go, have a great evening. Sophia, please come inside, I need to speak with you alone."

Sophia rolled her eyes at Natalia, who gave her a small smile and mouthed the words 'good luck.' Sophia entered the office and took a seat on the large leather sofa. "What's up?"

He waited for her to get settled as he turned in his chair to face her. He'd put off this discussion, and he felt the need to take a firmer hand with her. She'd not shown an interest in any of the suitors he'd arranged for her to meet.

"I have arranged a meeting with the Rothschild family in Germany. They are a powerful coven, not as old as ours, but still strong, well respected. Hans Rothschild is very handsome, so I am told. They are not a royal blood line, but his father is a powerful master. This union would be an opportunity for us to extend our reach into Germany. Hans has agreed to the meeting, quite willingly, I might add. So, you will meet with him, sit and talk, let him give you a tour of their castle and their vast estates. You *will* go, and you *will* conduct yourself according to your station. I will escort you, of course. And Sophia, by the fires of hell, you better change your attitude. You must stop turning up your nose at these males and acting as if they are all beneath you. I grow damn weary of your superior attitude, and that flippant mouth. Hans is wealthy, intelligent, and highly educated. You would want for nothing."

Sophia hung her head. "Well, I would actually want for something."

Shade drew his eyebrows together. "Well, I would certainly love to know what the hell that might be, princess. Because if there is something specific the previous sons have lacked, perhaps it would be helpful for me to know what it is."

She looked up at him, her face showing a tinge of sadness. "Love, Daddy. You have introduced me to dozens of eligible males, all from good families, all rich and powerful in their own right. And they see me as a ticket to expand their power, to merge their dynasties with that of the Medici's. Not one of them cares about me personally. Not one of them has shown any real interest in getting to know who I am, what I like, what I want in life. I think about a life with them, and it feels hollow and empty. I want someone to love me, like you love Mommy. And I found that person in Alfie."

Shade blinked several times, staring at her. She did *not* just say Alfie. He thought that crush was long over. A deep laugh rose up from his gut, and he threw his head back and howled with laughter. "Oh, no way is that happening, princess. Alfie is a warrior. He belongs to me, and his future is already set in stone, Sophia. You need a mate, not a damn warrior. Alfie is destined to be your brother's SIC. He will spend his life in servitude to your brother. Let it go. Let it go now!"

He walked to where she sat on the sofa and placed his hands on her shoulders, gently pushing her back against the couch, his face mere inches from hers. He locked eyes with her and held her in his gaze so she couldn't look away. "Let go of this ridiculous notion that you love Alfie. You have clung to this fantasy far too long, *figlia*. No wonder you cannot find the mate who will satisfy your hunger for love. Stop daydreaming. It is not Alfie, and it never will be, *si*?"

She struggled against his grip. "Daddy, you said you wouldn't force me into a mating. You didn't mate into a powerful family. You didn't even mate an immortal. And you can't tell me not to love someone I already love. I don't understand why this is so important to you. You can't just wave your hand and say stop loving somebody. It doesn't work that way. It is Alfie, it will always be Alfie!"

The growl that erupted from him was loud and blew the hair around her face. He let go of her, but he felt like taking her across his knee. "I promised you choices, Sophia, and that is what I am giving you. But your choice must be made from among the children of masters. *Cazzo*! What your *madre* and I did has nothing to do with this, so drop that subject right now, female!"

He walked away from her, his fists at his side. "You have no damn idea what love is, princess. And what the hell makes you think Alfie cares about you, beyond a sisterly adoration? His future is set. He knows his station in life, he is a warrior. Alfie would never walk away from his calling to become a great warrior. It is what he was born to. He is one of the best warriors I have seen in a long time."

He dragged his hands through his hair and over his face, flopping down in his chair he shook his head at her. "No! You will go to the Rothschild's, and I swear, if you do not behave as you should, I will lock you down so damn tight you will feel that leash and collar around your neck. There is no argument. You go."

Sophia jumped to her feet and stormed out of the room. "You don't know anything about me! I'm not some breed mate you can just pawn off to the highest bidder. I'm not some pawn on your chessboard, helping you to gain a strategic advantage. I won't go! Not now, not ever!"

She slammed the door behind her and ran to her room. Kate heard the screaming and came out of the bedroom to see her daughter running down the hall. "Sophia?"

Her daughter didn't answer but ran to her room, closing the door firmly behind her. Kate heard the lock slide into place, followed by the sound of her daughter's sobs. Natalia opened her door, peered out, and saw the confusion on her mother's face. "Mommy, you have to do something. I'm telling you I've seen Sophia's future. She's with Alfie, not any of these males Daddy is insistent she mate with."

Kate looked torn but nodded her head. "I'll talk to him." She headed down the stairs to find Shade in his office, angry, and slamming things around on his desk. "Lover?"

His daughter's angry screams had only infuriated him more when she stormed out of his office. Mumbling in Italian, he opened and slammed the desk drawer and realized he couldn't concentrate on anything at the moment. Standing to pour a Midnight, he sloshed it out of the glass, onto the bar. Slamming the bottle back down, it only angered him more. He heard *bel's* voice, and before he could reel in his anger, he barked out at her. "What!"

He turned to face his *bel*, realizing none of this was her fault. "I am sorry. She has a foolish heart, *mi amore*. Foolish dreams of love. She told me she loves Alfie. Well, I crushed that idea of a happy little mating to dust. Oh, and she is refusing to go to the Rothschild's with me, flat out said no. To me!"

Kate moved into the room, saying nothing as she let him blow off steam. She poured him a glass of Midnight, wiping up the mess on the bar, and handed him the glass before she took a seat on the sofa, curling her feet under her. She was caught in an epic tug of war, between two of the most stubborn people she knew, her mate and her daughter.

"Perhaps we can talk about this?" Her voice was almost whisper soft. "Sit down please, drink, calm yourself so we can talk."

He took a deep draw from the Midnight and sat back in his leather chair. His head remained down, trying to get control of his temper. "What is there to talk about? She won't have any of this. She has pushed me far. Word is getting around about Sophia, and none of it positive. And now, Master Burkhart Rothschild tells me his son is quite intrigued to meet with my infamously insubordinate *figlia*. Do you have any idea what this mating could mean?"

Draining the Midnight from the glass, he slammed it down on the desk. "You need to talk to her. You will talk to her. You will make her understand that Alfie is not an option. And if she does not obey me, there will be consequences, and she will not like them one bit."

Kate bit her lip and sighed, laying her head back on the sofa. "Do you remember that first night, when I saw you at Alec and Rissa's? I took one look at you and knew my life was about to change. I didn't know how exactly, but when your hand touched mine, when you helped me with my coat, I couldn't even find my tongue to speak. I can see every second of it as if it happened only yesterday. I rushed home, feeling overwhelmed in your presence, like I couldn't breathe, and as soon as I was inside my condo, I missed you. I wished I had the courage to stay and talk to you. I spent the whole night wondering where you were, and if I'd ever see you again. Do you remember that?"

His looked over at her, her brown eyes showing a sparkle as memories of love shined through them. "I remember that vividly, *bel.* But Sophia is different. You have to admit that. This is a different situation. Alfie is my warrior. He is not going to mate. Does she even know how he feels? He probably pays her no mind whatsoever."

Slamming his fist on the desk, he stood up and walked to the window, opening it to let in the cool night air. "I am sending him back to Castello. Out of sight, out of mind. I would have preferred he had more training here, but she leaves me no damn choice. I am tired of being ruled by my own daughter. I won't have this, Kate, you cannot change my mind. And when you speak with her, let her know one thing. I am done playing this little game. It is time for her to choose her mate, or I will choose one for her, and she will like it. I am not threatening her, I am dead serious."

"So, your daughter has no say in this? Why do I feel like this same conversation took place centuries ago, between your father and your mother? I can hear Christofano insisting you mate the Alizzi. Had your mother not stood up to him, you would not be here today, mated to me. And why can a warrior not mate? Luca is mated. It has not hindered his abilities to perform as a warrior. Do you see Shannon as beneath you? A mortal, so, therefore, only good enough for a common warrior? How do you think that makes me feel?"

He spun on his heels so fast it made the curtains billow out from the window. "I have never thought such a thing. Luca is not Alfie. And our daughter is royal blood, or have you forgotten that? This is serious. Alfie has a responsibility to this coven, and to our son. You and your memories, you seem to forget the nights of me coming home bloodied, and you wondering what I had done. Have you forgotten that? Is that what you want for our daughter?"

She locked eyes with him, "I have forgotten nothing. Not one night. I remember every battle, and every night you came home covered in blood. I remember some bitch in black leather that was prepared to remove me as if I was nothing more than an inconvenience that stood between herself and you, and this demon that crawled up from hell, and into my bedroom window, intent on ending my life. I remember the baby we lost, and the agony of being turned. Now, ask me if I would change any of it. Because I also remember the love, and the passion, and our children, and this life we have built. Neither of us planned this love. It made no sense for us to mate but love rarely makes sense. You have to let her go, Shade. You have to let her find her own path."

He watched as her beast rose up, and her argument was a fine one. But she'd been a mortal, and still didn't understand the full implications of their mating. The coven had expectations and needs that must be fulfilled in order to sustain them all. He raised himself to his full height, straightening his shoulders.

"I am the Medici, the King of the coven. Our daughter is the first-born Princess to the dynasty I rule. The decision is made. You will go talk to her and explain the following. She will travel with me to meet with Hans Rothschild, and Master Burkhart and his mate. We will stay there several days and nights, as their honored guests. She will conduct herself according to her station. If Hans makes a proposal for her hand, she mates. Hans was my top choice from day one and remains so. I refuse to see our daughter waste her life, waiting on a warrior to return to her when he has time. If she refuses to comply with my wishes, she will be assigned a personal protector, and Luca will be relieved of his duty to her. She will not move without her protector. Her path will be guided by me. Go talk to her."

Kate knew it was pointless to argue with him when he took a stand, but she knew this battle wasn't over. The only person more stubborn than Shade was Sophia. "I'll deliver your message, but don't be surprised when your daughter rebels."

"Like I said, if she does not comply, she will pray to the devil himself that she had. Our other two children know their path, and both will rise to exalted heights, providing power and strength to the Medici coven. Sophia has no clue as to what her destiny is. She is too busy fighting me at every step. Well, the fight is about to get real up close and personal."

He leaned over the sofa and kissed her. "I am going into D.C. tonight, Alfie is working the Dead House, and he is going to get his orders to leave Bel Rosso and return to Castello. I will be late coming home." He walked from the office, heading to the back door.

Kate leaned her head back against the sofa, her eyes closed. *How can a man who loves so passionately be so blind to what is happening right before his eyes?*

2-15

Shade teleported directly out of the house and straight to the Dead House in D.C. The exterior of the old house had remained unchanged, but throughout the years, the inside had been upgraded to include the latest in security and monitoring technology. Shade now used GPS monitors on every warrior when they were on the streets, so it was possible to see exactly where they were, tracking their movements on the grid maps that appeared on the monitors. It made the response time to any situation that developed much quicker, guaranteeing no single warrior could be ambushed. Once Alec had been banned by Council and forced to go underground for the next century, the D.C. territory, along with Alec's other territories in Connecticut, Maryland, and Delaware had become Shade's. As he took full ownership, he'd taken on the project of renovating the interior of the Dead House, including the addition of showers for the warriors to use when coming off the streets, as well as a bunk room for any warrior who chose to stay there for their slumber. The basement had been renovated to include steel-walled cells for any rogues, but few ever survived long enough to be held there. In his history of ruling the Medici coven, not once had he ever relinquished territory, and he had no plans to change that history.

He let go of his temper a bit while teleporting. Still, he hated the idea of having to remove one of his best warriors from the Bel Rosso training camp because of his daughter, but she left him no choice. He headed straight to the upper floors where the main control center was located and found his SIC, Theo, keeping a close eye on all the action. Theo turned as he entered the large room.

"Hey, Master. Wasn't expecting you tonight. Anything wrong?"

Shade shook his head no and flopped down in one of the chairs facing the grid monitors. Theo had been running the Dead House for so long he was a permanent fixture here, and Shade trusted him with his life. "I need to speak with Alfie, reel him in, get a replacement for him for his grid sector. He won't be coming back."

Theo looked a bit confused. "Damn boss, what the hell did he do? He's one kick ass warrior out there."

Shade smiled. "He didn't do anything wrong. I just need him back at Castello with Lorenzo as soon as possible." Shade stood and patted Theo on the shoulder. "I will be outside having a smoke, then heading back to camp."

As he strode outside, lighting up, Theo called in Alfie, telling him to move his ass, master was waiting.

***

Alfie was sitting on a rooftop near the campus of Georgetown University, keeping his senses peeled for anything unusual, although it was still a little early in the night for rogues to be out hunting. They liked to wait until the bars let out and they had easy pickings. He'd come to enjoy his assignments in D.C. It was so different than anywhere he'd ever been. As he heard Theo give him orders, he felt his heart leap to his throat. *Fuck, Shade has gotten wind of his and Sophia's secret meetings.* He teleported out, his mind racing as fast as his body, as he started to formulate an explanation. He circled several times and saw Shade outside the Dead House smoking. He landed in front of Shade, ready to face whatever wrath he laid before him.

Shade felt him circling, and when he landed, he sensed his fear. "Having a good night?"

Alfie took a deep breath and prepared for everything and anything. He calmed his breathing, but his heart was pounding. "Slow, always slow this early. But fine other than that."

Shade flung the butt of his cigarette to the ground and looked at Alfie. So, his daughter was in love with the warrior before him. He'd never understand it. "Look, I'll get straight to the point, I have things to do tonight, and so do you. I am sending you back to Castello. You leave tomorrow, as soon as dusk hits. I need you more there than here. Go straight back to Bel Rosso now, pack all your things and be ready to go, *si*? Your SICs have been informed."

Alfie felt the air leave his lungs. No! He didn't want to go back, not without his red. Questions rose in his mind. Why, what had happened? Did he know about Sophia, did something happen to Lorenzo? Before he could open his mouth, Shade disappeared. Alfie shook his head and wondered if he dreamed it, but his emotions told him this was all too real. He teleported back to camp to find Marcello.

Marcello was in the office, going over some schedules with Aislynn. He saw Alfie land on the training field. Shade had already told him Alfie was going back but offered no explanation as to why.

Marcello knew something was up, but he didn't question the orders.

"Aislynn, go out to the field. I need to speak with Alfie alone." She nodded and rubbed shoulders with Alfie as she left, feeling the tension in the room. Her gut told her this was related to Sophia.

Alfie entered and leaned on the desk in front of Marcello. "Why am I being sent back? What happened, what did I do?"

"Nothing that I know of, Alfie, master just said he needed you back at Castello, your training here is done."

Alfie paced around the small office. "Just like that, I'm done? He said nothing else?"

Marcello shook his head. "No. Does he have a reason to send you back?"

Alfie sighed. "No. But you'll tell me if you hear anything?"

Marcello shrugged. "Sure, brother. We got no secrets."

He teleported out, heading straight to Cory's workshop. Landing inside, Cory looked up, startled. "What in hell are you in such a hurry for?"

Alfie locked eyes with Cory. "Your dad is sending me back to Castello. Did he say anything to you? Does he know about me and Sophia?"

Cory sighed. "I don't know what he knows, Alfie, but he hasn't heard anything from me, or Madison. I don't know what's going on. So keep your cool, and do whatever he tells you to do, brother."

"Right, just keep my cool." He teleported out as fast as he flew in and landed inside his room in the barracks. How the hell was he going to let Sophia know what's going on? He needed to see her before he left. He couldn't just leave without saying goodbye to her. His heart was hammering and breaking, all at the same time. What had he done?

***

Shannon was going over the deeds for the new olive groves they had just purchased. They would start cultivation on existing property that Luciano had identified as being good soil for new groves but buying the established groves would allow them to enter the market quickly. It was all a part of their business plan.

"So, we have completed the purchase of these five groves. We only have two left that Luciano is still negotiating with the seller.

He said the negotiations were going well and he should have that wrapped up in a week or so."

Kate was staring out the window, biting her lip, when she realized Shannon was speaking to her. "I'm sorry, what?"

Shannon gave her a quizzical look. "Hello, earth to Kate. You haven't heard a word I've said tonight. What's bothering you, and don't say nothing? I know better."

She shook her head. "It's just...Shade, and Sophia."

Shannon laid the deeds down on the desk. "Okay, well, spill it, because clearly, we aren't going to get any of this stuff done until you do."

Kate turned and looked at her. "You know about Sophia's crush on Alfie, right?"

Shannon stared back at her. "Crush? Is that what we're calling it these days? Yes, I am aware that your daughter is head over heels in love with the warrior. And in case you haven't noticed, his feelings are mutual. Luca has explained to me that Shade is not happy about it, although, for the life of me, I can't figure out why. Who would be better for Sophia than Alfie?"

Kate sighed heavily, leaning against the desk. "Shade won't have it. He's insistent about her mating with the son from one of the great families. I think he's even more adamant now that he knows Natalia will be going to Council."

Shannon huffed. "Well that's just stupid. You know Alfie loves her, right?"

Kate looked at her, her expression showing the internal conflict of trying to please her mate and her daughter. "Does he?"

Shannon looked at her with exasperation. "Oh my god, Kate. I can't believe we're having this conversation. He can't take his eyes off her whenever they're in the same space together. She's been writing to him since she was four years old, for Pete's sake. He looks at her like he just discovered the crown jewels or something."

Kate closed her eyes. "Shade is sending him back to Castello, and I have to tell Sophia. He thinks if he sends Alfie back, she will get over it."

Shannon put both hands over her face and mock screamed. "Kate, this is crazy, and you know it."

She nodded. "He's made up his mind. He's sending Alfie back, and the arrangements have been made to visit the Rothschild's."

Shannon shook her head. "Well, good luck with that. But, just for the record, I think you're making a mistake."

Kate walked from the room to find her daughter. "I know we're making a mistake. I just don't know how to convince him otherwise."

Kate made her way up the stairs and stood at the door to her daughter's bedroom, tapping on the door.

Sophia yanked the door open. "Oh, my jailer. Come to let me out of my cell?"

Kate gave her a pained look. "Sophia, I'm not your jailer."

Sophia flopped down on her bed. "Could have fooled me."

Kate felt pushed to tears but knew she couldn't cry in front of Sophia. Shade had decided, and she was here to deliver the information. "I thought you should know your father is sending Alfie back to Castello."

Sophia leapt off the bed. "What! Why, Mommy? Alfie has done nothing wrong!"

Kate tried to calm her, but her daughter pulled away. "Alfie's not being punished. Your father thinks if he's sent back to Castello, you'll get over this attraction to him."

Sophia knocked the lamp from her dresser, watching it crash to the floor. "Get over him? Get over him? Like a bad cold or something? Mommy stop him! I know you can!"

Kate ignored the outburst, and the broken lamp. "Sophia, I can't. He's already decided. Alfie is leaving."

Sophia's eyes were wide with horror, as she rushed past Kate, almost knocking her down, as she left the room. Kate turned to call after her, but Sophia teleported out, with the cry of "Alfie!" on her lips.

Sophia teleported to the camp, desperate to get to him before he left. She had no idea where he was, so she landed in the middle of the training field, right into the middle of the warriors training. The warriors stopped on a dime, swords held above their heads, or mid swing as their master's daughter landed hard in their midst. Sophia looked around for him. She saw her father, looking back at her in anger, when she took off running for the barracks.

"Alfie! Where are you?"

She saw him emerge from the barracks, a look of confusion on his face, and she ran straight to him, throwing her arms around him. "Alfie! I love you. Don't let them do this."

Alfie saw her barreling toward him. *What the hell is she doing?* They were surely asking for their deaths now. Sophia ran headlong into his arms, sobbing, and he could see Shade heading for the both of them, full steam, and he knew only one thing, he'd protect her with his life.

"Shh, calm down. Come on, Red. Relax. Screaming and fighting is not going to help the situation, and certainly not going to calm your father who is heading right for us."

Alfie held her to his chest tightly and held up his hand for Shade to see. "Please. Let me speak to her, Master. I beg you. She'll listen to me. Please."

Shade was seeing red and his eyes were blazing with fire. His fangs had punched, and his beast was angry as hell. What the fuck was she doing in the middle of the camp? He was moving like a steam roller straight at Alfie when he saw his hand up and could barely hear his words for the anger boiling in his veins.

"She has disobeyed me. You are standing on thin ice, warrior. Do not push me. It will be your death."

Sophia screamed back at him. "Daddy, stop. Stop it! He didn't ask me to come here. He didn't even know I was coming. Please stop!" She was sobbing out of control and hated that the decisions that would determine the rest of her life were being decided by others. "Don't ever touch him! I love him! Why is that so hard for you to understand? If you want me to mate with that stupid Hans, I'll do it, but leave him alone!"

Alfie heard her words and knew she'd do anything to save his ass. And in that moment, he knew he'd do the same for her. She was his mate. "Sophia, stop talking. It's okay, let me deal with this."

Alfie's eyes never left his master's. "Master, I am a warrior, under your charge. Your daughter is upset, in tears. I ask you, as a Medici warrior, to let me speak with her alone. I am honorable, loyal and would never disrespect your orders. But if you don't let me speak to her, she will only keep trying, putting herself in danger. I know Sophia, I know how she is. So, please, allow me to calm her. It's all I ask before I leave."

Sophia sobbed against the warrior's chest, and Shade knew he was right, his daughter wouldn't stop. Reluctantly, he nodded his head. "Take her inside the house, speak with her. But this changes nothing. You are returning to Castello."

"*Grazie*, master." He picked up Sophia and teleported straight to the house, before she could open her mouth, and blow the one chance they had at saying goodbye.

***

Kate was on her knees in the hallway, sobbing, when Shannon came up the stairs. "What happened?"

Kate answered through her tears. "She left. To find Alfie, I'm sure. Do you think I should send Luca to find her?"

Shannon knelt down and hugged her friend. "Well, if she went to the camp, Shade will find her."

Kate looked up at her. "I don't know what to do, Shan. He's never been so resistant to even hearing another point of view." The air crackled around them, as Alfie landed in the hallway, holding a hysterical Sophia in his arms. The two women look up at him.

"Master gave me permission to say goodbye to her, and to calm her."

Kate nodded, and pointed to Sophia's bedroom. "There, you'll have some privacy."

He carries her into the bedroom, and kicked the door closed behind him. Shannon helped Kate from the floor.

"Come on, give them space. I don't know about you, but I could use a drink." She led Kate downstairs, and away from her daughter.

***

With Sophia in his arms, he carried her to the bed and laid her down. Stripping off his leather jacket, he lay down beside her as she curled into him.

"Don't say anything, Red. You need to listen to what I say. It's important." He tipped up her chin as the blood tears still streamed down her cheeks. Kissing her softly, he smiled at her. Taking her hand, he laid it across his heart. "Listen to my heart. Hear my words. We're never going to get anywhere if we keep fighting him. He's angry, and he can't see straight because of anger. So, here's my plan. I'm going back to Castello. Don't worry, you know I love you, I'm yours, Sophia. Stop resisting him, do what he asks, see who he wants you to see. This will buy us time to figure out what to do. You can do this."

She nodded her head as he spoke. "Just promise me that you won't give up on me. Once we're mated, he'll have to accept it. I know he'll come around."

He kissed her lightly. "We'll be together soon. I promise. I love you, Sophia Medici. Promise you'll never stop loving me."

"I'll never stop loving you, Alfie. I've always known you were mine."

Sitting up, he got off the bed. "So, come say goodbye to your warrior. It may be a while until we see each other again. Don't cry. We'll find a way."

She hugged him like it might be the last time she saw him. "I won't say goodbye. That's too final. I'll just say I love you."

"That's the spirit. Keep posting me letters, through Aislynn, and I'll send my answers back through her as well. No one will know. And you need to go to your mom, she's upset, she loves you both and is stuck in the middle."

He hugged her to his chest, his heart feeling like it would break, but hiding his pain from her. "I love you, Sophia." He walked to the door and teleported out, feeling like he'd left his whole world behind him.

2-16

Alfie reported to Marco immediately on his return. Marco knew to expect him, but had no idea why he'd been sent back, only that Shade said he'd completed his training. Alfie knew the real reason was to place distance between him and the master's daughter. But Alfie and Sophia had their own plans.

Marco assigned Alfie a bunk inside the barracks, apologizing, knowing he'd been given a private room at the Bel Rosso camp. Alfie shrugged it off. "Don't worry about it. I'll be fine." Throwing his gear down on the bed, he headed out to see his best friend. He needed to tell him what happened back in the States. Landing in front of the massive door to Castello, Antonio opened the door before he could knock, and escorted him inside. "Prince Lorenzo is on the upper floor."

Alfie took the marble stairs two at a time as he raced up to Lorenzo's room, and was startled to encounter him in the hallway. "Bro!"

Lorenzo looked up to see his best friend approaching. "Alfie? What are you doing here? Is everything okay at Bel Rosso?"

"No, everything is *not* okay. Don't panic, nothing's wrong with the family, except Sophia and your father are having it out. There are some things I need to talk to you about. I need a drink, a heavy one, and some of your time."

Lorenzo nodded, not sure he liked what he was hearing. "Sure, let's go back to my room. I'll have Antonio send up a bottle."

He slapped his friend on the back as he led him to the bedroom, and within seconds, a staff member was carrying in a tray of Midnight and a couple of glasses. Lorenzo plopped down in a chair. "I was just going over to see the Alizzi, but I'll send word something has come up. Take a load off, brother, and tell me what went down."

Alfie bristled when he heard the name Alizzi. He wished he could tell Lorenzo all he knew about her. But that was another time and place, and it had been years ago. "Why are you still putting up with Dona? I thought you said you wanted her to cut the apron strings?"

"I've been assigned to her territory. I had been assigned to all the posts in Tuscany, and Marco wanted me to be familiar with Umbria. It's our responsibility to protect her as well. Besides, Dona's not so bad. But we didn't come here to talk about her. What happened that ended your ass back here, brother?"

Alfie downed the entire glass of Midnight, and then refilled his glass. He took a deep breath, hoping he wasn't about to hang himself with what he revealed to Lorenzo. "I've fallen in love. She's the one. She's my mate. But there's one very large problem." He looked up at Lorenzo to gauge his reaction.

Lorenzo held up his hand. "Back up, brother. You're moving too fast. Who have you fallen in love with?"

Alfie couldn't keep the smile off his face, just saying her name made him happy. "Princess Sophia Medici."

Lorenzo wasn't completely surprised. He knew his sister had been chasing after Alfie for years, and he'd known Alfie had a fondness for her, but love? Lorenzo downed his glass. "Yeah, well, that explains a lot. You know my dad is going to push her to mate a master's son. He hasn't started on me yet, to the same degree as he has with Sophia, but he's told me when I think I'm ready to mate, I need to look at the daughters of masters, and if I can find royal blood, even better. I'll make sure I've sown my wild oats before I settle down, but I don't have a problem with it. I'm sure I can find a mate who will keep our bloodline strong. "He looked back at Alfie. "So, what are you going to do, bro? You look miserable."

Alfie bolted out of the chair, downing another Midnight and began talking. "I didn't mean to fall in love with her, Lorenzo, but it happened. We met when we could. I never did anything to her. I give you my oath. I never crossed the line with her, and I knew she was off-limits, we both did, but it happened anyway. I can't explain it. Cory and Madison offered to let us meet at their house when time allowed. It was close, and we could be alone, without being caught. Then everything just blew up, brother. Your father knows she's in love with me, and now he's pushing her hard to mate. She got angry at him, and he sent my ass back, trying to separate us. He's trying to drive us apart, but it won't work. He can't see she'll be happy with me. No one can get through to him, not even your mother. *Cazzo*, Lorenzo, I love her so much. Your crazy sister landed in the middle of the camp training field and he was standing right there. She was screaming for me, hysterical, when she found out he was sending me back. I thought he might kill me!"

Lorenzo poured himself another glass and took a long drink as he listened to his friend. "Wow. I don't know what to tell you, Alfie. Dad's going to stand his ground. You'd think after mating a mortal he'd have more tolerance, but I think it's the opposite. He mated with his heart, and not his head, and he thinks if he allows his progeny to do the same, the bloodline will become too diluted. He thinks the coven needs to see a strong bloodline to feel secure in the Medici leadership. My mom can usually soften his views on a lot of things, but I don't think she'll be much help to you on this one. This has been drilled into us since we were children, and with Natalia going to Council, that's one less of his children who will breed, so he'll feel even stronger about our choices for a mate. Maybe you'll get over her. I mean, it's not like we experience a shortage of females, brother."

Alfie felt his beast rise up. "Get over her? Great, I'm spilling my guts to you about the female who my beast already knows belongs to me for eternity, and you want me to get over her? Let me tell you something, Lorenzo, when the right one walks into your life, come talk to me about getting over her."

Alfie headed for the door, thinking this had been a really bad idea to tell his lifelong friend. He stopped at the door and turned. "You're my best friend, so I won't keep this from you, but we're going to mate. No one will know when or where, but it's going to happen."

Lorenzo stood up so quickly he spilled his drink. "Wait, what? Get back in here, warrior! What do you mean you're going to mate?"

Alfie spun on his heels, facing his best friend. They'd been through so much together, but now Lorenzo was pulling rank. "I thought you'd understand. I needed to tell someone I could trust. I know I'm only a warrior, believe me. But I didn't choose to fall in love with her. She's just Sophia to me, not a princess, not the daughter of a master, and we're going to mate. What is master going to do once it is done? I'll go to my death if I must, but I'll go there knowing she'll forever be mine. I need you to be my friend. I need you to help me."

Lorenzo was angry at being caught in the middle, he loved Alfie, but he worshiped his father. "Sit down, Alfie. Just because I'm pissed doesn't mean we're not still friends. I've never been in love, so I can't say I understand what you feel. I'm a pragmatist when it comes to love. I mean, I've grown up watching my parents, and I know what they have is rare. I don't expect to find it for myself. I mean, I won't mate someone I don't love, but look around, how many couples are bonded like my parents?" He paced the floor, running both hands through his hair. "I'll talk to my sister. If this is what the both of you want, then I won't stand in the way. I won't help you, but I'll keep my mouth shut. Jesus, Alfie, you know my sister is a handful, right?"

Alfie grinned back at him. "Yes, but she's my handful." He walked back into the room and flopped down in a chair. He was so tired. "I just need you on our side, Lorenzo, I'm not asking you to defy your father. I'm just asking that you not say anything. I promised her I'd make it happen."

Lorenzo shook his head. "I'll give you one thing, brother, you never choose the easy path. If this is what you want, if this is what my sister wants, then I'll stand beside you. Once the deed is done, he'll be forced to accept it, but don't expect him to like it. Shit, Alfie, he won't kill you, but you might wish he had. All I can say, brother, is you better produce some grandchildren for him really fast."

Alfie laid his head back and laughed. "I'll do my part, brother." Looking back at him, his face serious now, he responded. "I am so damn tired, Lorenzo. I have to let this take its course, let him calm down. But I appreciate you standing beside me. I never thought about how mating your sister would put you in the middle. How it would make you feel. But I know one thing, when we come home from battle, she's the one I want to come home to."

"Seriously, Alfie, you make me glad I only have to go through this once. But hey, it's your life. If this makes you and Sophia happy, who am I to judge?" Lorenzo laughed. "A whole world full of females, and you have to fall in love with this one. At least Sophia will be good training for my SIC."

They both stood and hugged, slapping each other on the back. "I heard what you said about being pragmatic, but someday, Lorenzo, the female you're meant for is going to knock your ass right out from under you. And you'll be beating my door down, asking me what the hell to do. I can't wait. I love her, brother, and she loves me. I'm heading back to the barracks. I need sleep, and I don't want to hold you up any longer from Dona. Tell her I said hello."

2-17

Kate had talked with her daughter, informing her that her father was moving ahead with his plans to set up a meeting with the Rothschild family. She knew, before she spoke the words, it wouldn't go well. Sophia had screamed, and cried, and slammed things around the room, yelling that it wasn't fair. And Kate agreed, it wasn't, but she couldn't say that right now. She'd argued with Shade on this issue until she was blue in the face, and he wasn't budging.

"Sophia, just go. Try to be cordial. Give me time to figure this out."

Sophia was near hysteria. "I'm running out of time, Mommy! He wants me mated."

Kate soothed her, but she was inconsolable, and asked to be alone. Kate nodded and left the room, closing the door behind her.

***

Shade walked slowly back to the house. It had been a very long night. He'd not expected the drama on the training field, when Sophia suddenly appeared, in hysterics over Alfie. He was certain Alfie's absence would be better for them both. It would give Sophia time to get over this insane idea she was in love with him and get her mind back in the game. He was determined she'd find the appropriate mate, and that mate would be Hans Rothschild. Shade would make sure of it. The sun was coming up quickly over the horizon and he hurried to the house, slamming the door a bit louder than usual. He was filthy, and bone tired. He stopped in his office and had a large glass of Red Moon before going upstairs to their bedchamber. All night, he'd felt the pain and frustration coming from Kate, and knew she was caught between him and their daughter. But she was his mate, and she needed to understand he was going to secure the Medici bloodline one way or another. As he topped the stairs, he saw her exiting Sophia's room. She looked up at him and their eyes locked. "I haven't changed my mind, Kate."

She looked back at him, her face not showing much emotion. "I'm aware, so is your daughter. You can force your hand here, if that's your decision, but you can't force her to like it." She walked past him and into their bedroom.

Sighing heavily, he followed her into their bedroom. "I don't want to fight about this with you. But you do realize securing our blood line is important, *si*? And she'll grow to love Hans, as soon as she gets this notion out of her head about Alfie."

Kate turned to look at him, and started to speak, but knew this was an argument she couldn't win. She shook her head and felt her daughter's pain. "I'm going to take a shower."

Shade stared after her as she walked to the bathroom. "Please, Kate, don't make this a wedge between us. I am going to speak with Sophia now."

He got no reply from Kate as she closed the bathroom door. Damn, the females had him in knots this night. He strode with a sure footing to Sophia's room and the closed door. Standing there for a moment or two, he didn't know what the hell he'd say. By the fires of hell, he wanted at least one of them speaking to him before the slumber took him. He knocked several times on the door. "Sophia, open the door, please."

Sophia got off her bed and wiped her tears, swinging open the door, she glared at him. "Seriously? You ask permission to enter my room, but you think it's okay to dictate who I mate? Say what you want to say, Dad. My opinion clearly means nothing."

He entered her bedroom and took a seat in a chair too delicate for his frame. He looked at her. She'd been crying and was disheveled looking. Her voice was angry and defiant.

"Princess, I know everything I am trying to do makes no sense to you. But I do this because I want you to end up being happy with your mate and making the Medici coven strong. I can sit here all night and speak, but you will not hear me. I have listened to you. And tonight, when you landed in camp, proclaiming your love for the warrior, I did not hear him say the same. He never asked me not to send him back to Castello, he never made a plea of me. Why? Because he is a warrior, and he knows his destiny. I will move forward with the plans to make your introduction to Hans Rothschild. I will escort you to Germany. Prepare yourself, and make sure this is a cordial visit."

Sophia muttered, “Fine.” She already had her plans in place with Alfie. They’d be mated, and then there would be nothing he could do about it. The harder she fought against him, the deeper he’d dig in his heels. Best to let him think she’d go along with his plan. "Whatever you say, Dad."

He sighed. Her compliance came too easy. Standing, he walked to her bedside, but she refused to look at him. Gripping her chin softly, she finally looked back.

"*Grazie*, princess. I love you very much. I know you don’t feel that right now, but I do. I’ve always loved you with everything I have, Sophia, I always will. Nothing you ever do will change that. Remember that." He kissed her on the cheek. "Good night."

Sophia didn’t respond, but buried her face in her pillow, hoping he’d leave her room. She felt him turn to leave. "Turn out my light, please." He’d slip into his death slumber soon, and maybe she could find a friendly shoulder to cry on in Shannon.

He flicked the light switch off and left her room, closing the door behind him. He thought being a *padre* was tough when they were just babies, but this was worse. Making his way back to the bedroom, he found Kate still in the shower. He stripped down quickly, tossing the dusty leathers aside and joined her there. The water cascaded over both of them, as he slid his arms around her waist, pulling her close. "I am sorry, *mi amore*."

“I know. I know you’re making the decision you think is best for her, but I disagree. I think this is a mistake, but I won’t fight you. I’ve always said you lead, and I’ll follow. You’ve made this a hard choice, placing me between two people I love more than life, but I’ll comply with your wishes."

He stood still as she soaped up her hands, and gently washed him. He felt the air go from his lungs. Her touch still had the power to leave him breathless. He lifted his face to the water, and felt it wash away the chaos of this night.

"She is a mature female, and yet I struggle every day with her. I cannot struggle with you too, *bel*, for it will break me inside. I need you like the air I breathe.”

She felt her daughter’s pain, but she felt his more, and wrapped her arms around him as he lowered his head to feed.

2-18

Lorenzo had been assigned to Umbria for over a month now. It was one of the most boring assignments he'd ever had. The last battle for Umbria took place when his grandfather was alive, and Christofano led the Medici warriors against the Borgia coven. The Borgia's remained an enemy to the Medici, but they had kept to themselves, ruling in Rome and Southern Italy. The two covens, being of equal size and power, reached a peace agreement that had survived for centuries, deciding it was in the best interest of their respective covens to leave well enough alone. So far, the treaty had held, and the Borgia's ruled most of Southern Italy, while the Medici's had stayed in Tuscany, providing protection to neighboring Umbria, and all regions to the north, while expanding their grasp in other lands, like France, Greece, and now, the United States.

At least once a week, he'd be summoned by Dona to come by and help her with some errand. Lorenzo was amused by the request, as the errand could easily be performed by her house staff. He knew the Alizzi was just lonely, and wanted his company, so he wasn't surprised tonight, in the middle of his shift, when he received a message from her to help carry down a trunk from the attic. He let his brothers know he'd be at her villa if they needed him and teleported out.

He landed at her door and the butler answered, bowing to him as he entered. Wearing his black leathers, his dark hair brushing his shoulders, he entered the hall, his boots clicking on the granite floors. The butler showed him to the parlor, and poured him a glass of Midnight, letting him know the Alizzi would be with him shortly. Lorenzo sat down and took a sip of the much-needed drink, before laying his head back on the chair, closing his eyes. He heard the click of her heels as she approached, and looked up to see her enter, wearing a white satin night gown, that clung to her figure, and dusted the floor. The white gown emphasized her dark skin, and even darker hair.

"I see you have a drink already. Do you need a second round?"

Lorenzo smiled back at her. "No, I'm good, and I'm on duty."

She waved her hand, as if it were nothing. "Nothing ever happens here. We'll be fine."

She sat across from him, crossing her legs in a deliberately slow movement that he didn't miss. "What did you need me to do, Dona?"

She clapped her hands. "I have this old trunk, it's in the attic. It is full of things I have collected over the years. Nothing of any real value. I had almost forgotten about it until I found an old photo in my desk the other day, and it brought back some memories, and then I remembered the old trunk. Do you think you could carry in down from the attic for me?"

He emptied the glass and sat it down on the table. "Of course, just show me where it is."

She jumped to her feet and grabbed his hand, leading him through the villa and up two flights of stairs to a musty attic. She flipped on a light switch to reveal the usual collection of discarded items that should have been thrown away centuries ago. "It's up here somewhere. Oh, there it is. The big wooden chest, see it?"

He nodded and lifted the heavy chest as if it weighed nothing and carried it back down to the parlor. She scurried along beside him, trying to keep up with his long stride.

"Where do you want it?"

She brushed past him into the parlor. "Just set it here, near the sofa."

She took a seat on the sofa, as he set the trunk in front of her and she started to grapple with the lock, lifting the lid, as the hinges creaked, and several hundred years of dust slid off the lid and onto the floor. Lorenzo was dusting his hands off on his thighs when she smiled up at him.

"Sit next to me, please."

He paused a moment. "Dona, I'm on duty. I should get back."

"Oh, pish posh, you're on duty protecting me. What better place to protect me than right here?"

She patted the sofa next to her, indicating she wanted him to take a seat, and called for the butler to bring him another drink. Lorenzo sat next to her as she started to dig through the trunk, pulling out old letters, invitations, and newspaper clippings. He sipped at the wine while she took a trip down memory lane.

"Look, Carnivale!" She pulled out a brittle poster, with a date in the 1700's, announcing the gala event. "Have you ever been to Carnivale in Venice?"

Lorenzo shook his head. "I've been to Venice, but never during Carnivale."

She laid her hand on his thigh. "Oh Lorenzo, we must go! I went with your father many times. We had such adventures there, the three of us."

Lorenzo scrunched his brow. "The three of you? You mean Marco?"

Dona threw her head back and laughed. "Oh heavens no. We would always go to Carnivale with Casanova."

Lorenzo almost choked on his drink. Why should he be surprised his dad knew Casanova? "Casanova? Really? He never speaks of it."

Dona leaned against his shoulder and giggled like a schoolgirl. "Well, of course not. He is mated, and I doubt, seriously, your mother would want to hear these stories."

Lorenzo shook his head, not sure he wanted to hear them either. Dona picked up an elaborate face mask and held it to her face. Only her eyes were showing, and she was instantly unrecognizable behind the alluring mask. "Your father learned much from Casanova."

Lorenzo took another sip of his drink, as he chuckled. "Yeah, I'm sure."

She set the mask aside and sipped from her own drink. "Casanova was a master of seduction. He made every woman feel beautiful and extraordinary, whether they were young or old, virgin or experienced. He reveled in sex, rooting like a pig looking for truffles. He was addicted to seduction, to the chase. Venice was ruled by the elite, but during Carnivale, the barriers between rich and poor would fall, and the entire city would dive headfirst into debauchery. The mask is a great equalizer," she held the mask over her face again to make the point, "allowing for plenty of anonymous sex. The mask conceals everything, your face, and your features. It even distorts your voice."

He listened to her muffled voice from behind the mask before she lowered it again.

"You can be anyone, Lorenzo, and you can *have* anyone. There is no more perfect celebration for a vampire. Once in costume, the wearer can shed all their inhibitions, and behave in a way they would never consider during their normal life. Even priests and nuns would sneak out, breaking their vows of celibacy. Anything and everything can happen under the cloak of a masquerade."

Lorenzo had seen enough debauchery in his young life, it wasn't hard to imagine. "How did you meet him, Casanova?"

Dona shrugged. "I don't recall the details. Some grand ball. Your father noticed him first, because Casanova was moving through the women even faster than he was." She laughed at the memories. "They became fast friends. Casanova loved he had met a vampire. It was all so exotic to him. Years later, when Casanova was imprisoned–"

Lorenzo looked up. "He was imprisoned?"

Dona fanned herself with a delicate lace fan she removed from the trunk. "Oh yes, darling. It was over something ridiculous, like cheating at cards and displeasing the government. I think the charges were just a front as he was, in fact, banging the judge's wife, but he was sent to the Doge's prison for five years. Of course, your father heard of his plight, and helped him escape. They left Venice on a gondola, and Casanova moved to Paris, and later, Amsterdam, and London. He never returned to Venice."

Lorenzo slapped his knee, laughing hard. "I never read that in Enzo's history books."

"It's all there, darling, the imprisonment, the escape, minus your father, of course."

Lorenzo couldn't stop laughing when he felt her hand on his thigh. "Oh, promise me, Lorenzo, you'll go with me to Venice. We'll go together to Carnivale. Please, it has been centuries since I have been."

Lorenzo smiled back at her. "Dona, I'd be glad to carry on the tradition, and walk in my father's footsteps. Carnivale it is." He raised his glass to her, and she clinked her glass to his. As she took a sip, she winked at him over the glass. He emptied his glass and set it down. "But right now, I need to get back on duty."

She stood up beside him. "Of course, I have kept you too long. Thank you so much for giving me something to look forward to."

He kissed her cheek and teleported out, as she lifted the mask to her face, and waltzed around the parlor, humming to herself, having completed the first step of her plan.

2-19

The whole family had traveled by jet to Castello. Luciano had planned to meet them there, so he could show them the properties he'd purchased. In addition to the conversion of some of their existing property that had been cultivated and planted with young olive trees, Luciano had also purchased a total of seven mature groves. Kate and Shannon had seen photos of the olive groves, as well as the land deeds, but had not seen the actual properties yet. They wanted ample time to visit, and coordinate with Luciano on the plans for harvesting, as well as plans for how the harvest would be processed. Both Kate and Shannon were interested in using the older methods of hand pressing the olives as opposed to the modernized factories.

This trip would also give them time to visit with Lorenzo, as well as arrange for Natalia to spend time with Ivor and Malachi, as she began her studies in preparation for joining the Council. Malachi had reported he'd found two more of the new Council members, Onyx, who was responsible for maintaining security for all covens, and Citrichi, their banker.

Sophia was both eager and reluctant to join in on this trip. She was hoping to be able to see Alfie, but her father had already told her at the end of their stay, when the family returned to Virginia, he'd be taking her to Berlin, to meet the Rothschild's. She felt the pressure to select a mate and was calculating ways to delay the inevitable.

Antonio was thrilled to have the castle filled, and he'd had the staff preparing for the visit all week. The rooms had all been prepared with fresh linens and fresh flowers. Lorenzo was there to greet them as the house erupted into chaos on their arrival. There was laughter, constant chatter, and hugs all around, as the staff worked efficiently to carry luggage to the appointed rooms. Shannon looked around the grand foyer.

"Wow, I always forget how big this place is. I can't imagine heating it in the winter. It already feels chilly."

Lorenzo laughed. "It doesn't get very warm, even with the central heat. I'd freeze if all the rooms didn't have a fireplace."

Lorenzo hugged Natalia who returned his hug with enthusiasm, then turned to Sophia, who appeared to be sulking. He gave her a hug. "What's going on? You're not happy to see me?"

She answered him quietly. "It's not you, Lorenzo. Dad is taking me straight to Germany from here, unless I can figure something out."

He felt sorry for his sister and gave her a tight squeeze. He hugged his mother, who noticed the new piercing in his nose, but said nothing. He gave Luca a fist bump, then turned to his father who gave him a bear hug and slapped him on the back.

Castello always felt welcoming for Shade, and he was glad Lorenzo occupied it full-time. He was aware of Sophia's attitude and Natalia's excitement. Sophia had been a bit more compliant but gave him the cold shoulder more often than not. Shade stood back from his son, shaking his head at the nose ring. "You know, son, I am beginning to dread coming back. Every time I do, you have added to your body art. What next?" He held up his hand before Lorenzo could speak. "Don't answer that."

Looking about at the chaos, he took charge, issuing orders. "All right, everyone settle in. Luciano will be arriving shortly to take us on a tour of the new olive groves. I suggest you all grab a jacket. Natalia, I requested that Marco provide one of our warriors to escort you to Council. Malachi is expecting you. Any questions?"

Shannon spoke in a whisper as she leaned into Luca. "So much for a luxurious shared bath after the long flight."

He smiled back at her. "Our master only has one speed, *mia bellezza*, and that is full throttle." He kissed the tip of her nose. "I promise you a bath in the marble tub together before this trip ends."

She winked at him, as the chaos swirled around them. A warrior from the camp appeared to escort Natalia to Council, and they were gone in a split second. Luca led her up the stairs to the room that had once belonged to Shade and watched as Shannon flopped across the bed.

"My kingdom for a nap."

He removed a leather jacket from his suitcase and pulled out a jacket for her as well. "I'm afraid your king does not have much use for naps. Here's your jacket, you'll need it tonight."

Shannon stretched out across the bed. "And apparently, he doesn't understand jet lag, either."

Luca laughed. "His sleep is dictated by the sun only. Come on, they will be waiting." He took her hand and pulled her up from their bed, giving her a kiss. "Later, I'll make it up to you."

She giggled. "Oh, I have no doubt."

***

Shade led Kate upstairs. "Let us go change. I'll just wear jeans since we'll be walking through the olive groves, but I'll still carry a weapon or two." Looking over his shoulder, he called down to Sophia. "Come on, princess, you will need a jacket."

Sophia looked back at him with dismay. "Why do I need to go? I don't know anything about olives. Can't I stay here and visit with Lorenzo? Please?"

Shade sighed. He didn't want to fight with his daughter this evening. "Sophia, Luca is going with us, you will have no protection. Lorenzo has his own schedule and things to do. You will come with us. No more argument."

Lorenzo spoke up. 'It's all right, Dad. Marco knew the family was coming, so I don't have an assignment tonight. Let her stay here with me."

Shade looked at them both. He didn't want to spoil the mood of the night ahead. "Fine, but you are responsible for your sister until our return. She is not to leave this house, *si*?" Lorenzo nodded, as Shade held his gaze a second before turning and heading back up the stairs.

As they entered their bedroom, they found their suitcases had been unpacked by Theresa, and fresh clothes laid out on the bed. "Thank you, Theresa. You make my life so easy. Lover, your things are laid out. Just give me a second to splash some cold water on my face, and then I'll change."

Kate walked to the large marble bathroom, and washed her face in cool water, brushing out her hair. Theresa followed behind her.

"Emma will see to the girls, my lady. And if there is nothing else you need, I would like to visit Marco."

Kate smiled back at her in the mirror. "Of course. We'll be gone most of the night. We have a lot of property to see, so take your time. And don't worry about being here for our return. I'll be joining Shade in his slumber."

She nodded, responding, "Thank you, my lady," as she scurried from the room. Kate returned to the bedroom, and pulled on jeans and boots, so they could walk the new property they'd purchased. They both grabbed a jacket and headed out, meeting Luca and Shannon in the grand foyer before piling into the Hummer, driven by Luciano.

Lorenzo stood in the doorway with Sophia and waved at his parents. "Well, that didn't take long. Less than an hour, and they're gone already."

Sophia walked through the grand foyer, looking up at the massive ceiling that scaled three stories. "So... how's Alfie?"

Lorenzo laughed. "And that took less than a minute. Alfie is fine."

She ran her hand over the bust of some long dead ancestor, as she asked nonchalantly, "Is he in camp tonight? Or has he been assigned elsewhere?"

Lorenzo followed her with his eyes. "He's in the camp. Sophia, you did hear what Dad said, right? I'm responsible?"

Sophia flashed him a look. "Well, he should have known better then. I mean, look at you. Cool nose ring, by the way."

He smirked and chuckled. "Hey, what can I say? The ladies like it."

Sophia wrinkled her nose. "Do they really?"

He laughed out loud, missing her sarcastic mouth. "They say they do, and that's all I need."

She walked over and sat on the steps. "So, I can count on you then? You know, what we talked about?"

He creased his brow. "Now?"

Sophia threw up her hands and looked at him incredulously. "Hello! He's taking me to Berlin at the end of this trip. It's sort of now or never, Lorenzo!"

Lorenzo ran both hands through his hair, and Sophia noticed how much he looked like their father, even his mannerisms were the same. "Okay, but listen. He can't know I knew in advance, understood? He can't know I was aware of what you planned to do. I mean it, Sophia!"

Sophia smiled at him. "I got your back, brother. Always have."

Lorenzo paced, knowing Marco would also be preoccupied tonight with a visit from Theresa. He sent a telepathic message to Alfie. **“Come up to Castello, brother. Sophia is waiting, and remember, I know nothing!”**

***

Alfie had been pacing all night. He knew she was here but had no idea how he’d manage to see her. He hoped Sophia didn’t pull another crazy stunt like she did at Bel Rosso, and land right in the middle of the camp. When he heard the message from Lorenzo, it didn’t take him long to respond. He teleported straight to the castle, landing in the foyer. His feet had barely touched the floor when Sophia ran into his arms. He held her like it had been a lifetime since he last saw her.

"I’ve missed you, red.” He looked to Lorenzo. "What’s going down? Where is everyone, and how much time do we have?"

Lorenzo shrugged. “Don't know for sure, brother, but they’re driving, not teleporting. I know there are seven separate pieces of property that have been purchased, and they plan to go to all of them tonight, so I’d guess they’ll be a while. You know my dad will need to be back before sunrise, though." He looked at both of them. "You're sure? I mean...fuck, this is forever, dude."

Sophia huffed. "Well, thanks a lot, Lorenzo."

Lorenzo looked at her, his apology evident on his face. “Come on, Sophia. You know what I mean. You're both rushing your decision. I mean, I understand the deadlines with the upcoming trip to Berlin, but...fuck, do what you have to do. I'm going to go visit the Alizzi. I'll tell him she summoned me, otherwise, I don't have an alibi for what's going down here tonight."

Alfie nodded. "Don’t worry, brother, I got this. Go to Dona. You know nothing. I’ll take the blame. There’s nothing he can do once this night is over. I love her. Now, go."

As Lorenzo teleported out, Alfie smiled down at Sophia. "We’re alone, this is our moment. If you’ve changed your mind, or want to wait, I’ll understand." He kissed her like it might be the last kiss they’d ever share. "If only I could take you someplace special."

Sophia smiled. "Well, Castello is special. My mother was turned here, and we were all born here, and my grandparents still roam here. Follow me." She led him to the kitchen where she collected a bottle of Midnight and two glasses and led him upstairs to her bedroom. As she poured the wine, she turned to him. "Make us a fire, will you?"

Alfie placed some of the logs stacked by the hearth into the fireplace, and willed the fire to begin, watching as it blazed up. "This place is very special to me as well. It is the stronghold of the coven I serve. I guess it holds meaning for both of us." He took the glass of wine she held out to him, and clinked glasses with her, looking deep into her eyes. "To Medici, to us, to our love, and its eternal flame."

She raised her glass to his toast and took a sip of the wine. Now that she was here, she was nervous. She'd never been with a male before. Her feeding had been limited to feeders, and even when Aislynn would take her to hunt, her father insisted she feed from female mortals. Alfie would be her first male lover, and her last. "You know I don't really, uh, know anything, right? I mean, I've never been with a male."

His smile was coy, but with a bit of cockiness to it. "Yes, red, I know. And you have no idea how happy that makes me. I'm your first and last. I will teach you. Just follow your heart, and your body will lead you." He kissed her cheek and let his hand slowly caress her cheek. "But you understand I've been with many. None have fed from me. Once we feed from each other, Sophia, it can never be reversed."

She didn't know the details of his exploits, but she'd been raised around warriors, and had overheard enough wild tales to fill a lifetime. She didn't need to know the details of his many conquests, but she did need to know it was behind him. She nodded her head.

"I understand. I don't want it reversed. But I do need your loyalty, your faithfulness. I know you're young yet, you and Lorenzo both. Are you ready to put the exploration behind you? You know your position as a warrior doesn't concern me. When we mate, you'll become a prince. But I need to know you're ready to commit to only me."

"Sophia, I've had my fill of sowing wild oats, hunting and whoring. Part of it was my training, learning to hunt, and to live among mortals undetected. I needed to learn those things to survive, and I did that. But my heart has always belonged to you. Now, you'll be my life. Your blood will sustain me, and our blood bond is sacred." He dropped down on one knee and took her hand, his eyes locking with her beautiful blue ones. "I'm your warrior. I'll be your mate. I'll give my life for you, Sophia. I love you and I need no other love but yours."

He stood and slid off his jacket. As he began to unbutton his shirt, he took her hands. "Help me undress. Explore my body with your hands, after all, it's all yours."

She'd held him in a close hug, and kissed him, but had never explored his body before. She'd never explored any male's body before. She wasn't a prude, and she'd grown up around warriors who paraded bare chested through the camp. She'd heard the sounds of passion in their house, as they echoed from her parents' bedroom, or from Luca's. She'd studied procreation in Enzo's classroom, as well as the basics of mating, and even turning mortals. But this was different, as he stood before her, unbuttoning his shirt, exposing the smooth, hard muscles of his chest. She reached out her hand, and placed her palm on his chest, feeling the heat from his skin. She helped him unbutton the final buttons on his shirt, and slid it off his broad shoulders, letting it drop to the floor. His skin glowed in the reflected light of the fireplace, and she couldn't think of ever seeing anything so beautiful.

Alfie felt his beast rise up, and he pushed him back down. There was no place for the beast this night. He must move slowly, and with patience. Her hands were soft and smooth across his skin. Closing his eyes, he felt her hands slide down, over his hardened abs. His breath quickened as she slid them inside the waistband of his leathers. Her movements were slow and tentative, as she explored, and it only fueled his desire.

"Unbutton the leathers, red. Slide them down my legs. Take me in your hand, feel how hard you make me, how much I crave you."

She dropped to her knees and untied his boots, pulling them free, before turning her attention to his leathers. The outline of his cock was visible through the supple leather, molded to his shape.

She looked at him and saw the passion in his eyes. She liked the feeling of power it gave her, knowing she could generate this response from him, and she smiled. She unbuttoned his leathers, and slowly lowered the zipper, as he helped her ease the supple leather down his narrow hips. He stepped free of the leathers, and stood nude before her, a magnificent specimen of manhood. She'd seen pictures of Hans, with his pasty white skin, his blonde hair, so pale it was almost white, and his pale blue eyes. Hans was tall, but thin, and he was no warrior. His life had been much like hers, living sequestered inside an estate. He wouldn't have the fine chiseled musculature of a warrior.

Sophia stood and walked slowly around him, letting her hand drag across his skin as she explored his back. She leaned in and kissed his spine, letting her tongue taste his warm skin. Her hand traced the tattoo that stretched across his shoulders, and she kissed his shoulder, near his neck and whispered, "No more tattoos. They only take away from your beauty."

As she moved slowly around him, he could barely breathe. Did she have any idea the effect she had on him? He felt her breath on his back before her lips grazed his skin, and his heart raced, and his cock became a rigid rod for her pleasure. Fisting his hands at his sides, he resisted the urge to take her. His voice was raspy and heavy. "Would you allow me to have one of your name?"

"Allow? Alfie, you'll be my master. I want you to include me in the decisions that will shape our life, but you don't need my permission. My sister and I have both been taught that we respond to the demands of our master, although, I admit, I've never been very good at it. Where would you put this tattoo of my name?"

She completed her turn and stood before him, and he pulled her against his chest, taking her hand and placing it over his heart. "There is only one place it belongs, over my heart."

She smiled back at him, pleased at his choice. "Then maybe one more."

He'd never seen her naked, and his body was on fire for her. He pushed her hair back from her face and slowly licked the soft skin of her neck, starting at the base and working up toward her ear. The desire to feed from her was so powerful, and once again, he must push down the beast. Nibbling on her ear, he whispered, "My turn."

He lifted the edges of the ivory sweater and carefully, slowly, pulled it over her head, letting it drop to the floor. She wore an ivory bra of the finest silk and lace. Her breasts spilled beautiful and plump over the scalloped edge. Leaning down, he kissed their fullness. Dropping to his knees, he left soft kisses along her ribs, moving his mouth slowly to her low-slung jeans that clung to the curve of her hips. She was made to be loved by a warrior and take his beast. He opened the snap on her jeans and lowered the zipper, sliding the jeans down her thighs. He removed her Italian made boots, before removing her jeans altogether. He looked up at the delicate ivory panties that barely covered the most gorgeous red patch of heaven he'd ever seen. Hooking his thumbs on each side, he slid them down as she stepped out of them. She wasn't shy. He kissed that sweet patch and moaned. Her perfume was a blend of roses and lavender. Standing, he kissed her lips, and the kiss was hot and tortured.

"You're so beautiful."

She felt his body pressed against hers, the searing heat from his cock, its hardness pressed against her abdomen. Her heart pounded as he kissed her, and he made it hard to breathe. When he broke the kiss, he told her she was beautiful. She'd heard that all her life, from her father and her mother, but the words meant nothing. But, on his lips, to know he found her beautiful, filled her heart. "Show me what to do, Alfie."

"Just breathe, red." Taking her hand, he led her to the bed where she laid down, turning on her side. He climbed on the bed beside her and took her hand, placing it on his cock. He heard the sharp intake of her breath. "Stroke me, slowly, like this. I'm already hard for you, wanting you, just feel me."

As she began the slow exploration, he reached around and unhooked her bra, freeing her breasts. Cupping one breast in his hand, he leaned his head to her and suckled her nipple, rimming the edges with his tongue. He felt her hand stop as he did so.

"Don't be afraid, Sophia. Don't hold back. Do whatever you feel, whatever you want. Nothing you do is wrong. This is about cherishing each other, discovering what we both enjoy, and bringing pleasure."

Her hand encircled his cock, and she felt the weight of it, it's hardness, and the smooth, slick head. She felt a ripple in her belly, as the heat built between her legs, her body responding to his. She caught her breath when she felt his mouth on her breasts. She'd felt this before with the feeders, but his mouth felt different. His hand slid down her back, and pulled her closer, their hips pressed tightly against each other. When he lifted his head, telling her to not hold back, her lips found his. She clung to him, inhaling him, as their tongues explored. She broke away to catch her breath and could only whisper his name. "Alfie."

His name was just a whisper across her lips, but he'd waited a long time to hear it. Rolling on top of her, he kept his full weight from crushing her. "Red, I can wait no longer, I need to be inside you."

He gently inserted his fingers to find her wet and loved the musky scent of her sex. He probed slowly, letting her get used to the sensation, and waiting until her hips respond. When he thought she was ready, he slid his cock slowly inside her, she gasped softly.

"Easy, just breathe. I won't hurt you. Your body will adjust to me once I'm inside you. It will become easier."

He guided his dick further into her, feeling the tight grip of her sex. "You're so tight and feel hot and beautiful around me." He moved slowly, waiting for her desire to overcome the discomfort. He felt her nails as she gripped his shoulders. "Relax, Sophia, relax your body and match your rhythm to mine." He felt her body start to respond, rocking with his, as he lowered himself on top of her, covering her mouth with his.

Even with the initial pain of his penetration, her body demanded him. As she relaxed beneath him, she followed the rhythm of his hips, matching his movements, and each stroke produced more pleasure. She slid her arms around his shoulders and loved the strength of him. She wrapped her legs around his hips, feeling the power of him. This felt nothing like the sex she'd had with the feeders, or the mortal females she'd been taught to hunt. She felt claimed by him, owned by him, and her fangs ached with the need to feed from him. She felt her fangs punch through. She'd never had to learn control when feeding, and she sank her fangs into his shoulder, feeling the hardness of his muscles as his blood spread across her tongue, and her body felt electrified.

Alfie was lost in the sensations of her body, when he felt her razor-sharp fangs pierce his shoulder, and he threw back his head, his beast emerging as she fed from him. As a warrior, he'd fed from many, but no one, except a mate, was ever allowed to take his blood. The power of the blood bonding was unexpected, and his roar could be heard throughout Castello. "Sophia!"

His beast responded as his fangs punched through, and his eyes glowed a vibrant red. He plunged deep inside and couldn't hold back his need to taste her. "You are mine."

He sank his fangs deep in the tender flesh of her neck, and the first taste of her blood in his mouth overpowered him. He remembered the first taste of the Alizzi, and the power that came from her, but it couldn't be compared to the extreme power of the Medici blood that was rushing through him. His veins literally crackled and popped, and he drew another mouthful, lost in the vortex of all that was Sophia. He felt her body begin to shake softly and he knew she was close, both of them feeding, sealing the blood covenant between them that would bind them, one to the other, for all eternity. He exploded inside her as her hips moved to meet him. Her fangs broke free and he held her in his arms as her orgasm took control of her body.

She felt him cum inside her, his body shuddering with the release, before feeling his body relax on top of her. Mated! She was mated. She belonged to him now, and there was nothing anyone could do to reverse it. "I love you, Alfie."

He looked down at her face, a light sheen of sweat on her pink cheeks, her hair spread across the pillow beneath her, creating a halo of red, and the bluest eyes he'd ever seen. She looked back at him with love. Yes, *this* was how she should be loved, by a warrior. He'd love her until the end of time.

"I love you, Sophia. How do you feel, being mated? Are you all right, I didn't hurt you, did I?"

Sophia looked back at him and smiled. She didn't know how much time they had before the whole family returned, and she'd have to face her father's anger, but she planned to make the most of it. "Are you sure we're mated? Maybe we should do it again, just to be sure."

A smile crossed his face, and he laughed out loud. "Oh, that's my Sophia!" He rolled over onto his back, pulling her on top of him.

"We are totally mated, red. But I think you should ride on top this time, to make damn sure."

He slapped her ass hard, as that red hair cascaded around him and her kiss took his breath away. He was going to make every minute count with her, because, soon enough, they'd both face the wrath of his master. He had no idea how that would play out, but for the moment, he had his Sophia atop his cock and smiling like a Cheshire cat.

2-20

It had been a long night, as the four of them, escorted by Luciano, had toured the seven new olive groves that dotted the Tuscan countryside. Kate and Shannon were pleased with the properties that Luciano had found. The amount of olive oil produced from these groves wouldn't make them major players but would allow them to make a noticeable footprint in the market. Shannon was suggesting they use a boutique-style marketing approach to the olive oil, producing an extra virgin olive oil, including sprigs of rosemary or basil inside each bottle, and position their product as a limited edition. Emphasize to the market there was a limited production, and when it ran out, it ran out, and wouldn't be available again until the following harvest. She and Kate were making notes, and getting excited about developing their brand, agreeing they'd only sell in Italy to start.

Luciano was driving fast, keeping an eye on the sky, to get his master back to Castello before sunrise. They drove past the outskirts of Florence, as the *duomo*, atop the Cathedral of Santa Maria del Fiore, was silhouetted against a pale pink sky, and reached Castello just in time. They stepped from the Hummer, and Kate stretched, lifting her hands to the sky. "Oh, it will feel so good to fall into bed."

Shade slid his hands around her waist, guiding her in the direction of the door. "Oh, you will do more than fall, *bel rosso*."

She was still laughing when Antonio, his face somber, opened the door for them. The four of them entered the grand foyer, their voices bouncing off the walls of the open space. The castle seemed unusually quiet, almost as if it was unoccupied. Kate looked to Antonio.

"Is Lorenzo not here? Did he go back to the camp?"

Antonio bowed his head, not making eye contact with her. "Lorenzo was called away by the Alizzi."

Kate creased her brow. "And left his sister here alone?"

Antonio pursed his lips but didn't answer. Kate turned to Shade. "Why would he leave her alone? I mean, I know the camp is nearby, but that's not like Lorenzo."

Shade instantly lost his good humor. By the look on Antonio's face, he was suspicious about the news of Lorenzo leaving the house. This wasn't like Lorenzo at all. Shade looked at Luca to see him wearing a confused expression as well.

"He would never leave her alone, *mi amore*. Something is wrong." As he was about to barrel up the stairs to find her when his eyes caught movement and he looked up to see her descending the stairs with Alfie. He fisted his hands at his sides, clenching and unclenching them several times as he tried to get his anger under control. He was hoping they had a good explanation. "Where is your brother, and why did he leave you alone?"

Alfie had his hand on the small of her back, and whispered to Sophia, "Don't be afraid." Making eye contact with his master, he answered. "Lorenzo was called away, and he asked me to stay with Sophia."

The two of them stopped halfway down the stairs, aware that if they got any closer, Shade would pick up the change in their scent, and know they were mated. Alfie was trying to find a way to break the news to him in a manner that would cause the least amount of drama. He looked at Kate, and locked eyes with her, gauging her mood as ally or foe, and he thought she'd stand with them.

Shade stared back at the warrior and spoke through gritted teeth. "Did he now? I was not directing the question to you, warrior, but to my daughter."

Alfie nodded, but continued to address his master. "He was summoned by the Alizzi and felt he must check on her as he's been assigned to Umbria. As his upcoming SIC, I volunteered to guard Sophia, as is my duty."

Shade huffed. "How honorable of you." His voice held more than a touch of sarcasm. His eyes locked onto his daughter. "The upper floors of Castello have always been off-limits to the warriors. They are our private quarters. You have some explaining to do." Shade casts a scathing glance at Alfie, pointing his finger at him. "I suggest you keep your mouth shut, warrior."

Sophia felt Alfie tighten his grip around her waist, letting her know they were in this together, and she wouldn’t face him alone. Sophia was nervous, but she knew going in that, at some point, she’d have to face her father's anger at the choice she’d made. "I invited him, Daddy. You left me no choice."

Shade took two steps forward and stopped. He could feel his blood ready to boil, but he was confused by her answer. "Explain what in hell you are talking about!"

They descended the stairs slowly, knowing each step brought them closer to him, and it would be only seconds before he knew. "You were taking me to Berlin, and I didn't want to go. I told you, and you wouldn’t listen. I won’t be mated to Hans. I’m already mated to Alfie."

Sophia heard the soft intake of breath from her mother, as Kate quickly moved to Shade's side, grasping his arm. Sophia knew her mother's quick move was one of a mother protecting her child, and she knew she was going to need all the help she could get.

As the words left his daughter’s mouth, her scent washed over him, and he felt Kate grab his arm. They’d outwitted him, and she’d disobeyed him. His beast emerged and his blood boiled, his heart hammered inside his chest. He stood rigid, as his fangs punched through and he threw back his head and screamed. "No!" Lowering his head, he growled loud enough to rattle the art hanging on the walls, as his eyes bored into the warrior. "You bastard!"

Alfie knew his fate lay in the hands of the people in this room. If his master attacked, or ordered Luca to take him, he’d not be able to defend himself. He felt his own beast emerge, but his posture was defensive. He pushed Sophia behind him. "If you’re going to kill me, don’t do it in front of my mate. It’s my only request. But I’ll die for her, she’s mine now. She came to me willingly. I love her. I always have."

Sophia clung to him. "Daddy, stop! You have to listen!"

Kate pulled at Shade's arm. “Shade calm down. Please."

Luca stepped closer to Shade. He knew better than to touch him, especially when the beast was out, but he spoke in a calm voice. "Master, Sophia won’t move away from him. Retract the beast."

Shannon threw both hands in the air. "Oh, for Pete's sake! Here we go, another testosterone-infused struggle for who is the most alpha male in the room."

Luca flashed his eyes at her, gritting his teeth as he spoke to her. "You're not helping."

Shade heard nothing around him. His beast was focused on Alfie. "You intend to challenge your master?" His voice was graveled and deep. "Get away from him, Sophia. Now! This is mine to settle."

Shade made a lunge to grab her, but he was pulled back. He growled loudly and spun to see his *bel*, whose crimson eyes locked with his. She had never stood against him, not in all the years they had been together. She could cajole him, and tease him, and use her feminine wiles to get him to see things her way, but when all that failed, she submitted to his rule, but not today.

Kate starred him down as her own beast emerged. She'd let him know he wouldn't hurt their daughter, and he wouldn't take away the male their daughter had chosen for her mate. "Enough! She's my daughter too. Don't lay a hand on him, or it's me you will fight!"

Shade bent down, going nose to nose with her, growling, when he felt his beast respond to her. There was nothing in this world that could bring him to ever lay a hand in anger on his mate. His beast felt covered in her absolute love, as her beast showed him what he'd forgotten. He could have mated anyone and had been pressured to do so. He could have mated out of expediency and produced the required heirs to the Medici dynasty. A vampire can choose to mate anyone, but only the beast can identify who the vampire was destined to love. The beast would choose, for the beast was the root of the vampire, and was ruled by emotion not logic. He felt the beast retreat, as he began to shake, and his eyes returned to their icy blue.

For the first time in their life together, she'd stood her ground against him and he didn't feel defeated or weak as her master. He felt whole, loved, and a fool for his actions, and fortunate that he had a mate who knew what it would take for their child's happiness. Grabbing her in his arms, he held her close.

Kate looked at both Alfie and Sophia. "Go, now. We will talk later."

The two of them took advantage of the break in the drama and hurried up the stairs. Luca took Shannon by the hand and started to lead her away, as Shannon whispered to him, “But this was just getting good!" Luca bit his lips not to laugh at her. The fire inside their master was not burning as hot, but the flames still flickered. He didn’t need Shannon to reignite the situation.

"Come, *mia belleza*. You've caused enough trouble for one day, *si*?"

She looks at him innocently. "Me? What did I do?"

He led her away, leaving Kate and Shade to sort out their differences. Kate caressed his face. "You can’t force your daughter to love out of convenience for the coven. You have a choice here. Embrace her decision, and welcome Alfie as her chosen mate, the new Prince of Medici. Or lose your daughter. She won’t bend to your will any more than you’d bend to your father's. You can't change this. Her path is sealed. Accept her, or lose her forever, because I promise you, if you make her chose between you, or Alfie, it’s her mate she’ll follow. You decide."

He listened to her words, but his brain still felt muddled. What had just happened? His daughter mated without his consent. The proposed mating should have been announced in advance to the coven, as it was cause for great celebration. But instead, he’d created this chaos, because he lost sight of his daughter’s needs over that of the coven.

"I wanted what I thought was best for her, to be mated to the son of a great master, who could provide for her more wealth, and expanded territories. Why did she choose a warrior? She knows, better than most, what the life of a warrior entails."

"Her heart found her mate, lover. She could have any male in the world, and she found the one she wanted. She mated against your will, because she had no other way to bond herself to Alfie before you arranged a mating she didn’t want. Stop pulling against your daughter. Embrace her spirit and accept that she’s chosen well. Alfie is honorable, and good. He’ll love her and take care of her. What more could you want for your daughter?"

His body felt heavy, as it was well past his death slumber. But there was one thing that repeated in his head, Alfie was made a prince by this mating, but it wouldn’t change his standing as SIC to Lorenzo, who’d reign as king. His beautiful princess would have to live here in Florence now. He felt like he'd lost them all. Lorenzo and Sophia, both called back to the land of their birth, and Natalia, destined to the seclusion of the Council. He turned and walked away from Kate, and into the office used more by his son now. He didn't bother to pour the wine but rather drank the Midnight straight from the bottle.

How ironic that he and Kate had often joked about the day when they'd have the house to themselves again, and it would just be the two of them. Now that the day was near, he wanted to grab them back to his chest, hold onto them.

"Be careful what you wish for, *mio figlio*."

He looked up to find his *madre*, Portia, smiling at him. Her long blonde hair braided atop her head, her gown of red satin trimmed in gold, looking as regal as ever. He went to her, taking her in his arms. "I love them all so very much, *Madre*. I have made many mistakes raising them, but Kate has always kept me in line. Tonight, she stood up for herself, and our Sophia. I seem to be a miserable fool when it comes to love and seeing it clearly."

Portia could only smile at him and took his face in her hands. "You were born of royal blood, but also born a warrior. You have a warrior's heart. I, too, stood my ground when it came to your happiness and future, and I would do it again. Above all things, your queen is your mate, and the mother to your children. She saw the love in your daughter's eyes. Stop fighting against her, *mio figlio*. Look deep into your daughter's eyes, and you will see for yourself. Sophia looks at her mate the same way your queen looks at you, with love and devotion, a love that is eternal."

She disappeared before him, as quickly as she'd appeared. He knew she was right. He left the office and walked back to the foyer, now empty and quiet. His feet felt heavy as he climbed the stairs and found her waiting for him. The death slumber pulled at him as he slid between the sheets, and his *bel* curled around him. He felt her hand on his chest as the slumber took him, and he knew there would be much to sort out tomorrow, as they dealt with the new reality of Sophia's mating. But for now, it was Kate's voice he heard as the slumber pulled him down.

"Sleep, lover."

2-21

Shade rose early from his death slumber, and felt Kate stir beside him. The house was still very quiet, when he left the bedroom and sought out Luca. He wanted all of his children here and sent Luca to gather Natalia and Lorenzo. He telepathically let Sophia and Alfie know they were not to leave Castello, and they'd meet as a family as soon as everyone was gathered.

He returned to their bedroom to find Kate sleeping lightly as he started to get dressed, pulling on his jeans and a black V-neck sweater over his head. As he was combing his hair, he heard her stir in the bed. There had been no time to talk with her last night before his slumber stole him away from her, but he'd felt her close, her head on his shoulder, her hand on his chest. He knew working this out was as important to maintaining the relationship with his mate, as well as it was to be maintaining the relationship with his daughter.

"How do I look?"

Kate sat up on her elbow to admire him. She knew how much he was troubled by Sophia's decision, but she knew this as well, was the right path for Sophia. "You look good enough to come back to bed."

"Still want me in your bed after last night?" He shook his head. "I am sorry, *mi amore*, for refusing to see what was before me. I still have a lot of questions. I have sent Luca to bring Natalia and Lorenzo home. I will meet first with Lorenzo in my office, and then I will meet with Alfie." He saw the look of doubt on her face. "It's okay. But I must address the issue with Lorenzo, father to son. He left his sister, he disobeyed me."

Kate reached out her hand to him, and he sat on the bed next to her. "Be kind. I don't know if Lorenzo knew what they planned, but I know they're close. If Lorenzo disobeyed you, it was out of love for his sister. I know you had a different path in mind for Sophia, but even Natalia saw this as her future. I know Sophia can be impulsive, but I do believe with all my heart she loves Alfie. And

Alfie loves her. He's a good and honorable warrior, and he'll love and protect her. If he makes her happy, then I couldn't wish more for our daughter. I hope you can come to accept this...and him. Look how loyal he's been to Lorenzo. We have seen his character already."

Squeezing her hand tightly, he looked into her eyes. "My response was out of anger. Not rational thinking. I need to thank you." He ran his thumb over her soft lips. "*Grazie, mi amore*, for reining me in, and standing your ground. I am grateful, because if you had not, I think I could have lost my daughter, and my mate. I do not intend to lose either one."

He kissed her then, and felt that passion burned bright, as it had from day one. Nothing had changed between them. "Will you do me one favor?"

"Whatever you need, lover."

"Once I am done meeting with Lorenzo and Alfie, I wish to have a family meeting. Will you please make sure the girls know I expect them to be there?"

"Of course. I need to check on Natalia anyway. I haven't spoken to her since she came back from Council."

Kissing her on the forehead, he stood to leave. "*Grazie*, I am off to meet our son. I do not wish to be interrupted."

He took a deep breath and headed down the stairs to the office that now belonged to Lorenzo. His son was already there, awaiting his arrival. "Good evening, son."

Lorenzo had missed the drama last night when his parents got home, but he'd heard all the details from Luca and Shannon. So far, his name hadn't come up, but he's pretty sure that was about to end. "Hey, Dad. So, it looks like our family has grown since yesterday."

Shade moved to the chair behind the desk. "Please have a seat. It does appear our family has gained a new son, not born a prince, but becomes one through mating." Shade leaned back in the chair and steepled his fingers together, staring hard at Lorenzo.

Lorenzo tread lightly. He'd heard how angry his father was last night, and that his mother was able to calm him, but that didn't mean he was totally accepting of this change.

"You know, Dad, Alfie has always had my back. When I came here as a boy, he took me under his wing. He took a lot of crap for it too. People saying he was sucking up to the Prince, giving him a hard time for sleeping at Castello some nights. He helped train me and guide me. We have battled together, and he stands at my side. I can trust him with my life, as you trust Marco."

Shade locked eyes with his son, now the warrior he'd dreamed of. "I have never questioned Alfie's loyalty to you, or this coven. He is one of the finest warriors I have seen come out of this camp, and that's saying something. I do question a few other things." He sighed and looked down at his desk. "Lorenzo, I am questioning your integrity as a warrior."

Lorenzo looked up surprised. "Mine? I don't understand."

Shade kept his temper at bay. He laid his hands on the desk. "We have a rule as warriors, one that is ironclad, and was probably the first thing you were taught. We never leave our post. I can think of no other warrior I would have assigned to remain here with Sophia who would have then left her, especially when that order was given by their King. Did you forget this rule? Did you think the Alizzi was more important than your own sister? Because, you see, son, I can't seem to make any sense of why you decided to leave her. Now, if I had been in your shoes, I would have stayed at my post, and sent Alfie to the Alizzi. So, you see my dilemma? This gives me cause to think you knew damn good and well what they were up to and became an ally to their mating."

Lorenzo sighed as he ran his hand through his hair and paused before he answered. "Okay, I knew. The Alizzi didn't summon me, although I did go there, to give myself an alibi. I knew they planned to mate. But Sophia was desperate. Dad, she has loved Alfie since she was a small girl, and no one took her seriously. I mean, believe me, I understand why. Sophia can make things difficult for herself. But she really loves him, and I know Alfie loves her. She was afraid if she waited, you would have forced her to mate with Hans. I'm sorry I deceived you, but I would be lying if I said I was sorry she and Alfie are mated."

Shade knew his son wouldn't lie if confronted, but he still had ground to cover here. He stood up and poured himself a Midnight before walking to the window. Standing with his back to his son, he lifted his hand and leaned against the window. "Lorenzo, let me make something clear to you. I am still the King of this coven. I am very disappointed. Your allegiance is to me first, and then this coven, not to your SIC. And trust me when I say, I would wish no other but Alfie to be at your side. I have not given you full command of this coven yet. You knew how I felt about all of this with your sister, and yet you let it all happen without my knowledge. I have accepted her choice and will acknowledge Alfie as the new prince." He took a long drink. "I am just disappointed."

Lorenzo laid his head back against the chair. His father had never once said he was disappointed in him. It was hard to hear, and yet Lorenzo knew he wouldn't change his course. If he had it to do over again, he'd still have helped Sophia achieve her goal.

"I'm sorry, Dad. I'm well aware I don't have full rule, and I've often wondered how I'll manage it all. I've tried hard to be a good son, and a good warrior, and to learn to lead this coven. But I'm a brother too. I love both of my sisters, and they, too, have a role in this coven. I can't tell you I'd change my mind if I had it to do over. I think Sophia needs to find her own mate, and follow her own heart, and I can think of no one I'd welcome more to the family than Alfie."

Shade listened as his son took a stand and spoke his truth. He knew he was close to being able to lead. "I am learning that you will each follow your own hearts. I learned a great lesson myself. My children are grown now and have minds of their own, and I need to open my eyes to their personal journeys and goals." He walked to Lorenzo and pulled him from the chair, hugging him, and slapping him on the back. "I love you, son."

Lorenzo returned the hug. There was no one he had greater love and respect for. "And I love you, Dad."

"Look, Alfie is outside the office, waiting. Send him in on your way out." His son walked out the door as Shade poured himself another Midnight, downing it quickly. *Just hold it together old man. He is your son now too.*

Lorenzo left the office to find Alfie, dressed in full leathers, pacing in the hallway. Lorenzo chuckled. "You look ready for battle, brother."

Alfie let his breath out slowly. "After last night, I wasn't sure what to expect."

Lorenzo slapped him on the back. "You'll be fine. Don't wimp out."

Alfie nodded and laughed nervously. "Easy for you to say. You didn't see his beast emerge last night."

Lorenzo winked at him. "Never underestimate my mother's power, my friend." Lorenzo laughed as he walked away, knowing Alfie would be fine.

Shade heard the door open, as he was pouring another glass. "Come in, Alfie. Take a seat. Would you like a drink?"

"Uh, a Midnight please, master." Alfie took a seat, happy to have a drink that would sooth his nerves.

Shade poured him a large Midnight and turned to see him in full leathers. He had to hold back the laugh. *Warrior came prepared, can't hold that against him*. He handed him the glass and kept his tone neutral. "Damn, you look as if you are expecting a war, son. Relax, just breathe. I need you to hear what I say."

Alfie took a gulp of the drink. "Yes, sir." He figured the best approach was to keep his mouth shut and listen.

Shade sat down in the leather chair and took another sip of his drink. "First of all, apologies for my behavior last evening. My beast does not listen to logic, but he does respond to my mate, something I'm sure you will experience from my daughter."

Alfie took a deep breath. "I want you to know, I have no ulterior motives in mating her. I love your daughter, master, and I always have. Sophia is headstrong, I'll give you that. But I love her spirit."

Shade nodded. "Let's get to business. As you sit here now, you have become a very wealthy vampire. It is custom for the bride to bring a dowry to the table. Sophia was to be given the estate that came to us following the death of Max. Kate turned it into an inn, and it is very profitable. It belongs to you and Sophia now, to use as you see fit. Since you are destined to become Lorenzo's SIC, it will be imperative you reside here in Florence. We will find you a residence befitting your station. Your family will be taken care of as well, as befits a Prince of Medici. Any questions so far?"

Alfie looked back at him stunned. He had to admit, he'd never really thought ahead as to what it would mean to be mated to Sophia. "I... I didn't expect this. I was prepared to live simply. I hope you don't think I mated her for her wealth. I assumed she'd live as I lived, not the other way around."

Shade laughed hard. "Son, I know you think you know my daughter, but she would never live simply. I assure you, you will want for nothing, and there will be no argument. You are now a prince. So, you must take on responsibilities as such. You will have a staff assigned to your household. Get used to it. I will have Enzo come spend some time with you. He will teach you our history, as well as help you to understand our role in supporting the coven. Lorenzo and Sophia can help you with that as well. It has been drilled into them since they were born." Shade stood up then, stretching his legs. "I love her, Alfie. When I held her in my arms that first time, she took my breath away. Don't ever let her come to me in tears over something you have done to her, I can't guarantee what will happen."

The magnitude of how much his life had just changed made his head swim, and he emptied the glass of Midnight. "You have my word, as a Medici warrior, and as...a prince of this coven."

The word prince didn't come easily to him. He was born poor and was grateful to live as a warrior. He'd been provided access to Lorenzo's lifestyle through their mutual friendship, but was never jealous of it, or saw it as something he'd ever attain for himself.

"I wouldn't have been able to give Sophia the material things, but she'd never have wanted for love and devotion. I've pledged to her my loyalty, my faithfulness. It's important to me you understand these things. I love Sophia for who she is. I would have loved her had she been a poor maiden in our village, working in a life of servitude."

Shade sat back down in his chair and gauged the truth to his words. He saw the devotion in Alfie's eyes, and knew, in that moment, his daughter had chosen wisely. Why had he fought so hard against it? Hans would never have loved her like this.

"You are a warrior, Alfie, a damn good one, one of the best. My son has attested to your valor and loyalty. Just make her happy. I can't ask anything more for her."

Alfie dropped to one knee before him. "You have my word, master."

Shade stood up, proud and tall. "Arise, son. Welcome to my *familia*. We will need to go to Council and have Malachi record the mating. There will be a ceremony to present you both to the coven. I suggest you inform your family." He hugged Alfie, slapping him on the back. "Go to your mate now. Spend some time with her before the family meeting."

He released him and strode back to his desk. "I have a phone call to make. Burkhart is not going to be happy with the news my daughter is mated."

2-22

Shade finished his call to Burkhart Rothschild with the news of Sophia's mating. The master was angry, and felt he'd been led on. Shade soothed him as best he could, stating his daughter had met another that called to her heart. Wrapping up the call, he checked his watch and figured Kate would have assembled everyone in the parlor by now. He followed the sound of the chatter and laughter to find his family, along with his new son-in-law sitting with his arm around Sophia. Kate was curled up on the sofa, her legs tucked under her, and a smile on her face, filled with love. As he walked into the room, a hush fell over them. He took a seat next to Kate and leaned down, giving her a kiss.

"Excuse me, my queen, is this seat taken?"

Kate scooted over to make room for him. "I was holding it for you."

He looked at the faces in the room, as they looked back at him expectantly. "Well, it is good to have you all here tonight. I have asked you here because we have a great deal to discuss, and I will need your help." He locked eyes with Sophia. "But my first objective is to speak with my newly mated daughter. Come here."

Sophia looked at her mother who shrugged and nodded her head, indicating that Sophia should follow his direction. Sophia got out of her chair and walked to stand before her father.

Shade took her hands in his. "I have made my apologies with everyone in this room but you. Congratulations, my princess. You have chosen well in your mate, and I love you with all of my heart."

She squeezed his hands. "Thanks, Daddy, for respecting my choice."

"It took me long enough, I know."

As Sophia returned to her seat, she snuggled into Alfie, as Shade addressed the room. "So, we now have a new prince. I have already discussed terms of Sophia's dowry with Alfie, and I have asked him to bring his family here before we present the new couple to the coven. I think it proper the two families meet each other." Turning to Kate, he smiled. "I will leave those arrangements for you and

Alfie to coordinate. Make sure everyone is present. I would ask that you get Cory and Madison here as soon as possible. They will need to be here for the celebration anyway."

"Yes, of course. They wouldn't want to miss it."

"Good. The first piece of business is to get to Council, and have their mating recorded. Once that is done, and the two families have met, we will schedule the grand ball and celebration for the coven, where the princess and her new prince, will be formally presented. Some of our coven travel great distances to see us. This is an important day and helps them to see their future is secured. Any questions so far?"

They all shook their heads no as Lorenzo inched his foot over and kicked at Alfie's boot, smiling broadly at him. "Too late now, brother. Welcome to the circus."

Shade laughed. "Oh, this is just the tip of the iceberg. I want you and Alfie to coordinate with Marco for the security necessary for this event. We will need all warriors onboard, call them in from whatever outpost they have been assigned. There will be thousands of people here. Marco is familiar with how this rolls, so follow his guidance."

Lorenzo leaned back in his chair. "Consider it handled." He and Alfie fist bumped each other.

"Now, we come to the ball. Kate, you will find Antonio and Gi can assist you greatly on the lists of masters that need to be present. They need to be officially invited. After the masters and their mates, each of you may choose whom you wish to invite. It is your party, so have fun." He addressed Sophia directly. "This celebration is all about you. So, decide what you want. Make it a day you will remember. You only mate once. Let them all know he is your chosen one."

She smiled back at him. "I will, Daddy."

"Now, the last order of business. I will begin immediately to find a villa suitable for my daughter and her mate, something nearby. Until then, Alfie and Sophia will reside at Castello. While the search for your new home is underway, I think you should take off for some time together. I have robbed you of the opportunity to spend much time with each other, and I am sad for that. I hope this will make up for it."

2-23

It had been a whirlwind of activity at Castello, with the formal presentation of the princess and her new prince to the coven, followed by the ball. The ceremony was well attended, although the masters' whose sons had been snubbed by the princess in favor of a common warrior did have their noses out of joint.

They'd been registered at Council, and Malachi made no comment as he recorded the latest entry into the family history. Once the Medici had mated a mortal, it seemed anything was possible with this family. It wasn't his place to judge. Well actually, it was, but it seemed to fall on deaf ears.

Sophia and Alfie had spent a week at the house in Paris, and then came back to Florence to look at the homes Shade had identified for them. They selected their favorite, a beautiful old Tuscan villa not far from Castello, nestled near a vineyard. It had a view that reminded Sophia of home. House staff had been selected, and Sophia's belongings from Virginia had been shipped over, as the couple picked out the furnishings for their new home together.

Kate and Shade had returned to Virginia, leaving two of their three children behind. Kate had sighed heavily on their return. "At least we'll still have Natalia for a few more years."

Still, the house felt empty now, as Shade resumed training the new recruits who showed up every spring, and Kate and Shannon continued to work with Luciano on the development of the olive groves. This year's production of olive oil was used to produce several experimental samples, as they decided on packaging design and their marketing launch. The first batch was sold in Tuscan markets only, as they got feedback on their product, and decided which herbs received the best response. It was life as normal, and yet, forever changed.

Shade found the camp running smoothly under Marcello, and activity at the Dead House under control. Natalia resumed her love affair with books. She'd always been quiet, and more interested in reading and learning than socializing.

They were moving into winter, giving Shade less daylight hours in his death slumber, and more time to spend with his family. He found he missed the controlled chaos of their home, as the children had moved away. He walked back to the house from camp, looking at the lights in the windows, warm and inviting. He saw smoke rising from the chimney, and knew *bel* was waiting for him.

He entered their home and found her snuggled up with a book, sitting in front of the fireplace. "I have always loved coming home from camp, *mi amore*, but I swear, it is quiet as a tomb sometimes. I miss the simplest of sounds."

She looked up at him from her spot on the sofa, setting the book aside. "I was thinking the same thing. I'm just as busy with the business, but it's so quiet. First, Lorenzo moved away, then Cory and Madison, and now, Sophia. Natalia was always quiet as a mouse anyway, so I hardly know she's here. I think we're experiencing what mortals call the empty nest syndrome. Come, sit with me before we must go to bed."

Throwing off his leather jacket, he kicked off his boots and stretched out beside her, his head in her lap. She ran her fingers through his hair, and he sighed.

"So, what is to keep me from throwing you down on that rug in front of the fireplace? We could snuggle and sleep there all night. Who the hell would care?"

She smiled down at him. "It wouldn't be the first time, but it's been a while since we had the freedom to make love without having to concern ourselves with where other people were inside the house." She kissed his forehead. "Have you heard from Marco? Lorenzo says things are fine, but I wonder how the other warriors are responding to Alfie now."

He kept his eyes closed, enjoying her feel of her fingers through his hair. "Oh hell, Marco loves Alfie. He's doing just fine. What news do you have from our daughter? How is mated life suiting her?"

"She's happy. She thinks she'd like to help Luciano with the vineyards over there and learn the wine business. That would be good for her and will keep her occupied while Alfie is busy in camp."

He thought about that for a minute or two. "She is smart enough. And she definitely needs something to keep her busy." He reached up and caressed her face. "I am a bit worried about her."

"Worried? Why are you worried about Sophia?"

He sat up then, throwing his arm around the back of the sofa. "I need to run this by you. Alfie will be away a lot. He has responsibilities as Lorenzo's SIC. That will leave her alone for more time than I am comfortable with. I think I would feel better if she had a protector."

Kate nodded. "I have wondered about it as well. The camp is near, and someone would respond quickly, but I think it would be a good idea."

"So, you thought about it too. I don't want to impose my will or offend Alfie. What do you think?"

She laughed. "Excuse me, but who am I talking to? This can't be my mate. I think you proceed as you always proceed, appoint her a protector, and tell them when he'll arrive. Just make sure their villa will accommodate him, so they still have their privacy."

"This is not funny, bel. I could appoint someone, and insist she have a protector. But I think I need to let her choose, as you chose Luca. It is important they both be involved and agree. I can put my foot down, but that's not how I want it to be."

"Then talk to Alfie first. He'd probably have the same concerns as you. See who he'd recommend from the warriors to be his mate's protector. Let him talk to Sophia. She'll listen to him."

"That's my thought as well. I can't lose her. I made that mistake with Cory and Madison, and I almost lost them. I'll be damned if I will make that mistake again. I think Sophia will be fine with it, she has had a protector all her life."

"Then it's settled. Talk with Alfie. Let him know you respect his opinion."

He grabbed her in his arms and rolled her to the floor, as they laughed, and he slapped her ass as she lay on top of him.

"I think we should make the most of the quiet while we can." He willed the fire to blaze brighter and put concerns about his children and protectors out of his mind. They were as alone as they could ever get in the house they built from love.

2-24

The winter had passed without incident, and now that spring had arrived, the family was returning to Florence. Kate and Shannon would meet the new manager that had been hired to oversee the olive business, Danilo. Luciano had found him working in neighboring olive groves, and Marco had checked his background. After interviewing and making him a substantial offer to join the coven, Danilo had accepted. Luciano was glad to be able to turn over this aspect of the business to someone who was an expert in the field. He knew the wine business, and had spent his whole life in the vineyards, but his knowledge of the olive business was limited.

Danilo had fit in quickly and was already directing the field hands as to what needed to be done to ensure maximum production from the mature trees, as well as how to nurture the new groves. He was fair minded, and a hard worker and the workers responded well to him.

Kate and Shannon were looking forward to the trip after the long winter, to be able to get outside, and walk the fields again. There was a lot of excitement and anticipation around starting this new business venture. And for Kate, it was also an opportunity to see her two children who now permanently resided there. During their last trip, Shade had wanted to see the property they had purchased, so they visited during the night hours. During this trip, however, Kate and Shannon needed to learn more specific details of managing the groves and would have Danilo give them a tour of the groves during the daylight. Luca would escort them, as would Marco, to ensure their protection. It seemed like overkill to take both of them, but Luca had been in the States now for close to thirty years, so Marco was much more familiar with the territory. With Shade deep in his death slumber, the four of them planned to gather in the grand foyer to head out. They'd meet up with Danilo at their first stop.

***

Marco shifted his weight from one leg to another, while he was waiting for the females to appear. Shade had asked him to escort the Queen and Shannon to the groves, but he wasn't used to being kept waiting. Luca was leaning against the wall, his feet crossed at his ankles, watching him fidget. Marco looked up suddenly when he heard their chatter as they descended the staircase. Damn, those females could chatter, and Luca's female talked so fast, he had a hard time understanding her half of the time. Clearing his throat to get their attention, he nodded. "If you are ready, my queen, we should be heading out to meet Danilo. There will be workers in the groves, so please, let's stay together if possible. Dante is waiting in the Hummer."

"Of course, Marco. Lead the way please." Kate smiled to herself, she knew he had a soft side, but one he rarely let anyone see. Dante was standing by the Hummer as they exited Castello. Shannon and Luca climbed into the back. Marco held out his hand, indicating to Kate to enter the vehicle before him. The running board of the Hummer was so high she could barely step up. "Give me a boost, will you?"

Marco looked discomforted by her request. Kate laughed. "Shade just grabs my ass and pushes me in."

Marco turned red and he could hear Luca's laughter from inside the Hummer. Luca extended his hand and pulled her in, saving Marco from the embarrassment. As Marco slid in beside her, she looked at him mischievously. "You missed your chance."

Marco gave Luca a grieved look. "Not to be rude, my queen, but I would like my family jewels to stay intact. If Shade knew I even touched a hair on your head, let alone..." he grinned, "let alone his most favorite part, I do believe I would not be able to resume my duties."

He looked at the back of Dante's head. "Drive on, Dante, and for hell's sake, we have females in this hunk of metal, so take it easy."

Dante grunted back at him, like he hadn't been driving, or flying, the queen all over the world for almost thirty years. He headed out to the first grove, where they were to meet Danilo. Dante stayed clear of the city, and the traffic. Within about twenty minutes, he was pulling off the main road and onto an unpaved road that ran through a mature olive grove. Stopping the Hummer under the shade of the olive trees, he jumped down from the driver's seat, as the four of them climbed out.

Danilo rushed to meet them. He'd met many people in his new coven, but he had yet to meet his new master or the queen. He was barely able to sleep last night, he was so excited. He saw the group exit the vehicle, and his queen was easy to spot. She was so small compared to the natural born vampires that escorted her, and her flaming red hair would be recognizable anywhere. He humbly approached. His former master was not of royal blood, and he wasn't certain of the protocol. He didn't want to mess up on his first meeting. The chance to work for the Medici fell into his lap, and it was a gold mine!

He kneeled before her. "My lady."

Kate rolled her eyes. "Please, Danilo, you don't need to kneel. I don't take this queen stuff too seriously."

As he stood up, he towered over her, and she extended her hand to shake his. "My name is Kate, and this is my best friend and business partner, Shannon."

He shook Kate's hand before turning to Shannon, who flashed him a big smile. Shannon shook his hand as well, as he seemed caught off guard. Kate introduced the men. "This is Luca, my protector, and Shannon's mate. Our driver, Dante, and, of course, you've heard of Marco, I'm sure."

Danilo was surprised when she introduced her protector, but even more so when she introduced their driver. Those who serve the master were rarely introduced. He'd heard the staff of the Medici was treated like family, but he didn't expect this.

"Yes, my lady...uh, Kate." He almost choked on her name. He'd never addressed a master or his mate by their given name. He glanced nervously at Marco. He'd never met Marco, but every vampire in Italy knew his reputation as SIC to the Medici. Danilo nodded at him, unsure of whether to extend his hand to the warrior.

Marco stood with his arms crossed over his chest and waited through all the introductions. He was used to the queen's casual attitude about her role, but he still demanded those meeting her for the first time to show respect, just as Shade would. Marco could sense his nervousness at once, and knew he wasn't used to royalty, or the proper protocol. Marco returned the nod and reached his hand out to shake. "Just a piece of advice, Danilo, always address your queen as such, or my lady, no matter her preference. She may not put much stock in her title, but I assure you our master does. You will follow my advice if you wish to keep your job. There is no offense at this time, as you are unaware of protocol. We will be escorting The Queen everywhere she is to go. Lead on, the females have much to learn and discuss." He looked at Shannon and then back at Danilo. "And I am sure they will ask more questions than you have ever heard."

Kate sighed and shrugged at Danilo. "No one listens to me."

She and Shannon both laughed, and Danilo seemed more confused than ever. The Queen said to call her by her given name, but the warrior said he'd better stick to protocol or lose his head. He swallowed hard. "Yes, my lady. If you'll all follow me, I'll be happy to show you what we've started."

He noticed the protector slid his arm around his mate, and Marco stood imposing and close to his queen. Marco wore an expression that looked like he was looking for any excuse to remove Danilo's head from his shoulders. He smiled nervously as he led them through the groves, pointing out how the trees had been pruned to ensure new growth, and talking about the health of the trees.

"It looks like it will be a very bountiful production, my lady. Of course, we must keep an eye out for the *mafioso*."

Kate creased her brow. "The *mafioso*? You mean the mafia?"

Danilo nodded. "*Si*, the mafia."

Kate shrugged. "I don't understand what they have to do with our olive groves."

Danilo looked uneasy, glancing again at Marco, wondering if it would mean his head if he ever delivered bad news to the queen. He wasn't sure of his place and hoped the warrior would give him some guidance as to whether to continue to speak or not.

Marco had trudged along as Danilo blathered on about the olives and pruning. He stayed close to his queen, keeping his senses keen but expected no trouble. He was only half listening to the conversation when he heard the word *mafioso*. "Hold up! Someone needs to explain to me exactly what we are talking about here. Did you say *mafioso*?"

Marco looked at Luca who shrugged Danilo looked as though he would piss his pants at any moment. "What the hell would the *mafioso* have to do with this land? Master bought this land outright. He owns it free and clear."

Danilo looked from Luca to Marco. The big warriors scared the piss out of him. "Oh, *si*! He owns the land. No question. But there have been problems, *si*? The *mafioso*, they have inserted themselves into the olive oil business. They force the farmers to sell their production to them, for a fraction of their value. Then they produce their own olive oil, but using contraband labels of known brands, diluting the pure olive oil with inexpensive seed oil. They cheapen the product, but sell it as pure virgin olive oil, making big profits." He wrung his hands. "I have not seen them in your groves, but I thought you were aware."

Marco growled. He spun on his heels, facing Kate. "My queen, were you aware of this? Does Shade know?" He could see her mind churning and didn't wait for an answer. "Medici has lived in Tuscany and ruled this land long before the *mafioso* existed. We are immortal, and I think a few damn warriors can handle some mob of mortals. No one interferes with the Medici, mortal or immortal."

Kate looked at Shannon who raised her eyebrows and said, "It's news to me. I didn't even know the mafia was still a thing."

Kate nodded. "It's news to me as well. But I'm sure we'll be fine, Danilo. The Medici has ruled Tuscany for centuries. I've never heard Shade mention any conflict with the mortal mafia. Have you, Marco?"

Marco paced, not worried, he just found this news interesting. "Never, my lady, but then we have never been in the olive oil business. I dare the bastards to give us one minute of grief, and I assure you, it will be my utmost pleasure to shut their asses down if we ever find them."

Kate smiled at Danilo. "See, no problem. Who would be stupid enough to go up against the Medici warriors?"

Danilo nodded, relieved to have shifted this burden to the warriors' shoulders. "Only a fool, my lady."

He wrapped up his tour of this grove, then climbed into the Hummer with them as he took them to one of the processing plants where the olives were pressed. Kate and Shannon inspected the first shipment of the bottles they'd ordered for their premier olive oil, as well as their new labels. Their oil would be sold under the brand name Liquid Gold and featured an image of one of their groves near harvest time, the trees loaded with olives ready for harvesting. They'd sell a plain olive oil, along with several varieties that would include a sprig of sage, basil, rosemary, and even lavender. The Medici name was clearly visible on the label, as it was with their wine, and their sunflower and lavender bath products. Everything seemed in place to launch their new product. As the day wrapped up, Danilo bid them farewell, and the group piled back into the Hummer, heading back to Castello.

Kate was quiet on the trip back, before turning to Marco. "You don't have any concerns, do you?"

Marco slowly turned his head to her and winked. "Have you forgotten who I am, my queen? Nothing is getting past me. My name is well known, as you so elegantly pointed out. Those bastards try anything they will never see us coming. We are vampire. I will rip out a heart and serve it to you on a silver platter. Never, my queen, do I have a concern over some pretend mortal warrior. But I would make a request."

She was relieved by his confidence. "And what is that?"

"When you return to Castello, you need to inform Shade. If it were me, I would call in Danilo and have a meeting. Find out how this *mafioso* operates. What they demand and how they go about their business. Danilo will know."

"Oh, of course, I'll tell him. I'm sure our warriors can manage the threat, if there is one, but it would probably be wise to assign warriors to the groves and the processing plants, just to be safe."

Marco was nodding his head in agreement. "I shall need to be in on this meeting. I think we should include the prince and Alfie as well. I do not expect any trouble, but better to be prepared. If they give us a hard time, it will be short and sweet justice." He turned his head and looked at Shannon. "You are very quiet, what do you have to say about all of this?"

Shannon smiled back at him. "I think anyone who would decide to stand against you, Marco, would have a very short lifespan. I'm not worried."

Marco laughed. "I like that one. Short and to the point."

2-25

Kate and Shannon had come home from their tour and informed Shade of the *Mafioso* and their rule over the olive groves. He and Marco discussed it briefly and decided they should meet and determine what precautions were needed. Danilo had been summoned to Castello to join them, and Shade took Marco's advice, inviting Lorenzo and Alfie as well. Although they'd have no say in the security measures, he included Kate and Shannon in the meeting. They'd need to hear what decisions were made.

They gathered in the office at Castello, awaiting the arrival of Danilo. The sun had set hours ago, and the men were enjoying a glass of Midnight, and a few cigarettes. Shade knew about the *mafioso*, but they'd never been a concern for him or the coven. He was relaxed, as was everyone involved. Preparation was always the best defense. Everyone looked up when Antonio entered the room and announced Danilo. Shade stood from behind the desk to greet their newest member to the coven.

Danilo was overwhelmed as he entered Castello for the first time. The inside of the great castle was even more impressive than the exterior. He followed the butler to his new master's office, where he was introduced. Danilo looked about the room full of leather-clad warriors, knives or swords strapped to their bodies. As a vampire, he was taller than most mortals, but the warriors in this room weren't just tall, they were built solid, as their bodies tugged at the seams of the form fitting leathers, they wore. He swallowed hard. His mouth suddenly dry. His eyes sought out his Queen who smiled softly at him.

Kate spoke softly to him, "Come in, Danilo. Antonio, pour him a drink, please."

Antonio responded immediately to her request, pouring the farmer a large glass of Midnight, served in their finest crystal. Danilo's hand trembled slightly as he accepted the glass. "*Grazie*." He took a much-welcomed sip, as the elixir soothed his nerves.

Shade immediately sensed this man's tension. They could be one intimidating lot, and he liked it that way. It amused him that

Danilo looked to *bel* for confirmation and not himself. "*Grazie*, for joining us, Danilo."

Shaking the vampire's hand, Shade felt the clammy palm and took note of the beads of sweat breaking out on his forehead. "Welcome to Castello, I am Master Shade, King of Medici. This is our son, Prince Lorenzo. This warrior is Prince Alfie, he is my son-in-law and my son's SIC. I do believe you have met the others. Please, take a seat and relax. Let me explain we are here to take some precautionary measures against the *mafioso*, and I am interested in what you know."

Danilo was tongue-tied as his master spoke and was asking for his advice. He was both honored and nervous as he took his seat. He looked around the room at the prince, who looked like a younger version of his father, except he wore his hair long and straight. He nodded to the prince, who acknowledged him. He looked to the male that sat next to him, also a prince, mated to the master's daughter. Danilo took a large gulp of the wine before answering, as the room of warriors stared back at him, waiting to hear what he had to say. My lady sat next to her master, and he found it less intimidating to address her.

"Well, as I was saying when we took the tour of the groves, the *mafioso* has inserted themselves into this business. My previous master was not affected. He only had a small grove and decided not to expand because of the *mafioso*. There are no other vampire covens that are involved in the production of olive oil that I am aware of. The mortals control this market, and the *mafioso* controls the mortals. The farmers are threatened to sell their harvest below market value to the *mafioso* families, or risk having their groves burned to the ground...or worse. I have heard their families are threatened. I do not know this to be true. It is only what I have heard. The *mafioso* takes the pure olive oil, and dilutes it with cheaper oil from other sources, like saffron, then sells it at a high price. That is all I know about it really." He emptied the last of his wine from the glass and wiped his wet palms on his thighs.

Shade listened carefully to Danilo's information. This was an easy task in his mind. "*Grazie* for your honesty and input, Danilo, it is vital. I do believe we will need to keep some warriors on guard, starting tonight. If they decide they want to burn us to the ground, I believe we have a great solution to that problem." His eyes slid to

Lorenzo, who grinned. Looking back at Danilo, he inquired. "Do they move about in the daylight, Danilo? I need to know if I will need day-walkers to patrol as well."

Danilo nodded. "Oh, *si!* They do not hide their activities. In fact, they are quite open about it. They will approach a farmer in broad daylight. Tell him what they will pay for the harvest. 'Take it or leave it', they say. And, of course, the mortal knows better than to say no to the *mafioso*. They only had to burn down a few groves to get the message across. Now, the mortals, they just comply. The land has been in their families for generations, and now they can barely make a living."

Shade drew his brows together and growled. "I do not like the sound of that. No one has the right to walk in and take what belongs to the people, those who struggle with hard work. I am a fair and honest master. We will not be intimidated or allow anyone to take what is mine." Shade looked at Lorenzo. "Anything you think we should do beyond what I have already planned?"

Lorenzo wasn't concerned. He was young, but he'd lived among warriors all his life and couldn't recall they'd ever battled against mortals. "I think the plan is sound. We assign protection 24/7 to every grove and processing plant, so our people are safe. If we're approached, the warrior can handle it, and notify us immediately if more help is needed. If they think I can be intimidated by fire, they will have a big surprise waiting."

The other warriors chuckled, knowing their prince could burn down much more than an olive grove.

"Agreed." Shade looked at Kate. "Are you concerned about anything dealing with this issue, my queen? I do believe your son has this well in hand. "

She shook her head no. "I think you and your warriors would make quick work of any threat, mortal or immortal."

Looking back at Danilo, he nodded. "Do not worry, Danilo, Medici warriors have this under control. Any problems inform the warrior on duty. I appreciate your time away from your family to assist us this night."

Marco moved to the door. "I'm on it, Shade." As he exited the door, Antonio appeared to lead Danilo out.

Shade nuzzled his nose into Kate's hair. "Well, I think we have that settled. Let's enjoy our night. I wish to spend time with our daughters."

As they all filed out of the office, Shade soon forgot the *mafioso*. Who the hell did they think they were? He was the damn Medici!

2-26

Sophia loved their new home, and she loved being closer to her brother. She'd always loved Florence, and had no trouble shopping for their home, or finding the fashion she was used to in the designer shops. She'd not been happy when her father insisted she have a protector. She felt perfectly safe with Alfie, but Alfie still had responsibilities to the camp and the coven, and was always on assignment, so she was frequently alone. Well, she would have been alone if not for Nickola.

Marco had pulled out five of his best warriors for her to review, and with some prompting from Alfie, she'd chosen Nickola. Their villa was large enough to easily accommodate the new protector, as well as the staff that had been assigned, with plenty of rooms left over. Her father never failed to mention those rooms were for his grandchildren, to which she'd always roll her eyes.

Nickola looked nothing like Alfie. He had dark hair, and darker eyes, and looked rather brooding, but had shown himself to be kind and respectful. He was the quiet type, but still, she felt safe with him when she was alone here at night. Walking into their bedroom, Alfie was dressing in leathers, and preparing to leave for the evening. Sophia flopped down across the bed.

"I need to pull rank and get Marco to assign you some time off. Where are you working tonight?"

"Pulling rank already, red? That didn't take long, you held out longer than I thought. Tonight, I'm heading to one of the olive groves just outside Florence. It's not far. I worked it a few times, and it's been a rather boring assignment. Lorenzo and I rotate to keep from getting bored out of our minds, but the *Mafioso* has yet to show their faces. Nickola will be here with you. You two getting along alright?"

She lifted herself up on her elbows, resting her chin in her hands. "Nick is fine. He's quiet, so I'm the one doing all the talking, but we get along fine. I feel safe, which is the whole point, I guess.

So, if there's no action, then maybe I can ask Marco to give you some time off? I mean, this princess crap ought to count for something!"

Alfie finished strapping up his boots and looked at her. "Sophia, I have a job, an important one. Remember, I'm new to this family. So, asking Marco to give me time off is not something I approve of, to be honest with you. You'd probably get better results asking your father to give me time off. He'd love that since all he wants to know is if I'm working on making *bambinos*. You need to talk to him about that."

She giggled. "Yeah, that won't work. I get the same inquiry every time I talk to him. It's like, 'Hey, Dad.' and he says, 'Are you pregnant yet?' No 'hello, how are you, are you happy?' He has a one-track mind. I just say we're working on it, and he says work harder."

Alfie shook his head and laughed "I used to think my most important role to the Medici was warrior, now I think I'm a stallion, retired from the races to breed more stallions. Lorenzo thinks it's hilarious, by the way. I keep reminding him his time will come. Give us a break. Not that I ever need an excuse to make love to you." Leaning down, he kissed her and playfully pushed her back on the bed. "I have to move now, or Danilo will wonder what the hell happened to me. Miss me?"

She smiled back at him. "A lot. Maybe I should get in trouble more. Then they'd make you stay home."

He grinned and shook his head. "If you do that, you have to deal with *my* punishment." He wiggled his eyebrows. "And I think your spunky ass might like that too much. I'll tell Nick I'm leaving. What are you going to do tonight?" He grabbed his leather jacket and slipped a blade into the sheath at his waist.

She sat up on the bed as he prepared to leave, shrugging her shoulders. "Not sure. I'll call my Mom. She had some good ideas for some things I could start planting in the gardens. Maybe see if Lorenzo is working tonight or not."

He walked to the door, sliding on his jacket. "I'm relieving Lorenzo, so I should see him when I get over there. He'll be home tonight unless he drops over to see the Alizzi."

She wrinkled her nose. "Is it just me or does that woman rub you the wrong way? I mean, she's always been very nice to me, nothing inappropriate, but it feels so...fake, or something."

He tried to avoid any references to the Alizzi, if possible. He'd never tell her of the relationship he'd shared with her, and he doubted seriously Dona would ever speak of it. He was smart enough to know there were some aspects of his past that were better left unshared with his mate. But he too felt the same discomfort with Lorenzo's friendship with the Alizzi. He'd tried to approach Lorenzo about it, but it was clearly an off-limits topic between them.

"Dona's lonely, that's all. Lorenzo is assigned to Umbria. He has a responsibility to her, so she feels an obligation to this family. It's nothing, I'm sure. She dotes on Lorenzo, they're pretty tight."

"Trust me, I notice how tight they are." She laughed. "Okay, now I'm starting to even sound like my mother. Go, the quicker you finish, the quicker you get back home to me."

Walking back to the bed, he lifted her easily in his arms and kissed her. "Take Nickola with you if you go to Castello. Please follow the rules, red. I love you. Easy night, so I won't be late." He set her down on her feet and teleported out in a flash before she could drag him onto the bed.

Teleporting inside one of the olive groves, there was a small building where Danilo could take care of paperwork, get the field hands their pay, and conduct business. Lorenzo was standing outside, looking bored as hell.

"Hey, brother, you look like it was a rough day." Alfie laughed and fist bumped his best friend.

Lorenzo was relieved to see him. "Brother. Glad to see you. Wish I had something to report, but nothing happening here. It's like watching paint dry...or olives grow...take your pick. Danilo is fine, the workers are fine, the olives are fine. I know that's a good thing, but damn, brother, a warrior needs a little action."

Alfie nodded his head in agreement. "I know we need to be on patrol, but this is such a waste of time. I feel like I haven't used my sword in weeks. By the way, your sister is thinking about visiting you later tonight."

Lorenzo grabbed up his stuff and prepared to teleport out, when they noticed a car pull onto the dusty unpaved road. Lorenzo squinted to see if he could see who was driving and didn't recognize the person. "Hang on, brother. Mortal. Could be lost or something."

The two warriors stood side by side as the car approached and came to a stop outside the office. The man behind the wheel was dressed casually, as he stepped from the car, a large cigar in his mouth. He stood and looked around the groves. Lorenzo looked him over and could pick up the slight bulge under his jacket, and knew he was carrying a gun. "You lost, *amico*?"

The guy walked slowly over to the two warriors, the cigar smoke billowing over his head. "Looking for the man in charge."

Lorenzo and Alfie stood shoulder to shoulder, creating an imposing wall, as Lorenzo answered. "You can talk to me."

The man looked him over slowly, puffing on the cigar, intentionally creating more smoke, which he blew in their direction. "You own this?"

Lorenzo stared him down. "My family owns this. What's your business here?"

The man looked about, as Danilo started to exit the door, saw the mortal, and quickly ducked back inside. The man chuckled to himself. Turning back to Lorenzo, he extended his hand and said, "Name's Sal, and you?"

Lorenzo didn't shake his hand but held his stare and didn't give him the information he sought. "What's your business here, Sal?"

Sal took in the both of them and noticed the knives on their hips. They were clearly security, but what the fuck kind of security armed themselves with knives? "I got a proposition, but I only talk to the person in charge. I'll come back another time."

The man climbed back in his car, and slowly drove back out of the olive groves. Lorenzo looked at Alfie. "Well, brother, looks like things just got interesting."

2-27

Lorenzo made sure everything was secure, telling Alfie to keep an eye on Danilo, he looked a little pale. Alfie laughed. "He's definitely not warrior material."

Lorenzo slapped his friend on the back. "I'll let Marco know what went down. Keep on your toes, brother."

Alfie leaned against the shack and lit up a cigarette. "Don't worry about me, brother. Just give my love to your sister."

Lorenzo made a face. "Uh, you're gonna have to do that yourself." He teleported out and headed straight into camp. The training field was in full swing, and Lorenzo walked among the new recruits as they practiced with swords, as he ducked and weaved between the mock battles. He could see Marco on the far side of the field, dressing down some poor recruit who was probably wondering why he ever decided to come to camp in the first place. Lorenzo smiled to himself, remembering his first days in camp. He stood to the side until Marco dismissed the young warrior, and then gave Marco a crooked smile.

"You finish wiping the floor with that pup? If so, we got something to talk about."

"Damn rookies. Every year, it is the same old shit. They come in here and think they know it all. Kids never fucking change." Marco lit up as they headed back to the office. He barked orders along the way. Entering his private quarters, he held the door open for Lorenzo. "*Cazzo*, I got two damn females now. Your father is going to be the death of me, insisting we bring females in this camp. Finding someone the caliber of Fiamma, you just don't see that very often. Most of them don't belong."

As he entered the office, Marco dropped the cigarette on the floor and crushed it under his boot, before he flopped down on a leather chair that looked like it couldn't withstand the weight of a cat, let alone his huge frame. "So, you saw some action in the middle of the Queen's groves, did you?"

Lorenzo straddled an old wooden side chair that had seen better days and looked about at the wreck that Marco called his home. "Jeez, Marco, who's your decorator? This stuff looks like you got it in a flea market at the end of the Spanish Inquisition. I'd be afraid to light up in here."

"Look, this is my blasted office and I don't need no fancy ass shit like you tiptoe around in that big castle. I'm a fucking vampire warrior, and my ass has worked the seat of this chair to perfection. Now, if you are done dressing my ass down with your sissy decorating advice, get the hell down to business."

Lorenzo chuckled to himself. Marco wouldn't be Marco if he didn't have a burr up his ass. "Just thought you should know we had a visitor at the main olive grove today. Mortal. Pretty sure he fits the bill as *mafioso*. He wanted to know who was in charge, who owned the place. I told him it was in my family, but he wants to talk to the person in charge. Said he had a proposition. He was carrying a gun, but it was subtle. He didn't flash his weapon or make any threats. Left peacefully. Thought you should know. Alfie was there when he came, so he's on top of it."

Marco pulled at the desk drawer, wiggling it back and forth to get it to open. Removing the flask of Midnight, he slammed the drawer shut with his booted foot. Taking a swig, he considered the information Lorenzo had just shared. "So, the bastard's decided to finally move in. You get a name? Give them any names on your end?"

"Sal. No last name. He asked who I was, didn't answer. But the whole region knows Medici owns the groves, so it won't take any effort on his part to find out who's running things."

Marco gulped down another mouthful of Midnight. "Let me tell you something, they already know, trust me. Sal, huh. Fuck, they are all named Sal or Luigi or Anthony. We need to figure out which family we're dealing with. That won't take long. Looks like I need to make an appearance out there, give them something to see." Marco took another swig and held out the flask to Lorenzo. "*Cazzo*, did Danilo shit his pants?"

Lorenzo laughed. "Cut him a break, he's a farmer, not a warrior. He looked a little pale and stayed inside the office the whole time."

Marco snorted. "That farmer better start keeping some clean drawers in the shack. This is just the beginning. He looked like a chicken with his head on the block when he came to the meeting at Castello. Looked at Shade like he had three heads and two cocks."

Lighting up another smoke, he grinned. "Truth be told, I'm ready for some action, but this has to be handled differently. As much as I would love to lop off a few heads, we can't let them know we're vamps. Everything we've worked for would be right out the damn window. We must approach them as mortals. Make sure all the warriors assigned remember that. Speaking of which, you left Alfie in charge." Shaking his head, he laughed "All he can think about is that redheaded pussy, not unlike your damn *padre!*"

Lorenzo gave him a hard stare. "My father never backed down from a challenge, or ever lost one that I'm aware of, and while we're on the subject, neither has my mother, and Alfie has his priorities straight. Watch your tongue, Marco. You still run this camp, but I'm the Prince."

Marco stared right back at him. He sat forward in his chair, leaning his arms on the desk. His voice was low, but he knew he could push only so far. "And you remember who taught you your skills. Your father tried that bullshit once, pulling rank. It was a long night, and we damn near killed each other, I suggest you don't repeat that, my prince." He walked to the door and opened it. "I will inform Shade of the information."

Lorenzo stood to take his leave and glared at Marco on the way out the door. "Careful how you refer to my sister."

Marco heard the pride in his voice and heard the unvoiced and inevitable outcome that he would one day rule this kingdom. They'd made him a warrior. Marco had watched him grow and knew his skills as well as anyone alive. Lorenzo was much like Shade in many ways, but he had his own path to follow. Marco had lived to see the changes that Shade had brought to the coven, altering the directions of Christofano, and he had no doubt things would change again under Lorenzo. Marco hoped he lived long enough to see the day Lorenzo's sons ruled these lands. Marco grunted at Lorenzo's back.

"Don't get your panties in a wad, kid. Your father and I may not have always seen eye to eye, but I have loved him like a brother, and I always had his back, just as I'll always have yours."

He followed Lorenzo back onto the field, where he barked out orders. It was just another night, with another bunch of punks to shape into warriors. It was what he was good at, and he'd never regretted one moment of his life.

2-28

Alec had just finished up a meeting with his accountant. He'd been running L'Adventure now for well over ten years and had turned a profit year one. At least he was making money, and a lot of it, but he hated the isolation. He'd had to add on to the facilities to accommodate the demand, but he could run this place with his eyes closed. Most of his clients were return customers, and had specific fantasies they liked to play out, over and over again. Occasionally, they'd get someone new. He only took new clients if they had a strong referral from an existing client. He had staff who set up the rooms according to the client's request and made sure whatever they needed to carry out their sick fetishes were there and waiting. Bree handled the door, and got them situated, and payments were collected before the client ever set foot inside the premises. That way, he never got stiffed on the payment, and in return, he provided protection and privacy.

Some clients came with their mate, others were unattached, but came with another immortal. If the client needed to be set up with a partner, Alec had a stable of females, and males, that the clients could choose from. He pushed the spreadsheet across the table as he drank the Red Moon, wondering what the fuck difference it made. What good was the money when he was stuck in this place 24/7? It was his prison. A very opulent prison, with a lot of perks, but a prison, nonetheless. A least he would have amassed a fortune by the time the Council lifted its ban and allowed him to live among mortals again. A century had never seemed like a very long time to him before, but then, he'd never been restricted in his ability to go where he wanted, when he wanted.

He drained his glass when Bree came crashing into the room, her eyes wide, and her face pale. "Master!"

He looked up, non-plussed. "What is it, Bree?"

"Uh, we've got a problem in suite six. I think you need to uh, check it out for yourself."

He looked at her with annoyance. "Isn't this something you can take care of? It's what I pay you for."

She shook her head no, a look of fear in her eyes. Reluctantly, he got up from the chair and followed her to suite six. Bree was walking briskly ahead of him but smiled nervously at a few clients she passed in the hallway. Alec nodded to them and mumbled something about hoping they were enjoying their stay. He tried to avoid dealing with the clients directly, if possible. Bree got to the door and waited until the hallway was clear of any foot traffic before using her key card to unlock it. Alec was getting impatient as she slid the door open a crack, and slipped inside the dark room, and motioned for him to follow. He rolled his eyes at all the drama and entered the dark room and heard her close and lock the door behind them. Only after the door was secured did she turn on the lights. What he saw was more blood and carnage than he'd ever seen on a battlefield. "What the fuck?"

There was a female, one of his, or what was left of her, strapped to an inversion table. She was clearly dead, her body mutilated beyond recognition. Sitting on the bed, drinking a Red Moon, and completely oblivious to his surroundings was the new client, Marchesa, or Marcus, or some damn name he couldn't remember. Speaking softly, under his breath, he asked Bree to bring a couple of warriors, and do it quietly. She nodded and slipped back out through the door.

Alec cautiously approached the client, unsure of his intent at this point. "So, Master, uh Marchesa, is it?"

The vampire looked up. Blood smeared across his face, as he smiled back at Alec. Alec could see his pupils were dilated, and he was high on something a lot more potent than Red Moon. The client nodded slowly. "Marchesa."

Alec looked around the room, hoping the warriors got here quickly. He spoke quietly. "Looks like you had quite an evening."

The client chuckled. "It would appear that way."

Bree returned with Robbie and Riley. Alec motioned for them to stand down, as they each had their hands on a sheathed weapon, ready to respond. Turning back to the client, Alec talked to him in a calm voice. "I'm going to have these two gentlemen escort you to a private room where you can sleep off whatever it is you took. For your own safety, okay? And we'll take care of this mess."

The client gave them a lopsided smile. “Of course."

Alec nodded and the two warriors secured the client in their grip, and lifted him off his feet, taking him to a secure room below ground. He’d face no consequences as a result of his actions, other than Alec would make sure he never returned here. His service thrived because it guaranteed absolute privacy, and the female he killed was no one of importance. She wouldn’t be missed, but the master, on the other hand, could cause big problems for him. He stood next to Bree as they looked at the carnage, and Bree asked, "What are we supposed to do about this?"

Alec shook his head. He’d never had to handle anything like this, not even in the sex chamber below Castello. “Not sure, but I know someone who does." Pulling out his cell phone, he scrolled through his contacts until he saw the one he was looking for, Jacks. He hit dial and hoped like hell it didn’t go to voicemail.

***

Jacks was currently taking an assignment on the east coast, for a master in Maine who was paying her a bundle to escort him on some high stakes business deals. He was a day-walker, and slept at night, so she was taking a break. Standing on the balcony of his mansion, overlooking the Maine coastline, she could hear the ocean crashing against the rocks. Her cell buzzed inside the pocket of her custom leathers. Pulling out her phone, she saw it is was a California area code, but didn’t recognize the number. "Jacks."

Alec sighed with relief. “Jacks, Alec here. I know we haven't talked in years, but I’ve got a situation. I mean a real situation, like, right now. Hoping you can lend me a hand here."

Jacks bit her lip. Alec Canton. That short and sweet job as Rissa’s protector landed her a nice chunk of change. Of course, she’d heard his fate through the rumor mill. She knew his Presidential bid had failed, and the Council had exiled him to live underground. She’d heard he was running an exclusive underground sex club, and it was doing quite well, but she hadn’t seen him in years. "What kind of situation?”

“One of my clients got out of hand. I don’t want to say too much on the phone.”

He heard silence on the other end of the phone for a few seconds before she responded. "Master or whore?"

"Whore, but still, I've got a mess on my hands. Need to keep this quiet, Jacks. It would be bad for business. Not to mention, this is Shade's territory. I'm here because he grants me the privilege to be here. I don't need to fall out of favor with him. Not sure where the fuck I'd go."

She looked up at the moon and almost laughed out loud. *My, how the mighty have fallen.* "I can help, but it will cost you, a lot. Send me the coordinates and have someone waiting to escort me." She ended the call and slid the phone in her pocket before going inside. She placed a knife inside her boot, four shurikens tucked inside her jacket and a loaded Glock. Once she received the coordinates telepathically, she teleported out, heading for California. She made a few flybys overhead to check out the activity. Seeing nothing unusual, she landed at the entrance, and was greeted by a few Medici warriors who escorted her inside, where Bree is waiting.

Bree looked at the tall, dark warrior. "You're Jacks?"

Jacks nodded, giving the blonde the once over. She wasn't impressed, but she did seem to be Alec's type. He had a thing for blondes, at least he used to. Bree motioned for her to follow. "I'm Bree. Follow me." The two females walked down the corridor and again, Bree used her key card to unlock the door as they both slid into the room. Alec looked up as the two entered.

"Thanks for coming. Hope you can help with this...mess."

Stepping inside the room, Jacks assessed the situation. The level of destruction was definitely caused by a master, one who'd lost all control of his beast. And not just any beast, but a beast juiced up on something. She walked close to the body, inspecting what was left of it.

"Get rid of the blonde. We need to talk."

Bree didn't need to hear any more to know she was being dismissed. She gave Alec a nod and left the room, securing the door behind her. Alec started to pour himself some Red Moon from the bottle in the room when Jacks barked at him. "Stop! Your client may have spiked the wine."

He stopped mid-pour and set the bottle back down. *Fuck! He could sure use a drink.* "Tell me you have a plan, Jacks."

"First, tell me the master's name and where the hell he is."

Alec watched as she examined the room, the blood splatter, and the ripped sheets on the bed. "Marchesa. Do you know him? We got a referral from one of our long-time clients, and he checked out okay. This was his first visit, and his last. I had the warriors take him below ground. He's in a secure room until I think it's safe to release him."

Jacks nodded. "Lock this room down, don't remove anything, and let no one else in. We need to go someplace private and talk." She slid one red painted fingernail down his cheek and kissed him lightly on the lips. "You need a drink anyway."

He nodded his head as he scanned the room one last time, turning out the light before opening the door. The two of them exited the room as he locked the door and led her back to his office. He flopped down in the chair behind his desk and poured himself a glass of Red Moon.

"How about you? Is your body still a temple and all that crap? Or can I pour you a drink?"

"No thanks, I'm perfectly fine. And yes, this is still my temple." She walked around his office and let him stew a bit as she took in all the expensive things in the room. She took a seat in a chair opposite the desk, crossing her legs. "So, let's start with Marchesa. He likes it rough, but nothing like what is in that room. There's a new drug in circulation, very expensive, so I've only seen it used by masters. They're the only ones who can afford it. The street name for it is Tainted Beast. It's a powder, white in color, and they snort it. It creates a high that goes straight to the core of the beast. The vampire has no control, no matter their age and how much they have learned to control the beast."

Alec creased his brow as he considered the implications. "I've never heard of it."

She shrugged. "Relatively new. I've seen it more on the west coast than on the east coast. The stuff is expensive, outrageously so. That has slowed the spread. Common vamps can't afford it." She stood up and walked to the bookshelf and perused the titles. She could feel his eyes on her ass. "I'll handle Marchesa, teleport him to his residence, and stay with him until the drug wears off. It's potent, but the high is short lived. As for the room, get your staff in there. Tear up the carpets, dismantle everything, and put it in the incinerator. Throw the whore in with the mess. There can't be any evidence of anything." She reached inside her pocket and withdrew a business card, tossing it on his desk. "Or, if you don't want your staff involved, call this guy. He's a cleaner. Quiet and discreet. You're not the only one who needs his services, believe me. It will cost you. And if I were you, I would tip heavily. This may be your first incident, but it won't be your last."

Alec took the business card, sliding it into his pocket. "I'll call tonight. You sure you'll be all right taking him out of here?"

She gave him a coy smile. "You worried about me, Alec?"

He stared back at her, knowing she could handle pretty much anything thrown her way, but avoided the question. "I owe you one."

She laughed as she left his office to gather up Master Marchesa. "Oh, you own me more than one."

2-29

Raven woke up alone in bed. He wasn't surprised. Micah had his hands full running the inn, and usually handled any guest requests personally. They'd worked together to ensure the success of the inn, but Raven's primary responsibly here was to oversee the warrior camp Shade had established on the west coast.

Raven's responsibilities had grown over the years, from providing security for the inn and the vineyards, to developing the west coast camp, and providing security for Alec's underground club, L'Adventure. It was a lot of territory, but they hadn't experienced any trouble, until tonight. Two of Raven's warriors had called him with an unusual tale of a killing by a master at Alec's club. Riley reported that Alec had called in Jacks to handle the cleanup. He dressed in leathers and braided his long black hair into a single braid down his back when his mate walked in.

"Need to make a quick run to L'Adventure, there's been some trouble and I need to find out exactly what the hell happened before I go to the boss-man. I may end up teleporting to Bel Rosso before the end of the night, depending on what I find out." Strapping on his sword, he had no intention of walking in there unarmed.

Micah gave him a goodbye kiss. They'd been blessed since they'd been living here, in that there had been no battles for territories, and their lives were peaceful. Micah was hoping it could remain that way. "Be careful. I never trusted Alec, but I agree, it's probably good to investigate. You'll let me know if you're going to Virginia tonight, so I won't wait up?"

Raven looked into his eyes and smiled. "I love how you still worry about me. I'll be fine. Canton is no warrior and he won't give me any shit. He's here on boss-man's good graces. I'll let you know if I'll be late."

He kissed Micah one more time, then teleported out to the club. He nodded to Riley and Robbie as they opened the gate for his entrance. They both looked nervous and that made him laugh.

"No problem, warriors, I'm just going to have a little tea party with Canton."

He strolled inside and looked around. Nothing had changed much. He'd been here many times, installing security, and checking on his warriors. The blonde at the reception desk looked up with surprise.

"Raven! I didn't know you were coming."

"Take me to Canton, now."

"Uh, of course. Was he expecting you?" She was flipping through her appointment calendar, looking to see if she'd overlooked something and stalling for time.

Raven put his fist down on the book and grinned at her. "No appointment, just take me to him, and I suggest we don't warn him." Raven kept the grin on his face and took her hand. "Shall we?"

Bree looked at the dark-haired warrior and nodded. He wasn't as physically imposing as most of the warriors she'd seen, and his eyes always had a playful glint, but she had no doubt he was as deadly as the others, if not more so. He took her hand and gripped it firmly, making it clear he meant business. **"Alec?"** She tried to send him a warning that she was coming, but as usual, he was blocking her.

"Yeah, okay. Follow me." She led him down the corridor, away from the private client suites to Alec's office. She tapped lightly on the door and heard him grunt a response to enter. Opening the door, Bree looked at him apologetically as he sat behind the desk, nursing a Midnight.

"Uh, Raven is here."

Alec barked, "Tell him not now!"

Bree's face turned red, as she realized he didn't understand her meaning. "Uh, no, I mean here, as in, right here."

Raven almost laughed as he strolled in and winked at Bree. "*Grazie*, close the door on your way out."

She left quickly, closing the door behind her as Raven looked around the office. "Well, nothing much has changed in here. So, how's business? Anything interesting happening?" He took a seat in the large leather chair across from Alec's desk, and draped his leg over the arm of the chair. Hell, he could still smell Jacks in this room. She hadn't been gone long.

Alec was smart enough to know Raven's visit wasn't a coincidence. His warriors had seen the carnage and had escorted Marchesa downstairs into a holding room until Jacks could get him out of there. He'd hoped to keep this from Shade, but he knew if he was caught in a lie it would play out worse for him. Alec poured another glass of Midnight and slid it across the desk to the warrior.

"Little incident. Everything's under control now, though. Your warriors worked quickly and discreetly, and I called in Jacks to handle the master. His name is Marchesa, first time he's been here, and the last, I might add. Jacks says he was on a street drug called Tainted Beast. Ever heard of it?"

Raven looked at the drink and pushed it back at Canton. Relaxing back in the chair, he pulled out a pack of cigarettes and lit one up, blowing smoke rings above his head. Watching as the smoke rings floated aimlessly in the air, before they slowly disintegrated, he took his time responding.

"Incident? Well now, in my day, a mutilated body and blood from floor to ceiling was called a kill. I haven't gotten a memo that it's now called an incident. And you let the master go? Interesting. You brought Jacks in but didn't inform me. Last I checked, I was still in charge of security here." Raven leaned forward across the desk. "What are you hiding?"

Alec gave him a hard stare. "Clearly, nothing. I brought Jacks in because she knows every master, works for most of them. I knew she'd know what to do with him, and she'd keep her mouth shut. This business demands discretion and privacy, regardless of what happens in these rooms. I didn't need a lot of warriors showing up. It was handled, and handled quickly, with none of my clients any the wiser. If I'd called you first, and you showed up with a battalion, there would have been no way my clients would not have been aware. Besides, it's done now. What does it matter?"

Raven stood up, placing both hands on the desk and leaning over the top to glare at Canton. "What does it matter? Maybe you called Jacks hoping Shade wouldn't find out. That fucking matters. I'm in charge here, not Jacks. And if I wanted her here, I would have called her."

Raven walked around the room, he didn't have the authority to threaten Canton, that was Shade's decision. "Tainted Beast. Don't know much about it and didn't think it would be a problem for us.

If this takes off, then Master needs to know about it. It won't take long for it to travel. I have every intention of telling him what happened here. You'll be hearing from him directly, I'm certain of that." He stopped wandering around the room and turned to Alec. "Next time, don't panic, call me."

Alec emptied the untouched glass he'd poured for the warrior. "Next time? There will be no next time, trust me. I will have your warriors strip search my clients if we have to, but that drug won't be coming inside these walls again. But I'll call you."

Raven nodded and said, "Glad we understand each other. You know I have to tell him. I'm out." Raven teleported out of the office, heading to the opposite coast. It was time to fill Shade in on what he knew. As he teleported, he let Micah know he was on his way to Bel Rosso.

2-30

Raven flew over the Bel Rosso camp and the memories flooded his heart. Except for his home with Micah, the camp at Bel Rosso had been the truest home to him. He'd never taken for granted his good fortune to be accepted into the Medici camp, and trained as a warrior. He was completely dedicated to his master, and his master's mate. He knew that his queen had always liked him, and he'd loved her from the moment he met her. She was the perfect match for the boss-man.

It didn't take him long to spot Shade standing in the middle of the training field, surrounded by the new recruits. He towered over the rookie warriors, as he led them in mock battles. Scanning the crowd, he singled out Cory, another person who he held close to his heart. Cory had just stepped out of his shop and Raven landed easily in front of him and grinned.

Cory was surprised, and his heart was lifted by his old friend. "Raven, my brother!"

They clasped each other in a tight bear hug, beating each other's backs. "Damn, it's good to see you, Raven, what brings you home?"

Raven could see that Cory was beginning to age. He looked younger than his thirty-six years, and as a half-breed, he'd live longer than any mortal, but he wouldn't survive as long as the rest of them.

"Little problem out in California, no big deal, brother, just came to inform boss-man. Damn, you're looking good. How is the beautiful Madison?"

"Maddy's great, couldn't be better. And Micah?"

Raven threw his arm around Cory's shoulders. "Best decision I ever made. But I never let him forget he's older, si, and I am the young hot warrior." They were both laughing when Raven heard that familiar voice float across the field.

"Leave my son alone so he can get back to work, punk, and get your warrior ass over here." Shade joined the two of them, as he fist bumped his California SIC. Although he was glad to see Raven, he knew this wasn't a social visit. Raven wouldn't show up unannounced without good cause.

"Can I speak to you alone, boss-man, delicate problem out at L'Adventure."

Shade stiffened, wondering what the hell happened that would have made his warrior make a personal appearance. "Let's head to the house. I am sure your queen would love to see you anyway." Shade shouted orders to Marcello and Skelk to carry on with training, as he walked off the field and toward the house with Raven.

Shade took him to his office and poured them both a Midnight before sitting down. Raven held up his hand, declining the drink. "On duty."

Shade laughed. "Since when did you ever follow the rules?"

Raven grinned. "Since you made me SIC and said not to fuck it up."

Shade chuckled, as he sat back in his leather chair. "Start at the beginning, don't leave anything out."

Raven kept it short and to the point, giving Shade all the details, he'd been given from Riley and Robby, as well as the conversation with Canton. "The thing that pisses me off is his attitude, like it was nothing. And then he fucking calls in Jacks. I don't think he wanted you to know. Did he really think Medici warriors weren't going to report to me what went down?"

Shade took it all in. "Not surprised he called Jacks. What worries me more is the drug, Tainted Beast. Have you seen it on the streets?"

Raven shook his head. "Right now, it's too expensive. We don't see the masters on the streets, and this is the first time the drug has shown up in Alec's club, but I'd be naïve to think it won't spread."

Shade stood up and ran his hands through his hair, his mind spinning. Immortals and drugs were a dangerous combination, and not an easy one to control if it became epidemic. "You did the right thing, Raven. I appreciate you coming here to tell me personally. I need to speak with Jacks and Alec. I will keep you informed. You do the same. Ramp up the security on the streets, especially around the clubs, see if our warriors can pick up any information on the source for the drug. See if we can figure out who's moving it."

Raven stood to leave. "No problem, boss-man. We have a good group of warriors out there."

Shade nodded. "Well, you never had a problem predicting the streets, so see what you can find out. Look, I won't hold you up any longer. I know you want to get back and spend some time with Micah."

Raven shook his head no. "If you think for one minute, I'm leaving here without seeing my queen, think again, boss-man."

Shade smiled. "She is all beauty and grace, until you piss her off, and I have done that a few too many times in our history together. She is my light, Raven."

"Mi amore, you have a visitor who won't leave my damn office until you make an appearance."

Kate had been on the phone with Danilo, getting an update on the progress with the olive groves. She and Shannon were finding that running the business remotely offered some challenges. She was wrapping up the call when she heard Shade speak to her in her head, letting her know they had a visitor. Running a brush through her long hair, she added a touch of nude lipstick to her full lips and hurried down the stairs to his office to greet the unexpected guest. Stepping inside the office, the lights had been kept dim and it took her a moment to notice him. Kate flashed him a smile that lit up the room, holding her arms open for him. "My second most favorite warrior!"

He walked to his queen and bowed elegantly with his dramatic flair before walking into her hug. "Damn, if only I had met you first, we would not have boss-man hovering over us. But I will take second place any day, my lady."

She returned his strong hug before breaking away. "How is Micah? No trouble, I hope?"

"No trouble. Micah is gorgeous as ever. He takes good care of me. But he works too hard, reminds me of someone we both know. He has to do everything himself. Master never brings you to California anymore. You should make him bring you there for a vacation. How are you? Is Natalia still living here?"

She laughed easily with him. "We're both too busy for a vacation, and yes, Natalia is still at home for now. She's spending more and more time in Florence in preparation, but we haven't lost her yet. I'm glad you're happy."

Raven shook his head as he looked her over, she hadn't changed a bit. "Imagine that, a Medici in the Council. Give her my love, will you? Well, I should be heading back, I promised Micah this wouldn't take long. He won't sleep unless I'm with him. Needs my young warrior ass to protect him." Grinning, he hugged Kate again, whispering in her ear. "Don't tell him I said this. But I love you, I always have, and I always will."

She kissed his cheek lightly, and whispered, "The feeling is mutual. Now go home to your mate. I know what it feels like to wait."

Raven fist bumped Shade and teleported out. Shade waited until he was gone before turning to Kate. "We have a problem, and it won't be long heading to D.C. Raven made a personal visit to inform me."

The smile left her face as she saw his expression of concern and her heart sank. Problems meant one thing to her. She'd see him less. "What kind of problem?"

Shade shared what he knew. Her opinion was always important to him. He moved from behind the desk and took a seat on the sofa, grabbing her hand and pulling her to sit next to him. "This could be a problem from coast to coast. I haven't seen it on the east coast yet, but it fell right in Alec's lap. I need to make a few phone calls to clear some things up."

She settled in next to him as she contemplated the idea of a drug that left the beast out of control. "Lover, you have to find the source. Once this spreads, your warriors will be tied up handling the individual outbreaks, and it will never end. You have to find the source and make an example of him."

"I agree. It will spread rapidly. The masters that visit L'Adventure come from all over the country. If they buy it on the West Coast, and take it back into their territories, it won't take long for it to spread out of control. I think Jacks knows more than she is saying. I can bet on it. I need to talk to her, and I prefer to talk to her face to face."

Kate bristled at the mention of her name. "I know I said she wasn't welcome here, but if you must see her...I understand."

Shade leaned back and looked at her. “No need for jealousy. I see her as warrior, nothing more. You should know that by now."

Kate sighed heavily. "You see her as a warrior. What she sees is quite different. She’s a warrior, yes, but she’s also a parasite. I’ve learned much from Aislynn about female warriors who work independently. Jacks feeds only from masters, even some who are mated. She sees nothing sacred in the blood covenant and takes their blood to add to her own power and strength. I didn’t trust her then, and I don’t trust her now. She manipulates and seduces. It’s her charm, and her gift. But I understand she may have information you need. At least meet with her here."

He could feel her flare of anger. "So, my queen has ruled, and her king shall abide her ruling. I will get word out to her tonight. I need to see her as soon as possible. I don’t know where she is currently, but she responded to Alec quickly, so not too far away. But then, those two seem to have a long-standing relationship."

"Oh, I have no doubt. I had my own issues with Rissa, to be sure, but Jacks was proud to wave Alec's infidelity in Rissa's face. Her heart is black as coal. And if Alec has something she wants, she won’t hesitate to take it. Just let me know when she’s coming."

He stood up from the sofa and returned to his desk. "Consider it done. I am going to call Alec first, feel him out. Then I will call Jacks and set this up. Not planning on teleporting to California tonight, but if I need to, I will let you know." Kissing her cheek, he nibbled her ear. "You have some nerve giving me instruction, when not thirty minutes ago, you had a warrior whispering his love to you in that beautiful ear of yours."

She laughed. "You know I'm not Raven's type. He’s like a lost boy from Peter Pan, who never wanted to grow up, and I’m his Wendy."

Chuckling, he nibbled at her ear, inhaling her rose scent. "Well, if I ever catch any other warrior whispering words of love in your ear, that fucking crocodile will have a delicious meal! Now, let me get this done before you become too much of a distraction. I have work to do, woman."

Shade watched her as she walked out the door, the subtle sway of her hips as tantalizing as the first time he’d seen her. "Damn, I love that woman." He adjusted himself in his leathers. She never failed to stir his blood. Grabbing a fresh Midnight, he pulled out his cell phone and checked the time before dialing up Alec. L'Adventure should still be in full swing with the time difference, and Alec had better fucking answer the call.

2-31

Alec had made the rounds tonight, checking with guests personally as they left, making sure they'd had a pleasant evening. If any of them were aware of the earlier disturbance, they didn't show it. He asked Bree to let him know if she heard anything, but so far, the rest of the clientele seemed oblivious to the drama that had played out here. He was just getting back to his office when his cell rang, and he saw Shade on caller ID. "Well, that didn't take long." He plopped down in the chair behind his desk and answered. "Alec."

"Well, hello, brother. Sounds like business is really kicking some ass out there. Funny thing happened tonight. I got a visit from Raven. Seems there was a bit of an incident with Marchesa. Care to fucking tell me what the hell that was about?"

Alec was in no mood for attitude. He poured another Midnight and lit up, giving himself time to process before he answered.

"You probably know as much as me then. This was his first visit, and he had a referral from a long-time client. We did a background check, and everything was clean. He's not mated, and didn't have anyone with him, so he picked a female from our stables. He'd asked for some heavy BDSM, so Bree had the room ready. His allotted time was up, so Bree went to their room to see if he wanted to pay for additional time. She knocked several times and got no answer, so she used her key card to enter, and when she did, she walked into a slaughterhouse. She was smart enough to leave, and lock him in, and came to me immediately. As soon as I saw him, I knew he was on something. I had your warriors isolate him underground, and I called Jacks. She was on the east coast, got here pretty quick, gave me the number for a cleaner, and then escorted his ass out of here. Said she'd stay with him until he slept if off. Jacks said he was on Tainted Beast. Never heard of it myself, but fuck me, if this takes hold, we're in for some real problems. I've been talking to clientele all night, and no one here seems to be aware of anything happening, so I feel good we have it under wraps."

Shade listened and threw his booted feet up on the desk, crossing his ankles. He could hear Alec light up, so he did too. "This is far from being under wraps. Why the fuck didn't you just call Raven, or me? Listen, I know you got something with Jacks, I don't give two fucks about that, brother, but this is my territory. I call the shots. I don't like outsiders coming in and seeing our business. Jacks only works for masters, and she hears everything, knows everything. She won't have any problems blabbing my troubles to other masters if it works to her advantage. Keep that in mind next time your cock needs a round or two with her. You ever call her again for anything other than a fuck and feed, and I'm shutting that club down!" Shade was getting worked up and threw his feet to the floor with a thud.

"Raven is amping up the security. I need you to keep your ears and eyes open. You hear one damn thing; you call me pronto. This is going to get real ugly, brother, real ugly. And to save both our asses, I need to find the source of this fucking nightmare. We clear?"

Alec bristled at taking orders, but knew he was in no position to argue. "Clear. If I hear anything about the drug, I'll let you know. And believe me, we'll be doing full body searches on any new clients before we let them in."

"My work is cut out for me and I need your assistance. For once, you need to help me out here, Alec. I don't want to be a bastard, but I will if pushed. Raven was certain the drug originated on the west coast, and the cost would prohibit it from being purchased by anyone other than masters. You're in the best position to figure out who's pushing it."

Alec ran his hands through his hair. It had been a long night and he was tired. "Whatever, brother."

Shade hit his fist on the desk. "Get your head out of your ass, brother, this is just the beginning."

He hung up and shook his head. No matter where the fuck Alec went, there'd be a shit storm stirred up eventually. He thought once he was underground things would be quiet, but he should've known better. He sat for a moment and thought about the masters in that area, but no one came to mind. He'd maintained a friendly alliance with all of them, but someone was cooking up this Tainted Beast. Before he drove himself crazy, he picked up his phone and ran through his contacts. There she was...Jacks. He was certain she knew more than she was saying. He dialed her up to invite her to a friendly meeting with him tomorrow evening at Bel Rosso.

2-32

Shade woke early and hurried to the camp. He had a lot to finish up before Jacks arrived. He kissed *bel* before leaving, reminding her about the meeting. She nodded but didn't respond, and he knew already she was less than happy about having to make this concession. Shade had never judged Jacks. She wasn't at the Medici camp in Florence for very long and wasn't considered a Medici warrior. She'd come to his camp when she was younger, at the behest of her master to improve some of her weapons skills. She'd later left that master and worked as a mercenary. He was aware of her practice of working, and feeding, from masters only, and had learned of her brief relationship with Alec. Apparently, there was still a spark between them. It meant nothing to Shade. She'd never presented herself as an enemy to him, and how she conducted her personal life was none of his business.

She traveled the world, taking the jobs that appealed to her, and it gave her access to a lot of information. She typically knew what was going on out there, and she called no one master. She'd flirted innocently enough with him before he was mated, hinting she was available, but had never made any serious moves on him. He had respect for her skills, but she held no attraction to him.

Returning from the camp, he checked back in with Kate to find she was stepping out of the shower. He informed her he had some calls to make and reminded her of the time. Glancing at his watch, it was 11:30 p.m., and Jacks would be arriving soon. Kate muttered that she'd be ready as he left her getting dressed. He chuckled to himself, wondering how this evening would go.

***

Kate wasn't looking forward to Jacks' visit. The last time she was here, Jacks was told she'd never be welcome here. Shade had been clear he'd honor her request to bar Jacks from their home, but had also said Jacks had been an ally, and their paths may cross. He couldn't promise he wouldn't have to deal with her again at some point. Now that he needed to talk with her, Kate hated she had to rescind her own edict, and invite this woman back into their home, but it was preferable to having Shade meet her somewhere else.

She'd showered and used her rose fragrance, and stood in her walk-in closet, wrapped in a towel, trying to decide what to wear. She had a closet full of designer clothes she rarely wore and felt ridiculous putting any of them on now. She settled on a pair of tight jeans, a cashmere sweater in black that fell off one shoulder, and her red knee-high boots with heels. She brushed her hair to a high sheen and put on her makeup. She was completing the finishing touches when she heard Shade call to her telepathically, letting her know Jacks was due any minute. She hurried down the stairs, sending a message to Aegis to stand down but stay close to the entrance, and headed to his office when she heard him in the living room. *So, he's receiving her like an invited guest, and not like the warriors he brings straight into the office. Well, isn't that interesting.* She gave him a look as she entered the living room.

"Are we serving wine too?"

His eyes took her in from head to toe. Her rose scent washed over him in a delicate yet erotic wave. The jeans hugged her every female curve and the black cashmere set off her crimson hair and exposed her lily-white shoulder. She was wearing his favorite boots, and the total affect made him want to eat her alive. It took him a moment to realize her question was a sarcastic one.

"That is what we do when we have guests, *si*? Are you angry about this, *mi amore*? You said you were fine as long as you were present."

She sighed and waved her hand. "Whatever. Let's just get this over with. The sooner that woman leaves, the happier I'll be." She walked with purpose to the sofa and sat down. "She better not be late."

Shade grinned. He was amused by her jealousy. If she only knew how little he cared about Jacks. He wondered if she'd ever lose those feelings, or even if he wanted her to. She kept his life interesting. "Jacks is a warrior, she can tell time. Would you like a Midnight or Red Moon?"

Kate snapped her head around. "Do *not* serve Red Moon, and do not offer it. Understood?"

Gi was entering with a tray that included bottles of each when he heard her comment and made a sharp U-turn to return to the kitchen to remove the bottle of Red Moon, and Shade had to stifle a laugh. The doorbell rang as Gi was heading back to the kitchen, and he paused like a deer in the headlights. If he answered the door now, their guest would see both bottles on the tray.

Kate waved her hand at him in exasperation. "Go, I'll get it!"

Gi was flustered as he hurried back to the kitchen. "Yes, my lady." It was so rare to see her in a bad mood, he was unsure how to handle her.

Kate stalked to the door, her boot heels clicking hard against the stone in the foyer and swung it open to greet Jacks. Jacks had her hair down, hanging long and loose on her shoulders. Her cat-eye makeup gave her an even more exotic look, and she was poured into the black dress that left nothing to the imagination. Even without heels, she'd tower over Kate, but her four-inch stilettos put her close to Shade's height. Kate stood with one hand on the door and the other on the doorjamb, blocking her entry as she took her in, pointedly looking at her from head to toe with disdain.

"Got a date tonight, Jacks?"

Jacks was taken off guard when Kate answered her own door. *My, we do live a country life when the queen must open her own door.* "It's nice to see you, my lady. I have an appointment with the Medici, his request, I might add."

Jacks knew she was jealous, and not happy she was being allowed back inside their home. She looked down at her attire and smiled. "I'm meeting a royal master. I dress appropriately when meeting any master of Shade's caliber."

Kate laughed. "You dress like the whore you are when meeting any master, you think might advance your purpose, so cut the crap, Jacks. I'm not impressed. Now come in. You have information my mate needs to get this situation under control, and unless you want an up close and personal visit from that wolf standing behind you, I suggest you tell him what he needs to know."

She swung the door open and turned on her heels, walking back into the living room without waiting to see Jacks' response. "Gi! Where's the wine?"

Gi was hurrying back into the room with the newly prepared tray, where Kate lifted one glass for herself and sat back down on the sofa, and took a sip, looking up at Shade. "Let the games begin, lover."

Shade had heard the entire exchange and sighed heavily. **"Back it down, *mi amore*, I need her help."**

Jacks was left to close the door, and saw the wolf staring her down, her teeth bared. Pushing the door closed, she walked, unescorted, into the living room.

Shade turned with a smile on his face as Jacks entered the room, Gi scurrying behind her like a befuddled old man on the first day of a new job. Damn, this was going to be a long ass night. His eyes scanned the dress Jacks had chosen to wear, and knew Jacks picked her attire specifically to aggravate Kate. He shook his head.

"Welcome, Jacks. Good to see you again."

Jacks looked him over, as he stood there in jeans and a blue dress shirt that matched those glorious eyes, his most startling feature. He could rule the world with those eyes. "Thank you, Shade, I'm most honored to be invited to Bel Rosso again."

Walking to him, she decided not to push any more buttons this early, so she settled for taking both his hands in hers.

Shade squeezed her hands and smiled. "Can I get you a Midnight, Jacks?"

She released his hands and smiled back at him. They were almost eye to eye. "You forget, I don't partake of wine. My body is my temple." She casually sat in the armchair positioned across from the sofa. "I must say, the estate looks beautiful this time of year. A full camp as well, I saw it when arriving."

Shade took a Midnight from the tray and sat beside Kate, throwing his arm across the back of the sofa, and around her shoulders. "Yes, the camps have grown over the years. But I cannot take credit for the beautiful grounds. That is Kate's doing."

Kate silently claimed him, as she slid her hand down his thigh. Speaking in a quiet voice, meant for him, she answered. "Thank you."

Shade was aware of her hand on his thigh, and its meaning. It was Kate sending a 'back off bitch' message, but if it registered on Jacks, she didn't show it. Jacks responded with a counter move of slowly and seductively crossing her legs, as the short, tight skirt rode up high on her bare, toned thighs. He could feel Kate's grip on his thigh tighten, and he leaned into her, nuzzling her hair and kissing her cheek as he whispered softly, "Pay her no mind, *mi amore.*"

Looking back at Jacks, he relaxed. "So, there was a killing out at L'Adventure. I have spoken with Alec. You should know, I dressed him down for not calling Raven instead of calling you. I did not appreciate that. Just getting that out in the open."

Jacks returned his stare and nodded. "I understand the breach, Shade. Alec is in your territory through your good graces. But I have to tell you, I think he was in a bit of a bind. He knew I'd know all the masters, and I handled it as best as I could. He didn't want to create a disturbance or draw the attention of his other clients. I saw immediately what the circumstance was when entering the room. I've seen the kind of violence Tainted Beast brings out in a vamp. The drug works quickly, creating a rapid and uncontrolled rage and blood lust, followed by a hard crash, where the beast retreats and the vamp is left feeling drained and tired."

Shade nodded. "Understood. But if he calls you again, consider yourself warned, Jacks. Decline. Are we clear?"

Jacks nodded, her eyes never leaving his face. "Perfectly, master."

Shade drank heavily from his Midnight. "I don't like this Tainted Beast. It can wreak havoc on all of us. You know more than you let on, Jacks. I want some details."

Jacks cocked her head slightly, letting her long raven hair fall across her cheek. She casually pushed it back behind her ear. "If you're implying, I've told Alec more than I've told you, you'd be wrong, Shade. I may know a few things, but probably not the details you're looking for. Shall I tell you all I do know?"

Shade sighed loud enough for her to hear it. "Jacks, do not play games with me. It doesn't suit you. We have a serious problem here that could affect all of us. I asked you here because I intend to end this. You can either help me, or I can consider you on the wrong side of this epidemic. Be careful which side you choose, warrior."

Jacks sat up straight. Was he threatening her? She stared at him without flinching. "Master Medici, I'm a mercenary warrior of the highest degree. Our world is very important to me, and to those I protect from such evil. Don't misjudge my purpose. When it comes to my livelihood, I play no games. This drug is designed to give the beast an uncontrollable high. It's a powder. It has no smell. It's short lived, maybe an hour at the most. Just enough time to do immense damage. The drug is typically snorted, and from what I hear, it can be injected. I haven't seen the substance myself, but I've heard masters speaking of it, masters whom, I may add, are against its use, just as you are. Everyone thinks its origin are in California, or close by. It's very expensive, so no one has yet to see it on the streets with rogues or your average vampire. I couldn't, at this point, tell you if it's addictive, but I'd assume that it is. And that's all I know."

Kate had been listening to the exchange between them as they bantered back and forth, when she spoke up. "So, this master you took away from L'Adventure, what was his name? He obviously came in with the drug. Did you ask him where he got it?"

Jacks' eyes immediately went to Kate. "It was Master Marchesa. He's from Canada. Montreal. When they take the drug, its after affect leaves them quite drained. He was all but unconscious when I returned him to his home. I was already on another assignment to a master in Maine, and I couldn't wait around for Marchesa to wake up. It's a very good idea to question him, though, if he remembers anything."

Kate rolled her eyes. "So, you took the money to escort him home, and that's it? What he knows could be invaluable to us."

Jacks held her head up and smiled softly. "No offense, my lady, but you're not warrior. I was paid to do one job, make sure he arrived at his home safely. I wasn't asked to interrogate him. A warrior has to make a living, but I know my place." Her eyes went to Shade, ignoring Kate. "I'm sure you'll understand I had an obligation to the master in Maine. I know a little about Marchesa. He travels a great deal, and he does like a bit of rough entertainment. It's not my place to intercede further, unless asked to do so. I leave that to you, as this incident was within your territory and under your command."

"You did fine, Jacks. Your obligation to another master is understandable, and the situation was handled well enough this time. Going forward, things will definitely be different, as you and Alec well know now. I appreciate your assistance, please understand that. I will handle this from this point on."

Jacks looked to Kate and nodded with a smile, before turning back to Shade. "I'll email you the coordinates for his home. If you wish for my assistance in any of this, Shade, I'll help you in any way possible. I come in contact with many, and gossip is very thick."

Shade stood and walked behind the sofa, standing behind Kate. "Would you agree to let me know if you hear anything? This drug is going to travel, and I cringe to think of it in D.C. I have already spoken with Raven, and we have ramped up security in California."

Jacks nodded with enthusiasm. "Of course, Shade. If you can find the source, we could all come together and get this finished. I'd be honored to be of assistance. You can count me in."

Kate muttered under her breath. "I'm sure he can."

Shade walked around the sofa and shook her hand. "I appreciate this a great deal. We will handle it, and I want you to contact me personally if you hear anything."

She laid her free hand on his arm. "Understood. Take my card, it has my personal number on it as well. The number you have is my business line. I'll answer my personal calls on any occasion, in any situation. It's always a pleasure to assist you, Master Medici. I wouldn't be here today without you. You've been a great master in my life." She smiled and tucked the card into the pocket of his jeans.

He ignored her bold move and was hoping Kate didn't come off the sofa to choke her. "It is always good to see warriors from my camp succeed. And we need a good ear out there."

Jacks looked up at him coyly and smiled before turning to Kate. "Thank you again, my lady, for entertaining me in your home. I know we've had our moments, but I hope you see I only wish to assist your mate and do what's best for our society."

Kate gave her a stare that could drop a lesser immortal to their knees. She stood but didn't extend her hand and led Jacks to the door, opening it for her. Aegis paced outside with Night-Stalker close at hand. They'd felt her anger and moved closer to the house. Kate did nothing to calm them. She heard the flutters of wings and looked up to see Danica land in the tree near the door. Kate held up her hand and the falcon swooped down, landing on her hand, careful not to sink his powerful talons into her tender flesh. The falcon squawked loudly. She felt the snake wind itself around her ankle of her red leather boots and didn't need to look down to know it was Harley. Turning to Jacks, she gave her a coy smile. "Be careful out there."

Jacks knew Kate was getting her retribution. There was no vampire alive who hadn't heard of her rare gift. "They're beautiful creatures. You're a powerful queen, you not only have these animals to fight for you, but a mate who is wanted by every female in the vampire world. And from what I hear, your son, the prince, becomes more like his father every day. The Medici prowess is still alive and well, apparently."

Without another word, she teleported out without taking one step outside. Jacks was laughing the entire way back to Maine. Her goal for the night had been met. Shade would need her for the information she could provide, and that would keep her close to Alec.

Kate released Danica who flew skyward, and the snake slithered from around her ankle. She slammed the door so hard it rattled every window in the house. "I hate that fucking bitch!"

Shade ran his hand through his hair and began to chuckle. "You know, *bel*, you really bring this on yourself. If you'd just relax, she wouldn't give you so many digs." Shaking his head, he poured another Midnight and slung it back, emptying the glass.

Kate was still muttering under her breath as she walked back into the room and threw back the rest of the wine in her glass. She was almost out of breath she was so angry. "Do you need her personal number? Really? Don't kid yourself. She treats the mates of all masters the same, looking down her nose at them. She wants to make her intentions clear and make them feel there's nothing they can do to stop her. I know her type from the mortal world. She's just more powerful. She may be your ally, but let me be clear, she's not mine."

Shade leaned against the small glass front cabinet used as the bar, his arms crossed. "Damn woman, you are fired up. But in this situation, she is best positioned to hear the gossip, and benefit me in finding who is producing this drug. Besides, it isn't me she is interested in, but Alec."

She closed her eyes and took a deep breath, calming herself. "I know she has her sights on Alec. But she's a predator, and if Alec isn't available, she'll go after whoever's in her path." Setting the glass back down on the table, she turned to him. "Just make sure you're not the one in her path. Her personal number?" She held out her hand, palm out, waiting for him to hand over her personal card.

"I was never in her path. As for the personal number..." He left the sentence hanging and walked up to her, towering over her. He took her outstretched hand and clasped it to his heart. "Be careful sticking your hands in my pockets. You are already making my beast sit up and take notice tonight. He loves to tangle with you, *mi amore*. You speak boldly to your master, and I would take you over my knee and smack that beautiful ass, but I think you would enjoy that as much as me. So, let's not push your master too far, my Queen."

He willed on the music, as Van Morrison's "Into the Mystic" filled the room. He slid his arm around her waist and began to dance with her across the floor. "I only want to rock one gypsy soul...yours."

She allowed him to lead her in the dance, knowing she'd pushed him as far as she could. Her battle wasn't with him anyway, but the bitch that always found a way to put herself in his path. This situation with the drug would mean he had more reasons to meet with Jacks. And Jacks knew it. She'd been blind to the manipulations from Rissa, and it had cost her their first baby. She wouldn't make the same mistake twice.

2-33

Marco walked out of the small shack sitting in the midst of the olive grove, slamming the door behind him. He needed a smoke. It was late evening, and Lorenzo would be arriving soon for his shift of guarding the groves. Marco was more bored than tired, as not a damn thing had happened. He normally didn't come to any outpost. But after the visit from Sal, he felt he should make himself visible. Danilo was busy with the migrant workers, so Marco was left to watch absolutely nothing happen. He knew eventually the *Mafioso* would show their face again. As he lit up, he leaned against the shack and knew this was the easy part of his day. He'd finish up here, then go back to camp to work with the new recruits. Before he finished his smoke, Lorenzo and several warriors appeared, ready for their duty.

Lorenzo approached him and asked how the shift went. "Nothing. Not a damn sign of this Sal or any other *Mafioso*."

Lorenzo lit up with him, using Marco's cigarette to light his own. "Well, maybe that's a good sign. Maybe they've moved on. Bigger fish to fry. Not sure what the *Mafioso* would want with us anyway. I always thought they were focused on drugs and prostitution. Not sure why they'd be interested in olives."

As he spoke, the same black car pulled into the groves. Lorenzo turned his head to watch the car as it drove slowly toward them over the unpaved road. He chuckled to himself. "Good timing, Marco. Looks like we're about to find out. This is the same guy that showed up the last time."

Marco bristled and checked his weapons. "All they want is money. Everything they do is about money." Marco watched as the man got out of the car and strolled casually in their direction. He was packing and made no attempt to hide it. "Let me do the talking." Marco stepped forward to address Sal. "You got business here?"

Sal stopped short as the older man stepped forward. He recognized the young punk with the long hair from his earlier visit. "Depends, you in charge?"

"*Si*, state your business. You are on private property."

Sal took his time and looked around the property as he lit up the stub of a cigar. "Been looking around. Lot of new groves under development, and some old ones being worked. They belong to you?"

Marco stood at his full height, easily towering over the man in the expensive suit. He knew this wasn't the boss. The *Mafioso* worked a lot like a coven. There was a hierarchy, and everyone had their role to play. "Well, let me get one thing straight, you keep answering my question with another question, your ass will be escorted out of here in a hurry, *si*? So, let me inform you, I am in charge here. And no, they do not belong to me and it is none of your business who they do belong to." Marco stepped a bit closer to the man. "Why don't you just tell me why your ass drove way out here? State your fucking business."

Sal didn't back down as the taller man approached him, standing close. "My boss wants a meeting, but if you aren't the person who can make the decisions, then don't bother. Are you the guy?"

Marco chuckled as he felt Lorenzo and the warriors move up behind him, establishing a clear line of defense. "Oh, I'm your man." Marco crossed his arms over his chest. "But meetings take up my precious time. Who the hell wants a meeting, and why?"

Sal gnawed on the stub of his cigar and leaned against the hood of his car. Removing the stub from his mouth, he spit on the ground, aiming just shy of Marco's booted foot. "Gonna cut you some slack, because you're obviously new to the business. Realize you probably don't understand how things work. I work for the Benito family, and they have an interest in your business. There's a restaurant in town, Solo Toscano, in the San Lorenzo district. You need to be there tonight, around ten. I suggest you not be late. The boss don't like waiting."

Marco grunted and looked up at the sky, it was about eight now, that would give him two hours to tell Shade what was going down and get his ass to San Lorenzo. "We will be there."

Sal spit on the ground one last time before getting in the car and backing it down the dusty road. He didn't speak again. He'd done his job, delivered the message and got an answer for the boss. After the car pulled away, Lorenzo stepped in closer to Marco.

"You want me there? I don't think you should go in alone. You'll be surrounded by mortals. Can't pull any vampire shit. Alfie's on duty tonight too."

Marco tossed his cigarette to the ground. "Let's head back to camp, just you and me, leave these warriors on duty. We just stepped into some shit. We need to call Shade; see how he wants us to roll with this. Trust me, mafia work like we do, no one goes alone. I'll have warriors stationed inside and outside the restaurant."

Lorenzo smiled to himself. *Fuck yeah*. Things just got real. He was tired of fighting fake battles and was looking forward to a confrontation, even if it was with mortals.

2-34

Marco and Lorenzo teleported back to Castello, leaving the warriors to patrol the olive groves. Lorenzo suggested they make the conference call from inside the office at Castello. Marco made a quick detour to the camp and gave out instructions for the evening, selecting the warriors he wanted to send into Florence to patrol and surround the restaurant. All warriors were informed they were dealing with mortals, so no leathers were to be worn. Everyone was to blend in and remain low-key. He wasn't expecting any trouble on this first visit, but he knew better than to go in unprepared. He teleported back to Castello and walked into the office to find Lorenzo and Alfie waiting for him.

"Well, the gang is all here. Let's wake up your old man and get some instructions. You got any ideas how to do this?"

Lorenzo shrugged. "I'll call my dad's cell, he'll still be in his death slumber, but Mom will answer." Putting them on speaker, Lorenzo dialed his father's number and heard the phone ring a few times before he heard his mother's voice.

Kate was sleeping next to him when she heard his cell ring. She sat up in the darkened room, and switched on the bedside lamp, momentarily confused. It was rare for his phone to ring during his death slumber. She reached across him to the table on his side of the bed and grabbed for the phone, seeing her son's name on the caller ID. Her heart skipped a beat, wondering if he was in trouble, but she didn't feel any anxiety from him. "Lorenzo? Are you okay?"

He reassured her that everything was fine. "Mom, I hated to call now, but I'm here with Marco, and we have a meeting set up for later. We need to let Dad know what's going on."

Kate was silent for a moment, working through the details in her head. Her son may not be in immediate danger, but whatever was happening was critical enough to notify Shade immediately and that concerned her. "Of course, I'll wake him. Hold on."

Kate set the cell phone down on the bed, as she leaned over him, stroking his face, speaking softly. "Shade, I need you to wake up." She could count on one hand the number of times she'd had to pull him from his death slumber. Leaning closer to his ear, her lips grazed his skin. “Lover, hear my voice, I need you with me."

Shade felt his beast stir as he heard her call to him. His heart began to slam harder in his chest as he felt her anxiety. His eyes flashed open, and he felt a momentary panic. "*Bel!*" He wrapped both arms around her, and rolled her to her back, protecting her with his body as he honed his senses, trying to detect any threat to her. "*Cazzo*, are you all right, what is wrong?"

“I'm fine. It's not me, it's Lorenzo. He’s on the cell." She picked up the phone from the bed and handed it to him, as he sat up, and cleared the cobwebs from his head.

"What is going on, is he in trouble?" Shade grabbed the phone. "Son, what the hell is going on, do you need me?" He was already getting out of bed, balancing the cell phone on his shoulder as he pulled on a pair of jeans, getting ready to leave if necessary.

Lorenzo could almost visualize the scene taking place in his parents’ bedroom as he heard his father scrambling around. "Chill out, Dad. I got you on speaker. Marco’s here. He wants to give you an update on the little mafia situation."

"You woke me from my death slumber to talk to his old leather ass? This fucking better be good!" Shade looked at Kate and grinned, as he took a seat in the large chair by the window and put the phone on speaker.

Marco laughed. "Somebody has to work while you sleep.”

Shade grunted. "What the fuck is going on over there? Give me the details, brother, before I teleport over there and bust heads."

Marco looked at Lorenzo and Alfie, and they were both grinning. "We had company out at the groves. Sal, same grunt as before. At least we know now it is the Benito family. He was asking who’s in charge. Boss wants a meeting tonight at ten, local restaurant in town. I’m guessing we’ll find out what they want. I got warriors heading out there now. Lorenzo and Alfie both want in, itching to go along. That’s your call, brother."

Shade took a deep breath and ran his hand through his tousled curls. "Doesn’t sound like they will cause much trouble tonight. They picked a public place for a reason. Marco, you take the lead, do all the talking. See what they want. Don’t argue, don’t start anything.” He thought for a minute about sending his son into this situation. "Lorenzo, give me your thoughts, son."

Lorenzo looked at Alfie and threw up his hands. "Dad, I'm not a kid anymore. What did you train me for? I need to be there, hear what's said. So does Alfie. I'll follow Marco's lead, but don't tie my hands here."

Kate had left the bed and sat on the arm of the chair, biting her lip. He took her hand and winked at her, letting her know everything was under control. "Okay but keep your damn wits about you. They are mortal, but they are still dangerous. Alfie, you make sure Nickola is with my daughter. Let me know what the fuck happens." Shade heard them all agree on their end and he ended the call.

He leaned his head back against the chair. "His first assignment as a warrior, *mi amore*."

"But it's just a meeting, right? And they're in a public place. You don't think there's any real danger, do you?"

"No, I do not expect any trouble. Lorenzo is right, he needs to see the faces, hear the words. I know I have given him all the tools he needs, and Marco is with him. Is it just hard to know he is now facing a real threat?" He pulled her into his lap. "They will be calling us back in a few hours with the results, so I need you to keep my mind occupied. Any ideas?"

She was reassured by his words, and his confidence that Lorenzo was safe. "Ideas? I have a long list. Should I just start at the top?"

"Oh *si*, and do not miss a one!" He laughed as he lifted her up and carried her back to their bed.

2-35

Teleporting into Florence, Marco and the boys knew exactly where the restaurant was. They landed easily out of view and blended quickly into the crowd of mortals. Marco scanned the plaza, and saw his warriors strategically placed.

"Let's fucking get this over with. Let me do the talking. If I get my temper up, someone nudge me or kick me or something. These *bastardos* have me pissed off already." Walking inside the busy restaurant, Marco made brief eye contact with the few warriors sitting inconspicuously inside.

Sal saw them when they entered, the older man who was in charge, and the two young punks, one with long dark hair, and the other looking clean cut. It was the same two boys he'd seen on his first visit. He stood up and walked in their direction. "Boss is over here," he muttered to the three of them and turned to head back to the corner table, where four other men sat waiting. It was clear which one was the boss. He sat in the center, flanked by muscle, as he ate a steaming plate of pasta. Sal sat down and motioned for the three men to sit.

Marco eyed the bastard, Benito, filling his gullet with pasta. His fat fingers were covered in diamond studded rings, and his hand-cut Italian suit was the best money could buy. Marco and Lorenzo took a seat at the table, while Alfie stood to the side, within hearing distance. Marco nodded to Benito and waited for him to chew and swallow, but what he really wanted was to shove the fucking plate up his ass.

Benito looked up from his plate. "You want macaroni?" Without waiting for a response, he yelled out to the waiter. "Hey, Tony, bring my friend some macaroni! And fill his glass." Looking back at the older man, he nodded. "Sal says you're the one in charge of the olive groves. Already know the land belongs to two women. Saw the deed. What was the names, Sal? Katherine and Shannon Medici. They your sisters? Your old lady? How do you fit into this picture, *paisan*? You a Medici too?

Marco narrowed his eyes. Before he could answer, there was a plate of pasta in front of him, and a glass of red wine. He lifted the glass to his lips and pretended to sip. Pushing the plate aside, he made direct eye contact with Benito. "I'm the man you need to speak to, Second-in-Command to the boss. Medici is the name. Olive groves are deeded to the ladies, little business to keep the womenfolk happy, *si*? What business is it of yours?"

Benito dragged the cloth napkin across his mouth and swallowed. "Didn't catch your name, *paisan*? What am I supposed to call you, Mr. Second-in-Command?"

"Marco, Marco Medici."

Benito lifted his glass. "*Salute*, Marco. Welcome to my table." He downed the wine and held his glass up as a sign to the waiter, who rushed forward and refilled his glass. "See, I thought we had a problem, but this isn't going to be a problem." He looked at Marco's untouched plate before proceeding. "You don't like the macaroni? Listen, this little business you got going. Seems like it's just something to keep the women occupied, am I right? So, here's the deal, Marco. Around here, we got a, what do you call it, a monopoly. We control the olive oil business. Now, your women? They just keep doing what they doing, *si*? You let them run the business. But when you get ready to sell the harvest, you sell to me. I set the price. Understand?"

Marco snorted. "You do have a problem. The females, *Americanos*. They don't take lightly to someone stealing their profits, and neither does the boss."

Benito threw up his hands. "Whoa, whoa, Marco. You misunderstand me. We pay for the harvest. We just decide what to pay, *si*? Your ladies, they still make money. See, the Americans, coming over here, messing in our business. This is how we do things, am I right? Now, you go back to the ladies, you explain how things work over here. You do that, okay *paisan*? You do that, and we got no problems. Last thing I want is problems, you know what I mean?"

Marco had to grip the sides of the chair to keep from ripping this fool's head off. Instead, he sat there like he gave a good shit, and listened to this pasta eating bastard pimp around his business. "I don't tell the ladies anything. Boss-man deals with it all. I am just the messenger and I will relay your message."

Marco stood up, and Lorenzo did the same. One of the Benito grunts started to stand, and Alfie casually laid his hand on his shoulder and pushed him politely back in his chair. The three of them turned their backs and walked out the door, knowing their backs were well covered by the other warriors in the room. As they got outside, Marco nodded in the direction they came from, and they wove their way in and out of the crowd, making sure they weren't followed. Teleporting back to Castello, they landed outside, and Marco shook his head. "Fucking damn mortals. What do you two make of all that bullshit?"

Lorenzo couldn't stifle his laughter. "Are you kidding me? They think they can just take over? I've read about the mafia. I mean, what can they do to us, Marco? We have enough warriors to provide protection to the groves. Mom and Shannon can sell to whoever they want. You know Dad's not going to back down."

"Dumb fucking *bastardos*. They make me ashamed to be Italian. They aren't taking anything from us. Nothing. We will be on that bastard like fire in hell. He won't know what hit him. I got some real work to get to. Call your old man. Tell him what went down." Turning to Alfie, Marco barked at him. "And get your ass home to your mate. She is already begging me to give you time off. So is Shade, he wants grandbabies at his feet." Teleporting out, he headed for camp, and left Alfie and Lorenzo standing there.

Lorenzo looked at Alfie and laughed. "First time I ever heard Marco issue an order for a warrior to go get fucked. Better take advantage of it, brother. I'll call my dad; let him know how the meeting went."

Alfie laughed and slapped Lorenzo on the back. "With pleasure, brother. Never turn down time with red!"

2-36

Raven sat in his office at the warrior camp, located on the far side of the vineyards, out of view of the inn. He was waiting on Matteo, the newest warrior from Bel Rosso to arrive. Raven had worked with him extensively during the time he'd lived in the Bel Rosso camp, and patrolled the streets of D.C., but this would be Matteo's first assignment to the California camp. Raven had been in conversation with Shade off and on since the incident at L'Adventure, and they had decided to try to infiltrate the club scene in San Francisco to see if there was anyone selling Tainted Beast. San Francisco was a big city, but Raven figured the best place to start their search was in the area known as the Tenderloin. If there was anything going on, it would start in the Tenderloin. He'd already had warriors scouting the streets, looking for any sign of the drugs, but the Medici warriors were known in this area now. No one would sell to them. His plan was to get someone inside the clubs, and they'd have to be unknown on the California circuit, and Matteo fit the bill.

Matteo had arrived in California the night before and had gotten settled into the new barracks. The layout for the camp was very similar to the camp at Bel Rosso. He knew most of the warriors here, as they had all trained at Bel Rosso or Castello at some point. Tonight, he was meeting up with Raven to get an undercover assignment. Since his last big assignment had been serving as a bodyguard to Canton during his Presidential campaign, Matteo had reverted to letting his hair grow back to its shoulder length. He made his way to the office that Raven maintained inside the camp. He'd already been given strict instructions to steer clear of the inn. He tapped at the door before opening and stepped inside. He had to grin when he saw him. California had only enhanced Raven's fashion style.

"Nice outfit, boss. Mind if I sit down?" Without waiting for a response, Matteo dropped into a chair in front of the desk, and threw his feet up, crossed at the ankles. He pulled a pack of cigarettes out of his pocket and lit up, offering the pack to Raven. "Smoke?"

Raven grinned when Matteo walked in. Matteo was big and bulky, perfect for this assignment as he'd be dealing with a rough element. "Hey, brother, I got style, what can I say?" Grabbing the smokes, he nodded and lit up. "I know boss-man informed you of what the hell is going on out here. You already know about Canton, and that whole situation. Master is afraid this drug will go mainstream, and we're trying to stop that before it happens. I want to get someone inside, snoop around, see if we can find out who's selling this shit, or better yet, who's at the top. Whoever it is, they're immortal. My warriors patrol nightly, and none of them have seen any evidence of the drug. We need someone who can get inside they won't recognize as being Medici. That's where you come in, brother. You up for a little fun?"

Matteo took a deep drag on the cigarettes before exhaling the smoke. "Things have been quiet in D.C. for a long time, brother. I'm ready to mix it up a little. You want an undercover sting? I can start hanging out in the clubs, try to score some drugs, ask about this new stuff, see if anybody knows anything. I'll need some front money. I'll have to make some legit buys of heroin and cocaine to establish my rep. If this stuff is still underground, no one's going to come forward to me until I've made some buys, shown my face, let them get to trust me. It will take some time. Breaking into drug rings takes patience, brother."

Raven waved his jeweled fingers in the air and pushed the long black hair out of his face. "Money's no object. And I understand where you're coming from. I grew up on the streets of Florence. It doesn't matter where you hang your cock, brother. Drugs are the same on every continent. There's a section in San Francisco called the Tenderloin. I highlighted it on the grid maps I left in your bunk. That's the best place to start. Clubs there are hopping with immortals. Drugs and feeding are easy. We have a lot of coverage there, so we'll have your back. My warriors won't interfere unless you need them. They'll steer clear of you, treat you like a stranger. Giving you free rein, brother. Do whatever you think you need to. So far, this Tainted Beast is only being bought by masters, still too expensive for the street. Just stay in touch and let me know whatever you see or hear."

Matteo nodded, and leaned his head back on the chair, looking at the ceiling. "So, what's my cover? I can't be Medici. You want me to just play a freelance warrior? A mercenary?"

Raven nodded. "Mercenary is a good cover and you look the part. But you'll have to be under contract to a master. No names. If someone asks, you'll have to say he doesn't want his name out there. Say you're making the buy on his behalf. That shouldn't be hard to sell. I'd think a lot of masters wouldn't want their name associated with it. Have to find the source, brother. That's the key. Find the source and eliminate his ass. Boss-man wants this nipped in the bud before it spreads to the east coast. Sounds to me like your asses are getting lazy out there, maybe they need some action."

Matteo took another drag from the cigarette. "Nah. You know master. He won't let anyone get stale. He rotates assignments, keeps everyone on their toes. He moves the warriors around Virginia, D.C., plus Canton's old territory in Connecticut. Plus, we keep a close watch over what's going on in Maryland and Delaware. That's Max's old territory, and Shade doesn't trust Fan Chen. We stay busy, brother."

Raven laughed. "Yeah, boss-man hates lazy ass warriors. Hey, you know Jacks, right?"

Matteo nodded. "I remember her. Don't know her personally. Why, is she involved in this?"

"Not sure, brother. When this went down at Canton's place, he called her in to clean up the mess. We've got Medici warriors on duty 24/7, but Canton called someone from the outside to handle the cleanup. She's a mercenary to the big boys, and I'm not sure she's sharing everything she knows."

Matteo nodded. "I'll keep an eye out for her. Bitch is hard to miss."

"She's got something going on with Canton. But I think that's her gig. She only feeds from masters, and then they share a little pillow-talk. I doubt she shares what she knows with Alec unless it's to her benefit somehow."

Matteo dropped his feet to the floor. "Look, if it's being sold on the streets here, I'll find it. I'm going to study the grids, but I need to go in green. Don't want to look too much like I know what I'm doing. I'll see if Jacks' name ever comes up, if it does, I'll follow those leads. Give me some time, Raven. No one is going to start talking to me right off the bat."

Raven stood up. "Hey, brother, do whatever you need. Just keep me in the loop, cause boss-man will be up my ass. I'll start you out with 250 grand. Let's see how that green roles."

Matteo fist bumped him. "Not a problem, bro. Unless you got something else, I'm heading into the city. I'll spend some time just scouting the clubs, see who hangs out where, and figure out where the deals go down."

"Move out, my brother. I got my own agenda tonight." Raven watched as Matteo left and he knew he could count on him. All they needed was one solid lead and they'd be set. Raven let Micah know he was on his way out for the night and would see him later.

2-37

Lorenzo headed to his bedroom, ready to crawl into bed, when his cell phone rang. Thinking maybe it was his dad calling back, he answered without looking at the caller ID. "Hey. Did I forget something?"

He heard the familiar female voice on the other end. It wasn't Dad but Dona. "Well, you tell me?"

Lorenzo chuckled. "Sorry, I thought you were my dad."

She giggled like a schoolgirl. "Surely there is no comparison, warrior."

He dropped down on the bed and stretched out on his back. "Yeah, my bad. Definitely no comparison. Everything okay, Dona?"

He heard her sigh through the phone. "Oh, I'm fine. You haven't been to see me in a while. Don't forget your promise."

He scrunched up his forehead. "My promise?"

"Don't tell me you have forgotten, Lorenzo Medici. You said you would join me for Carnivale in Venice. I've been picking out our costumes."

Lorenzo moaned. "You're not really going to make me wear a costume, are you?"

She was adamant. "Of course! That is the whole purpose of Carnivale! Please don't worry. I will find something perfect for you. I know your schedule is busy. I'll take care of everything. All you have to do is take a few days off. You won't forget, will you?"

Lorenzo was fighting to stay awake. "I won't forget. I made you a promise, and I'll keep it."

"You sound tired, warrior."

"Yeah, a little. I was just getting ready to get some sleep."

"You know, Lorenzo, if you ever need to get away, escape from the camp for a few hours, you are always welcome here. I'd take good care of you."

"I'm sure you would, Dona. Thanks for the offer." He was ready to say goodbye, but she continued talking.

"So, how about tonight?"

"You're kidding, right? I'm literally lying on my bed right now. The only thing keeping my eyes open is the sound of your voice."

"So, teleport to me. I'll bring you a feeder, whatever you need." Her voice was soft as a lullaby, and it soothed him. "I promise to send you home refreshed. Come see me, Lorenzo."

He wondered if he had the energy to teleport, but he had to admit, Castello could be lonely. "Yeah, all right, I'll be there."

Sliding off the bed, he put the phone in his pocket, and teleported into Umbria and the Alizzi's villa. Donatella was waiting for him, wearing a silk robe, tied at her tiny waist. It showed her bare legs when she walked toward him, giving him a hug.

"You don't know what this means to me, Lorenzo."

"Yeah, well, I won't be much company. I'm dead on my feet."

She brushed his long hair back from his face. "But I can take care of you. Come on, I'll show you your room, and summon a feeder."

She took his hand and led him upstairs to a bedroom where the bed linens had already been pulled down for him. The windows were open to let in the cool night air of spring, and a small fire burned in the hearth. "Sit down, warrior."

Lorenzo took a seat and Dona knelt before him, sliding off his boots and massaging his feet. Her butler rushed in with glasses of Midnight on a tray, and offered the tray to Lorenzo, who lifted a glass, and swallowed it down before leaning his head back on the chair. Dona continued to knead her fingers deep into the balls of his feet.

"This is how a prince should be greeted. You should never come home to an empty house. Now stand up for me."

Lorenzo stood, and she proceeded to unbutton his shirt, pulling it loose from the waistband of his jeans, and tossing it aside. She unsnapped his jeans and started to slide them down his slender hips, when he placed his hands over hers. "I got this."

She smiled back at him. "Of course, you do." She waved her hand at the door and the young feeder entered. Lorenzo stepped out of his jeans and crawled between the sheets, and the feeder climbed in bed next to him. Dona turned out the light, so the room was lit only by the light of the flickering fire and slid into the bed next to him. She stared with envy, and jealousy, as he started to feed from the young female, and his body responded to her. She watched as he rolled the feeder on her back, his mouth still latched to her neck, his cock plunged deep inside her as he rode her orgasm. She slowly ran her hand down his back, feeling the strength of him, his muscles flexing under her hand. When he'd had his fill, he rolled away, catching his breath, as Dona shooed the feeder away.

"There, there, so much better, *si?* You will sleep better now, and wake with more energy now that your body has been nourished." She rubbed her hand over his smooth, hard chest. "You need to let me take care of you, Lorenzo."

With his need for food and sex satisfied, he was feeling the pull of sleep. With his eyes closed, he answered her. "You do take care of me, Dona."

She watched as he drifted into a deep sleep, then curled around him, keeping his body warm.

Lorenzo slept like a log and woke early to find the Alizzi curled tight against him. He carefully slid from beneath her arms, trying not to wake her, when she stirred. Looking up at him with her tousled hair, and eyes still heavy with sleep, her voice was almost a whisper. "So soon?"

Lorenzo was stepping into his jeans. "Dona, I've been here all night. I have duty today. Need to move my ass." He sat down in the chair and started pulling on his boots, as she sat on the side of the bed, holding her silk robe to her breasts. He casts a quick glance at her. He couldn't believe she'd slept next to him all night. He knew she was lonely, he just never realized how lonely.

"You'll be back though, right?"

He shook his head. "Probably not tonight, but soon, okay? And we have Carnivale."

She gave him a coy smile. "I guess it will have to do." She eyed him as he stood and put his shirt back on, tucking it into his jeans. He was about to teleport out when she said, "Not even a kiss?"

He paused a moment and gave her a demure kiss on the cheek. He teleported directly out to the olive grove in the Tuscan countryside he'd been assigned to patrol today. It was the primary grove where Danilo had his small shack of an office and directed the efforts of the migrant workers. Lorenzo landed softly, and Danilo nodded, always glad to see the warriors.

"Anything going on?"

Danilo shook his head. "Not so far. A good day. The workers have their assignments. We are running some irrigation pipeline today."

Lorenzo wandered to a shady spot beneath an olive tree and sat on the ground, his long legs stretched out in front of him, feet crossed at the ankles. He took out a pack of cigarettes and lit up, thinking this would be a long day. He was wondering if he should mention the unusual encounter with Dona to Alfie, when he saw Marco teleport in.

Marco landed in the groves, and saw Lorenzo sprawled under a tree smoking. "Well, now. Either you had one hell of a great night carousing or you had some intense duty." Crossing his arms over his chest, he shook his head. "You look like you slept in your fucking clothes. I take it you were whoring."

Lorenzo laughed. "I got a good night's sleep; I'll have you know. Just not in my own bed."

"You get more like your old man every damn minute. So, anything going on out here, or haven't you been here long enough to find out?" Before Lorenzo could answer, Marco saw the familiar car coming down the dirt road toward the shack. "Well, looks like someone is paying a visit."

Lorenzo jumped to his feet, taking a final drag on the cigarette before tossing it to the ground. The car pulled to a stop, and Sal emerged, his trademark cigar held between his teeth. He pulled a handkerchief from his pocket and wiped his brow. "Gonna be a hot one today, *si*?"

Marco strolled forward. "Oh, it is about to get a little bit hotter. You here to deliver a message?"

Sal removed the cigar and studied it. "Actually, he is waiting for your message. Ball's in your court. He needs to know. You in, or you out? Think carefully before you answer."

"Well, I don't have to think. Boss says we're out."

Sal shook his head. "Wrong decision, *paisan*. But I will deliver your message." Sal looked across the horizon at the rows and rows of olive trees. "Too bad, too. Nice grove you got here." Sal pulled a business card from his pocket and handed it to Marco. "If you change your mind, you'll know where to find me, but don't wait too long." He climbed back in the car and cranked up the air conditioning before backing down the dirt driveway.

Lorenzo stepped up next to Marco. "You think this means trouble?"

Marco shoved the card in his pocket without looking at it. His eyes never left the car as it backed away. "Trouble only they can muster. Nothing we can't handle. I need to call your old man, though and let him know things just got real. We have now dropped the proverbial gauntlet on the *Mafioso*. They haven't seen that in a while, I am sure. Keep your head in the game, warrior. Eventually, they are going to try some scare tactics."

Lorenzo smiled. He was eager to engage, even if they were mortals. "About fucking time."

Marco looked over at him and laughed, shaking his head. "That's my prince. Just remember, no vampire fun, unless absolutely necessary. "

Lorenzo nodded. "No fireballs, I get it."

Marco teleported out, back to the camp at Castello. He had a phone call to make.

2-38

Matteo was wearing jeans and a t-shirt featuring a local rock band, as he sought to integrate into the crowd. It wasn't an easy task as he stood six foot four, with broad shoulders, and muscular chest and arms. His dark brown hair hung past his shoulders, and he preferred his facial hair to a clean-shaven look. He wasn't built to blend in. He walked the Tenderloin, randomly selecting bars and clubs, quickly slipping inside, and finding a seat where he could sit and observe. Some of the bars attracted a rough trade, and more than a few bikers. He saw a few drug deals going down, but every transaction he'd seen had been mortal to mortal and involving street drugs like ecstasy and molly. The bikers were moving heroin and cocaine. It was still early, and the vampires didn't come out to play until the mortals had had time to consume the drugs and alcohol, and their defenses were down.

He moved on, checking other hot spots, until he started to find the more popular vamp playgrounds. He stumbled on Under the Coffin and could smell the vamps from outside the building. Raven had told him about this place, and Matteo had been told Shade frequented here himself in the past. The music was so loud he could hear it in the streets. He approached the doorman who looked him over.

"Haven't seen you here before."

Matteo nodded. "Never been here before." He pulled a hundred-dollar bill from his pocket and slipped it to the doorman. "Is that going to be a problem?"

The doorman smiled and said, "Not tonight," as he cleared the way for Matteo to enter. Matteo walked into the dimly lit club, with pounding music and strobe lights, and stood a minute to get his bearings. He was immediately approached by a hostess. She was vamp, as was most everyone in the club. She shouted at him over the music.

"Hi. I'm Katrina. You meeting someone?"

He shook his head. "Nope. Can you find me a table?"

She eyed him up and down and gave him a coy smile. "I can find you about anything you want. Follow me."

He followed her through the crowd to a wall booth located more centrally and giving him a good view of the club. "This okay?"

He nodded his head and slid into the booth. "Who owns the place?"

She leaned in, giving him a view of her ample cleavage. "Baby, I just work here, pick up my paycheck, know what I mean?"

Matteo nodded. "Vamp or mortal?"

"Oh, definitely vamp."

He slipped her a fifty, which she quickly pocketed. "I'll send the waitress over." She turned and walked away, as Matteo enjoyed the parting view. Within a few minutes, another female approached with dark hair and leather, tattoos, piercings, and all vamp.

"Well, aren't you the bonus size. I'm Tatiana, call me Tat. What can I get for you?"

Matteo asked if they carried Red Moon and she made a pouty face. "No, we can't get it yet. We're working on it, though. I can keep the Midnight flowing." He nodded, and she hurried off to fill his drink order. He took the time to scan the room. The strobe light made it hard to single out any one individual, as the bodies writhed on the dance floor.

Tatiana returned with his drink. "Haven't seen you in here before. Pretty sure I'd remember you."

He smiled at her. He'd need to cultivate every possible contact. He never knew who would provide a lead. "First time. You gonna show me the ropes?"

Tat's eyes twinkled. "Oh, I can show you ropes, and a whole lot more."

He laughed, as she flirted with him, and he encouraged the conversation. "How long you worked here."

She rolled her eyes. "Forever?" She laughed. "Seems like forever. What did you say your name was?"

He stared back at her, holding her in his gaze, she was definitely sending him signals she was interested. He had no doubt he could feed and fuck, and he may have to play her game to get the information he was looking for. "Name's Matteo."

She smiled. "Matteo, I like the sound of that."

He slid the cigarettes from his jeans pocket and lit up, offering her a smoke. "Nah, can't smoke on duty. Maybe later?"

He nodded, never breaking eyes contact. "Later sounds good. So, who owns this place?"

She shrugged her shoulder. "Don't know."

"That's a little strange, don't you think?"

She leaned her hip against the table. "See, here's the thing, they don't pay me to think, just make sure people keep buying drinks."

He laughed with her as she turned to leave, looking over her shoulder at him, flashing him a smile. "Don't leave, now!"

He sat back in the booth. "I'll be right here." He sipped at the Midnight and watched the crowd. It was a mixture of vampires from every station in life, including a few masters, and a smattering of mortals. The alcohol and Midnight flowed freely, as he saw a few drugs, but not what he was looking for. He watched vamps seek out the mortals, lure them into booths, where feeding and sex were exchanged easily and openly, while the crowd moved around them, dancing to the pulsating beat of the never-ending music. This wasn't an environment Matteo would ever seek out, but it sure looked like his best bet of finding Tainted Beast. Tat continued to bring him drinks throughout the night, and he downed them, sliding a hefty tip to her with each trip. He watched her work the room. She knew every patron by name, and he had no doubt she'd provided them with more than her skills as a waitress. As her shift came to an end, she sought him out.

"You waited for me."

He smiled back. "Told you I would."

"So, you following me home, or what?"

He stood up and left the club with her, as she took him to her small apartment. She wasn't his type, but sometimes a warrior had to do what a warrior had to do, and Tat looked like his best ticket to getting the information he needed.

2-39

Lorenzo was waiting for his shift to end, and tonight he'd be relieved by Alfie. He'd moved from grove to grove today, and all day he'd seen the big, black car, cruising slowly past the groves. The car never stopped, and no one ever got out. The windows were tinted, so he couldn't see the occupants, but he knew it was the *mafioso*. Lorenzo stayed alert, but thought to himself, they're going to have to do a lot more than that to intimidate the Medici. He teleported back to the main grove, and landed outside Danilo's shack, waiting for his friend.

Alfie was running a bit late. Nickola had been fully advised of the situation with the *mafioso*, and he was keeping Sophia on a tighter leash. Her father had always kept the family on lockdown during crisis periods, and she understood the drill. He grinned to himself. He'd at least kept her well occupied when he was home. Landing in the groves, he saw Lorenzo waiting for him.

"Sorry, brother, running a bit late. Any action out here?"

Lorenzo was leaning against the side of the shed that gave him some shade from the sun, smoking a cigarette, when Alfie dropped in. He shook his head. "Not unless you call that car driving by behind you 'action'. They've been doing that all day. I checked the other groves, and it's the same thing. No one gets out, though. They just want to make sure we know they're there. I'll talk to Marco when I get back to camp. How about you, brother, you doing okay?"

Alfie turned his head to see the black car moving slowly. "I don't like this at all, Lorenzo. I've talked to Nickola, and he knows what's going down. He's on Sofia all the time, and she isn't real happy about that."

Lorenzo chuckled. "Yeah, Sophia doesn't like rules much." As the two warriors stood together, Danilo exited the shack, clearly distressed. Lorenzo looked him over. "What the fuck, Danilo. You look like you've seen a ghost."

Danilo nodded. "*Si*, I would prefer a ghost. This is like at the other groves where I worked. Same thing. The *mafioso*, they are scaring away the migrant workers. Most of them are mortal, and they fear for their families. The *mafioso* threatens them, and they are leaving. I had four quit yesterday, and another six today. We need to get the irrigation pipes done soon before the summer heat. We are getting behind schedule."

Danilo looked with fear in his eyes as the black car circled around again. Lorenzo threw his cigarette on the ground, grinding it out under his boot. The Medici had never had to provide protection to mortals before and doing so would surely expose them as vampires over time. Losing the workers was going to be a big problem. “Fuck! We need to let these fucks know we're not playing their game."

Alfie knew that look. Lorenzo was very levelheaded, but like his father, he had a short fuse and it could jump start his blood fast. "Slow down, brother. Let’s think this through. You do anything rash, you may put the mortals in more danger. This isn’t just about the workers but their entire families. The *Mafioso* means business, and bucking their rule is not something they’re going to take laying down. What did you have in mind?"

Lorenzo couldn’t hide his agitation. If these were rival vamps, they’d just confront each other, face to face, and battle it out. He didn’t like having to play by their rules. Nothing in his experience had prepared him for battling mortals and concealing his true nature. "I don't have a fucking clue, brother. Hoping Marco will have some ideas. You and me together could take these sick fucks out in a minute and a half, but our hands are tied."

Alfie agreed, but he knew he had to keep his head in the game. "Look, I think you need to talk to Marco, and your dad. They’ve had more experience in dealing with mortals than the two of us put together. Get out of here. I’ve got this for now. Hell, we can’t just sit back and let this shit happen!"

Lorenzo stood upright and fist bumped Alfie. “I'm out of here then. You okay, brother? You want me to send backup?"

"To be honest, I like the idea of more visible warriors." He turned to look at Danilo who looked like he wanted to run off and quit at any minute. Nodding to Danilo, Alfie raised his brows. "Might help Danilo relax a bit. Having more warriors visible may help the workers, too."

Lorenzo nodded. "Consider it done. I'm going straight to camp, talking to Marco. First thing we'll do is increase our presence. Let them know we see them, and we're ready for them." He turned to Danilo. "You let the workers know we got this covered."

Danilo nodded, but he knew Lorenzo didn't understand. The *mafioso* were integrated throughout the mortal culture. Unless he sent a warrior home with each migrant worker, the workers would never feel safe. *"Si*, I will tell them, but if the *mafioso* stick around, the workers will leave."

Lorenzo nodded, letting him know he got the message. Glancing at Alfie one more time before he teleported out, he said, "I'll call you as soon as I meet with Marco."

Alfie looked at Danilo. "Relax, believe me, The King and Queen will never let them hurt any of the workers. I know this is hard for you to make the workers understand, since they are mortal, but try to reassure them. We are going to be here 24/7, and very visible. Go home to your family. Medici has got this."

2-40

Marco was about ready to walk out on the field when Lorenzo barreled through the office door. He knew his blood was up and there could only be one reason, the damn *mafioso*. Lorenzo paced back and forth, giving him the details of the day. Marco got more and more annoyed. "Sons of bitches. This is just the beginning, scaring off the workers. We need a more solid plan, and we need Shade and your *madre* involved. But right now, I need to get more warriors out there with Alfie. Give me three fucking minutes to make some re-assignments. As soon as I get back, we need to call Shade, wake his ass up, and see what he has to say on this."

Lorenzo dropped into a chair as Marco marched out on the field, grabbing a few warriors by the collar as he reassigned them to the olive groves. Lorenzo laughed to himself. Marco would never win any humanitarian awards for his people skills, but he was one bad ass warrior. As soon as he'd finished barking out orders, he returned to the office and poured himself a Midnight.

"You got that fancy phone in your pocket?"

Lorenzo smiled as he pulled the cell phone from his jeans pocket. "This fancy phone?" Marco grunted at him as Lorenzo called his dad before Marco blew a gasket.

Kate heard Shade's cell phone ring again as she struggled awake. "Well, this is getting old." She turned on the lamp and looked for his phone on the nightstand, but it wasn't there. "Crap." She slid out of bed and followed the sound to his jeans, tossed across the chair by the window. Fishing the phone from his pocket, she tried to get to it before it rolled to voicemail. "Hello? Lorenzo?"

"Mom? Everything's okay, I'm here with Marco and we need to talk to Dad again. Can you wake him please?"

"Is this about the olive groves again?"

"Yeah, afraid so."

Kate sighed and returned to the bed, sitting on his side of the bed, and gently shaking him awake. "Lover, I need you. Wake up for me please."

From deep in his slumber he could hear her voice, and it stirred his beast. He felt himself slowly surfacing, as she gently shook him. He pulled her to his chest, snuggling into her hair, he licked her neck. "*Mi amore*, hell of a time to need me."

She shushed him. "Your son is on the phone, with Marco."

Growling, he looked at her. "Fuck." As she handed him the phone, he sighed. "Damn it, Lorenzo, what the hell is going on now? What could possibly happen that you and Marco can't handle?" He sat up in the bed and looked around the room for his clothes. Kate pointed to the chair where he'd left them before crawling into bed. He made his way to the chair, pulling on his jeans.

Lorenzo chuckled, hearing the frustration in his father's voice. "Hey, good morning to you too. Listen, Marco just wanted to make sure you were in the loop. The mafia is making their presence known. They drive around the groves all day, scaring the fuck out of the workers. Danilo says the workers are being threatened, and he's lost ten so far this week. Marco just sent more warriors out. We're going to make the security more visible, for the mafia, as well as to maybe give some peace of mind to the workers. You got any other ideas?"

"*Cazzo*! Now we are losing workers? This is really starting to piss me off. Other than their presence, are they threatening the workers?"

"Not that we're aware of. Danilo says this is what they did at the olive groves owned by the mortals. He says the threat is implied. The migrant workers aren't bound to any one place anyway, so they just move on to a farm that's already under mafia control. We already pay them more money than the groves run by the mortals, but they aren't going to risk their lives for it."

Shade lowered his head and ran his hands through his hair. What in the hell was he going to do about this? "This is going to hold up the work. If those irrigation pipes don't get installed, we could lose the new plantings, as well as affect the harvest on the existing trees. I approve the idea of putting more warriors out there, making them visible. We can't keep them from driving on the public roads, but we can make sure they don't set foot on our property. Arm them and make it visible. Right now, we need to show power and strength to ease the workers' concerns. And for hell's sake, don't go on the offense. We will not make the first move. Maybe beefing up the security will be enough to show them we're not playing their game."

Marco listened to his master and best friend's direction. "We'll get the warriors out there, and we won't make the first move. But if you think for one minute any of our boys are gonna take a hit and not respond, you better think again. I don't train them to sit around playing with their balls. They need to be able to defend themselves if someone gets an antsy trigger finger, *si*?"

Shade already knew what Marco was saying, but he was hoping like hell it didn't come to that. "I am not backing down, Marco. Let me get that straight right here and now. If they come at us, we will respond, but they need to make the first move. And if it comes to that, our warriors must be armed with guns, fight with guns. No swords or shurikens, are we clear?"

Lorenzo answered. "We get it, Dad. Fight like mortals, only better. We got this."

Shade slumped down in the chair, laying his head back. "If you had this, you would not be waking my damn ass up every other fucking day. I know this is tricky. I am not angry, just frustrated. The situation is complicated since we are dealing with mortals. Both of you get busy. I want this in place now!"

Marco shook his head. "Look old man, the Prince isn't the one who wanted this call, that was me. Relax, he knows what he is doing, chain of command, just like I taught him. So back off, we will take care of it. Damn, you're getting grumpy as fuck in your old age when you don't get your slumber. I don't have time for chatting; we've got a lot to do." Marco looked at Lorenzo. "Hang up."

Lorenzo chuckled to himself as the two men sparred with each other and disconnected the call. "Good thing you're friends. Hate to see the two of you if you were from rival covens."

Marco cuffed him upside the head. "Get the fuck outta here, pup. Go get some sleep."

Shade heard the phone go dead and looked at it, then at Kate. "He hung up on my ass!"

Kate had listened to the whole conversation and didn't like the direction this was going. "Maybe this was a bad idea, this whole thing with the olives. The land wasn't rich enough for developing into vineyards, but it would support the olive groves. It was a way to put the land to use and produce more income. But I'm wondering now if it was worth it. Maybe we should just abandon this. We haven't got a lot invested yet. We're just beginning. Maybe we just leave well enough alone."

He stared at her in disbelief. "Did I just hear you say you wanted to quit? That's not my queen talking. *Bel,* I am not letting anyone, mortal or immortal, tell me how to run my coven. These bastards need to be taught a lesson. I will not stand by while others force us off our own land, and neither should you."

Kate drew her knees to her chest as she sat on the bed. "I know you're right. We can't give in. It's just you have that stuff going on with Tainted Beast on the west coast, and now this. I don't want to see any of our warriors hurt."

He smiled at her. "Our warriors know what they face. They can survive a bullet wound if it is not in the heart or head. As for the Tainted Beast, we will get it under control." He got up from the chair and went to her, curling around her. "Be honest with me, you are worried about Lorenzo getting hurt."

She nodded her head. "I'm a mother first. I'll always worry about my children. The title of queen will never remove my fear for their safety, or for yours. Our coven is strong, stronger than it's ever been. I need to place my faith in them."

He tipped her chin up, looking into those amber eyes. "You once told me I needed to let our children have their wings. He needs to fly, Kate. This is just the beginning of his reign. He will need to prove to the coven, and the warriors, he can lead them. He will be fine. He is smart, brave, and born from a long line of warrior blood. And he has Alfie, just like I have Marco. Have you heard from Sophia lately?"

Kate smiled. "She texts me every day, usually with emojis, a smiley face, a heart, or a most inappropriate eggplant, to remind me they're trying to get pregnant."

Flopping back on the bed, he moaned. "Well, they are not trying hard enough. They are young, what the hell is the problem? We never had a problem getting pregnant. Damn, what is wrong with the younger generation? Whenever I confront either one of them about it, they just shrug and roll their eyes at me."

She laughed as she lay down beside him. "It's only been six months. It will happen."

Tickling her softly, he rolled her over. "Well, I have two things I want done and done soon. One is a grand babe from my daughter, and the other is to see my son mated, so he can start giving us an heir. But for right now, I think I will settle for us laying in this bed until the sun sets and entertaining each other, *si*?"

2-41

Matteo had spent the last week scouting all the bars frequented by the vamp community, and he kept coming back to Under the Coffin. It was the only club that drew masters, and there was a steady stream of them from all over the country passing through here. He'd shacked up with Tatiana since he'd been here, and she'd confirmed most every master worldwide had passed through here at some point or another but acknowledged Alec's new business had drawn some of them away. He didn't grill her about things, but worked his inquiries into their conversation, moving slowly. She'd worked there a long time, and she'd have a lot of information that might be useful, but he had no doubt she'd clam up if she felt like he was using her. She could easily blow his cover, so he took it slow.

He dropped into the club tonight, near dawn, approaching the end of her shift and slipped into his usual booth. It wasn't hard for his practiced eye to spot the occasional drug deal, but so far, he'd not seen or heard any reference to Tainted Beast. He winked at Tat as she hurried from table to table, closing out tabs, and stuffing her tip money into her bra. As the club closed, and the crowd thinned out, she made her way to his table.

"You didn't need to wait for me."

He scooted over in the booth, making room for her. "You're worth the wait."

She beamed back at him. She'd had a very long list of one-night stands under her belt, from the revolving roster of clientele, but it was nice to have this warrior in her life. She slid into the booth and rested her head on his shoulder, sighing deeply. "Long night. I'll be glad to get home."

He kissed the top of her head. "You look tired. I saved you my last Midnight." He pushed the glass in her direction, and she gratefully accepted it. He looked around nonchalantly. "Lot of drugs in here. Couldn't help but notice the deals going down."

She laughed. "You telling me you never indulge?"

He chuckled as he nudged her shoulder. "Not me, I'm pure as driven snow."

She laughed hard and he joined her in the joke. Truth was, as a Medici warrior, he'd never touch drugs, and he was careful never to feed from anyone who did. "You heard about this new stuff? Tainted Beast?"

She finished off the glass of Midnight. "Yeah, we've all heard about it. Heard it brings an intense high, but the beast can get really violent. We haven't seen anything happening in the club, so if it's being sold here, it's not being used here. We have good bouncers. They move people out pretty quick if any trouble starts. The club has an "anything goes" policy, but that refers more to sex. It wouldn't be good for business to turn the place into a slaughterhouse. Why, you looking to score Tainted Beast?"

He shrugged. "I was curious about it."

She dragged him out of the booth, and back to her place. "Well, I'll keep my ears open, and let you know if I hear anything. Just don't take it in my place if you score."

He gave her a squeeze. "You're safe with me."

She smiled up at him. He was massive, and she had no doubt any female would be safe with him.

The next day, he teleported out to Marin County and the California camp, to touch base with Raven.

"Hope you're finding something, brother. Boss-man has been up my ass."

Matteo flopped down in the chair which creaked under his weight. "Not sure, but my instincts say Under the Coffin. It's the only place that makes sense. You know who owns it? If we can find the owner, I'd like to follow that lead."

Raven flipped his hair back. "You know, I've been there a million times, and I don't have a fucking clue who owns it. I'll put some feelers out, though. Somebody will know."

Matteo nodded. "Other than that, brother, it's a dead end. Most of the vamps I've talked to never heard of it, so that's good. We know it's not on the street. But the waitress at Under the Coffin has heard of it. Said she'd never seen it, and I believe her."

Raven gave him a questioning look. "You trust her?"

Matteo nodded as he chuckled. "I've been banging her for the last few weeks. She's in lust, brother, and not used to any male sticking around for very long. She's my best lead right now."

Raven laughed. "Tatiana? You're banging Tatiana? I think she's on our master's long list of conquests, so be sure you never mention Medici."

He shook his head. "Nah, I'm good. Everyone thinks I'm freelance."

Raven asked about the money, and Matteo told him all was well, he'd only scored some cheap street heroin and some weed, mostly to get information.

"Cool, brother. Just let me know what you need. I'll give Shade an update and see if he knows who owns the club."

2-42

Shade got a call from Raven saying he wanted to meet. He obliged, without hesitation, and asked Raven to meet him at the Dead House. He didn't want Raven coming out to Bel Rosso. He knew Kate was already worried about the *Mafioso* in Florence, and he didn't want to add to her concerns with this drug nightmare in California. He could meet with Raven, see what had happened first, and let her know if it was necessary.

Shade teleported into D.C., where Theo, his long-standing SIC, had already made the assignments for the night. His warriors in D.C. had been warned about Tainted Beast, but fortunately, they hadn't seen any sign of it here. Theo was at the command center, which looked a lot different than the situation they'd started out with twenty-five years ago. Their security system tapped into every external security camera in the district, whether it was a government owned camera, or owned by a private business. Theo could enter the coordinates and had a visual of practically any street in D.C. on the massive wall of monitors. The old beaten up furniture had been removed, and their command center looked like NASA headquarters.

Theo was giving him an update when Raven teleported into the house. Shade picked up his scent long before he saw him and could hear his boots stomping down the metal stairs to the control room.

"I hope the hell you weren't trying to sneak in, because I could hear you from a fucking mile away in those damn boots. If I fucking look up and they have bells or some bullshit on them, you are going down to the floor, runt!"

Raven tossed his hair over his shoulder and laughed. "Hell boss-man, I was just breaking in these new boots. They have a three-inch heel and you still wouldn't be able to catch my ass!"

Raven and Theo fist bumped, as Shade rubbed his hand over his face. *A fucking warrior in high heel boots.* If it had been anyone other than Raven, they wouldn't still be standing. He sat while Raven and Theo shot the shit, as Raven got caught up on the most recent happenings at the Dead House and what had been going down in D.C.

Shade looked at the two of them with annoyance. "You two need a private room?"

Theo chuckled as he got up to leave so Shade can have his discussion in private, slapping Raven on the back. "See you later, brother. Master is getting impatient."

Raven took a seat beside Shade and stared at the screens lining the walls. "Nothing like coming home, boss-man. Different than it used to be, though."

Shade leaned back in his chair and threw his booted feet up on the table. "I was just thinking the same thing. Damn, I miss the smell of this place sometimes."

Raven threw his own high-heeled boots up on the table, his legs crossed at the ankle, and pulled a cigarette from behind his ear and lit up. "You smell Medici glory in here, from real street battles. Perfume of the warrior."

Shade grunted and shook his head, looking at those fucking boots. No warrior in his lifetime had ever been like Raven, he was fast as lightening and quick on his feet, but he'd glam up any place he entered. "So, I am hoping you have some good news for me. Talk, warrior."

"Matteo has been out on the streets a few weeks now, and he keeps going back to Under the Coffin. He says it's the only place in the city where he sees masters congregate. He hooked up with Tatiana, been bleeding that source dry. He says he trusts her. She hasn't seen any Tainted Beast in the place, but she's heard of it, and knew enough about it to understand how it worked."

Shade chuckled. "Matteo and Tat? Well, if you want to know what's going on, she is a good source. She's been at the Coffin a long time, she's well connected."

Raven blew a few smoke rings. "He's staying at her place a lot of nights. Said she's not his type but tapping her seems to be his best bet for getting more info."

Shade pushed the ashtray across the table toward Raven who put his cigarette out in it. "Damn, in the old days, I would have ground that butt out on the floor and left it there."

Shade stood up and walked around the table. "Look, you didn't come all the way out here to tell me Matteo was tapping Tat. What the hell is going down over there, Raven?"

Raven held up his hands. "Damn, don't be so fucking aggressive, I'm getting to the point. Matteo asked Tat who owned the place. She didn't seem to have the goods on that. Matteo thinks the owner may be a link to Tainted Beast, but he can't find anyone out there who knows. We both thought you might know since you've been going there since there were dinosaurs."

Shade paced a bit, hands on his hips. "I'm not sure who owns it now. Hell, come to think of it, never really knew before, wasn't important when I was going there. Last time I was there was when I first met Kate."

Ravens eyes widened. "You took the Queen to that dump? And you think I'm crazy?"

Shade grinned at the memory. "We were mated, but she was still mortal. She needed to see what she was getting into, and what I was walking away from."

"Well, isn't that an interesting bit of history."

Shade stared into space, racking his brain to recall if he'd ever known anything about who'd owned that property. California had belonged to Alec once, but Alec didn't own that club, and Alec had never kept a tight rein on any of his territories. Hell, it could be anybody in there.

"You got me thinking, Raven. If Alec doesn't now, then I only have one source who might know who owns that place. If she doesn't know, no one will."

Raven followed him with his eyes as he paced. "And who might that be?"

"Jacks. Let me give her a call, and I'll let you know what I find out. In the meantime, tell Matteo to keep up this charade, and never mention Medici in that place!"

Raven laughed and winked. "Oh no, we wouldn't want him tapping Tat while she's dreaming of lying on her back under the Medici."

Shade took a swing at him, but Raven teleported out faster than he could blink. "Damn punk!"

2-43

Finding himself alone in the Dead House, Shade pulled out his cell. No time like the present to call Jacks. She'd slipped her business card into his jeans pocket on her last visit, much to Kate's dismay. He'd destroyed the card but memorized the number. Dialing it up, she answered almost immediately. He heard the deep, seductive purr of her voice as she answered.

"Medici. So glad to hear from you. I noticed you called on my private line. Is this business, or pleasure?"

Shade would have to tread carefully with her to get the information he needed. "Hope I am not disturbing you, Jacks."

Jacks smiled, as she stood on the wraparound deck of the mansion on the water. What a perfect vampire to speak to while standing alone, watching the moon reflect on the water. "For you, Shade, I'd always stop whatever I was doing. So, business or pleasure? Please don't break my heart and tell me this is business."

Shade shook his head. Oh, she could get a male worked up easily. "The call is business only, Jacks, nothing more, never anything more."

He heard her soft sigh through the phone. "Never say never, master. But, how can I help you?"

"Just curious if you know who might own Under the Coffin?" He listened to the long, silent pause from the other end of the phone.

Jacks heard the club name and her mood changed immediately. If he was asking about Under the Coffin, he was getting too close to the source and she set her mind quickly to the task. "In San Francisco? My, I thought you'd given up that lifestyle once mated. Doesn't surprise me, though. I mean, I certainly understand the need for a little variety."

Shade bristled and narrowed his eyes. "I don't have any interest in that lifestyle. But I may have a lead on Tainted Beast. Answer my question, Jacks."

She walked slowly along the deck, letting her hand run along the polished railing, stalling for time, trying to figure out how much he knew. "Well, give me a second to think on it. It's been under numerous ownerships throughout the years. So, you have a lead, at the club?"

Shade was getting impatient with her, but he knew he couldn't push her, or he wouldn't get any answers. She was playing games and he hated games. "Look, Jacks, my warriors have been scouting the area and Under the Coffin is the only place where the masters congregate. It is the perfect place to sell the drug. Give it up, who owns it?"

Jacks grinned to herself. Oh, she'd love to give it up to the master who taught her how to fight, kill and defend. He was on a short list of masters she'd yet to conquer. He was mated now, but that wouldn't stop her if she put her mind to having him.

"I remember now. His name is Master Lovell, he hails from Vancouver, British Columbia. Apparently, the club came to him when the last owner had some cash flow problems, and Lovell had the cash to take it off his hands."

Shade scribbled the information onto a notepad. "Don't know him, never heard of him. British Columbia? Isn't Marchesa from Montreal? Are you thinking what I am thinking?"

Jacks bit her lip as Medici fell hook, line, and sinker. "It could be a connection, both from Canada. Vancouver isn't that far from California. You may have a good source there. I'd definitely check it out. Do you need any help with that, Shade?"

Shade unconsciously shook his head no, even though he was on the phone. "*Grazie,* Jacks, but no, let me handle this. I have my warriors on this. But if I need you, you still in with us?"

Jacks licked her lips. "You can always count me in when it comes to you, Shade."

Jacks ended the call and looked up to the moon. *That's right, Medici, run across the border and snoop up there*. She looked down at her phone, time to make another phone call.

2-44

Jacks waited for him to answer his call, and then heard the familiar voice on the other end. "I just had a call from Shade Medici. He wanted to know who owns Under the Coffin."

She could hear him breathing on the other end, and knew he was thinking, wondering what she'd told the Medici. She let the silence hang in the air. The Master of Nevada was no fool and knew if Medici ever found the source of Tainted Beast, his life was over. "Don't worry, Colin, I sent him on a wild goose chase that will take him nowhere and will lead to a dead end."

Colin paced the floor of his Las Vegas mansion. He was making Tainted Beast here in Nevada, but had purposely distributed it in California, hoping to throw people off his trail. There was a lot of money to be made in drugs, but it sure as hell was a controversial business model. The Council could exile him, and there'd be plenty ready to kill his ass if they discovered the source.

"You have as much at stake here as I do, warrior. If Shade takes me down, you're going down with me. You better make fucking sure he never figures it out. You've been shaking me down for months now, so don't think you can walk away from this without a penalty. How much does he know?"

Jacks laughed to herself. *You stupid, ignorant master.* Colin wasn't a warrior and she'd found it easy to push him around. Besides, Shade would never believe Colin over her. She'd trained under the Medici once, and she knew he felt a sense of loyalty to her, despite the misgivings of his meek little mate. Once she got her hooks into that beautiful male, he'd side with her no matter what went down. She was damn sure that little mate of his could never truly satisfy him like she could. She could make Alec howl, and she was damn sure Shade wouldn't find her a disappointment.

"Relax, Colin!" *Such a twitchy master!* "Medici has his warriors on the streets in California. They've figured out the best bet for the distribution of Tainted Beast is your club. Right now, he doesn't know who owns the club, or who's making the drugs. I've sent him across the border to Vancouver. His little warrior out in California got no information out of Marchesa, trust me. He doesn't remember enough of the evening to provide any valuable information to Shade or anyone else. Shade is now looking in Vancouver for a Master Lovell. There was a Lovell coven there a long time ago, but it will take him a long time to figure out there's no such master. Beyond that, he's clueless."

Colin hated that this warrior has her hooks in him. He'd hired her originally when he was setting up the lab to produce Tainted Beast. He'd tried a similar drug in Amsterdam, and he'd been trying to replicate it for sale here in the U.S. Jacks had some great contacts in Europe that helped him gain access to the ingredients he needed. The drug he created was not the same as the drug he'd taken in Amsterdam. It created the same high, but it also released the beast in a violent rage. It was an unexpected side effect, but one that wasn't totally without merit. There were many masters that loved the opportunity to release the beast, freed of all constraints. But still, it was a dangerous path to follow. Jacks had seen the opportunity and cut herself in by threatening to expose him unless she got a cut of the action.

"Yeah, well, you make damn sure he remains clueless. Do whatever the fuck you need to do to keep him distracted and sniffing down the wrong trail."

"Oh, dear Colin, you suddenly doubt my skills? I have the Medici and Canton in my back pocket. If anything happens at L'Adventure, I'm the first-person Canton calls, and look who Shade came to when he needed help tracking down this drug. Neither of them will do anything without my knowledge. In two days' time, I'm released of my duty with this master in Maine, and I can focus totally on this situation. I have your back, Colin. Just remember, you owe me."

Colin was seething. "I owe you? I must admit, warrior, I appreciate how your twisted mind works. You're blackmailing me, so trust me when I say, if you try to double cross me, I won't hesitate to expose you. Your little game of mercenary to the masters will be over quick when they realize you'll use their secrets against them."

Jacks snarled and felt her own beast rise up. She didn't take well to threats from anyone, not even a master.

"Don't you threaten me, Colin. That would be the biggest mistake of your life. I kill those that get in my way. You wouldn't be getting filthy rich without my assistance, and you'll share the profits with me. Keep your mouth shut, keep a low profile, and let me deal with the big boys. It's what I do best."

Jacks ended the call. Colin may be the Master of Nevada, but he was nothing compared to the masters she dealt with, and she could easily manipulate him. She'd keep him on a tight lead, while she went after her main objective...Shade Medici.

2-45

Raven landed outside of Bel Rosso and looked about. It had been awhile since he'd visited here, and the property was as beautiful as he remembered. He saw Aegis and Night Stalker approach and Aegis eased into him, nudging his hand. Raven scratched behind her ears and smiled. "Don't worry, girl, just here to see the boss-man."

He heard the loud cawing as Poe landed on his shoulder. The raven had been given to him by the queen as a gift and he had a deep attachment to the bird, who was his faithful companion. Sometimes, Poe would come with him when he visited Bel Rosso, which seemed to be a lot lately, thanks to Tainted Beast. Gi welcomed him inside, as Poe flew skyward, taking a perch on the eaves. Raven entered the house and walked to the open doors of Shade's office, finding him at the large desk, covered in papers. Sliding into the chair opposite the desk, he grinned as Shade looked up.

Shaking his head, Shade looked at the outfit Raven had on. He was wearing a kilt made of a hodge-podge of leather patches, sewn together like a quilt, hanging at angles along the hem, along with his popular fingerless leather gloves, studded across the knuckles. He had on a black t-shirt, and his heavy combat boots, along with his trademark jewelry.

"What the hell are you wearing?"

Raven looked down and admired his own outfit. "Boss-man, you need to get with the times. I call this urban warrior. Cory made it for me. I'm fashionable and stylish. Besides, the kilt is very practical in the hot weather."

Shade sighed. "Right, well, this vampire is sticking with traditional leathers. Look, I didn't fucking call you here to talk the latest fashion. I called Jacks and got some information. She knows who owns Under the Coffin." Shade lit up and pushed the pack of smokes to Raven. "She informed me it is a Master Lovell from Vancouver. Now, I never heard of him, but it got me to thinking.

Marchesa is from Montreal. Maybe there is some Canadian connection. I need you to go up there and find him, check it out and get all you can on this Lovell."

Raven lit up and blew smoke rings. "Well, Marchesa was no help. He didn't seem to remember a damn thing about that night. He was still afraid, didn't want any information getting out that he'd used Tainted Beast, and didn't have a clue about who'd made it. Said he bought it from a stranger who approached him before he entered L'Adventure, which may or may not be true. All I know is, he won't ever be trying it again. He seemed terrified when I was asking for information. I'll check out this Lovell. Hell, why not, I've never been to British Columbia. If he's your vampire, I'll know."

Shade pushed the folder with the coordinates toward Raven. "I can't find out shit on this Lovell, so there isn't much to go on, but find whatever you can. If you need to take another warrior with you, that is your call. Keep a low profile. Don't mention who or where you are from, and try to blend in." Shade knew he was wasting his words telling Raven to blend in.

Raven rolled his eyes to Shade and grinned. "Blending in, not exactly my forte, but' I'll tone it down."

Shade laughed and shook his head. "Get moving and take that damn bird with you."

2-46

Carnivale was fast approaching, and Dona had been contacting him almost daily to remind him of his promise. It had been a few weeks since the warriors had been re-assigned to provide the added protection to the olive groves, and they appeared to be at a stand-off with the *Mafioso*. The black car would occasionally drive by, but they'd only see it once or twice a week now, instead of multiple times a day. The workers seemed relieved to have the warriors standing guard, and Danilo hadn't lost any additional workers. The irrigation pipes were back on schedule, and everything seemed relatively calm. Lorenzo figured this was as good a time as any to ask Marco to give him some time off. Before teleporting out to the olive groves, he stopped by Marco's office.

"Got a minute, Marco?"

Marco looked up from his desk with a grunt and waved him in. Lorenzo pulled a chair up close to the desk and sat across from him as Marco inquired, "Problems?"

Lorenzo shook his head no. "Nothing new. Still see the car. It's like they're just checking to see if we're going to let our guard down. No more visits from Sal, and Danilo says the situation with the workers had stabilized."

Marco stretched both arms above his head, yawning. "Then what the fuck you need, warrior?"

Lorenzo smiled to himself. Marco wouldn't be winning any Mr. Congeniality awards. "I wanted to take a few days off, go up to Venice for Carnivale."

Marco laughed. "Oh, you really are a chip off the old block, aren't you? I went to Carnivale a few times with your father and the Alizzi." He smiled as the long-ago memories play out in his head. "You going alone?"

Lorenzo wondered if he should tell him but figured Marco would hear about it eventually. "No, actually. I'm going with the Alizzi too."

The smile disappeared from Marco's face, as he creased his forehead. "You sure that's a good idea? You're not fucking her, are you, kid?"

Lorenzo looked shocked that he'd even ask. "Aw gross, Marco! She's like a mom to me! No! Hell no! She just told me about the days when she'd go there with my father, and how much fun they had. She wants to go again and wanted me to take her. I told her I would. I didn't think much of it, but she's been calling me all week to remind me. She's lonely, you know? That's all it is."

Marco stared him down and paused before he answered. "Yeah, get out of here for a few days, but be careful with that one."

2-47

Dona had worked feverishly to have their elaborate costumes made for Carnivale. As was standard practice, the masks were custom made works of art, and molded to completely cover the wearers face, exposing only the eyes. No two masks were ever the same. She'd carefully overseen every detail of their costumes, obsessing over the fabrics and the embellishments. When she used to go to Carnivale with Shade, they always had the grandest costumes. She couldn't remember the last time she'd been this excited.

Lorenzo arrived at her villa, ready to escort her to Venice. He was wearing jeans, a t-shirt, and a sports jacket, his hair pulled back into a loose ponytail at the nape of his neck. "This look okay? You said casual."

She looked him over, and it took her back a few hundred years, when she was a young girl, and she'd thought maybe, just maybe, Shade Medici was still within her reach. She smiled at him and ran her hand along the lapel of his jacket. "You look wonderful. So much like your father."

Lorenzo shrugged; it was a comment he heard frequently. "Do you need me to do anything, Dona?"

"No, my darling, it is all taken care of. I packed a trunk for us and had it sent ahead, along with our costumes. You just need to teleport with me. You'll hold my hand, please? It has been a long time since I teleported any distance."

He bowed slightly. "I'd be delighted. But I need some directions."

Dona clapped her hands. "The Gritti Palace Hotel. It's off the Grand Canal. I have stayed there before with your father. The building has been there since the 15th century. Only the best for you, Lorenzo."

He laughed and took her hand. "Hang on then."

She gripped his hand and laughed as he carried her away. It had been so long since she'd been on an adventure, she was giddy with happiness. They landed easily on the narrow and crowded passage in front of the hotel, their sudden appearance among the tourists and other passers-by unnoticed. Lorenzo looked up at the massive front to the palace, its walls a terra cotta color, with the trademark Venetian balconies at each window.

Dona led him through the doors as she asked, "Have you been here before?"

He shook his head no, as he took in the elaborate tile floors, the dark wood paneling, and massive marble counters that lined the reception.

"Good," she replied. "I want every experience about this trip to be new for you."

She led them to the registration desk, where she gave their names and informed the hotel clerk, they had reservations. The clerk pulled the information up on the computer and flashed them a bright smile.

“Of course! We have Mr. Medici in the Hemingway Suite, and we have you in the Pisani Suite. Excellent choices. Your baggage arrived earlier and has already been taken to your rooms. I'll have the bellman escort you."

Lorenzo was pulling out his wallet, ready to pay for their rooms, when Dona placed her hand over his. “It is already paid for. My gift to you for bringing me."

He knew the Alizzi's fortunes were fading, and she couldn’t afford this extravagance. "Dona, this is too much."

She waved her hand. "Don't be silly, and do not reject my gift. You will hurt my feelings. Allow me this please, Lorenzo."

He smiled at her and offered her his arm as they followed the bellman to their respective suites. The bellman took them to her suite first, where she turned to him. "You'll find your costume in your room. Everything you need. Please join me in the ballroom at midnight."

He laughed. "What will you be wearing? How will I know you?"

She laid her hand on his chest. "Oh, my darling, but that is the fun! You won't! Go, put on your costume, and see where the night takes you. Tomorrow we will meet up and share our stories. That is what we would do when we all came together, your father, Marco, and me. Sharing the stories, the next day was the best part."

"I'm not sure how I let you talk me into this." He laughed as he left to follow the bellman to his own room. She blew him a kiss and closed the door to her room.

Donatella walked through the magnificent suite, to the corner of the room which was flanked by floor to ceiling French doors that opened onto a balcony overlooking a canal. She opened the doors and stepped out into the night air, watching the gondolas glide through the dark water of the canal below her. She could see the silhouette of the buildings in St. Mark's Square against the night sky. She grasped the banister around the balcony and let her mind travel back to those days when she'd visited here with Shade. A tear fell down her cheek, as she wondered for the millionth time what her life would have been like had he mated her. She'd never gotten over his rejection of the marriage contract, especially since he'd spent time with her, and bedded her on numerous occasions, as she allowed him to feed. But her request to feed from him was always denied. She should be the queen of the Medici coven, merged with her own, but maybe it wasn't too late to change her fate. Heading back into her room, she showered and prepared to dress in her elaborate costume.

Tonight, she'd go as the Queen of Hearts. She tied back her dark hair, and took the long, red satin scarf and elaborately wrapped it around her head and neck, so only her face was exposed. She pulled the heavy red velvet gown over her head and stepped into the low-heeled red satin slippers. The bodice was fitted and had a high neckline. The sleeves were long and the skirt full, dusting the floor. She attached the elaborate gold collar that spread across her shoulders, and set atop her breasts, each point of the collar ending with a jeweled heart. She looked in the mirror, and applied her makeup, the kohl heavy around her dark eyes, and the false eye lashes expertly applied. She slipped on the face mask of purest white, with blood red lips, and a single red heart painted under the opening for her left eye. She placed the gold crown on her head, each tip on the crown encrusted with a red ruby heart. She stared back at herself in the mirror. She was unrecognizable, even to herself. Picking up the fan, she gave a snap of her wrist as it spread open, its gold foil catching the light, as did the small heart-shaped jewels. Tonight, she'd change her fate.

She left the suite, and swept down the long hallway, and down the staircase leading to the ballroom where the revelers were already gathering. She entered the ballroom, and within minutes, had drawn the attention of several mortal men. She laughed and encouraged their flirtations, as she waited.

***

Lorenzo admired the opulence of his hotel suite, granting him a view of the canals. He was wishing Alfie could have joined him for this little adventure, but he knew Sophia would never have approved. If Dona's tales of the sexual debauchery that took place here were accurate, this was something they should have experienced when they were both unattached. After he showered, he unpacked the costume Dona had made for him, seeing it for the first time. He could tell from her tales of her times here with his father, this costume was a slight variation of the one his father used to wear. He shook his head as he laughed out loud, glad none of the warriors at Castello would see him in this get-up.

Sitting on the side of the bed, he pulled on the white silk stockings that come just above his knee, followed by a pair of gold brocade knee britches that buttoned just under each knee. He put on the shoes, which were black, and polished to a high sheen. The shoes had a slight heel, as were worn by gentleman in the 15th century, and topped with a gold buckle. He put on the long-sleeved white shirt, with large ruffled cuffs, and a scrunched high neck collar. He slipped on the long, gold brocade waist coat, which was nipped in at the waist, then dropped to about mid-thigh. The cuff ruffles on his white shirt extended beyond the sleeves of the brocade coat. He pulled the lush black cape from the box, and draped it around his shoulders, securing it at the neck with a large pearl broach, set in gold. There was a small drawstring bag inside the box, which he opened to discover eight gold rings, all lavishly designed, and he slipped a ring on each finger. Tying his shoulder-length black hair into a loose ponytail once more, his hair was secured by a gold ribbon. "Well, don't I look dandy."

Finally, he lifted the mask from the box, and he knew instantly, it would change the tone of the costume. The mask wasn't that of the human face, but a human skull, gilded in gold, with a moon and a star on the forehead. Like all Venetian masks, it would completely conceal his face. The only feature visible would be his intensely blue eyes, which looked eerie when seen through the mask. He stood before a full-length mirror and studied the effect. His own mother wouldn't recognize him. He laughed to himself, and the sound of his voice was muffled behind the mask. "I'll be sure to save this for Raven." Satisfied with the final results, he turned on his heels and headed for the ballroom.

Lorenzo walked through the corridor, his already tall height increased by the heeled shoes, and despite the grandiose design of the clothes, they still show off his physique. His broad shoulders, narrow waist, slender hips, and muscled legs. As he approached the dimly lit ballroom, several women locked eyes with him through their own elaborate masks, as they peered back at him. He could sure use a smoke, and a Midnight, but neither were possible through the mask, and Dona had told him under no circumstances could he remove the mask. There was an orchestra playing classical music, and couples were waltzing across the ballroom floor, but there were also couples at the tables that lined the walls, some already engaged in a variety of sexual acts, making no move to hide their activities. Quite the contrary, the whole point seemed to be to put your sexual conquest on display but do it in full costume.

He felt a soft hand at his back and turned to see a mortal female who barely stood at his shoulder height. She held her finger to the lips of her mask, as if to say "shh", and beckoned him to follow her. He smiled behind the mask and followed the female back to her table where she offered him her seat. Lorenzo took a seat as the female, dressed all in pale blue and white lace dropped on her knees, kneeling between his legs. Her porcelain mask hid her face, and any emotion she might be feeling, and Lorenzo found the interaction odd to not be able to read the face of his sexual partner. The female placed her hands on his knees, and slowly slid them up his thighs, as Lorenzo leaned his head back in the chair, and let her have her way. She stroked his cock through the gold brocade, until he was hard and long, then she unbuttoned the britches, and took his cock in her hands, stroking slowly. He heard the rustle of her long skirts as she stood, lifting her full skirt above her hips, and straddling him on the chair. He felt the heat of her hot, wet sex as it slid down the full length of his dick, and she proceeded to ride him, as a crowd gathered to watch. He gripped her hips and guided her as she rode hard. She held onto his shoulders, and he could hear the moans escaping from behind the mask. As the small crowd gathered, Lorenzo was aware of the many eyes watching, as the men's erections under their own costumes became evident, and the women shifted their weight uncomfortably from foot to foot. The effect was electrifying, as the sexual energy from Lorenzo and the anonymous female fed the crowd. Lorenzo heard a male voice in the crowd growl, "Fuck the bitch." The anonymous female was crying out now with each stroke, as they both drew closer to orgasm, Lorenzo thrusting his hips upward. He felt her grip tighten on his shoulders, her fingers digging deep into his flesh, as she dropped her head back, and the long, open wail echoed in the room as she reached her orgasm.

Lorenzo was aware that several of the men were now masturbating as they watched, and their breathing had become labored, when he released into her. As the female collapsed on his chest, the small crowd that surrounded them gave a smattering of applause, and he heard a few respond with, "Good show." As the crowd dispersed, the female in blue sat upright, staring back at him from behind her mask. She gently stroked the side of his skull mask, before standing up, and straightening her skirt, and disappearing into the crowd.

Lorenzo adjusted himself and was in the process of re-buttoning his britches when another female, dressed in all black with porcelain white face approached and said, "Don't be in such a hurry."

Lorenzo held up his hands and answered. "Never let it be said I disappointed the ladies."

The mortal female in black began to work her magic, as Lorenzo thought to himself, *Alfie, my brother, we seriously screwed up not coming here earlier.*

2-48

Lorenzo hadn't been able to make his way across to the other side of the ballroom without being accosted by another female. He'd lost count of the number of sexual encounters he'd had. There were a few vamps, but mostly mortals. His biggest problem had been the inability to feed. The venue was quite public, and he couldn't remove his mask and sink his fangs into the succulent flesh of the beauties who had been bouncing on his cock all night. Actually, he laughed to himself, he had to imagine they were beauties. He had no idea what they looked like behind their mask.

There was the one incident, when the four mortal women removed their masks, as they had a contest to see which of them could best swallow his sword. His job was to just lean back and keep an erection, while the four of them competed in who gave the best blow job. The one who finally made him cum won the game, and they giggled together as they finished up, and wandered back into the crowd. Lorenzo knew he'd been here for hours now, and he hoped Dona's evening was as successful as his, when he was approached, once again, by a female dressed as the Queen of Hearts. She curtsied deep before him and remained bowed at his feet until he reached his hand down to her. Even though it was heavily masked by her perfume, he knew from her scent she was vamp, as she silently placed her hand in his, and stood before him. With her free hand, she beckoned to him to follow, as she turned, still holding his hand, and leading him across the ballroom. He had no idea what she had in mind, but so far this evening, the females had been in charge, initiating all the contact, so he allowed himself to be led to a side entry. He heard the moans of the other females in the room, begging him to stay, or admonishing the female who was leading him away to not be so greedy, and be sure she returned with him. Lorenzo was wondering if he'd need to fuck them all before the night was over. If so, he'd need to feed soon.

The Queen of Hearts led him down a narrow corridor and into a large linen storage closet, where the hotel stored the crisply folded sheets, towels, and tablecloths. She closed the door behind them, as she slowly backed away from him, beckoning with her finger for him to follow. He smiled behind his mask as he watched her lift her skirt, and expose her shapely legs, and the dark patch at their apex. He unbuttoned his britches, his cock responding to the scent of her heightened arousal, as he walked to her and easily lifted her up, so her legs wrapped around his hips. He pushed her against the shelves of linen, as he penetrated her, and she dropped her head back, the gold crown tumbling from her head, as her moans filled the room. He pounded her hard, and she returned his thrust. He didn't need to hold back with her. She was vamp and would give as good as she got. He felt his fangs punch through behind the mask, his need for blood overwhelming him, and he clawed at the red scarf around her neck until he dislodged it. The Queen turned her head, displaying her neck, inviting him to feed. He ripped off his mask and sank his fangs deep into her soft flesh. The blood hit his parched tongue and fueled his appetite for more of her. Her moans spurred him on, as his guttural growl filled the room. He braced himself on the shelving unit, as her legs tightened around his hips, and she clung to his shoulders. He fed by the mouthfuls, replenishing his energy, and fueling his desire at the same time, as his cock pistoned in and out of her. She was wet, and hot and welcoming. She was just what he needed.

He heard her whispered plea behind her mask, "Cum with me." He released into her, his moans loud in the enclosed room, as he felt her respond, her hips bucking wildly to drain every drop from him. He leaned into her, supporting his weight against the shelving, as he caught his breath, and she dropped her legs to the floor, but hung on to him for support. They stood in their embrace while their bodies returned to their normal rhythms. Lorenzo was aware that, for many vampires, the lure of the mortal was irresistible, but for him, there was no comparison. He loved the raw power of fucking another vamp, and this one was practiced and perfect. He stepped back from her, letting his eyes take her in. Even through the heavy velvet gown, her womanly curves were most evident. He bowed to the female in the elaborate costume.

"I hope you won't find it necessary to continue to hide your identity, Queen. I promise I'll be your humble servant."

She0 reached out to him as he bowed before her, running her hand through his hair, and releasing the gold ribbon that bound his hair into the ponytail. His dark hair fell free around his face. It was the face she'd seen in her dreams for centuries, Shade's face. He looked up at her, and locked eyes with her, as she slowly peeled away the mask.

Lorenzo watched as her hand went to the mask, and he couldn't wait to see the beauty behind it. She lifted the mask from her face, and he was momentarily struck dumb. He stumbled backward, almost falling. "Dona! I'm so sorry! I had no idea."

As he spoke, the puzzle pieces fell into place. He'd no idea, but she had. She'd chosen his costume. She knew full well who was behind the golden skull mask, similar to the one his father used to wear. "You tricked me!"

Dona smiled at him coyly. "Tricked you? My darling, I simply seduced you. I have watched you all evening, as the mortals toyed with you. I pleased you best. I had you bow at my feet and beg to be my humble servant. Does that not tell you something? Do not be ashamed, Lorenzo. This was meant to be. We were meant to be."

Lorenzo recoiled from her, shaking his head no, and holding his hand out, keeping her at a distance. "You were like a mother to me. Stop it!"

She tried to approach him, and he dodged her, heading for the door. "Lorenzo, wait!"

He stepped outside into the corridor, closing the door behind him. He felt repulsed and conflicted. She'd tricked him, betrayed his trust! He needed to escape her, and in a split-second decision, he teleported back to Castello. Donatella collapsed in tears on the floor of the closet, picking up the gold skull mask he'd left behind, her last chance for a Medici mating having disappeared.

2-49

Lorenzo landed in his bedroom at Castello and started ripping the costume from his body and tossing it aside. He was disgusted with himself, and with her, and his roar could be heard throughout the castle.

Antonio rushed in. "Master! We were not expecting you back so soon." He looked at the remnants of an elaborate costume, ripped and shredded on the floor, and started to pick up the torn fabric.

Lorenzo barked at him. "Get it out of here. All of it!"

Antonio had never heard his master raise his voice to him before, but he knew he wasn't the source of his anger. As Antonio picked up the torn garments, Lorenzo marched nude into the bathroom and turned on the shower, as hot as his skin could tolerate, and stepped under the flowing water. The steam rose around him, and he punched the tile wall hard, as the cracks spread out like an intricate spider web. He roared in anger again, as he started to scrub away at his skin, trying to remove the scent of her perfume, and her betrayal.

Antonio was at a loss as to how to appease his master. He knew he'd been to Venice, to Carnivale. He couldn't imagine what had happened there to have his master so angry. He thought about calling out to Marco, but Marco wasn't exactly the type to lend a sympathetic ear. He decided to call to Alfie, and hoped his master wasn't angered more by his decision. **"Master Alfie, the Prince is back from Venice, and something has gone terribly wrong."**

***

Alfie was on patrol in the olive groves. He tried to stay close to the shack where Danilo worked, and where the workers checked in, as it seemed to give them a sense of security to have him there. Things had been quiet ever since they increased their presence here, which made for a long, boring shift. Lighting up, he leaned against the shack and closed his eyes, thinking about Red. Damn, he couldn't wait to get home to her. He heard Antonio's voice in his head, and he answered him. **"On my way."** Calling to another warrior to take his post, he put out his smoke and took off for Castello, landing inside the grand foyer and taking the steps two at a time. He saw Antonio in the hallway near Lorenzo's room.

"What happened?"

Antonio was shaking his head and wringing a torn piece of silken cloth in his hands. "Master came back from Venice, upset and yelling. He had these torn garments on the floor and wanted them removed. He has already rattled the house with his bellowing and now is in the shower. Something happened in Venice."

Alfie took a deep breath. "Bring up some Red Moon, but stay clear, I'll handle this." Antonio nodded and scurried for the drink. Alfie walked in and found Lorenzo coming from the shower, his skin red and rubbed raw.

"What in hell happened? Antonio called for me, he said you were upset."

Lorenzo looked up in surprise to see his best friend. He walked to the dresser and pulled out a pair of jeans and slipped them on, then ran his hands through his wet hair, brushing it back from his face. He shook his head as he walked to the nightstand and grabbed a pack of cigarettes, lighting up. He exhaled the smoke before answering. "Fucking Alizzi! She betrayed me, brother."

Alfie stood there stunned, but not surprised. Antonio walked in with the tray of Red Moon and rushed back out. Alfie held up the bottle. "You just want the bottle, or a glass?" He wasn't even sure Lorenzo heard him as he continued to pace the floor non-stop. Alfie poured him a glass and handed it to him, before filling a glass for himself. "Betrayed you how?"

Lorenzo accepted the glass and downed it in one gulp. Setting in down, he continued to pace. "We went to Carnivale. She'd gone with my father, and with Marco, when they were all young, and she wanted to go again. She'd told me it was a sexual feast among mortals and vampires, and that part was true. She'd chosen our costumes, and I didn't see mine until I arrived. She told me it was similar to the one my father used to wear. I wasn't allowed to see her before the ball, so I didn't know what she looked like in her costume. She was right about the feast. I could barely make it across the room without having to stop and fuck. The females were plentiful, and they ruled the night. I was getting drained because I couldn't feed. The males couldn't remove their mask, and the females could choose to keep their mask on or not. The night was almost over when she lured me away, into a linen closet, her face hidden by the mask. I fucked her, and fed from her, and only afterward did she reveal herself."

He swung his hand and knocked the wine glass to the floor, watching it shatter. "I've known her since I was a small boy of ten. I thought of her as my mother! She watched after me in my own mother's absence. She couldn't have been unaware of how I saw her. She tricked me. Betrayed me. She wanted us to be together. How can I face her again? I want to kill her!"

Alfie listened to him spill out his anger and knew he had to calm him down. He'd never seen him this pissed off. "You need to calm down first, brother. You can't just kill her. Fuck, she really thought you two would be together? Has she lost her damn mind? Did she ever approach you before in a sexual way?"

He shook his head. "Not really. She brought me feeders and laid beside me while I feasted on them. One night, I fell asleep, and she slept by my side, but she never made any sexual advances toward me. You know Dona, she's a bit eccentric, but I always chalked it up to her loneliness. I can't forgive her for this, though. She's crossed the line. I don't know what to do, Alfie. The Medici has protected her territory for centuries. Maintaining an alliance with the Alizzi provided greater protection to the Medici coven, as Umbria is on our border. I never want to see her face again! How do I explain this to my father?"

"Alright, let's think this through." Alfie refilled his glass. "As difficult as it may be, you need to tell your father. The alliance with the Alizzi's was established by Christofano and honored by your father. Marco won't withdraw his protection of Umbria unless your father directs it, and as long as the Medici is expected to protect her, you'll have to face her. Look, as I see it, you need to let him handle this all the way around. It's complicated, brother. Umbria is on our border, and protecting Umbria also provides another barrier for Tuscany. And like you said, your father has a past with her."

He poured another drink and handed it to Lorenzo. "Listen, brother, you don't need to be worried about your father, he'll know, once you explain that none of this is your fault. Your father knows you, Lorenzo, better than anybody."

Alfie got Lorenzo to sit on the bed. "For now, you need to rest. You're depleted in more ways than one. We'll tackle this tomorrow, head on. You'll feel better once your energy returns and you have time to wrap your brain around all that's happened. I'm here for you, whatever you need."

Lorenzo picked up the bottle and swallowed down the wine. Her blood was inside him. He wanted to slit his wrist and drain every vile drop of her blood from his system. He felt shame and didn't want his father to know.

"I don't want to tell him. I don't want to see that look of disappointment in his eyes."

He felt the exhaustion in every cell in his body as he lay across the bed. He felt Alfie's hand on his shoulder, and knew his brother had his back. "But you're right. I need sleep. Thanks, brother."

Alfie patted him on the shoulder. "I'm going home. If you need me, call."

He watched as Lorenzo's eyes began to close. He walked out of the room, closing the door. As he left, he instructed Antonio that the Alizzi was not to be allowed to enter, and if she showed her face here for any reason, he was to contact him immediately. He stepped outside and took a deep breath. The sun was already coming over the horizon. Damn, it was morning. He teleported quickly back to Red.

2-50

Raven had been in Vancouver for over a week now. He'd scouted the area, checked out the few clubs, but had found nothing that would lead him to Master Lovell. The place wasn't exactly a bevy of vampire activity. The weather sucked and he kept running into nothing but dead ends. He missed the California weather of warmth and sun. This place was bleak, and rainy. He missed Micah and sleeping with his mate. He'd already gone back home once to feed and be with his mate, and he wasn't used to being away this length of time. All that aside, he had a mission to accomplish for the boss-man. If this Lovell was anywhere around here, he was sure keeping a low profile.

His surveillance had revealed the vamp activity in Vancouver was minimal, but he did identify the few clubs where they gathered. He'd tried to avoid drawing a lot of attention to himself in the clubs, and wore jeans, or traditional leathers. Still, he was a stranger here, and drew stares from everyone whenever he entered. Every vampire in the place turned to check him out. It was clear they were locals, and they didn't get many visitors. He needed to find at least one vamp who'd open up and talk.

Walking to the bar, he checked out the bartender who eyed him suspiciously. "You got Midnight, brother?"

The bartender nodded, still giving him the once over. Raven paid in cash and sat back, sipping at the wine as he checked out the other vampires. The music wasn't to his taste, and the mortals seemed unaware that there were vamps in their midst. Hearing a bit of a ruckus at the door, he saw a noisy group of six vamps walk inside, four of them female. He watched as they found their table and eyed him suspiciously. The brunette was wearing heavy makeup and sidled up next to him, ordering a Midnight.

"Haven't seen you here before? You new in town?"

Raven didn't look at her but sipped his drink. "New to this place, and I'm going to be leaving soon, no action around here."

She laughed and slid her hand along the supple leather jacket that covered his arm. "There's action, but you aren't going to find it above ground, handsome. You looking to feed and fuck or something a bit wilder?"

Raven turned to look at the group still sitting at the table who seemed intrigued by the stranger that had wandered in among them.

"I could be enticed. Never turn down a little action." He flagged down the bartender, and ordered her a Midnight, slipping the money across the bar. He was aware he might have to fuck her to get the information he wanted.

She curled up to him, letting her hands run through his long hair. "Where you from?"

Raven played her game, letting her lead the seduction. "Italy, but I've been scouting out the states. Thought I'd come north. Looking for a place that suits me. Can you help me out here?"

She almost purred into his ear. "Anything you want, I can make sure you get."

Her hand dropped from his arm to his thigh and slid in the direction of his cock. Raven was quick and stopped her hand, taking it in his own and kissing her palm. "Not looking for that tonight. You ever heard of a Master Lovell? I heard this was his territory."

She looked back at him and shook her head. "Lovell? Never heard of him. You sure you got the right name?"

Raven shrugged. She looked genuinely confused by the inquiry. "Maybe I got it wrong. Hey, where can I find the underground? There's got to be more vamps up here that what I've seen." He snuggled into her ear, hoping she'd talk. "Come on, you're much too sweet not to help me."

She giggled and whispered back, her lips grazing his cheek. "The underground is about twenty-five miles north of here. That's where the action is. The vamp community here is small, and they stay very low key. But if you decide to go there, you'll experience things you never encountered before."

Raven almost laughed out loud, if she only fucking knew! "Now you're talking. Can I score some coke over there?" Raven was taking a risk asking her for a drug lead, but she didn't flinch at his request, which was a good sign.

"Sure, anything can be had over there. You need something now?"

Raven nibbled at her ear, he wasn't going to be here long enough to tackle her sexually, but he needed her to think he might. "I'm looking for some Tainted Beast, actually."

She backed up a bit and looks confused. "Tainted Beast? Never heard of it, what is that? Would I like it?"

Raven winked. "You probably would, just something we have in Italy."

Her eyes lit up. "Do you have some on you now? I'll make it worth your time to share." She nodded in the direction of her table where her friends sat and watched. "You could have all of us females. We'll make it a great night for you."

Raven looked at the four hungry females. "I'm sure you would." He leaned in and kissed her, and she returned the kiss. "Thanks for the information. I have some things to check out, but another time." He left the club and immediately teleported back to his hotel.

Gathering up his gear, he headed directly north. He scouted for hours until he finally saw enough vampires going to the same building. It was an old music store, now closed down. There were steps leading down to a basement entrance at the back of the building, near the dumpster. Every damn person going in was a vamp. He knew he had at least found a possible source for information. He could hear the music blaring from where he stood and watched the activity. He took out his cell and dialed up the boss-man.

***

Shade had just returned from camp and tossed his phone on the desk when it vibrated. He picked it up and saw it was Raven. "Your ass better be giving me some news. You've been up there a fucking week."

Raven grinned. "Nag, nag, nag. Look, this place is like a vamp desert up here. I found a female in Vancouver who'd talk and got a lead on a place about twenty-five miles north. She never heard of Tainted Beast or Lovell. It's late, so I'm going to hit this joint up tomorrow night. If that bastard's around here, maybe this is where I can find him, or find someone who knows him. So far, I haven't encountered anyone who's ever heard of him. If he's the master in Vancouver, he's sure as fuck keeping it to himself."

Shade sighed. "Whatever it takes, Raven, keep at it. If he is the one making the drug, then maybe he has reason to stay low profile. Keep me informed."

Shade hung up just as Kate entered, and wrapped herself around him. "Problems?"

He caressed her hair and closed his eyes. "No problems, just Raven doing some investigating and coming up empty handed. Nothing for you to worry about."

2-51

Alfie landed outside the villa he now called home. Every time he came home, he still couldn't believe he actually lived here. Being a prince's second had its perks. The sun was already up. He figured it was mid-morning by now, but he decided to have a smoke before going inside. His mind was in a whirl and he wondered if he'd be able to sleep. The Alizzi had betrayed his best friend. He remembered how she'd seduced him so easily when he'd first reached his sexual maturity, and he never saw it coming.

Nickola stepped outside and sat down with him at the table under the portico.

"Is she waiting on me?"

Nickola nodded as he lit up. "Oh yeah, she's wondering where the hell you've been. She's a bit riled up, nothing you can't handle. But, brother, you need to call her when you're going to be late. She worries about you."

Alfie sighed. "Yeah, brother, I know." Nickola wasn't much of a conversationalist, but Alfie was damn grateful he'd chosen him to protect Sophia.

Nickola stared at Alfie and knew something wasn't right. He was usually happy to come home to the redhead, but he seemed in no hurry to go inside. "Something wrong? If you need something, brother, I'm here."

Alfie grunted. "There is something, but seriously Nickola, I can't talk about it."

Nickola didn't want to pry. He knew the *Mafioso* was putting the heat on Medici, and Alfie was out every damn night patrolling the groves. "Look, brother, if it has anything to do with Sophia, if you think she's at risk, you need to keep me in the loop."

Alfie put out his cigarette and stood up, slapping Nickola on the back. "No, has nothing to do with my mate. Don't worry. Once the sun goes down tonight, I'm sure it will be handled by the master. *Grazie*, I appreciate you taking care of Sophia."

Alfie walked inside and went straight to the bedroom. He knew she was there waiting for him, and knew he'd need to have an answer for why he was so late. He just wasn't sure he could tell her the truth.

Sophia looked up as he came in. She was well aware of the tension between the Medici and the *Mafioso*, and when he was late, she immediately thought the worse. "Alfie, what's going on? Is everything okay in the groves?"

"Relax, everything's fine, red. Just got sidetracked. I'm sorry, I should have called, but I didn't have time."

She looked him over, and he didn't look the worse for wear. No battles, anyway, but she could read the concern on his face. "So, what's bugging you? Something's on your mind. I can read you like a book."

Sitting down on their bed, he knew she'd pry until she got an answer. After all, this was his Red. He began to unlace his boots. "Look, Sophia, everything's fine in the groves. Lorenzo needed to talk to me, that's all. I stopped at Castello before coming home. It doesn't concern you." He stood and began undressing so he could get in the shower, but he could feel her anger rise and knew he hadn't worded that right. He was fucking tired. It had been a long night.

"Uh, wait. He's my brother. What do you mean it doesn't concern me? I thought my brother was in Venice. Is something wrong with Lorenzo? What's going on, Alfie?"

He paused and turned to her in frustration, as he was walking to the bathroom. "Sophia, I'm tired. I need to rest. Lorenzo was upset and he needed to unload. He isn't injured or anything, okay? Look, I'm gonna be honest, I can't talk about this with you. Please don't push me. Right now, I need to shower and rest." Walking back to her, he took her in his arms. "Please, I don't want to fight with you, so I'm asking you to shut this down. Your brother will tell you in his own time. Let me take a shower, and then we can go to bed."

Sophia put her hands on her hips, as he turned to walk to the shower. "Excuse me? Who do you think you're talking to, Alfie Medici? I'm not one of your warriors you can just order to step down! You can either tell me what's going on, or I'll pick up the phone and call my brother. Now get back in here and tell me what's going on."

Alfie balled his fists at his sides and took a deep breath. She wasn't going to back down. He turned and stared at her. Battling Sophia was a lost cause. "You want the truth? Your brother went to Carnivale with the Alizzi. The fucking bitch tricked him. She was in costume and seduced him, she fucked your brother and let him feed from her. She removed her mask when the deed was done. She wanted to mate him. She betrayed him. It was her whole damn plan from day one. The bitch is insane. Now Lorenzo feels tainted, embarrassed and doesn't know how he'll tell your dad. There? You happy now?"

Sophia heard his explanation and was fighting to control her rage. It took every ounce of her limited self-control not to teleport out to the Alizzi's villa. "That fucking bitch! I knew she was up to no good, and so did my mother. I'll kill her, Alfie! I can't believe she'd do this to Lorenzo. He's always trusted her. Oh my god, poor Lorenzo." She paced the floor of their bedroom. "Poor Lorenzo. Maybe I should go to him. He has to tell Dad."

"Oh no! You sit your ass down. I'll talk to him again after he's had some time to sleep." Alfie threw his hands up in the air, now he had another damn Medici to calm down. "You're just like your brother, you know that? He wanted to run out and kill the Alizzi too. Keep out of this, Sophia. I mean it. This is something Lorenzo must deal with on his own. "

He watched as she was still pacing and fuming, her face red as hell. "You *will* not go to Lorenzo. Are you listening to me?"

Sophia stopped her pacing. She didn't take direction well, and she never took orders, not even from her mate. "Oh, I'm listening, Alfie. I heard every word you said. Now go take your shower."

"Sophia, I mean it. Stay put, don't wake him. He was depleted and he needs rest. And for that matter, so do I." He turned and headed to the shower.

"Don't worry, Alfie, I promise I won't wake my brother. I'm sure he's upset, and he needs to sleep now."

Alfie looked back at her and she seemed calmer. "That's my red. I won't be long." He stepped in the shower and turned on the water. He just wanted a hot shower and some sleep.

Sophia picked up her cell phone and called home as soon as she heard the water running in the shower. She heard her father's voice on the other end. "Daddy? I think you need to get over here.

No, I'm fine, it’s not me. It's Lorenzo. I wouldn't ask if it wasn't important, and I can't talk right now. Just come, please."

2-52

Shade had no fucking idea what was wrong with Lorenzo. He'd felt his emotions earlier in the evening, but they didn't convey any danger, and then he'd immediately shut down. Shade knew, at that point, Lorenzo was blocking him, but that wasn't unusual from any of his children. He understood their need for privacy in their personal lives. Then he got the phone call from Sophia, telling him something was wrong. Shade could feel that Lorenzo wasn't in any life-threatening situation, and he wasn't injured.

He had to wait until sunset before he could teleport, and in that time, he'd run every conceivable possibility through his brain. Kate wanted to go with him, but he'd told her all he knew, and convinced her to stay until he found out what was going on. He'd done nothing but pace to wait out his time to teleport to Castello, and the hours passed slowly. He kept trying to tune into Lorenzo from time to time, but Lorenzo was still blocking him. "I fucking hate this!" He threw the glass of Midnight across the room and the glass and wine splattered everywhere.

Kate heard the glass shatter and rushed into the room. "Shade, please. We don't know what's wrong, but we know he's not in any physical danger. He wasn't harmed, and he's under no threat. We'd both have felt that. Marco would have contacted you. Whatever's wrong, you'll discover soon enough. He's troubled, but he's safe."

Shade spun to look at her. "Is he blocking you? Is he talking to you? Is Sophia talking to you? I can't deal with this, Kate. Fuck the time and the sun. I am going to Castello now."

Kate rolled her eyes. "Really? And you wonder where Sophia gets her stubbornness from. You'll wait here, and if that's not good enough, then call Marco. Have him check on Lorenzo. Or send Luca ahead. Lie down. Stop fighting your death slumber. You'll need your strength when you go to him."

Shade knew she was right, but he was losing patience. "If I lie down, you wake me as soon as the sun sets, and not a minute longer." He walked back to their bedroom as she followed him. So far, the adrenaline rush had kept him awake. Flopping down on the bed, fully clothed, he willed himself to go down and out.

2-53

Kate woke him, he felt startled and confused. Clearing his head, he was glad for the rest. He felt calmer and was ready to teleport the distance. His goodbye with Kate was a short one, but they made a promise that whatever the outcome, they'd tackle it together. He teleported out, and traveled as fast as he could, making record time. He landed in the grand foyer at Castello, and Antonio rushed to greet him.

"Master, we were not expecting you!"

Shade nodded. "I'm sure you were not. Where is Lorenzo?"

Antonio was wondering who'd notified him but knew better than to ask. "In his room, master."

Shade didn't acknowledge his response but teleported straight outside the closed door of his son's bedroom. He knocked hard on the door. "Lorenzo, get the fuck up and open this door."

Lorenzo woke to the sound of someone pounding on his door, but he was confused by the sound of his father's voice. "Dad?" He slid out of bed and grabbed a pair of jeans tossed over a chair and pulled them on as he was walking to the door. Opening the door, he looked surprised. "Dad? Is everything okay?"

Shade looked him over from head to toe, making sure he wasn't hurt. He took a deep breath. "No, everything is not okay. You have been blocking your mother and me for a very long time. I felt your turmoil, and then you shut us out. Sophia called me." He looked him in the eye and raised his brows. "Whatever this is, you need to talk to me. Not like you to shut us out, son."

Lorenzo opened the door for him to enter, and muttered "fuck" under his breath. "Sophia called you?" He was processing the information in his head and knew Alfie must have said something to his sister. Turning, he walked back into his room, wondering what, if anything, he wanted to tell his father, and how much he already knew.

"I assume you confided in Alfie, *si*? Did you forget he is mated to your sister? Sophia is like your mother, nothing gets past her for long. Get used to the fact, that once mated, your female knows it all. They sense everything eventually, no matter how much you try to lock it down."

Shade took a seat and looked at him. Something was definitely eating at his son. Something he didn't want to talk about. "I can feel your reluctance to talk to me. I understand that. I had no parents to confide in, to guide me or even console me when I was your age. We raised you to come to us. I may not always approve of your actions, but I will never stop loving you, Lorenzo. And you know how your mother feels."

Lorenzo dropped down in the armchair and slung his leg over the arm of the chair, as he looked out the window, unable to look his father in the eye. "It's just...embarrassing. I feel like a fool. I gave someone my complete trust, and they betrayed me. It's not the end of the world, Dad. I mean, I'm fine. I'll get over it. I wish Sophia hadn't called and gotten everyone so worried."

Shade looked at his son's expression of shame. "Lorenzo, if someone betrayed you, it is not your fault. The fault lies in them, and their black heart. You have your mother's heart. She is kind and trusting, she believes there is good in everyone until they prove otherwise. So, if you gave this person your trust, then I believe their betrayal is an evil thing. And do not blame your sister, she loves you and is concerned for you. Now, tell me who betrayed you?"

Lorenzo bowed his head. He hated to speak the words. He answered softly, almost a whisper, "The Alizzi."

Shade sat dead still. His mind went back to every moment he'd ever witnessed his son and Dona together, trying to remember if he'd missed any signs. He shook his head to clear his mind. Kate had warned him so many times. She didn't trust her or the lavish gifts, and always questioned her motives in mothering him so closely. *Cazzo*, when was he going to start listening to her? He kept his voice calm. "Tell me everything. No matter what it is."

Lorenzo laid his head back against the soft chair and closed his eyes. It was easier to speak of it if he didn't have to look at his father, afraid of seeing disappointment in his eyes. "Dona asked me to take her to Carnivale in Venice. She was telling me all the times she went there with you and Marco. She said she'd take care of everything and selected our costumes. We checked into the hotel, and we had separate rooms. I dressed in my costume and went to the ball. I never saw her in her costume, so I had no idea what she looked like. Near the end of the night, she approached me, and led me away from the ballroom to a linen closet, where we had sex. I was drained from the night's events, and desperately needed to feed, and she made herself available to me, and I fed from her. Only afterwards did she remove her mask." Lorenzo covered his face with his hands. "Dad, I was never attracted to her. She was like...my mom. She has looked after me since I moved here when I was ten. I felt...used or violated. She betrayed my trust. I think she thought if she could seduce me, I'd see her in a different light...and I do, but not the one she wanted. I can't face her again. I don't think I can bear to look at her again."

Shade felt his shame. She'd seduced his son, hoping to lure him in, and finally mate with a Medici. Did she love Lorenzo, or see him as a means to an end? Either way, she'd used their past together to get her final revenge on him. He stood up, and his heart felt betrayed as well. He'd protected her lands, her home, and her name for so long.

"This is my fault. All of this is my fault, not yours, son." There was no anger in his voice. He too felt like a fool, and an even bigger one than Lorenzo, for she'd been fooling him for much longer. "You will never face her again. She has betrayed me, my name, my honor, my respect, my protection, and now my family. Her fate now lies in my hands."

He walked to the window and looked toward Umbria. "I am proud of you, Lorenzo. You are an honorable warrior. You are the son I always dreamt of. This shame belongs to her, not to you. You are no fool. I am the fool."

He closed his eyes and asked his *madre* to send him strength. Her wisdom had kept Dona's black heart from his own so many years ago. "Stay here. Do not follow me. I have some business to take care of."

2-54

Dona had left Venice shorty after she realized Lorenzo had teleported back to Florence. She'd packed up their things and arranged to have the trunks shipped back home before checking out of the hotel. The clerk had slipped her the receipt for the one-night stay, and Dona looked hard at the exorbitant amount of money she'd spent. Money she couldn't afford to squander. She'd hoped his attachment to her, his fondness for her, could be shifted to something more. That once he'd had sex with her, fed from her pure bloodline, he could be coaxed. She hadn't anticipated his anger. She returned home and retreated to her bedroom, wondering if she should call on him and apologize, but her instincts told her it was too soon.

***

Shade teleported into Umbria and straight for the Alizzi villa. He landed just outside the front entrance and picked up her scent. He knew she was inside. As he opened the door, not bothering to knock, he felt his beast emerge. He'd held down the beast during his conversation with Lorenzo, but he couldn't restrain him any longer. Her butler rushed to the door, and Shade brushed him aside, as the smaller vamp stumbled backward. Shade knew he wouldn't interfere.

He followed his nose as he walked through the villa, in search of her. He noticed most of the elaborate and expensive furnishings were gone. The paintings that used to hang on the walls were also gone. There was no silver, no gold. It looked like the house had been robbed of its very soul. He crept silently toward the upper floor and found the door to her private suite.

She was lying in bed when she picked up Shade's familiar scent, and she cowered beneath the covers.

His heart raced and he was enraged for his son. His breathing was rapid, and he narrowed his eyes. He kicked down the door and found her lying in the bed, the room bare but for the simplest necessities. He gave her no time to think, but rushed at her, grabbing her long dark hair, and wrapping it around his fist. He yanked her head back, almost taking it off her neck and rattled the house with his roar. He glared into her bewildered face, as his fangs dripped with saliva. "You fucking bitch!"

He came at her so fast she had no time to think. He grabbed her by the hair and held her immobilized, as he screamed at her.

"I'm sorry! Shade, I'm sorry! I meant no harm. I thought he would welcome me if he knew my true feelings for him. Please..."

Shade trembled, his anger was at a point of wanting to slay her dead, but he was warrior first and foremost. She wasn't a warrior but female and held no weapon. Killing her would bring him momentary satisfaction, but also dishonor in the long run. He shook her hard by the hair, as she struggled to try to get away.

"Oh, you should beg for your useless life. You disgust me! You have brought shame and disgrace to the Alizzi name."

Donatella started to sob, a deep, heart-wrenching sob because she knew she'd lost it all now. She'd lost Shade's friendship, and she'd lost whatever affection Lorenzo held for her. Her coven had all but disappeared, as had the fortune left to her by her father. She wouldn't be able to hold on to the estate much longer. Everything she was born to inherit was gone. She could claim to be the daughter of a royal master, but she'd lost everything that came with it.

"It is a useless life. I have nothing now. There is nothing you can take from me that can push me lower than I am right now. You did this to me! If you had mated me, like your father wanted, we could have had everything. Why couldn't you love me? I could have brought you so much more than the mortal!"

Shade dropped her on the bed and recoiled from her. He couldn't stand to touch her. "Shut up, Dona! You will listen to me now and heed every word that comes from my mouth. You betrayed me, my son, my warriors, and my good graces. Never mention my queen again. She is too pure and good for any reference of her to roll off your tongue. Our fathers created this alliance long ago, but it is no more. My *madre* knew your heart was black and cold, and saved me from you. This obsession, this jealousy, it ends now. You can never touch me, you never could. And my son, he was born from a love that is eternal and pure, and that is something you can never understand. Never show your face in my territories again or you will be slaughtered. My warriors will know you for what you truly are. There is no more protection from the Medici."

He shook the bed hard, dislodging the mattress that slid to the floor with her on it. "I hate you, Donatella! I have never hated anyone more in my life. You betrayed my son, yet you claim to love him? I spare your life for one reason. So, you can sit here and die alone, broken, and penniless with nothing. I hope your enemies bear down on you and destroy whatever is left. All the warriors in the world could rain down on you, and I would rejoice in their ending your life."

He walked over to the door that now lay off its hinges, splintered and broken. He stepped over the wreckage as he turned to her one last time. "Never fuck with what is mine! You so much as look at my son, I will behead you, and proudly ride through the streets of Florence, holding your head high for all to see."

Donatella curled into a ball on the floor. What would she do without the protection of the Medici? She had no warriors, and no money to pay for mercenaries. Her territory would be completely vulnerable now. She hid her face and sobbed, knowing she'd truly lost him now, for all eternity. He'd never forgive her for this.

He walked back through her villa, reaching the outside air, and gulped in deep breaths of the night. He'd never in his entire life berated and belittled a female in that manner. But then, none had ever violated his son before. He teleported out of Umbria. It was time he let Kate know what had happened. He'd blocked nothing from her or his children as this went down, and she would have felt his rage.

Shade teleported over Tuscany, instead of going straight back to Castello. He wanted some time to clear his head and calm down. His emotions were rolling inside him. He finally landed inside the camp and saw Marco on the field. The warriors in training stopped in their tracks, even before the dust from his boots could clear the air. Marco took one look at him and knew something major had gone down. Marco was aware that Lorenzo had gone to Venice with Dona, and had come home earlier than expected, but Lorenzo hadn't shown his face in the camp. He looked at Shade, his face expressionless as he spoke, "Alizzi?"

Shade nodded. "Give me fifteen minutes alone with Lorenzo, then come to the house." Shade didn't wait for a response. He knew Marco would be there. Teleporting inside the grand foyer, he walked to the office on the ground floor and found his son and Alfie inside. "I need a fucking drink."

Antonio appeared from nowhere with a tray of both Midnight and Red Moon, and a collection of glasses. He bowed his head before Shade. "Master."

Shade took the Midnight, while the two boys preferred the Red Moon. Lorenzo was still finding it hard to look at his father. He felt like he'd let his family down. Lorenzo gulped down the wine and turned toward the window. "So, you saw the Alizzi?"

Shade downed the glass, then picked up the bottle and drank straight from it. He turned to his son, who still couldn't look at him. "*Si*. Marco is on his way, once he gets here, I will give my instruction." He felt the tight grip on his heart. His son still couldn't face him, and he hated her even more for doing this to them. "Don't let her win an ounce of your pride. If you can't face me, she wins. I won't give that bitch one second of what we have built as father and son."

Lorenzo remained with his back to his father. "I feel like I've let you down. All my life I have strived to be like you, to make you proud of me, to be worthy to lead this camp, and this coven. I feel like I've failed you, and Mommy."

Shade felt his heart crack, and he wished like hell Kate was here right now to make this right, with her gift of love and light. His eyes strayed to Alfie who shook his head. Whatever words he said, they would have to reach inside his son's wounded pride. He closed his eyes and let every ounce of his love and pride for Lorenzo pour over him.

"Son, no one is judging you. If there is any fault to be had, it would fall on my head. You are so much like me that my legacy follows you. I regret parts of my life and for that I apologize, but I sure as hell won't apologize for building up this camp, or making warriors out of ordinary boys, or making this coven one of the strongest. I fell in love with a female I am proud to call my queen, and proud to have as the mother of my children. But more than anything else, I will never apologize for the warrior who stands before me, that I proudly call my son. I have made a lot of mistakes, some you will know, and some I hope you never know. I lived a warrior's life, and the privileged life of a royal and a master and took every advantage. The Alizzi is nothing, Lorenzo. But I am still here, so are you. If we can't get past this, then we betray our own. We betray Medici. We are family, and we will survive and conquer. Look at me, Lorenzo."

Lorenzo turned and looked at his father. "I'm sorry, Dad. She knew I cared for her, and I even felt sorry for her. I knew she was lonely. But I really thought she was my friend. I won't be so foolish again."

Shade held up his hand. "No more talk of this. I love you. I have achieved more as master and king once I found my true mate and was surrounded by the love of the family we created. I may be a legend to the world of immortals, but I am no god, Lorenzo, just a vampire warrior trying to do the best I can. I learned from my mistakes, and you will learn from yours, and be stronger for it."

Marco stood outside the door and waited, listening for the conversation to conclude before entering. He'd never heard his best friend be so humble. He strolled in then, grabbed a Midnight and looked at each of their faces. "Fuck me, who the hell died. Like a damn graveside service in here."

Alfie had to bite his lip not to laugh out loud. Leave it to Marco to lighten the mood.

Shade grunted. "Subtlety never was your strong point, you old coot. Listen up. We have had a breach of trust with the Alizzi. We will not discuss the details, but from this moment on, that bitch is dead to us all. We are removing our protection, and our alliance with the Alizzi is over. This now leaves our border to Umbria exposed. I need to have that border heavily guarded. Let them be seen. Let her know she is now my enemy, for now and all time. Any questions?"

Marco kept his emotions hidden. *What the fuck did Dona do to spark this?* If Shade was breaking the centuries old alliance, then something definitely went down in Venice. "No problem. Are we expecting resistance? I will have to recall some warriors from other posts to do this. We are already covering the olive groves heavily."

Shade turned to look at him. "She has nothing, no warriors, and her coven is almost gone. The house looks like she sold everything that had any value."

Marco took a long sip of Midnight and gauged Lorenzo's reaction over the rim of the glass. "You know I am the fucking SIC here, and I have been covering Umbria my whole fucking life. So, could one of you assholes tell me what the hell went down?"

Lorenzo answered him. "It's my fault. Well, not my fault exactly, but I'm responsible. I went with her to Carnivale as you're aware, but she betrayed me. She picked our costumes, and I wasn't allowed to see them, so when I went to the ball, I had no idea what Dona looked like. She used the disguise to seduce me and didn't reveal herself until afterward. She wanted us to mate."

Marco slowly lowered the glass to the table and looked at Lorenzo. "You know, I always thought she was a twisted female, hell I thought they didn't come any more fucked up than Sabine. But I was wrong. That bitch is going to go down one way or another, Lorenzo. Her time will come."

He slapped Shade on the shoulder. "I got this, Shade, I will put out the word. Send some warriors out there tonight." Marco walked to Lorenzo and stuck out his fist to bump. "No honor lost on me, brother."

Lorenzo returned the fist bump. "Thanks, brother."

Shade was grateful for the brother he had in Marco. As Marco left the room, he decided he had one more issue to address. "I could not have made it where I am today without the support and loyalty of my SIC. Marco has been a true brother to me. So, I need to know if there is a rift between the two of you. Lorenzo, I know you confided in Alfie, but it is Sophia who called me."

Alfie grinned. "No rift that I'm aware of. Lorenzo and I have been together long enough to know each other pretty well. We're brothers first and foremost."

Lorenzo shook his head no. "If there's one thing I know for sure, it's that nothing gets past Sophia. Besides, I'd never expect Alfie to keep secrets from his mate. If Sophia called you, she called out of love for me. I get that."

Shade nodded. "Good. I'm glad that is settled. So, get your ass home to my daughter and make some *bambinos*. Tell her I said so, and it is a direct order."

Alfie chuckled. "Yes, master." He fist bumped Lorenzo and headed out the door. Shade stood up and paced around the room, dragging his hand through his hair. "I am sorry this happened, son, but it has made us stronger. I have to go to my slumber before I can go back to your *madre*. I can't lie to her, Lorenzo. And I know she felt every ounce of my anger and pain. Yours as well. I will leave it up to you if you want to tell her, or if you want her to hear it from me."

Lorenzo nodded. He knew his mother had always been suspicious of the Alizzi, but he'd grown up watching her respond to every female that showed any interest in his father, he'd never paid it any attention. "It was my doing. I'll call her while you slumber. She'll be worried, and she shouldn't have to wait for an answer."

Shade stopped his pacing and looked at his son. "I stood in this room many times and felt my own *padre's* wrath for my mistakes. But there was always someone else who made it all right, kept me from fearing him, to keep my faith in Medici. It was my own *madre*. I hope, someday, Lorenzo, you find the mate that is like your *madre*, because that love is something to be cherished."

He walked to Lorenzo and hugged him tight. "I loved you, from the moment you were born, and even before that. It is okay, it's over now. Don't beat yourself up anymore." He walked out of the room and headed up the stairs.

2-55

Kate had received a call from her son, giving her the details of his encounter with the Alizzi and she was ready to rip someone's head off. Lorenzo had explained the Medici coven had broken all ties with her, and she'd no longer be under their protection, but Kate was fighting the urge to go there and choke the life out of her. She'd been stomping around the house all day. Shade was still in his death slumber in Florence and wouldn't be able to return for several hours yet.

Shannon emerged from her room. "Want to tell me what's going on? You've been stomping around all day."

Kate unloaded on her, and Shannon was shocked, but not completely surprised. "You know, you had instincts about her all along."

Kate nodded. "I know, but I always feel so much jealousy around women I knew he'd been with, it was hard to separate those emotions. I never know if I'm just over-reacting to the fact they slept with him at some point, or if their motives are still suspect. I hate that this has happened to Lorenzo."

Shannon soothed her. "He'll be fine, Kate. Just one of life's hard lessons. He'll learn not everyone who presents themselves as a friend can be trusted."

Kate sighed. "A hard way to learn a lesson."

Shannon gave her a hug. "We've all been there, my friend, and eventually, the betrayer pays the price."

Kate shrugged free of the hug. "It's the eventually part that's pissing me off."

Shannon chuckled. "Remind me to never get on your bad side. Listen, I have some work to do. You know where to find me."

Kate nodded as Shannon left, and Kate stomped back upstairs to the bedroom.

***

Shade had checked in with Lorenzo and Marco before leaving Castello to head back to Virginia. Lorenzo had told him he better be prepared for a rough homecoming. No one had to tell Shade that Kate had always been suspect of any of the females in his life, and now Donatello's actions weren't going to help the situation any. He landed inside the house and Gi came out to greet him, asking him if he'd like a drink.

"No, Gi, I think I will just go to *bel*."

Gi cringed. "Are you sure, master? I think, perhaps, you should have one. My lady is very angry, and I am surprised the doors are still on their hinges. The animals have also been howling most of the night."

Shade took a deep breath. "*Grazie,* Gi, but I will pass. The sooner this is over the better."

Shade walked up the stairs, hoping in the time since Lorenzo's call she'd have calmed down a bit. But he understood her anger. He'd felt much the same. He stepped inside the bedroom and didn't get far inside the door. She was waiting for him.

Despite her best efforts, she hadn't been able to calm down. She spun on her heels when he entered the room. "Is Lorenzo okay? Did you talk to Dona? I never want to see her face again, do you understand? If she sets foot in Castello, I will kill her myself! What was she thinking? That she could mate this...this...child?"

He knew he'd be bombarded with anger, and his old *bel rosso* poured out a million questions at once. He held up his hands in a calming manner. "I know you are angry. You have a right to be. I was as well. Ask one thing at a time, *mi amore*. I will answer everything. But can I have a kiss and a hug first? I need it. I need you to hold me, before I tell you all of this. You are my light and my rock, please."

She took a deep breath, knowing he wasn't the source of her anger, and went to him to be wrapped in his embrace. "I'm sorry. I felt so bad for Lorenzo. I could feel his pain, his embarrassment. I wanted to hold him and tell him everything would be alright. Please tell me this woman won't be able to get to him again."

He led her to their favorite chair near the window and sat with her on his lap. He snuggled into her neck and breathed her in. Her rose scent calmed him like nothing else could. "Lorenzo has had his pride bruised. It is a hard lesson for him to learn, but he will be fine with time. We talked, and he understands he needs to tell me when anything like this happens. He was afraid to tell me, he couldn't even look at me. He felt as though he disappointed both of us. I assured him he had not. As for Donatella..." He left the words hanging.

Kate lay with her head nestled against his shoulder as his arms held her. His nearness calmed her. "He told me you'd withdrawn protection and Dona's on her own now. I'm glad for that, but I can't promise you I can control myself if I ever cross paths with her."

"What I did was break the alliance. I have warriors posted on the border, well seen and armed. She has been told to never step foot in Medici territory ever again or I will slaughter her without batting an eye. She actually thought Lorenzo would fall for her. This is my fault. I should have listened to your instincts. I should have cut all ties with her, and I did not. I regret that with all my heart." He laid his head back and closed his eyes and sighed. "I have never spoken such vile words to a female. I wanted to kill her."

"Lover, you trusted her, and our son trusted her. She abused that trust and used it to manipulate us all. In the end, she is the one who will pay."

"She will never face us again, nor step foot anywhere near us. If nothing else, she knows she has broken all the rules. This is over and so is she. This is done, *mi amore*, we speak of her no more. She does not exist to me." He stood with her still in his arms, carried her to the bed, and laid her down. He put his finger to her lips, "No more talk, just love. Let us love each other and the rest of the world be damned right now."

2-56

Raven waited until the night had descended. He landed near the club in the outskirts of Vancouver and observed the activity, watching the crowd of both mortals and immortals as they came and went inside the club. He could hear the pounding beat of the music from his position across the street. The club drew a fairly big crowd, and he decided it was time to go inside. He'd dressed more traditionally, and tried to blend in, but kept all his senses on alert. Any new vampire in a community would automatically be suspect.

It was easy to see the immortals inside the club knew each other, he was expecting that. Watching the small groups congregate to fuck or feed, and exchange drugs, was normal. He kept a close watch for the bimbo he ran into the previous night. He sure as hell didn't want to run into her again. Raven didn't want to engage with anyone yet. He was here to watch, listen, and gather information. For the most part, everyone left him alone, but his presence didn't go without notice. Throughout the night, his attention kept returning to the male vampire who sat alone. Like Raven, this vampire was extremely interested in watching the comings and goings of the club crowd. Was this Lovell?

Moving to another table to get closer and perhaps get the attention of the vamp, Raven ordered another Midnight. As expected, it didn't take long for the vamp to notice him, which was what he wanted. The vamp raised his glass to Raven and nodded. Raven nodded back and once the waitress came around again, he ordered the vamp a drink. The waitress looked at him and smiled.

"You're new here." She nodded her head toward the other vamp. "And you're just his type."

Raven lit up a smoke. "What type is that?"

She ran her fingers through his long hair. "A pretty boy. Sexy, and new, and if you're looking for a sugar daddy, Frenchy is your ticket."

Raven leaned around her and eyed the vampire. "Frenchy?"

She sat down on the edge of the empty chair. "That's what everyone calls him. He's fucking older than Satan himself, I think. Been here forever. You want me to tell him you're interested when I deliver his drink?"

Raven smiled at her. "No, I can handle the pickup myself. Hey, you know a vamp called Lovell by any chance?"

She stood up, taking the cigarette from his fingers and taking a long drag. "Lovell? Nah, never heard of him and you won't need him if you get Frenchy." She winked and walked off, still puffing on Raven's cigarette.

Raven waited until she delivered Frenchy his drink. The old vampire eyed Raven and smiled at him. Raven smiled back, letting his long black hair do its own talking, flinging it back over his shoulder. The old vampire licked his lips and Raven almost laughed out loud. Well, at least he knew he still had it. They played a little cat and mouse game from their prospective tables, and Raven knew he had him. He stood and stretched. His small but muscular frame enhanced by the tight leathers and giving Frenchy an unobstructed view. He grabbed his drink and walked over to his table. "Mind if I sit down?"

The old vampire motioned for him to take a seat. "I would be delighted to have some company, especially one so beautiful and well-mannered as you."

Raven took a seat and noticed the old vamp didn't miss a thing. "Most obliged. Name is Raven."

The vampire raised his hand in the air and snapped his fingers several times, and the waitress returned quickly with two more drinks. "You're new here, so tell me, what is your business here tonight? Or are you just scouting for some fun and enjoyment, *mon bel immortel*?"

Raven knew this vamp had been here a long time and was hoping he'd be able to give him some useful piece of information. He didn't want to spend any more time in this place than necessary, and boss-man was getting antsy for something tangible. He had to take a shot.

"I'm looking for someone specific. Can't seem to find him. I was hoping I'd see him here, but this club scene needs some help. Pretty damn lame, if you ask me, present company excluded, of course."

Frenchy chuckled. "I think you would be quite the challenge for this old vampire, Raven. But you do amuse me and bring pleasure to these old eyes. Who are you looking for?"

Raven leaned back in the chair and decided to go for it. "A master, name is Lovell. Heard he was in the Vancouver area. Just curious where I might find him."

Frenchy's face remained expressionless, giving away nothing as he answered. "If I tell you what I know, *mon beau*, what do you plan to do for me?"

Raven already had a feeling the old bastard knew something, and he wasn't about to fuck him to get what he wanted. "I'm not here for a date, I'm on business. In the past, I would have easily accepted your more interesting plan for me to reward you in exchange for information, but I'm mated. I came here to find someone for a business deal, not cheat on my vampire."

Frenchy laid his hand on top of Raven's and smiled. "Honor and faithfulness are a lost art. I admire that in the young. The name Lovell has not been heard by these ears in many centuries. The last Lovell's in this area were here in the 1700's and died out. The coven was never very large. Whoever gave you this information was misinformed."

Raven sat for a moment thinking, something wasn't right. He believed the old vamp, but Jacks had given the boss-man this information. Raven couldn't imagine her sending him on a wild goose chase, but hell, maybe she didn't know either.

"Thank you, Frenchy. I appreciate the information."

Frenchy took a long look at the beautiful, young vampire as he stood, and knew he'd never know the glorious feel of his hard body. "I wish you well, Raven. Perhaps, a kiss then, as a reward for the information? It would make this old vampire happy."

Raven smiled down at him. He wondered, for a brief moment, if this would have been his own fate had he never met Micah. He leaned down and kissed him on the lips, a kiss of appreciation and respect. Frenchy moaned softly when Raven broke the kiss.

"Safe journey, *mon bel ami*."

Raven walked outside and stood looking up at the moon. "Time to head back to the boss-man. He's not going to like this bull shit."

2-57

The new camp warriors had been chosen from the spring recruits, and Shade was busy working with Marcello to direct their training. He was invigorated by the new talent that came to the camp every year and loved the challenge of molding them into warriors, the caliber of which was unmatched in the vampire community. He wrapped up for the night, giving out orders to Marcello, Aislynn, and Skelk for the following night's training.

Walking back to the house, gave him time to clear his head. He felt the light breeze then picked up his scent, Raven had arrived. He continued walking toward the house and saw him sitting on the patio, smoking a cigarette.

"About time your ass got some information for me. Hell, if I knew it would take you a damn week or more to find one master, I would have done it myself."

Raven watched him stroll up to the house. He never changed in his appearance, always the same black tee shirt, old style leathers and boots. But Raven knew that while he looked the same on the outside, he'd changed a lot on the inside, thanks to his queen. She'd filled the hole in his life to capacity, and Raven understood that now more than ever.

"You know, for a wealthy old vampire, you're one grumpy and impatient ass master. One would think you aren't getting any fun time with the queen. You're almost as bad as Marco."

Shade stopped and stood with his hands on his hips. "You mind your own damn business about *bel*. Do not take liberties, Raven. She is still your queen. Now shut the fuck up, give me a smoke and tell me what you learned."

Raven laughed. "You want me to shut the fuck up or talk? I'm good boss-man, but damn, make up your mind."

Shade flopped down in the lounge chair near the pool and lit up. "Look, I'm in no mood. I just got back from Castello and the alliance with Alizzi is over. As far as I am concerned, she is now our enemy. She betrayed Lorenzo, took him to Carnivale in Venice, while in disguise, she tricked and seduced him. I wanted to rip her damn head off and shove it up her ass. The *Mafioso* is trying to take control of the olive groves. I got more warriors in Florence on guard than ever before. And the camp here is getting under way with new warriors. It never stops. All the children are grown. You would think by this time in my damn life, I would be spending every moment with Kate, but here I am up to my ass in shit. And now, I've got this Tainted Beast fiasco looming, and I need to find the source and destroy it."

Raven was shocked at the news of the Alizzi. That was one old alliance, reaching back centuries, and now it was broken. Shaking his head, he looked at his master. "Damn, sorry about the prince. But I'd think all this activity would make you happy. You're a warrior, and you're keeping all of us busy as hell, feels good to be useful."

Shade closed his eyes. "What I want keeping me busy is my female. We are both so busy. I sometimes wonder why she puts up with me."

Raven laughed. "We've all been wondering that since she walked into your life!"

Shade sat up and slapped him hard against the shoulder. Raven pulled away, but too late to avoid the slap. "Okay! Damn, grumpy and agitated."

Raven proceeded to relay to him the entire conversation he'd had with Frenchy. He left nothing out and explained to him he was pretty damn sure the old vamp was telling the truth. As the conversation went on, Shade sat up, leaning forward as his interest was piqued.

"So, you think Jacks fed me bullshit information, or you think she was misinformed?"

Raven shrugged. "That, I can't say."

"*Cazzo*!" Standing up, Shade paced. "If there is no Lovell, we need to know who the hell owns Under the Coffin. She is the best informant I have when it comes to masters. All right, thanks Raven, get back home, and keep your eyes and ears peeled. Let me know what Matteo finds out."

Raven stood up and looked at him with a cockeyed grin. "You owe me, boss-man, a big one. I had to kiss an old, decrepit vampire to get this useless information. The things I have to do for Medici."

Shade crossed his arms over his chest and grunted. "Well, suck it up. The last time I looked, you liked older vampires!"

Raven nodded. "Low blow, boss-man, but true." He was gone in a second, and Shade stood in the cool night air, wondering what the hell to do next.

***

Natalia had been in the stables and was walking back to the house when she saw Raven and her father on the patio talking. She could overhear much of the conversation and knew Raven hadn't been successful in tracking down the vampire her dad was looking for. As Raven teleported out, Natalia stepped onto the patio and joined her father. "Maybe I can find him."

Shade was so distracted by his own thoughts he didn't hear his daughter approach. "My beautiful Nattie, how, exactly, would you propose to find him? You are much too young to be wandering around looking for vampires."

She sat down across from him. "Daddy, I have no intention of chasing after vampires in seedy clubs. I leave that to your warriors. But, you know, the Council has archives that go back centuries. Technically, I'm not Council, and therefore, I'm only allowed access to the Medici records. But Jasperion keeps records of all coven territories and land deeds. It might be a stretch, since Under the Coffin sits in your territory, but you never know, we might get lucky. Let me go to Florence and see if I can convince Malachi to allow me to dig through the records. You can send one of your warriors with me."

Shade looked at her, his mind taking in what she was telling him. It was a logical and fast solution if there were records to be found. "Nattie, I have some reservations about this. First of all, there may be no record and it may be a wild goose chase. Secondly, Malachi will not be inclined to let you look through the records of other masters. Those documents are private and distinctly reserved for use by the Council. It will be a challenge to convince Malachi to make a concession."

Natalia shrugged. "What have you got to lose? I can do a better job of convincing Malachi if I show up in person. Besides, I can stay at Castello a few days. Lorenzo could use some company."

Shade smiled at her with so much love. "Lorenzo definitely needs some family around him right now. You are right. Malachi needs to know about the drug, he needs to know I am doing all I can to get this under control. You will have to convince him, Nattie. He really does take to you, and besides, I can tell you are itching to get back in the archives." He hugged her to his chest. "How did you get so grown up and smart right before my eyes. Come on, let's get inside. We need to tell your *madre* you are heading for Florence."

2-58

With Aislynn in tow, Natalia left for Florence. She'd never teleported this distance alone, so she'd allow Aislynn to lead her. They landed in Florence, outside the Council compound, and she was immediately admitted and shown to a parlor. Malachi appeared shortly, the hood obscuring much of his face.

"Young Natalia! This is most unexpected. To what do we owe the pleasure of this visit?"

Natalia stood when he entered the room and bowed her head slightly. "Good evening, Malachi. I apologize for not requesting a visit, but this matter is rather urgent. My father is faced with a situation in the States that he's trying to get a handle on. There's a new drug called Tainted Beast, have you heard of it?"

Malachi shook his head no. "We have not. Is this another drug from the mortals?"

Natalia approached him. "No. It appears to be a drug made specifically for the vampire, and it has serious repercussions. It releases the beast in a rage of violence, and he destroys without restraint. My father thinks it's being produced by a master. It's being sold to masters only, right now, as it's very expensive. My father is trying to track down the source before it gets out of control. He has only seen it in his California territory, but if it spreads, it could wreak havoc on our kind. I'm here to ask a favor."

Malachi nodded. "I'm not sure how we can help you, my child, but what is it you seek?"

Natalia continued. "My father's warriors believe the drug is being sold out of a club in California called Under the Coffin. We've been unable to find the owner of that club. I was hoping, with Jasperion's help, I could go through the land deeds, and see if, perhaps, we could find the owner."

Malachi bowed his head as he mulled over her request. According to their bylaws, only Council had full access to their records. She'd only have access to records relating to the Medici, but then again, the club was inside Medici territory, and a drug like this could expose them all.

"I will grant your request, child. Come with me."

Malachi sent a message to Jasperion to join them in the archives, and he arrived there as they were approaching the massive doors. "Take the princess inside and assist her in her search."

Natalia quickly explained what she was looking for. Jasperion nodded and opened the door, allowing Natalia to enter. He led her down the aisles of dusty records, until they reached the section containing land deeds for California. Natalia looked at the long shelves and high stacks of documents and sighed. This could take her days. Jasperion started pulling the documents from the shelves, as she sat at a table and started to sort through the deeds, and deed transfers.

"Don't guess anyone ever thought about putting this stuff in a computer."

Jasperion lifted his hood as he looked back at her. "A computer? Child, it would take an army of people to key all this information into a computer. We do research the old-fashioned way."

Natalia muttered to herself, "Tell me about it", as she continued to sort through the documents. After ten straight hours of searching, she finally pulled a property deed from the stacks for Under the Coffin. She scanned through the document, searching for a name, and gasped when she reads it. She didn't know him personally, but she'd heard her father mention him numerous times...Colin Vos. "Colin!"

She turned to Jasperion. "Can I get a copy of this document?"

He nodded as he took it from her hands, and returned in a few minutes with the copy, tucking the original back into their archives. She rushed from the room, shouting over her shoulder as she left. "Thanks, Jasperion!"

She practically ran into Malachi on her way out. "Did you find what you were looking for?"

She nodded her head yes as she caught up with Aislynn and shouted, "Let's go!"

Malachi watched as she teleported out and he shook his head. The new Council in the U.S. would be a very different place with the Medici's daughter.

Aislynn took her home, as Natalia clutched the paper to her chest, and they landed inside the house at Bel Rosso. Natalia's feet had barely touched the floor before she called out to him. “Daddy!"

Shade was in Luca and Shannon's suite, informing Luca of all that had happened in Florence with the Alizzi, as well as the drama surrounding the olive groves, and what little he knew about Tainted Beast. They both heard Natalia at the same time, as she called out for her father. Both of them jumped up and ran out of the room and into the hall, and damn near ran into her head long. Shade halted and looked at her.

"Nattie! Are you all right? What is going on?"

Natalia held the piece of paper up in the air, as Aislynn stepped back. “I've got it, Daddy! The deed for the owner of Under the Coffin!"

Shade picked her up and swung her around in circles. "Malachi actually let you go through the records? Let me see! Who is it?"

She handed him the paper, not sure of how he’d respond. “It's Colin, Daddy."

Shade set her down gently on her feet. He didn’t take the paper she held but looked at Luca. In unison, they both said out loud, “Colin?”

Shade turned back to Natalia, taking the copy of the deed from her. Luca and Shade both scanned the document. "Damn, he does own it. I knew he spent a lot of time there, but Colin and Elana have always been visible in the club scene."

Luca looked at the name on the deed. "We can't jump to conclusions. We know he owns it now, and the fact he kept that information hidden is suspicious, but he could have many reasons for not wanting people to know he owns Under the Coffin. Just because he owns the club, doesn’t mean he’s the one making and selling the drug there. I think we need to keep this information to ourselves. Tell Raven and Matteo, no one else. If Colin’s the one, we don't want to expose our hand. He’ll just close shop and move somewhere else if he feels we’re getting too close."

Shade was nodding his head. "Good point. I need to tell Raven, so he can relay this to Matteo."

As Luca returned to his suite and Shannon, Shade saw Kate coming down the stairs. Hugging Natalia close to his chest, he kissed the top of her head. "You have such a beautiful mind,

Princess. *Grazie*, for doing this for me. What the hell do I have warriors for when my own daughter gets me answers in a day?"

Kate joined them at the foot of the stairs. "Did you find what you were looking for?"

Natalia nodded her head yes and showed her mother the document. Kate looked at it and looked up at Shade. "Colin? Why would Colin..." Her sentence hung in the air, as Donatella's betrayal played across her brain. "Never mind, I'm learning I trust no one that isn't named Medici."

Aislynn still stood in the corridor, she hadn't been dismissed. "Aislynn, thank you for your service, but please return to camp. If you need to rest tonight, do so. Do not repeat anything you have heard."

She nodded and left for camp. Shade smiled at Kate, his face beaming. "She is brilliant, our Princess. And I do believe she has Malachi in her back pocket already. Go, get some rest, my beautiful Nattie. I am proud of you!" She kissed him and headed upstairs.

"I need to contact Raven, *mi amore*. This is vital information. Then I am going out to camp. It never ends."

Kate held on to him. "Are you going to confront Colin about this? He never came to you once you assumed control of California, but are you sure Alec never gave him permission to have the club there when the territory belonged to him?"

"*Bel*, right now, I want to keep what I know under wraps. I will not confront him, nor tell Alec what I know. This needs to be kept quiet until we can figure out what is happening. Believe me when I tell you, if I find out he has anything to do with Tainted Beast, his head will roll. Now, don't worry. Raven and Matteo will follow up on this. I need to call Raven, then get to camp, but I will be back as soon as I am done."

He kissed her and pulled her close. "Don't look so worried. We'll figure this out." He smiled at her and walked into his office. Calling Raven, he gave him the details of what Natalia had found. He instructed Raven to tell no one other than Matteo. Shade didn't know if Colin was involved, but he didn't want anyone to have a jump on this. Whoever was responsible was sitting in his territory, and he alone was going to take them down.

2-59

Matteo was preparing to go out again for the night. Raven had shared the news from their master that Colin owned Under the Coffin. Matteo had seen him in the club a few times, but he looked like any other patron, not an owner. He didn't want to jump to conclusions, though. Just because Colin owned the club didn't mean he was making Tainted Beast. Still, the fact he'd kept his ownership a secret did seem curious. He'd observe Colin with fresh eyes.

When Matteo arrived at the club, the doorman waved him in. He'd become a regular now. Katrina winked at him as he entered, and he made his way to his favorite booth to find it occupied by a couple of mortals. He stood close to the table and glared at them, never speaking a word and watched as they scrambled from their seats. He chuckled as he slid into the booth and looked up to see Tatiana bringing him a Midnight. She slid the glass onto the table and rested her hip on the edge.

"Missed you the last few nights. You tired of me?"

He laid his hand on her hip and gave her a firm squeeze, as he chuckled. "You know, I do have to work for a living and these drinks aren't free. You want company when you get off tonight?"

She smiled back at him. "Of course. I've missed you."

He patted the seat next to him and she sat down for a minute. "I can't stay. I have a lot of tables to wait tonight."

He draped his arm around her shoulder and pulled her close, nuzzling her ear. "I understand. Don't want to get you in trouble. You noticed any drug deals? I haven't been able to find anybody who knows a fucking thing about Tainted Beast."

She shook her head. "Nothing new. Just the usual, but I'll let you know."

He gave her a kiss, and she gathered up her tray and left the table. Matteo propped his feet up in an empty chair and took a drink of Midnight as his eyes scanned the crowd. He sat for hours, listening to the pounding beat of the heavy metal music, as Tatiana made sure his glass stayed full. It was close to 2:00 a.m. when he saw Colin walk in with his mate. They took their seat in one of the masters' booths, and he watched closely as Tatiana rushed to take their drink order. It didn't take the two of them long to attract a couple of mortals who joined them in the booth for a little fuck and feed. As the feasting ended, Colin excused himself, leaving Elana to continue to entertain the mortals.

Colin disappeared down a dark corridor. Matteo watched the corridor closely, and within a few minutes, another master disappeared down the corridor. He saw the bartender flag Tatiana down, and sent her to follow the masters. Within minutes, she was back, and loading the tray with a bottle of Midnight and returning back down the corridor. When she returned, she carried the cash to the bartender then made her way back to Matteo. She was standing close but holding her serving tray as if taking his order. She looked about nervously then leaned in closer.

"The two masters in the back room...when I went in to take their drink order, I overheard them discussing Tainted Beast. They stopped talking when I came in."

Matteo nodded. "Which one was selling?"

She looked over her shoulder before continuing, "The light haired one. Master Colin. He comes here a lot."

He winked at her. "Good girl."

She looked at him expectantly. "You want me to say something to him?"

He shook his head. "Not tonight. Might spook him. He doesn't know me."

She smiled. "Okay, well, don't go anywhere."

He smiled back at her. 'I'll be right here."

Matteo took her home at the end of her shift, just as the sun was coming up. Tatiana was a day-walker, but she worked nights, and slept during the day. He bedded her, and fed, and slept restlessly, waiting for her to wake. By late afternoon, he felt her stir beside him, and he stretched and yawned, as if just waking. She jumped from the bed and headed for the shower.

"Want to join me."

He slid from the bed and grabbed his leathers. "Another time, babe. Got some things I need to take care of tonight."

She stopped in her tracks. "But you'll be back, won't you?"

He gave her a hug and kissed the top of her head. "You worry too much. I'll see you later."

She smiled at him as he finished dressing and teleported out to the camp in Marin County, where Raven was waiting for him.

***

Raven kept looking at the time. Something was definitely up. Matteo was usually back by now. He was getting ready to leave the camp when Matteo walked in, looking worse for wear. "She's riding you hard, brother. You been up all fucking day?"

"I do sleep sometime, you know. Sit down, brother, and quit complaining. My cock has finally paid off. Colin was in the club last night. He disappeared into a back room, and when Tat went back to get their drink order, she walked in on a Tainted Beast deal. She confirmed that Colin was the one selling. He comes in maybe twice a week, but not on any kind of schedule. I think I can get Tat to approach him, he knows her, and would probably trust her if she set something up. But that means you and Shade will need to be on call and get your asses here in a moment's notice."

"Nice! So, that crazy bastard Colin is selling in his own fucking club. We need to call boss-man. He'll let us know what the hell he wants us to do." Pulling out his cell, he dialed up Shade. He looked over at Matteo, scrunching up his face. "Your cock isn't getting attached to that female, is it?"

Matteo lit up a cigarette, exhaling before answering the question. "Nope, but she's sure getting attached to me. It won't be pretty when this sting is over. I've got to think about this. Don't like to burn bridges, you know?"

Raven shook his head. Females were never his thing. Shade answered and Raven looked at Matteo and rolled his eyes, as Shade started talking, before he had a chance to even say anything.

"Raven, you better fucking have something for me because my own daughter got information in a few days you couldn't find in a week. Talk!"

Raven relayed Matteo's information to Shade and heard nothing coming from the other end. "You still with me, boss-man, or are you so old, you writing this shit down now?"

Shade was thinking through what he'd just heard. So, Colin was the root of all of this. He must be making the drug in Nevada, and hauling it into California, pushing it at the club. But there was still something that didn't settle with him about Jacks. She'd known Colin for centuries and taken a few jobs for him as well. Something wasn't adding up.

"Good job. Okay, both of you need to be ready to jump when this opportunity goes down. We have one shot and I don't intend to fuck it up. Set up a sting and contact me once Matteo lets you know it's going down. This kill is mine, and mine alone. I want warriors on the outside hidden around that place. Only the three of us are going in. Matteo, you make damn sure Tat doesn't know a thing."

Matteo responded. "Consider it done. I got Tat under control."

Raven answered. "We got this. Be ready to teleport out here as soon as we know it's going down."

2-60

The sting had been planned, and Matteo continued to make nightly visits to Under the Coffin and kept Tat close. The next time Colin appeared, he'd notify Raven and Shade, and have Tatiana try to set up the buy. Tat would have to be kept in the dark as to their real intentions as it related to Colin.

Matteo had grown tired of this club, and the hours he spent there. He didn't like the pounding music or the constant pulsing of the strobe lights, and he preferred to hunt his prey than to have it served on a platter like these mortals who offered themselves up so readily, seeking a thrill. He entered the club again tonight, after a ten-day stretch with no sign of Colin. Tatiana had come to expect he'd leave with her every morning, and he hated that she was being used unwittingly. He had no feelings for her, but it was clear she'd become attached to him, and he regretted she'd be hurt by his sudden and unexplained disappearance from her life when this was over. He slid into the seat at what has become his regular booth, and within minutes, Tat was there with a Midnight. She leaned in and kissed him as she placed his filled glass on the table.

"This one's on the house, but I can't sneak more than this, the bartender will notice."

"You don't have to do that, Tat. I can pay."

She smiled at him. "But I want to. See you later."

She winked at him as she turned away, rushing off to wait tables. He couldn't imagine living her life, stuck in this club every night, and he was once again reminded of his good fortune at being born warrior, and trained by the Medici. He sat by himself at the table, turning away the mortal females who always approached, which only endeared him more to Tatiana. If she only knew the real reason for his lack of interest was, he must remain attentive and couldn't afford to be distracted by some dalliance with a female.

Matteo sipped at his drink and kept an eye on the activity in the club. It was close to 3:00 a.m. when he finally saw Colin enter, and take his seat in the reserved booth. Matteo immediately notified Shade and Raven of his presence. Both would teleport in, but neither of them would enter the club unless they could set up a buy. They'd both be recognized here. Matteo subtly lifted his finger as Tat scurried by, indicating he wanted her to stop at his table. As soon as she'd delivered her tray of drinks, she made her way back to him, sliding beside him in the booth.

Matteo slid his hand up her thigh. "Want to help a warrior out?"

She smiled slyly. "If you're the warrior, then yes."

Matteo nodded in Colin's direction. "You know him, right? Use your charms and see if he'll meet with me in that back room."

She looked at him quizzically. "You want me to set up a buy? He only deals with masters."

Matteo nodded. "Tell him I'm here to represent my master, who wishes to remain anonymous. My master wants Tainted Beast, and he says price is no object."

Tat nodded her head, eager to please him. She left his table and made her way across the crowded floor, expertly weaving between the patrons. It wasn't long before Matteo heard Raven's telepathic message in his head, letting him know he was outside the club and Shade was on his way. They would wait for him to summon them.

***

Shade had returned suddenly from camp, to find Kate and Shannon hunched over his desk together, talking with the manufacturer in Italy who'd be converting the olives into the virgin olive oil. She looked up when he entered and could read the expression on his face. She excused herself and went to him, leaving Shannon to continue with the call. "Lover, what's wrong?"

"Nothing wrong, *mi amore*. Matteo has a lead on Tainted Beast. I need to leave for California now. If things go smoothly, I will be back before sunrise. If not, I may have to stay in California for my death slumber. Either way, I will let you know."

She looked at him with concern. "You're going alone?"

He shook his head no. "I will meet Raven and Matteo there. Your warrior will be fine, *bel*."

She nodded as she bit her lip, and he smiled at her, taking her in his embrace. "You do not hide your worry well, *bel rosso*. I will be back soon, and Luca will remain here with you, *si*?"

His kiss was deep, and conveyed his love, as she clung to him. She whispered, "I love you," and he locked eyes with her before kissing the top of her head. "And I love you. Now go, finish your work with Shannon, and I'll be home before you know it."

He let go of her and tapped on Luca's door, informing him of his plans, then teleported out. Luca looked at Kate and could see the worry on her face. He smiled as he shook his head. "He always returns, Kate."

Kate looked back at him. "I know, but I just had a feeling...like a chill."

Luca stared back at her. After the incident with the Alizzi, they were all learning to have more respect for her feelings. "I'll tell Raven. Ask him to have some back-up. Will that make you feel better?"

She smiled and nodded her head. "Thank you, Luca."

***

Shade landed softly next to Raven on a rooftop across the street from Under the Coffin. Raven was sitting quietly, his back against a heating unit for the building, as he smoked a cigarette. "Took you long enough."

Shade grunted and squatted down beside him, removing the pack of cigarettes from Raven's pocket and lighting up. Raven looked up at him, "Oh, would you like a cigarette, master? Why yes, Raven, I would, thank you very much."

Shade cuffed him upside his head and Raven laughed, just as two more of the California warriors landed on the roof. Shade eyed the two, recognizing them both from the training camp in Napa. "Didn't know we were having a party."

Raven shrugged. "What can I say? My queen worries about you, and I always listen to my queen."

Shade instructed them to remain on the rooftop unless they were summoned, and the two nodded and took a seat on the roof. He looked at Raven. "This could all be for nothing, you know. If Colin won't meet with him, it's just a waste of time, and we'll have to figure out another way to trap him."

Raven took a deep drag on his cigarette before answering. "He'll bite. He'll be suspicious, but Colin's ego will get the best of him. Sit down, boss-man. This may take a while."

Shade sat next to him, resting his back, and looked into the night sky. **"You requested additional warriors, *mi amore*?"**

She heard his voice in her head and paused. **"Don't be angry with me, lover."**

He smiled to himself. **"I find it nearly impossible to remain angry with you for any length of time. Your warrior is fine, *bel*."** He felt the softest brush of her lips across his and caught the slightest scent of roses. **"And you manage to distract me, even when we are separated by three thousand miles."**

He heard her voice in his head. **"Glad to know I haven't lost my touch."**

He chuckled out loud, and Raven looked at him with one raised eyebrow. Shade took a deep drag on the cigarette before crushing it on the rooftop and smiled back at him.

***

Inside the club, Tatiana approached Colin, placing a Midnight in front of him. "Good evening, Master Colin."

He looked up at her. "Tat, good to see you again."

She looked around the room quickly before leaning in closer. "May I sit for a moment?"

He looked back at her, trying to guess her motives. He was here without Elana tonight. Perhaps she thought he'd like to feed. "Of course, sit, please."

She slid into the booth next to him, sitting close so she could speak into his ear and be heard over the music. "There's someone who's requested to meet with you, you know, in the back room."

He looked around the club as he answered. "A master? I didn't see any masters when I came in."

She shook her head. "Not a master. He's here for his master who wishes to remain anonymous."

Colin looked at her suspiciously. "Point him out to me."

Matteo was watching the interaction from across the club and saw when Tatiana nodded in his direction. Colin looked over at him and the two of them locked eyes. Matteo nodded ever so slightly.

Colin responded. "A warrior?" He huffed. "You know I only meet with masters."

Tatiana nodded her head. "He asked me to tell you his master said money is no object. He'll pay whatever you demand."

Colin took a sip from the glass of Midnight, as he considered the request. What the hell, it's only a meeting, and maybe he could find out how this master learned about his drug. Colin nodded his head as he slipped from the booth. "Bring him to the back room. Give me five minutes before you follow."

Colin headed down the dark corridor marked private. Tatiana winked at Matteo from across the room, and he smiled back at her. He sent a message to Shade. **"Colin took the bait."**

Tatiana returned to his table and told him what he already knew. "Be careful, Matteo."

Matteo chuckled. "Don't worry about me, little one."

2-61

Tatiana led Matteo down the long, dark corridor to a door marked 'Private. Personnel Only'. She tapped lightly on the door then opened it, sticking her head around the door. "Master Colin?"

Colin sat comfortably on the large sofa and waved his hand, indicating she may let the person enter. Tatiana opened the door wider as Matteo walked in, quickly scanning the room, and assuring himself that Colin was the only other person present. Colin didn't stand, and Matteo towered over him.

"My master is looking for Tainted Beast. I heard on the street you might be able to hook me up?"

Colin took a sip from his drink, licking his lips. "And who is your master?"

Matteo shook his head no. "He wishes to remain anonymous. Using drugs would not enhance his reputation in the business world."

Colin nodded. "Certainly, you understand my reluctance, warrior. I'm taking a risk here. This drug is very expensive to make. How do I know you have the money? I only deal in cash."

Matteo nodded. "He said money was no object, and I wasn't to come home empty handed. How much you asking?"

Colin looked at the massive warrior before him. He was well dressed, and well cared for. He belonged to a master of means. "I usually charge $100,000 an ounce. That's good for about four hits. It's the real stuff. I make it myself...but I don't like working with a third party. What's your name again?"

Matteo stared back at him. Colin would have no reason to know him, or who he belonged to. "Didn't say...but the name is Matteo."

Colin pulled out his phone and dialed a number as Matteo sent a telepathic message to Shade and Raven that the deal was about to go down and they needed to move inside. Raven and Shade teleported inside the club, landing in the corridor and positioning themselves on either side of the closed door, waiting for Matteo's signal. Inside the room, Colin started talking to the person on the other end of the call. "Jacks, I got a warrior here, says his name is Matteo. You know who he belongs to?"

Jacks had completed her assignment in Maine and was about to head out to Annapolis when her phone rang. She smiled when she saw it was Colin, but her mind went into a whirl when she heard the question about Matteo. She didn't know Matteo personally, but she knew he was a Medici warrior.

She was walking a thin line here and looked for more information. "Where are you, Colin?"

"Under the Coffin. Warrior wants a drug deal, but says his master wants to remain anonymous."

Jacks was caught off-guard. *Fuck! If a Medici warrior is inside, that means Shade knows everything.* He may not know she was involved yet, but he would. Her survival was at stake. She'd be hunted and killed. It wouldn't take Shade long to figure it out. She struggled to control her breathing and had to think fast. She'd deny she knew who Matteo was. It would buy her time. Time to do something she never thought she'd do. "Never heard of him. Are you concerned? Do you need help removing him?"

"No, my delicious Jacks, I don't need your help. I was just hoping you might know his master. Sorry to have disturbed you." Colin ended the call and turned back to Matteo. "Tell you what, since you want anonymity, that's going to cost you. Double the fee. Two hundred thousand."

Matteo opened his jacket slowly, to show the master he wasn't pulling out a weapon and pulled out the roll of thousand-dollar bills, counting off the two hundred thousand on the table. Colin smiled broadly as he reached to scoop up the money, and Matteo placed his large hand over top of it. "The drug?"

Colin sighed. "I'm a master. You think I wouldn't keep my word?" He pulled the one-ounce bag of white powder from his pocket and tossed it to Matteo as he scooped up the cash. "Be careful with it. Remember that's about four doses."

Matteo let Shade and Raven know the deal had gone down, and Colin had made a phone call to Jacks to ask about his identity.

Shade didn't barrel in, hell, he could take Colin without breaking a sweat. What really disturbed him was hearing that Jacks was involved. He signaled Raven he was going in, and to stay at the door making sure no one followed him inside. Opening the door slowly, his body blocked the doorway. He wore a grin, but he was in warrior mode, and this kill would be a pleasure. He locked eyes with Colin. "Hello, Colin. Sitting in my territory, pushing Tainted Beast?"

Colin looked up as Shade entered the room, and his mouth went dry. "What? Shade, no, I uh...this warrior. He was snooping around. I was just yanking his chain. I don't deal...you know I don't deal."

Shade looked down at the table. "You seem to forget who I am, and what I do. You just told my warrior you make it and deal it. I heard every word while standing outside the door."

Shade could smell Colin's fear fill the small room. He closed the door and leaned his back against it. "Now, my only decision is how to kill you. Because I have one more task to accomplish before the night is over, your partner in crime, Jacks. So, what shall it be, Colin? I don't think I should make this easy for you, hell, you have made a drug that could destroy our race."

Colin stuttered over his words. "No, you don't understand. I made sure it didn't get on the streets. See, by charging these fees, I kept it...safe. Only masters, with the means to, uh, cover up their deeds. You understand, of course."

Shade moved so fast it was just a flash and he grabbed up the bag of Tainted Beast and held it in front of Colin. His eyes blazed red, and his fangs punched through. "Oh, I understand. This little white powder you concocted, just for masters, is now going to be just for the master in front of me."

As Shade grabbed Colin by the throat, Matteo stood behind Colin, and Raven walked in, closing the door behind him. "Open up, Colin, and meet the beast you never knew existed inside you."

Matteo yanked his head back and Shade grinned. "Open wide."

Colin struggled but was powerless to free himself from Matteo's grip, as he pulled his head back so hard it forced his mouth open. Shade poured the powder down his throat and clamped his mouth shut, holding it closed. Colin had no choice but to swallow. Matteo dropped him to the floor as they waited for the beast to arrive.

Colin's heart pounded in fear, knowing they had force fed him a lethal dose. He'd only taken very small portions to test the purity of the drug, and even then, his beast went mad with rage. The one-ounce bag they just emptied into his mouth was enough for four. He felt the drug enter his system, as he crawled on his hands and knees, gagging, and trying to spit out what he could. He felt his fangs punch through and could see the red glow from his eyes reflected on the floor. His heart raced in his chest at an unnatural rate, and he felt the adrenaline surge through his system. He started to stand when he felt Matteo's heavy boot on his back. He quickly rolled away and leapt to his feet as he charged the massive warrior. Matteo could take him down with a single slash of his blade across the throat, but they'd let this master die by his own hand, and his own doing. Matteo tackled him, and took him down, as Shade and Raven joined him, holding Colin flat on his back as he writhed and roared in anger, his teeth snapping at them, as he swung his head from side to side, the saliva turning to a white foam, that he flung from his mouth.

Shade held him steady and watched as the drug took hold. He'd never seen this drug work before. His gut wrenched at the thought of one of their own wanting to make their fortune selling this outrageous drug. "Having fun yet, Colin, you fucking bastard?"

Colin tried to sink his fangs into Shade and felt Shade's fist crushing his jaw. Shade had to hold his own beast at bay, he didn't want to kill Colin, but watch him die a painful death of his own doing. Colin's eyes bulged out of his head, and his heart was visibly beating out of his chest. Shade knew it wouldn't be long now.

Colin clawed at the arms that restrained him, trying to find something to sink his fangs into. His body started to seizure and jerk uncontrollably, and his mouth filled with the white foam, blocking his airway. He spit and shook his head, flinging the foam onto the three vampires who tried to hold him immobile. His heart beat faster in his chest, as he gasped for air, and he couldn't focus his vision. He blinked his eyes rapidly, as the room went dim. He screamed at the Medici, his eyes wide with fear. "Elana? Who will take care of Elana?"

He felt his body jerk violently, before he was overcome with a severe pain in his chest as his heart ruptured, and the blood poured from his mouth. He sank into a black void, his vision fading. The last thing he saw were the angry blue eyes of the Medici, and then his body lay still and lifeless on the floor.

The three warriors let go of his body and stood in a circle around him as the pool of blood beneath Colin seeped across the floor. Shade looked at them and shook his head. "I will never understand how one of our own can do these things, no matter how long I walk this earth. Raven, get warriors out to Colin's place. Find the lab, and destroy it, and the drug. Look for any kind of logs or paperwork, anything that looks like it might be instructions on how to produce the drug, or who it was sold to and bring it to me, as well as any cash. Get it done tonight. I am now the Master of Nevada." He turned to Matteo. "Is Elana here tonight?"

Matteo shook his head. "Don't think so. I never saw her, and he was at the table alone."

Shade nodded. "She is probably at the house. Raven, make sure she knows what's going down. Assign a warrior to her, but don't kill her. I will figure out what the hell to do with her later. Right now, I have important things to finish. Go!"

Raven nodded and headed out, taking the warriors from outside the club with him. Shade turned back to Matteo. "I need to find Jacks before word gets out this went down. Get Colin out of here. The cash on the table is yours. Make sure this room is cleaned..." Before he could finish the sentence, Shade felt his heart slam hard in his chest. Kate was feeling fear, anger, and surprise. He felt his beast rise up instantly. "Kate! Fuck, I need to get to *bel*." He launched out immediately, only one thing on his mind.

***

Jacks teleported directly to Bel Rosso. She came in fast and hard, knowing she'd be surrounded by warrior and time wasn't on her side. She had one option to use as a bargaining chip with Shade for her life, and that was Kate. It was the only shot she had, and she had to get there fast and take his mate. Shade would have to decide, her life, or Kate's. She ignored the unbreakable vampire code of teleporting uninvited into another vamp's home and landed inside his office. The penalty for breaking the code was death, but if she didn't secure Kate as a hostage, she was dead already. She landed behind the two females who stood gazing over papers on the desk. She grabbed them both before they could even react to her presence, realizing she had Kate, as well as her protector's mate. She easily towered over them both, pulling them to her chest, as she held a long blade to their throats. "Time for a little fun, bitches. Jacks is in the house." She leaned into Kate's ear and purred. "I only came for you, but you fight me, and I'll slit her throat without a blink."

Luca felt the rush of panic from both Kate and Shannon and rushed into the office to see Jacks, holding them both with a long blade knife at their necks. He locked eyes with Shannon, her fear palpable. It was his worst nightmare. He could easily save one, but he knew if he moved, the other would be sacrificed. Shannon's eyes were pleading with him, and he looked at Kate, who stared back at him with a look of defiance. He hoped she didn't try to put up a fight because Jacks would slit her throat without hesitation. "Don't move. Either of you. Drop the knife, Jacks."

Kate couldn't believe this bitch had entered their home! She was struggling to keep her beast at bay, knowing her actions could endanger Shannon as well. She saw Luca enter and pause, faced with the decision of who to save. Kate telepathically called out to Aegis and she could hear the scratching at the back door. Luca held up both hands, as he moved slowly into the room. "Don't do anything stupid, Jacks. Just drop the knife. You know if you leave a scratch on her, Shade will spend the rest of his life hunting you down."

Jacks saw Luca's face, and knew he had to make a choice. She knew his code of honor would force him to save Kate over his mate. "I have no need for this one." She nodded her head toward Shannon. "But Kate is coming with me, and if you move one more step, I will take out your little beauty."

Jacks held the knife closer to Shannon's throat, just enough to nick her neck and watched his eyes follow the blood trail that ran down her shoulder. "Rough decision, your mate, or your master's. But I know you'll choose your beloved red-haired queen. I know you, Luca, loyal to the fucking end. But I'll spare you having to make the choice."

Luca stalled for time, but his beast emerged when he saw the blood trail down Shannon's neck, and heard her soft whimper. Luca called out to Shade, and locked eyes with Shannon. **"Don't move *mia belleza*! I will not let her hurt you!"**

Shannon held perfectly still and blinked her eyes in acknowledgement. He looked at Kate, her own beast had emerged, and Luca warned her to stay calm. "You're right, Jacks. I will save our queen. And in doing so, maybe you will kill my mate, but you will never leave here alive. Do you think Shade, or I would let you live after this?"

***

Natalia was upstairs in the room that used to be their childhood classroom, now converted to a library. She was sliding a book back on the shelf when she felt her mother's fear. She crept silently down the stairs and could see Luca's back through the doorway into the office. She overheard enough of the conversation to know her mother and Shannon were in danger. She looked down the hall to see Gi, his face pale, as he waved to her to follow him. Her instincts were to go to her mother, but she followed after Gi. Now she could hear it too, the insistent scratching at the back door. Gi grabbed her and held her close as he opened the door and swung it wide.

Aegis leapt forward, followed by Night Stalker, Riparo, and Danica. The wolves and the cat scrambled across the tile floor, the sounds of their claws scraping across the tiles. The falcon flew in low, his screech deafening inside the confines of the house. The animals rushed to the defense of the queen who ruled them. Luca heard them approach and timed his response, as the herd came crashing into the room, teeth bared. The falcon swooped forward, her talons extended as they grabbed Jacks by the hair, sinking her talons into her scalp and yanking Jacks off balance as the long knife clattered to the floor. Luca raced to grab both women and rolled with them across the floor as Riparo leapt and sank her teeth into Jacks' neck. Jacks tried to push the mountain lion away, but the animal's grip on her throat was too strong. She issued a strangled cry, as she tried to roll away from the mountain lion, when she felt a searing pain, as the two wolves ripped and tore at her body, disemboweling her. She felt her strength fading as the blood pooled beneath her, and she feared this battle was lost. She struggled to find the gun in the holster at her waist, when she felt the sharp bite of the black wolf, crushing the bones in her wrist. She heard the sound of her own screams and looked on with horror as the two wolves played a game of tug of war with what must be her intestines. She felt her heartbeat slowing, as the strength ebbed from her body, and she went limp on the floor, as she watched the animals feast on her flesh.

Shade landed inside the office, in time to see the light disappear from Jacks' eyes, as the animals fed on what remained. He knew there would be nothing left of Jacks. He looked over to see Luca, holding both females. He smelled Shannon's blood, but knew Kate was fine. Without blinking, he grabbed her into his arms, crushing her into his chest. "*Cazzo*. Are you all right? Damn it, I am so sorry, I never thought she would do this!"

"I'm fine." She looked up to see Gi and Natalia standing in the doorway and knew Gi had pulled Natalia away from the danger and opened the door for her own warriors. She nodded at him and he silently bowed his head. She looked down at the dwindling remains of Jacks, no longer recognizable, as the animals continued to devour her.

"I had Luca, and Gi...and of course, Aegis." The wolf looked up at her, her snout covered in blood as she licked her lips before returning to her meal.

Shade turned to his daughter. "Are you hurt?"

"I'm fine. I'm no warrior, Daddy, but I was raised next to a warrior camp. I would be disappointed to see anything left of our enemy."

"Well, your *madre* now has two vampire assassin kills under her belt. When she does it, she does it right." He kissed the top of Kate's head, and looked at Shannon and Luca. He knew his warrior had been faced with a hellish decision. "Luca..." The words got stuck in his throat. He knew the two of them needed to be alone. "Is Shannon all right? How much blood has she lost?"

Luca lifted Shannon in his arms. "She's fine. It is just a flesh wound, made to taunt me." He licked the small slash made on her throat by Jacks' knife and watched as it healed. "Master, if you no longer need me, I'd like to take her back to our suite."

"Of course. *Grazie*, Luca. Go, take care of your mate." As Luca walked out the door with Shannon in his arms, Shade looked down at his crimson haired beauty and wondered, for the millionth time, how he ever lived without her. Tipping up her chin, he looked into her beautiful amber eyes.

"Colin is dead. You are now Queen of Nevada. Our territory grows, my Queen, but I'm looking at the only thing I live and breathe for."

2-62

Before Raven arrived with the goods from the raid on Colin and Elana's house, Shade decided it was time he informed Alec of the situation. Raven had let him know that Elana had been in the lab cooking up the drug when they arrived, and they had taken her out. Shade knew Alec had ties to Jacks, and he wanted to make damn sure Alec wasn't involved in the scheme. Gi and Theresa had already started to clean up the mess that was Jacks out of his office, so he walked outside on the patio and lit up a smoke. It was quiet outside, as he heard only the sounds of the crickets and tree frogs and felt a breeze off the mountains. He dialed up Alec and waited...fuck only knows what the hell he was doing.

It was a busy night at *L'Adventure*, and all the suites were filled. Alec had just dismissed Bree, who was showing him the full calendar for the rest of the month, when his phone rang. He saw Shade on the ID and picked up. "Hey, brother. What's up?"

"Medici was a little busy last night, West and East coast had a few things to clean up. Just thought I should keep you informed. How are things on your end?"

Alec leaned back in his chair, swallowing down the last of the Midnight in his glass, distracted as he looked for his cigarettes. "Couldn't be better, brother. Bree was just showing me we're booked for the entire month. I may need to expand again."

Shade chuckled out loud. "Glad to hear you're turning a profit. I see, from my accountant's figures, the Red Moon is flowing. Seen Jacks lately?"

Alec scrunched his brow, trying to remember when he'd last heard from her. He had fed from Jacks, and she from him years ago, and he'd felt a spike of fear from her earlier, but that was nothing unusual. He'd feel her emotions from time to time when he wasn't blocking her. He paid them no mind, Jacks was a warrior, and prone to frequent confrontations.

"Not since she carried Marchesa out of here, why?"

Shade listened carefully to his tone and didn't notice any deception. Besides, Tainted Beast wouldn't be good for Alec's business. "Well, brother, I hope you had one last hoorah with Jacks, because she's dead."

Alec sat up straight in his chair, knocking over the empty glass on his desk, and unable to mask the look of shock on his face. "What? What are you telling me, brother? What happened?"

Shade couldn't help the smile that was on his face. *That got the bastard's attention.* "Well, like I said earlier, it was a damn good night for Medici. Let me start at the beginning. Turns out, Colin owned Under the Coffin. He was cooking up Tainted Beast at his house in Nevada and shoving it out to the masters in the club in San Francisco. Jacks was in some kind of partnership with him. Not sure of why, and I may never know now. My warriors set up a sting at the club, caught Colin red-handed, and gave him a dose of his own medicine, so to speak. I sent Raven and a few of my warriors to Nevada to take out the drug lab, and Elana was home. I had asked Raven to spare her because I wasn't sure she was involved in Colin's business, but she was in the lab when Raven got there. She'd been helping him make the drug. Collateral damage. Raven burned that bitch to the ground. While all of this was going down, Jacks got wind of it and went to Bel Rosso. She thought she could take my mate hostage as a bargaining chip for her own life, but that little plan didn't quite work out. She seemed to have forgotten my mate has warriors of her own, and they took her ass out royally. Now my fucking office needs a makeover."

Alec's hands shook almost imperceptibly as he lit up a cigarette. "Jacks was working with Colin? She knew about Tainted Beast? The bitch stood in front of me. Helped out with Marchesa, and all the time she knew?" He took a deep drag on the cigarette and exhaled as he reached for the bottle of Midnight on his desk and poured another glass. "Colin? I've known Colin for longer than I can remember. He's always lived in the clubs. Didn't know he was involved in drugs, but that doesn't surprise me. Jacks...that surprises me."

Shade could hear the shock in Alec's voice. "You're not the only one, brother. Jacks was the last person I would have thought would betray our kind. But I am glad to hear you didn't know. So, I am now Master of Nevada. I am shutting down Under the Coffin permanently. You may see an influx in business, brother. I'll expand Raven's responsibility, so he'll monitor Nevada now as well. I have more than enough warriors coming out of my camps now, and I'll get them assigned out here. One more thing before I go."

Alec's head was spinning as he tried to process all the information. "One more thing?"

"Tell Bree to check the fucking fax machine. I had Raven confiscate all the paperwork and the cash when he burned the house. Raven tells me the bastard kept some pretty good records of who bought from him and when. As soon as Raven gets here tonight, I'll fax the records over to you. Some of these masters are bound to be clients of yours. You will have a heads up of who might have been using. I suggest if they have purchased this drug within the last few weeks, maybe cancel their visit. If you need extra warriors on hand, just let Robbie know."

Alec nodded. "I'll tell Bree. We'll check our client list and clear out anyone who was buying from Colin, just to be on the safe side. Any more earth-shattering news for me?"

"I don't think so, brother. At least for tonight, who the fuck knows what tomorrow brings. I've got to go. Have you ever seen what a mountain lion, a bird of prey, and two wolves can do to a vampire? It is one hell of a blood splatter. Catch you later, brother."

2-63

Raven had left Bel Rosso and teleported into California. Shade wanted Under the Coffin shut down permanently. Matteo and a large group of warriors met him outside. Under the Coffin was a well-known establishment and had been in business for a long time. The place was packed every night, and tonight, it would be shutting down for good. As he landed outside, he saw Matteo and the others waiting on him.

"What's going down, brother?"

Matteo stepped forward. "We put up signs that said the venue was closed, and I stationed our warriors at every entrance so the clients couldn't enter, but the staff was already inside getting ready to open. Do me a favor, brother. Let me handle Tat. She's innocent in all this, and she helped us set up the sting."

Raven nodded his head. "Fair enough." Raven led the warriors inside and ordered the staff to the stage area. He informed them the club was being shut down permanently, and their jobs here were done. They were to submit their timecards to him, and he'd see they were paid for the time they'd worked. He let them know the master that owned the club had been dealing Tainted Beast, and he'd been removed.

Matteo stood behind him as he listened to Raven tell the staff they no longer had jobs. He saw the look of fear then betrayal on Tatiana's face as she looked at him, and he held her gaze. Raven told them to get their stuff and clear out, and Matteo made his way through the disgruntled vamps to reach her. He took her hand and she pulled away.

"You used me?"

He shook his head no. "I'm sorry. I never meant for you to get hurt by this."

Tatiana grabbed her bag, as the tears flowed down her cheeks. "But you knew this meant something to me, and now you come in here and tell me my job is gone? And I was just a pawn? This is all I have, Matteo!"

Matteo pulled her to his chest, feeling more pain than he'd expected. Maybe he cared more for her more than he wanted to admit. "In the beginning, I needed a way in, and you were it. But it wasn't all...I did feel something for you."

She pulled away from him. "Something? You felt something? Well, something isn't good enough." She stormed out of the club and into the night.

Matteo turned to Raven and shrugged. "Tell me what you want me to do, brother."

Raven couldn't help but overhear the exchange between Matteo and Tatiana. Tatiana had been at this club for as long as Raven could remember, and Matteo was probably a dream catch for her. She'd lost her man and her fucking job in one night.

"We've got things under control here. Go fix that situation with Tatiana if you want. You can't just let her go out on the fucking streets in that condition, brother. She might really do something stupid. Don't just let her go, like some one-night stand." Raven poked him in the chest. "You know she hurts."

Matteo sighed. He'd never been good at relationships. For him, it was always easier to walk away, but he did like this girl. "Yeah, okay."

Matteo headed out of the club and found Tatiana on the street; her backpack slung over her shoulder. "Can we go somewhere and talk?"

She looked up at him, wiping away the tears. "And say what, Matteo? Let you tell me how sorry you are?"

Matteo looked up and down the street as clubbers started to arrive, seeing the signs that the club was closed and walking away grumbling. "Look, Tat, I'm no good at this stuff. You're right; I did use you to get inside. But the longer we were together, you know, I started to really care about you. Maybe we have something. I'm willing to find out if you are."

Tatiana turned and looked at him. His voice was sincere. "I don't want to be hurt again, Matteo."

He shook his head. "And I don't want to hurt you. I need to help Raven right now. We need to close this place down, and then I'll meet you at your place. If you want me."

She looked at him for a long time before she responded. "Yeah, okay. I'll wait for you." She teleported out, and Matteo returned inside, where the warriors were busy boarding up windows and collecting the receipts and cash from the safe.

Raven saw Matteo when he came back in. “You good?” Matteo nodded as Raven stood with his arms crossed. “Don’t fuck it up with her, just fix it. Damn, now I’ve got to bust heads and be a damn counselor. No damn wonder boss-man is always cranky as hell!"

Matteo was in no mood for his crap. "Yeah, well, don't go hanging out your shingle as a couple’s counselor yet. You're not the sympathetic ear I was looking for, brother."

2-64

Shannon lay curled up on their bed. Every time she closed her eyes, all she could see was the savage attack on Jacks. She had no remorse for Jacks' loss. She knew if Kate's warriors hadn't intervened, she might not be here. This was the first time she'd felt her life was at risk, and the first time she'd had to face the reality of Luca's role as Kate's protector. She'd felt his pain and conflict, as he'd felt her fear. Would he have let her perish to save Kate? Thankfully, it wasn't a choice he was forced to make, at least not this time.

He whispered to her softly, as he slid into their bed, molding his body to hers as he pulled the blanket over both of them. "Are you all right, *mia belleza*?"

She nodded but didn't speak. He kissed her lightly on the back of her neck, and gently stroked her shoulder. "I'm sorry you had to see that. I try so hard to shield you from the violence in our world."

"I know you do. I'm always aware of just how protective you are of me."

He slid his arm around her and pulled her closer; her back nestled against his chest. She felt a tear escape and roll down her cheek. He gently wiped it away. "You're safe now. I won't let anyone harm you."

She answered him, her voice a whisper. "You can't promise me that."

Luca squeezed his eyes shut, as her hurt rolled through him. "You're right, I can't. Any more than I can promise the safety of the Queen. I can only promise you I will use every resource at my disposal. I'd already summoned Shade, and knew he was responding. I could hear Aegis, but didn't know if she'd be able to get in. I was stalling to buy time. Don't think I wouldn't have fought for you. I'll fight for both. I'll always fight for both."

She knew he would. His devotion to her had been unwavering since the day they met. It was unfair to place this burden on him, when she knew he'd die trying to save her. "I never want to lose you, Luca."

"You can't lose me, *mia belleza*. I'm a part of you, as you are a part of me. This, I promise you."

2-65

Lorenzo had returned to his regular duties of working in the camp, or guarding the olive groves, but he still felt the guilt and humiliation of his tryst with Donatella. His father had disavowed her, and now there were Medici warriors on the border between Umbria and Tuscany, where the borders had been open for centuries. He couldn't help but feel like that was his fault. Alfie had tried to cheer him up, but Alfie was mated now, and had his own obligations to Sophia. Lorenzo's life had become a routine of completing his assignment, returning to Castello, and having Antonio send him a feeder. He didn't show much interest in the hunt. Tonight, he was scheduled to work in the camp, and walked slowly through the formal gardens until he picked up the well-worn path. He saw Marco on the field and walked in his direction.

"Do you have a special assignment for me tonight, or do you want me to work with some of the new recruits?"

Marco saw him coming, dragging ass as usual. He was damn tired of watching that kid with his tail between his legs over the ordeal with Dona. Kid needed to get the hell over it already. "Well, that depends. Are you going to keep moping around here, or are you going to do some fucking work? Need to get your act together, Lorenzo."

Lorenzo was annoyed with the constant reminders to 'get over it.' "I do my job, Marco."

Marco stood with his arms crossed over his chest, staring at him. When Shade was young and got his head messed up, he'd go on the hunt. Marco didn't think that suggestion would help Lorenzo. "Look, you need a fucking break from all your responsibilities. You do your job, but you sure as fuck aren't doing it with any enthusiasm. Nothing's happening with the *Mafioso*, and I don't expect any change, at least not until the harvest. Why don't you go home to Virginia? You need to kick this thing, get yourself in order."

Lorenzo shrugged. He and Alfie used to take off for Greece, but Greece wouldn't be the same without Alfie. "I don't know, I could go check on the vineyards in Burgundy, stay in the Paris house."

Marco slapped him on the back. "That's the idea. Do something away from here. Hell, your father and I used to travel the world. You took a bit of a fall, Lorenzo, no shame in that. But you can't let one fucking night bring you down to a level where you can't find your way out. It happened. No one holds it against you. Just go to Paris and take some time off, and don't fucking come back here until your ass is ready to be a warrior."

Marco walked away, out into the middle of the training field. He didn't wait for Lorenzo's response. The kid needed some time to put his life in perspective.

Lorenzo stood in the middle of the training field as Marco walked away. "Now? You want me to go now?"

Marco didn't respond but started barking out orders to the recruits. Lorenzo looked around, wondering what the fuck he was supposed to do tonight, and apparently, it was go to France. He shook his head and started walking back to Castello. He had Antonio help him pack up a few things, and then sent Alfie a message he was leaving for France to check the vineyards there and would be at the Paris house if he needed him. Lorenzo teleported out, as Antonio informed him, he'd send Carlos along with him to attend to his needs, and his belongings would be shipped, and would be there by daybreak.

Lorenzo landed in the foyer of the Paris house and Carlos landed several minutes behind him, carrying a small duffle bag of Lorenzo's belongings. His mother would bring them here as children, and he and his sisters would play on the stairs, and in the small courtyard behind the house. He climbed the stairs to his bedroom on the third floor and stood in the doorway. The rooms were elegantly appointed, and the furnishings decidedly French. This house looked nothing like Bel Rosso where he'd grown up in Virginia, and while it was ornate, it couldn't compare with the ostentatious opulence of Castello.

Carlos stepped up behind him. "You should change from those leathers, master. Let me lay out some clothes for you. The rest of your things will arrive tomorrow, but this should do for now."

Carlos quickly moved about the room, opening the windows to let in the night air and scrambling through the duffle bag, laying fresh clothes on the bed. Lorenzo nodded but walked away from the bedroom, exploring the house. It had been a long time since he was here last, and he enjoyed the memories that filled his head. He poured himself a Midnight, and wandered from room to room, ending up back in the foyer. There was a stack of un-opened mail on the table and he picked it up, shuffling through the envelopes.

Carlos appeared on the stairs. “Master?"

Lorenzo looked up. "How long has the mail been here?"

Carlos answered, "Only a week. Someone comes by every week to clean and collect the mail. It is then forwarded to your mother at Bel Rosso."

Lorenzo nodded as he read through the hand-written addresses on the envelopes. “Bills?"

Carlos shook his head no. "All bills are automatically sent to the accountants. The mail that comes here is usually personal communications from other masters."

Lorenzo ran his hand over a thick envelope, ivory in color, addressed to the Medici family, and bearing the Valois Coat of Arms on the envelope. He opened it to find an invitation to a grand ball in their home here in Paris. Lorenzo had heard his father speak of Henri over the years. Henri was the Master of France and had a strong relationship with his father who owned vineyards in the Burgundy area of France, by the grace of Henri. Lorenzo kept the invitation.

“I should go. I’ve never met Henri, and the French vineyards are now under my rule."

Carlos nodded. “Of course, master. I’ll make sure you have the proper attire. When is the ball?"

"Tomorrow, I'll check the vineyards during the day, then tomorrow evening, attend the ball."

Carlos nodded. "Very good, master. Perhaps, for now, you should sleep?"

Lorenzo nodded and made his way back up the stairs, determined to get this ordeal with the Alizzi out of his head. He slept soundly and woke to a bright, clear day, and teleported out to the vineyards, where he toured the land, and met with Luciano. The weather had been favorable for them, and they were expecting a good harvest from the crops this year. He watched the time, and teleported back to Paris, showering, and donning the tuxedo Carlos had lain out. He tied his hair back in a loose ponytail at the base of his neck.

Dante had been summoned to drive him to the Valois chateau, which sat on the outskirts of Paris, along the Seine. As the car approached the grand chateau, Lorenzo stepped from the car, and saw many familiar faces of the masters who had visited Castello for his and his sisters' Coronation ceremonies. They politely bowed their heads to him, and he walked up the stairs to the entrance. He was greeted by Henri, who introduced himself.

"Bon soir. You must be Lorenzo Medici. You look exactly like your father. We are honored to have you with us this evening."

Lorenzo bowed, as Henri, like him, was royalty. Lorenzo laughed. "My father is so well known, and we look so much alike, it means I can't get away with anything."

Henri laughed, and introduced his mate. "This is my mate, Queen Amelie."

Lorenzo bowed low, and took her hand, brushing the back of her hand with his lips. She curtsied slightly. "Please, come in. It has been a long time since a Medici has graced our home, and we share so much history."

Lorenzo looked at her quizzically. Amelie slid her arm in his and led him away. "You are aware, are you not? The mortal, Catherine de Medici, was wed to King Henry II of the Valois family. They ruled France as mortal king and queen in the 15th century. So, you see, our families share a bloodline."

Lorenzo nodded, remembering his History classes from Enzo. "Ah, I do remember."

Amelie led him into a ballroom. "Have you met our daughter, Chantal?"

Lorenzo shook his head no. "I have not had that pleasure."

She waved her hand for her daughter to join her, and Lorenzo looked up and was dumbstruck. Chantal walked in their direction, her ball gown brushing the floor. Her dark hair was pulled back from her face, and collected in a tight bun, a hair style that would be too stark for most, but her face was a vision of loveliness. Her skin was fair and flawless, and her eyes were large, and blue as the sky. Her lips were full. She wore very little makeup and needed none. She had a long neck, and her composure was regal. She approached her mother, but her eyes were locked on Lorenzo. Lorenzo had never seen a female as lovely, and he was wondering if she was out of his league. Her mother introduced her. "Chantal, this is Lorenzo Medici."

Lorenzo bowed low to her, and took her hand, planting a kiss on the back of her hand as he looked up at her.

***

Chantal had been greeting people for what seemed like hours, but the smile never left her face. She had been raised as an aristocrat, and never broke protocol. She mingled among the invited masters and friends of her parents. It was her duty to represent the Valois family style and grace. She found herself momentarily alone and glanced in the direction of her parents and felt her heart skip a beat. The young male standing before them was tall, and even beneath the tailored tuxedo, she could see the definition of his toned body. His hair was almost black, and he wore it long, but tied back with a silk ribbon, and even from here she could see the piercing blue of his eyes. Behind all the finery, she couldn't help but notice the pierced ears, and the subtle nose ring. She smiled to herself, recognizing the rebel under the expensive tuxedo. He was speaking to her mother and looked like an Adonis chiseled from stone. This was no ordinary vampire, and no one she'd ever seen before. She felt her breath slowly escape her lips, not realizing she'd been holding it. Her mother called to her and she quickly straightened the elegant blue gown without notice. As she walked toward him, he turned to her and their eyes locked onto each other. His eyes were like the clearest blue ocean and made her gasp, they were so stunning.

When he bowed, he kissed the back of her hand and it felt like a lightning strike traveling up her arm and her heart hammered in her chest. Medici, she'd heard her father speak of the Medici's often. "It is a pleasure to meet you, Lorenzo." She looked him in the eyes and found herself quite intrigued with this male.

Lorenzo couldn't take his eyes off her. "The pleasure is mine, I assure you, Chantal, is it? A beautiful name. You wear it well."

Amelie looked from her daughter to the Medici and smiled to herself. Even she could see the sparks fly. "The night is young, why don't the two of you scurry off. Chantal, take him out on the balcony overlooking the river."

Lorenzo smiled at her. "Lead the way. I'm at your disposal."

Chantal had been introduced to many young eligible males, all carefully screened by her parents to ensure a good match. But this one, if she was correct, had a reputation as a real Romeo, much like his father. Their fathers were allies and longtime friends. She was enticed but surprised by her mother's suggestion that the two of them retreat to the balcony. She smiled at Lorenzo and led him across the room, around the dancing couples and out to the balcony. The view of the city in the distance was beautiful, and the air was light and cool, a soft breeze blowing softly off the river Seine. She was grateful for the cool breeze, as she could feel her face was flushed. A butler holding a tray walked out and they each took a glass of the deep red Midnight. Chantal looked into those beautiful eyes and clinked her glass to his. "*Santé*". Taking a sip, she was grateful for the drink, as she found her mouth suddenly dry.

"I'll drink to your health, and to mine. May we both live long and prosperous lives. You still live with your family, yes?"

"*Oui*, I still live at home. I would venture to say we have much in common, being from royal families. But I do expect the Medici lifestyle is very different than my own."

"Perhaps not as different as you think. My parents are very strict, and my sister Natalia still lives at home. She's not mated and would never be allowed to live on her own. It's true my father is a warrior, as am I, and that has made for a different life. But my father honors the traditions of our culture and holds true to the values of honor and integrity. That is more than I can say for many of the vampires I encounter."

He stood close to her, and she found it hard to concentrate on her words. "My father admires those traditions. He is much the same. I have no siblings, so I envy you that. There are some things I know about your family. My father tells me Castello is a very elegant and historical place. We have a number of horses from your stables. And then there is the wine." She peered over her glass at him, distracted by his handsome face. She'd never met a warrior before. "What is it like to be a warrior?"

He sipped from his glass, and never took his eyes off her. "It's a job. That's a hard question to answer because it's all I know. My father was born warrior, as was his father. As is tradition, I left my family home in the United States at the age of ten to live and train in the camp in Florence. I have lived at Castello ever since." He looked about the chateau. "I imagine your home holds as much history as mine. There's art in our home from the Renaissance, pieces that have never been seen by the outside world, by the artists of the time, Botticelli, Michelangelo, Da Vince, and Varsari, to name a few. I would be most happy to show you, should you ever find yourself in Florence."

She watched his mouth as he spoke and found herself wishing to kiss his lips. She'd never felt any such feeling from the many males her father had introduced her to. His conversation was relaxed and easy, and yet she sensed a wild streak. She admired that he loved his home and family, so evident in his words. She gave him her best smile. "I would be delighted and honored to visit Castello. It would be nice to journey away from France. Of course, I am not allowed to travel without my protector. My father is so protective over me." She laid her hand gently on his, the smile leaving her face. "It must be very lonely living away from your family."

Lorenzo looked out over the river, her voice was soft, and it soothed his soul. "It can be lonely. I'm afraid as a warrior I'm more accustomed to the gruffness of males, and a warrior's life can be solitary. I try not to dwell on it. I'm close to my family, my sisters, and my parents. You'd like my mother. She has a gentleness about her. My father says she has a soft heart, and that is true, but she is strong too."

Lorenzo wondered how much she knew of his family history. She was royal blood, but her blood lines were pure. He wondered if she'd be disapproving of his. He decided to put it out there and see how she reacted. "My mother was mortal once."

Leaning her back against the balcony railing, she faced the open doors of the ball going on inside. She looked up at the stars and bit her lip softly. She lowered her head and looked at him, he was so handsome. "We are stuck in the traditions of our culture, and yet the world changes around us. My father controls who I am introduced to. He wants to ensure I am only exposed to males from a strong lineage. But mortal or immortal, love is love in either world. I think your mother is brave to take on this life we live."

The sound of a waltz streamed out the doors as the orchestra played. Looking to the crowd inside, she saw her parents dancing together. "I should get back inside and join the party. At least let my presence be seen."

Lorenzo offered her his arm. "Then I hope you will allow me the first dance?"

Taking his arm, she smiled coquettishly. "I thought you would never ask. I didn't want to be rude, but I was not sure warriors could dance."

He chuckled. "We are not completely lacking in the social graces, my lady."

Taking her into his arms, she felt the strength and bulk of him. For the first time in a very long time, she felt happy. He was an excellent dancer and she didn't want the night to end. They talked while dancing; their eyes never left the other.

"Are you staying close by, or do you return to Castello?"

"I'm staying here in Paris for a few days. My father has vineyards in Burgundy, and my family owns a home in the city. Perhaps you'd like to visit? I understand it wouldn't be proper for a female of your station to travel alone. I would welcome you and your protector."

Chantal felt her heart leap. *He wants to see me again!* "I would like that very much. Being a proper prince, before you leave, please ask my father. He will be pleased by such manners and respect for me."

As the dance ended, they spent the rest of the evening separated as she had obligations to entertain their guests, but their eyes met often across the crowded room. She watched closely when he approached her father and knew he was leaving for the evening. Her hopes were high that she'd see him again soon. She knew, deep in her heart, the admiration her father held for the Medici and she hoped that would play in her favor.

2-66

Lorenzo had seen Chantal every evening he was in Paris. She'd not been allowed to leave the chateau, but her family was most welcoming of him. He'd been back in Florence now for well over a month and had spoken with Chantal every day. He'd shared the information with his parents, and his father insisted it was now time for the two families to formally meet. The Valois had been invited to Castello, and the staff was rolling out the red carpet. His whole family had come from Virginia, in addition to Sophia and Alfie.

Still keeping his hair long, Lorenzo had cut a few inches off the length at Alfie's suggestion. Antonio had arranged for them to gather in the parlor and had brought in a quartet to play music. Lorenzo thought it was a little over the top, but whatever. He was wearing a suit and tie, and he kept pulling at the collar as he stopped at his parents' bedroom door and tapped lightly before hearing his father say he could enter. He opened the door to see his father in a suit, and his mother in a summer dress of the palest pink. Lorenzo continued to pull at the necktie.

"Is this thing on right? Who invented this? It's like a noose around your neck."

Shade chuckled as he turns to *bel.* "Our son has finally turned into a true warrior, his leathers more comfortable than anything else he wears."

Kate went to him with a smile on her face and helped him adjust his tie, as Shade reassured him. "Being well dressed shows respect. Trust me when I tell you, your little French pastry will be dressed to impress as well."

Kate gave him a scowl as he referred to Lorenzo's love interest as a French pastry. "You look quite handsome, Lorenzo. I'm afraid growing up at Bel Rosso you never had much opportunity to wear suits, and since you've been living at Castello, you're like your father, jeans or leathers." She brushed her hand through his hair. "You cut your hair? It looks nice. Chantal will be impressed. Don't look so nervous." Turning back to Shade, she inquired, "Are you ready, lover?"

"So, our son gets all the glory tonight, is that it? You do not even find your own vampire handsome?" He laughed and took her arm, whispering in her ear. "I wonder if she knows he has tattoos everywhere?"

Kate slapped at his arm. "Since he's only been with her in the company of her parents, I seriously doubt it. Behave yourself tonight! This girl seems important to him. Let's go downstairs to greet them and pretend like we know what we're doing."

Shade couldn't help but laugh, and he's pretty sure his son was in love for the first time in his life. As they entered the parlor, he felt a great warmth roll through him to see his family gathered. Alfie and Sophia, Cory and Madison, and Natalia were all laughing and talking together, as the classical music from the quartet drifted through the formal parlor. Antonio entered and announced the Valois had arrived. Lorenzo looked at him as if he'd never greeted people before. "Introduce them, son, and just relax."

The males all stood as Antonio returned with the Valois. Lorenzo went to Chantal's side immediately, and shook Henri's hand, kissing both of Amelie's cheeks. "Thank you for accepting our humble invitation. Antonio, bring them some Midnight, please. Allow me to introduce my family."

Lorenzo turned to his father and mother first. "You know my father, of course, but you may not have met my mother, Queen Katherine Medici. Mommy, this is King Henri of France, and his mate Queen Amelie."

Kate curtsied to the king and queen and they both nodded in her direction. Henri spoke up. "We did not meet formally, but we did attend your Coronation some years ago. It is a pleasure to meet you finally. You have gained a powerful reputation among our culture and have proved a most worthy queen for the Medici."

Kate thanked him for his kind words, and Lorenzo was relieved they didn't appear to hold her once mortal status against her. Lorenzo directed them to his siblings. "This is my sister Sophia, and her mate Alfie. Alfie is my SIC here in Florence."

Henri had heard the daughter of Medici had married a warrior, but then, Shade had married a mortal. The Medici seem to have some very relaxed ideas about keeping the bloodlines pure. Henri took Sophia's hand. "Princess, I must say, you are truly your mother's child."

Sophia smiled back at him, as she curtsied. "I can only hope to be as strong as my mother."

Henri shook hands with Alfie and was impressed with the respectfulness of the Medici children. Lorenzo directed them to Natalia. "And this is my youngest sister, Natalia."

Henri bowed. "Ah yes, the single one, but a beauty. You should have no problems finding a mate."

Natalia smiled and curtsied before him. The world wasn't yet aware of her fate to spend her life in service to the Council. Lorenzo turned to Cory and Madison, and Henri was momentarily caught off-guard, as he picked up their scent. He'd heard the Medici had accepted a half-breed but wasn't aware that he was presented as family among the vampire community, and with a mortal in tow. Lorenzo saw the flash of hesitation on Henri's face, but it quickly disappeared.

"This is my older brother, Cory, and his mate Madison."

Cory bowed his head to the King, and Madison curtsied. Lorenzo watched Henri closely. This was his family, and anyone joining this family would need to accept them as is.

Henri noticed that Lorenzo didn't introduce him as a half-breed, or even as his half-brother. He extended his hand to Cory and shook his hand. "It is a pleasure to meet you." He nodded his head to Madison, not sure how to address the mortal. "And to meet your mate."

Antonio returned with the tray of wine glasses and made sure everyone was served as they all took a seat. Henri sat next to his mate, and noticed his daughter sat next to Lorenzo. "It would appear, Medici, that my daughter and your son have made a connection."

Shade observed closely as his longtime ally met his family. If Henri had any objections, he hid them well. "I must say, Henri, *mon amie*, I was pleased to hear our children had met, and *si*, a connection is good for us." Shade turned his attention to Chantal. "I am honored that you grace us this evening, Princess, you have made quite an impression on our son."

Chantal was a nervous wreck. This meeting of the two families was a big step for them both. "It is I who is honored to be here in this beautiful palace. My father has told me much about it, but words could never describe its beauty. Lorenzo has told me so much about his family I feel as though I know all of you already."

As the evening progressed, everyone relaxed, and the conversation flowed easily. It was a relaxing night and Shade was glad it seemed to be going so well. They had all been talking for several hours, as the Midnight flowed, when Shade suggested a change. "Lorenzo, perhaps you would like to give Chantal a tour of Castello. And I do believe, *mi amore,* that Amelie has a great interest in the rose garden. As for my children, if you would not mind, I wish for some privacy with Henri."

Shade looked at Henri. "What do you say to a cigar, Henri? I do believe we have some things to discuss."

Kate stood and took Amelie's hand, leading her outdoors into the rose gardens. Sophia laughed as she stood and turned to her siblings. "Well, that's a not so subtle hint." She exited with Alfie, as Natalia, Cory and Madison followed.

Lorenzo took Chantal by the hand. "Come, I'll show you the art pieces here, and the murals."

Chantal was glad to leave with him, and finally have some time alone. As the room emptied out, Antonio refilled the men's wine glasses, and displayed a cigar humidor, allowing them each to choose the cigar of their choice. As the men lit up, Henri leaned back in his chair. "It would appear my daughter is quite taken with your son. I want you to know, she has not been allowed outside the chateau without her protector, or her mother or me at her side. She has been raised in the old traditions and has not been with a male. There are not many of the royal families remaining, Medici, and she is my only child. I refused to allow her to meet with anyone who was not of royal blood."

Shade wandered around the room, wondering if Henri was unsure about this union. "Say what you mean, Valois. My mate is mortal, but she was turned. My blood runs through her veins, and she remains loyal to this coven. Lorenzo is pure Medici. I have learned quite a lesson through my own children. Love makes no distinction of breed or blood. Your heart will choose for you."

Henri puffed on the cigar. "The times are changing, Medici, I don't always like it, but I must move with the times. Your choices have been controversial, especially with the half-breed. It is not a path I would have followed for myself, but I see your family, and they have been raised with the old values. Please do not see my hesitation as a sign of disrespect, for it is not. We are all aware of what you have achieved, and your queen has shown us she has more than earned our respect. You can appreciate my protectiveness for my only child. I must say, I did not envision her with a warrior, even one that is a royal. It is not an easy life for a female, mated to a warrior. But I will not stand in the way of her happiness if this is the path she chooses."

Shade took a seat across from Valois. "*Si*, being mated to a warrior is not easy for any mate. But I assure you, your daughter will be provided with every protection. My coven is growing every day, and this is Lorenzo's home, and my territories in Europe will be his to rule. Your daughter would be loved, and well provided for. Lorenzo has not yet spoken to me about a mating with Chantal. If he does, I assume you are in agreement to their union?"

"*Oui*, I have discussed the matter with Amelie, and she is also in agreement. My daughter does not speak of it, but I know the look of love in a young woman's eyes, *mon amie*. If your son is inclined, and if it is love that draws him, and not power and money, then I will give my daughter's hand."

Shade stood and shook Valois' hand. "It will be a good union, Henri. Let us have our lawyers draw up papers. If they decide to mate, we will be prepared. Now, I suggest we gather up our two families and spend a little time together."

2-67

Lorenzo was happy to have some time alone with Chantal, or at least as alone as her father would allow. He thought *his* father was strict with Sophia and Natalia, but it was nothing in comparison to how sheltered Chantal had been raised. He was very much aware this female he was falling in love with, had never been with a male. She'd been given a single feeder when she reached her sexual maturity, and her father had even limited the males she was exposed to. Vampires that weren't of royal blood weren't even introduced to her. Like him, she'd been well educated, but her travel had been extremely limited. Her father wasn't a warrior, and he was aware of the dangers in their world. His priority was to protect his daughter and ensure a mating that preserved the bloodline. She'd been raised in the traditional values, and like her mother, was completely submissive to the male. He wouldn't speak of it yet, but he knew all the females in his family were much more outspoken, and Chantal would learn her voice could be heard as well.

He walked with her through the halls of Castello, pointing out portraits of ancestors long dead, and explaining their place in history. If her father agreed, and he was allowed to mate her, this would be her home. He watched her face closely. Castello was as grand as the chateau where she was raised. It was just a different architectural style. He stopped before the portrait of his grandparents, Portia and Christofano, and his father at age ten. Added to the gallery now was a portrait of Shade as an adult, along with Kate, and the three children. Chantal smiled as she looked at the portrait of Lorenzo as a young boy. Lorenzo laughed. "I remember having to stand still for this portrait. Sophia kept running off, and Theresa would have to run after her. The artist would shout at the rest of us not to move while Theresa wrestled with Sophia to get her back in place. My mother would scold her for not standing still, and my father was muttering under his breath. So, you see, those smiles on our faces don't tell you everything."

"Well, I hope the smile on your face now is telling me the truth of how you feel. This place is beautiful, Lorenzo. I love the portraits of your family. Your sisters are so beautiful, and I had to stifle a laugh when Sophia spoke her mind about being dismissed earlier. You were right, she holds nothing back. I am not so outspoken."

Lorenzo slid his arm around her waist and pulled her close to his side, as he continued to walk with her. He laughed out loud when she referred to Sophia as outspoken. "Oh, believe me, Sophia was on her good behavior tonight. Our mother was mortal, and not raised in our culture, and my father saw her as his partner and mate. My mother has been very involved in developing the family businesses, and my father respects her opinion. She has learned what's acceptable in our culture, while pushing the boundaries. My mother will disagree with him, and stand her ground, but she does it in private. Sophia was raised in that environment, where she saw my mother speak her mind. She was raised by a strong woman. My father found it difficult to be strict with Sophia, so I'll warn you now, do not be surprised at anything when it comes to Sophia. My friend Alfie adores her, but he has his hands full. I'd say the females in the Medici household have strong opinions and don't hesitate to share them."

As he pulled her close, she felt her body quiver slightly and her breath left her body in a soft gasp. No male had ever held her this close. His body was muscular, and she was lost for a moment in the feel of him against her. "Your family is so different than mine, Lorenzo. Your mother laughs easily, speaks easily. My own mother holds her tongue, as do I. When the males are in the room, they hold the floor. Your parents are very much in love, it is so evident. My own parents have been together a very long time and are in love." Shaking her head, she moved away from his grasp slightly and stopped to look at a portrait on the wall. "Business is left to the males. Women belong in the house. It is a saying I have heard so much in my life, a mantra. Your sisters and mother must make me sound so weak and lame."

He slipped his hand in hers. He'd never met a female so delicate. "Chantal, I promise you, no one in my family sees you as weak or lame. I'd love to be the male able to show you the world, and all the adventures it holds. And the females in my family would welcome you in. If you wanted to be involved in the family businesses, there'd be a place for you. But if that's not something you desire, then you can explore your own path. My father is a warrior, and I'm a warrior. That lifestyle would be quite different for you. There's much violence in our world, but you, and those like you, are protected from much of it. The warriors are the guardians who protect our kind from those who would expose us, both mortal and immortal. It's not a life without risk, but you'd be well protected. You'll need to think about these things should you choose to follow me."

Chantal had become close to him, in a short period of time. He listened to her, really listened. He was strong yet gentle in his manner and speech. The more he spoke about his own family, the more she realized she was nothing like the women he'd grown up with. Looking down at the floor, she felt embarrassed and inept in his world. "You said your father saw your mother as a partner. She has her own businesses. How do I become a partner to a warrior? I know nothing of that life."

She let go of his hand and strolled a few feet from him before turning to look at him. "Lorenzo, I am not sure I could ever fulfill what you need in a mate. Being protected is something I know well. I have been sheltered all my life. I have never traveled. What I know, I learned from books and tutors. I care about you so much. You are a wonderful, handsome male. But now that I have met your family, seen them together..." Biting her lip softly, she was losing hope of them together, she felt like a square peg in a round hole. "I have no idea how to be a partner in a warrior's world."

He stepped up behind her and wrapped his arms around her protectively. "Chantal, my mother and my sister Natalia have a protector at home in Virginia. Luca has been at my mother's side even before she was turned. And Sophia is mated to a warrior, and still she has a protector. My mother isn't a warrior, although I'm sure you're aware of her gifts, and neither of my sisters were born warrior. Even my half-brother Cory and his mortal mate must live on the property in Virginia and have their own protector. I don't need a warrior at my side. I have a camp full of warriors. I need a female who'll love me, one who understands the demands made on a warrior, and can be my soft place to fall. My father calls my mother his light in the darkness. Can you be my light in the darkness, Chantal?"

Chantal felt his arms around her, and it was like a cage of hope, happiness, and love. She could feel his heart beating, and she inhaled his masculine scent. She wanted to love him. "I feel no darkness from you, Lorenzo, but I would like to be your light." She turned in his arms, looking up into his beautiful face. Hesitantly, she laid her hand on his cheek. "I want to be your soft place."

Lorenzo leaned down and kissed her with tenderness and passion and wondered if his lips were the first. He felt her respond to the kiss when he heard footsteps in the hall and broke away. He wouldn't rush her, and he wouldn't jeopardize his chance to be with her. She was a female who'd be worth the wait.

She'd been lost in the moment when he pulled away and she heard the footsteps. She patted her hair and turned quickly to the portrait on the wall, trying to stop her heart from pounding like a drum. She looked up to see Alfie and let out the breath she was holding.

"Brother, just a heads up, the mother's are coming back in from the garden and rejoining the males. It might be a good idea to head down that way. Maybe keep from being sought out if you get my meaning."

Lorenzo slapped his friend on the back. "Thanks, brother."

He took Chantal's hand. "Shall we head back to the parlor? Let's see if your father has decided to let me hang around."

2-68

Throughout the summer and into early fall, Lorenzo had teleported to Paris to see Chantal. Her father would still not allow him to see her without a chaperone. He felt drawn to this girl in a way he'd never experienced before, but he was still young, and he wondered if he was ready for the commitment of mating. His father waited several centuries before mating, but Lorenzo found the process of hunting tedious and empty. The feeding satisfied his hunger, and the sex still provided a thrill, but it was empty and vacant. When he came home after the hunt, he was even more aware of how alone he was at Castello, and he envied Alfie, who had a mate to come home to. He showered quickly and put on his leathers as he teleported out to the groves. He landed softly in the dusty soil just outside the shack Danilo called his office. Danilo had been hiring new migrant workers in anticipation of the fall harvest. Alfie had been making rounds, saw him coming in, and walked in his direction.

Lorenzo gave him a fist bump. "Brother. Anything new I need to know about?"

Alfie returned the greeting. "There's something stirring, not sure I like it. There's been an increase in the number of cars driving by, as well as their frequency. Sometimes, they stop and watch the workers, and occasionally, one of those goons even steps outside the car to watch. I think the harvest season is going to get interesting. Workers seem to be getting real nervous again." Alfie lit up a cigarette and passed the pack to Lorenzo. "So, anything happening with Chantal?"

Lorenzo took a cigarette and lit up. He took a drag before running his hand though his hair. He chuckled as he answered. "Not much can happen when her protector, her mother, and her father are all within hearing distance. They expect to hear a conversation, and if things get quiet, someone manages to find an excuse to come into the room. I thought my father was strict with Sophia. It makes it hard, brother. We can sit together and talk, I can kiss her, but not for too long."

Alfie bent over laughing and shook his head. "Oh yeah, brother, you got it bad. At least you weren't attracted to a female whose father had the reputation of being the most bad-ass warrior alive, and didn't think you were worthy of his daughter. Don't even fucking talk to me about how hard it is!"

Lorenzo laughed as he leaned against the shack. "I probably wouldn't be so different if I had daughters." He took a drag on the cigarette and exhaled slowly, as the smoke caught on the breeze. "How did you know it was real? The love I mean. I know you're happy with my sister, but is it what you were looking for? My only frame of reference is my own parents. I love Chantal, but I don't think I feel what they feel."

Alfie looked at his life-long friend. "Every relationship is different, defined by the two people in it. Don't try to measure what you feel by what you see in your parents. Sophia suits me. She gets me, and I love her spirit and her stubbornness. We just fit, but we're nothing like your parents. That doesn't mean we settled or made the wrong choice. Your parents are..."

"Different."

"Yeah, different." Alfie paused, looking skyward. "Don't take this the wrong way, brother, because I mean it in the sincerest way, but I'd describe their love as obsessive. Like no one else exists for them or something, you know what I mean?"

Lorenzo smiled as he dropped the cigarette to the ground and crushed it under his boot. "Yeah, I do know what you mean. And I think you're telling me I'm not going to find that."

Alfie punched him in the arm. "I'm trying to tell you to find what fits you Lorenzo. You're not your parents. Don't try to measure your happiness by someone else's measuring stick."

Lorenzo chuckled. "When did you become so wise?"

Alfie looked at him and grinned. "Since I mated your sister."

Their conversation came to a sudden stop as Lorenzo nodded his head in the direction of the road as another black car drove by slowly. It was the second one he'd seen, and he'd only been here a few minutes. He could see the workers in the field pause and look up each time a car rolled by. "Fuckers just trying to intimidate."

Alfie turned to look at the car "The mortals get spooked really easy. If these crops can't be harvested, your mother is going to get mighty pissed off. Sophia says it takes a lot to make her angry, but when she goes there, everyone should take cover." Alfie threw down his cigarette butt. "So, it sounds like you're getting pretty serious with the Valois. Talked to your dad about it yet?"

Lorenzo followed the car with his eyes. "Sort of. I know he met with her father, and the two of them have reached an agreement as to her dowry. I hate that part, though. Makes it sound like a business deal, you know? My father didn't have to deal with that when he fell in love with my mother."

"Well, you're both royal blood, and there are territories on both sides, and a lot at stake. I'm pretty sure your grandfather ensured there was a dowry agreement between Shade and Dona when he and Dona's father agreed early on to their mating." Alfie regretted the words as soon as they left his mouth. Lorenzo seemed to have left that incident of the trip to Venice with Dona far behind. "Sorry brother, I didn't mean to bring her up."

Lorenzo shrugged. "Oh, there was a deal all right. It would have given the Medici control of Umbria. It was why my grandfather, Christofano, fought so hard against my father's decision to disregard the contract. Christofano was trying to put more distance between our territory, and the Borgia coven. But that's all water under the bridge, brother. She's out of my mind."

Alfie slapped him on the back. "Good to hear. I need to get back to your sister. Things should quiet down with the cars as soon as the workers leave the field, but don't let your guard down." Alfie started to teleport out and paused. "Lorenzo, don't play with Chantal if you're not serious. I know you're taking it slow, but it won't take long for word to get out that the two masters have a deal on the table, and her suitors are going to come out of the woodwork. I don't want to see either of you get hurt or lose each other. I think she's a great match for you, brother. Don't over think it. Let your heart lead for once."

Lorenzo grinned back at him. "Misery loves company?"

"Hell, I didn't say anything about misery. I love your sister. I think, deep down, I always have. Your ass is the one in misery. I'm going home to my mate." Alfie teleported out.

Lorenzo chuckled as he headed into the shack, checking on Danilo. The man seemed in a panic. "What's eating at you, Danilo?"

He looked up frustrated. "Have you seen the cars? Every fifteen minutes. You could set a clock by it. The workers are scared. I am having trouble hiring enough migrants. The other farmers are telling me to just pay them what they want, it is better than nothing, and nothing is what we will have if we don't play their game."

Lorenzo sat on the edge of the desk. “The Medici don’t play games. Haven't you figured that out yet?"

2-69

Lorenzo had come back from Paris, and Antonio had a feeder waiting for him in his room. Lorenzo made quick work of her and sent her back to the compound. He was finding the time with the feeders to be less and less satisfying, as it was Chantal he saw in his head when he fed and had sex with the feeders. He showered quickly, changed into leathers, and teleported out to the groves. He could tell Alfie was agitated when he dropped in. Alfie let him know the black cars had been driving by about every fifteen minutes. Lorenzo lit up a smoke and looked up the road. "Stick around for a while, brother, let me get a feel for this before you take off. The workers are agitated. I feel a real negative vibe."

"Not a problem. This is starting to get ridiculous. I'm waiting any minute for one of these mortal assholes to do something stupid and set off the warriors." Alfie kept his eyes peeled for the next car, as it would surely be there soon. "You look tired, brother, teleporting to Paris wearing thin?"

Lorenzo chuckled. "Is it that obvious? I really like her, Alfie. There's a part of me that keeps saying I'm still so young. I mean, look how long my dad waited." He shook his head. "I don't know, the hunt seems weary to me. How about you? You miss the hunt? The weekends in Greece when we picked up mortals by the armfuls and feasted until we couldn't move?"

Alfie smiled, remembering their exploits together, and shook his head no. "Let me ask you something, Lorenzo. When you're with the feeders, no matter how much you take from them in nourishment or sex, do you still feel empty inside? Like it's not enough?"

Lorenzo nodded. "It's never enough, and empty is a good word for it. The hunger is gone, but I still feel...empty."

Alfie stared at his best friend. How could he be so smart and not have figured this out yet. "That's a good sign you won't be missing the hunt. That's when I realized Sophia was all I wanted. Nothing else filled me like being with her." Alfie looked up as the black car approaches. "Fuck, right on schedule."

Lorenzo looked in the direction of the slow-moving car as it pulled to a halt at the end of the dirt road. The warriors who were standing guard stepped forward and the tinted window was slowly lowered. Lorenzo could see one of his warriors lean forward, speaking to someone in the car, then the warrior turned in his direction and called out. "He wants to come talk to you."

Lorenzo nodded, and waved his hand. "Pat him down. No weapons."

The warrior turned back to the car, and Sal stepped out, holding his hands in the air as the warrior patted him down, removing the luger and tossing it on the front seat before nodding Sal in Lorenzo's direction. Sal walked slowly down the dirt road toward the shack, the overweight man already wiping sweat from his brow with a handkerchief. Lorenzo stood shoulder to shoulder with Alfie.

"Well, this should be interesting."

As Sal approached, he looked red in the face and was huffing and puffing from the walk. He stood a minute and wiped his face again before speaking. "Boss sent me to make one final offer."

Lorenzo smirked at him. "Well, since you walked all the way down here, let's hear it."

Sal pulled out a stub of a cigar, asking for a light, and Alfie flicked out his lighter. The man puffed away, the acrid smoke swirling above his head. "Boss says he'll pay $500 a ton. Can't go higher because that's what he's paying the other farmers. Take it or leave it, but I suggest you take it, son."

Lorenzo shook his head. "You're kidding right? Market price is $1,000 a ton. $500 is barely breaking even."

Sal puffed on the cigar. "Is it your call? Where's the other guy? Marco...the one that came to the restaurant. I need to tell him."

Lorenzo stepped closer to the man, pushing into his personal space. "Marco? I'll tell him, but don't expect the answer to change."

Sal nodded. "Give you twenty-four hours. I'll be back tomorrow, but seriously, son, you need to consider the offer."

Lorenzo stared back at him. "I'm not your son. I'll deliver your message, now get off our land."

Alfie stepped up next to Lorenzo as the two of them towered over the man, and he turned and waddled back up the dirt road to the comfort of his air-conditioned car.

Lorenzo muttered under his breath as the man walked away. "Fat fuck is about three minutes away from a heart attack."

They both waited until the black car pulled away before Alfie spoke up. "$500 a ton? Why doesn't he just slap us in the fucking face? You want me to go with you to tell Marco?"

Lorenzo laughed. "Oh, Marco is going to love this. I pity the warriors in the camp tonight. Come on, brother, let's get this over with."

Alfie slapped him on the back. "Let's roll!" They both teleported quickly to Castello and found Marco in his office. As they walked in, Marco looked up.

"Well, if it isn't the twins. What the fuck happened now? And don't take all night to tell me, I have a lot of heads to bust tonight." Flopping down in his old leather desk chair, it creaked loud under his weight. He pulled a bottle of Midnight from the desk drawer and poured himself a drink.

Lorenzo sat on the corner of the desk as Alfie leaned against the door. "Got a visit from our friend, Sal. He stopped by to make their final offer; with a strong suggestion we take it. $500 a ton. I politely told him to fuck off, but he insisted I had to tell you, and get your decision. He's coming back tomorrow. So, what do you want me to tell him? Fuck off, please?"

"So, let me get this straight. That pasta eating fuck wants to give us half of what the crop is worth?" Leaning back, he threw his booted feet up on the desk. "Good damn thing I wasn't there, I would have ripped that bastards head off his shoulders. Well, call your father. I already know what he is going to say. But I told him we'd keep him in the loop."

Lorenzo pulled out his cell phone and checked the time. It was early evening here, so it was early morning in the U.S. If he called now, he could probably catch his father before he went to his death slumber. He hit dial and waited for his dad to answer.

***

Shade and Natalia had just finished discussing her plans for spending more time with Malachi in preparation for her eventual move to Council. They were both tired and about to head upstairs.

He loved the kinship he had with Nattie, in that she too was called to her death slumber, but he regretted she was denied the sunlight. Shade felt his cell phone vibrate as they reached the top of the stairs. He kissed his daughter as she headed down the hallway to her bedroom. Pulling out his phone, he saw it was Lorenzo and kept walking toward the bedroom.

"Son, good to hear from you. How is Chantal?"

"She's good, Dad, and I want to talk to you about that, but not right now. We got a visit from Sal just a few minutes ago. He said their final offer was $500 a ton. Alfie was with me, and we told him to take a hike, but he insisted we inform Marco. We're all here with Marco now. Listen, he didn't say what he'd do, but it was a veiled threat if we declined the offer. How do you want us to handle it?"

Shade listened as he entered the bedroom and found *bel* sitting on the bed, her laptop balanced on her knees. He quickly informed her of the information Lorenzo had called to share. "Son, you just keep doing what you are doing. If Marco thinks we need to beef up the amount of coverage from the warriors, then do it. But those bastards are not getting a damn thing from us. You can tell him in those exact words. Be mindful they are mortals. I will not go on the offensive here, and I sure as hell don't want to expose our coven, but they have no fucking idea who they are messing with."

"No problem, Dad. He's coming back tomorrow, and Alfie and I will personally deliver the message. We'll let the warriors know what's going on, just so they can be more alert to anything suspicious."

"Keep me posted, no matter what happens, any time. We need to keep our identity tight, Lorenzo. They cannot have one suspicion. If you need me, I can be there. Do what has to be done."

"We're good. I'll call tomorrow after we deliver the news. Tell Mom I love her."

"Will do, son. Keep your mind in the game. Call me when you know more." Shade hung up and looked at Kate. "I think it might be show time in Florence. Your son said to tell you he loves you."

Kate closed the laptop and pushed it aside with a sigh. "I am beginning to regret this decision to pursue the olives. I understand we can't back down, but this is turning into more trouble than it's worth."

Flopping down in the chair, he started removing his boots. "No, it is worth it. *Bel*, this is your business, and it is a good opportunity for the coven. I won't let anyone take this away. Besides, this is good experience for Lorenzo. Sooner or later, he was going to have to tangle with something outside the safety of Castello, and I prefer his first experience be with mortals."

Kate pulled her knees to her chest as she sat in the middle of the bed. "Don't underestimate the evil of mortals, lover. They don't have the strength and power of the vampire, but their capacity for evil is equal to any vampire I've encountered."

Sitting back, he grinned at her, cocking his head to the side. "I don't know about that."

Kate bit her lip, hoping he wasn't taking the threat from the mortals too lightly. She rolled off the bed and pulled back the blankets, making room for him as he joined her in bed.

2-70

Lorenzo completed his watch and returned home to catch a few hours of sleep. Other than the cars driving by at fifteen-minute intervals, they didn't see any additional activity from the *mafioso*. That might all change once they give Sal their answer. He'd called Chantal before reporting back to the groves and told her how much he loved her. He'd need to have a conversation with his dad about her soon. He teleported out to the groves and quickly found Alfie. The two of them waited for the car that carried Sal.

"I think I'm going to ask Chantal's father for his permission to mate his daughter. What do you think, brother?"

Alfie knew Lorenzo had been taking it slow. Lorenzo was royal blood, but born a warrior, and he'd led a very different life than Chantal, who'd remained sheltered. "There are only two things you need to ask yourself. Do you love her? And do you think she's prepared to help lead this coven. She'll have responsibilities, Lorenzo. Have you talked to her about that stuff at all?"

He nodded. "She's well aware of her responsibilities. Her parents have a very large coven in France. It incorporates an area larger than Tuscany, and includes Burgundy, Loire Valley, Champagne, and Paris. She's an only child and has been raised with the understanding she must provide for the coven, whether single or mated. Her parents have prepared her well for the role of queen. And yes, I do love her."

"Then I have no idea what you're waiting for. It's obvious your parents like her. And I'd assume, since her father has met privately with yours, this dowry has already been discussed. It will be the best thing you ever did, brother." Alfie saw a cloud of dust on the road. "Looks like Sal is arriving. Ready to throw down the gauntlet?"

Lorenzo looked up to see the car pull to a stop, and the warriors pat down Sal again before letting him walk down the dirt road. His suit was expensive but looked dumpy and wrinkled on his oversized frame. Lorenzo chuckled. "You know he hates that walk down here."

Sal was sweating again and wiped his face as he approached. "You got an answer for me?"

Lorenzo nodded. "Yep. Same answer as yesterday. We've already got a buyer for the harvest. You're wasting your time here."

Sal stood still and stared at Lorenzo as he chewed on the unlit cigar. "Big mistake, kid. I'll take your message to Benito, but he won't like it."

Lorenzo shrugged. "I'm sure he'll survive the disappointment."

Sal spit on the ground. "Oh, he'll survive it, kid. He's not the one you need to worry about."

Lorenzo leaned his shoulder against the shack, and caught a glimpse of Danilo through the window, as he watched the encounter through the dirty glass. "That a threat, Sal?"

Sal shook his head no and stuck the cigar back in his mouth. "Nope, that's a promise. Watch your back now, you hear?"

He turned and started the long walk back to his car as Danilo exited the office, wringing his hands. "Master, you don't understand what these people can do."

Lorenzo calmed him. "I have no doubt they'll try something, Danilo, but our retribution will be swift, and disproportionate. If they harm one, we harm many."

Over the next few days, the cars kept coming, and Danilo's anxiety level climbed with each passing car. The migrant workers had been informed that the Medici had refused the *mafioso's* offer. Some came back to work, others didn't, but the harvesting continued. Lorenzo told Alfie he might be late, but he'd arrive after sunset and relieve him. Alfie wasn't bothered about staying longer. Sophia wasn't always happy when he worked late, but she understood. He sat down against the shack and was ready to light up a smoke when he heard Lorenzo's voice in his head. **"I'm teleporting in. We have a fire in one of the groves."**

Alfie jumped up and teleported straight up in the air, allowing him to pinpoint the direction of the fire, and then took off in that direction. The flames and smoke were billowing into the night sky.

The warriors and the workers moved quickly, but they didn't have the means to put out the fire. They turned on the irrigation system, but the spray was focused on the ground. They beat at the flames with their jackets, and Danilo had called the fire department, but the olive groves were in a rural area, and it would take a long time for the fire response people to arrive. It didn't take long for the fire to spread from tree to tree, and soon, the entire grove was engulfed. Wetting the ground had at least helped to keep the fire from spreading to the next grove, and thankfully, there was no wind.

Lorenzo looked up to see the black car parked on the side of the road, and Sal standing next to the car, his cigar tip glowing red each time he drew on it. The fire truck arrived, and the fire was put out, but this grove was destroyed. Their message was clear. They'd burn down each grove until the Medici gave in to their demands. Lorenzo started in his direction and Alfie grabbed him by the arm. "Not now, brother."

Lorenzo paced, and had to fight to hold back the beast. He looked at Alfie. "They want a war? They came to the right place."

"Keep your wits about you, brother. Don't expose us. We need to get Marco out here. What's the next move?"

Lorenzo looked around at the smoldering olive grove. It was one of the smaller groves but had been well established. It would take years to replant and have the trees reach maturity again. He shook his head, as he left another warrior in charge of overseeing the mess and sent the others back to guard the other groves. "Let's get to Marco now. We'll need to beef up the coverage and see what he wants to do about this."

They were about to teleport out when one of their warriors approached. "Master, we've got another problem."

Lorenzo looked at him, already agitated. "Well, spit it out."

"We encountered one of the mortals in another grove trying to start a fire. The mortal pulled a gun, and we had to slit his throat. We dragged the body back to the mortal's car and left him inside. What do you want us to do now?"

Lorenzo slapped Alfie on the arm. "Let's go, brother. We need to take care of this before going back to Marco. Last thing we need is some dead mortal on the side of the road."

As they teleported out to the road, the car was pulled off to the side, the dead mortal slumped in the driver's seat. Alfie walked around the car before stopping and crossing his arms over his chest. "Looks like it's time to start a little fire of our own, what you think, brother? Would you like to oblige me with that?"

Lorenzo looked around to make sure there were no other mortals, then rolled up the sleeve on his left arm. He held his hand palm up and concentrated as the flame started to blaze in his palm. He watched as the fireball grew, and then threw it inside the car. They both heard the loud whoosh as the flames washed across the interior of the car and engulfed the mortal. They both stepped back from the heat as the flames grew, reaching skyward. The Medici warriors watched with awe as the prince threw the fire into the car. They'd heard of Lorenzo's gift, but had never seen a fire-thrower before. It didn't take long before the body of the mortal, and the interior of the car was reduced to ash, and all that remained was the bent metal frame of the car.

The warrior who slit the mortal's throat stepped forward. "I had no choice, master."

Lorenzo slapped him on the back. "You did the right thing. Now get back to your post. Anyone even sets foot across the fence line, I want them dead, understood?"

He nodded. "Yes, master."

Lorenzo turns to Alfie as they both teleported out to give Marco the unwelcome news.

2-71

Once again, Lorenzo and Alfie teleported into the camp to find Marco on the field, barking out orders as the new warriors scrambled to follow his commands. They landed on the soft dirt of the training field, a few feet from Marco, kicking up a small cloud of dust. Lorenzo's feet had barely touched the ground when he started talking to Marco.

"We got trouble."

Marco looked at him, he could see on Lorenzo's face this wasn't something small. "Tell me now. Because whatever this is, I need to handle it so I can get back here and finish up for the night."

"The *Mafioso* burned down the small grove near the village. It's gone. While we were there getting the fire under control, they tried to get into another grove. Our warriors intercepted him and the *Mafioso* pulled his gun. They cut his throat and dumped him back in his car. I burned the car, so no one could recognize the body. I ordered the warriors back to their stations, with instructions to kill anyone who steps foot on our land, but this is just the beginning, Marco. They're not going to stop."

Marco sighed heavily. He knew it would come to this. "Fucking bastards. All right let me give these punks some orders for the night, and then I'll go out with you and see the damage. Your old man is going to want details." He turned and barked orders to the warriors and gave instructions to his Lieutenants before grabbing a sword and strapping it on his back. "Take me to the grove. Move!"

The three of them teleported out, riding low over the burned-out grove so Marco could survey the damage. They landed near the torched car, still smoldering. It wouldn't take long for the mafia to miss whoever had been driving this car. Marco slowly circled the car. It was burned beyond recognition, and there was nothing left of the mortal. He was about to suggest they get one of the tractors from the equipment shed and drag the car out of sight when another black car pulled to the crest of the hill and stopped.

Lorenzo looked up. "Looks like we got company."

As Marco and Alfie turned to look in the direction of the car, Lorenzo saw the long barrel of a gun through the open window and shouted, "Get down!"

Lorenzo dropped to the dirt, just as he heard the shots ring out, and saw Alfie hitting the dirt beside him, muttering "Shit!" He lifted his head and saw Marco face down in the dirt a few feet away and heard the spinning tires of the car as it sped away. Lorenzo stood up, brushing the dust from his leathers, and reached his hand down to pull Alfie to his feet.

"Guess it was a warning shot, letting us know what's coming. We're going to need to re-arm the warriors. They can keep their knives, but they need to carry guns now."

He walked over to Marco who was still on the ground. "You can get up now, old man." Marco didn't move and Lorenzo squatted down next to him, placing his hand on his shoulder. "Marco?"

He turned him over, to see a bullet wound in the center of his forehead, and Marco's eyes still open, staring out at nothing. He was dead. Lorenzo stumbled backward and landed hard on his ass. "Fuck! Mother fuckers!"

Alfie stood dumbfounded, staring at the man who'd dedicated his life to training him, and the thousands like him, gone in the blink of an eye. He dropped to his knees next to Marco's body, leaning over him, checking for a pulse, or the tiniest evidence of breathing, but there was nothing. Marco was gone. Alfie looked back at Lorenzo, who had tears in his eyes.

"I'll kill them all! All of them! Do you hear me?" Lorenzo stood up and shouted into the night sky. "All of them! I'll kill all of them!"

***

Shade climbed from bed as the blinds rose, preparing for another long night at camp. It was fall, and he loved this transition to the colder months for one reason only, less daylight. *Bel* had slipped on her robe, and was searching for her slippers, complaining that her feet were cold. He pulled on his leathers before grabbing his boots and sitting down to lace and buckle them up. He loved watching her as she made the bed, humming to herself. He stood up and pulled the shirt over his head when, from nowhere, the pain struck him, and he fell to his knees. "Nooo!"

The house rumbled with his scream. Connected by the blood oath that was sealed centuries ago, he felt the bullet that struck his oldest friend, followed by Lorenzo's anger and overwhelming sorrow. He couldn't move for a moment, stunned with the loss that slammed his body. Marco was gone.

Kate turned quickly when she heard his scream, her heart in her throat as her thoughts went to her children, and she felt Lorenzo's anger and panic wash over her. "Shade! Tell me he's all right!"

She called to him, **"Lorenzo!"**

And heard his response in her head. **"I'm okay, Mommy. It's not me, it is Marco."**

She felt the depth of pain from both Shade and Lorenzo, and he didn't need to tell her Marco was gone. She heard a wail from the bedroom down the hall and knew Theresa felt him now as well. Kate stumbled over to Shade, and knelt beside him, draping her body over his. Their bedroom door opened as Luca and Shannon both rushed in, and Kate looked up to see the question in Luca's eyes. She looked back at him as the tears rolled down her cheeks, and simply answered, "Marco." Luca dropped to his knees, as he had lost the second most important male in his life.

The pain washed over the house like a cloud of black shadows and death. Shade could feel the light in his darkness cover him, and he knew she tried to protect him, but nothing could stop this pain. Marco was like a blood brother to him in every aspect of his life. Shade felt like he'd lost a part of himself. Standing slowly, his body began to shake, and his beast roared to the surface. He looked at Luca in his grief and heard Theresa's wails. His growl of revenge began slowly and built until it poured out of him like a raging wind. He looked at Kate, and they spoke no words. She knew his beast would seek revenge. She knew what he wanted, and where he needed to be.

Teleporting out, he moved with a speed he didn't know he possessed and was soon soaring over the groves. He had one goal, and that was to destroy them all, every mortal that had a hand in his brother's death, would die this night. He landed with a hard thud to find his own son, in much the same condition as himself. Kneeling beside Marco, his heart screamed with the raw pain of his loss, but there was much to be done before he'd rest. Reaching out, he gently closed Marco's eyes. Speaking softly to his dearest friend, he whispered, "I will avenge you, brother." Turning back to his son, he issued orders. "Gather every warrior in Florence. We have a score to settle. No one remains alive."

The word of Marco's death was spread from warrior to warrior along the fence line, and they heard their master shout that no one would remain alive. They all started walking in the direction of their master. One of the warriors was ordered back to the camp, and delivered the devastating news, and sent every warrior to the groves. All the warriors from every outpost in Tuscany was called back in, as they gathered, several hundred strong, in the olive groves. The warriors all dropped to one knee before the King and Prince. They'd avenge the death of the one who'd trained them, or they'd die trying. A lieutenant trained at Marco's hand stepped forward. "You have only to whisper your command, master, and it will be done."

Shade looked up to see them arrive in droves, every warrior ready to do what they'd been trained to do, for the man at his feet. "This is a mortal's doing. This death is personal. And we kill every one of the *mafioso* and their families. No one stays alive. We can leave no witness to the carnage we bring on them tonight. You are hereby commanded to unleash your power, and leave no mortal standing." Turning to Lorenzo, his face was a reflection of his own. Pain and revenge is a dangerous mixture, but together, they'd end this battle permanently, and avenge the death of Marco.

"Lead me to Benito. This is my kill. You burn the house to the ground." Looking at Alfie, he issued further orders. "Split up the warriors into teams and take them all out. When you're done, we return back here to the groves. All will die!"

As Shade and Lorenzo teleported out, Alfie split up the warriors into smaller groups as each headed out to destroy all the members of Benito's mortal thugs. No one would be left standing by sunrise, not one man, woman, or child. They made no attempt to disguise the fact they were vampire as they descended on each household, and with speed and precision, ripped through each mortal, beheading with their swords, and shredding with their teeth. The bodies were left for the local police to find, all except Benito's. Shade attacked him personally, making sure he saw the face of the beast before plunging his fist through his chest, and ripping out his still beating heart. Lorenzo made quick work of his wife and children. They were innocent sacrifices, and he didn't make them suffer, but they had seen the faces of the vampires. The message to any of the other mortal *mafioso* families was loud and clear. Fuck with the Medici, and they will answer with a scorched earth policy.

When his father emerged, both arms covered in blood to his elbows, he simply nodded his head. Lorenzo extended his left hand and summoned forth the fire for the second time tonight. As the fire grew in his palm, he tossed it into the room, and watched as the drapes and furniture immediately caught fire. He left with his father and stood in the street as they watched the flames lick through the windows, and up to the roof line. They heard the screams of neighbors as they too rushed outside but stopped in their tracks as they saw the two men standing shoulder to shoulder in the middle of the road. It was no secret that Benito was *mafioso*, and the neighbors didn't take long to figure out someone had finally extracted their revenge. The house burned out of control, as the beams started to collapse in on itself, and the crowd stood back, in fear of the fire, and the two men who stood illuminated before it.

Lorenzo tugged at his father's arm. "Time to go." They turned and walked away, the crowd parting to let them go, as they heard the wail of the fire engine in the distance. Once they were out of view, they teleported back to the groves, where, one by one, the Medici warriors returned, having accomplished their mission to exterminate every member of the Benito family.

Shade waited until every warrior had returned. Alfie approached him as the warriors stood lined up before him. "Master, all have returned. Orders followed."

Shade looked him in the eye and nodded. Alfie took a stand to one side of Shade, as Lorenzo stood on the other. Shade looked out over the warriors before him, their bodies covered in mortal blood. "Return to Castello or your outpost. I will give further orders once I have settled the affairs of my brother. *Per sempre*, Medici!"

The warriors all dropped to one knee; their heads bowed in honor to the male who trained them. Shade lifted Marco's limp body into his arms. "This is your last flight, you old leather ass. I will miss you. Know that every fight and every sword I raise from this moment on, you will be with me in my heart."

Crushing Marco to his chest, he teleported back to Castello. He landed inside the foyer and found the house staff already gathered. He carried Marco's body past them all, through the halls, and out the back of Castello into the rose garden. Unstrapping the sword from the warrior's back, Shade laid his body among the roses and placed the fallen warrior's sword across his chest and positioned his hands around the hilt. He walked back into Castello and climbed the stairs to the highest room, looking out over the garden. He stood in silence as the sun peeked over the horizon, and the rays of the sun slowly stretched out to his brother. He was gone in a small cloud of smoke; his remains reduced to ash as the sword remained, laying on the ground. Walking away from the window, he fell to his knees, his bloody arms and hands reaching over his head, as his blood tears rained down.

***

Theresa appeared in their bedroom door just as her master teleported out. Kate stood unsteadily and opened her arms to her. Theresa clung to Kate and sobbed. Looking up at Luca and Shannon, Kate said quietly, "Leave us, please."

Shannon had her hand over her mouth, as her tears flow silently, and Luca wiped the tears from his face. He led his mate out of the room, and softly closed the door. Kate lay down on the bed with Theresa, as Kate rubbed her back. She closed her eyes and let Shade's and Lorenzo's emotions roll over her. She felt like a tiny boat being tossed in a turbulent sea as she rode the waves of their collective pain and anger. She knew when they left to take revenge, she felt the rage from their beasts as they killed, and she felt when her son released his gift of fire in a rage. She held tight to Theresa, but her mind was with her mate and her son, as she opened herself to their every feeling. The door opened, and she felt Natalia slip into the bed, so she was now sandwiched between Theresa and her daughter.

"Mommy."

Kate stroked her cheek. "They're okay."

Natalia nodded; her tears silent. Kate heard the roar from the warriors in the camp, as the news reached them, and Marcello struggled to keep them all here. Kate felt Shade's pain and anguish as he bent over the lifeless body of his oldest and dearest friend and lifted him gently in his arms. **"Lover. I am with you."**

She knew when he laid Marco down in the rose garden, in the very spot where his father and mother took their last breath, and she knew when the sun struck his body, turning him to ash. She heard the plaintive wail from Theresa, as she too knew Marco was no longer on this earthy plane.

2-72

The office was dimly lit from the full moon, and the huge castle echoed with quiet. The days since Marco's death had passed at a torturously slow pace and left only hollowness inside him. Shade had arranged the memorial for his fallen brother. The family had all come from Bel Rosso, including the warriors who'd served under Marco, trained by his hand. The memorial had been held inside the camp where Marco had dedicated his life in service to the Medici. His sword now hung on the wall inside the office where Marco had spent much of his time at camp. Shade couldn't force himself to go through his friend's belongings. It was too painful, and he already had enough memories screaming in his brain. Theresa had taken on that task, saying she needed to touch his things, to feel his essence through the few belongings he kept in his private quarters.

Castello was filled with his family and their mates, but it still felt empty to him. Kate had been at his side throughout, but he was numb to it all. Nothing could replace Marco's laugh, his gruff voice or his insistent nagging and teasing. It had been a week since his death, and yet it seemed as though years had passed. He hadn't left the office for three days, sequestering himself inside, sleeping on the worn leather sofa. The empty bottles of Midnight were lined up on the bar and strewn across the room. Shade knew the others suffered as well, he could feel their pain, but their pain seemed like a scratch compared to the gaping wound in his heart. Marco had been a constant in his life, and Shade had never allowed himself to envision a future where Marco didn't play a leading role.

He stood in the darkened room, staring out the window toward the camp. There was no activity there, no sound of clashing swords, or the loud whoops of the warriors. Nothing, and no one, was moving there. He hadn't issued any orders, and the warriors remained in the barracks. He couldn't remember a night when the camp wasn't bustling with activity. He didn't hear Kate when she entered the room until she spoke, her voice shattering the silence, and breaking him away from his thoughts.

Kate had allowed him to sequester himself in his grief and pain, and she felt the depth of his loss, and saw it in the faces of all the warriors who walked aimlessly around the camp. She stood silently in the doorway and looked at him, his back to her as he looked out the window. "Lover?"

Shade wondered how long she'd stood there watching him. How many times had she called his name and he was so lost in his thoughts he didn't hear her? "*Si, mi amore*."

She walked into the office and turned on the lights as she went. She made her way to the leather sofa, and noticed the empty bottles strewn across the table, the desk, the floor, but said nothing. She curled up in the corner of the large sofa. "Come sit with me, please."

He knew she was trying to pull him out of his grief, but he wasn't ready to leave yet. He remained standing, staring out at the lifeless camp. "Say whatever you have to say, I know you mean well, but I am not ready."

Kate sat silently, letting his words hang in the air before she spoke to him again. "Your coven grieves his loss, and your warriors wander aimlessly. You don't honor the spirit of your brother through your actions. This is Marco's legacy, what he devoted his life to, and you're letting him down. The coven needs you. The warriors need you. They need their king. They look to you for direction. They look to you to lead them out of the dark. You dishonor Marco by leaving his camp in shambles, and his warriors leaderless. If the roles were reversed, and it was you who'd been lost, do you think Marco would have let this camp go? I can tell you the answer, he would not. You'll feel his loss for all time, you'll grieve for him with every breath, but this isn't the warrior I know. This isn't the warrior I mated. Push through your pain, and deal with your son. He's much too young for the burden, but the responsibility for this camp lies on Lorenzo's shoulders now, and you must transfer that mantle of responsibility, and direct the warriors to move forward, keeping everything Marco taught them in their hearts. You've vanquished one enemy, but there are others, and you leave your coven weak and exposed. You're the King, and you aren't afforded the luxury of waiting until you're ready. Do what you were born to do."

Shade felt the sting of each word, her voice was soft but firm, and he felt the truth in what she said. He turned to her slowly and could only imagine how he looked to her. He hadn't left this office for days to shower, or shave, or even comb the mop of curls on his head. He knew he probably smelled of cigarettes, Midnight, sweat, and pain. "You think, because I am King, I am not afforded the luxury of my grief? What did you expect me to do my queen? Go on as usual? I have spent hundreds of years with Marco at my side." He walked to her and sat beside her on the couch, placing his head in his hands. "I know this is not the warrior you mated. I have stayed here, out of sight, for that very reason."

Kate leaned into him, her hand stroking his back. "Don't you know I feel the same pain? The same loss? I see that pain reflected to me in the eyes of every warrior in this camp. Every ache in your heart, I feel in my own. And I have watched Theresa, unable to rise from her bed. But while we wallow in our grief, our enemies celebrate our loss. As we become weaker, they become stronger, and I won't allow what we have built and bled for to be laid to waste. If you don't take control, then Marco died for nothing. His life, and his sacrifices to you, were all for nothing. Don't make his time on this earth meaningless. We don't have the luxury of time, my king. The coven waits for direction, as do the warriors. If you can't step forward, then I will. If they don't have their king, then they will at least see their queen. Tell me now, who will stand on the parapet tonight and address the coven. You? Or me? Because I refuse to let our coven suffer alone any longer."

He knew her strength, and her stubbornness, and had no doubt she'd stand on that parapet alone. Throughout their time together, he'd pushed her to accept her role as queen, and her responsibilities to the coven, and he saw in her now the complete acceptance of who she was, who she'd become. She understood, maybe better than he, that the coven came first. The coven must survive. He whispered softly, "You have always been my greatest strength, and my greatest weakness. It is your love that keeps me going. Without you, *bel*, there is only darkness." He turned and pulled her into his chest. "We stand together, or not at all."

She held him tight, not wanting to lose him again to the depths of his grief. "We'll stand together. Now come, take a shower with me, and then meet with your son. The Florence camp is his now, and he must step into Marco's shoes. Your prince is now a king."

She led him through the halls and up the stairs to their bedroom, where she undressed him. Together, they stood under the hot water of the shower, where her hands healed him, washing his hair and his body. She dried him off, and shaved his face, and laid his clothes out on the bed. She was there with every step he took, leading him back to their life as she prepared him to face the future, and lay the groundwork for his coven.

For the first time since Marco's death, he opened himself up to feel the emotions of others and reached out to find his son. He could tell he wasn't inside the castle, and extended his reach until he felt Lorenzo outside, alone in the rose garden. He felt his son's black grief and doubt. Kate had been right, this hell had to be put to rest, and it began with his son. He kissed her, and held her to his chest, speaking in a whisper, "Lorenzo."

She nodded her head as he released her. "Go to him, lover."

He walked through the empty halls of the Castello, and out to the rose garden where his son sat, secluded on a stone bench. His *madre* would often sit there when she needed to be alone with her thoughts. "Lorenzo? We need to talk, son."

Lorenzo looked up at his father. "Was it my fault? Was I not fast enough? He was standing right next to me. I should have been able to do something!"

Shade sat next to him, crossing one leg over his knee. His arms stretched across the back of the bench. "It is no one's fault. You cannot stop a bullet. This was a hit, and Marco was their target. Son, in your life, you are going to lose many warriors. I know I have, and each one is painful, and every time, you will question yourself. Being a warrior means even when you win, the loss of those that fall feels more than you can bear. It is an ugly world we live in. Marco had a good life, he lived to serve me and this coven, and he went out doing what he loved. None of this is anyone's fault."

Lorenzo nodded. "The camp is like a tomb. Every warrior feels his loss. They all complain about how hard he pushed them, but they all know they're better warriors because of him. And they loved him. He helped train me, and Alfie, and now he's gone. He makes me realize our gift of immortality is a fragile gift and can be taken away in a fraction of a second. I'm your only son, and the responsibility lies on me now."

"This is your birthright. You were born a prince, and a warrior. With the loss of Marco, you must step forward now, just as I had to step forward. You are a king now and will rule all our territories in Europe. Marco and I taught you all we know. You will never be more ready than now. Marco can't lead you anymore, Lorenzo, but you still have an advantage I never had. I am still here for you, two kings of this massive coven on two continents. You worked hard, earned your birthright. I am proud to give you your just rights to rule as King."

Lorenzo lit up a cigarette and exhaled the smoke in a cloud above his head. "What if I'm not ready? I'm not sure...I'm not Marco. I don't know if they'll follow me, trust in me, the way they did in Marco."

"Hell, son, no one will ever be like Marco. That fucker was one of a kind." Shade laughed at the thought of anyone being even remotely close to his best friend. "He didn't start out as that old leather ass grump you knew growing up. He was young once too, and full of doubt about whether he could command this camp. But for all the bitching and complaining, he loved every warrior that ever walked through here. He learned from his mistakes, and grew into the role, just as you will grow into yours."

Shade pulled out his smokes and lit up. "You have Alfie, you know his heart, just as I knew Marco's. You will learn to transfer some of the burden to him, and the two of you will become even closer through the years. As our coven grows, Alfie will be there for you, assuming additional roles, training your warriors. Give the warriors you trust a chance to prove to you what they can do. It will make your reign much easier. Follow your gut."

Lorenzo nodded at his father's advice. "Speaking of following my gut, there's something else I think I need to do. Losing Marco makes me understand that no matter how big our coven is, we are just one battle away from extinction. I want to mate Chantal and have our own children. I know you took a grave risk and waited a long time before you mated. You've told me before you had your reasons, but whatever they were you hold them secret still. The hunt doesn't have the same appeal to me. I love Chantal, and she's royal blood. It will be a good mating. I hope I have your blessing."

Shade took a shaking breath and his heart flipped inside his chest. He sat a long time before answering. He *had* taken a risk in waiting so long to mate, and leaving his coven without an heir, but he'd had his own selfish reasons for the delay. His son would never face that same dilemma. Creating a strong line for succession was crucial to their survival, and his son would mate and bring forth a new generation of Medici. His legacy would live on. "Love is something I have learned I cannot live without. If you love Chantal, then you have our blessing. Henri has already told me if you ask for her hand, he will not deny you. I think she will make for a beautiful and loving queen. Together, you will give me some grandsons."

Lorenzo's smiled. "Well, at least I'll take some pressure off Sophia." He looked at his father. He knew he'd been absent from them all for the last three days. "We're going to be all right, though, Dad, right? I need to know we're going to be all right. That you're...that you and Mommy...I need to know we're all going to be all right."

Shade looked at his son, locked eyes with him, and saw a reflection of his own face in his son. "Son, two things you need to remember. First, your mommy and I, no matter the circumstance, hold each other up. We reign together. We can never be separated. And secondly, the coven will follow you. Cherish your mate. Fight, love, and become one soul, and let nothing come between you."

Lorenzo stared back at him. His father had been the role model for his entire life, and there was no one he respected more. "Then let's see what lies ahead for the Medici."

As they stood together, Shade threw his arm around his son's shoulders and they walked back to the castle. "You have risen in the shadow of a king, but it is time for you to now step from the shadow and rise on your own. Let the world see what King Lorenzo Medici can do."

About the Author

Emily Bex is an avid life-long reader, and a first-time writer of the epic six book Medici Warrior Series. As she says, "Why start small?" She worked for over twenty years in marketing, developing ad campaigns, catalogs, product launches and promotional literature. She figured if she could write creatively about products, then surely she could write something about these characters that were rattling around inside her brain. She currently lives in Virginia, but has used her extensive love of travel, both foreign and domestic, to create the backdrop for her characters to play out their story.

View the Medici Warrior Series Here:

https://www.emilybex.com/books/

Make sure to stalk me!

Instagram:

https://bit.ly/3dAaO5k

Facebook:

http://bit.ly/3k5GHUC

Goodreads:

http://bit.ly/3ukYcVU

Twitter:

https://bit.ly/3s6m3GG

Bookbub:

http://bit.ly/2ZBJ9ZM

Website:

https://www.emilybex.com/

More From This Author

"Blood Covenant combines the hedonistic jet-setting pleasures of ***BILLIONAIRE ROMANCE*** *and the dirty little secret thrills of a* ***DEAD SEXY VAMPIRE!"*** **- Katalina Leon, USA Today Bestselling Author**

"This series is going to ***HIT THE CHARTS****... what an epic tale. Thank you Emily from a* ***NEW FAN!"*** **- Cheryl, Amazon Reviewer**

When he met her, he knew how it would end.

Shade Medici, a warrior king and sole male heir to the dynasty, is expected to mate and produce an heir to secure the continuation of the Medici coven. He's waited over 500 years for the right mate, and when he meets Kate Reese, his

attraction is more than primal - it's merciless.
She's also mortal.

Kate is fresh off a broken engagement and reluctant to open her heart, but her hesitations are no match for the unrelenting pursuits of the vampire King. Their passion for each other is searing... and not everyone is happy about it. Namely the ruling Council.

As they fight against deceit, treachery, and those who aim to see their love fail, Shade also struggles to control his impulses as Kate is immersed into his dark and dangerous world, but it's imperative he prepare her for the changes that will be demanded of her should she choose to bind herself to him through the blood covenant. All that scorches and glitters isn't gold, and she quickly learns that falling in love with a vampire King comes at a hefty price:
It may just cost her everything.

"Riveting", "electric", and hailed as "the NEXT BIG THING", The Medici Warrior Series follows the exploits of a vampire dynasty that spans four generations in a multi-genre novel with elements of paranormal, smoldering slow-burn romance, and historical fiction. Get your copy today! Your vampire king is waiting...

JR Ward and Christine Feehan fans will become enchanted with this deliciously dark and scandalous tale by International Bestselling Author Emily Bex. It's everything vampire romances should be made of!

*The **DANGEROUS ELEGANCE** of these worldly, wine and blood loving Medici warrior vampires and their mates is **TOTALLY ADDICTIVE**. I cannot wait for more."* **- Katalina Leon, USA Today Bestselling Author**

Unable to escape crushing grief, Kate needs an outlet to channel her anguish. Turning to Luca, she pleads to be trained to fight like a warrior, but such a thing is in direct violation of Shade's commands.

If she can get Luca to agree, her training must be done in secret.

Unfortunately, any training is too little too late. Intent on crushing Shade, the Aries coven is pressing in on him from all sides. Shade's only weakness is Kate, who becomes their perfect bait.

While Kate has been made stronger, as long as she's mortal, her life is in peril. But going through the turning to become immortal would be a big gamble to her survival.

So many decisions, too many obstacles. This second installment in a vampire saga will draw you in from the first page to the spellbinding end.

"Scorching", "riveting", and hailed as" the NEXT BIG THING", The Medici Warrior Series follows the exploits of a vampire dynasty that spans four generations in a multi-genre novel with elements of paranormal, smoldering romance, and historical fiction. Get your copy today! Your vampire king is waiting...

AUTHOR'S NOTE: This is a series that must be read in order. New to the Medici Warrior universe? Start at Book One!

JR Ward and Christine Feehan fans will become enchanted with this deliciously dark and erotic tale by International Bestselling Author Emily Bex. It's everything vampire romances should be made of!

There are new beginnings for the ancient Medici vampire coven.

The sexy, powerful King Shade Medici intends to increase his coven and territories to include the U.S. The new Medici Queen proves she can hold her own beside her king. She carries rare abilities believed extinct by the vampire community. She also possesses something never seen in the vampire world. What will it mean to their kind?

A male heir must be produced to carry on the Medici line.The royal couple has many new plans in business to advance their hold in the States...but not everyone is happy about it. The sprawling Medici estate is a threat to its neighboring coven, controlled by

Max. Their lifestyle is Rissa's greatest envy. Secrets will be revealed, old scores will be settled, and many will fall.

"Scorching","riveting", and hailed as" the NEXT BIG THING", The Medici Warrior Series follows the exploits of a vampire dynasty that spans four generations in a multi-genre novel with elements of paranormal, smoldering romance, and historical fiction. Get your copy today! Your vampire king and queen are waiting...

JR Ward and Christine Feehan fans will become enchanted with this deliciously dark and scandalous series by International Bestselling Author Emily Bex. It's everything vampire romances should be made of!

Continue the journey in this dark fantasy with Shade and Kate Medici.

Lorenzo discovers his mother isn't the only one born with unique powers.

Alec makes his final bid for political power and is prepared to take down anyone who stands in his way.

There is nothing more dangerous than a vampire with nothing more to lose. You won't believe what happens when he returns to exact his own revenge.

"Scorching", "riveting", and hailed as "the NEXT BIG THING", The Medici Warrior Series follows the exploits of a vampire dynasty that spans four generations in a multi-genre novel with elements of paranormal, smoldering romance, and historical fiction. Get your copy today! Your vampire king is waiting..

Foundations Book Publishing

10-9-8-7-6-5-4-3-2-1

Lorenzo's Rising
The Medici Warrior Series: Book 5

ISBN: 978-1-64583-061-0